Despite her exultation she felt a trickle of dismay. What would she do if he did not love her enough – if he would not marry her? She rolled on her back again, her eyes wide and unblinking. Her future would be grim; seeing Daniel every day without having him, cooking, ironing and cleaning for her family with no children of her own, and ruining Becky's chances into the bargain.

Unexpectedly, an answer came to her. *I'd marry Chaim Cohen!* And as soon as the thought crossed her mind, she was appalled. Suave and elegant though he was, she could not think of marrying him. The idea was ludicrous. She laughed softly to herself. What was she worrying about? Daniel had invited her to visit Sheik Suliman with him to choose a colt. Of course he loved her, of course he planned to marry her. Why should she even think of Chaim Cohen?

The SCARLET THREAD

MANDY RiceDavies

SPHERE BOOKS LIMITED

A *Sphere* Book

First published in Great Britain by
Michael Joseph Ltd 1989
This edition published by Sphere Books Ltd 1990

Printed and bound in Great Britain by
Cox & Wyman Ltd, Reading

ISBN 0 7474 0028 8

Sphere Books Ltd
A Division of
Macdonald & Co (Publishers) Ltd
Orbit House
1 New Fetter Lane
London EC4A 1AR
A member of Maxwell Macmillan Pergamon Publishing Corporation

DEDICATION

To my daughter DANA
and in memory of her grandfather
Captain Shalom Dulitski

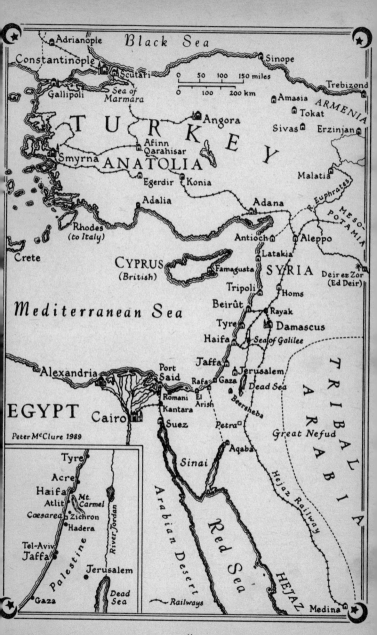

Peter McClure 1989

vii

Author's Note

Although this is a novel, the story is inspired by a true one and many of the events are a matter of history and public record.

During the first world war in Palestine, a pro-British group of young Jews with dreams for the future of their ancient homeland did exist. Convinced that only the British could wrest Palestine away from the tyrannical Ottoman rule and help the Jews establish their own state, they set up and operated an intelligence network behind Turkish lines. Their role in the preparation for Allied advance into Palestine was vital.

Against this factual backdrop I have introduced my fictional characters. These are a creation of the author and live only and entirely in my imagination. The exceptions of course are the public figures associated historically with that period, such as Jemel and Enver Pasha, Field Marshal Edmund Allenby and others. Their activities as portrayed in *The Scarlet Thread* are based on fact, as indeed are their sentiments.

I am extremely grateful to Sophia Watson who typed and retyped her way through endless drafts of my handwritten manuscript, and briskly marshalled up my syntax whenever it stepped out of line. Her patience and reliability as the novel grew and changed did much to keep me going.

I am equally indebted to Susan Watt of Michael Joseph for her forbearance in listening to my half-formed theories and for providing me with many hours of crucial suggestions regarding the structure of *The Scarlet Thread*.

And my greatest debt is to my husband, Ken, for his support, interest and understanding.

In the vast wilderness of the Sinai desert there is a date palm grove. It is said that the tallest tree grows from a human skull. The Bedouin call it 'Kabr Yehud' – the Jew's Grave.

PROLOGUE

Sinai Desert: November 1967

In a concealed fold beside a date palm grove a small group of wandering Bedouin camped. The fires that had burned all night through were now low in the light of early morning and flickered circles of warmth in front of the black goatskin tents. On the ridge, just above the camp, a bearded elder sat toying with a string of amber beads. Now and again he pressed them to his lips in silent prayer. Two boys standing higher on the ridge suddenly cried out and ran down to the elder. Immediately he was surrounded by children who pulled at his sleeve, pointing into the distance and eagerly demanding his attention. The old man, his concentration broken, rolled himself onto the balls of his feet and narrowed his eyes, searching the horizon. Far across the desert he saw a pair of headlights, the faint beams swinging and dipping as they zig-zagged their way across the rough ground towards him.

'Rawi, storyteller – who are they?' the children chorused. The strangers could be anything – Egyptians, Syrians, Jordanians. After a war there was no certainty.

'Jews.' The storyteller said after a long pause.

'The infidel.'

The jeep stopped only a few paces away. A Lieutenant-Colonel of the Israeli Army jumped out of the dust-whitened vehicle. He was followed by three regular soldiers carrying spades and trenching equipment. He approached the elder and greeted him in Arabic.

'*Salam alaikum*' [Peace be with you].

'*Alaikum wa salam*' [Peace to you too].

'*Yak, la bas*' [No evil to you].

'*La bas, hamdullah*' [No evil thanks to God], answered the old man, raising his eyes to the heavens.

The ritual exchange of courtesies over, the Lieutenant-Colonel left the elder and quickly walked across to the tallest date palm in the grove.

'This is the one,' he said firmly to his men.

'Dig here.'

The old storyteller sat and watched, inscrutable and omniscient as an ancient god.

'Why are they digging up the palm, Rawi?' a child whispered. The children were all much quieter now, awed by the presence of the infidel.

The storyteller sighed, shifted his weight and settled back on his haunches. He smiled very slowly, gently clicking his beads and said nothing. The children recognised the beginning of a story and quietly gathered in a huddle around him.

'That is the Kabr Yehud – the Jew's Grave,' the old man said finally. He breathed hard and his expression changed, becoming a blank page on which the story would be written. With the opening traditional among nomadic storytellers, he began.

'Allah be my testimony and Allah be witness to what I say. In a day of the days there was a spy for the British. She was as beautiful as the moon's tears . . .

BOOK ONE

CHAPTER ONE

Palestine: 1914

Under the scarlet and gold banner of the Ottoman Empire stood Haifa railway station, its stone façade cooled only by a few dusty palms, its stillness total in the dense autumn heat. A man in his late thirties stepped out from under the narrow wooden awning and, shading his deep blue eyes from the unrelenting mid-morning glare, he stared into the horizon.

The platform was crowded with a diverse collection of waiting passengers and visitors: Turkish officials, in full dress uniform with scarlet sashes, fezes and revolvers at their hips, mingled with Carmelite nuns trapped in their voluminous habits. One or two of the newest arrivals, the Imperial German officers, sauntered up and down the platform in their polished calf-length boots and grey field jackets, all sporting a pomaded moustache in honour of their Emperor. And the Arabs were of course everywhere: a rag-tag collection of children at the base of the water tower tormented a lizard; a woman in a black embroidered gown balanced a tray of pitta bread on her head, steadying the load with a richly hennaed hand.

Aaron Levinson, gazing hard at the skyline, stood out distinctly from the rest of the motley crowd. This was not only because of the fine cut of his blue serge suit but because he had a natural dignity of bearing which set him apart from the casualness of the Arab and the fussy pomposity of the countless officials who served Turkey's crumbling Empire. Levinson was both scholar and farmer, both immigrant and Palestinian; a rare man indeed and by now a very impatient one. He turned to the station-master.

'She's late,' he said to the short, plump man who stood in the shadow of the awning. The station-master shrugged, pulled out a large steel pocket-watch and consulted it with an air of importance.

'Only an hour, Your Honour,' he said, shaking the watch as if it were at fault rather than the train.

'Which makes her early, I suppose,' answered Aaron with an exasperated smile. He turned back to stare into the distance, watching the thin shimmering line where the sand met the sky. A dark smudge appeared on the horizon. Shielding his eyes with both hands, Aaron concentrated even harder, as though willing the train to appear. The smudge took form; the train was coming.

The station-master emerged from the shade. Huffing and panting he began to trot briskly up and down the platform, turning this way and that to throw orders at the scurrying clerk who, knowing full well that duty came a poor second to his master's comfort, was trying to keep a black umbrella between the sun and his chief's head.

Aaron turned his attention back to the horizon. The Sultan's Donkey, as the Bedouins nicknamed the Hejez train, was chugging slowly through the soft yellow sand dunes in a cloud of steam, bucking wildly on the narrow single-track line. Aaron gave a grunt of satisfaction and, lifting his deep-brimmed Panama, carefully mopped the beads of sweat from his forehead. His thick hair was bleached a pale gold by the fierce Palestinian sun, and his fair skin was the colour of rare beef. Deep lines cut harshly down from the corner of his nose to his square, clean-shaven chin – lines that spoke of the determination which had carried him to the position he held today.

Aaron was no simple farmer, but founder and director of the Jewish Agricultural Research Station, a station unique not only in Palestine but throughout the Empire.

Aaron tilted his hat forward over his eyes again and smiled to himself. How long had Daniel been away . . . was it four years? It seemed like a day and a lifetime.

Daniel Rosen sat quite still in the railway carriage, his eyes half closed. In the dirt-smudged window he could see the reflection of the woman opposite him. She was in her late thirties, he supposed, a blonde with magnetic blue eyes, which seemed oddly familiar. Obviously a German officer's wife on her way to join her husband, he thought. She was reading a German novel – or pretending to; he saw her steal yet another glance at him over the pages of the book. Daniel knew only too well what was going through her mind. He had often been gazed at with just that mixture of

6

curiosity and lasciviousness and he was used to responding with an easy charm. A few months ago he might even have struck up a conversation with her, arranged a clandestine meeting and left the rest to chance. But things were different now. Ignoring the woman, he closed his eyes and fell into a fitful doze.

Shifting slightly in her seat, the woman adjusted her geranium-red hat hoping that the movement would attract his attention, but his eyes remained firmly shut. She glanced at the young man opposite her. By no means inexperienced with men – you could almost say she made a living from them, but then who didn't one way or another – she found her eyes drawn back to him every time she tried to look out of the train window and take in the monotonous view.

She had changed carriages an hour earlier when her wagon had cracked an axle and from the moment when, settled in her new compartment, she had raised her eyes to his she had cursed fate that the accident had not happened earlier.

His suitcases were cardboard and on close inspection the cloth of his well-cut suit turned out to be cheaper than she had at first thought. But it was not the face of a poor man. She took advantage of his closed eyes to appraise him once more. He must be in his late twenties, she thought, tall and dark with a lean, spare body. His looks were exceptional but there was more than that to him. His face, shadowed by the white Panama hat tilted over his eyes, showed an uncompromising strength and virility that marked him out from other good looking men she had known and admired, Then the sudden shriek of the whistle drowned out any further thought and, feeling her cheeks flush, she fanned herself crossly.

Cat-like, Daniel Rosen opened his eyes and stared at the woman opposite him. The nagging feeling of familiarity returned. Then he remembered.

He turned his head and gazed out of the train window, hardly aware of the countryside passing by. The rich blue eyes staring so persistently at him were curiously like those of Aaron's sister, Sara. His mind went back to her, not for the first time on this long journey home. She was the one weak chink in the armour he had built around himself during the last four years in France.

Daniel had gone to France to take up the scholarship given by Baron de Rothschild.

In the lush comfort of the French countryside Daniel often thought of his home village, Hadera, and the situation in Palestine.

He remembered his father's arguments in favour of living peacefully under the Turk. While conceding that the Jews, like all other minorities, were maltreated by their Moslem rulers, his father would say that with persistence and bribery a Jew could buy as much land as he wanted and live happily on it. His father had died with that belief intact.

But even then Daniel had been frustrated by the slow immigration of Jews, by the way they were forced to buy swamp land at exorbitant prices from absentee landlords who were only too happy to offload the near-useless ground to the new arrivals. He believed then – and the more he read, the more convinced he became that he was right – that only by overthrowing the Turk could the Jews restore the Jewish State.

In Daniel's view there was only one way to achieve this: guerrilla warfare. The Jews were a tiny minority in the Empire, so any armed conflict or uprising would lead to instant defeat. The Turks, with their vast network of police agents, informers and petty civil servants, dealt with subversive elements ruthlessly. To oppose them openly would be suicide. But Daniel fantasised that he might one day reorganise some of the existing political parties and workers' unions into secret cells that would fight the Turk underground. At the same time as holding this dream, he knew that most Jews wanted only to live in peace and would not be drawn into battle. Somehow Daniel had to find a way that would make Palestine more trouble than it was worth for the Turks. After all, he reflected, the only real enemy of the lion is the tiny louse.

Inevitably, Daniel had drifted into the French Zionist movement, but before long he had found himself at odds with them. The majority of the leaders had never even visited Palestine and had no real conception of the problems Jews living there faced. They talked endlessly about the future, held endless meetings, and endlessly frustrated Daniel by the constant bickering between themselves. Daniel couldn't stand their air of sanctity and virtue – that wouldn't rid the Jew of the Turk. He wanted action.

More and more often Daniel found his mind wandering home. He would hold up his hands to the light, inspecting the callouses he'd built up working in the fields of Palestine. He would daydream about those days when he and Aaron worked together in the vineyards of Zichron and he read Aaron's letters with pride and envy as he followed the progress of the experimental project at Atlit, begun just after Daniel had left for France.

But he still could not bring himself to pack up his bags and return home. He felt his destiny was of a high order, more sacred than the slow painful process of redeeming the land. Corn and grapes were no protection against the myriad laws designed to muzzle his people, to restrict their movements and to disarm them. Farming would not restore compassion and justice to a land materially and spiritually bankrupted by the Turk. Nor would it restore the Jews' inherent right to their motherland, Israel, given them by God for all time.

And so, with these hopes and aims, he remained in France, marking time with a burning impatience, but confident that one day soon his ambitions and desires would become real. He would await the call of destiny.

Another image came to Daniel whenever his thoughts turned to Palestine: the unwelcome but persistent image of Sara. She was so lovely, so warm and loving, so entirely what he had always dreamed of in a woman. At the oddest moments her face would drift into his mind, and he would remember himself sitting in the Levinsons' comfortable drawing room listening to her playing the piano with a passion and technique amazing in a girl so young. He had always been a little frightened of her beauty, those dazzling eyes and the shining gold hair. But when she played the piano her beauty underwent a subtle change: she no longer seemed untouchable, unreachable. There was something earthy and passionate about her at those moments and Daniel would feel something akin to a stab of pain as he remembered.

He wanted her. But it would have been so irresponsible to marry her. He could not imagine a greater happiness – or a fate more appalling. But he would not allow himself to think of her. Not now, now that the winds of fate were at last blowing in his direction.

Less than five weeks ago, he thought with an increasing sense of wonder, his political energies and hopes were at the lowest ebb of his life. He was almost exhausted with talking, planning, talking. But now it had all changed. And all because a schoolboy, resentful at the annexation of his country by the Hapsburgs had shot dead Archduke Franz Ferdinand, heir to the Hapsburg monarchy.

The assassination at Sarajevo would ultimately bring Germany and Russia into conflict, and this sparked Daniel's imagination. Russia was Turkey's traditional enemy and it did not take much to guess that Germany would do its best to inveigle Turkey into its war. And Daniel was convinced that Turkey *would* be brought into the war very soon. He *knew* it. The thought made his skin tingle and raised the hair at the nape of his neck. In a clairvoyant flash he realised that this was the moment he had been waiting for.

Then and there he had decided to return to Palestine immediately. He would do everything in his power to nudge 'the sick man of Europe', as Turkey was nicknamed, towards its deathbed.

Daniel turned his face to the woman again, and smiled to himself. Yes, she had a hint of Sara in her eyes, but he was not going to let that have any effect on him. A man that fears nothing can do anything, Daniel thought. If he allowed himself to get entangled with Sara, he would be reluctant to take risks. It might be difficult at first but he would stand guard over his heart with deadly resolve. There was nothing he would not do to further his political aims and, if the price was his personal feelings, so be it.

They must be nearing Haifa now and he was longing to stand on the soil of Israel again. He was looking forward to seeing his mother, his friends and Aaron's work at the research station. With that strange rush of excitement that a traveller feels on nearing his destination he rose and, with a smile and half bow, left his disappointed admirer and made his way to the observation platform at the back of the train. He looked with undisguised joy at the stark Palestinian landscape through which the train was jolting. The beige linen suit flapped briskly around him in the breeze. He was home. Like a dog sniffing the air, he raised his face into the wind, breathing deep gulps. On impulse he tore off his expensive hat and threw it high up in the air. Caught on the wind, it hovered for a while, turning and rolling, until it fell in the dust behind the train. Daniel smiled.

The wolf had returned to the forest.

The engine ground to a halt in a cloud of steam, the carriages buffeting into each other one by one before they came to rest. Aaron scanned the train door by door, his view impeded by the sudden flurry of activity as porters reached for baggage and passengers were greeted by friends.

Daniel, standing on the lower step of the train, saw his friend first and, tossing his suitcase and carpet bag on the platform, leapt the few paces that separated them. 'Aaron,' he exclaimed. 'By

God, it's good to see you.' The two men embraced, then momentarily caught off guard by their own emotions, held each other at arms' length.

'Welcome home,' said Aaron, putting an arm around the younger man's shoulder.

'Soon to be the only place I am welcome,' Daniel replied. They laughed together and the uneasy moment passed. A bare-footed Arab retrieved the suitcase and stood silently beside them. 'Abdul?' Daniel queried, stooping and staring into the myopic eyes of the old porter.

'Why, it's His Honour Mr Daniel,' Abdul replied, staring back and grinning to reveal naked gums. 'Peace be with you.'

'Peace be with you too,' said Daniel automatically and then, chuckling, added, 'Still got your head on your shoulders, I see.'

'Thanks be to Allah,' said Abdul, lifting the suitcase on to the head in question.

The old porter was a local legend. For want of an efficient signalling system, the station-master had made it Abdul's job to sleep with his head on the rails and warn of approaching trains. He had never missed one yet.

Aaron led the way through the crowd to an open space at the back of the station where carts and horses baked in the heat despite the light wind which blew the sand around. The only car was a Ford 'Tin Lizzy', resplendent in brass and sparkling black paintwork, standing like an orphan in the sunlight.

Aaron walked over to claim it with studied nonchalance. Daniel raised his eyebrows in astonishment and whistled through his teeth.

'Is that yours?'

'She belongs to the research station,' said Aaron, patting the bonnet with satisfied affection. 'She's a perk from Aunty America and her name is Jezebel.'

'I hope she's less trouble than her namesake.'

'Get in while I crank her up and we'll see.'

On the third crank the engine spluttered into life and a smiling Aaron signalled thumbs up. He slid into the driving seat and pushed the gear stick into first.

'We're going straight back to the house. There are a couple of young ladies just dying to see you.'

'Sara! Help me wind up my hair, you know how much better you

11

do it than me.' Becky turned her pale-green eyes imploringly on her older sister. 'Please!'

Rebecca was almost sixteen; she made a pretty picture, standing in front of the looking-glass with three-quarters of her face turned towards the mirror, and her left hand holding up the thick stream of coppery hair.

Sara, sitting on the bed tying a blue ribbon around the crown of a broad-rimmed straw hat, gave a sigh of resignation. 'Heavens, Becky – they'll be here at any moment and I'm not dressed myself yet.' But she put down the hat and shaking out her linen petticoat walked over to the mirror, took the silver-backed hairbrush from her sister and began to wind up the thick tresses.

Becky peered anxiously at her reflection.

'Oh my nose, my nose! If only it weren't so snub. Why isn't it as perfectly straight as yours, Sara?' She wailed.

'Don't be such a goose,' said Sara good-naturedly. 'You've never looked half so pretty. Call it retroussé not snub and you'll like it more.'

Becky was not convinced and wistfully compared their two reflections in the glass. 'Next to you he won't even see me,' she said despairingly.

'Nonsense, of course he will.' Sara fixed the final pin in place. 'There,' she said and stepped back to check Becky's final appearance.

Basically, the sisters looked very alike – with the same strong square jaws and pointed chins. Even their skins were the same creamy magnolia. But there the similarities ended. Where Becky's hair was a glossy chestnut, Sara's was a thick deep gold with glints of ash blonde. Her eyes, long and tilted up at the corners, were a dark, clear blue and framed with unusually dark and thick black lashes. Her sleek brows were perfect arches in a high, fine forehead.

Sara had just turned twenty but her height and natural poise made her seem older than her years. From childhood people had remarked on her ability to turn heads but Sara, who had no streak of vanity in her, was genuinely unaware of her beauty. She would occasionally gaze into the mirror hoping to find that 'special something' reflected there, but she had never really managed to define it. She thought her face quite pretty, but otherwise perfectly ordinary and had no real notion of the attention she attracted.

Becky's voice burbled on.

12

'Oh Sara, I'm so excited. I do so want to make a good impression. Tell me – are you sure this dress doesn't make me look like a schoolgirl?' Becky squirmed and twisted for a better view of herself in the looking glass. Sara glanced at her sister over her shoulder. Becky, even sharp, pretty, confident Becky, sought her big sister's reassurance. Sometimes Sara longed for a day with no responsibilities.

'You look young, lovely ... and audacious,' she added, knowing full well how the 'audacious' would delight Becky.

'Oh, do I?' said Becky, obviously flattered.

If only Mama were alive to see you today, thought Sara, her heart clenching in sudden pain. Miriam Levinson had died unexpectedly of a heart attack three years before, leaving her large family shocked and grieving. More than all the others, Becky, the 'baby' of the family, had turned to her sister for the love and attention which had been so generously forthcoming from her mother. It was a task Sara rose to with all her strength, but for which she often felt inadequate. Sometimes she felt that Becky's need for love and security was endless.

'Thank you, my darling sister.' Becky stood on her toes and kissed Sara lightly on the cheek.

'Becky!' Fatma's voice echoed down the corridor like a whip cracking. Becky turned, mildly irritated. Her visions of herself as a beautiful heart-breaker faded and she was left a schoolgirl needed for an errand.

'I suppose I'd better go and help Fatma in the kitchen – I did promise,' she sighed. And, always quick on her feet, she was gone leaving nothing behind but a faint smell of honey-suckle toilet water and a rustle of skirts.

Sara glanced around the room. Discarded garments lay everywhere, on the floor, the bed and the chair, in soft mounds of colour. She bent automatically to pick up a petticoat, then, checking herself with a smile, sat down at the dressing table and began skilfully to braid her luxurious profusion of blonde hair, twisting it into a chignon high on her head. From a silver box she chose four tortoiseshell bodkins and pushed them in to hold the knot in place. The pins had belonged to her mother, and Sara thought of her every time she wore them. She still missed her terribly – her warmth, her common sense, the wonderful smell of her that Sara would always associate with childhood.

Miriam had been the force that kept her wild and passionate

family stable and, try as she might, Sara was finding it increasingly difficult to follow in her mother's footsteps. As the eldest daughter, she had been left in sole charge of the house and family – a heavy burden for one so young. Even with the help and loyal support of Fatma, occasional help from the nearby Arab village and even more occasional help from Becky, Sara found it very hard to do a woman's work – the washing and ironing, the cooking and cleaning. Sometimes the domestic drudgery seemed endless. Thinking of it now, Sara sighed wearily. It was the harder as, although she wanted so very much to be like her mother, she was just not cut from the same cloth.

Sara was an intelligent girl, and had sailed through her school years with ease. Had she been given a full education she could well have attained the same excellence as her brother Aaron. As it was, she knew she would be much happier if she were allowed to work with him at the research station, or were given the chance to accompany him to America as her middle brother Alex had often done. She would even be content with doing the general work of the vineyard and farm along with her youngest brother Sam.

But Sara was also practical and knew that, as a girl, she was most needed at home and here she had to stay. She did not complain, but sometimes she dreamed.

Today would be different. After four years in France, Daniel was finally coming home. Her heart began to pound in anticipation. She had loved Daniel Rosen since she was fourteen years old and she had first seen him riding into their courtyard at Zichron.

Although their hillside village was a world in itself, and a good two hours' ride from Haifa, the nearest town, it was not that rare for strangers to ride in looking for her brother Aaron. His encyclopaedic knowledge of agriculture, botany and geology was already recognised and respected throughout Palestine, and he was much sought after for advice.

But Daniel was different from any visitor Sara had ever seen. He couldn't be real, she thought, and stood gaping at him in genuine astonishment. He was without doubt the most handsome man she had ever seen in all her life.

He drew up his horse and leaned forward over its withers towards her, fixing his eyes unblinkingly on her for a moment. They were a deep amber – no, gold – she thought, and felt a strange trembling inside her.

'Why, it's true,' he had said, his eyes still riveted on her. 'Angels do indeed walk the earth.'

Sara, rooted to the spot, blushed inexplicably and, wishing not to appear foolish – or even worse, immature – had responded sharply. 'I am *not* an angel. I'm Aaron Levinson's sister, Sara.'

'Sara,' he had repeated thoughtfully and then laughed – a laugh that for some reason put her to shame.

'Well, Sara,' he had said with good-humoured ease. 'Go and tell your brother Aaron that Daniel Rosen would like to see him.' He smiled and his eyes crinkled at the corners, which made him seem more human and less of a god. But from that moment on he was Sara's Prince Charming and she remained totally entranced.

She later discovered that he was just twenty-two and was from Hadera, a two-hour ride south and one of the closest settlements to their own. His parents were Russian and, like the Levinsons, had been founder members of their settlement. Daniel's father had died recently of malaria – a common fate among the early settlers – and Daniel had come to Aaron in the hope that he could work with him for the next couple of years until he was ready to take up a scholarship to France.

Aaron had been one of the first local youths to be awarded a Rothschild scholarship to Grignon and he took to Daniel immediately, giving him a job on the spot. Within a few short weeks Daniel had joined the small group of devoted disciples that worked with Aaron, and had also become one of the family.

Everyone who knew Daniel loved him, although no one more than Sara and the next few years passed like a dream for her. She saw Daniel almost every day, and the more she knew him the more she loved and respect him. He had the relaxed charm which had first attracted her, but he also possessed a fiery vitality that often made him reckless. He was frequently careless of his own interests and always put the needs of his people above his own. Sara loved him for it, and the not infrequent nights he spent in jail for insulting the septieh (the local Turkish Police patrols) only strengthened her admiration. The septieh's power over the citizens of Palestine was almost total and they were universally feared and loathed.

Sara spent hours dreaming about Daniel, sitting in her little bedroom or in the quiet of the garden and letting her imagination roam over all the possibilities the future held. What it would be like to be married to him, she wondered. They would sit together in

the evening, reading to each other, holding hands, kissing. She painted a romantic picture and lived in the certainty of its coming true.

She was not entirely ignorant about the facts of life – a large
family and living on a farm had seen to that. But she was definitely
hazy about exactly what happened. She would creep into Aaron's
little study which he had built for himself in the courtyard and
surreptitiously turn the pages of the medical books, looking for
pictures and information about what really did happen between a
man and a woman. But wherever she looked, the mechanics of the
act remained tantalisingly obscure.

Finally, lacking the courage to ask her mother, Sara had gone to
Fatma with her question. The old Arab servant had never married,
but she must know a thing or two. Fatma's answer was not
comforting. According to her the whole ritual was a nightmare.
Along with the pain was the dire danger of pregnancy and, even
worse, a disease that ate away at your flesh. This was very
confusing, and conflicted with the glee Sara was sure she detected
when she overheard other women discussing the subject. But
Fatma had told her something else, which worried her most of all.
'After they have had their way with a woman they lost interest in
her – the randy tom cats!' *If Daniel loses interest in me, I'll die,*
Sara thought.

But did he have an interest? Sara was sure that he did. In the
evenings he would sometimes read poetry to Becky and her, and
then beg Sara to play the piano. Sara imagined married life as an
extension of these happy evenings, but without Becky. Sometimes
when she was playing a particularly moving piece of music she
would catch Daniel watching her in a way that warmed her whole
body and brought the blood to her cheeks. At moments like that
she knew with intuition as old as time that he wanted her as much
as she did him. But more often than not he seemed to keep a tight
control on his feelings and a distance between them. His carefully
cultivated control had only failed him once.

Daniel would often accompany Aaron on his field trips and very
occasionally Sara would be allowed to go with them. These
outings with the two men she loved most in the world were to her
the pinnacle of happiness. A few weeks after her sixteenth
birthday she had accompanied them both on a trip to Galilee.

While Aaron was busy in the tent sorting out the day's
collection of rock and plant specimens, she and Daniel sat together
watching the sun slip down behind the Golan mountains. The sky

16

above them was a heavy crimson, the stars just appearing, the valley below a rich green coil with the sea of Galilee a glowing silver mirage far beneath them. The colours were so violent and beautiful in their intensity that Sara, intoxicated by the beauty, sat in awed silence.

'I'm leaving next week for France,' Daniel had said abruptly. Sara, stunned, watched the colours drain out of the scene below her, dissolving into a meaningless palette of black and grey. She turned and stared at him in disbelief. Over the last few years she had managed to forget about the scholarship that was bound to take him away to Grignon. Then she shrunk back as though at a physical blow as the full impact of what he had said sunk in.

'No – never. I don't want you to go – ever,' she had blurted out, scrambling to her feet and staring down at him, her eyes blazing.

Daniel had looked at her in surprise for a moment, then smiled. 'It's only for four years,' he said gently.

'But that's for ever!' she had cried.

Daniel, laughing, had risen to his feet. 'Yes, and when I return you'll be an old maid.'

'I wish – I wish,' Sara began, but did not go on for she suddenly felt very shy.

'What do you wish, Sara?' His voice had been low and hot as he stood facing her, his meaning unmistakable. She had stared at him, knowing that at any moment he was going to bridge those last few inches between them. Then he reached out and seized her, almost roughly, and pulled her to him. She met his advance swiftly and they found each other's mouths eagerly. Waves of feeling swept over Sara, so powerful she felt her legs give way.

As suddenly as he had pulled her to him, Daniel had pushed her away. There was a brief, awkward moment in which the only sound was Daniel's breathing. Then he had sighed. 'I'm sorry . . . I'm so sorry . . . I don't know what happened. I think for a moment I lost my mind. There is no excuse for what I just did. You're . . . you're only a child.'

'You're only a child.' The words echoed in her ears. Why didn't the hill fall into the lake, carrying them both with it? She couldn't speak to tell him what was in her heart so she had looked blankly at him, nodded and, fighting back the tears, turned and ran back to the tent. From then until he had left for France, Daniel had kept as large a distance as possible between them.

* * *

Not a day had passed in the next four years without her dreaming of Daniel and yearning for his return. Many young men had asked to call on her, many possible husbands had been thrust under her nose by her father and brothers. She had just become used to putting them off and hiding what she really felt in her heart from everyone. She had not met one other man who made her heart twist and her knees weaken when she looked into his eyes.

Whenever Daniel wrote to Aaron he always included a few lines to the whole family, but there was never any special message for Sara, never a word more than he might have written to a sister. Sara had been too shy to write to him herself, and she had begun to wonder if he had forgotten her. Then three weeks earlier the long-awaited news had come from France – he was coming home.

Sara's feelings for Daniel had not changed since the day she saw him ride into the courtyard. The fact that Daniel had never acknowledged any love for her only doubled the value of the prize. For the last few weeks Sara had been unable to think of anything except today – and now today was here.

Sara rose from the dressing table, her body taut with excitement. She crossed to the bed to put on her gown. It was the same deep blue as her eyes and she had started cutting and sewing it for this moment the day she knew Daniel was returning to Palestine. The material was a gossamer light muslin embroidered with tiny white flowers and was from one of the precious and jealously-saved lengths of cloth Aaron had brought her back as a present from America. As she did up the final hook she caught sight of her full-length reflection in the mirror at the other side of the room. The simple cut of the frock emphasised her tall, shapely figure and the style of the bodice drew attention to her high, full breasts. She gazed at herself in the mirror, and a smile of unrestrained happiness lit her face. When Daniel had left she had been a gawky sixteen-year-old 'skinny-bones'. What he would see today, she realised, was a woman. He would no longer be able to say to her, 'You're still such a child.' She was a woman, and a woman who knew what she wanted.

She wanted Daniel Rosen and she was going to do everything in her power to make sure she got him. The next few months were going to be the most important of her life – she would try everything to make her dreams come true. They had to come true. Her eyes darkened at the thought of failure. She had waited four years and now, aged twenty, was by the standards of the village too old to be single. *They will come true*, she said to her reflection in the mirror. She straightened her back and threw up her head. Nothing and nobody could interfere with her plans.

'I am going to marry Daniel Rosen, I just know I am,' she whispered. Her eyes sparkling, she swept her hat from the bed and left the room radiating happiness, determination and all the optimism of untried youth.

'So it takes the threat of a war to bring you back!' said Aaron as he negotiated the treacherous road leading south from Haifa. An obstacle course of potholes and boulders, it was one of the only two roads in the whole of the country fit for wheels.

'The promise of war,' Daniel corrected with a wide grin. 'I was worried I might get stuck for months in Constantinople, but as it turned out it took less than a week to arrange my internal passport. A record if ever there was one.'

Aaron nodded. He knew only too well the time consuming bureaucratic problems of every Ottoman citizen. Without the 'Teskeres', the passport for the interior, which gave its owner freedom to move as he pleased within the vast Empire, a subject had (in theory at least) no right to move around at all – even from one village to the next.

'So what's the gossip in Constantinople?' asked Aaron, looking over at his friend.

'Look at it this way,' Daniel began, 'Serbia will take a crack at Austria, Germany at France, and then England will go in with France. Russia will, of course, have another go at Turkey and Turkey . . .'

'. . . will join Germany,' Aaron interrupted quickly.

'Precisely. And to the British, Serbs, French and Russians we will be . . .'

'The enemy,' they concluded together and their laughter broke the earnestness of the conversation.

Aaron took his eye off the road for a moment and turned smiling to Daniel. 'Perhaps we should prepare for a British invasion?'

With a loud grind the car's offside wheel mounted a boulder and came down with a crack. Aaron braked hard, swearing. He got out and looked down at the wheel, quickly checking the axle. 'No damage done,' he said with relief and, starting the car up again, he got back in and drove off more cautiously. 'But if the British do

19

intend to invade, someone ought to tell them to forget about motors and bring large numbers of donkeys with them.'

'Well, I for one, would welcome them with flowers,' said Daniel and then, suddenly intense, he added, 'The war is our only hope.'

Aaron was quiet for a moment. 'You do mean a British victory?' he asked, negotiating his way around another potentially lethal rock.

'Precisely,' replied Daniel firmly. 'The Turk is weak, over-stretched. If the British were to strike at Constantinople through Palestine, Turkey's whole provincial structure would collapse.'

'You've been gone a long time,' said Aaron pensively, 'the Jewish community here is split. Not everyone thinks it would be bad for us if Turkey sided with Germany. Don't forget that it is only about ten years since the Kishnev pogroms. The Russian settlers will never forgive the Tsar for that. If Turkey decided that joining up with Germany would break the Russians, many of the settlers would feel no compunction about joining in. You know the theory – the enemy of mine enemy is my friend.' He laughed but was immediately serious again. 'Many of the Russian settlers have already taken Turkish citizenship and are proudly proclaiming their loyalty to Turkey whatever side she takes.'

'God Almighty,' Daniel exploded. 'Why are we always playing into the hands of our enemy by disagreeing among ourselves. Has nothing changed?'

'Well, you certainly haven't,' Aaron was amused at seeing the same old Daniel under the sophisticated suit. 'Europe's done nothing to cool your head. We may live uneasily with – or, I grant you, under – the Turk, but don't forget that at least we live. If Turkey did join in, you must see that we would have no choice but to fight with her.'

'Personally, I'd rather strangle the Turk than salute him.' Daniel's voice was still fiery with passion, but he abruptly turned his head to look out of the jolting car at the peaceful shores of the Mediterranean. The gesture signalled that the subject was closed, and Aaron knew Daniel better than to press the point. He gave his old friend an affectionate look. Daniel, in a calmer frame of mind, was a lovable man – wise, witty and fearless with a warm nature that drew loyalty from all those close to him. But he was born of a line of men who had burnt their fires on great heights and his very qualities could make him a danger not only to himself, but also to those he most wished to protect.

The landscape they were driving through was unchanging and harsh. The road was edged with a nettle and thorn scrub which clung tenaciously to the sides of the road. Pale and dry, the life was all but sucked out of it. The two men drove through a small Arab village where a group of barefooted and ragged children ran after them shouting playfully in Arabic. Aaron waved gaily to the children and shouted back greetings. The parched brown outline of the Carmel Mountains rose to their left – to their right the sun threw a white gleam on to the motionless sea. In the overbearing heat even the water seemed still and promised no relief.

'Look!' Aaron exclaimed suddenly, jerking Daniel out of his reverie, 'there it is! The Jewish Agricultural Research Station.' Daniel narrowed his eyes, blinking into the sun. Ahead of them a refreshing patch of green was appearing out of the ochre browns of the scenery. Gradually, he recognised the outline of tall deferential palms snaking across the horizon in a ribbon of green. The scene had the shimmering coolness of a mirage. He turned to Aaron and looked at him incredulously. Aaron smiled a slow lazy smile which did not disguise his triumph.

'All it took was persistence,' he assured his friend. And then added, 'I hope you still remember what they taught you at Grignon. I could really use your help.' He waved airily towards the green miracle. 'We'll come down tomorrow and I'll show you round,' he promised as he swung the car left and they started climbing up into the blue hills of Ephraim, 'but first you'd better meet your reception committee.'

Sara, shoes in hand, crept silently down the tiled hallway, pausing only to be sure she was not seen passing the kitchen where Fatma was drawing hot loaves of bread from the oven. She knew from experience that Fatma would have no care for her newly arranged hair and fresh dress, but would have her at work in the sweltering kitchen the moment she set her shrewd black eyes on her.

Fatma had been with the Levinsons since Sara's parents arrived from Romania over thirty years earlier, and she was utterly devoted to the family. Her father had been a 'fellahin' – a peasant who worked the land around Zichron for an absentee Arab landlord. When the land was sold to an unknown group of Jews, Fatma, with a courage unheard of in an unmarried Arab girl of only twenty, had been the first to offer her services to the new landowners. Before very long she had become Miriam Levinson's

21

right-hand woman and the one person with total control over their wild children. With an affectionate but dictatorial eye she had watched over them as they climbed trees, fell into water, argued and played and stood no nonsense from any of them.

Sara heard Fatma complaining in rapid Arabic about the demon which, all morning long, had been trying to stop the bread from rising. Poor Fatma found djinn everywhere – she was djinn riddled. They were under the bed, in the fireplace, in the parlour and the dairy. They forced the milk to curdle and the wine to sour. They were at the bottom of every little thing that went wrong in her life. As a background to Fatma's monologue, Sara heard Becky sympathising automatically with Fatma and the bread.

Smiling fondly at the scene, Sara quietly let herself out on to the back veranda, and ran down to the courtyard. Alex and Sam were carrying a flagon of wine over to the front of the house.

Alex, the elder of the two, noticed her first and dropping the flagon to the ground, bent his broad, tanned body into a mock bow.

'Your servant, madame,' he said with an insolent twinkle in his blue eyes. Sara grinned back at him; his manner always won her over. Sam looked over to her and gave a low whistle of appreciation at his elder sister's appearance, brushing a lock of reddish hair from his forehead with a rather grubby hand. He could have passed as Becky's twin and shared much of her bold and impetuous nature.

Abu, the Arab coachman, came shuffling into the light and looked at Sara in silence but with full approval. No one knew what he wanted to say, but on this occasion it was easy to guess. At some stage in his sixty-odd years his tongue had been cut from his head, a punishment for some minor breach of an implacable law.

'Oh stop it! All of you!' Sara's voice was sharp but her eyes sparkled. She was not sure how much proper maidenly resentment she really felt. Sultan, the farm dog, sloped lazily out of the comparative cool of the stables, eyes shut against the sunlight and tongue as far out as it could go. Sara turned her back on the three grinning men and strode off, not without a hint of pride in her step, to the front of the house.

It was one of the oldest and largest in the settlement and curiously beautiful. Built of soft, mellow, hand-hewn stone, it was two storeys high and stood well back from the road. The gardens that surrounded the house were a testimony to Aaron's genius with plants. Even though it was autumn and the sun's heat was pitiless, the land was vibrant with colour and the air fragrant with the mingled scents of the varied flowers and shrubs. The Levinsons' house was on the very outskirts of the village and their garden was edged by several acres of olive and almond groves. Perched high on the hill, the view from the windows was magnificent and covered the entire region. Many years earlier the Levinsons had built a wide, shady veranda that ran all round the house. In the New Land it was a permanent reminder of Mr Levinson's native Rumania – and it had the advantage of keeping tolerably cool in the hottest part of the day. Today it was full of friends of Daniel's from the village, all of whom Sara had known since childhood, and who were looking forward eagerly to Daniel's return. They were a small, close-knit group and all worked for Aaron at his agricultural research station down on the plains, as well as doing their share for the communal vinery in Zichron. It was a hard existence, but a peaceful one, except when the Turkish authorities decided to make life difficult.

Among the men, Sara saw Lev Salaman. He was her brothers' contemporary, nearer thirty than twenty, and a boyhood companion of both Sam and Alex. Sara noticed once more how distressingly short his dark hair was cut and how earnest the set of his expression as he tried to engage Sara's father in conversation. He was a young man who took his duties in life seriously and loving Sara was one of them.

Abram Levinson seemed hardly to notice his daughter. He glanced quickly at her as she stepped on to the veranda and reached out a gently restraining hand as Lev started towards her. Sara noticed the gesture and was grateful for her father's intuition. Not Lev, not now, now of all times. Abram knocked his pipe into an ashtray and turning back to Lev resumed the discussion. Levinson was a grand old man of the village, one of its founders and a source of strength to all. He had the calm and contented air of a man who has lived an active and useful life, despite the unhappiness of his wife's sudden death.

Sara greeted the guests quickly, not wanting to get involved in more than a brief greeting. Ruth and Robby Woolf were standing close by, so involved with each other and oblivious to everyone around, that Sara, in her emotionally charged state, felt a twinge of envy.

Ruth had been her best friend ever since they had had desks next to each other at school. The other children had thought Sara stuck-up, but this was not true at all. Sara was reserved by nature which set her apart from others. Luckily, Ruth had instinctively understood this and walking to and from the school together they used to 'chatter like magpies' as Sara's mother would say. Since her mother's death Ruth had been Sara's only confidante, and she alone knew quite how much hope for the future Sara pinned on Daniel's return. Sara caught Ruth's eye and the two girls exchanged a conspiratorial glance.

Ruth was exquisitely tiny, just over five feet tall and her daintiness was exaggerated all the more next to her husband Robby. He was six feet two inches of hard muscle with strong masculine features – a large hooked nose and wide-set dark eyes with a hard flinty gleam – except when he was looking at his wife.

Only Manny Hirsh detained Sara for more than a moment. He shared her sense of heightened expectation and Sara felt the warmth of the unacknowledged bond between them. Manny, she knew, adored Daniel and was as excited as she was about his return – and he had the advantage of not having to suppress his greetings in front of his friends. Manny was small and wiry, the quintessence of pent-up energy and charm. Sara kissed him lightly on the forehead. He squeezed her arm in understanding and she skipped down the steps to walk to the end of the drive. She wanted to be the first to see Daniel arrive. She was too excited for small talk. She looked quickly over her shoulder and saw the group on the veranda with pleasure. The girls wore bright summer dresses, the men polished riding boots, breeches and loose white Prussian shirts with Arab kaffiyehs tied rakishly around their necks. It was a colourful blend of east and west that had evolved into a distinctive style.

Sara sat down on a low terrace wall at the end of the drive under a large green pepper tree. Through eyes half-closed against the glare of the sun she kept an eager watch for the first sign of Jezebel. From here she could see for miles over the entire region. The main road in front of her was no more than a dry, wheel-rutted track running down the mountain to the coastal plain of Sharron. The surrounding hillsides were rock-encrusted buttresses rising aggressively into the sky but which changed abruptly as they descended to a vista of endless vineyards that produced a robust red wine, famous throughout the Empire, and which had even won a gold medal in Paris. The rolling foothills were terraced, the precious earth shored up to keep it from washing down to the arid, swamp-infested plain which stretched like a scar to the sweep of the sea. From her vantage point she could even see as far as Atlit, its bay dominated by the ruins of the old crusader castle, and to the right of the bay Aaron's research station stood in its proud patch of green. The scene had a certain beauty and peace and gave out a comfortable aura of prosperity – not of great wealth but of solid ease and warmth. It was a land to love and Sara loved it passionately.

She was growing restless and, her eyes smarting in the harsh sunlight, she pulled the brim of her hat down to shade her face. They were late in coming and she searched the land below her again. Then she saw the little black motor car and heard the strained put-putting of its engine. Sara suddenly felt a little flicker of anxiety and self-consciousness. What might Daniel think seeing her standing waiting for him at the top of the drive, alone? All her courage suddenly deserted her and, gathering up her skirts in both hands, she fled back to house and the safety of the guests.

The little car swung into the lane, swept into the courtyard and came shuddering to a halt. Daniel sat in the front seat for a moment, looking through the smeared glass of the windscreen at the tableau in front of him.

He saw the Levinsons and all his old friends from Zichron standing on the lawn, looking expectantly towards him. Daniel stepped out of the car, but even then nothing seemed to move. He felt as if time had stopped and frozen this scene into a picture painted by one of his Paris friends. After four years away they all looked so different . . . and yet so familiar. For a moment Daniel felt as awkward as a stranger at a family gathering.

Sam, he noticed, had grown a few inches taller than his older brother Alex. Becky, who had been a little girl of twelve when he had left, was now a very pretty young lady and could almost be Sam's twin they looked so alike. Their chestnut hair was exactly the same rich shade and they were both looking towards him with the same impudent, humorous expression in their green eyes.

Alexander, too, had changed. The smooth look of youth had left his face and, with his blond hair and high colouring, he looked very like his brother Aaron – although without Aaron's air of

25

authority. He now looked the soldier Daniel remembered he had longed to be.

Daniel's eyes roamed over the scene. Where was Sara? He saw a blur of blue topped by thick blonde hair towards the back of the gathering: there she was, hanging back a little. Daniel felt deeply curious about what time had done to her.

Then the silence, which had seemed to last an eternity, but could only have been for a moment or two, was broken by Sultan, the farm dog, who suddenly recognised the new arrival and came barking across the lawn, his whole body twisting and writhing in welcome as he wagged his greying tail ecstatically. Then Manny came running across the lawn crying 'The boy-chick's back, the boy-chick's back!' and all at once everyone was around him shouting words of greeting. Robby Woolf was wringing his hand and Ruth was kissing him on the cheek. Lev Salaman's dark and gloomy face was for once cracked with a smile and Sam was hugging him with all his strength. Old man Levinson, who seemed to have shrunk a little without losing any of his gentle strength of character, was smiling in quiet welcome. Alex was thumping him on the back and Becky was hanging on to his arm as though she would never let go.

'I'm so glad you're back, Daniel, you can't imagine how we've all missed you,' she said, her voice shrill with excitement. And then a worried frown creased her forehead and she added more soberly: 'This time you're staying for always, aren't you Daniel?'

Daniel grabbed her under the arms and began to swing her around him as he had when she was a little girl. 'Always and for ever, monkey face,' he said, the laughter burbling up into his throat now that the spell was broken. 'Always and for ever.' And he whirled her round and round, Becky screamed half in delight and half in horror at the collapse of her carefully arranged grown-up appearance.

'I'm so giddy,' she laughed as he set her on her feet and collapsed, giggling on to the gravel.

How beautiful, how wonderful to be back, Daniel thought with a sense of relief. The desperate weariness that had haunted him over the past few months seemed to fall from him like a heavy cloak and he wondered what had kept him away from the land that was so much a part of him for so long.

Why hadn't Sara come forward to greet him?

As soon as her name came to his mind, she was in front of him,

26

even more beautiful than he remembered. She was no longer a child-woman, but was possessed of a new poise and confidence. Looking at her he felt that familiar feeling of awe. He kissed her on the cheek self-consciously.

'My God,' he said. 'What a beauty. Haven't you grown up.'

Sara blushed and hoped the great gush of love she felt for him wasn't obvious to everyone.

'Well,' she said lightly, 'you have been away four years.'

He smiled gently and looked around with satisfaction. 'Do you have any idea how wonderful it feels to be back here?'

'Do you have any idea how wonderful it is to have you here?' she said, and took him by the arm. 'Come,' she said, pulling herself together, 'I expect you will want to wash off the dust of travel.'

Manny pressed a cup of wine into Daniel's hand. 'Wash it from your throat as well,' he said with a grin.

Abu grabbed Daniel's luggage from the back of the car and Fatma, who had been alternately laughing and crying into her skirts, flapping around everyone in her robes like an immense black crow, took his carpet bag and led the way into the house.

Daniel stood at the window of his old room, overlooking the lawns in front of the house. After the hubbub of his welcome he wanted to spend a few moments on his own, taking stock. The buzz of his friends' conversation rose from the veranda below and made a happy background to his homecoming thoughts.

He had quickly abandoned his suit in favour of his old riding breeches, a bleached, colourless shirt, and calf-length brown boots. Perhaps it was the change back into these clothes, but already he felt better, physically stronger and harder as though his body as well as his soul was being nourished by the return to the land of his birth.

He picked up the mug and took a sip, revelling in the taste of the wine grown a few miles only from where he stood. How little things had changed in four years. The house still smelt of beeswax and he could even smell Miriam's lavender water. Poor Mama Levinson, how he wished he could have seen her again, and his thoughts turned guiltily to his own mother in Hadera. He knew he should really have gone to her first, but Aaron had told him that his two cousins, Ben and Josh, would meet him tomorrow at the research station and would ride shotgun with him on his way home.

27

It was not just the good things that had not changed, he reflected. A man travelling alone was still an attractive target for the warrior Bedouin tribes, to whom robbery was an honourable profession and the greatest heroes were the most daring thieves. He had hoped some order might have been instilled, but apparently the war between the Bedouin and the peaceful Arab and Jewish farmers whom they regarded as cowards raged as ferociously as ever.

So Daniel would have to be accompanied back to Hadera, where he would stay a few days before returning to start work for Aaron.

He sipped at the wine again. He doubted anyone would understand quite how much he was looking forward to riding across the parched scrubland and working under a sun so violent that it dried up the blood, purifying the men who worked long, hard hours under it. It was a clean, pure heat, as clean and pure as his friends in the garden. He had learned a lot in Paris and had made many good friends, but none of them had the refreshing simplicity and faith that made these people so special to him.

A sudden joy flooded through him as memories of all the best moments of his life here rushed to his brain. *It's all just beginning*, he said to himself, finishing the wine in a gulp. *It's only just beginning.*

During the course of the meal the conversation inevitably turned to the research station.

'What do you think of it?' Daniel asked Sara. 'It's an amazing achievement. You must be proud of your brother,' he went on, looking down at her with his usual directness. She had not forgotten his gaze which, after four years' absence, still tightened her heart and shortened her breath.

'Aaron loves it,' she answered, looking fondly at her brother, who was draining a glass of wine. 'He spends so much time down there I half expect him to come home with a spot of greenfly himself.' Aaron, overhearing, joined in their laughter.

'This land has always flourished under the Jew and turned to stone and dust under the conqueror.' He made the comment in semi-jest but Daniel took it literally and his brow darkened. Lev Salaman followed his train of thought.

'Stones and dust – that's exactly what we will be eating if the Turk goes to war,' Lev muttered to anyone who would listen.

'Oh no! Not fig tea again – I couldn't bear it!' interrupted Ruth, patting the thick braids of her hair coiled twice around her head. They all laughed, remembering the difficult times of their childhood when there was little food and there were no luxuries.

'Don't you worry,' said Robby, drawing his adored wife towards him. 'The Turk has everything to lose and nothing to win: even Enver Pasha can't be stupid enough to get caught up in a war.'

'I for one don't underestimate Enver Pasha's appetite for power,' Daniel interjected drily. Enver Pasha, the Ottoman Minister for War, was one of the three men who had ruled supreme since the young Turks' rebellion five years before. 'Our debonair champion of freedom has grown into an all-powerful military dictator,' he added bitterly.

The men's faces brightened and the women's dropped as talk turned to war. Sara, hoping to make the point that the women just weren't interested, took her glass of wine and headed towards the shade of a eucalyptus. Abu had spread colourful rugs and cushions around the foot of the tree and Sara settled herself comfortably in a spot from where she could see but not hear the men debating.

'Oh Daniel, am I? Do you really think so?' Becky's voice floated over to Sara. She was chattering eagerly to Daniel, her eyes shining with passionate admiration as she plied all the tricks of the flirt.

'Let him come to me,' Sara thought perversely, and lay back on the rug, her arms cushioning her head: a picture of perfect tranquillity. Daniel drifted over to her and Sara felt her heart give its customary lurch.

'This is the life,' he said, lounging next to her on the rug. 'I can't understand why I stayed away so long.'

Sara propped her head up with her hand, resting on her elbow. 'Tell me about France,' she demanded. 'Was Paris fun?'

Daniel smiled. 'Cold, wet and terribly dull.'

She made a face and laughed. 'You're teasing me.'

Daniel nodded and laughed with her. 'Of course I am. But tell me about you – what are you doing with your life?'

'The same as always – looking after the house, the family . . .' she tailed off with a shrug. She didn't want to talk about herself. 'Nothing important really.'

'Still reading those novellas you used to be so fond of?' he asked, smiling down at her.

'You're teasing me again!' she said reproachfully, looking so serious that Daniel could not help but laugh at her.

'Still the same Sara!'

'Still the same Sara,' she agreed, leaning towards him slightly. She longed to touch him but confined herself to picking some grass from his shirt. 'Really, tell me about Paris,' she urged. She didn't want him to stop talking and felt as though she could listen to his voice for ever.

'Paris is wonderful – modern, busy, very exciting. Mind you I was hungry most of the time and broke for all of it,' Daniel launched into a description of life abroad, telling her of the paintings he had seen, some old masters, some by artist friends he made during his stay. 'There was one by Renoir that I particularly liked,' he wound up. 'Every time I looked at it I was reminded of you.' He stopped and looked at her for a long moment. He tried to draw away but could not break his eyes from hers.

Sara saw such love in that heart-stopping stare that she ached. 'I'm glad you thought of me sometimes,' she said softly. 'I was beginning to think that you were never coming back.' But as she spoke an odd expression came into Daniel's eyes, she saw them harden and become cold. In one easy movement he rose to his feet, effectively breaking the spell. Sara was left looking up at him, shocked by the sudden change.

'Well, here I am, and here I'm going to stay,' he said lightly without really knowing what he was saying, but simply obeying an impulse to put distance between them.

Becky ran up to them burbling happy nonsense. Sara could have killed her, but Daniel blessed her for interrupting them. *I've been here only a few hours and the sacrificing has begun* he thought, with a flash of intermingled pride and self-pity.

Sara watched thoughtfully as Daniel's tall, lean figure made its way back to the veranda. She realised she was going to have to make some plans. In a moment Ruth was beside her and had thrown herself down on the rug, questioning her excitedly.

'To tell you the truth,' said Sara, 'he's still as much as mystery to me as darkest Africa. Mind you he did say he had thought of me sometimes,' she added, turning happily to Ruth. 'And tomorrow I plan to give myself a day off and ride down to the research station with them. I have a feeling that Daniel Rosen is going to need a little encouragement.'

'A huge push, more like,' said Ruth, and both girls collapsed in helpless laughter.

CHAPTER TWO

'Wake up, sleepy-head!' Sara wriggled her feet and at last opened her eyes to see her sister bent over her and squeezing her toes. A second later she was wide awake.

'What time is it?' she asked, sitting bolt upright. She and Daniel had sat up very late the night before, talking about everything that had happened to them in the last four years. It was not until the first signs of dawn showed over the horizon that they had at last given each other a peck on the cheek and had made their ways to bed.

'Nine o'clock – Daniel and Aaron have had breakfast and left for Atlit.' Sara leapt from bed and ran to the window, her heart in her mouth. 'Only joking,' Becky added, making for the door before her sister could catch her. 'It's seven and Daniel's waiting in the kitchen.' She banged the door behind her, leaving Sara to get ready in a panic.

Seven o'clock! In spite of her late night she couldn't believe she had slept so late, and she washed and dressed as fast as she could, although not without carefully checking her appearance.

Sara reached the courtyard and found Abu and Daniel tightening the horses' girths.

'Good morning, Abu,' she said. 'Good morning, Daniel,' and she gave him a sisterly pat on the cheek.

'You look wonderful,' he said admiringly and led her Arab mare to the mounting block for her. Sara patted Bella's neck and sprang gracefully on to her back. 'Thank you.' She smiled, 'You're not looking too bad yourself.'

She was not flattering him. Dressed in local clothes and with his skin already slightly darkened by a day in the sun, he bore little resemblance to the pale sophisticate who had stepped out of the car only the day before.

'Where's Aaron?' Sara asked.

'He went on an hour ago by car,' Daniel answered and Sara felt a surge of happiness at this unexpected bonus.

Daniel mounted the chestnut Aaron had lent him for his journey to Hadera and together they set out down the road to the research station.

The countryside had never looked as beautiful to Sara as it did that morning. The early morning air was unusually crisp and clear and on the slopes the men and women bending to pick grapes gave the scene a feeling of unreality, like an almost too perfect watercolour. Dotted along the roadside were huge wicker baskets, already full of juicy purple grapes, and the horses picked their way delicately between them.

A handful of men from the village walked past, shouting greetings to Daniel and whistling playfully at Sara. She lowered her eyes so that Daniel would not see the gleam of pleasure in them; the sooner he realised how men admired her the better. With a little laugh she spurred Bella on ahead and let Daniel catch her up.

Forty minutes later they reached the main Haifa to Jaffa road. Sara had deliberately skirted the research station and taken the slightly longer route.

'I know it's silly but I want you to ride in through the main entrance the first time. It's the best way to see it,' she explained.

Now, as they reached the main gates, they reined in in front of a large sign, which Daniel read aloud, 'The Jewish Agricultural Research Station. Managing Director Aaron Levinson.'

'You've said it!' Sara urged Bella down the long, Tarmac drive lined with double rows of tall, slender Washington palms. 'Now get your passport ready – we're entering America!' They both laughed at the ludicrous situation.

Years before, when he was still in power, Sultan Abdul Hamid had been forced to pass a law that said that properties or nationals of another country remained under the jurisdiction of their own government for an indefinite period of time. When the Young Turks snatched power from the Sultan they did not rescind the law and so the research station, bought by Jewish-American sponsors, remained as American as Manhattan and as immune to Ottoman law as Philadelphia.

As they crested the small hill Sara and Daniel saw a two-storey building and, close by, a windmill, some barns, and a fine stableyard. On all sides the buildings were surrounded by huge fields of wheat and corn, orchards of fruit and nut trees, and even fields of cotton. Daniel paused for a moment on the edge of a wheat field.

'*Triticum hermonis*,' he said, turning to Sara with a smile. She nodded proudly.

'Aaron's baby,' she replied. The wild emener wheat was Aaron's discovery. For years there had been a world-wide search for this wheat in its ancient form. The cereal cultivated since the dawn of civilisation had degenerated, becoming susceptible to climate and disease, and so the hope was that if the original wheat could be found and crossed with a modern strain it would produce a hardier species. Aaron had discovered the ancient wheat seven years earlier along the slopes of Mount Hermon and it had made his name world famous.

Sara and Daniel went to the stable-yard where they dismounted and handed their horses to a helper.

'His study's on the upper floor. And he'll be somewhere behind all the paper,' Sara said and settled down for a long chat with Frieda, the Hungarian cook.

Aaron's office was a study in organised chaos. It took up at least half of the upper floor and two of the four walls were lined with books. Through the open windows came a fresh smell of grain and sea.

Aaron was at his desk, just visible behind the agricultural pamphlets piled high on the worktables all around him. Printed in the five main languages of the area – Hebrew, Arabic, English, French and Turkish (all of which the Levinsons spoke fluently) – the pamphlets and scientific journals were sent to Aaron from universities all over the world. In contrast with the mess everywhere else, Aaron's own desk was pin-neat.

Aaron jumped up as Daniel came into the room.

'Are you ready for a tour of the most unique establishment in the entire history of Palestinian agriculture?' he asked with a broad smile.

Daniel laughed. 'Lead the way, big head.'

'Right! Let's start in the labs. They should get your agronomists' juices on the run,' Aaron said, ushering Daniel out of the study. Happy knowing that their friendship had survived the four-year gap intact, the two men went in to the laboratory happily discussing *phanerogamic herbaria*.

*   *   *

Daniel stood on the flanks of a hillock, his back to the stone building, looking out over the fertile fields Aaron had coaxed out of the arid land. He was still under the spell of the tour of the station, and he needed a pause as he looked towards the blue of the Mediterranean to collect his spinning thoughts.

The research station was unique in the Middle East. Daniel had, of course, been kept informed of developments by letter, but it was not until he had seen the station that he fully appreciated the enormity of Aaron's achievement, and the great significance of what he had done for the economic development of Palestine. In only four years Aaron and his team had created five different species of wheat and barley that showed strong powers of resistance to the diseases that had until now ravaged the cereal crops in Palestine. One species was particularly rich in gluten which made it especially suitable for making pasta – 'and you know how we Jews like our lockshen', Aaron had said with a wink.

As well as working on cereal crops Aaron had succeeded in acclimatizing a table grape that ripened three weeks earlier than any grape grown in Cyprus or any other neighbouring country. Those vital three weeks meant that this year Palestine had succeeded in cornering the valuable Egyptian market in grapes and had already made an impressive economic impact.

The grapes, the wheat and a great deal more had all been grown on just over a hundred acres of land widely known for its sterility. Aaron, 'obstinate as usual', as his brothers and sisters teased him, had specifically chosen the site to prove that there was no such thing as 'used-up' soil. His Arab labourers, most of whom had worked alongside him for years, were convinced that 'Sheitan' (The Devil, which was their affectionate Turkish nickname for him) had finally gone mad. Allah must have mixed sheep's urine into his brain, they muttered among themselves. But they had set willingly to work on the sand dunes and malarial marsh, directed by Aaron and a few of his devoted disciples. And it had worked. He was indeed a devil. Daniel stood bounded on all sides by an area so green and fertile that it might have been the Garden of Eden, not a patch of desert and swamp. And it had not been done with fertilisers and endless tanks of water but by dry farming techniques. A secret, Aaron maintained, known up to now only to the Biblical cultivators of the region. His friends in the US Department of Agriculture and the members of Aaron's sponsoring committee in America were delighted with the results.

The American sponsorship had not been entirely altruistic: Aaron's experiments, if successful, would prove useful in their own land. The techniques with which Aaron brought fertility to Palestine would be used on the vast and arid deserts 'back home'.

Just think what could be done if Palestine were ours, Daniel thought feverishly. It was a rich country, Aaron had shown that, but ruled by weak and foolish people who had squandered its wealth through either stupidity or greed. The must rid themselves of the Turk.

'Well, Aaron,' he said at last, turning to look at his friend with a grin. 'Even you can't improve on that,' and he waved his hand at the blue sweep of sea.

'Don't you bet on it,' Aaron laughed, and the two men strolled back down a path shaded with apple and fig trees.

They rounded a corner between the greenhouses and suddenly saw Sara, standing in the milky-green light of an enormous pine tree. Cushions and rugs were spread at her feet and a white cloth covered with tempting-looking baskets and jugs was laid out on the ground. She was beckoning them over.

'It looks as though we're being invited to a picnic,' said Aaron. 'But I'm afraid you're on your own – I have a few things to discuss with the men over lunch.'

Sara watched Aaron shake Daniel's hand and walk away, and was thrilled by the success of her scheme. Although she had ingeniously provided enough for three and carefully laid out three glasses, she had banked on Aaron having to eat with the men.

Her face an expression of smiling innocence, she went forward to meet Daniel.

'Where's Aaron going?' she asked, leading him forward to the shade of the tree and dropping to her knees on the rug. 'I especially arranged this picnic for us,' she pouted prettily. 'Don't you think it's nicer than being inside?'

'Oh, much nicer,' he agreed, smiling, but scrutinising her face closely; he suspected that she had arranged to be alone with him.

He cleared his throat. 'Have you seen Ben and Josh yet?' They were the Shushan cousins who were to accompany him back to Hadera, and Sara was surprised to hear a note of anxiety in his voice as he moved restlessly from one foot to the other.

'No,' Sara looked up at him, wondering what on earth was making him so nervous. 'But I wouldn't worry – it's still early and don't forget it's harvest time. Daniel – how long are you going to stand there? Sit down, do.'

He sat down opposite her, his arms around his drawn-up knees. 'I'm still in a daze after the tour, I'm afraid. To tell the truth I just didn't imagine it would be so – well, so *grand*.'

Sara laughed, her face suddenly aglow with pride. 'I don't think any of us did – except, of course, Aaron. Nothing he sets out to do is anything but.' She poured them both some wine and raised her mug. 'To the vine,' she said and they clinked mugs in a toast. Then Sara opened up the baskets and set about arranging the feast.

'All my favourite things,' said Daniel, greedily watching as she put out a bowl of humous and *tehrina* dribbling with olive oil. Sara handed him a pitta bread, still warm from the oven.

'We might as well tuck in,' she said, dipping a piece of the bread into the thick chickpea mixture.

She looked up and saw him watching her. For a moment their eyes met, and then as if by some optical trick she saw right through him. *He's falling in love with me*, she thought, *and he doesn't want to*. The idea was so surprising and so sudden that she quickly pushed it out of her mind.

They did not talk much while they ate; both were hungry after their ride and Sara had missed breakfast. But their silence was the companionable silence of old friends, and both felt happy under the tree. Daniel watched Sara surreptitiously as she ate. The sunlight shone through the leaves, casting dappled shadows on her face and throat. For the first time Daniel had the quite ridiculous wish to be a painter like his friends in Paris so that he could keep this picture always.

Sara felt Daniel watching her and bit delicately into an apricot, wondering where they could go that was less public. She took a quick look round; under another pine tree an Arab was leaning on his spade – why wasn't he at lunch like everyone else? Irritated, Sara felt that everyone was conspiring against her plans.

Daniel was chatting lightly about his tour of the research station, but Sara was not listening. An idea came to her. Standing up, she gave a shout of laughter and ran off, heading in the direction of the stables. Daniel gazed after her in astonishment, but in a moment was by her side.

Bella was grazing beneath the trailing branches of a huge eucalyptus tree, and for a moment Sara talked to her, patting the powerful neck and treating her with a sugar lump from a hidden pocket. Then, narrowing her eyes for a moment she vaulted swiftly and easily on to the mare's unsaddled back.

'Race you to the fortress,' she shouted at Daniel and galloped off down the palm tree avenue which led to the beach.

'After all that lunch?' he laughed, but he had no intention of ignoring the challenge. As quick as she, he leaped on to Aaron's chestnut gelding and rode hard after her. Riding was one of Sara's greatest joys and she was fast and fearless with a firm hand.

With Daniel still just behind, they crossed the coastal road, giving the horses full rein. Sara's mare was fresh after her rest and, always light on her feet, she kept the lead over the sand. Sara's hair had worked free and flew out behind her, stray ends whipping her cheeks. Atlit's ruined fortress loomed up ahead of them, stark and forbidding against the curve of the bay. Sara reached it first and, jumping to the ground, ran into the shaded interior, her breath coming in quick gasps.

Moments later Daniel followed, but he paused in the archway, his eyes accustoming themselves to the dim light. Sara peered out from her hiding place, waiting to see what he would do. Her heart was beating quickly, and not just from the chase. Daniel moved forward cautiously, sure there was a trap but unaware what form it would take. Suddenly, like a whirlwind, Sara was in his arms, laughing deep in her throat, a husky breathless sound. She looked so beautiful in the thick gloom that he thought his heart might break.

'You witch,' Daniel said softly, and for a moment they stood staring hungrily at each other. Then Sara swayed towards him, her eyes closing. Daniel's arms tightened around her waist, drawing her to him. She arched her head back to meet his mouth and raised her arms around him. Daniel's last traces of restraint vanished. He was as lost as she as her mouth opened to receive his kiss. It was several moments before he released her. As she drew back and opened her eyes Sara saw him looking at her with faint surprise.

She wished he would say something – tell her that he loved her – and waited in silence, watching him. She began to feel a little less sure of him again, he was looking at her closely but from the expression on his face he might never have kissed her. After what seemed like a eternity, he kissed her cheek.

'Ben and Josh will be waiting for me; we want to get to Hadera before nightfall.' They stood and stared at each other for a moment and then Daniel led the way out into the sunlight.

They rode back to the station in silence at a slow walk, Sara feeling confused and vaguely cheated – of what she wasn't really sure.

When they neared the courtyard the sounds of Goliath the research station dog's barking and people shouting made it quite clear that Ben and Josh had arrived. Daniel spurred his horse forward and clattered into the yard to see from the excitement on the men's faces that something important had happened. *It's war*, he said to himself, and he felt suddenly breathless at the idea. *War!*

'There you are,' Ben shouted, hurrying across to Daniel. 'Where the hell have you been?'

Daniel ignored the question and flung himself off his horse.

'What's happened?' he asked, searching the faces around him. Ben was red with excitement.

'Germany has declared war on Russia!'

'When?'

'Yesterday.'

'And Turkey?'

'General mobilisation.'

Daniel let out a jubilant shout.

'Don't get your hopes up, Daniel,' said Aaron, practical as usual. 'Mobilisation does not mean war, whatever the European generals may think.'

'No, of course not,' Daniel felt drunk with enthusiasm. 'But it's a beginning.' He wanted to scream and shout, to yell out that at last a new era was beginning for them all. All thoughts of Sara were pushed to the back of his mind, if not abandoned completely, and he mounted Aaron's gelding in seconds.

'I'll be back in two days,' he promised and, hardly waiting for Ben and Josh to remount, he set off at a tearing pace, his horse's hooves throwing up gravel and dust behind them.

Sara watched him disappearing, and it seemed to her as if he was riding off to war. She was suddenly aware that the war – and all it stood for – would be her chief rival. She had seen the look in his eyes when he heard the news; never before had she seen such a glow in anyone's face. She half understood now why he was fighting against loving her, but was still determined that that was one battle he would lose. She felt an icy cold creep over her and she shivered in spite of the heat. For the first time the prospect of war seemed real and close, and she realised the intrusion it would make into her secure and happy life, into all their lives.

Aaron had not noticed Sara in the general commotion, but he now saw her sitting pale and dishevelled on Bella. He went up to her and helped her dismount, giving her a big hug as she reached the ground.

'It doesn't necessarily mean that Turkey will enter the war,' he said gently, trying to calm her. To his surprise as well as her own she burst into tears.

'I hate all this talk of war,' she spluttered between sobs.

Aaron soothed her, holding her tightly against him, but she was not crying because of the threat of war; she was crying because, less than fifteen minutes after kissing her, Daniel Rosen could so completely forget her. Her sobs subsided and she gritted her teeth. *Damn him*, she thought, *damn all men and all their shallow masculine pretensions*. Quietened, she leaned into Aaron's shoulder and through narrowed eyes watched Daniel disappearing from view.

Well, Daniel Rosen, she said to herself as, with a watery smile, she disengaged herself from her brother's arms, *if you think war is going to make a scrap of difference as to whether or not you marry me, you're mistaken. Wholly mistaken.*

CHAPTER THREE

Constantinople

Abdul Hamid II, deposed Sultan of the Sultans, Commander of the Faithful, Lord of Two Seas and God's Shadow on Earth, stood peering through a delicately-latticed window into the grounds of the Beylerbey Palace. His long pale face was bathed in melancholy as he contemplated his kismet, the will of Allah no man can strive against. Try as he might he could not blind his eyes or blur his vision to ignore the heavy bars on the other side of the lattice work. Once a ruler feared and obeyed throughout a vast Empire he was now as powerless as a rabbit.

His gaolers certainly allowed for his whims. By his own command Abdul Hamid only occupied rooms that faced the Aegean shore, thus sparing himself the constant mental torture of the sight of the gilded cupolas and gently rocking cypresses of his former home, the Topkapi Palace. His former home – his former life.

Footsteps of the soldiers who were now his guards floated up from the courtyard below. What use was luxury without power, he thought angrily and vented his frustration by banging his fist on the window casement. He slammed his fist down again and a small piece of the majolica, which encrusted the walls of the reception room within the harem, crumbled and fell to the floor in a small heap of brightly glowing dust.

'Dust to dust – like my Empire,' he muttered and turned sadly into the room.

The Sultan was bored. Deeply and terrifyingly bored. For thirty-three years he had ruled the Ottoman Empire with an iron fist. Now he ruled a few servants and a handful of women and gradually, even they, like his Empire, like his 'loaned' Palace, were crumbling away. Even Selena, the Armenian concubine who had so faithfully followed him into exile and back again to Constantinople, would soon be gone.

40

If anyone deserved freedom, it was Selena. Abdul Hamid was the first to admit that. But her very departure was another example of his powerlessness. The women of the harem were no longer Abdul Hamid's slaves. If they asked permission to leave, he was duty bound to grant it.

Clasping his hands behind his back, the ex-Sultan paused and contemplated his reflection.

He was seventy-one years old. His beard, by nature grey, had that morning been retinted black by his favourite wife, Mûzvicka. He knew the dye made him look paler than ever but, as he constantly reminded himself, a Sultan — even an ex-Sultan — should give the illusion of immortality. He turned his mind back to the present and the German Major who was to visit him this evening. Hans Werner Rilke remained one of the few men that he had kept up acquaintanceship with and was the only European he was still allowed to receive. Doubtless everything — their conversation, his health, his state of mind — would be reported back to the Triumvirate, the German High Command, and then on to Kaiser Wilhelm. Abdul Hamid's thoughts turned to the impending war and he allowed himself to dream. If that vain dog, Enver Pasha, were to draw his Empire into the war, it would surely be on the side of the Germans. After all, they could hardly take up arms against their old allies and tutors. Perhaps it might just be possible that at the end of hostilities his old friend Kaiser Wilhelm would have him reinstated. Perhaps. He had no doubt that were Germany to win she would take all the Empire's provinces, vast domains that stretched from the Caucasus to the Persian Gulf, from the deserts of Mesopotamia to the Nile, but that would still leave him with Turkey.

He forced himself to stop this train of thought. He was a man with dreams, but above that he had been born an Emperor and his duty was above all to his Empire. He had no power, but the Triumvirate must in some measure appreciate the experience of his long reign, and he must somehow try and make the three rulers see the dangers of entering the war. He had been informed that Jemel Pasha and Taalat Bey were fiercely opposed to an alliance with the Germans but he suspected that the fiery Enver Pasha was hell-bent on a pact. Major Rilke, a true German but with sympathy and friendship for Abdul Hamid, might well be the channel through which he could communicate his views.

*   *   *

Selena's apartments were in a state of complete chaos. The harem, normally so neat and elegant, was at sixes and sevens. The ebony doors, extravagantly inlaid with mother of pearl, which led into Selena's rooms, stood wide open and through them the servants and pampered concubines of the diminishing harem trotted busily back and forth, giggling. That morning Abdul Hamid had ceremoniously presented Selena with the papers necessary for her life outside the Palace, and with a leather purse containing fifty, softly-chinking gold Turkish pounds. Since then she had not had a moment to herself. Perhaps that was just as well, she thought. For a second she drew back and stood, partly hidden, behind a curtain, and watched the scurrying that was happening all around – and all for her.

Her emotions were mixed as she watched the scene. For so many years these women had been her companions and her friends. And now they were all rejoicing in her good fortune and joy. Any one of them could leave, but Selena was one of the youngest and most of the older women preferred to stay in the luxurious prison rather than to face the unknown 'real' world.

Now, for the first time, she felt fear. Abdul Hamid had assured her she would be looked after – but for how long? She was saddened at the thought of her master. He had always been so kind to her, gentle and understanding. After Selena had made the decision to leave the harem, Abdul Hamid had generously offered to help her secure a good position elsewhere.

It was some months before he came up with one for her to consider: secretary to Annie Lufti, an American heiress and widow of a Turkish officer who had been killed in the Balkan War. She ran one of the best salons in Constantinople and the élite of the town fought to be accepted by her. Her reputation remained unblemished despite the string of spirited and brilliant young men that passed through her doors. Major Rilke, a close friend of Mrs Lufti's, had suggested the arrangement and Abdul Hamid knew enough about Annie Lufti to be able to rest easy on Selena's behalf.

Selena had agreed as soon as the job was suggested to her by 'Baba' Hamid. He had given a small, resigned shrug, then smiled at her with obvious fondness and told her that he planned to place her under the protection of a friend of his, the German Major Rilke. He had pointed out to her the advantages of Rilke's having a foot in both camps.

42

Rilke was due to visit the Palace in a few hours' time. If all went well, she would be leaving with the Major that very evening.

Selena instinctively trusted the Major. She had often seen him at the Palace, although she was always heavily veiled and kept her distance. Most important of all, he too was a Christian and so there was no danger of his selling her to the slave traders.

Even Selena, who was far more intelligent than most of the women in the harem, found it hard to take in the momentous changes in the world since she had entered the harem. It seemed almost impossible to believe that seven years after her enforced entry into the harem she was leaving it a free woman.

A wave of exhaustion overcame Selena and she slumped on to a cushion in one corner of her dismantled rooms. She realised that she was holding in her hands the very jacket she had worn all those years before on her arrival at the harem. Turning the richly embroidered brocade over in her white hands she fell to dreaming of things far removed from what should have been occupying her mind.

Selena, aged fifteen, was walking to the American Mission School in her native American village when she was spotted by slave traders with a licence as purveyors to the Imperial Harem. Even at that age Selena was a rare beauty and, although brought up to behave modestly, was used to being crudely ogled. She was not used to what happened next. The man so openly assessing her qualities saw in Selena a face and body worthy of the Sultan's bed. He swooped down on her and, before she even had a chance to scream, bundled her into his closed carriage and bore her off to his home. There, drugged but unviolated, she was to pass the days until her fate was decided.

Her companion in those opium-dazed days was another Armenian girl, slightly older than she and infinitely more knowledgeable about the ways of the world. She had been kidnapped three weeks earlier in much the same way as Selena and was more than grateful for a friend in her captivity. In whispers she told Selena her probable fate and the two girls wept, clinging to each other in the dark. Selena had often heard of the slave-catchers – who hadn't? – but it was Okra who told her just where the girls who occasionally vanished from the mountain villages ended up.

'You're lucky,' Okra whispered. 'I think you are destined for the

Imperial harem. It's the Sultan's birthday next month and I've heard say that you are to be presented to him as a gift. It is a great honour.'

Okra's voice sounded wistful in the half dark but Selena could not comprehend the idea of herself as a *present*, or that it should be an honour to be a concubine. 'And you?' Selena asked desperately.

'I think they're sending me to a merchant in Constantinople but I don't know.' Weeping again, the two girls tried to draw comfort from each other's presence.

After two weeks Selena was dressed in embroidered brocades and sumptuous silks and satins, given another dose of opium, and shipped off to Constantinople.

She was still half-drugged as the carriage stopped just outside the Gates of Felicity at the Topkapi Palace. The door of the carriage opened and Selena shrank involuntarily from the sight of the monstrously fat black man staring sternly down at her. She was pinched and pushed from the rear, and pain alone forced her to descend from the carriage. The man took a waddling step towards her.

'I am Kislar Agha. His Excellency the Sultan Abdul Hamid – God's Shadow on Earth – has seen fit in his goodness to appoint me his chief eunuch.' The man's voice, though soft and high, was exquisitely courteous, but nothing could quell Selena's spiralling fear. Kislar Agha's towering frame was draped in an ermine-edged pelisse. An enormous turban quivering with brilliant flamingo plumes added inches to his height. Selena looked past him to the gates and knew she was at the point of no return. Once through those so-called Gates of Felicity she would spend the rest of her days in the jealousy-guarded Imperial harem. Only God could free her, and only by death.

Struck by the horror of her fate and exhausted from the drugs and the journey, Selena fainted into the eunuch's voluminous embrace.

She came round to see the loveliest pair of blue eyes looking into her own. With a sinking feeling she realised it was now too late – she was in the harem. As she was about to black out again she heard a low, sweet voice soothing her, and felt strong dark coffee being pressed to her lips. The woman urged Selena to drink and introduced herself as Mûzvicka Sultane, a name Selena quickly came to recognise as that of the Sultan's favourite wife. Kislar

44

Agha had told Mûzvicka that he thought the new odalisque had spoken a few words of English before collapsing and she, eager as always to be of assistance to her much loved royal master, had rushed to find out if this was true. It was a lucky chance for Selena. It was thanks to this Georgian beauty that the first few months of harem life were made bearable for her.

Mûzvicka Sultane, the long reigning royal favourite, had nothing to fear from this new girl. Burdened with worry and affairs of state, the sixty-five-year-old Sultan's waning physical energies were devoted to keeping his crumbling Empire together. Political events disturbed even the most sanguine people that summer in 1908. Britain's Edward VII had signed a friendship treaty with his nephew Tsar Nicholas II of Russia, one stroke of a pen bringing together Turkey's old enemy and the world's greatest power.

Rumour running rife within the Empire was even more disquieting. The recent activities of a group of disgruntled army officers calling themselves the Young Turks had come to the Sultan's attention, as had the secret political organisation, known as the Committee of Union and Progress, which backed them. In spite of the Sultan's 20,000 strong army of spies and informers he could not discover the identity of the men leading and preaching this new brand of Nationalism and fanning the flames of revolt.

So the Sultan had no time to take much interest in bejewelled, voluptuous beauties who swelled the Imperial harem. And Mûzvicka Sultane had another strength: she knew that Abdul Hamid was touchingly faithful and still passionately in love with the peasant girl who had become one of his four legal wives. She returned his love with equal ardour.

When Mûzvicka Sultane became aware of the sharp intelligence and superior education of the 'Nasrani' Christian girl, she realised how valuable the concubine would become to her beloved master. The Sultan trusted women more than he did men and instructed the more intelligent members of his harem to carry out his secretarial duties.

With all this in mind, Mûzvicka had helped nurse Selena out of her early misery. When she would not eat Mûzvicka sat on her bed feeding her spoons of milk and honey-sweetened rice. Most importantly, she kept the eunuchs, who were on the whole full of bitterness at their fate, at bay.

It was not long before Selena emerged from her swollen-eyed grief and, as the months passed, she gradually recovered her spirits. Some days she still lay reminiscing about the flat-roofed houses of her mountain-village home. She missed the American Mission School where she had been the star pupil but her mother, father and brothers had all died in a typhoid epidemic the year before her kidnap and an old great aunt had taken her in. So, although Selena had felt fond of her aunt, it was for her friends at the mission, for the way things had once been for which she wept.

Her common sense resurfaced after a while. Selena was blessed with a happy disposition and a practical nature: it was this, coupled with her natural intelligence that helped her cope with her problems. She realised immediately that escape was not feasible so as she recovered she tried not to dwell too much on the past. None of the other odalisques seemed to have any memories and Selena began to understand why the women of the harem seemed to adapt so ably to their existence. After all, if your home, family, husband, children were all taken from you there were only three choices – suicide, madness or adjustment.

Selena determined to make the best of her new life. She began to notice, observe and finally absorb the people around her. Awed at first by the extravagant splendour of the women's quarters, where even the dustpans were made of solid gold, she soon came to realise that life in the Imperial harem was in a sense not so different from that at school – and a great deal more comfortable.

Only a very few of the eight hundred or so odalisques had ever been called to the Imperial bed (and in recent years none but Mûzvicka), so Selena's fears of lying with a man outside marriage soon subsided.

At this time Mûzvicka, confident that the Christian girl had settled in, ordered the attendants to make Selena presentable for his majesty. She was bathed twice a day, massaged with scented oils and had her hair brushed to a satin sheen. Her missionary education was abandoned for a more sensuous training. Every day she was given lessons in the theory of giving pleasure to men in the unlikely event that her royal master would one day call her.

Once she was deemed presentable, Selena joined the ranks of perfumed and pampered harem beauties. Holding herself in the prescribed court pose, hands across her breast, Selena stood next to Mûzvicka as the Sultan passed among them. When he reached Mûzvicka, she gave an almost imperceptible nod and, as he moved in front of Selena, he dropped an embroidered 'kerchief at her tiny hennaed feet. A ripple of surprise followed, for this meant that

Selena had been chosen for his favour that night. Selena was 'in the eye', but not in the way the others imagined. Nevertheless, the rituals were kept to.

After the Sultan retired, Selena was taken to be massaged, shampooed and perfumed by the keeper of the baths. Next she was 'dressed' by the keeper of the lingerie and finally led, with great ceremony, to the Sultan's bed by the chief black eunuch. Selena stood trembling at the foot of Abdul Hamid's bed. This was the great moment when the charade would end.

But Abdul Hamid lay motionless under the silk, watching her closely through his black eyes. Shaking badly now, Selena lifted the coverlet at the bottom of the bed, and kissing it humbly, praying that she had not been duped, crept timidly up the bed until she was face to face with him.

To her amazement and great relief he had given one of his rare, illuminating smiles and, holding a finger to his lips to silence her, his Imperial Majesty slid from the bed fully clothed and checked the doors were securely locked.

He returned to the bed with a pile of newspapers and despatches in German and English. All night long she translated them into Turkish for him. She soon realised that this was the only way the Sultan, surrounded by sycophants who feared his displeasure, could glean the truth.

For months they kept up the same ritual pretence, and Selena became his confidante. By day she opened all his letters and petitions, by night she translated documents.

But then the unthinkable happened: the Young Turks seized power and Abdul Hamid was deposed. His weak brother Rashid ascended the throne under the name of Mohammed V, from where, manipulated like a puppet by the Young Turks, he ruled. The New National Assembly took upon itself the personal security of the Sultan and his family.

Selena was among the women who chose to follow him into exile, but she was no longer a slave or concubine, she was now his salaried personal secretary. She thought she would never want to leave him.

Selena rose from her reverie at the sound of her old slave coming in with the coffee. She carefully packed the jacket which had sparked off so many memories and waited as she watched the slave pour coffee into a delicate jade cup and put a gold spoon into a little dish of rose-leaf jam. Then the women gathered round, breaking into tears, until only Mûzvicka was left dry-eyed, supporting Selena with a firm hand on her arm, until she had a moment to herself. Finally, Mûzvicka succeeded in leading Selena aside to a quiet corner where, taking her protégée's hand, she pressed something cold and hard into it. Selena looked down and saw an emerald as large as a pigeon's egg nestling in her palm.

She drew Mûzvicka's hand up to her face and kissed it gratefully.

'It is most exquisite,' she said softly. 'Thank you.' Then, looking down at the emerald, 'How did you manage to hide it?'

'Women are always cunning where their men and their jewels are concerned, little one,' Mûzvicka replied, smiling down into her friend's eyes. 'Remember that.'

Selena carefully wrapped the emerald in a silk 'kerchief and laid it with the Sultan's gold and her hoarded wages, which she hoped would ease her passage into the outside world.

'I love you, Mûzvicka,' Selena spoke in a whisper. 'It is because of your kindness and noble heart that I am able to leave here today. I shall think of you and pray for you daily. You – and the Sultan.' Mûzvicka looked down on her as she would have on a child.

'No, Selena. When you leave the Palace you must look ahead – never behind. Look back only to remember how much we all loved – still love – you.' Now even Mûzvicka was fighting to keep back the tears. She kissed her friend for the last time. 'To sever such a bond is – painful,' she murmured, drawing Selena into one last embrace. She held her close for a moment and then, with a tiny sob, fled from the room.

Left alone again, Selena crossed slowly to the long Venetian mirror which hung on a wall covered with a gold tapestry.

She must look her best the last time the Sultan would see her. Picking up a small gold pot, she began to outline her huge, dark eyes with kohl. The slave placed a small, flat pillbox cap, blazing with gold embroidery, at a jaunty angle on Selena's shining black hair. Then, fixing one end of the yashmak to the cap she passed it over the bridge of her mistress's straight little nose and fastened it at the other side with a gold and amethyst bodkin. The veil was so fine that Selena's features could be seen through it without offending the laws of modesty. She looked utterly beautiful.

48

She slipped on the embroidered velvet waistcoat which was the same shade of green as her cap. When it was in place she gave herself a generous dab of attar of roses and was ready just as the towering frame of the faithful Kislar Agha appeared to escort her to Abdul Hamid's apartments. As she left the room Selena snatched up the copy of the latest Sherlock Holmes which she had promised to finish reading to him that afternoon. There were only sixteen pages left.

Night was falling fast and the air was still. No breeze alleviated the enveloping heat, but the thickening darkness brought the promise of respite. Within an hour the air would be cooler: people would move faster and breathe more easily. The sentry standing guard at the entrance to the Turkish Ministry of War was longing for the darkness. His uniform, he thought for the thousandth time, had not been designed with its wearer in mind, although it certainly worked wonders with ladies.

A sleek grey motor car bearing the standard of the German military mission, turned into the turretted gateways. The sentry, standing stolid at his post, saluted with his rifle, moving with military precision, his eyes showing none of the resentment he felt. Forty-five degrees, dressed in a red jacket with the gold braid of the collar sticking into his neck, and he was expected to salute the bastards too. By the beard of the prophet, he would live to see every German dropped into the Bosphorus and drowned one by one. He stood to attention, fingers to his forehead, motionless in a heat-induced reverie. Then, looking into the back of the car, he recognised its occupant and broke into a smile which banished his sullen expression and transformed his features.

The Turkish soldiery was unanimous in its dislike of the Germans brought in to Turkey by the ex-Sultan Abdul Hamid. The Germans' brief had been to carry out reforms in the Turkish Army. In retrospect, it was conceded that reforms had been needed and that the Germans had carried out their job with their customary humourless efficiency. But their high executive authority over the native Turks exacerbated an already delicate situation. The Turks found the Germans stubborn and overbearing: the Germans believed (and showed that they believed) the Turks to be corrupt and incompetent. The Germans domineered; the Turks were sullen in carrying out their orders.

The German officer in the car was one of the few who was popular with both the Turks and the Germans, and the sentry's spontaneous grin was met with a bright gaze and a friendly smile.

'An exceptionally hot day, wasn't it?' The Major spoke in Turkish from the back seat of the car.

'By Allah, it certainly was, sir,' answered the still-sweating sentry. The two men smiled again and the car drove slowly on through the gates.

The huge courtyard was still. A few Turkish officers idled in the gathering darkness, they saluted the car as it drove up to the magnificent main entrance of what had once been a palace and was now the prison of Abdul Hamid.

Major Hans Werner Rilke leapt from the car, too fast for the driver who was hardly out of the car by the time the long booted legs had carried their owner to the top of the shallow steps. One hand on the sword at his side, Rilke paused as he always did before entering this beautiful building. He turned away from the door and looked across the courtyard to the distant skyline. As always, the view reminded him of his first visit to this palace fifteen years before, when he arrived in Constantinople as a junior aide of exceptional promise in the suite of Kaiser Wilhelm. Now, as then, he caught his breath at the beauty of the scene before him. If ever he wondered at how completely the Levant had seduced him, this scene at this hour answered his questions. Pencil thin minarets and motionless palms were silhouetted against the amber glow of the sky as the deep orange sun slid down into the Bosphorus. From a mosque close by the sweet voice of a muezzin calling the faithful to prayer gave life to a scene which so entirely captured the insidious attraction of the East. An attraction which far outweighed the possible charms of any Fraulein back home.

The slam of a car door below him brought Rilke back to the present and in a second his abstracted expression was replaced by an alert, soldierly look which made him appear so much younger than his thirty-six years. He moved quickly into the cool of the marble hall, his blue eyes adjusting to the dimness of the interior.

'Major Rilke.' The duty officer walked across the hall towards him, stopping in front of the Major and saluting ceremoniously. 'His Highness Abdul Hamid is expecting you. Please follow me.' Rilke nodded perfunctorily and walked after the chief of staff up the ornate staircase with its great marble pillars and through several long ante-rooms, saluted as he went by members of Enver Pasha's personal guard. Dour faced men, they stood sentinel at every doorway, hands on their long, vicious daggers.

Hans Werner bit back a smile. The war minister was obviously still taking no chances with this prisoner. Doubtless Enver Pasha wished his charge at the bottom of the Bosphorus but the new government, hailed as liberal and progressive, could hardly resort to the methods used by its autocratic predecessors. Abdul Hamid, with his cynical sense of humour, might well derive a certain pleasure from this irony, the Major thought as they waited for a heavy iron door to be opened.

A sergeant peeked through a grill at them and nodded. The door swung open and the staff officer saluted smartly and walked quickly away. The door clanged behind Rilke and was noisily bolted and locked, leaving Hans Werner marooned in another world, another age.

In front of him stood Abdul Hamid's chief eunuch who bowed respectfully before leading him down the long corridor which connected the men's quarters with the harem. Despite himself, Werner always felt a mixture of reverence and fear when he entered what only five years ago had been a secret and forbidden spot. Abdul Hamid might now be a prisoner in his own palace, but he still inspired a degree of respect and dread even among his friends.

The eunuch ushered Rilke into a charming waiting room with pink marble walls and a fantastically tiled ceiling, and Werner paused a moment to collect his thoughts and say a little prayer to himself. He knew so little about the girl he had so willingly recommended to Annie Lufti. Hans Werner had noticed Selena and knew that she had acted as Abdul Hamid's confidant for many years, but he had never exchanged a word with her or seen more of her than her eliptical eyes and the hint of grace which even her heavy veiling could not hide. He sighed quietly, hoping he was doing the right thing.

The chief eunuch once again bowed respectfully and disappeared through the heavy crimson curtains, sewn with thousands of seed pearls, which covered the doors to the reception room. Another eunuch stood dutifully guarding the entrance and he smiled as he caught the Major's eye.

Werner turned away, the sight of these wretched creatures with their wrinkled skin always made his flesh crawl. He knew both the chief eunuch and the one now guarding the door were 'clean shaven' and as always his hands had moved subconsciously over his crotch at the thought. Werner was a strong and brave man but the idea of having his organ and testicles cut off with a curved blade and being buried up to his armpits in hot sand made him feel faint.

Werner opened his eyes to see Kislar Agha holding the heavy curtain aside to allow him to pass into the presence of his Imperial master.

'Ah, Major Rilke,' Abdul Hamid's gentle voice rose above the racket of Kiki the parrot's screeching. 'How are you, my dear friend?' Werner bowed before accepting the outstretched hand and warmly shaking it. Abdul Hamid was dressed in a plain black frockcoat with gold buttons and his fez was pushed far back on his head, accentuating the high brow and sunken temples.

Selena, standing slightly behind the Sultan with arms crossed on her breast, lowered her eyes for a second to allow the two men a moment of private greeting. Then she returned the Major's bow. Although they had seen each other often, it was the first time they had acknowledged each other. Selena studied the Major surreptitiously from beneath her eyelashes. He was not conventionally handsome – his nose was a little too short, and his lips too thin – but the overall impression was a pleasant one. Tall, he carried himself well and his light blond hair was neatly parted to one side. But his finest characteristic was his light blue-grey eyes that were lit with kindness and sincerity. She decided that she would feel safe with any person such a man recommended.

Hans Werner noticed the apprehensive look in her dark eyes as she raised her little head and was for a moment taken aback. Assured as she had so often appeared to him, she now seemed like a tiny defenceless child. He responded with a broad friendly smile and Selena looked back gratefully, blushing crimson, and retreated with a bow.

Under their heavy lids, Abdul Hamid's eyes missed nothing of this exchange and he watched the girl as she left the room. There was a brief silence after the door closed behind her, both men thinking about the girl who had just left them.

Abdul Hamid waved an arm at a chair. 'Do sit down, my dear Major. I have a favour to ask you. Selena is leaving my palace but she has a place in my heart that she can never leave. I ask you to look after her – to protect her – until she can look after herself.' The ex-Sultan smiled wistfully.

'I give you my word,' the good-natured German assured him. 'She will be cared for. I cannot speak highly enough of Madame

Lufti. She is a unique woman, generous and warm and with the kindest of hearts.'

'Good, good,' said Abdul Hamid and studied his small, dry hands thoughtfully for a moment before lifting his shoulders in a resigned shrug. 'I am most sorry to see her go – but there you are.' The ex-Sultan raised his eyes, half smiled and continued in a livelier tone. 'Well, well. Here we are thinking of women when the whole of Constantinople is thinking of nothing but war.' Abdul Hamid briskly fitted another cigarette into his amber holder and called for coffee. Once the coffee was poured and the servant dismissed, the Sultan asked Werner for news of the war. His questions were acute and penetrating and for the first time Werner realised that the royal aviary was more than decorative: its constant chirpings and warblings, and Kiki's shrieking, ensured against any listening ears.

'Ah war – what folly.' Abdul Hamid stood up and began to pace the room, his good humour vanishing. He paused a little and looked at Werner solemnly. 'Throughout my years on the throne one thing stood above all others – the wish to keep my Empire intact. No sooner did the smart young men depose me than they lost most of our European possessions and the cream of our fighting force in the Balkan fiasco. But Enver Pasha and his arrogant Young Turks knew best – what else could you expect? That war would never have happened had I still been in power.' Abdul Hamid was no longer the courteous host; he was speaking so forcefully his eyes glittered. 'Enver Pasha – bah! The Turkish people have been taken in by that vain poppycock, much as a girl is taken in by the first handsome officer who pays her a compliment.' Werner, who secretly agreed with the ex-Sultan, began to feel uneasy. He folded one booted leg over the other and looked studiously at the floor. Abdul Hamid grew more and more animated and bore no resemblance to the frail, if dignified, old man who had greeted him earlier.

'Mark my words, Rilke,' he said, pausing for a moment and looking fiercely at the Major, 'mark my words. Enver Pasha will bring us into this war as sure as the Black Sea whips up the Bosphorus. And with a more lasting effect. We have no business in this war. It is not of our making. Our interests should remain here, in the East. We must protect our borders from the Russians in the West and from the English in Egypt. If we enter this foreigners' war we will fight, we will die, and we will lose our lands. I have seen it happen before, and it will happen again.' He seemed to lose energy and sank wearily down on a divan. 'Even if we win, we lose.'

'But what can I do?' he continued with a sigh. 'No one asks the opinion of a weak old man. "All reason will be clouded by ambition as fire is by smoke",' he quoted bitterly and held out his hands. 'Look at them,' he ordered. 'There was a time when a whole Empire trembled before me – now it is only my hands.'

Then suddenly he felt very weary. All he wanted now was to be left alone with Mûzvicka ... no country ... no ambitions. Standing rather shakily, Abdul Hamid reached for Rilke's hand. 'Please excuse me, Major, but I am feeling rather tired.'

As he was about to leave the room, Abdul Hamid turned and addressed Rilke once more. 'Major,' he said, casually, 'please inform the Kislar Agha of Madame Lufti's address so that Selena's belongings can be sent on to her.' The Major bowed to the Sultan's departing back.

The chief eunuch was waiting for him in the pink marble room, and with him was Selena. She gracefully rose to her feet and, offering him her slender hand, thanked him in a low sweet voice for the trouble he was taking on her behalf. Seeing her face closely for the first time Werner was struck by the perfection of Oriental beauty in her heart-shaped face. She reminded him of a delicate, exotic flower and for some reason he was suddenly overcome with the desire to shield and protect her – a desire far stronger than his wish to please his old friend Abdul Hamid.

'It will be my duty and pleasure to escort you to the house of Madame Lufti,' he said, his voice elated. Selena smiled at him gratefully and, putting on a black cloak, followed him into the night.

CHAPTER FOUR

Palestine

Sara swept into the kitchen, threw herself into a chair beside the huge, scrubbed kitchen table which was laid ready for breakfast and kicked off her shoes.

'I've finished hanging out the washing,' she told Fatma, who was busy at the range banging pots and stirring pans. 'And thank goodness – it's hotter than hell out there.' She wriggled her bare toes appreciatively on the cool tiled floor. Even with the heat from the range the kitchen was cooler than the outside air; the thick stone walls and shade from the veranda outside made all the difference.

'We need some more oil and sugar,' said Fatma, unscrewing a glass jar and throwing a pinch of herbs into a pot.

'I'll add them to the list,' answered Sara, more irritably than was normal for her and, taking out her handkerchief for the tenth time that morning, she wiped away the perspiration that was trickling down her neck.

Fatma, looking concerned, glanced at Sara and picked up a huge brass pitcher from the range. 'Now you just sit there and drink up this coffee and eat before the men come in,' she scolded, crossing the kitchen.

'I'm too hot to drink coffee,' said Sara crossly.

'Eat, Sara,' she ordered, prodding the girl's shoulder firmly and pushing a basket of sweet rolls towards her. 'Since Mr Daniel came back you've been pecking at your food like an old hen. If you don't eat, you'll get sick. If you get sick, Allah knows,' she said, rolling her eyes to the heavens. Sara knew Fatma's implacable will too well to argue and so she broke open a roll and chewed at it listlessly. Fatma, pleased at having won her way, turned back to the business of cooking breakfast for the hungry men who would shortly fill her kitchen.

Leylah, the skinny little Arab who came each day from the village to help in the house, was standing day-dreaming at the window. She should have known better. With surprising speed Fatma was on the other side of the kitchen and had given the girl a good hard pinch. Leylah yelped like a cat and hurried back to her job of pumping water up to the sink. Fatma, muttering about worthless monkeys and invoking the help of the spirits, returned to her cast-iron stove and the frying eggs.

Sara rested her elbows on the table and pressed the heels of her hands into her eyes. There was truth in what Fatma had said: she had lost her appetite and it was because of Daniel. Each morning since his return eight days ago she had put on a pretty dress, taken care over her toilette and waited for Daniel – who never came. The bubbles of excitement she had felt for the first few days were now well and truly burst. What Fatma took as a malaise was simply the outward sign of the waning excitement.

'Why doesn't he come?' she thought, desperately digging her fingers into her hair. She doubted he was even thinking about her while she spent every waking – and sleeping – moment full of thoughts of him. He was probably making plans for the war and the future; she wondered whether she was to be included in them. But then her mind swung back to that hope-filled moment when he had desired only the present, and that present had been her. She felt a glow on her lips at the memory of his kiss and burned with impatience to see him again, to give him – and herself – another chance.

It was then that she conceived her plan. Daniel had still not returned the horse he had borrowed on that day. After lunch, when the household was asleep, she would ride over to Hadera with some eggs for Daniel's mother and tell him that she had come for the horse. It was perfectly reasonable: it was harvest time and they had constant need of the horses. She would be gone without anyone realising and back before nightfall. Her spirits rose at the thought of action. It was reckless but she would face the music and happily dance to it – later.

With a guilty start Sara realised that Fatma's eyes were sternly fixed on her, and quickly buttered some bread in an effort to divert her attention.

'After breakfast I'll pick the tomatoes for bottling,' she said sweetly. The household was undergoing preparations for winter but this year, with the threat of war, everyone was more frantic than ever. Fatma, whose ability to read into Sara's and Becky's minds was almost uncanny, was not completely deceived. Narrowing her eyes suspiciously she turned back to stirring the huge pot of *fuhl*, a powerful mixture of broad beans, mutton fat and garlic.

'I hear the Zabiah tribesmen are back in the area, may their fathers be cursed,' she said, making as if to spit. 'Mind you stay close. They are thieves and murderers and don't know Allah.' With that she shook a plump arm at the window, her gold bangles jangling musically. The armful of bangles represented her entire fortune and it often amused Sara to think that on Fatma's arm her riches were as safe as they would be in the deepest vault.

Fatma's announcement about the Zabiah took Sara aback, but she was determined to let it make no difference to her plan. The Zabiah were much feared bandits who attacked lone travellers and stole their horses. But Sara would be back well before dusk and would take a rifle just in case.

It was only eight o'clock but the air was thick and humid and the temperature had already reached 100°F. At the pump Leylah irritably plucked the damp material of her black robe away from her chest and wiped her forehead with the back of her hand. She carried a large bowl of water to the veranda and, putting it on a low footstool with a clean towel beside it, leant on the doorpost, trying to catch a stray breeze.

Sara jumped up from her chair and put out the big white plates. The men had been out in the vineyards since dawn at four, helping with the harvest. They would come in as hungry as wolves. Fatma piled the centre of the table with cast iron pans of fried eggs, potatoes and an enormous bowl of tomato and cucumber salad, diced Arab-style and sprinkled thickly with parsley. The pot of *fuhl* took place of honour in the middle.

The kitchen, a large, friendly room, always relaxed her and today, the sun streaming in through the open windows, casting flickers of light over the cream walls, would have raised anybody's spirits.

A clatter of footsteps on the veranda's stairs announced the arrival of the men. Sam was first through the door, face flushed and red hair darkened with sweat. He stopped to wash his hands and rinse his face in the bowl of water and then, with a mischievous laugh, threw the damp towel into Alex's beefy red face – he had never been able to cope with the sun. Alex flicked the towel back at him, catching Sam a stinging blow on the fore-arm.

Abram watched the horseplay and raising his eyes murmured a short prayer as he dipped his hands into the water. Crossing over to Sara, he kissed her fondly on the top of her head before he took his place next to her.

The noise level in the room had already risen dramatically. Sam and Alex were still teasing each other and Fatma was busy scolding Leylah from that rich store of verbal insults that garnish Arab abuse. Sara had livened up at the prospect of her secret excursion and talked eagerly to her father. Another burst of clatter outside and Aaron burst in, followed by Manny Hirsh.

Manny sniffed appreciatively. 'Mmm – *fuhl*. I guessed as much. You can smell it all the way down the terraces,' he said impishly. Fatma shook her spoon at him, but was not really angry. She prided herself on making the best *fuhl* for miles and was smiling again as she ladled an extra big spoonful on to Manny's plate. As soon as she put it down in front of him he attacked it hungrily. 'Killed more Jews than the Tsar of Russia, this has,' he said through a mouthful of food, and set the table laughing.

The men had brought the soft aroma of sun, wind and warm earth into the room with them, and everyone was noisy and cheerful. Sara was happier than she had been for days and even managed to be civil to Benjamin, a neighbour whose adoring looks and sighs only irritated her.

Becky, last as usual, ran into the kitchen, slamming the door behind her. She ran round the table kissing everyone – even a rather startled Leylah – and then made a break for the door.

'Oh no you don't, madam.' Once again Fatma showed her capacity for speed, and was standing firmly in Becky's way. 'You sit down and have some breakfast before you go anywhere.'

'But I've helped with the laundry,' Becky wailed, shifting restlessly from one foot to the other; 'and besides I'm not hungry.'

'Hungry? Who said hungry?' Fatma asked, steering Becky firmly towards the table. 'Appetite will come with the food.' Becky wrinkled her nose at the over-powering smell of the *fuhl*, but sat down obediently and picked up a roll. 'How you going to get a husband, looking like a plucked sparrow?' Fatma snorted, squeezing the girl's skinny shoulders.

'Oh I'll get myself a husband, don't you worry,' she retorted, shaking Fatma off and tossing her head proudly.

'Who'd want to marry a broomstick?' Sam teased from across the table.

'Adam Leibovitz, that's who,' said Becky slyly, mentioning a lanky boy from the other side of the village.

'When you two bone bags get together who'll need flints?' Sam shouted to a roar of laughter. Abram smiled, shaking his head and wondering as he so frequently did how he and Miriam had bred such a wild, rowdy bunch. It reminded him of the old tale of the hen who hatched ducklings he thought as he knocked his pipe into a brass dish that served as an ashtray.

Becky, determined to have the last word, cut in on the laughter. 'I've plenty of time to look – I can't marry until Sara does, and Sara won't marry anyone but Daniel, who won't marry anyway.' She tailed off slightly – she had not meant to sound so malicious. Suddenly subdued, she wolfed her bread roll, her eyes on the table.

In the short silence that followed, everyone carefully looked at anyone but Sara. But she was thunderstruck at her sister's words. Staring down at her plate, she realised the truth of what Becky had said. Tradition demanded that the older sister marry first; if Daniel would not have her, she would have to find someone else. But the thought of marrying anyone except Daniel made her blood freeze, and she shivered slightly in the heat of the kitchen.

If anyone mentions Chaim Cohen now, I'll scream, she thought. Chaim Cohen was a rich Turkish Jew, purveyor to the Turkish Army, whom Aaron was expecting to visit Zichron soon. Aaron was hoping to sell him significant amounts of barley for the army *and sell me too*, Sara told herself bitterly. Like so many others of his background Cohen was hoping to find himself a wife in Palestine and his forthcoming arrival had been much heralded in the local community. With varying degrees of subtlety Sara's father and brother had kept her well aware of the advent of the expected guest.

Abram gave Sara's arm a squeeze and she looked at him gratefully and gave a wan smile.

'And talking of Daniel – where is he? He promised to bring the horse back days ago.'

'And we need him now the big grey's gone lame.' Alex's systems of organisation were so complicated he practically ran the horses to a timetable.

'If I can finish my chores by lunch time I'll ride over to Hadera and bring the gelding back,' Sam volunteered. 'I could do with a ride.'

Sara's face did not change. 'Same here. I'll come with you,' she said, rising nonchalantly from her chair, plate in hand. 'I'll take over some eggs for Daniel's mother.'

Voices shot back at her from all over the room.

'Sara, you promised to pin up my new dress for the dance.'

'Don't you realise – with the threat of war the Turkish patrols will be out. You'll be raped.'

'Ox, ox, an ox remain. What did I tell you about the Zabiah?'

'What about the Zabiah?' Aaron asked, looking swiftly at Fatma.

'I hear they took sheep and goats from Faradis,' she said, naming a nearby Arab village.

'Then Sam, Sara is not to go with you and make sure you're back before nightfall,' Aaron said. 'And stay on the coastal road. No short cuts.' He was still advising Sam when the towering frame of Robby Woolf lumbered into the kitchen and banged a crumpled newspaper on to the table in front of Aaron.

'Read that,' he said excitedly. 'I got it off the supply cart.' The men's thoughts all turned to the war. For once the newspaper took preference over the *fuhl* and Sam, quick as always, snatched up the copy of *Tanin*, the official Ottoman paper.

'It's dated the 5th August – it's only six days old!'

A silence fell in the kitchen as the men all read the paper over Sam's shoulder.

Sara did not move from her chair. She knew she couldn't go to Hadera and her heart sunk in disappointment. Now she felt both deflated and frustrated, as though everyone were united against her. She sat listlessly, watching the men read the paper with such eagerness.

'So the Turk is mobilising,' said Alex, straightening up.

'Yes, but "as a precaution against an act of aggression by Russia",' quoted Sam excitedly. ' "This does not commit Turkey to war: we intend to remain neutral," said War Minister Enver Pasha yesterday,' he read on.

'Yes, but for how long?' Aaron asked sarcastically.

Becky looked at Aaron, her eyes big and bewildered. 'What does it all mean, Aaron? What's going to happen?'

'It means, my sweet little ignoramus,' Sam answered, tweaking her hair, 'that, God willing, the Germans will drag the Turk into the war with them.'

'But we are the Turks,' said Becky, biting her lip and determined to understand now that the war seemed a reality.

'Well, subjects of the Turk, yes,' began Sam.

'Then why do you want war?'

'Because we're Jewish, stupid,' Sam was beginning to become exasperated.

'Because it might change things for us here in Palestine,' said Alex, and he suddenly sounded much older.

'What's wrong with Palestine as it is?' Becky was sulky now. 'I like it.'

'Oh, nothing's wrong as long as you don't mind being beaten, tortured or raped, for no better reason than being a Jew – by a gang of thugs who pass themselves off as police.'

'That's horrible,' Becky cried, covering her ears.

'Horrible, but true. And you know it,' said Alex, shrugging his shoulders. 'We are entirely at the mercy of a handful of capricious men. Becky, we pay not to be beaten, nor to be *butchered* even. Does that sound right to you?'

'Of course not,' said Becky, indignantly.

'Well, that's why we want the war – so the British will come and take us out of the Middle Ages and into the twentieth century, where we belong,' Alex finished triumphantly. Manny looked up from the newspaper and nodded in agreement.

'But Nelly Jacobson,' said Becky, mentioning her best friend in the village, 'says that her father hates the British because they are allies of the Russians who killed his entire family.'

'Find ten Jews and you will have ten opinions,' said Robby Woolf, helping himself to a bread roll and disposing of it in two mouthfuls.

'Oh dear,' Sam shook his head sadly. 'You can't expect Becky to understand – she's a girl and since when have girls understood politics?' Becky snorted and threw a roll at Sam who ducked, chuckling.

'Stop this nonsense, will you,' said Abram wearily. He only had five children, but they often seemed like twelve.

Sara, to hide her increasing agitation, got up and began clearing the dishes from under their noses. 'There is only one problem,' she said sarcastically, banging the plates down on top of each other. 'Before the British arrive on their white chargers to transport us into the present, we – or at any rate you – will have to go and fight against them.' And she marched over to where Fatma was pouring water into a galvanized tub for the washing-up.

The men looked at Sara but chose to ignore her comment and Sara picked up a cloth and dried the dishes. The conversation was still on the theme of the approaching war and the words 'Austria' 'battle' and 'the Hun' floated around her ears like motes of dust in the sunshine. Much as the idea of war frightened her, Sara had to concede that a lot of what Alex said made sense. She noticed that Aaron and her father had said nothing, but had merely exchanged looks; this had all obviously been discussed between them before.

Sara knew that Aaron, like Daniel, was very pro-British. She also realised that the Levinsons were in a very privileged position, mostly thanks to Aaron and his access to American dollars. Zichron itself was also well-off compared to other settlements because it was one of the oldest and best established. But despite this, not even Aaron himself was above the power of the utterly ruthless Turkish police patrols, the dreaded septieh who arrived once a month to collect their baksheesh, the bribery that stopped them from at best slicing down the vines and, at worst, beating the men and raping the women.

The Ottoman Empire was almost four hundred years old and it was tired and corrupt. Its subjects had become used to accepting the unacceptable. Five years before there had been cause for hope: when the Young Turks deposed the Sultan, the Jews had rejoiced along with the Armenians, Greeks, Arabs and other minority subjects. They had all soon been disillusioned. Their original hopes for an Empire 'of free and equal members' as the Triumvirate had promised, had soon been dashed. Five years into the new regime, nothing remained of those words of hope. The three rulers were more and more preoccupied with petty squabbles, squalid intrigues and struggles for their own survival. It was becoming increasingly, and alarmingly, clear that 'Ottoman' meant Turk and millions of Jews and Christians throughout the Empire were beginning to fear for their lives. Indeed a few weeks before, a new police chief had arrived in Palestine and his reputation as a Jew-hater had already reached the northern settlements. It was said that his first act on arriving in Jaffa had been to hang the first Jew he had seen walking innocently past his headquarters. 'As a warning.'

No, Sara mused, it was not difficult to imagine that Palestine under the British would be a better place to live than it was now, under the Turks. It was even widely known that several members of the British Parliament were greatly in favour of Palestine becoming a Jewish state, an idea so glorious they hardly dared dream about its coming to fruition. But war! War meant starvation and slaughter: it would mean her brothers all being taken from home and maybe some or all of them never coming back, but dying, killed like pigs fighting for the Turk, whom they loathed. As Jews they would be thrown to the battlefront like Christians to the lions. Sara was drying the plates faster and faster as the men's conversation became more and more heated. Fatma's normally cross face was now looking petrified and Leylah was practically in tears.

'Will you all be quiet!' she exploded, unable to contain herself any longer. 'Do you want the entire world to hear you? Don't you realise it's treason that you're talking – you could get us all arrested long before your precious war even begins!'

'Put your hat on, Becky, and we'll go and collect eggs for Daniel's mother. You come too, Leylah,' she added, taking pity on the girl. Sara collected her hat from the peg on the door and turned her full gaze on the men. 'Quite frankly, I'm fed up with hearing about war,' she snapped. 'But if you really think it's going to happen, shouldn't you stop talking and start preparing for it? We will need to start buying in supplies like oil, sugar and salt. And we must build secret places to hide them. I also suggest that we increase our number of chickens and maybe start breeding rabbits. I may be only a woman,' she finished with all the contempt she could muster, 'and my life utterly worthless, but I have every intention of hanging on to it.' She wheeled round and stormed out of the door with Becky and Leylah hard on her heels.

All the men looked at each other silently. Abram tapped his pipe into the bowl, looking at the door through which his daughter had made her exit. 'She sounded just like her mother then,' he said wistfully, and not without a certain amount of pride.

Sam lifted his eyebrows. 'Rabbits aren't a bad idea,' he said thoughtfully. 'I might try and buy a few over in Hadera.'

'Take the Winchester with you, would you?' Aaron asked. 'Nissim Aloni ought to take a look at it – the trigger keeps jamming.' Sam nodded. Nissim Aloni was ostensibly a blacksmith, but he was also the best gunsmith in Palestine.

'Buying some more guns might be a good idea too,' said Alex

quietly. Aaron looked around; only Fatma was in the room, brushing around the range, and she was family. In theory Jews were only allowed to own a few guns per settlement. Now, when spy fever would obviously take off, buying guns would be an even more delicate business than normal.

'I'll try and get hold of Joe Lanski,' Aaron volunteered after some thought.

'Are you sure we can trust him?' Robby was dubious.

'I think so – for this. Some people say he collaborates with the Turk; others that he is an intelligence agent for the Americans. Either way, he is a Jew and whatever our differences, we don't denounce each other.'

He looked around the table and everyone nodded agreement. 'Then I'll get in touch with Lanski as soon as I can.'

As soon as Sam arrived in Hadera he made his way to the blacksmith and was told the reason for Daniel's silence.

'Malaria,' said Nissim Aloni, squinting at the jammed trigger of the rifle. Sam shook his head sympathetically. Few in this part of the country escaped the suffering caused by the swarms of mosquitoes that thrived in the fetid black mud of this swamp-ridden region. 'It seems he's not had an attack for a long while and you know what they say, the longer it stays away the harder it hits when it arrives.' The malaria in these parts was recurrent and often fatal. Indeed so many of the original settlers had died from it while draining the swamps that the Arabs had nicknamed them 'children of death'.

'Can you fix it?' Sam asked anxiously as Nissim Aloni inspected the barrel of the gun.

'Sure. Come back in an hour or so and it should be ready,' and the blacksmith disappeared back into the darkness of his forge.

It took Sam ten minutes to reach the Rosens' neatly whitewashed two-storey house. The Rosens had arrived from Russia in 1882, the same year as the Levinson parents came from Romania, and were among the original half-dozen families to pioneer the settlement, so their house was in the oldest, and most picturesque, part of the village.

As Sam rode up the street to the house he saw Maya Rosen sitting sewing at an open window. She waved at him in welcome and by the time she opened the door to him he had dismounted and was tethering his horse to the gatepost. Sam could never look at Daniel's mother without marvelling at the beauty she must once have possessed. Now her fine Slavic features were ravaged by the inhuman demands of a settler's life; a few teeth were missing and her cheeks were rough and sunken, but her bone structure was still noble and her liquid dark eyes, Daniel's eyes, were untouched by hardship and the passing of time.

Mrs Rosen took Sam's hands in hers and shook them warmly. 'You've come to see Daniel? He's been ill with malaria again. He's in his room, but Sam, no politics; he's not strong enough yet!' Smiling, Sam promised to keep off inflammatory subjects. 'And how are you all?' she asked, letting go of his hands at last.

'Oh, everybody's fine,' he answered cheerfully.

'I've brought you some eggs from Sara, with her love. How has the patient been?'

'Difficult, of course. Brooding like a caged snake,' Maya sighed. 'Go on up, I'll brew you some tea.'

Sam took the narrow stairs two at a time but paused before he knocked at Daniel's door. He would hardly admit it, even to himself, but the truth was that Sam was always a little in awe of Daniel and was never completely at ease when they were alone together. As a child he had hero-worshipped his older brother's friend and some of the awkwardness of that feeling remained.

He tapped at the door, but there was no reply. Opening it he saw Daniel stretched across a bed in the far corner of the room. He was breathing in shallow gasps, his head sideways on the pillow, one arm trailing on the floor. The window was open and a winey fragrance of grapes and sugar floated in on the breeze. Daniel had lost weight and the light from the whitewashed walls made him look even paler and thinner than he was.

Sam drew up a chair to the bed and gently patted Daniel's arm. He felt like a kitten trying to attract the attention of a panther by pulling on his tail. Daniel opened his eyes, which still had the hard, bright unfocused glare of fever in them. He tried to sit up but collapsed back against the pillows.

'Forgive my bad manners, Sam, but I'm still very weak.'

Sam nodded. 'Yes, I know. Lie back and rest – you'll be fine in a day or two.'

'I expect you came for the horse – I'm sorry to have kidnapped him.' With an effort Daniel propped himself up against the wall. He gave a long tired sigh. This persistent weakness infuriated him, and what strength he had was wasted in raging against it. 'He's stabled at my cousins. Josh said he or Ben would try to ride him over, but I guess they've both been too busy.'

'If you need the horse you can keep him for a while,' Sam volunteered quickly. 'I really came to find out what had happened to you. Aaron was worried.'

'Can't manage without me, eh?' said Daniel with a glimpse of his old grin. 'No, take the horse – I've been promised an Arab colt by Sheik Suliman.' The Sheik was Daniel's spiritual father and old friend. At the age of thirteen, Daniel had been sent to live with the Suliman family to learn Arabic and the Arab way of life. 'If there is to be any hope for the future, the Arab and the Jew must learn to live together' had been Daniel's father's often-repeated maxim. After six months Daniel had earned the Sheik's love and, more importantly, his respect. Daniel was looking forward to riding out to pick up the colt.

'Don't let him out of that bed,' a voice from the doorway warned, and Sam turned to see Mrs Rosen coming into the room with two glasses of tea. She put them down on the bedside table and smoothed Daniel's pillow with the air of a professional nurse. 'You listen to me,' she urged, shaking her finger, and with a smile for Sam she left the room, shutting the door softly behind her.

'Poor mother,' said Daniel thoughtfully. 'It's been lonely for her since father died and I've not been much support to her.'

'Sara wanted to ride over with me, but Aaron wouldn't let her,' Sam blurted, anxious to break the silence which had descended on the little room. 'She sent your mother some eggs,' he added lamely.

Daniel, sipping his tea, thought it safest not to answer. He did not want to start discussing Sara. During the last five days she, along with the fever, had been troubling his mind.

'Why didn't you take your malaria pills?' asked Sam, noticing a bottle by Daniel's bed. Daniel shot him a contemptuous look. Sam laughed. The little yellow pills made you feel as ill as the disease itself.

'We got a copy of *Tanin* this morning,' Sam tried a new subject of conversation. 'Only a few days old. It said that . . .'

'You don't expect to find any truth in that rag, do you?' Daniel interrupted, glaring at Sam. 'Truth is a dangerous weapon in this part of the world.'

Sam wearily thought that he should have known better than to mention *Tanin*. 'I'd better be going.' He rose to his feet. 'Leave you to sleep and rest.'

Daniel closed his eyes against the weakness that suddenly invaded him and passed a hand across his forehead. 'I have centuries of rest ahead of me,' he said with frosty humour. Despite himself, the familiar weakness was overtaking him once more. 'But of course you're right – I must sleep,' he conceded. 'Tell Aaron I'll be over in a few days,' and he settled back into the bed. He was in a deep sleep before Sam had closed the door behind him.

It was nearly four o'clock when Sam, leading the chestnut gelding, turned on to the rough stony cart track that led to the forge. He would have to hurry to get home before dark, but it would be quicker once he was out of Hadera. His ride back from Ben and Josh's had taken some time. At this hour of the day everyone was sitting at open windows or on their verandas, and he had had to keep stopping and greeting people. As he rode, Sam mused on the single-minded energy of these people who had arrived with nothing and spent years developing the settlement. They had built houses, cultivated land, married and produced a new generation. They had ignored the temptations of a more worldly life and worked and prayed. Their only luxury was the books, and later the musical instruments, they ordered from Europe to keep their minds as well as their bodies active and strong. Sam was flooded with a warm love for his people and a deep peace. Lulled by the clopping of the horses' hooves and the distant tinkle of a piano he rode quietly on. A pair of Arab workers were squatting in the dappled shade of an ancient olive tree sharpening scythes, and they saluted him cheerfully as he passed.

The track petered out just ahead, and Sam turned off it into the big courtyard in front of the forge. He slid off his horse and led the two animals to the trough to water them in readiness for the journey home. Loosening the girth, he tethered them under a tattered palm tree and, kicking aimlessly at a scrawny chicken that clucked across his path, he turned to look for the blacksmith.

Nissim Aloni emerged from the shade of the smithy, squinting in the harsh light. 'I've fixed your rifle. You'll have to watch for . . .' He stopped suddenly and seemed to be listening intently. Sam started to speak but Nissim motioned him to be silent. Then Sam heard it too and the two men exchanged a grim look of understanding. 'The septieh,' the blacksmith said bitterly. 'And it sounds like a troop rather than a regular patrol. God damn them!' and he spat into the dust.

The peace of the afternoon was shattered by the strident calls of bugles and, lower but more insistent, the sinister tapping of drums. And drums always brought bad news; they meant that the Turkish police were coming for more than their regular collection of baksheesh. Sam's stomach tightened. Everyone from these parts had an instinctive fear of the septieh: their power was total and indiscriminate. They would arrest people for no better reason than the cast of their features, and could beat their victims senseless for nothing more than a moment of excitement.

'What do you think they want?' Sam stuttered, aware that his hands were trembling slightly.

'They're probably posting a new edict, something anti-Jewish. No doubt it's our new police chief's opening move against the settlements. I hear Hamid Bek's leather bastinado is covered in strips of flesh from his prisoners' feet.'

'For God's sake spare me the grisly details. I'm frightened enough as it is. I don't have a travel permit on me. If they want to make things difficult . . .'

'Your gun, is it registered?'

Sam felt a rush of fear. 'I don't know – perhaps not.' Nissim hurried back into the forge with Sam close behind him.

'Stick it in here,' said Nissim, grabbing a bulky sack of coarse fodder wheat. In a moment Sam had snatched up the Winchester from the gun rack and buried it in the grain, his fingers clumsy in his efforts to move quickly. 'I came to this country to shoe horses and find myself repairing guns, making ammunition and acting as arbitrator for the accursed Turk,' said the blacksmith with a wry grin, and wiped the trickling sweat from his forehead with a muscular forearm. 'Come,' he added, taking Sam's arm; 'we had better get to the square, where I suggest you lose yourself in the crowd – you should be safe there.'

The sound of galloping horses took them quickly out into the courtyard. It was Ben and Josh. They pulled their horses to an abrupt halt when they saw Nissim and Sam coming out of the forge.

'It's the septieh,' Josh shouted, his face furious and streaked with sweat after his ride up from the fields. 'And they want more than baksheesh this time.'

'Damn them,' Ben roared, his boyish face crimson with heat and rage. 'They've tied old Uri up with rope and are leading him up to the village square for interrogation.' Uri Golan was one of the

68

village elders and the man with whom the Turks usually negotiated. 'And what the hell are you still here for?' he added, surprised at seeing Sam. 'Well, you'll just have to come with the rest of us. It's too late to make a run for it now.'

'Are all the guns in the slick?' asked Josh, dismounting and dousing his head with water from the trough. Every settlement had its arsenal of illegal weapons hidden away, and Nissim Aloni was in charge of Hadera's.

Nissim nodded, his face suddenly looking very old.

'I'll meet you in the square.' Ben wheeled his horse round and galloped back up the cart track to the village. For a minute the air was filled with the furious shrieks of chickens who had been disturbed by his flight.

'I expect we're in for another display of animal brutality,' said Nissim with a sigh. He went back to the forge to pick up a small pouch of gold coins just in case they could buy their way out of potential trouble, and then wearily saddled his horse. The three men set off together.

'Where's Daniel?' Josh suddenly wondered. 'Still too weak to lift a gun, I hope?' Sam's thoughts had been running along the same lines.

'Or his voice. I left him blissfully asleep just over an hour ago.'

'Let's hope he stays that way. After four years of freedom of speech in France he's probably forgotten how to conform. Not that he ever really knew. All we need now is one of his little speeches and we'll be picking him up in pieces: they've become very touchy lately.'

They rode on in gloomy silence.

When they arrived in the village square it was already filling up with a stirring, restless crowd. Bitter murmurings could be heard below the approaching scrape of hooves, the clink of horses' bridles and the short, sharp orders shouted out by the troops. Despite the insistent beating of the drums, which meant that every single person must present him or herself before the troops, the unmarried women and children remained locked indoors. Only the older women were there, in an attempt to curb any protest their men wanted to make. They wanted their husbands and sons alive.

Rumours about the new police chief in Jaffa had been circulating for weeks, and any slight change in the septieh's routine was bound to cause distress. The devil you know is preferable to the devil you don't and everyone had grown used to the old chief. Now, with a new commandant, new tricks would have to be learned, new ways to avoid disaster.

The village councillors stood in a little group on the steps of the synagogue. They held themselves with dignity but could not disguise their worry as they waited to receive the unwelcome guests.

Finally, the septieh rode up: twenty troops riding in single file were led by a handsome, brash-looking sergeant. The bright scarlet of their uniforms contrasted strangely with the clean, white lines of the village. The scene could not have been more different from the one Sam had ridden through so recently.

An unnatural silence fell over the square, broken only by the whimperings of a rabid-looking mongrel that had followed the soldiers into the village. Everyone stared at the dog, using it as an excuse to look away from Uri, the town's oldest surviving settler, who had been tied up to the sergeant's saddle with a length of rope. Despite his bondage Uri contrived to look both dignified and defiant: a proud old man challenging the power of the Turkish Empire with his stare.

The sergeant rode straight up to the elders of the village but did not dismount. He spoke to the septieh, who immediately took up positions with their rifles lying at ease across the pommels of their saddles; their relaxed air was an insult in itself. The dog, which had been quiet for a moment, broke into wild barking running in and out of the horses' legs. The sergeant's attention was drawn to it and it irritated him as it detracted from his authority. The cur was interfering with military order.

'Shoot it,' he snapped, his eyes, yellow as the dog's, shifting uneasily. A single shot rang out and a pool of blood spread out from the dog's twitching body. The horses fidgeted at the sudden noise and then were still.

'Clear it away,' the sergeant ordered and, as one of the men leapt lightly from his horse, he turned back to address the elders. But the echoing of the shot had disturbed a flock of crows, which flew up from the trees and circled above the square, cawing so noisily that his first words were drowned. Behind one of the closed doors a baby started to cry.

Sam felt almost sorry for the sergeant who, under normal circumstances, would have been drinking coffee with the very man

70

who was now his prisoner. The sergeant too was wishing himself elsewhere. Until Hamid Bek's appointment his life had been simple – he rode around the villages, drank coffee and collected baksheesh. No one could be expected to live on his meagre wage and his relations with the locals had been, if not friendly, at least civilised. Now he could sense a silent hostility against him. Damn and curse Hamid Bek, he thought disrespectfully. And then: serve them right; why on earth did these educated people want to live in this cesspit desert of a land anyway. They deserved what was coming to them.

He pushed out his chin and spoke to Nissim who, apart from being the tallest of the elders, spoke fluent Turkish.

'I have come with orders and an edict issued by the glorious Enver Pasha himself.' He paused for a moment to give effect to his words. Then, taking a flimsy-looking document from inside his uniform, he unfolded it and held it high so all could see. The paper was of such poor quality that it fluttered in the slight breeze, annoying the sergeant who remembered that under the Sultan all edicts had been written on parchment. This skimpy little thing seemed in some way to undermine his importance, so he straightened his back and spoke harshly to increase his authority.

'This edict states that the Jewish settlements in Palestine must deliver up all unregistered arms – all illegal weapons – do you understand?' The sergeant glanced around at the crowd and saw a sea of impassive faces. 'If they are not given to us willingly, we have orders to search.' He grinned maliciously, his teeth white against his dark skin.

'Why arms from the Jewish settlements, Effendi Sergeant? Why not Arab or Greek arms? We Jews are all loyal citizens of the Empire.' Nissim spoke with a studied calm politeness that he was far from feeling. The sergeant shrugged; he was as much at a loss for an answer to that as they were. The Jews caused his men and him fewer problems than any of the other minority races in Palestine and, to give vent to his frustration, he tugged viciously on the rope, pulling the old man closer.

'What do you have to say about illegal arms, Effendi Uri? What answer will you give me?'

The old man raised his eyes to the sergeant's, his face full of a sudden fury, but he saw his wife's imploring expression and remained silent, lowering his eyes again.

71

'We have no illegal arms, Effendi Sergeant. Only a few registered guns, kept to protect the village from bandits.'

'I most urgently recommend you to think again.' The sergeant's voice was tight and furious. 'Colonel Hamid Bek, the new commandant of Jaffa, is most anxious for me to return with Jewish arms. I have orders to collect them at any cost. I am prepared to sit here and wait several times round the sun. Although I don't think that will be necessary.' As if to emphasise his leisure the sergeant took a handful of sunflower seeds from his pocket and began cracking them between his teeth, sucking out the sweet centre and spitting out the husks. The crowd was uneasy, each man waiting for a lead.

'Why are there orders to search for arms at all, Effendi Sergeant?' asked Nissim. He was still scrupulously polite but a tick beat in his cheek, a sure sign of his suppressed anger. 'Do you, sergeant, know why?' This challenge to his importance nettled the sergeant, but he too kept his self-control.

'It does not concern you.'

'My dear Effendi, it concerns us very much indeed. Without the few arms we have to protect us, we are open to attack from bandits and murderers alike.' Nissim's self-control was waning and his clenched fists showed his feelings: he was longing to beat the sergeant's brains out.

The sergeant, too, was beginning to lose his air of calmness. He was filled with a rising irritation. After all, he was in charge and it was time these people knew that once and for all. Swift as a snake, he took his bastinado from his belt and flicked it back and forth over the heads of the crowd. His horse, which had been half dozing in the sun, woke and pranced a little. The sergeant's upper lip was beaded with sweat.

'You will deliver the weapons to me – now – each and every one – now!' he shrieked, and brought the tip of the bastinado down on Uri's head. A thin line of blood appeared on the old man's face, widening and spreading until his beard was crimson with the stain. The silence was all at once broken by the angry muttering of the crowd, and the wailing of Uri's wife. Sam, who had been witnessing the scene with mounting horror, suddenly caught sight of Daniel's mother, her hands nervously twisting her apron, and her eyes constantly looking back towards her house, thanking heaven that it was so far back in the village and that her son was confined to his bed.

Uri did not flinch. 'Don't do anything on my behalf,' he warned the councillors, with a contemptuous look at the sergeant. 'He can torture me until I die – or until he sees what is so plainly the truth. *There are no arms.* And that is the end of the matter.' The sergeant, angry with himself for losing his temper, drew his mouth into a thin line. In spite of himself he knew anger would not lead him to the truth; he could torture this man until he was half dead with pain without learning a thing. Experience had taught him that the men who knew the secrets were the ones who could withstand the slowest torture to the death. More worrying than this, torture as a means of extracting information was routine, but to cause the death of a prisoner was a criminal offence. Torture was a very precise art. This was not a good day.

He still had his trump card left to play and now was the moment. 'Well, well. No arms. A disappointment, I admit,' he said, turning to address the square and then looking back at the committee. Suddenly he was the fanatic they had all suspected him to be. 'I don't notice any young women here to greet us,' he said conversationally, and added with vicious glee; 'if you can't bring us the guns, bring us your virgins instead. My men have worked hard recently, but they will give the girls a good time, won't you, boys?' The troops, delighted with this turn of events, gave an appreciative snigger, and shifted in their saddles.

The sergeant knew what he was about. Within seconds crazed mothers, fearful for their daughters, were begging their men to give the guns. Nissim realised he was beaten, or at any rate, almost. A few weeks before, some premonition had led him to split the community's secret cache of arms and relocate half of them. His pleasure at having outwitted the Turk was balanced only by his worry over the new edict. Carefully composing his features into a study of defeat, he turned towards the fields and told the sergeant to follow him.

Sam rode at a fast trot. The light was fading but he was secure in the knowledge that his horse knew the track even better than he did. Furthermore, the events of the last few hours had left him in a turmoil. For the first time he would be the man of the family, the one to bring home the news and suggest action. It was urgent that he should tell Zichron that the Turks had started to confiscate weapons – and that they were using every means to get at the hidden guns. Zichron had one great advantage over Hadera in that the research station was American territory. If they could only get their guns there before the Turks arrived they would be safe. Even now, in their present aggressive frame of mind, the Turks would not dare invade American property.

Sam was riding the chestnut gelding that had been resting at Hadera. After its break from farming, it was restless and skittish. The bay he had ridden over was pulling at the leading rein, unwilling to keep pace. The night was falling faster and faster: the blues of the sky were now pinks and purples; darkening clouds swept across the horizon. Sam made a quick decision – to leave the highroad and take a shorter route, along the foot of the mountains and through the swamps. Riding there at night carried some danger, but he knew the route well and after the events of the day he was both exhausted and concerned. He wanted to be home, safe in the bustle of the kitchen being fed by a nagging Fatma. And he wanted to be in bed.

The coastline was practically invisible now. Only in the far distance could he see a reddish light reflected in the moving sea. The black mountains loomed above him, blocking out the light from the few stars that had already appeared. Sam picked his way steadily along the tortuous bridle-path, through stunted shrubs of thorn bush, until he reached the thin line where cultivated land ended, ringed by straggling eucalyptus. On the other side of the trees was the swampland, almost dry now in the August heat. Giant reeds, thorns, and rushes grew in sad clumps on each side of him. The air was fetid and brackish. The horses never liked this part of the journey; the foul air made them uneasy and they breathed fast, snorting nervously. Sam urged the gelding on. Even in the dark he could find his way around every twist in the path and knew where every swampy patch threatened him.

The clouds parted and a big, bright moon floated over the man and horses. The pools of stagnant water were transformed into glittering silver ponds. The only sound was the horses' breathing and the slight creaking of the saddle.

Pushing a path through the thick scrub that grew halfway up the horses' chests, Sam caught the smell of woodsmoke hanging in the breeze. He was suddenly worried, remembering Fatma's warming that the Zabiah were in the district. He rode on a little faster, praying that he hadn't made a foolish mistake in taking the short cut. The horses also sensed something and, ears pricked, began dancing from left to right. Sam reassured them in a low whisper, but he could feel the tell-tale sweat break out on his face.

Something flashed like lightning in the scrub to his right and immediately disappeared. Sam reined in his horses and began listening hard in the moonlight, his eyes searching to make sense of the grotesque shadows which spread out before him. A slow shudder passed over the horses' flesh and Sam, his sense heightened, heard the cracking of a twig. Something was moving behind him. He sat stock still on the horse, praying that it was only tension that was making his ears play tricks on him.

And then he heard a sound that he recognised instantly and that sent ice cold terror down his spine. It was the cocking of a rifle. In that spinning second, the adrenalin racing, he knew that he had two choices: to fight or to flee. To fight was to die. Without thinking twice, he dropped the leading rein, leaving the bay to its fate, dug his heels hard into the chestnut's flanks and, lying close along his neck, urged him to gallop like the wind. The gelding gave a curious little arched hop before plunging wildly straight ahead into the scrub.

He slithered and stumbled in the soft dead earth, but Sam's panic had communicated itself to him and he flew with the wind. Until a gunshot cracked out into the night air, and with a hoarse wheeze he pitched forward and fell, throwing Sam over his head.

Dimly, Sam registered a group of Bedouin standing over him, their long daggers drawn. Sam felt a warm flow of blood run down his face.

'The dog is dead.' The voice sounded so far away. He saw, rather than felt, the boot come out and roll his head over. Then, merciful darkness began to overtake him and he fell into a deep black abyss.

It was ten o'clock before the Levinsons finally admitted that something serious might have happened to Sam. The first worry had been raised when he had not come home in time for dinner, as he had promised, but they reassured themselves that he could easily have set out a little late and would soon arrive, hungry for his supper. As the meal progressed they began to think that maybe he had been held up and had decided to stay the night and to set off at first light. Deep down they knew that this was unlikely as it was a rule of the community that, if a member did not return within a couple of hours of the time he had specified, a search party would be sent out. In a community as isolated as theirs, it was the only way to ensure everyone's safety. No one was to travel alone except in broad daylight, and even then the only safe roads were those patrolled by the septieh. The last vestiges of light had left the sky over two hours ago now.

'He ought to be back by now,' said Alex, running his fingers through his blond hair and pacing up and down the length of the drawing room. The others sat tensely, watching his long strides in silence.

Sara was almost feverish with concern. The trip to Hadera had been her idea, and had been for the most selfish of motives. It had already backfired on her when, furious, she had had to watch Sam ride away without her. And now, if anything had happened to him, she would never forgive herself.

'I feel something terrible has happened.' Her voice was almost a whisper and she twisted her skirt between her fingers as she tried to blot out the horrifying images that had invaded her mind more and more persistently over the past couple of hours.

'What do you think we should do?' Lev asked morosely, cracking his finger joints.

Sara looked at him irritably. It was by now obvious what they should do, and his habit of cracking his knuckles maddened her at the best of times.

Aaron stood up. 'I think we should go and look for him. He may have fallen and injured himself, or he may have lost the horse and be trying to make his way back on foot.' He looked to his father for approval and Abram, who had been sitting silently until now, nodded. 'Lev, would you call in Manny and Robby,' he asked. As it was the harvest they were staying in the village, rather than at the research station. It would not take long to gather a search party together this evening.

Sara looked at her father and suddenly realised how much he had been hiding his worry for their sakes and how relieved he was by the action.

Aaron immediately took command and began to plan the routes they would follow. 'Alex and I will go in Jezebel and cover the coast road – it will be quicker and easier by car. Lev, when you've raised Manny and Robby, go ask Abu to saddle up four horses. Then you, Abu, Manny and Robby can ride the Carmel ridge and swamps. If he's hurt he could be anywhere.'

'I'll put on my riding skirt and come with you,' Sara said,

determined to be of some use, but Aaron put out a restraining hand. 'Please, Aaron. He's my brother too,' she pleaded.

'If something has happened, we will need you here,' he said gently and Sara, seeing the sense in what he said, reluctantly gave in.

Twenty minutes later they were all gathered in the courtyard, ready to set off. The four riders were mounted and Alex and Aaron were standing ready by the car, which Alex had just cranked to unwilling life.

'Right,' Aaron said; 'are you sure you've all got plenty of ammunition?' They all nodded. 'When you reach the fork in the swamps, pair off. Four is too many together and two can keep an eye on a small area and on each other. Anyone who finds him, shoot three shots into the air. If we hear more – or fewer – shots, we will know that you are in trouble and will try and reach you.'

He looked up at the clear sky. 'Luckily it's a moonlit night. Good luck and God help us,' he said, and watched the four riders set off before climbing into the car.

The four mounted men rode in near silence towards the silhouette of the mountain. They heard the put-putting of the car gradually dying away as it headed down the hill to the coast. Despite the moonlight, the going was slow and hard on the stony track, and by the time they reached the fork in the road the moon had almost disappeared behind a milky layer of mist. Abu drew up and motioned that Manny and he would take the track due west while the other two were to follow the ridge – these were the only routes, apart from the coast road, that Sam could have taken back from Hadera.

'Don't call out for Sam,' Manny said as they straggled apart. 'If he was ambushed by Bedouin they could be lying in wait for the search party.' They nodded and, rifles at the ready, lost sight of each other as they separated.

The air became thick and hot with the foul stench of the swamps as Manny's horse fidgeted under him, communicating its nervousness to him. His rifle lay across the pommel of his saddle and he fingered it for reassurance. 'If only I could see clearly,' he whispered to Abu who motioned him to silence, nodding agreement. The dry cough of a scurrying jackal made Manny jump

77

and he cursed himself for his cowardice. His ears and eyes stretched to their limits, he rode warily on.

They came to a twisted stretch of track, strewn with rubble and broken branches. Manny, working over the trail like a hunting dog, was the first to see Sam, his bone white face glistened in the moonlight. He leapt off his horse and bent over him. Sam was lying so still that for a few heart-stopping moments Manny thought he was dead.

He dropped to his knees, frantically feeling for a pulse. 'He's dead – he's got to be dead,' he said, on the verge of hysteria. Whispering a prayer he gently turned Sam over and noticed a large, ugly gash across the side of his head. Then he felt it and let out a heavy sigh of relief; there was a pulse.

He looked up at Abu, who had also dismounted, and nodded. Abu's eyes were misty, but his face was dark with a rage Manny had never seen there before. Abu raised his rifle and fired one shot, then another and, reloading, a third.

'Help me get him across one of the horses – we'll take turns riding back,' Manny said; and added, looking down at the wound, 'he must have fallen and knocked himself out on the rock.' Abu shook his head. Even in this dim light he had made out the tracks of more than one horse.

'Your brother's a very lucky young man,' said Doctor Ephraim, stepping back to admire his handiwork with the bandages. 'He's got away with nothing worse than a slight concussion. Not many wander off into the night and live to tell the tale.' He shook his head reflectively as he neatly packed up his case. Sara smiled to herself at his words. She well knew that he had more than once been guilty himself of 'wandering off' into the Arab areas, curing the sick in outlying villages or doing his best to help stem an epidemic in a Bedouin tribe. But he, like all the best of his kind, was protected by unseen guardians wherever he travelled. No one would harm the old doctor with his mane of white hair; Sam, unfortunately, had not yet earned the same respect.

'More luck than brains,' said Sara, gently squeezing Sam's still, cold hand. He opened his eyes, smiled weakly at her, and closed them again.

'That's right, sleep. Don't try to talk any more,' commanded Doctor Ephraim. 'Everything is under control.'

Sam had gained consciousness almost as soon as he had been

laid on his own bed and had managed to mumble his story before passing out again. The search party had immediately disbanded to wake up and warn the villagers, and by now, Sara assured Sam, whatever weapons the villagers owned that were not registered with the Ottoman government would be well on their way to the slicks at the research station.

'Now Sam must have complete rest, and he will recover quickly.' Doctor Ephraim said as they left the room. 'I trust you to make sure he gets it.' Sara took his hand in thanks.

'I'll try, Doctor Ephraim. I know how important rest is,' she promised, as she showed him to the door. 'And many thanks.'

Dawn had already broken and when Sara returned to Sam's room he had a little colour in his cheeks again. Tired from all the fear and emotion she had experienced in the last ten hours, Sara settled herself into the chair by Sam's bed. *Those swine*, she thought. *They left him for dead. And took our horses. May they rot in hell.*

Despite herself Sara's eyes began to close and, for the first time since the worry about Sam had started, her thoughts turned to Daniel. At least he was safe in Hadera with his mother. And before long he would be safely with them. They would all be safe as long as the Turk stayed out of the war.

Please God, don't let it happen. I'm frightened. Please. Why was it that, as soon as things looked set fair in life, something always intervened?

She reached for Sam's hand. It was warmer now and as soon as she felt his fingers close round hers she fell asleep in her chair like a small child.

CHAPTER FIVE

Sara's hair, still slightly damp after being washed, hung loose to her waist. She paused for a moment, hesitating in the shade of the barn before venturing out into the sunlight that was still blazing defiantly for the last hours before dusk. The potted plants and small trees that lined the courtyard had been recently watered and Leylah was just finishing her twice daily job of spraying water over the paving stones to settle the dust. The result was a brief respite of coolness in the air, a fresh smell of damp earth and a buzzing of insects come to take advantage of the water.

Despite the recent trauma over Sam, Sara was in a very good mood. This had always been her favourite time of day and she shook her hair back over her shoulders with a rare and inexplicable sense of freedom as she crossed to the group of meterological instruments ranged against the southern wall. Every day since she was eight Sara had performed this little ritual for Aaron and had religiously noted down the temperature and atmosphere humidity. As a child it had been, to her, her most important responsibility and she had crossed the courtyard with an important step, her notebook and pen held tightly in small, hot hands. Now she took a different, but no less keen, joy in the chore. Once trusted with this job, Sara had progressed to the task of labelling all the rock and plant specimens Aaron brought back from his field trips. Palestine, at the crossroads of three continents and placed between two seas and three deserts, had a rich and varied plant life – so much so that the discoveries made throughout the country were astonishing botanists and agronomists worldwide.

Sara shared Aaron's interest in botany, if not his passion, and in the study he had built himself in the courtyard Sara and Aaron would pore over the expensive European reference books. The Latin names were easy enough to find but then came the more difficult task of finding the Hebrew and Arabic equivalents. For centuries Hebrew had been reserved almost entirely for prayer; Sara's generation was the first to try and revive it as a living tongue. But, if encouraging people to speak the language was hard, scientific classification was almost impossible. Slowly and painstakingly, they made their way through the Bible and found that by listening to the Arab fellahin employed at Zichron they could hear an echo of the ancient Hebrew names in the Arabic nomenclature.

As they began to trace the names, they wrote them down on a card, together with a note of the place the plant had been found. Four years before Aaron had arrived back from a lecture tour in America with a new invention, a typewriting machine, and for the following year Sara had been tied constantly to the Remington, typing out three thousand different cards for the plant section alone. The collection, by now famous all over the world, had for some time been housed at the research station: Sara could never look at it without a sense of pride.

The job done and the temperatures recorded, Sara strolled over to the stables. Apollo, Aaron's vicious black stallion, snickered when he saw her and shifted restlessly in his loose box. Sara reached in and cautiously patted his head. Alex had tried to mate Bella – Sara's little Arab mare – with Apollo, but Bella would have none of it.

Sara had every sympathy with her mare. She was uncomfortably aware that her family considered her to be in the marriage market. The thought of this brought her mind back to Chaim Cohen. After much heralding and blowing of trumpets, this latest prospective suitor was expected for dinner that evening. After such a build-up Sara almost expected him to arrive in a puff of smoke and with an accompanying clap of thunder.

The reminder of Cohen's presence at dinner dampened Sara's lighthearted mood. Not only would she have to act the perfect hostess, but there was another, more important guest expected – Daniel.

Daniel was now working for Aaron and living at Atlit, but tonight he was staying with the Levinsons in preparation for the dance, thrown annually by the settlers, they were attending the following night. Sara's hairwash had been both to prepare herself for the next day and to get out of the way of the preparations for dinner, which had already reached frenetic proportions.

Abu, sitting cross-legged under some bougainvillea-covered wattling which afforded a little shadow, looked up at Sara and smiled in welcome. He and Hamid, Leylah's brother who helped around the farm, were busy mending some leather harnesses. Abu's dark, ancient eyes gleamed in the shade. Sara reassured him, responding to his unarticulated question:

'Sam's just fine,' she said. 'He was up for a few hours this morning and is staying up for dinner tonight.' Sara and Abu had a strong relationship, based on an almost mystical communication between them. It had always been so. When Sara was six, Abu had mysteriously appeared from nowhere and helped her father with a difficult horse; he had not asked if he could stay but permission was not needed – a man with Abu's skill would be welcome anywhere in the Empire.

Abu had taught Sara many of his secrets about horses, how to track wild animals and find water in the most arid landscape and, also, how to understand him. He was very protective about the Levinsons, and Sara in particular, but no one had ever seen him angrier than when he had returned to Zichron with Sam's bloodied body a week earlier. During that week Sam enjoyed the status of village hero. The only people who had had quite enough of the hero were Fatma and Sara, driven mad by the stream of girls and by the hero's constant demand for attention. Fortunately for their sanity, Sam had today been given permission to get out of bed, but he was still confined to the house until the next night.

Sam's speedy recovery was lucky for all, but it had not assuaged Abu's fury. He had an Arab's single-mindedness about honour and saw the attack on Sam and the loss of the horses as an affront to the Levinsons' – and hence his own – honour. The morning after the attack he had set off to track the horses and had returned with the chestnut on a leading rein. He was lame and had been abandoned by the bandits but, lame or not, Abu was tremendously pleased about finding him, which superstitious Fatma had, of course, taken as a good omen for Sam's recovery.

Giving the stallion a farewell pat on his proud nose, Sara followed the winding path back through the orchard towards the kitchen garden and clicked the white gate shut behind her. The peace in the garden was absolute: countless butterflies, bright as paint, flickered in and out of the lavender and thyme and the steady hum of the bees provided a musical backdrop.

Sara wandered towards the purple-stained stone bench under the mulberry tree and, remembering Fatma's shrill request for mint for the fruit salad, picked a large bunch from the herb garden. The flower garden itself had been laid out by Sara's mother over thirty years before when the Levinsons first arrived in Zichron, and Sara could only marvel at her mother's persistence in cultivating the white roses that now bloomed profusely throughout the area. Indeed, everything around her was a testimony to the enthusiasm and hard work of the original fifty families – including Sara's parents, and a six-year-old Aaron. The Levinsons had come to Palestine to escape a life in Rumania that had become intolerable for Jews. They had arrived filled with dreams of the redemption of the Holy Land and the revival of the Jewish state.

Even with these dreams to nourish them, they had been dismayed by the tree-less, barren hillside that greeted them. The only houses had been a few primitive Arab huts, set precariously into the side of the hill. But, with a determination and vigour that neither the Arabs nor the Turkish overlords could begin to comprehend, the families had set to work, built themselves huts of mud and wattling and begun the never-ending task of clearing the land of rocks and stones.

Despite their hard work it became more and more apparent that the rocky land was totally unfit for farming and the settlers could well have met with total disaster had it not been for the timely appearance of Baron Edmond de Rothschild. The French Baron had begun to take a deep interest in the development of Palestine and, when the settlers needed it most, he stepped in with generous financial assistance and, just as importantly, agricultural experts and vines from his own vineyards in France.

The years passed and the land took on an order and a beauty that it had not had since Biblical times. Life for the immigrants of Zichron – and other, newer settlements around – improved steadily and their earlier harsh existence became gradually easier and more pleasant.

Aaron, who could just remember life in Rumania, took to Palestine from the very beginning. He treated the discomfort as adventure and lived in a world of his own, searching out the secrets of nature and even as a child making endless notes on small pieces of paper. He soon outgrew the village school. 'Your boy's a genius,' the schoolteacher said to Miriam Levinson and, although she demurred politely, the teacher was not the only person to point out her son's remarkable qualities.

Aaron was not liked by everyone: he was a man of science in a farming community and as such subject to the petty jealousies of small-minded people. Soon it was being put about that Aaron Levinson had grandiose ideas and, when the research station was opened, it was suggested that he was 'feathering his own nest'. By the meaner-minded his success was taken almost as a personal insult. The Levinson family began to close in on itself more and more and relations with the village – now nine hundred strong – grew steadily worse. On the whole, though, they remained on good terms with the older settlers, especially Doctor Ephraim and his wife, who were among the guests expected for dinner tonight.

Sara often came to sit on the stone bench for a moment of privacy, a short break from the hectic routine in the house. A muted clatter of pans from the kitchen was a pleasant reminder that she was avoiding work for a time and, the branches making shadowed patterns on her closed eyelids, she allowed the evening sun to soak into her bones and warm her skin. She was filled with peace and a quiet joy. Life was good again: Sam was alive, Enver Pasha had refused to join in the war, Daniel was working with Aaron and tonight . . .

'Dreaming of your future husband, little maiden?' Sara snapped open her eyes to see Sam looking down at her, hands in his pockets and a teasing look in his eye that spoke volumes for his improved health.

'Little maiden indeed!' she retorted. 'Little slave more like, resting after a week of dedication to Pasha Sam. And anyway you're not supposed to be in the sun,' she added.

'Nelly tells me Chaim Cohen is not only very rich, but also very attractive,' Sam volunteered, carefully ignoring her last remark.

'Nelly Jacobson is a gossip and has no sense at all – proved by her choice of you as a beau. Added to which,' she said, rising haughtily and collecting her scattered bunch of mint, 'I have no intention of throwing myself into matrimony, however varied – and rich,' she stressed, with a glint in her eye, 'the charms of Mr Cohen.'

'Then you had better hide your own not inconsiderable charms under a bushel,' Sam laughed, bowing sardonically. 'As the word is out that Mr Cohen is very keen to meet you.'

Sara gave her brother a withering look. 'Don't bore me with such rubbish,' she said and, with a swirl of her skirts, strode off to the kitchen to deliver the mint.

Damn Aaron for forcing this unwelcome man on them this evening. By now the whole village – if not the whole of Palestine – would know about this evening's dinner and would be waiting to hear its outcome. Sara knew it was not only her brothers who thought it was time she was married. She wondered what Daniel thought about a wife-hunter coming to look her over, but supposed with a sigh that he would not even notice. Mind you, if this man was as attractive as it was rumoured – Sara had to admit that she was the smallest bit curious – it might not hurt Daniel to feel there was some competition for her. Now that was a thought worth playing with.

Sara had one more job to do before it was time to change for dinner and she ran into the house and up the stairs to the attic office where all the farm and vinery records were kept. She opened a big black ledger on the desk and neatly copied the details of temperature and humidity, which she had noted down earlier.

The room was stuffy and Sara opened the small, round window in front of the desk, leaning out of it for a breath of air.

Chin on hands, she gazed down into the valley. Suddenly her eye was drawn back from the familiar view of the Crusader castle and the sea towards the station. Now, at the end of the day, it should have been quiet, but there seemed to be a hive of activity. Sara reached for the field glasses that hung by the desk and focused them on the courtyard in front of the station. Sure enough, a group of ten or twelve men was there and, as she watched, Sara saw the men mount up and ride off. Near Jezebel, Sara could make Daniel out, and saw him talking to a horseman that she was sure was Lev.

Puzzled, she laid the glasses down. Something was going on and, whatever it was, they certainly did not want her to know about it.

Aaron stood at the window of the research station looking out at the courtyard, his mind still working over the afternoon's events. The air in the room was heavy with the smell of cheroot and cigarette smoke, but despite the staleness there was still a feeling of excitement in the atmosphere. It had been a very constructive afternoon.

The idea had come from Daniel who, like everyone else, had been incensed at Sam's beating and was deeply concerned over the

Turkish campaign to deprive the settlements of their only means of self-defence against marauding Arab bandits. This was the first time the Turkish authorities had taken serious measures against the Jewish settlements; until now they had confined themselves to harassing them, sometimes quite viciously. But this time the Turks seemed to be motivated on racial grounds. What frightened the farmers and worried the community leaders was the discrimination between the weapons of Jews and those of the other minorities.

'Perhaps this is just the beginning of real persecution,' Alex had said over lunch one afternoon.

'I believe it is,' Daniel answered, and paused for a moment before turning determined dark eyes on Aaron.

'And that emphasises the need for us to do something about it – and as soon as possible. Despite Enver Pasha babbling on about the Empire being the Switzerland of the Levant, we all know that Turkey is planning to enter the war. The Turks fear that we will conspire with the Allies against them – so they are confiscating our weapons to crush any possibility of domestic rebellion, or treason, as they would call it.'

Aaron rose and silently closed the door. 'Talking of treason, you could be hanged for saying as much as you just have,' he warned. 'But you are right, of course. Unless we put some sort of plan into action the future in the northern settlements is beginning to look very bleak indeed.'

'There is a lot of evidence to show that our Arab watchmen are becoming more and more unreliable,' Lev put in, cracking his knuckles agitatedly. The watchmen who guarded the more isolated Jewish farms and settlements were Arabs – quite often Bedouins who were supposed to protect the livestock and harvest from their fellow tribesmen. Up to now the system had on the whole worked rather well. 'They know there is no justice in the land,' Lev went on, 'and don't seem to fear the Turks any more. We've all seen how futile it is to try and bring known wrongdoers to account, and now it's even been known for a whole herd to disappear in the middle of the night – along with the so-called watchman. We are now caught between the Turk and the Arab like some tasty morsel between the jaws of a crocodile.'

'Perhaps we should reconsider calling in the Hashomer,' said Manny, very quietly.

Some years before a security group, the Hashomer, had been

formed, the first Jewish attempt at self-defence. That group had won itself a formidable reputation, but from the beginning had allied itself with the socialist and Zionist movements in Palestine. In return for its protection, each settlement had to employ fifteen immigrant workers. Zichron, like the majority of the older settlements, had refused, believing that men and boys with no farming experience could not possibly compete with the Arab workers.

Aaron shook his head. He had nothing against most of the members of the Hashomer personally, and would happily have used their services had he not felt so deeply alienated from their ideology. He had no time for the many émigré Europeans who had recently arrived in Palestine carrying the banners of communism and socialism, and trying to force their ideas on the farmers. None of them had anything to do with farming, which was the priority for the building of Palestine into a Jewish state. He maintained a polite relationship with people like Ivan Bernski, but he was not going to have other people's beliefs forced upon him.

'No,' he said. 'We must handle this ourselves.'

Daniel nodded agreement and put forward his plan, which seemed well thought out and sensible. He proposed that they form a small group of loyal friends who would work together to protect the settlement and to piece together information and rumour until they found a pattern that would keep them one step ahead of the Turk.

This afternoon the eighteen men invited to form the nucleus of the group had met for the first time. Alex had dubbed them the 'watch group' and it looked as though the name would stick for they had jokingly used the nickname throughout the meeting.

Still thinking hard, Aaron noticed Alex and Daniel in the courtyard, deep in conversation with Paul Levy, an enormous English Jew who had stopped at Zichron on his way to Cairo five years ago and had stayed. The Englishman and his wife Eve were trusted and popular members of the community and Aaron smiled as he saw Paul heave his twenty-one-stone body on to his massive bob-tailed carthorse. It was the only horse Abu had been able to find that was large enough to bear Paul's weight.

Alex waved as Paul rode off at a lumbering canter, and Aaron watched him from the window until all he could see was a spiral of dust. Aaron was particularly pleased that Paul had agreed to join them – he was sure that he would prove a valuable member of the group and would more than pull his not insignificant weight. Paul was different from the normal run of settlers and effortlessly attracted admirers and followers from a wide range of people. He had achieved near immortal status among the Bedouin as a result of having once, with a single blow, felled a camel, which had tried to grab his shirt-tail in the Beersheba market.

Aaron consulted his pocket watch and turned back into the room. The maps of Europe and the Empire that papered the walls suddenly took on a new importance. Until now they had been there purely for research purposes. That afternoon they had served a more ominous one.

True facts about what was happening in the war were not easy to come by in such remote settlements as Zichron. The only information about the battle fronts of Europe and passed by the censor came via the German in Constantinople. But a few days ago a piece of luck had arrived in the shape of Chaim Cohen, a Turkish Jew who had come from Constantinople in search of barley for the German Army. Cohen was well-mannered but rather pompous and too aware of his own importance. Aaron had soon put him at his ease. Although intelligent he was easy to flatter and it had not taken too much diplomacy to learn a great deal of interest from him.

Over a glass of Aaron's carefully-hoarded French Cognac at the research station, Cohen told them that, despite official denials, mobilisation in Turkey was being pushed forward at a great pace. Troops in and around Constantinople were constantly seen drilling and there was a visible increase in the number of German officers in the city. In the last six months the average citizen had become very much more aware of the military presence, and it seemed that the Germans were arming the Turks as fast as possible. Ship-loads of munitions arrived weekly and left the city immediately – presumably to be distributed throughout the Empire.

'Surely that is in direct defiance of international law?' Aaron asked.

Chaim shrugged fatalistically. 'Of course it is, and Turkey is certainly flouting its obligations as a neutral power. But the German Ambassador, Baron von Wangenheim, is a man of amazing energy and is very pushy. Beside which, he has years of experience in Turkey and is very thick with Enver Pasha. All the cards are in his hand.'

'But what of the British and French – aren't they lodging complaints?'

'The British Ambassador arrived here only last year. He knows little about Turkey and not even a word of the language. The same goes for his three under-secretaries. He knows just what he is told, which is that Turkey has no intention of joining the war and intends to remain neutral.' Chaim was obviously enjoying being a man of the world, with a wealth of confidential information. His type was always the easiest to milk.

'What do you think will happen?' Aaron asked. 'Things get around.'

Chaim smiled knowledgeably. 'In Constantinople we know preparations are being made – our only question is against whom? At first we thought it was Greece, but when we realised that the emphasis was being placed on the army, we wondered if the intention was to push the British out of Egypt. When I left ten days ago opinion had switched; Russia seemed to be the target. If that is the case then, of course, Turkey will be joining Germany and Austria. But I've been away for over a week – I could be out of date by now.'

Aaron and Daniel exchanged glances.

'On the whole I think no one would be surprised if Turkey did join forces with Germany – except perhaps Talaat Bey and Jemel Pasha, who are friendly with the British and French – and trusted by them.'

All this and more was discussed at that afternoon's meeting and one conclusion was obvious: Palestine was in for a difficult period, which would be more easily faced if certain precautions were taken now. The settlement's problems were already being sorted out, but Aaron had other responsibilities to think about as well and he now turned his mind to these.

He had no doubt that, with troops running round the country looking for trouble, Becky and Sara would be safer elsewhere. He had already given some thought to this, and had come up with a solution as far as Becky was concerned. She might not like it, but she would have no choice. He had written to his friend Henry Morgenthau, the American Ambassador to the Empire, and had asked for his help in finding a place for Becky at the American College in Beirut. He had also asked Henry to find her a good family with whom to lodge. Aaron had every faith in Henry and knew that, once Becky was sent off, he would have little need to worry about her. She had a happy nature and was bright – and if she did have any doubts, the lure of the bright city lights would probably help change her mind.

Sara was the major problem. Her infatuation with Daniel was becoming increasingly obvious and, if it went any further, would put her chances of a good marriage in jeopardy. Aaron loved and respected Daniel as a friend but had no illusions as to what sort of husband he would make. Daniel was impulsive and contemptuous of any kind of authority: characteristics that might make a good revolutionary, but would not make Sara happy in the long term. Aaron was also fairly sure that Daniel had no intention of marrying Sara or, for that matter, anyone else.

He heard Alex's voice calling up at him and moved back to the window. 'Come on, Aaron, we're going to be late for dinner.'

Aaron crossed over to his desk and locked away a few papers. He did have one answer to the problem of Sara. Chaim Cohen had a second reason for coming to Palestine – he was looking for a wife. For that reason Aaron had invited him to dinner this evening: he could be Sara's last chance before the war overtook everything. With this in mind he made his way slowly down to the courtyard. Who knew, with luck Zichron might fulfil both Cohen's needs.

Sara came downstairs at seven to find the guests already gathering on the veranda drinking one of Fatma's special punches. Sara had not been able to resist the temptation of making an entrance – and she had done it in style. Sarah Bernhardt herself could not have made a more dramatic effect than Sara as, head held high and back straight as an athlete's, she came through the double doors on to the veranda. There was a brief silence before she held out her hand to Mrs Ephraim, apologising for not having been downstairs to greet her. Sara's hair, held back by combs, shone with the healthiness of youth. Her dress was a soft silk, a watery violet, which changed from blue to grey to the softest purple in the light. She was aware that something new in her appearance was creating an impression, but she did not know what it was. Daniel caught it immediately, a voluptuousness that hinted at some inner awakening.

Even Doctor Ephraim was momentarily dazzled by this girl he had known ever since he had delivered her over twenty years before. It confused him a little, but he bowed and kissed her hand warmly. 'You look lovely, my dear ... more like your mother than I would have expected – don't you think so, Irma?' His wife, a bird-like woman nodded.

'It's something in the way she holds herself – you should be proud, Mr Levinson.'

'I am.' The old man was beaming at the sight of his daughter's beauty and then, with a start, he added: 'But how rude of me. Mr Cohen, this is my daughter Sara. Sara, Mr Cohen.'

Sara had wanted to look pretty tonight, but was startled by the effect she was having on the company, all of whom – except this stranger – knew her well. She had been watching Daniel out of the corner of her eye ever since she had come on to the veranda. He was certainly looking at her with an intensity he had not shown since the day of his return – but in the meantime she must pay attention to the new guest.

Chaim Cohen was standing next to Aaron. At the moment, though, Cohen was showing no interest in him, but was looking at her with open admiration. Sara gave him her hand, meeting his eyes directly, and he bowed courteously. She had to admit that he was a good-looking man. Tall and well-built, the elegance of his suit did nothing to disguise his muscular arms and shoulders. His eyes were bright and black, his nose perhaps slightly on the large side. His hair was dark and attractively curly, though a little too carefully arranged. His mouth was firm, but the lips were slightly too thin – a feature Sara always distrusted. But, all in all, he was a handsome man, even if he was too aware of it. Sara quickly formed the impression that he thought himself a good match; this was not a man coming cap in hand to a girl's guardians, but a man who looked as though he thought he was offering a good deal.

Sara stole a glance at Daniel, who was leaning against one of the columns of the veranda and scowling at her. For the first time Sara experienced the true power of womanhood. It was obvious that Daniel was jealous; he did admire her as much as Mr Cohen and old Doctor Ephraim – but his admiration mattered to her so much more than theirs. Perhaps he was seeing her afresh as a strange man might, and was liking what he saw. Her earlier instinct had obviously been right – the idea of competition was not one which appealed to him. Now she knew what game to play.

Over dinner Sara carried out her part to perfection. She had placed herself in between Aaron and Chaim and had plenty of time in which to study her suitor. He was unfailingly polite and easy to talk to, slightly too sure of himself, and almost inhumanly calm.

91

She had the strange feeling that it would be almost impossible to ruffle him; it was as though he was untouched by any emotions – even perhaps love.

As they ate the *borsch*, which Fatma had spent much of the day preparing, Aaron chatted to Mrs Ephraim on his other side, leaving Sara to talk to Chaim. Daniel was on the same side of the table as her, sitting between Becky, who was teasing him unmercifully and giggling a lot, and Sara's father. Sara tried to hear what was being discussed at the other end of the table, but to no avail, and Daniel's face was out of her line of vision. Sara fell silent as she watched his long brown fingers toy with the bread and then play with a silver spoon. The pale yellow light of the candles lent a strange intimacy to the scene and this, coupled with the wine Sara had drunk, made her mind wander. She could not help but imagine Daniel's hands on her body . . .

'Some more wine, Sara?'

She was so startled at Aaron's voice that she temporarily lost her own.

'Oh yes, thank you,' she muttered and quickly rang the bell for Fatma to bring in the next course. With an air of a magician proud of his latest trick, Fatma came in carrying a huge dish of lamb stuffed with apricots. She set it down with a flourish on the sideboard, leaving Sara to serve. Behind her Sara heard Aaron and Chaim discussing the merits of the wine, which came from their own vineyards, and she wondered if her brother were trying to sell some of that too.

'Rather good,' he said with a certain modest pride. 'Of course, we don't claim that it can compare with any of the great wines of France – but I think we can honestly boast that our Cabernet Sauvignon surpasses many of their table wines.'

Chaim Cohen raised his glass to the light to inspect the colour and, pleased with what he saw, took another delicate sip. He nodded appreciatively. 'It is certainly very drinkable,' he said with a faintly, patronising air. 'And I must say it seems to provide the village with a healthy living.'

'Oh, it wasn't always like this,' Mrs Ephraim interjected. 'You would not believe it if you saw the land when we arrived – how long ago now?' she turned to her husband.

'Thirty years,' he told her, eyeing his plate of lamb with satisfaction.

'Thirty-one,' Abram corrected him with a smile. 'Nearly thirty-two now, and we arrived with nothing.' He looked round the room with pride at what they had achieved. 'There was nothing here and the land – the land was just a strip of rocky nothingness. I almost wept with despair when I first saw it.'

Well, that's done it, Sara thought irritably as she sat down with her food and nodded acceptance for a refill of her wineglass. Now for the millionth time we are going to have to hear what a hard time they all had, how they had to live in mud huts and dig the rocks out with their bare hands until we get to the bit where they would all have died had it not been for the extraordinary generosity of Baron de Rothschild. She could not even start a conversation with Cohen as presumably this was all being aimed at him.

'Ah, the Baron,' Mrs Ephraim sighed. 'He sent us seeds and medicine and vines and hope.'

Becky, as bored of these often repeated stories as Sara, made a great play of accidentally knocking over her almost empty wineglass and successfully diverted the conversation. As Leylah came in to clear the plates and Fatma brought in the fruit salad, Sara realised that she had not participated much in the conversation and was not really doing her duty as a hostess. After another failed attempt to hear what Daniel was talking about, she turned with an effort to Chaim.

'Do tell us about Constantinople, Mr Cohen,' she said. 'Is it as exciting as we are led to believe?' Chaim was relieved at her move to open a conversation with him. He had found her silence disconcerting as most women he met needed little encouragement and looked on him with a keen interest. He cleared his throat and relaxed in his chair; one thing he did know how to do was talk and soon he had everyone's attention.

'It is very exciting indeed, Miss Levinson,' he assured her. 'It is a beautiful and cultured city. Just as the West looked to the East for inspiration and beauty in the last century, so we now look to the West. We have an opera that is not bad, and many touring European companies come to play in our theatres. In Pera, which is just across the bridge from Stamboul, our streets are full of smart carriages and the shops are stocked with the latest fashions from Paris and Vienna.'

'I doubt that will last long, with the war in Europe,' Daniel said with a sudden and startling vehemence. But Becky was having none of this.

'Daniel, do stop going on about the war,' she groaned and turned immediately back to Chaim. 'Please continue, Mr Cohen. I do so want to hear more about the lights, the music and the actresses.'

The atmosphere relaxed again and everyone laughed. Chaim waxed lyrical about the charms of Constantinople, answering Becky's eager questions with perfect politeness, but addressing himself pointedly to Sara. Sara was beginning to enjoy being the centre of attention. She had no interest in Cohen, although she admitted freely to herself that he was handsome and, of course, rich. But all this was as nothing compared to the presence of Daniel and the knowledge that, despite himself, his outward gaiety was concealing a very jealous mood. Chaim, working hard to charm this Palestinian beauty, was unaware that it was because of Daniel that her eyes were sparkling such a deep and dangerous blue and that, by playing court to her, he was playing right into her hands.

Daniel, meanwhile, was in an agonising dilemma. For the first time he was forced to admit the power that Sara had over him. He wanted to stick to his principles, but more than that he wanted to love and be loved by Sara and to see Chaim Cohen at the bottom of the Red Sea. He found himself confused, hating himself and loving Sara. He had not realised how difficult it would be to be so close to Sara and wished he had never agreed to stay in the house over the holiday period. He would be glad when the next few days were over and he could get away from the distraction of her company.

Becky, by now in a state of high excitement, turned her most bewitching gaze on Chaim.

'Is it true that you are looking for a wife, Mr Cohen?' she asked saucily. Doctor Ephraim laughed into his fruit salad and, not for the first time, thanked heaven that he had been blessed only with sons.

'Becky!' Sara had blushed crimson. For a fleeting second, Cohen placed a kind hand on her arm and smiled serenely round the table. As she had suspected, nothing seemed to fluster the man. He looked back at Becky.

'Yes, young lady, that is perfectly true. But after this evening, if fortune smiles,' and he turned again to Sara, 'I may not have to look any further.'

Sara stiffened involuntarily and looked down at her plate. She felt Chaim leaning towards her. 'You are a very beautiful young lady, Miss Levinson,' he said in a low voice, 'and I believe you are not spoken for. If my request has not been pre-empted by some other lucky man, may I have the honour of escorting you to the dance tomorrow night?'

Sara was filled with conflicting thoughts. She wished she dared say no, but knew it would be rude and embarrassing. Even more, she wished that it were Daniel speaking to her like this – why hadn't he formally invited her to the dance? But no, he had expected her to tag along with the others and to spend the evening waiting for him to ask her to dance. She dug her fingernails into her palms, furious at her impotence in the face of the unfairness of life. Well, to hell with him.

She looked up at Chaim, nodded her head and smiled bewitchingly.

'Thank you, Mr Cohen. That would be wonderful,' she said.

'Well,' said Becky in an approving tone and sounding more like an older than a younger sister, 'I think he's very nice – very nice indeed.' The party had broken up and the family and Daniel were drinking coffee on the veranda, discussing the dinner as hosts always do after their guests have been seen safely off.

'Very nice indeed,' Daniel echoed ironically. 'The rich – like the devil – have all the best tunes.'

Sara gave a self-confident little laugh.

'You're all talking nonsense,' she said, tossing her head indifferently. Secretly, though, she was very pleased with herself. She had had her first taste of sophisticated flattery and also of jealousy and it was sweet to her inexperienced youth. Humming a few bars of *Faust*, she bid everyone good night and waltzed happily upstairs to bed. Tomorrow was the dance.

As soon as Sara opened her eyes she could tell from the sunlight streaming into her room she had overslept. She listened for any movement in the house but could hear nothing. It was unlike Fatma to leave her to sleep, but she supposed that the fit of kindness had been brought on by the late night before and the prospect of the dance ahead. Added to which, Sara knew that whenever a prospective suitor loomed on the horizon Fatma treated her like a pampered young lady rather than a household skivvy. The likes of Chaim Cohen had their compensations.

She lay for a moment, luxuriating in the silence and in the comfort of her bed. On the whole she had enjoyed the evening before; Chaim had been nicer than she expected. And, of course, Daniel – she smiled at the thought of his jealousy, pleased that she had discovered how to arouse it . . . and him.

Stopping her thoughts there, Sara leapt out of bed and ran to the window. It was another glorious day. Perhaps she would slip off for a ride before it became too hot. Spurred on by the prospect, Sara washed and dressed hurriedly. She was just brushing her hair when she heard the familiar choking noise Jezebel always made when she was first started. That reminded her: what had been going on at the station yesterday? She had not had a chance to ask Aaron before dinner, and it was not really a subject she could raise in front of a stranger, but now it was time to find out.

She dropped her brush and ran down the stairs. Just as Aaron had got Jezebel going he was surprised to see an eager face thrust through the car window.

'Good morning, Sara – you slept late.' Then, in spite of himself, he couldn't help asking: 'What did you think of our friend Cohen?'

'He was perfectly nice,' she said smiling non-committally, but then her expression grew serious. 'Aaron, I meant to ask you last night – what was going on at the station yesterday evening?'

'What do you mean?' Aaron was obviously being evasive, which always irritated Sara and she answered impatiently.

'You know what I mean. When I was logging the temperatures last night I looked out of the office window and saw half the men of Zichron milling round outside the station. Jezebel was there, so I presume you were also and I saw Daniel, and I'm sure Lev was there too. What were you all up to?'

'Nothing.'

'What do you mean, nothing? The more furtive you are the more mysterious you make it. Come on, Aaron, tell me.'

'It was just a group of us from Zichron and round about. After what happened to Sam we thought we ought to form a protection group – just to take turns to patrol the area and keep a watch on the settlement. Nothing of outstanding importance. Look, I've got to go now,' he said, putting the car into gear. 'I'll have to stop work early because of the dance, and I've a lot to get done. See you later.'

He drove off trailing a cloud of smoke and leaving Sara curious and not entirely pleased. It was unusual for Aaron to treat her in such a cavalier fashion; he normally told her what was going on and included her as much as a girl could be. This 'shut up and be pretty' attitude was something new. She watched him drive off, a small frown on her face, and turned back to the house.

CHAPTER SIX

'Are you girls ever going to be ready?' Aaron's voice boomed in mock fury from the other side of the door. 'The dance will be over by the time we get there.' The only answer he got was a great deal of giggling and rustling followed by Becky's quick step across the room.

'Don't come in, Aaron darling. I'm not dressed yet, but we will be ready soon.' Her voice was high with excitement and Aaron smiled at his sister's pleasure. He kept his cross voice for their benefit.

'If you're not down in five minutes we'll all be on the carpet. Mr Cohen and Sam have already drunk half a bottle of brandy between them!' And purposely heavy-footed, he stomped off down the stairs.

Becky's giggles showed how little notice she took of her brother's grumps and she ran back to Sara, who was still in her petticoats and kneeling on the floor. Ruth, who wanted to surprise her husband with a new dress, had come over to the Levinsons' to dress with the two girls, and was the only one of the three who was ready. She sat on the edge of the bed, her hands demurely folded and smiling prettily. Her thick black hair was braided in a shining coil around her head and she was dressed in a gown of pale yellow silk. Yellow rosebuds made of a slightly darker silk cascaded over one shoulder and circled her small waist. Ruth was an attractive girl, but tonight she looked magnificent. She had not told her two friends her second surprise for Robbie – they thought her luminous happiness was due only to the excitement of the dance and the dress. But that morning Doctor Ephraim had confirmed that she was pregnant and this was the secret that gave her a new and shining beauty.

In marked contrast with the three girls, Fatma was sitting in a low chair by the window. Not for anything, even such a grand event as the yearly dance, would she change either her black gown or her cross expression, but she was eager for the girls to enjoy themselves and only her noisy fussing showed how excited she was.

Becky had managed to break the heel of one of her slippers and Fatma was hurriedly sewing green bows on to another pair. The replacement shoes were half an inch shorter than the others and Becky was convinced that the dress was now too long but Sara, examining her critically with her head to one side, finally declared that Becky was quite wrong and that the change was, if anything, an improvement.

'Are you sure – are you sure?' Becky asked anxiously, pirouetting in front of her sister.

'Yes, I'm sure. What do you think, Ruth?'

'Yes, you look lovely, Sara,' Ruth answered absently, barely moving her eyes.

'Oh good – then I'll go in my petticoats!' Sara laughed, wondering what had come over her friend. Satisfied at last that the other two would not need her for anything else, Sara finally slipped her own dress over her shoulders. Both she and Becky had dresses of white muslin, Sara's decorated with pale blue ribbons and flowers and Becky's with green. Sara had tamed Becky's wild copper curls into a smooth elegance and had highlighted her own blondeness with a few camomile rinses. The three girls could not have looked more different, but each was looking her best.

Half the fun of the dance had been in the preparation, as for months the girls had been looking through recent fashion journals from France. In the event they had all chosen well, to suit their own individual styles. Sara's and Becky's dresses cleverly echoed each other, while being distinctly different. Becky's hinted at the old-fashioned Empire line, giving an impression of charming simplicity, while Sara's was slightly more sophisticated, reflecting the fact that she was a young woman while Becky was barely out of the schoolroom.

'Well, are we all ready? Can we put the gentlemen out of their misery?' Sara asked. 'Ruth?'

'I'm going to have a baby,' her friend answered. Sara looked stunned. 'Well, I did mean to tell Robbie first, but I'll die if I don't tell someone soon,' Ruth explained.

'So that's what all this day-dreaming is about. Oh Ruth!' Sara cried, and she and Becky swooped down on Ruth, hugging her wildly.

'Careful – don't kill him before Robbie even knows he exists!' Ruth laughed, her face alight with happiness. 'And whatever you do, don't spoil your dresses!' For one bitter moment Sara realised that she felt an overwhelming envy for her friend whose life seemed to be going so well, so according to plan. But then this unworthy feeling was immediately swallowed up by her genuine happiness for Ruth and Robbie.

'Well, I thought you said something about going?' Ruth asked innocently.

'You're right – they're probably all flat out on the carpet, drunk as Cossacks,' said Sara and, laughing, the three of them made their way down to the men.

Aaron had decided that Jezebel would not do the girls justice on such a night – they would be squashed into the back like cattle on the way to market and, even before he saw them, he knew they would look too pretty to appreciate such treatment. So tonight Abu was driving them in the carriage. Sara thought her heart would burst as they drove up to the large, lofty stone barn, which usually housed the communal farm equipment. This evening it was ablaze with light and the sweet smell of hundreds of flowers wafted out to them as they arrived. Sara had purposely not gone into the village today as she knew that to witness the transformation would be to destroy some of its magic, and her self-discipline was rewarded.

The tradition of the dance had been kept up for the last twenty years – at first it had been simple enough, but now it was a full-blown affair and reflected the growing prosperity of the community. No longer a purely local affair, dignitaries now came from miles around – Turk, Arab and Jew mixed in what was for once a genuinely informal and friendly manner. All generations looked forward to this meeting – the old for a chance to gossip about the past, the young in the hope of a romantic encounter.

The party arrived to find the dance already in full swing. Sara, proudly sweeping in on Chaim Cohen's arm, found herself the centre of attention; nearly everyone seemed to want to steal a glimpse of her with the eligible bachelor. She could not help feeling a small surge of pride as she noticed how many of the pretty girls, and their mothers, were looking enviously at her.

'Congratulations,' Cohen whispered into her ear. 'You're the most beautiful woman here.'

Sara looked up at him, a smile of amusement on her lips. 'To be honest,' she said with a soft laugh, 'I have the feeling that it is your distinguished presence that is causing such a sensation.'

'There you are!' Robbie Woolf rushed over to meet them and gave Ruth a long, admiring look. 'My, you look magnificent!' he said, and took her straight off for a dance.

Becky's excitement was obvious. 'Isn't it wonderful,' she kept whispering to Sam as Aaron led the party over to a long table where Manny Hirsh and Nelly Jacobson were sitting talking.

'Been waiting for me to dance with, have you?' Sam joked, but was prevented from taking Nelly off by Becky's enthusiastic greeting. The two girls fell on each other, giggling and admiring each other's dresses, though each was secretly convinced that her's was the more successful.

Sam sat down next to Nelly, who had been his most devoted nurse during his recent confinement to the house. Every day she had tripped up the path carrying chicken soup, causing Sara to laugh and wonder where all the chickens came from. Sam had been delighted with the attention and secretly blessed the Bedouins for hurrying along the romance. He made room for Sara and Chaim beside him and, as soon as she was comfortably seated, Sara's eyes started searching the room for Daniel. Everyone in Zichron was there it seemed, some dancing, some talking, some walking in pairs round the room, looking for friends or refreshments. She saw her father standing in a group of men against the far wall and gave him a little wave. Talking about old times, I suppose, she thought affectionately, and her eyes swept the room again. Then she saw him. She was standing at the far end of the room talking to Alex. Their eyes met and she waved happily.

'How pretty she is – in fact, without being biased, I'd say she is turning into a fully-fledged beauty,' Alex said.

'Who?' Daniel asked, although he knew perfectly well whom Alex was talking about.

'My sister, of course.'

Daniel smiled. 'I agree,' he said coolly, but feeling much more than he would show. From the moment he had seen her walk into the room on Cohen's arm he had felt his temperature rise and the jealousy, sparked off last night, now raged like a bush fire. She had never looked lovelier.

101

Sara noticed the exchange and the dark look on Daniel's face with joy. *He's as jealous as Othello*, she thought.

'Would you care to dance?' Chaim asked, interrupting her train of thought. 'Though I'm afraid I don't do it very well,' and he offered her his arm and led her on to the dance floor.

Chaim was right, he was not a good dancer; he trod on her toes and continually propelled her into other dancers. After an agonising ten minutes of bumping and apologising, the dance finally came to an end. 'That can't have been of much pleasure to you,' Chaim said sadly. Sara smiled sweetly and thankfully took her seat again. 'Perhaps I could be more successful in getting you a drink,' he offered.

'A glass of wine would be lovely,' Sara said, and watched him make his way through the crowd to the long table laid out as a bar.

Lev, slightly the worse for drink, lurched into view and gazed adoringly at her.

'Come on, Lev, let's dance,' she said and he, unable to believe his luck, led her out on to the dance floor. Just as they stepped out, Becky with her lanky admirer, Adam Leibovitz, rushed up and joined the dance behind Sara and Lev. A lively mazurka started up and the two couples, their faces flushed with happiness and high spirits, easily picked up the rhythm and swung into the dance.

'I'm only a Russian peasant, I can't dance this,' Lev gasped out, but Sara only smiled. His feet were already giving him the lie, beside which it was well known that Lev was one of the best dancers in the district. After two dances Sara had to beg Lev to let her rest, and he led her back to her seat at the table.

'Thank you, Mr Cohen,' Sara said, lifting the glass that glowed ruby red in her hand. 'I need it after that dance.' She sat, fanning herself slowly, and looked contentedly around the room. She saw many friends and many new faces, but her attention was soon drawn to a man she had certainly never seen before, but who stood with an arrogant ease, entirely at home in this roomful of strangers.

He was tall and aggressively masculine with careless dark hair and green eyes. Ivan Bernski, whom she knew by sight, was talking to him, but the man was staring at her. Bernski was the Russian grandee from Haifa who served on countless committees and was a passionate communist. The stranger did not seem to be paying much attention to Bernski; even when Sara met his eyes he refused to be stared down but continued gazing resolutely.

Sara felt resentment at the way this man was measuring her up. For a moment she stared back and then turned her head haughtily away and looked down at her fan. To her fury she heard a burst of amused laughter, and she had no doubts it was his. Hot with fury, she bit her lip. But, in spite of herself, she could not resist sneaking another cautious glance at him. Their eyes met again. He raised one eyebrow and smiled, showing perfect, white teeth. For some reason he challenged her, she was curious.

'You know everyone,' she said to Doctor Emphraim who had wandered over, 'who is that tall dark man with Ivan Bernski?'

Nelly interrupted at once. 'That's Joe Lanski,' she said, happy to be the one to give information. 'He's terribly glamorous – don't you think? He's a horse dealer.'

'And gun runner,' Lev muttered darkly.

'They say,' Nelly continued, 'he will sell anything to anyone – as long as they have the money. He's very rich and apparently something of a lady killer. Mind you, I'd happily die in his arms any time,' and she tailed off into giggles.

A lady killer, is he, thought Sara coldly and turned slightly in her chair so that her back was towards him.

'So you've found a woman you like the look of, Joe?' Bernski asked, noticing his friend's interest in the Levinson girl.

'Never could resist a beauty,' Lanski said slowly.

'So now we've found your weakness – cool blondes with blue eyes?'

'Hers are worth hanging for,' said Joe, keeping his own eyes on Sara. He had noticed her as soon as she had walked into the room. She was not a girl he could have passed indifferently in any city – Constantinople or Cairo, or in any European one. But in this room of provincial beauties she had a quality that made her stand far above the others.

'Try any tricks and you could well find yourself hanging – she's Aaron Levinson's sister.' Bernski warned.

'I fancy she's the kind of woman who would fasten the noose herself.' Joe mused, and turned to make his excuses to Bernski. 'At a dance, one must dance,' he said, and moved off.

Sara's question about Lanski had led to a flood of gossip about him, some totally scurrilous, more mildly funny. She wished she had not asked about the man; the rumour that obviously surrounded him made him even more mysterious and exciting to her.

'He sounds an out and out scoundrel,' she said to end the conversation, and leaned forward in her chair to look for Daniel again. He was sitting with Alex and a very slim, dark girl with bobbed hair and the face of a madonna. Sara felt a sharp twinge of envy: Isobelle Frank was undoubtedly a fascinating woman. She was an exiled Russian revolutionary who had, according to hearsay, a very racy life style. The whole of Palestine rang with stories of the countless adventures and scandals in which she was involved. Isobelle Frank was also the sister of Aaron's mistress, Hanna, a married woman who lived in Haifa. Of course, Sara was not supposed to know that Aaron had a mistress, let alone that she was married, but the affair had been public knowledge for years.

Sara, watching Daniel and Isobelle talk, felt her heart drop. Isobelle looked like the sort of woman men find it easy to become infatuated with and Daniel was bound to be impressed by the combination of her radical beliefs and fragile beauty. With a stab of annoyance she noticed how animatedly he was talking to her.

Just then the band struck up with a waltz and, looking up from the brunette, Daniel looked at Sara. With a word to Alex and the girl, he stood up and began to walk across the room towards her. *He's going to ask me to dance*, Sara thought.

Somebody touched her elbow. She turned and saw Lanski smiling down at her with an irritatingly self-assured expression on his bronzed features. She looked wildly back towards Daniel but he had stopped in his tracks and was watching hesitantly. Her face, when she looked back at Lanski, was neither sweet nor welcoming.

'I don't believe we have been introduced, Miss Levinson,' he said. 'But I fear my reputation may have preceded me.' Nelly collapsed in guilty giggles, Sam and Robby smiled with polite interest, and Lev glowered. Chaim Cohen nodded politely. Out of the corner of her eye Sara saw Daniel smile, then move back to his chair beside the brunette. She was furious with this arrogant man for his untimely display of interest and turned cold blue eyes on him.

The man bowed with over-polite exaggeration. 'My name is Joe Lanski,' he said and held out his arm. 'May I have the pleasure of this dance?' Sara felt herself grow hot with embarrassment at the attention they were drawing. She wished she could refuse and dismiss him with the words that were springing into her mind, but Chaim Cohen was hovering above her and she felt duty-bound to be polite. She looked up at Chaim and he smiled in assent, although a little frostily, so she rose and took Lanski's arm. He bowed courteously to Cohen, led her on to the dance floor, put a hand around her waist and swung her into the waltz. Sara noticed how easily and confidently Lanski moved and despite herself found this attractive.

Joe was taller than Sara had realised, and danced very well indeed – a relief after her ordeal with Cohen. He had the look of robust good health and animal strength and, although his features were irregular and his looks rather dark, she had to concede that the overall impression was of a very handsome man. Indeed so much so that Sara realised they were creating a minor stir on the dance floor among the other women, many of whom ceased to pay any attention at all to their partners as soon as Joe came near.

'How lucky that I stopped by here this evening,' said Lanski after the briefest silence. 'Meeting you was an unforeseen pleasure.' Sara threw him a withering look but he only laughed. 'My, my, you look as though you are about to bite my head off – but I like a woman with spirit; a challenge has always attracted me. It brings out my masculine instincts.'

He spoke with a curiously attractive drawl that hinted at an American background and he smiled at her as his eyes roamed boldly over her. Sara had the uncomfortable feeling that he knew exactly what she looked like undressed and her cheeks burned red. She glared at him fiercely, loathing him more than ever. 'Well, you can take your masculine instincts elsewhere. I for one am not flattered by your attentions,' she snapped, trying to break free. But he immediately tightened his grip and manoeuvred her adeptly round the dance floor.

He laughed again. 'How pleasant to meet a pretty girl who speaks her mind. To be honest, Miss Levinson, were you not here I would be bored. May I claim all the waltzes this evening?'

'No, Mr Lanski, you may not. And would you please not hold me so tightly,' Sara said sharply, suddenly acutely aware of his physical proximity, of the heat of his body against hers. She felt her heart rate quicken and stiffened like a wary cat. *It is just anger* she told herself as he leaned forward and whispered provocatively: 'That is not a request I am used to hearing from my dance partners,' before loosening his hold on her waist.

He spoke with an irony that Sara, in her flustered state, mistook for conceit. 'I suppose that most women fall swooning at your feet,' she said with bitter contempt.

enerally speaking, yes,' he said with a lazy smile on his lips
and an undisguised challenge in his eyes.

She noticed how intensely green they were and, unnerved, gave
a little laugh. 'Well, that just goes to show what fools most women
are.'

He threw back his head and laughed. 'I couldn't agree with you
more, Miss Levinson.' Then his expression changed and all trace
of mockery vanished as he looked at her thoughtfully. 'Look, let's
stop this silly bantering and call a truce. We are spoiling our first
dance together.'

'And our last,' she snapped, refusing to be won over.

'And how can you be sure of that?' he retorted, the mocking
look back in his eyes.

Her blood pressure rose again at the egotism of the man. 'Just
take my word for it,' she said and for the rest of the dance kept her
eyes studiously on his tie pin.

At the end of the waltz Lanski led Sara back to her table where
she found that Daniel and Paul Levy had joined the company.
Aaron greeted Joe easily. 'I see you've met my sister Sara – good.
While you are here, do you mind if we have a brief talk? Could
you come outside for a moment?' Joe bowed to Sara, who nodded
at him in a parody of good manners, and he left with Paul and
Aaron.

'Will you excuse me a moment?' asked Chaim, and followed the
other men out of the room.

'What on earth could Aaron have to say to Joe Lanski?' Sara
asked Daniel, startled to see her brother on such amiable terms
with him.

'Guns.' Daniel explained seriously, in a low voice. 'It was Aaron
who invited him here this evening. He's hoping to rearm the
settlement with Lanski's help.'

'Oh dear,' Sara was suddenly confused, 'I'm afraid I was rather
rude to him.'

'I shouldn't worry.' Daniel smiled thinly, 'Lanski will sell to
anyone who pays.'

Sara was relieved. 'That's what Nelly said, but she's such a
hopeless gossip . . .'

As Nelly's name was mentioned, she and Becky reappeared at
the table, carrying plates loaded with cold chicken and salad.
'Poor you,' Nelly squeaked, her eyes rolling with a mixture of
horror and envy. 'Fancy having to dance with that terrible man.'

'Terrible,' Becky echoed obediently, her expression a mirror image of Nelly's until it broke into a big grin, '– but exciting.'

'Oh Becky, do shut up,' Sara said, irritated at the combined silliness of the two girls. 'It's very warm in here – would you mind taking me outside for a moment, Daniel?' She looked at him and their eyes locked. For a second the mask fell from his face and the customary remoteness in his eyes slipped with it.

'Of course,' he said politely, giving her his arm. Sara took it quickly; she wanted to be out of the room before Chaim returned.

The terrace was dark and deeply shadowed except where the light from the open doors fell in sharply defined strips over the paving stone. With unerring instinct Sara led Daniel towards some outbuildings and into the deepest shadows. Snatches of music and laughter floated out from the half open windows and the air was heavy with the scent of tobacco plants and jasmine.

Daniel was uncharacteristically acquiescent as he followed Sara round the corner of the building. Her beauty, and the wine had seduced him. Like some inexperienced virgin, a part of him was whispering that this was folly, that he should have stayed inside . . . but there was an excitement emanating from Sara that thrilled him. Never had she seemed so purely sexual, so much a creature for animal loving. Left alone he could banish all thoughts of her but now, with her nearby, feeling the strength of her passion for him and, he had to admit, of his for her, he had no force to do so.

They stood quietly for a moment and then, recklessly, for she was now sure of herself, Sara moved close against him. 'Kiss me,' she said, her voice warm and anxious.

He looked into her eyes, into all that beauty. 'Oh Sara,' he said hopelessly, and pulled her roughly and almost desperately into his arms. For a few moments they were lost in each other's embrace, then Sara felt him pull away from her.

Daniel stood back, hoping to ease his heartbeat by distancing himself from her. The physical rage to possess her did not worry him as much as his love for her did; he fought against it fiercely and, when he was away from her, thought he was succeeding. But she moved him as no other woman ever had, although he could not quite grasp what it was about her that filled him with this unspeaking tenderness.

She was beautiful, and he had always been susceptible to

107

beauty. There was her abundant golden hair which he could never see without longing to run his fingers through. There were her eyes, her most spectacular feature, which were vivid and startling and framed by long, curling lashes as black as if they had been dipped in ink. And she was not just a beauty – she was a girl of character, which was reflected in the determined tilt of her chin. He knew that Sara would be as relentless in pursuit of her dream as he was in his . . . but he also knew there was no future for them – he had to put his dream before hers.

At the same time he recognised that Sara filled a void in his heart that all his dreams and ambitions left empty. She was a warm, passionate human being, and at this moment he longed more than anything to be able to make a triumphant declaration of his love. He fought it. He knew two things that made Sara dangerous: she was not the sort of woman a man could play around with; and she was Aaron's sister. That in itself was serious business.

Sara, who had been watching him, moved close again. 'What's the matter, Daniel?' Her voice was small, the confidence gone.

The terrifying tenderness crept into him again and he felt his control slipping. He took her chin in his hand and stared down at her with a suppressed sigh. He looked at her, wanting to return to that dizzying, responsive mouth, but frightened of her passion and his own, and of the responsibilities that unleashing it would bring. He smiled and gently traced the rounded curve of her lip with a finger.

'What would you do to me if I let you?' he said lightly and laughed, wishing to diminish the importance of the problem.

She smiled, her eyes glinting in the dark. 'Make you happy,' she said.

He looked at her long and intently, then turned from her abruptly. 'Come, we had better return to the dance before your suitor comes looking for you.' He spoke with deliberate indifference, although in truth Chaim Cohen irritated him.

Sara laughed and linked her arm through his. 'Why, I do believe you're jealous!' she said, light-hearted in response to his changed mood. Daniel gave a soft, rich laugh.

'Yes, I probably am,' he admitted ruefully. 'Let's find ourselves a drink.'

He guided her across the noisy, crowded room to a table where wines, beers and spirits were being poured out in great quantities and with a total lack of ceremony. Judging by the general demeanour and the energetic Round dancing going on most of the company had already helped themselves generously.

Daniel handed Sara a glass of lemonade, which she sipped thankfully, feeling the almost suffocating heat of the room after the cool of the outside air. He turned to talk to Alex and, as she could not hear what they were discussing, Sara moved to a half-open side door and waved her fan gently back and forth, savouring the feelings evoked by Daniel's kiss. The touch of his lips on hers had aroused so many disturbing, beautiful sensations. She had wanted to stay locked in his arms, electrified by his kiss, for the rest of her days.

Remembering his passion she smiled to herself. 'I've got him,' she murmured softly. 'He's mine.' A peal of laughter made her jump and she snapped open her eyes to see a dark figure detach itself from the shadows and float towards her. It resolved itself into the unwelcome shape of Joe Lanski.

'I'm sure you have,' he smiled, 'if that poignant little scene on the terrace was anything to go by.'

Taken by surprise, Sara gaped at him, infuriated by the thought that he of all people should have witnessed her raw emotion. 'You might have made your presence known,' she snapped, happy that it was too dark for him to see her hot blush.

'What? And miss the opportunity of seeing the real you?' he drawled and laughed again.

Sara had to hold herself back. This man really succeeded in getting to her. She felt an overwhelming desire to slap his conceited face but, instead, fixed her gaze steadily on his. 'Excuse me, I must return to my friends,' she said coolly.

Joe bowed mockingly. 'Until we meet again.'

Sara smiled sweetly, hiding her antagonism, and walked away without another word.

Joe leaned against the door jamb and thoughtfully bit off the end of a cigar as he watched her go. Her friends greeted her as she approached them and the tall, carefully groomed Chaim Cohen rose to offer her a chair as the undeniably handsome Daniel Rosen murmured something in her ear.

They don't deserve anything half as good, he thought to himself, blowing a small smoke ring. He wondered what was so special about Sara Levinson. She was very beautiful, but he had known many beautiful women and had never desired one so passionately; Sara was something different. But she was bound to be a virgin, and he had a horror of virgins. Not that she'll always be one, he thought, laughing to himself at the possibilities the future held. He had a feeling that they would run into each other again and they would come to know each other well – very well indeed.

Sara lay in bed looking blankly at the soft halo of light the lamp cast on the ceiling. All she could think about was Daniel. At least she knew one thing for certain now – Daniel desired her as strongly as she desired him. In spite of her inexperience, she had felt him stiffen as his mouth had lingered on hers. She shivered, feeling goose pimples rise on her skin. Turning on her side, she wrapped her arms round her body and hugged herself. Pressing her face into the pillow an image of Daniel leapt before her closed eyes as she remembered the moment he had looked down on her speculatively.

Despite her exultation she felt a trickle of dismay. What would she do if he did not love her enough – if he would not marry her? She rolled on her back again, her eyes wide and unblinking. Her future would be grim; seeing Daniel every day without having him, cooking, ironing and cleaning for her family with no children of her own, and ruining Becky's chances into the bargain.

Unexpectedly, an answer came to her. *I'd marry Chaim Cohen!* And as soon as the thought crossed her mind, she was appalled. Suave and elegant though he was, she could not think of marrying him. The idea was ludicrous. She laughed softly to herself. What was she worrying about? Daniel had invited her to visit Sheik Suliman with him to choose a colt. Of course he loved her, of course he planned to marry her. Why should she even think of Chaim Cohen?

She leant over and turned off the lamp. Sinking back on to her pillows she started to count the days until the visit. Next Thursday – five days, she mused drowsily, five days.

CHAPTER SEVEN

At five o'clock on the morning Sara had been looking forward to so eagerly, she and Daniel swung out of the courtyard in Zichron on to the lane that led through the village to the Ephriem hills. Bella seemed almost as excited as Sara and pranced skittishly beside Daniel, who was riding Aaron's stallion, Apollo. Sara's buoyant spirits soared even higher as she laughingly checked her eager mount. Abu had lovingly polished both horses' harnesses and had decked them for the occasion with gaily-woven saddle-cloths hung with coloured tassels, which swayed in the early morning breeze.

Sara too had dressed with special care for the outing and wore her best black riding skirt and a crisp white blouse with starched ruffles down the front to add a touch of femininity. Her boots were shining as they had not since they were new; she had polished them herself, not trusting the servants on this occasion. To add a touch of colour to her severe costume, she had wound a long, peach-coloured chiffon scarf around her straw hat and tied it under her chin. She was totally unaware of the enchanting picture she made; but Daniel, to his irritation, was all too aware of it. Her eyes sparkled with excitement at the adventure and she sat on her jittery mare with total ease and control.

For Sara this outing was a poignant reminder of her childhood, when she had accompanied Aaron on field trips miles away from home. But now Daniel was there. He had told Sara a great deal about his adopted father, but this was the first time she had ever been invited to meet him. She could not help hoping that Daniel's invitation held some further meaning.

Sheik Suliman belonged to the Anazeh tribe and his ruling house, the Beni Shalan, bore one of the proudest names in Syria.

111

His 'golden' mares – the ostensible reason for the visit – were among the best in all Arabia. Every spring Sheik Suliman, like many Bedouin, came from the Syrian desert to benefit from the rich summer grazing, which fattened his livestock. Soon before the winter rains he would return to his headquarters in the desert. Sara knew how Daniel adored his 'spiritual father' and was curious to see how he fitted in with his extended Bedouin 'family'.

Sara checked Bella and looked adoringly at Daniel. Her happiness knew no bounds today, she felt carefree and invigorated. 'You look more like an Arabian prince than a Jewish farmer,' she said teasingly. Dressed in traditional Arab clothes – a white keffiyeh held in place by a twisted gold headband and a newly-sharpened dagger hanging from his waist – he certainly looked the part.

'Perhaps I am, not the Daniel you think you know but a prince luring you away to an uncertain fate in the desert.'

'I'd be an easy captive,' she laughed.

That was all too true, Daniel thought wryly, and once again questioned the wisdom of taking Sara off into the wilderness. He had given the invitation on the spur of the moment and knew he could not go back on it. The danger did not worry him; he knew that the Sheik's men would be waiting for them less than an hour away on the other side of the mountain. The first leg of the journey was safe enough and with the Sheik's escort no one would dare attack them. He nonetheless touched the Browning pistol for reassurance, fingering the ornately-carved butt with affection. No, it was of himself that he was afraid. With every day that passed Sara became a greater threat.

Soon they were well clear of the village, following a rocky path – little more than a bridle track – that gradually climbed the mountainside. The horses picked their way cautiously and Daniel let them choose their own pace. They finally reached a wide plateau after which the path dropped again. Daniel drew rein for a moment and wheeled Apollo round, waiting for Sara to catch up. She urged Bella up the last few feet and turned her round so she was side by side with Daniel, looking back down into the valley they had ridden through. Daniel's face was transformed.

'I'll be damned if this isn't paradise. I don't believe there is a more beautiful spot in the world,' he said at last. Sara followed his gaze.

A pearly-pink glow still suffused the eastern sky where a soft, yellow sun had risen above the horizon. The mirror-calm sea far below was the colour of honey. A light breeze floated up from the sea, carrying with it the first fresh smells of the morning, the pine and the wild herbs that thrived on the rocky slopes adding their own sweet scent. The only sound in the dead calm was the creaking of their own saddles, the quick breathing of their mounts, and the occasional twitter of birds.

Sara closed her eyes, breathing it all in and after a moment felt Daniel touch her sleeve. 'Are you all right, Sara?'

'Of course I'm all right.' She caught his hand on her arm. 'Thank you for bringing me with you, Daniel. I don't think you realise what a treat it is.' He surveyed her fondly for a moment before raising her hand to his lips and kissing it like a gallant cavalier of old.

'The pleasure is all mine, ma'am,' he said in a tone suspiciously like Joe Lanski's. Sara shot him a questioning look through her eyelashes, but he had already wrenched Apollo round and taken the stallion to the other side of the plateau, ready to move on.

'Look, down there,' he pointed to a large rock formation below them. 'That's where the Sheik's men will be waiting for us.' He looked anxiously up at the sun, squinting into the rapidly brightening sky. 'We had better get going if we don't want to keep them waiting,' he said and, kicking Apollo on, he began the descent along a narrow track beaten smooth by the animals that had for centuries travelled down it.

Lulled by the steady click of the horses' hooves they rode on in silence until, reaching the valley, the horses suddenly became aware of the space around them and broke into a canter, and then a fast gallop, following the course of the dry river bed. They raced on for a few wild minutes, Sara laughing into the wind, until Bella settled down to a steady canter again as her hooves met the hard, rock-strewn valley of Armageddon. The summer lasted longer here and, among the sun-licked grasses and thistles, a few late blooming flowers still sprang up on the hillside.

The emptiness was supreme. It was possible to ride for hours across this wild landscape and meet nothing save a lone Arab shepherd boy standing guard over a scattered flock, gripping a long-barrelled rifle. Nothing moved apart from a few birds that soared into blue sky and then settled again among the wild almond or silvery olive trees.

The peacefulness was deceptive, as both Sara and Daniel well knew. Drawing rein for a moment Sara pulled her rifle free from its sling on the saddle and, holding it across the pommel, set off again. They would soon be coming into an area where Bedouin scouts lurked in hidden caves and hollows. Some, like Sheik Suliman, were peaceful and accepted the Jewish settlers. Some, like the Zabiah, were fierce warriors and hostile to Jew and Arab alike. The Bedouin were divided into numerous tribes, each with their own cultures, dialects, alliances – and emnities.

'Look!' said Daniel suddenly, pointing up to his right. High above them, floating easily on the thermals, was a flock of migrating white pelicans stretching out against the stark outline of the mountains of Gilboa. They watched in companionable silence until the stillness was broken by Bella, who gave an excited whinny.

Turning sharply, Sara saw a Bedouin on a sleek black horse galloping towards them. 'It's Yusef! My brother!' Daniel said excitedly as the youth came closer.

Yusef was about Sara's age with clear-cut features and a keen intelligence in his eyes. Sara liked the look of him at once. Both men threw themselves from their horses and into each other's arms. After much laughing and hugging Daniel turned to Sara.

'Yusef is not just my brother – he is my blood brother. He once saved me from a sticky situation.' Both men laughed at the memory. Something to do with a woman, I bet, Sara thought with a stab of jealousy, but greeted Daniel's 'brother' with a smile as they both spoke rapidly in an Arab dialect that Sara could not easily follow.

'Come,' said Daniel, remounting. 'The others are waiting for us in the shadow of the rock.'

As they rounded the outcrop they came across another three men squatting in the purple shadow. A further wild hubbub of greetings left Sara feeling slightly lost as Daniel plunged effortlessly back into the dialect of the nomad as though he had never spoken anything else. After a short pause and a long drink of water they set off again in a close group. Sara kicked Bella on and was surprised as Yusef overtook her and laid a hand on the bridle. He smiled, baring his even, white teeth.

'Lady, you are committed to my charge. I must ride first.' He spoke courteously, not in the patois of his tribe but in the standard dialect of the towns and Sara, pleased by his manner, fell back slightly and rode in the middle of the men, who were all carrying cocked rifles. Although they were now riding under the protection

114

of the Sheik, every now and again one of the men would let out a warlike whoop and fire a shot into the air or into one of the bushes. Sara knew they were doing little more than letting it be known they were there and were holding on to their advantage by loudly proclaiming their strength.

The sun was now high and the flies were beginning to plague both the horses and the riders. To her left Sara spotted a jackal skittering towards some scrub and, responding to some ancient instinct, raised her rifle and fired. The shot echoed across the hillside and the animal, hit square in the head, fell in the dust. The men paused for a moment and looked at Sara, obviously impressed.

'Good, good,' Yusef grinned. 'You shoot like a man.' Daniel looked away, but not before Sara had seen his face and caught the admiration in his eyes.

'Don't waste bullets, Sara,' he said calmly and kicked his horse on. Sara reloaded, feeling pleased with herself.

Not five minutes further on they saw three horsemen in the distance, riding straight towards them. The Sheik's men tensed and automatically gripped their rifles. As the strangers drew closer Sara could see they were armed to the hilt and their faces were black-browed and menacing. They drew to a halt a little distance away and after a moment threw them a sketchy salute.

'Ha!' said one of the Sheik's men laughing and slapping his saddle triumphantly. 'They think our lady is a Cookie.' 'Cookie' was the Bedouin term for all European travellers, whether or not they arrived courtesy of Thomas Cook.

'Bah!' said another with a grin. 'They are Zabiah. Like sheep they are when they meet one of us. Wallah!' he laughed madly. 'Like sheep!'

'Zabiah!' said Sara hoarsely, thinking of her brother and the missing horse and fiercely fighting down the urge to raise her rifle and shoot them as she had the jackal.

'Cowardly Arab scum,' said Yusef, spitting emphatically in the dust.

Sara rose in her stirrups and brought her hand up to shade her eyes, trying to focus. And then she saw what she had suspected was true.

'That's our horse those scum are riding!' she gasped, almost voiceless with indignation. There was no mistaking the white blaze that ran the full length of the bay's head. 'Look Daniel, look,' she edged Bella up beside him. 'It's our horse – I know it is.' She set her chin determinedly. 'We must get her back.'

'It would take the Turkish Army to get a horse out of their camp,' he answered and then, seeing her look of disappointment, added, 'I'll mention it to the boys when we get back, I promise.'

Sara nodded and let Bella fall back.

'The boys.' By that she guessed Daniel meant the newly-formed watch group. She had watched with envy as rotas were fixed, wooden platforms set up as watch towers in carefully-chosen spots and future plans discussed – the last usually behind her back. Lev, always her staunch ally, had never been able to keep a secret from her and it had been he who had told her the reason for the mysterious meeting at Atlit on the night of the dinner party. After the beating Sam had taken, Sara approved fully of the scheme, wishing only she were allowed to play some part. It was still the same old story, men right in the centre of things, women in the kitchen, she was bored in the kitchen she thought grimly to herself as she watched the Zabiah draw away.

As yet she did not know how she was going to worm her way into the watch group. She had tried the direct approach, choosing to ask Aaron and Alex first, hoping that they would be sympathetic. Neither had actually said no, but then neither had seemed very enthusiastic, and the decision had been left to Daniel. She looked at him now thoughtfully, but knew that this was not the time or the place to mention the subject. She brightened at the thought of the dead jackal – at least she had shown Daniel that, despite her femininity, she could shoot with the best of them. That must make a difference.

'They stole your horse, lady?' Yusef was riding beside her again.

'Yes,' she said furiously. 'And but for the will of God would have killed my brother at the same time.'

'Bah, they are fart-eaters,' said Yusef contemptuously, hawking in the dust again.

Sara choked back a laugh at this description of the fierce warriors.

'Let me tell you how fierce they are,' Yusef continued with a grin animating his thin features. 'The other night, for a joke, a brother of mine hid in some acacia bushes and, stark naked, jumped out at one of them in the dawn mist.' The escort party chuckled appreciatively at the picture. 'Faced with my brother, he ran back to the camp screaming that he had seen a djinni and no one should go near the bushes.'

Sara joined in the general laughter at the story. She knew that, however brave or fierce he might be, there are certain places an Arab will never go near if he believes it to be inhabited by an evil spirit.

'Are the Zabiah camping nearby?' she asked thoughtfully.

'They have pitched their tents just over there,' Yusef answered, pointing out a large rocky outcrop with two ancient alad trees casting a wide and heavy shade under their thorny branches. Sara strained her eyes in the direction of the camp.

'With brains and a little luck,' she mused, 'it could just be done.'

The countryside was changing now, the rocky ground giving way to scrubland. Suddenly, a volley of shots rang out in front of them, followed immediately by an uproar of blood-curdling yells. Riding directly at them on horses and camels galloped about thirty of the Sheik's men, whooping and letting off shots into the air. Nearer and nearer they galloped, showing their spectacular horsemanship at its best. They held their rifles high above their heads, twisting and turning in their stirrups, with the reins between their teeth, and flew across the open plain, the air echoing with their war cries.

Sara had never seen such a magnificent sight as she, along with Daniel and the men and horses of their party, were caught up in the drama and galloped forward to meet the welcoming party. There were noisy greetings as the two groups met up and then, joining together like two bands of brigands, they set off on the last stage of the journey, following the curve in the land until at last they reached Sheik Suliman's camp.

It was the largest Sara had ever seen. There, spread out before her in a wide fold in the land, were the black goatskin tents – the tribe's 'houses of hair' – and flocks of sheep, goats and camels covered the land for some way around. Sara was so overcome by the excitement at her new surroundings that she even forgot Daniel for a while and, when he rode up beside her, he was quite taken aback by her wild dishevelled beauty, so different from her normal immaculate appearance.

'Enjoy your welcome?' he asked.

'Oh, yes. I've never seen anything like it,' she replied, her voice husky and cracking with happiness. 'I've never seen the djerid ridden before.'

'And I hope you never will again,' he laughed. 'It's usually reserved for battle and plundering.'

A delighted group of small boys approached, falling over each other in their eagerness to lead in the horses and be the first to greet and touch Daniel. As they were led in Sara noticed some women dyeing cloth and laying it out over the tamaric bushes to dry. They did not look at the newcomers directly, but stole furtive glances, whispering to each other as they did so. Only one of them stood up, staring at them boldly. She was young and veiled, with black braided hair. For the briefest of moments she let her veil slip and looked into Daniel's eyes, giving him a forbidden sight of herself. Her face was a perfect oval, decorated with blue tattoo lines along her cheekbones and Daniel gave her a wide smile of greeting. Having achieved her aim she coyly drew the veil back over her face, provocatively jangling the silver bangles on her wrists.

'Who was that?' Sara asked, concealing her jealousy.

'Wanda,' said Daniel. 'My sister.'

'Sister my foot!' Sara retorted with a laugh and a curious look backwards.

They were now nearing the centre of the camp where the tents were larger and decorated with brightly-coloured tassels. Sara was about to dismount when an ageing Negro bent down beside Bella and offered Sara his back. Horrified, she looked to Daniel for guidance, dismayed by the idea that she should step on a man's back. But Daniel had already dismounted and his Negro attendant was leading Apollo away. She leapt off the other side of Bella, pretending not to have noticed the old man's offer and Daniel, seeing this, laughed.

'They're the Sheik's slaves bought specially for that use by his father.'

'Slaves!' Sara said, appalled. 'But that's illegal, isn't it?'

Daniel, amazed at her naivety, gave her a sideways look but did not pursue the subject.

Water-carriers offered them foot baths, which Sara refused, although she gratefully washed the journey's dust from her face and hands and eagerly drank the water flavoured with buttermilk. Feeling refreshed, she followed Daniel and Yusef to the largest tent of all where a tall, lean man rose immediately to greet them. Sara was silent as the Sheik laid his palms on Daniel's head in the traditional greeting of the nomads to their sons and embraced him affectionately.

118

Sheik Suliman had finely-formed features with a great hawked nose that betrayed his Semitic origins. His skin was smooth, the colour of weak tea, and a thin black beard followed the line of his jaw, coming to a point in a silver tuft. Sara judged him to be about sixty, but his eyes were sharp and clear.

After the long ritual of greetings and courtesies, the Sheik turned to Sara and welcomed her gravely, calling her an honourable lady and asking after her father and brothers. He placed his hand on the central pole of the tent, with the traditional words of welcome: 'This is your house, do as you please, we are your servants.'

Then he led them to the large goatskin rugs laid out under the awning, where about ten men sat in a circle. One by one they rose and greeted Daniel, some embracing him, some kissing his hand, and then they all sat down again, shifting round to make room for the guests.

Within seconds Wanda, Daniel's 'sister', appeared with cushions and Sara made herself comfortable with them, jamming them up by a chest and leaning back against it. Stealing a look at Daniel, she was sure his eyes were distinctly moist and was pleased to see him betray his emotions for once. There was much laughter in the group and Sara become aware that she was attracting a great deal of attention and curiosity. She caught the word 'wife' from one of the men and thrilled to it. This visit must be the prologue to her dreams coming true, she was sure of it. He would not bring her here unless it meant something – she would be his wife and they would be united in perpetual bliss. Her own eyes were misting over now and she forced her thoughts back to her host, who was preparing to make coffee, the essential ingredient in nomad hospitality.

In the middle of the rug was a circle of embers on which the Sheik was blowing in an unsuccessful attempt to produce more than a faint glow. Dissatisfied, he clapped his hands and an old woman in a shapeless black gown appeared with a few handfuls of scrub to build up a flame. Daniel rose and caught hold of her hands.

'Uma,' he greeted her with affection, and explained to Sara, 'my mother.' The old lady was obviously delighted and giggled shyly. Then, overcome at being looked at by so many people all at once, she let out a shrill squawk and rushed back to the safety of the women.

Sara joined in the laughter and the Sheik smiled and shrugged his shoulders apologetically as Daniel sat down again. 'What did I say?' Daniel asked ruefully and the look in the Sheik's eye said 'women!'

Sara settled back as the company fell quiet, as was usual during the preparation of the coffee. She felt drunk on the thick, rich aroma of coffee that rose from the long-handled brass pot, which nestled in the glowing embers. Mingling with the smell of the coffee was the tantalising scent of a sheep roasting in Daniel's honour, and the only sounds to break the silence were the small explosions from the thorns burning under the spit. The acrid smoke from the fire was carried away from Sara on the breeze, but the smell of the meat made her realise how hungry she was after the early start and the long ride.

At last the coffee was poured, the necessary phrases of politeness exchanged, and then the men could start exchanging all the nomadic gossip. They told each other stories involving the familiar themes of blood feuds, camel- and horse-thieving and this naturally led round to the war.

'Bah! The Turks are a curse to the world,' said the Sheik. 'To them murder and thieving is as sweet as the drinking of milk, by God. They make a mockery of our lives with their endless certificates and passes. And now they have leagued themselves with these godless Germans who try to trap us into their army. Their days are numbered if they enter into this bloody warfare.'

Yusef lifted his head and leaned forward confidentially. He began to speak of the advantages of British protection in Egypt. He himself had never been there but his cousins had told him that the desert was peaceful. 'Feuding and raiding has almost ceased.' He finished admiringly.

'By Allah, did they really say that?' an old man said approvingly. Daniel smiled to himself. He knew Rashid well and although today he was sitting with his cup of coffee, looking the picture of innocence, Daniel knew quite well that he was an old devil with many an adventure to his name. Blood feuding and raiding were the true sport of the desert, and Rashid was a true sportsman.

'There may be no feuding, but I have heard they have enforced registration of livestock,' another man chipped in disapprovingly.

Sheik Suliman listened carefully but gave no sign of his own views about the system under the British.

'We live in a state of war anyway,' he said at last. 'There is no knowing when raiders will visit from afar and descend on us. And

120

when they do, what happens? The Turk comes to take our weapons and leaves us like blind camels left to roam the desert. And how many years has this state of things lasted? My father's father could not remember the beginning of it. There is no certainty about anything now and by Allah it is getting worse.'

'Honourable father,' Daniel said slowly. 'If the Turk does enter the war and the British offer Arabs independence in return for assistance – as I have heard it said they would – whose side would you take?'

'Officially, I am neutral,' said the Sheik blandly.

'And by the face of truth, father?'

The Sheik paused only a moment and then a fleeting grin crossed his face. 'The English, of course,' he said. 'Even the Moslem hates his Ottoman brother. I would infinitely rather we were ruled by the infidel British – they offer us prosperity. The Arab and the English are one. We are both fighting races who, when evil bares its teeth against us, fly out to meet it.'

'But, father,' interrupted Yusef.

'But, but, but! Ever since they were small my children have always been full of buts!' exclaimed the Sheik, waving his hands impatiently.

Yusef ignored the rebuke and continued, 'We have no conception of nationhood – the world of the Prophet is split. Of what use is it if the Arab is like fine steel? Even the finest of steels is no good until it is tempered and beaten into a sword blade.'

The old man nodded, pleased with his son's turn of phrase. 'By Allah, you speak the truth,' he said. 'But have faith, my son. Allah will send us a great leader to rid us of the evils of the Turk, may Allah curse them!' The Sheik clapped his hands peremptorily. 'Come, it is sin to talk of warfare on such a day,' he announced and, turning to Daniel, rose in one easy movement.

'Now for the business of the colt, my son.' He yelled something to a small boy and strode out into the dazzling noonday sun, followed by the rest of the party. A few hundred yards from the tent a large, high circle had been formed from the tangled thorns of the lucium bush, which grew profusely in the region and was widely used to enclose animals.

The Sheik, his sons, brothers and Daniel and Sara stood together to inspect the three colts that had been driven in for Daniel to choose from. To Sara's eye one stood out immediately.

'The black,' she said firmly to no one in particular. The Sheik turned to her with a smile.

'We are of one mind,' he agreed. 'Look how proudly he stands – like a bridegroom.'

'Who am I to disagree with you both?' Daniel said with a laugh and shouted to a boy who ran out with a bridle.

In one smooth movement Daniel had the bridle over the black colt's head and the next second had vaulted on to its back. The colt stood stock still as though in shock, only its eyes twitching, white in its dark face. Then as suddenly as if a switch had been pulled it gave a huge, twisting rear before leaping and bucking round and round in the great circle of thorns. Daniel, his legs locked around the horse's body, remained on its back to the cheers of the men and children who had gathered round to watch.

After perhaps fifteen minutes it was all over, and the turbulent spirit of the desert seemed to fade from the colt. Sara thought she could almost see its spirit bending to its fate, and it saddened her.

Later, the women brought trays piled high with savoury rice and succulent chunks of roasted mutton to the tent. After satisfying their hunger and finishing the meal with curds and coffee the Sheik bid them a regretful farewell.

'Go in peace,' he said, embracing Daniel. 'And may God will us to ride together someday.'

They set off in the late afternoon with a new escort, who took them to the rocks and then returned to the camp. Daniel and Sara rode on slowly, Daniel leading the colt carefully up the bridle path until they reached the plateau where they had paused that morning. Here they stopped again, dismounted and tied their horses to a crippled tree.

Sara, confident that Bella was properly tethered, found herself a smooth stone ledge jutting out over the hillside and settled herself comfortably on it. Daniel took a little longer to tether his two horses. Once sure that they were securely tied up, he came over and joined Sara on the rock, offering her a drink from his water bottle. Thankfully, she took a long draught while he took out his tobacco pouch and rolled himself a cigarette.

Sara watched him furtively as she took long, greedy gulps of water. He really was extraordinarily handsome, with his dark golden eyes and deeply tanned face. Every inch of him exuded vitality, rugged glamour and even – though she was reluctant to admit it – a highly sensual appeal. She shivered as she remembered the passion of his kisses. Did *he* remember them as she did? There were so many facets to his nature, that she wondered if she would ever really know him.

She watched Daniel lift the cigarette to his lips, his fingers trembling slightly, but his eyes never leaving the distant view of the sea. Sara followed his line of vision and despite her preoccupation was entranced by the sweeping stretches of horizon before her. Below them the evening lay thick and hot over Zichron and her home valley. A dark red sun lay on the calm blue waters, its dying blood seeping a crimson river and a flamingo pink lake into the drowsy depths. The soft coastline ran away into the Mediterranean which in this light was shaded from aquamarine to midnight blue. If she had thought the view beautiful that morning, she had had no intimation of the glories of dusk.

'Isn't this beautiful?' she murmured, softly loosening her hat and throwing it on to the ground behind her.

Daniel had no eyes for the magnificent sunset; looking at Sara he was dry-mouthed at the tumbling golden silk of her hair. As she shook her curls free they were mingled with russet from the sun and Daniel knew he had never appreciated Nature until he had seen this.

He did not trust himself to speak, but drew calmly on his cigarette as he kept his eyes on the middle distance. While his whole body yearned for her, his mind still feared his own emotions and he knew that if he looked at her he would betray his mounting passion and would be left a victim to his lust. How he wanted that mouth, that wide, tender, generous mouth. His body was fired with desire while his eyes stayed resolutely on the horizon.

Sara moved closer to him and settled comfortably against his shoulder. All resistance evaporated as he felt her warmth against his side and he tossed his cigarette over the hillside, crushing her to him in the same movement. Her teeth gleamed between her lips and before he could stop himself he pulled her hard against him and pressed his mouth fiercely on hers, their teeth grazing in their eagerness to taste each other. Almost without realising it, Daniel's hand found the soft fullness of Sara's breast and cupping it in his palm he could feel its hardening point as her excitement mounted with his.

One hand buried in her hair, his mouth ran the length of her long, smooth neck, down to the base of her throat and up again to her mouth, pressing and probing greedily with the purest lust he

123

had ever felt. The blood hammered in his head and he was torn between his urge to continue what he had begun and his mental desire to stop. One half of him hated his weakness: the other longed to pander to it.

Then suddenly Daniel pulled himself away. His head back, he looked down at her almost dispassionately. He could not draw his eyes away from her but he willed himself to break the spell she had cast. As he forced his desire to fade, he almost regretted that he had not unburdened his heart. But then the cold, logical side of him triumphed, and, sighing with relief, he willingly released her hair.

Sara leant back, overcome with a sharp feeling of rejection. Once again his dreams had proved more powerful than her. Daniel had never looked so remote, so dispassionate, as he did at that moment. Daniel shifted sideways, took her chin in his hand and studied her averted face.

'We must never start that again, Sara,' he said gently, wondering if she realised that his pain was so much greater than hers. He stared into her face, but her eyes were lowered and she refused to raise them to his. He dropped his hand and moved away from her restlessly.

Sara looked at him as though she hated him, her eyes hard and bright. 'Why?' she almost spat out the word.

Daniel looked at her for a moment before he answered, knowing that the greatest sin he could commit would be to delude her or himself.

'Because I couldn't love you . . .'

She interrupted him before he could finish, her eyes flying desperately to his face. 'You won't give me the chance,' she flared. 'For goodness sake, Daniel, stop sheltering in your world of make-believe. I *know* you love me. Admit it, Daniel – to yourself.'

He remained silent as he watched her eyes glinting in the fading light.

'Very well, say you don't love me.' Her voice was triumphant suddenly as though she had found an answer.

Daniel groaned and rubbed his eyes with one hand. Then he turned to face her again. 'All right,' he said slowly, 'perhaps I do love you. But there is nothing to be done about it. Just because I have these feelings it doesn't mean I am going to act upon them. Don't you see, it doesn't change anything.'

Her unhappiness hit him like a wave but he continued, relentless and strangely calm. 'You are free to think romantically – I am not. I cannot float above the material consequences of marriage. I may be wrong, but I can't. And besides, what I have decided to do with my life is, in a way, more important than loving you.' He shrugged casually. 'But yes, I love you – in the way it is possible to love the impossible. I love you, but I can't marry you. Do you understand?'

Sara jumped to her feet and glared at him. 'Somewhere inside you is a sanctimonious idealist taking refuge from the world in his dreams. What a shame there isn't such a thing as a Jewish priest,' she mocked. 'It would suit you down to the ground, then you could put your God and your vows before me too.'

She turned and walked quickly to her mare, then, mounting in one, smooth movement she set off down the track towards Zichron without a backward glance.

Sara got up the next morning determined to greet Daniel with a cheerful smile and scrupulously to avoid any reference to their quarrel of the previous evening. At breakfast she did nothing to betray her disappointment and frustration towards him but, as the morning passed, the feelings lingered on. Resolutely, she tried to push aside all her negative thoughts and concentrate on the most important fact of all: Daniel loved her. He had said so and that was worth more than every other word he had said. He loved her.

Sara's mother had always told her she was strong; strong and determined, and Sara repeated these words to herself as she pushed the heavy iron back and forth over the freshly-washed sheets. But, in spite of all her strength, the terrible emptiness that she had felt since last night persisted and she could not lighten the strangling pain in her chest. Unexpectedly, her throat tightened and she felt the tears that had been threatening all morning rise behind her eyes.

She put the flat iron down with a bang. She had had enough of this for one morning. Fatma, who was scrubbing the kitchen table with salt, looked up surprised. 'I'm hot,' Sara said, her voice sounding surprisingly normal in spite of her closeness to tears. 'I'm going to see Ruth. I won't be long.' Without giving Fatma time to protest she grabbed her sun hat from the peg and almost ran out of the kitchen into the sunshine.

As she walked briskly down the lane towards the Woolfs she told herself to stop being so stupid, not to let her emotions rule her life. But all her hopes and expectations for the future were so bound up with Daniel she could not imagine life without him. And yet he had told her that it was not meant to be.

Sara pushed open the fly door of Ruth's small, neat house and let herself in. The kitchen was bright and welcoming, fragrant with the smell of the newly-baked bread, which was cooling on the table, and the tang of the lemons Ruth was squeezing for lemonade. Ruth looked up surprised as the door opened and then saw her best friend in the doorway.

'Sara, what a lovely surprise! Sit down – there's some lemonade ready if you want some, help yourself. I've just got these last few to squeeze and I'll be with you.' Sara helped herself to lemonade from the clay pitcher covered with a beaded muslin cloth as Ruth turned back to the sink.

'Well?' Ruth chattered on, 'how did it go yesterday? I've been looking forward to hearing all about it.' Surprised that Sara did not answer she turned and looked at her friend.

'Sara, what on earth is the matter? What's happened?' She wiped her hands on her apron and sat down at the table beside Sara, looking at her worriedly.

Her concern was, of course, fatal. At her friend's kind words all Sara could do was to give in to her despair and, her eyes filling with tears, she broke into sobs and told Ruth the entire story. 'And I've tried to cut him out of my life – I really have,' she finished. 'But try as I might I just can't imagine any sort of future without him.'

Ruth sat up straight and stared hard at her friend, frowning to herself. To her mind Sara, who was usually very perceptive about people, was totally blind about Daniel Rosen. However clearly she thought she was looking at him, her view was always blurred by the strong physical attraction. Ruth reached out and took hold of Sara's hand, squeezing it affectionately, choosing her words carefully before she spoke.

'I think,' she began, 'that the problem is that you're both strong minded – and strong willed – and so you're bound to be in conflict often. If you could only relax a little, give him the time to get his bearings here again, feel secure, then I'm sure he would relax too and come round. They always do, you know,' she added with a flicker of a smile.

Sara looked at Ruth through tear-bright eyes, but the new hope she felt lasted only a moment before she remembered Daniel's words and his set face as he had said them and the tears started again.

'He won't,' she mumbled, 'you don't understand. He's just like Aaron – or Alex for that matter. More interested in his ideologies than he ever will be in me, or in any other woman. He will never marry me. He told me so and I believe him, although I don't understand why. It doesn't make sense – he loves me but won't marry me. All those years I've loved him, wanted no one but him,' she began to sob again but choked them down. 'I'm like a moth – I'll keep going back and back until my heart beats itself to death. I have to stop wanting him, but I don't know how.'

Ruth wrapped her arms round Sara in a huge hug. 'Sara, Sara, be patient. At the moment Daniel is still young and self-centred. He's looking for something he feels is far greater than the ordinariness of love – something glorious because it can only be won romantically on the battlefield, not on the hearth.'

Sara smiled a little. 'He called me a romantic,' she said. 'Perhaps that's all I am, a foolish one with a schoolgirl crush. But I'm not a schoolgirl, I'm a woman who needs a husband so that I can enjoy the pleasures as well as the duties of love. I need a husband to give me the children I want so badly – Daniel's children,' she added in a whisper and then hurried on. 'Daniel would probably dance with joy at my wedding if it were to Chaim Cohen,' she finished bitterly.

'Only because he would be out of danger from your love,' Ruth answered. 'Although you could do far worse than marry Chaim Cohen.'

Sara was very dear to Ruth's heart, but Ruth kept a strict curb on her tongue where Daniel was concerned. She could see that there was much that was admirable in him, but still she did not believe he was really the man for Sara. She thought that despite his charm he was emotionally insecure and therefore potentially dangerous to her friend. She hugged Sara again until her friend remembered Ruth's own happiness and pushed Ruth gently away.

'I've been so selfish!' she exclaimed. 'Boring you with all my silliness and I haven't so much as asked how you're feeling.'

'I'm feeling splendid – never better,' said Ruth, going back to the sink happy that Sara's mood seemed to have turned.

'And Robby?'

'He fusses over me as though I were at death's door. I've told and told him that pregnancy is not a disease and pointed out quite how many people have had babies before, but he still seems to think I'm the first,' she laughed. 'Mind you, I must admit I fuss over him just as much with this watch group business. He was out again last night and I can't help worrying.'

Sara's mind went back to the bay mare, still at the Zabiah's camp and now likely to remain there. Daniel had told Aaron about the sighting over breakfast but the general consensus had been to cut their losses as they felt the danger was not equal to the reward. Sara was not so sure.

'I deserted Fatma in the middle of the ironing,' Sara said, rising to her feet and draining her lemonade. 'I'd better get back. Thank you for everything, Ruth.'

At the door she paused and turned back. 'Aaron has left the decision about my joining the watch group to Daniel. What do you think his reaction will be?'

'I don't know – and there's only one way to find out,' said Ruth cheerfully.

As the door closed behind Sara, Ruth shook her head. She had a very strong feeling that Sara was heading for yet another rejection and fervently hoped that Chaim Cohen would be around to catch her when she fell.

CHAPTER EIGHT

The Zabiah's camp was pitched in a hollow of scrubland, protected on one flank by a vast, natural shelf of rock. Sara, crouched among a few acacia trees less than a stone's throw from the sleeping bandits, was as still and watchful as a leopard as she stared hard through the darkness. The stars shed enough light for her to make out the motionless forms of the men who lay, wrapped in their blankets, exhausted, she hoped, by a day's thieving. So far everything was just as Sara had planned. She was slightly unnerved by the glinting of weapons – daggers thrust into their belts, swords and rifles close to hand – but she had come armed and knowing what to expect.

The clear night air was poisoned with rich, heavy smells of the camp, dung, urine and coffee, which, combined with the strain of searching the darkness, made Sara's eyes water. The adrenalin was flowing and she could feel the blood rushing through her veins, but the thought of Bella close behind calmed her. The mare was loosely tethered to a tree, her jaws tightly bound with cloth so no sound should escape. Sara had complete confidence in Bella's speed should the need arise.

Sara had found the camp easily enough and had now been hiding for half an hour, waiting until instinct told her the right moment to move. She had waited for the last grumble and first snore from the Zabiah, and was now certain that they were all asleep. The only sound now was the grinding teeth and munching of the camels, which were drawn into a crescent round the men. Their grunts were a useful cover for any slight noise Sara or Bella might make.

Her resolve momentarily weakened at the prospect of being caught by the bandits, Sara had almost given up halfway through her vigil. She knew they would rape and kill her as easily, and with about as little compunction as they had in urinating – it was not an encouraging thought. But the memory of the morning came back to her and her courage rose with her fury.

In the morning, Sara had ridden down to Atlit to put her case to Daniel. His reaction, although not totally unexpected, had enraged her.

'Defence is no job for a woman,' he had said coldly.

Sara stared at him, first in surprise and then in anger. The meaning behind his words was obvious – your place, my sweet, is in the kitchen.

'And why not?' she asked hotly.

'Because I say so,' he answered shortly and walked off without another word. Sara was so angry she could hardly breathe.

'All women aren't such fools as you like to think,' she shouted after him, her voice rising hysterically. She felt like a beaten dog. Resentment and hurt pride welled up in her.

'Damn him,' she muttered through clenched teeth. 'I'll show him. Defence no job for a woman! I'll show him.'

For the rest of the day she had turned over ways of proving her point – and by the evening she had decided that the answer was to get back the stolen bay single-handedly. This was how Sara came to be hiding in a clump of trees on the edge of a Zabiah camp.

Suddenly, Sara's fears evaporated and every nerve in her body told her that now was the moment. She lifted her chin determinedly and jabbed a stray lock of hair back into place. Then, silently and very cautiously, she began to leopard-crawl out of her hiding place. As wary as an assassin, drawn dagger in hand, she crept on, camouflaged by the shadows.

Careful to stay upwind of the dogs that were curled up by the men, she moved in among the camels. Ghostly and regal in the dark their heads swayed above her, like a nest of weird snakes. With sure, easy strokes, Sara severed the she camels' hobbling ropes. So skilful was she that not one camel let out a cry or one of the dogs a bark. Abu had taught her well.

This was now the most dangerous moment. One false move and she was dead. Sure footed and stealthy, she circled the men, her heart beating thickly. Still not hurrying, she reached the horses, hoping desperately that the bay would give no whicker of recognition. Sara cut the mare loose with one slice of the dagger and waited, still as a shadow.

One of the camels, finding itself free from the ropes, remembered a juicy patch of scrub and ambled off in search of a snack. The other camels soon followed and started feeding noisily. As they began to scatter across the scrub Sara gently coaxed the bay away from the other horses. She was only a few yards away from Bella when a bull camel, furious and confused at being hobbled while the females were happily browsing, bellowed out his anger.

Within seconds the camp was in total confusion. Dogs barked hysterically, the Arabs leapt to their feet, rifles in hand, and raced after the camels. Sara did not pause for an instant. Leaping on to Bella she dug in her heels and rode off like the furies, the bay in tow, sure in the knowledge that the Zabiah, caught unawares in the darkness and chaos, could not follow her in time.

She rode hard for an hour, and only then did she feel secure enough to stop and change horses. When she dismounted she realised quite how weak she felt: her lungs were burning, her teeth chattering and her limbs shaking feverishly.

She slid the saddle from Bella and lifted it to the bay's back but, suddenly, overcome by elation at her success, she dropped it to the ground and began to laugh wildly. Then the idea of what she must look like made her laugh even more. She was covered in camel dung, her hair was bound back in ugly snarls and she reeked of sweat – her own and the horse's. She thought of Chaim Cohen's face over the tea-cups and imagined how it would change if he could see her now – he would certainly be less keen to rush her into marriage.

Sara was still laughing weakly into the bay's mane when she felt a long, slow shudder through its flesh and, jerking at the reins, it raised its head whinnying and cavorting in sudden panic. Sara's laugh died in her throat and she straightened up at once, listening hard. Bella, as though from some hidden signal, gave a queer little jump and trotted on the spot, prancing round the bush to which Sara had tied her. She tossed her head and blew down her nostrils, looking out through the dim light.

What on earth is going on, Sara wondered, listening hard in mounting panic. They couldn't have caught up with her. The morning mist made it hard for her to see more than a short distance so she strained her ears until they felt they would burst with the effort. She heard a faint crackle in the undergrowth a few yards away and her heart began to beat violently. Someone or something was hidden there, in the bushes. She could sense it now.

She drew her shotgun from the saddlebag and aimed it towards the area of dense undergrowth. The bay plunged and reeled suddenly, knocking the rifle out of Sara's hand and sending her stumbling awkwardly into a patch of bushes. Before she could regain her balance the bay had bolted off into the mist. Sara lay painfully in the bushes for a while before the realisation of what had happened hit her. After all her daring, to be defeated by a nervous horse!

She pulled an arm free from the thorns, ripping her shirt in the process and almost weeping in vexation. She had risked her life in order to end up in a thorn bush with the horse maybe miles away!

'Damn, damn, damn!' she cursed, on the verge of tears, as she struggled to free her hair and clothes from the grip of the thorns that seemed to hold her in a vice.

Then, through her confusion, she became aware of approaching hoofbeats. In one last, futile effort to reach the rifle she almost tore the shirt off her back but it was hopeless. Dishevelled and close to breaking, she distinguished a figure on a white stallion. His face was bound in a cloth, and he was leading the bay horse meekly in tow.

Sara's first thought was that he was from the Zabiah. She tried to move but had no strength at all, both mind and body failing her. The back of her neck felt icy cold and terror rose in her throat as she fought against the wave of panic. Taking a deep breath she closed her eyes, she could not bear to face her fate.

Only a few feet from her, the rider checked his high-stepping stallion. A moment passed and then a laugh rang out, breaking the pre-dawn silence. It was a sound she instantly recognised.

'Well, well, if it isn't Miss Levinson,' said Joe Lanski, his voice and eyes betraying the same lazy amusement that had so irritated her at the dance. One hand held the bay's leading rein, the other rested easily on the pommel of his saddle as he slowly looked her up and down.

'You've changed your hairstyle, I see,' he said laughing again.

Sara, temporarily speechless, could only stare as Joe unwound the cloth from his face. 'I must say, I rather like it,' he added, dismounting and tethering the stallion and the bay beside Bella.

The relief of the stranger being Joe rather than a bandit set on revenge made Sara feel oddly light-headed. Her first reaction only seconds ago had been to fall on his neck and kiss him wildly – she now felt an irrational desire to shoot him dead. Why did this man annoy her so?

'Oh, stop your nonsense and for goodness sake help me out of this dratted bush,' she said as crossly as though he were being slow in helping her out of a pony trap at a picnic.

'Tut tut. The face of an angel and the heart of a shrew.' He said, moving to where she lay, ignominiously caught in the bush. Then, halfway towards her, he froze for a moment, all humour gone from his eyes and with a movement so fast that it seemed like an illusion, he bent and picked up her rifle, aiming it towards the scrub to her right.

'What the . . ?' she demanded furiously, thinking he was up to some new game.

'Shut up and for God's sake, don't move,' he commanded, his voice low and firm.

Then she saw it, fifty paces away. A wild boar as large as a heifer, its tusks curving upwards to the early morning sky as it lowered its head, preparing to charge. The horses whickered, prancing nervously on the spot as the beast stood, perfectly still, its malevolent little eyes glinting in the first light.

'Shoot it,' she said in a voice that she did not recognise as her own.

'Stay still,' Joe hissed. 'I need a clear shot,' and he dropped on one knee to steady himself. He knew that once the boar charged there would be time only for a single shot and at the range Sara's rifle was too light; he would have to fire once in the hope of scaring the beast off and if that failed let it come in close where the shot would be conclusive. Joe braced himself, brought up the rifle and fired.

Sara heard the sharp retort of the Winchester echoing round the mountains and saw the pig turn sharply on its short, powerful legs and speed off into the undergrowth. Joe lowered the rifle – he had fired well over the animal's head.

'My God, it would have ripped me to pieces,' Sara said in a shaken whisper. 'Why didn't you shoot it?' She was suddenly angry, glaring at Joe as though he had meant the boar to kill her.

'I wanted to give it a chance to change its mind,' he said nonchalantly, hooking the rifle into its sling on Bella's saddle.

'Pigs don't have minds,' Sara said meaningfully as Joe helped extricate her from the bush.

He only laughed. 'Well, that one did – it knew that it would take more than a pair of tusks to get you on your back.'

Joe's face resumed its customary mocking expression, but Sara sensed it concealed a personality much more interesting and dangerous than the idle façade he chose to present to the incurious, outside world. She cast round for something clever to say but to her frustration could think of nothing, so fought against the bush instead.

'Don't struggle, you'll only make it worse,' Joe said as, with surprising gentleness, he untangled the last thorns from her hair. 'What in the devil are you doing out here anyway?' he questioned as he helped her to her feet.

'It really is most inconsiderate of Daniel Rosen to arrange a lovers' tryst in the middle of the wilderness.'

Sara snorted indignantly, and threw him a scathing look. The effect was slightly spoiled by her efforts to hold her wrecked shirt together and smooth down her riding skirt. Joe looked at her silently as she fumbled with the rags of her blouse and Sara suddenly felt awkward and uncertain as he studied her face solemnly. She raised her head and looked up into his eyes. He was so close she could feel his body warmth reach her through the thin morning air and her limbs were suddenly stupified. The habitual mockery disappeared from Joe's eyes and Sara gasped as he reached out and gently stroked her arm from the elbow to the shoulder. Her lips parted and her breathing quickened as his hand slid to the nape of her neck. Then, without warning, he grasped her hair and brought his mouth down on hers. Sara was so overcome that it was a long moment before she was conscious of what was happening: that Joe was kissing her and that she was returning his kisses, her mouth soft and open to his.

What was she doing in the middle of the wilderness with a man she hated, kissing and being kissed by him? She tore her mouth away and he struggled to free herself but Joe held her easily by the wrists.

'I've been wanting to do that since I first saw you,' he said softly. Sara gathered all her strength and kicked Joe hard on the shins. She pulled away and glared at him from the safe distance of a few feet.

'You bastard,' she spluttered. 'Touch me again and I'll make a gelding of you.'

Joe threw back his head and laughed, the old taunting look on his face. 'Miss Levinson, I will keep my distance,' he said. 'I will make any sacrifice you ask of me,' and he bent and picked up the saddle. She snatched it from him and saddled the bay, silent with rage. Then she nimbly mounted and grabbed Bella's reins from Joe, who had been politely leading the mare over to her. He looked at her without expression and turned, whistling softly to his stallion, who trotted obediently to him.

'I won't say thank you,' Sara said through gritted teeth and, digging her heels into the bay's flanks, pulled at the leading rein. But for some reason Bella, usually the most docile of animals, would not obey. She was playing up to the stallion who was responding with gentle nuzzles. Tug at the reins as Sara might, Bella would not move.

'I think your mare has taken a bit of a fancy to Negiv,' said Joe, mounting and patting his horse's arching neck.

'Nonsense,' Sara snapped, pulling almost cruelly at Bella.

Joe grinned. 'I am sorry I can't accompany you home but I have to get some horses to the garrison at Afula.'

'I'm much safer on my own,' she replied smugly, ignoring the fact that he had found her struggling in a thorn bush.

'It's light now,' Joe said, softening for a moment. 'Go to the coast road and you should be all right.'

'I do know my way around,' she answered.

'Then there's no problem,' he said and, wheeling Negiv round so sharply that the stallion's forelegs pawed the air, he nodded and rode back into the mist.

Sara sat listening to the sound of hooves dying away, furious that the low-down swine had not offered to ride her home. I hope he breaks his neck, she muttered to herself and urged the bay into a canter. More than anything she wanted to be home. Pushing all thought of Joe Lanski out of her mind, she encouraged the horses, which were almost as tired as she was, to keep up the pace.

At least she had the bay, she told herself. She also hoped that her brothers would be proud of her, that Daniel would let her into the group and that Cohen, when he heard about her exploits, would be on the next boat back to Constantinople.

She could not have been more wrong on all counts.

'Whatever made you do such a stupid thing?' Daniel demanded furiously, his eyes blazing at Sara in real anger. He shook his head vehemently. 'My God, Sara, what can you have been thinking about?' Six hours after Sara's return they were all sitting around the kitchen table at Zichron shouting at each other.

Sara had come back so late in the morning that there had been

135

no hope of arriving unnoticed, so she had been bold about it. Proudly handing the bay to Abu she had told him the story – or at least as much of it as she thought he needed to know – and, encouraged by Abu's pride in his teaching and joy at being reunited with the mare, had marched defiantly into the kitchen. For some reason, she decided to tell no one, not even Aaron, about her meeting with Joe Lanski.

She was soon disillusioned by Fatma, who made her feelings quite clear. Sara had expected amazement, but not such fury. 'It's the first time a horse has ever been stolen by a donkey,' Fatma shouted, stamping heavily around the kitchen in her bare feet.

'I didn't steal it! It was ours. And besides, what I do is my own business.'

'That's what you think,' Fatma scolded and gave the unlucky Leylah, who happened to be in her way, a clip on the ear.

Sara turned her back on the kitchen, marched up the stairs and fell into bed, asleep in a deep and dreamless sleep within seconds.

When she woke up and went back downstairs she was overwhelmed by the family reaction to her jaunt. She found them all sitting round the kitchen table, each with something to say and each saying it at the top of their voice to whomever would listen.

Sam and Becky, if no one else, looked on the whole 'escapade' as it was now slightingly referred to, with blind and whole-hearted admiration. But Daniel, at whom the whole incident had been aimed, was siding with Aaron and Alex – a double blow as she had been sure Alex would see her point of view. Sara found herself being treated like a problem child, which considering she had been running the household for years, ensuring that they were all fed and looked after, and was at this very moment being pushed towards marriage, was more than a little insulting.

To Sara's chagrin, her father seemed to take the adventure the worst. He did not say much but suddenly looked greyer and appreciably older. His newly shadowed face showed a vulnerability that made Sara genuinely guilty. She felt a surge of tenderness for him and bowed her head silently in the face of his reproaches. This sad gentleness from her father was not what she had intended.

But she would not be told what to do by Daniel, and when he started to give her his views her self-control boiled over.

'From what I hear, your friend Isobelle Frank is hardly a model of docile femininity!'

The corners of her mouth turned down and her eyes, bright and hard, challenged Daniel's. She had recently heard rumours that Daniel was seeing the Russian revolutionary whenever he visited Haifa with Aaron. What drove her to fury was the certainty that they didn't spend the evenings discussing Karl Marx.

'Why, she dresses like an Arab, smokes cigarettes, has countless affairs and, apparently, you admire her deeply.'

'Isobelle Frank has nothing to do with this matter,' said Aaron stiffly, hoping to put a stop to this line of discussion.

Sara drew a breath and took control of herself. 'All right, you win,' she said softly. 'I'm sorry.' She said it with all the grace she could, but for her father's sake only. She was not remotely sorry. She rose and walked round the table to her father. Putting her arms around him, she brought her face down to his cheek and kissed him. 'I'm sorry, Papa. Will you forgive me?'

Abram took her hand and held it against his face. 'Yes, Sara,' he said quietly. 'But I beg you not to act so rashly in the future. Will you promise me?'

'I promise, Papa,' she said, kissing his cheek again and giving Daniel a cold, sulky little glance.

Well, that was that. They wouldn't let her into the watch group now, but she now did not care. She had had enough of living her life by other people's rules: from this moment on she would make her own.

Daniel's eyes followed her as she walked towards the door. He had always known Sara to have guts and courage but now he saw something else in her extraordinary blue eyes; a cold determination that left him for a moment with a tremendous sense of loss. He was already aching with regret for the offer of love she seemed to have withdrawn.

'If nobody minds my leaving the house,' Sara said archly. 'I'm going to visit the stables.'

And without a backward look, she strode out of the kitchen, the fly door rattling in its frame behind her.

CHAPTER NINE

Constantinople

The library, a large, airy room overlooking the lovely gardens of the Rose Palace, had been the obvious choice for Selena's workroom. The walls were booklined, circular tables were scattered with the latest magazines and as well as an enormous Chippendale desk, there was a scattering of comfortable sofas and chairs.

Selena clipped some bills neatly together and sat back with a satisfied smile as she looked at the uncluttered desk. The correspondence and ledgers were arranged in files and bills and receipts were pigeon-holed: it was just the way she liked it. Only six weeks before, the desk had been stuffed full of letters and drafts from lawyers, bankers and the companies in America in which her new employer had such huge investments. Selena had stared at them with amazement.

'Aw – just chuck them out and start over,' Annie Lufti said with a dismissive wave of her hand. Of course, Selena had done no such thing. She had carefully gone through every piece of paper and gently encouraged Annie to explain them so that she could file or answer them. Annie considered her a miracle and marvelled daily at Selena's ability to make easy sense of a column of figures. 'Far too clever for a girl,' she would say with her throaty chuckle.

For her part convinced that her employer had been sent her by the gods, Selena never for a moment forgot her luck in meeting Annie. Selena recalled fondly how she had stood with the Major in the pink marbled hall; her back ridged with nerves and her heart palpitating wildly. Her eyes darted about nervously through downcast lashes as she wondered what kind of woman could live alone in such splendour.

The Rose Palace, although huge, was not on the monstrous scale of some palaces she had lived in, and here everything seemed to match: the costly jades, porcelain and finely-wrought silver complemented each other perfectly. The marble floors, half-hidden by magnificent Persian rugs, the oil paintings in ornate gold frames and the deep bowls of flowers resting on lacquered Chinese cabinets all threw off a comfortable atmosphere in spite of their opulence. Selena had felt oddly awed and at home at the same time.

Hans Werner Rilke was apparently well known to Akiff, the impressively large Sudanese major-domo. Resplendent in a navy-blue galabya edged with gold braid, white gloves and red fez, he solemnly introduced himself to Selena and then, as though deciding he liked the look of her, he beamed broadly, took her cloak and the Major's hat, and pressed a bell.

A door slammed upstairs and a small, lithe woman, dressed in rich moiré with bright red hair swept up and away from an eager, attractive face, had appeared at the top of the stairway. Annie Lufti bore no resemblance whatsoever to the image Selena had conjured up of her new employer who, flying down the stairs to meet them, her greetings and apologies for keeping them waiting echoing round the vast hall, had immediately appealed to Selena.

Madame Lufti had paused on the last step and, as though remembering her manners, had held out a hand to Selena. 'My dear child,' she had bubbled in a voice that gave her away as an American and a heavy smoker, 'my dear child. I am so happy to have you here. Hans Werner has spoken so highly of you, given you such a glowing reference – I can see at once that he has not exaggerated.' Then, darting forward, she had embraced Selena warmly. 'And you are so pretty – I never could abide ugliness – we are going to get along famously. I just know we are.' She had paused a moment, looking at Selena anxiously. 'I do hope you will be comfortable with us at the Rose Palace.'

'I am sure I will be, Madame Lufti,' Selena had replied in her soft, courteous manner.

'Oh don't call me that – my friends call me Annie,' she had said, her brown eyes twinkling. 'And I shall call you Selena if I may.'

Selena had smiled and felt herself relax instinctively. There was something so open about this woman. 'I should be honoured,' she had said. And Annie, grasping her arm and chattering eagerly, had led her into the drawing room and so generously into her life.

No one could fail to respond to Annie's warmth and Selena was no exception. Despite their differences in age and experience, the two women struck up a friendship from that very day. Selena had spent the first days of her stay struggling to overcome her shyness and to adapt her self to the new pattern of her life. Her pangs of longing for the solid assurance of Mûzvicka and Abdul Hamid had been so intense at first that they had threatened to turn her back into the abducted fifteen-year-old child. But then she was angry with herself for her weakness and, as the days became weeks, she had begun to feel more at ease in this new world and she, who had not drawn a free breath in years, began gulping them down in lungfuls.

Gradually, coaxing her gently, Annie had drawn her into her own world. Selena learned that everything about Annie Lufti was out of the usual. She had been an American heiress who, when many of her country women were turning to Europe for romance and marriage, had gone East. She had found all she dreamed of the day she met Omar Lufti, an absurdly handsome hero, son of one of the most important Turkish families. Within a month of meeting him, Annie had 'bedded and wedded him' as she liked to say. The vast fortune left her by her father had helped reconcile her Moslem in-laws to their son's choice of bride. In the event, the marriage was one of the very few examples of cross and crescent living happily together.

Omar had been killed in the Balkan Wars leaving Annie a childless widow and terribly bereaved. Letters from her staunchly Catholic family in America urged her to come home, but 'home' was now in the East. 'Once one has lived among the palms one cannot live anywhere else,' she misquoted, and stayed.

After three years of widowhood Annie now had a perfectly adjusted and happy life. Everyone who knew her loved her – her spirited chatter and satirical sense of humour made sure of that. She led a whirling social life, into which Selena was increasingly drawn. It had started two weeks after Selena's arrival when Annie had cornered Selena in the library. She was going out visiting shortly and would Selena like to accompany her? Selena's first instinct was to refuse, but before she had opened her mouth Annie was pressing her invitation.

'Of course, you must come, darling. You can't spend your days wandering around this house or sitting with your nose in a book. Now be a good girl and be ready at four o'clock,' she had finished firmly.

Selena's days were filled to the last minute. Every morning she worked at her desk until eleven o'clock. Then she took a long walk in the Palace garden, which was of a rare splendour. After luncheon, there were visits to the houses of other wealthy women in the city, and then back to more work in the library followed by tea. In the evening, more often than not, there were grand dinner parties to give or go to. At first, Selena, shy and nervous, had tried to avoid these, saying she preferred to read. But as usual Annie was firm. 'You're not just a servant here, darling, besides which you read too much. It will harm your eyes.'

Fortunately, Hans Werner was a frequent visitor and, being the only link with her former life, he gave her some sense of security among the familiar-looking strangers with familiar-sounding names. She was learning to put names to faces, and told herself that when she had achieved this she would be much more at home.

Selena's thoughts were interrupted by the chiming of a clock and she stood up, quickly locking the bureau and pocketing the key. She would be late for tea and today Mrs Morgenthau, the wife of the American Ambassador, was visiting. Reaching the door, Selena instinctively put her hand up to pull her veil down then, remembering that she had abandoned it with the old life, laughed softly to herself as she rushed out of the library.

'Ah, there you are,' said Annie as Selena came into the drawing room. 'I thought you might be hiding again.' Selena laughed at Annie's silliness. 'This is Emma Morgenthau, who has come, as usual, to relieve me of some of my hard-earned fortune.' Annie turned to a small, middle-aged woman with a genuine and very charming smile.

'For the orphanage, I might add,' said Mrs Morgenthau, 'although I'm quite sure Annie's fortune is quite large enough to considerably reduce America's national debt.' She looked up at Selena warmly. 'Come, sit next to me,' she said, patting the quilted chair next to her. Selena smiled shyly and dutifully sat down.

Atiff, followed by liveried footmen, brought in tea and cakes. Annie dismissed them with a nod and, carefully lifting the heavy silver teapot, poured three cups. 'Cake, Emma?' she said, indicating the plates of rich confections.

Mrs Morgenthau smiled and took the cup being offered her: 'No thank you. Once I start on your cakes I can't bring myself to stop.'

'Oh, do try the chocolate *torte*,' exclaimed Selena. 'It's delicious.'

'Well, just a tiny slice,' Mrs Morgenthau capitulated with a smile.

Annie nodded to herself as she watched the girl lean forward and slice the cake. She was opening up like some lovely exotic flower. There were already many changes apparent in Selena; the growing confidence and poise she was just beginning to display. 'No no, not me,' said Annie, recoiling in mock horror as Selena offered her a piece of the cake. 'I shall be a dollop of lard.'

Selena laughed and sat back in her chair. Mrs Morgenthau turned to face her. 'Now, tell me about yourself,' she insisted. 'Your family?'

Selena crumbled her cake with a fork. 'I am Armenian. My parents and brothers died before – well, before I joined the ... household ... of the late Sultan.'

'So you are Armenian!' Mrs Morgenthau cried delightedly.

'Yes,' said Selena, surprised at this sudden interest in her nationality. Most people she met were more intrigued by her years in the harem. 'Why?'

'The orphanage is for Armenian children, run by a very capable Quaker lady. Perhaps you would be interested in visiting?'

'I would like that very much. Please, tell me about it.'

'There's really very little I am able to – mostly I collect funds,' Mrs Morgenthau said with a smile in Annie's direction, and she went on to tell Selena about the orphanage and scheme for the children and the problems of malnutrition, ignorance and poverty they encountered daily.

Selena listened attentively to Mrs Morgenthau's account. It aroused all manner of longings within her. 'I can see you have compassion,' said the Ambassador's wife, leaning forward intently and patting Selena's hand. 'I am going there tomorrow afternoon. Can you come?'

Selena looked at Annie. 'With forty-eight servants I have no doubt I'll survive an afternoon without you,' she laughed.

Selena turned back to Mrs Morgenthau, 'Oh yes, I wouldn't miss it for the world.'

The orphanage was in the Armenian quarter of Kum Kapu. The people knew Mrs Morgenthau and smiled and called greetings to her as they passed. The air was hot in the dark alleys but, although the area was obviously very poor, the streets and houses were clean and well looked after.

Selena was very excited and hearing her native tongue all round her was suddenly transported back to the Mission and her home mountain village. 'How many children are here?' she asked as they arrived at the orphanage.

'Oh, around fifty. Most of them are very young,' said Mrs Morgenthau, pushing open a gate in the wall. Selena followed her in, but was totally unprepared for her feelings on entering the garden. The moment the gate opened they were surrounded by sweet little faces, laughing and begging for the boiled sweets the American lady always carried in her pocket. Some of the children just stared at them with wide eyes and solemn faces. Most appeared to be six or seven years old, although at least half a dozen were only just toddling. Selena's heart went out to them in compassion and tenderness.

'I really must apologise,' said a small, stout woman with rosy cheeks and grey hair in a neat bun, as she came forward to greet them, 'but we are so short-staffed.' Her voice was tight and clipped: very English.

Clapping her hands together she ordered the children back into the house and, after introducing herself to Selena as Miss Rushton, followed the children indoors, shooing the stragglers before her.

'Where do the children come from?' asked Selena.

'Some are sent to us when their families are killed in the epidemics and, of course, after the purges there are always many orphaned children.'

Selena nodded knowingly. Fortunately, there had not been a pogrom against the Armenians for many years now.

Two girls began squabbling over an ancient-looking rag doll. 'Oh dear,' said Miss Rushton, flustered, but Selena bent down and in the Armenian which she had thought she had almost forgotten she ended the argument in seconds. 'My goodness,' said Miss Rushton. 'I don't suppose you would like to come and help out here would you?'

Selena, suddenly conscious of her heart growing lighter, smiled serenely. 'Oh yes,' she said. 'Nothing would please me more.'

CHAPTER TEN

Palestine

'Wouldn't it be wonderful to be rich,' said Becky with a sigh. 'I know that I would look staggering if only I were dressed by Worth or Molyneux.' She thumbed wearily through a fashion journal Daniel had brought them from Paris and looked sadly at the high fashion she so envied. Sara and Ruth exchanged smiles. The three girls were sitting in the drawing room, catching up with their sewing and listening to Becky chattering on about her future. Since Aaron and her father had told her she was going to Beirut in January, Becky had taken herself very seriously. She constantly pestered Sara – and anyone else who would listen – for details of smart life. Everyone was beginning to tire of Becky's preparations and although they knew they would miss her they began to long for her to launch herself on society and leave them all alone.

'Of course,' Becky continued, looking at her sister slyly. 'If only you would accept Mr Cohen's offer you would have the most exciting life – clothes, jewels, the theatre . . .' A dreamy expression came over her face.

Sara sank back on the sofa and groaned. 'Becky, will you please shut up about Chaim Cohen. Apart from anything else he hasn't even asked me.'

One of the most irritating results of Sara's midnight adventure was the increase in comments about Chaim Cohen and marriage. Everyone in the house had his own opinion and everyone endlessly – and more often than not surreptitiously – gave her advice. Every time Chaim arrived, Fatma would whisper, 'Here he is,' with as much fervour as if she were announcing the Second Coming and, when he left, she would pad around the house mumbling sly remarks like: 'A woman without a husband is like a bird with one wing.' Sara's father, whom she longed to please, told her how happy he had been in his marriage, adding, almost as if by chance, that he thought Cohen a real gentleman, a man who could get on with everyone and offend no one. Even Doctor Ephraim had found an opportunity to tell her he found Cohen a fine-looking man and one no one could despise.

To Sara's surprise, far from being put off by her midnight gallivanting, Chaim had visited almost every day since, never once arriving empty-handed. Although he brought flowers or bonbons, his manner to her changed and he began to treat her less distantly, more as a friend than a suitor.

As the days passed Sara realised that she looked forward to his visits. She was touched by his thoughtfulness, his solicitude, and by his attitude which had been so far from what she had expected and so much more understanding than that of her brothers – and Daniel. Chaim made Sara feel good, and she began to feel proud that she could be admired by such a man of the world. Chaim took her out of the small, confined world of Zichron and made her feel part of something wider and more glamorous. At a time when her self-confidence was badly shaken, Chaim did much to build it up again, and she appreciated that.

For all these reasons her opinion of Chaim had changed in the past few weeks; but she could not stop comparing him with Daniel Rosen. Sara still clung on to her love for him with all her heart, but in the coolness of her mind she knew that Daniel had rejected her. So she began, almost against her will, to consider other possibilities. The idea of another world, without Daniel, invaded her mind. A world of smart clothes, visits to the opera and theatre . . . a world she had conjured straight from romantic fiction and which beckoned to her increasingly seductively.

Perhaps Chaim Cohen was the answer. For this reason alone Sara was drawn to the idea of marrying him. If he could deliver her from the dreary insignificance of a life without Daniel, perhaps she should take the opportunity while she still had it. He was not disagreeable, in fact she liked him very much indeed. Her family was allied in trying to convince her that he was a good match. He was not the first man who had been pointed in Sara's direction, but he was certainly the best so far – maybe no one better would come along.

And perhaps the cynics were right – that the world conspired against love; that love did not last but was driven away by boredom, poverty and the passing of the years. Maybe she ought to settle for less than love. And yet some rebellious part of her still refused to lend itself to this obvious conclusion. She felt that, after all she had been through recently, there was nothing she wanted more than to be able to stick to her dreams and hopes, however unlikely they now seemed.

She looked secretly at Ruth, and yet again ached at the thought of her friend pregnant. It really was time she was married, she longed for a family of her own. Daniel's family, but that was an impossible dream. Ruth, catching her friend's look, put down her magazine.

'Becky, be a darling and make some tea, would you?'

For once tactful, Becky jumped up cheerfully, scattering magazines all round. 'All right,' she said, moving casually towards the door but looking, in her light cotton dress, anything but the *femme de monde* she was imagining herself.

Ruth watched her leave the room and then walked over to the open doors that led out to the garden. She stood for a moment with her back to Sara, thinking.

'What will you say when Chaim asks you to marry him?' she asked quietly.

Chaim was coming to call this evening and everyone was convinced that he would ask Sara to marry him. He had successfully concluded his business with Aaron and was due to leave the area in less than a week. It was already the beginning of October and he had to get back to Constantinople.

'I shall have the pleasure of refusing him,' Sara said with a tight little smile, but suddenly wondered whether she was as set against him as she pretended.

'What would you say if Daniel Rosen did not exist?' Ruth persisted.

Sara thought for a moment, trying to be honest with herself. 'I would accept,' she answered, almost in a whisper.

Ruth spun round to face Sara: 'Then you're a damn fool not to,' she said, her voice hard and cold. Sara, shocked by the earnestness in her friend's voice, just stared at her.

'You're not looking at this straight, Sara,' Ruth continued. 'You must know that if you turn Chaim Cohen down, you'll be making a big mistake. If only you would let yourself see that.'

Sara bit her lip and shook her head dejectedly. 'But I want Daniel.'

Ruth snorted in exasperation, her self-control finally snapping.

'It's time you abandoned your silly pride. Admit defeat, Sara. What is the use of clinging to someone who doesn't want you?'

Sara knotted her fingers together and paced the room searching for an answer. 'It doesn't matter that he doesn't want me – I want him.'

'Sara! You're living for some futile hope. For God's sake admit it!' Ruth crossed to her friend and laid a hand on her arm. It calmed Sara immediately and she sank back on to the sofa, Ruth sitting close beside her.

'Perhaps Daniel does love you, Sara,' Ruth said more gently. 'But you need more than some vague, spiritual, one-sided romance.' She paused for a moment, knowing how important it was to express herself properly. 'You have a great chance. You have met Chaim Cohen, who by some miracle is giving you a chance to pick up the threads of your old life and weave a new one. Think of it!'

In spite of her emotional confusion, Sara realised that Ruth was speaking sense. She struggled for a coherent thought. 'I don't think marrying Chaim will make me any happier.' She looked down at her hands, which she was still twisting in knots. 'I'd have to go and live abroad . . . hundreds of miles from here . . . and all of you,' she trailed off, and her eyes filled with tears. She had never felt more at a loss. She blinked away the tears and brushed at her eyes with the back of her hand, swallowing hard. '. . . it's so *frustrating*,' she finished wretchedly.

Ruth took Sara's hand in hers, willing her to feel the warmth of her friendship. 'I know you'll be leaving a lot behind and giving up a great deal, but I'm sure that in the end it will be for the best. You are twenty years old, and you know everyone around here too well – it's unlikely you'll ever fall in love with anyone here. Salvage what you can of your emotions. Leave behind your memories, your hopes – *Daniel Rosen*.'

Sara drew a deep breath, thinking about what Ruth was saying, and then answered slowly: 'I do want my own home . . . with a husband . . . and children.' She looked at Ruth, filled with love for her and suddenly glad that she had brought up the subject of Chaim Cohen. Talking to someone else certainly helped clear her thoughts. She smiled weakly. 'I'm sure you're right, it would be the best solution.'

Ruth stood up, giving Sara a quick hug. 'I'll go and see what happened to the tea. Think about our conversation, won't you?'

As she reached the door she turned: 'In the meantime, Sara, stop cursing the whims of fate – things are simply meant to be.'

As Sara watched Ruth walk out of the room her heart sank once again. The time for making up her mind was drawing terribly near. 'I must decide,' she thought and got up, vexed and restless, and totally confused again.

She sat at the piano and ran her fingers up and down the keys for a moment before settling into Liszt's B minor Sonata. She played until she and the instrument were exhausted and then, feeling calmer and full of self-pity, switched to Sibelius's haunting *Valse Triste*. Under the music's spell her frustration faded and her long fingers overcame the old piano's deficiencies. Her head went back and her shoulders up and she lost herself in the music.

Gradually, she became aware of a presence in the room, and turning abruptly saw the tall, elegant figure of Chaim Cohen, immaculate in riding boots and breeches. 'Good God, how long have you been there?' she demanded, rather sharply in her sudden awareness that he had caught the emotion reflected in her playing.

'Since you began,' he said with a slow smile. 'Where on earth did you learn to play like that? Your technique is superb.'

'I had a good teacher – my mother,' she said, mollified by his genuine admiration. She closed the lid, smiling to make up for her shortness. 'You like my playing then?'

'I don't think I have ever heard Liszt play better.' Once again, he was sincere, and Sara realised he was not paying a drawing-room compliment.

She looked at Chaim quickly. 'I'm glad,' she said, rising and offering Chaim a chair on the other side of a table from the one she chose. Her heart was beating annoyingly fast and she wished Becky or Ruth – anyone at all – would come into the room and break up the tête-à-tête. Chaim's attention was wholly on her and she felt compelled to say something but did not know what. Chaim broke the silence.

'You probably know that I have concluded my business with your brother and am going back to Constantinople next week.'

Sara realised with sudden apprehension that the moment had come when Chaim would ask her to be his wife, and felt the panic rising in her. Oh God, what was she to do? She looked down at her hands, unable to meet Chaim's darkly-penetrating gaze. Then she took a deep breath, willed herself to keep calm and, raising her head, looked straight at him.

'We shall be very sorry to see you go. I – we – have become very fond of you.' As she spoke, she was amazed at the steadiness of her voice.

Chaim stood and in a few long strides was around the table and standing over her. 'Sara, there is something I must say to you – and in truth I don't know how to begin.'

'Then don't.' Sara laughed to take the sharpness from her words. She felt flustered and confused, totally out of control of the conversation.

Chaim only looked down at her appreciatively. God, she was pretty this afternoon, dressed in a demure gown of blue crêpe de Chine that brought out the extraordinary colour of her eyes. Chaim was not a man much given to introspection but he was sure that Sara Levinson would make him the best of wives. She was perhaps a little flighty – and there had been the matter of the horse, although he had felt a sneaking admiration for her over that. But all that side of her would disappear when she was his woman – his wife. All she needed was her own home to run and she would settle down nicely. He cleared his throat.

'May I sit here?' He indicated a low chair close beside her own and Sara nodded, not trusting her voice. She shifted slightly so that she would not have to meet his eyes, cursing herself for her cowardice and Daniel Rosen for existing. How could she find the words to turn him down?

'Well, Sara?' he said, his eyes fixed on her face. 'I don't have much time left.' A tinge of pink crept up into her cheeks and, seeing this, he spoke more gently.

'The last thing I should wish to do is to find myself a bore. You know what I want to ask. Is there any hope for me? If not I should like you to tell me so, and I promise I will just leave.'

To her own surprise Sara felt a jump of alarm at the thought of him leaving and, looking into his face, allowed herself a small smile.

Chaim leaned forward and took her hand lightly in his.

'Sara, please let me be direct. I would like to ask you to be my wife.' His look was tender, but he said the words carelessly as though the answer was assured – or as though it didn't really matter. Sara was momentarily speechless, then Chaim lifted her hand to his lips and kissed the palm softly.

Sara struggled to keep her expression bland as she tried to fight against the turmoil of feelings sweeping through her mind. She opened her mouth to speak but, terrified of saying the wrong thing, closed it again silently. Chaim patted her hand and returned it to her lap.

'Of course, you will want time to think, and to discuss it with your family,' Chaim said, crossing to the fireplace. Sara, almost giddy with relief at not having to come to an immediate decision, practically told him that her family had discussed little else since his arrival.

'I don't want to press you into a reply right now. I want you to think about it – and then agree to marry me. I know you may be worried about moving so far from your family and home, but I promise you that you can come and spend every summer here. Marry me, Sara, and you will have whatever you want.'

Sara laughed, suddenly feeling alive and flirtatious. 'Anything?' she asked.

'Anything within my power to give you,' he assured her gently, hoping that this girl, with her sense of humour, her spirit and her many other varied qualities would agree to be his.

'And I have a surprise for you,' he said, crossing back to her and sitting beside her again. 'I have invited Aaron to bring you all to Jaffa the day after tomorrow. A German company is to perform at the Alhambra and I thought it would be a good way of thanking you for your hospitality and kindness to me. Oh, and I invited Daniel as well. I hope that is all right.'

Sara felt the muscles in her face tighten and her pulse immediately began to race at this news, but she kept her gaze firmly on Chaim and her glance did not waver.

'How kind of you,' she said carelessly, her eyes suddenly clear and bright. All the possibilities that a day with Daniel would afford rushed through her mind in dizzy succession.

Chaim looked at her seriously, then took her hand and, standing, drew her up with him. 'Perhaps, Sara, you can have an answer for me when we meet in Jaffa?'

Sara nodded and their eyes met for a moment before he bowed, kissed her hand, and strode out of the room. After the door closed Sara stood for a second and then sank into the nearest chair, her legs shaking and her mind racing. She closed her eyes, trying to calm her thoughts. Chaim was certainly charming. He could not have approached her in a better way – had he spoken of love she would have frozen, and she appreciated his silence on the subject. But why, instead of considering her first ever serious proposal of marriage, was she once again wondering about ways to trap Daniel Rosen? A wave of self-pity washed over her and a lump rose in her throat. Oh, maybe Ruth was right, but she loved Daniel so much: she would never stop loving him. Why, oh why, hadn't it been Daniel asking her to marry him, to be his wife?

With a major effort she decided she must concentrate on the priority, which was to give Chaim an answer. He deserved that much at least. But she had a couple of days – she didn't have to hurry into a decision this very moment. And if she was sure of anything she was sure that in the next few days she must use every trick, every womanly wile in the book to secure Daniel, to capture his love for ever. She knew she could do it, but she also knew that time was running out and that now was the moment when all would be lost or won. A comforting thought was that maybe Chaim's having declared himself would make a difference to how Daniel felt about her.

Her worried frown disappeared as she smiled, suddenly light-hearted. Of course, he will come round, she murmured to herself, trying to convince herself that she could bend life to her will. Ruth said that men always came round in the end. And what did she have to lose by trying? Nothing, she answered herself. Nothing at all.

CHAPTER ELEVEN

Sara stood at the open window of her hotel room looking out at the view. The room she was sharing with Becky was on a corner: one window overlooked the sea and the ships lying at anchor a mile out from the coast; the other had a view over the Jaffa rooftops. Many of the stone houses were crumbling and defaced; nearly all with a blue hand-print over their doorways to protect the house and its inhabitants from the evil eye.

A cold moon shed light over the inky dark sea and shone harshly on the minarets and the lighthouse. A light breeze was blowing in from the sea, bringing with it snatches of music, laughter and the sporadic cries of the street hawkers below, who were always the last to call it a night. Sara loved the noises of the city, the sense that all races were netted together, living, loving and fighting.

Behind her she heard Becky kick off her slippers and jump into the high brass bed they were to share. Sara turned to see her sister sink into the feather mattress, pulling the cotton sheet around her.

'Do you think Daniel will come back?' Becky murmured softly.

'Yes, of course, he will,' Sara went over to the bed, took off her dressing gown, and sank into the mattress, bending her knees up to her chin.

'I bet he went back after those women,' said Becky smugly. 'You know, those ones outside the theatre. I think they were . . .' her voice faded off.

'You do talk nonsense,' Sara exclaimed, crunching her pillow behind her neck, and then added more gently, 'Go to sleep now. It's late. He'll be back before morning.'

She spoke with an assurance she did not feel. If Daniel had not gone after the trio of girls who had called hoarsely after him as they had gone into the theatre, girls whose intentions were made clear with every obscene movement of their belly-dancing hips, then there would no doubt be others. Why did he have to spoil everything always, she thought vehemently.

'I don't care what you all think,' said Becky with a tired sigh. 'I think Daniel was wonderful – far more dramatic than the characters in the play.' She turned noisily to face the wall.

'That's because he was the only one who wasn't acting,' Sara replied with incisive irony. Becky giggled, then after a moment blew Sara a kiss, threw her pillow to the floor and within seconds was asleep.

Sara looked over at her sister, sleeping like a child, her long chestnut hair plaited loosely for the night, and felt like weeping with disappointment over the evening. The day had begun so well, so happily. All the young Levinsons and Daniel had travelled together in the train from Haifa. Sara had a seat next to Daniel and they had sucked sugar cane like children on holiday, while he had talked animatedly about Paris, the plays he had seen, the people he had met. The journey had passed all too quickly for Sara.

Chaim had been waiting for them at the station and then had taken them on a tour of the city. They had wandered through the narrow alleys crowded with stalls selling spices, sweetmeats and amulets, dodging the laden camels as they swayed along the streets, and finally sitting in a sidewalk café drinking lemon sherbert and watching the old men sucking on their long narguiles. Daniel had bought Sara a proper fan from a stall and the two girls had taken it in turns to fan a breeze on to their hot faces.

The men had even waited while Sara and Becky visited a fortune-teller. They had laughed at the girls' wish to peek into a hidden world, but were just as curious as to what the old woman would say. The girls' hearts had been beating wildly as they climbed the worm-eaten stairs. They heard rats scurrying in the shadows and were both secretly grateful for the other's company. When they entered the room Becky would have fled right back out again if she had not been spellbound with fear.

Crouched on a mat in the middle of the small dark room was a raddled old hag. Her ravaged face was thickly painted, her eyes so heavy with kohl that they seemed almost inhuman. The woman looked up sharply as the girls came in and hurled a vicious oath at Becky, who was giggling feebly and clinging on to Sara's hand. She beckoned Sara towards her and motioned her to sit, her eyes never leaving Sara's face. As Sara sat beside her on the mat, she grabbed her hand in her own claw, turned it over and deftly filled the palm with black ink, mumbling incantations in a voice that was oddly melodious.

Becky, as superstitious as any illiterate peasant, watched fascinated as the old woman hung over Sara's palm, tracing her destiny. Even Sara, who normally pooh-poohed what she called superstitious rubbish, trembled a little as she felt the old woman's hypnotic power. She fixed her eyes on the aged gnarled hands, tattooed with the symbols of Islam. After a silence the diviner put two brown fingers on Sara's arm and leant close to her ear as though she were about to tell a secret.

'It is Allah's blame,' she said softly, 'that you will not marry the one you love. Oil is poured over the well of sweet waters and many suns will cross the skies before you may drink of them.' She bent over Sara's hand again, frowning slightly in concentration. Then, sure of what she saw, continued: 'But you will marry, very soon. And cross many deserts.' Sara's heart jumped and she looked into the old woman's eyes, which burned like live coals.

'But all things pass and as the world moves towards the tomb and the night to the dawn – you will return. Allah wills this.' Then, uncurling her claw from Sara's hand she said thickly, 'The light will pass from your hair and Allah will save many lives through you.'

'What lives,' began Sara, 'and when shall I return?' But the old hag was suddenly breathing heavily.

'Mighty is Allah,' she said, closing her eyes, and her head lolled wearily to her chest. Her jaw hung open and a thin trail of saliva made its way down her chin.

Sara, who took the reference to her light hair to mean the Arab superstition that fair hair is unlucky, doubted the old hag's vision of her future. She didn't want to believe it. She rose to her feet, waiting politely for the woman to look up. After a long pause she put some coins on the mat and the two girls left the diviner slouched on the floor.

Back in the street the men and Becky, who had strained her ears in vain to hear the fortune-teller's words, begged to know her future.

'She said I was to marry a tall, dark, handsome man,' Sara answered with a gleam in her eye. How lucky it was that the description fitted both Daniel and Chaim she thought, amused.

Chaim had smiled delightedly and looked at her with pride. She could not return his look, but suggested it was time they move on.

Up to then it had been a lovely day. Sara picked up the paper fan from the night table by her bed. It was small and painted with large gaudy flowers, which she could still just see in the half-light of the room. She fanned herself lazily, listening for the footsteps that would herald Daniel's return. It was no good pretending to go to sleep; she knew that she would dare anything to see him tonight. She must speak to him before she talked to Chaim. She must hear him say that he loved her once again. The only chance she ever had of talking to him was always in company and the frustration of never being able to tell him what was on her mind was driving her to desperation.

On the train journey up Sara had decided that she would make one last attempt to ensnare Daniel. She knew that if she could get him to compromise himself – by making love to her – he would marry her. It was a trick as old as love, and if it had worked for others it would work for her. It did cross Sara's mind that it was a cheap trick, but she brushed the thought swiftly aside. She would sneak into Daniel's room that night, after the play . . . But once again fate had obstructed her.

They had been standing and chatting in the interval, discussing the play, all of them excited and enjoying this special treat, when Hamid Bek, the new police chief, had come up and greeted Chaim effusively. He had, of course, been heavily bribed to ease the passage of Aaron's barley so they knew they should be civil to one another.

Chaim shook his hand and turned to introduce him to the party, 'Excellency, Daniel Ros . . .' he began to say but froze as he caught the stubborn, malicious look on Daniel's face. Sara caught it too and was paralysed by fear as she heard Daniel, his voice rising, fiercely address Hamid Bek.

'I don't shake a hand that beats Jews.' Those standing nearby gasped, then everything froze into a rigid silence.

A look of amazement appeared on the police chief's face, then he gave a curious little jerk, as though he were trying to dislodge a fly and smiled, his eyes boring into Daniel. 'The lamb is eager to feel the jaws of the lion but when he does he will squeal.'

Daniel's eyes gleamed cold and hard: 'I would prefer to die in the jaws of a lion than live on my knees.'

Sara could not believe her ears: Bek was as dangerous as a

rattlesnake and here was Daniel, antagonising him. *Oh my God, he's going to kill him*, she thought and, unable to stand the strain any longer, heard herself laugh sardonically and say, 'I'm afraid Mr Rosen has a worm in his head that is devouring his brains.'

Everyone gaped at Sara as Bek swung round and looked at her appraisingly, the rage wiped from his face. 'I hope you will accept my apologies for any discomfort this appalling little interlude may have caused you,' he said courteously. Sara blushed and murmured something, then, turning to Cohen Bek said with studied boredom: 'Are you going to remove this man from the theatre or shall I?'

There was no mistaking the threat behind the polite tone and Aaron immediately took Daniel's arm and, with a few whispered words, hurriedly moved towards the exit with him. Chaim, to his credit, did not bat an eyelid.

'Daniel Rosen,' Bek said thoughtfully, flicking his ebony-handled fly whisk against his leg. 'I will not forget that name.' It was said almost to himself and then he added, in a more conciliatory tone, 'Well, Effendi Cohen, we shall meet tomorrow at eleven as arranged.' Then, with a nod to the company and a deep bow to Sara, he strode off.

Of course, the evening was ruined. They had all taken their seats for the second half of the play, pretending to themselves and each other that the atmosphere was unbroken. Sara felt sorry for Chaim, who had made such an effort to give them all a lovely day. Midway through the last act Aaron had returned and told them that he had left Daniel in a bar halfway into a bottle of arak. He looked as though he had had a few glasses himself. The party had broken up immediately after the theatre, with everyone thanking Chaim a shade too effusively.

Sara plumped up the pillow behind her, beginning to give up hope that Daniel would ever come back. Then she heard footsteps in the corridor outside. She jumped out of bed and ran silently to the door. Daniel's room was diagonally across from hers and when she heard his door open and close she knew it was definitely him. She rushed to the dressing table to tie back her hair, then decided to leave it loose. She reached for her dressing gown, but decided not to bother with it and dabbed a little attar of roses between her breasts instead. She was going to need all the help she could get.

She glanced at Becky, who was still sleeping peacefully, her face calm and untroubled. Then, trembling a little, she crept barefoot from the room, closing the door softly behind her. Listening hard for sounds from the other rooms she crossed to Daniel's door. She was becoming very adept at creeping around in the middle of the night.

Sara rapped lightly on the door and opened it slightly. She did not want to be seen in the corridor and, after one last swift glance round, she let herself into Daniel's room. The only noise was the faint hiss of the gas light and Daniel's heavy breathing.

He was slumped sideways on the small iron bed, fully dressed in what remained of his clothes. His white shirt was torn, his hair was ragged on the pillow and there was no sign of his jacket. As I suspected, he is drunk and has been brawling, Sara thought, feeling a wave of affection for him.

She tiptoed across the cold tiled floor and sat gently on the bed in the hollow made by Daniel's knees. She had never seen him so vulnerable and watched, fascinated, at the gentleness of his sleeping face. Her eyes followed the curve of his closed lids, with the dark sweep of eyelashes and his straight nose. How handsome he was, how impossible it was not to love him.

Her eyes moved down to the smooth brown skin of his chest and she noticed a bluish stain spreading over his ribs. Without thinking she unbuttoned what was left of his shirt and with unsteady fingers peeled back the torn material. She lent over and gently pressed her lips to his bruise, her fingers moving slowly and sensuously up his chest until she felt the damp heat of his neck. An accomplished coquette could not have done it with more skill.

Daniel woke aching, and throbbing with pleasure. For a moment he lay, revelling in sensuality, until with sudden horror he realised where he was and what was happening.

'Sara,' he whispered, and closed his eyes, trying desperately to think of anything other than her mouth on his flesh and her full-pointed breasts pressed flat against him. His mind told him to pull her away, but his body dragged her into his arms as he searched hungrily for her mouth. She seemed locked into him, her body, beneath the thin cotton nightdress, warm and melting. He kissed the smooth, glossy skin of her shoulders and felt her heart knocking against his ribs. He was drowning, sinking with guilty pleasure.

Sara clung closer, desperation as well as hunger making her

bold. She coiled her arms around his neck and again his mouth closed on hers.

'Go on,' she whispered passionately. 'Go on – make love to me – please.' Her voice was urgent and with glittering, imploring eyes, she leaned into him once more, her body stretching along his like a cat's . . .

The strap on her nightdress had fallen from her shoulder and her bare breast lay against his chest. The nipple, so delicate and pointed, was unbearably close to him. All he could think of was his desperate wish to kiss it.

'Don't,' he said frantically. 'Don't. For God's sake stop or I will take you.'

'But I want you to Daniel, I want you to take me.' It was the voice of a stranger; the voice of a woman.

A shock passed through Daniel and with a start he wrenched her arms from round his neck. She tried to lean into him again, but he kept her away, his eyes, still full of longing, staring intently into hers.

'Daniel,' she urged, 'you don't understand . . . I don't care.' She paused, conscious that she was not finding the right words and terrified that she was about to lose her advantage.

Daniel ran a hand over his face and heaved a weary sigh. 'Oh Sara, don't say things that you may regret.'

'Never! I love you and I want you.' The blood rushed into Daniel's face and, grasping her by her shoulders, his fingers pressing hard into her white skin, he shook her hard.

'And don't you think I want you?' he whispered, his golden eyes dark with pain. 'For God's sake, Sara, you are enough to try any man's reason.' He dropped his arms, feeling as drained and weak as if he had, in fact, made love.

Sara did not look away or drop her gaze. A change came over her face, a change so subtle but so full of emotion that it startled him. He had not realised until that moment quite how deeply the girl – the woman – in front of him could feel.

'Then why won't you marry me,' she challenged him. 'You love me – you have told me so yourself.' Her face softened and a pleading entered her voice. 'Oh Daniel, don't you know I would do anything for you. I'd work beside you, fight beside you, but please, please let me into your life.' She argued with the desperation of the vanquished. She felt she had to convince him or die.

'I can't marry you, Sara. I can't do it. I have to try to do something other with my life than fulfil my own selfish desires.' His face was tender and he searched for the words that would ease her painful sense of humiliation. 'We can't just live for ourselves and not care.'

'Why not? Others do – all over the world others do just that. So why can't we?'

He shook his head slowly and crossed to the washstand. Now that the adrenalin had stopped running through him he was beginning to feel the consequences of the arak. He poured a pitcher of water into the flowered basin and splashed some over his face.

'I can't do it,' he said finally, almost to himself.

Sara's mood switched completely and a malicious gleam came into her eyes. 'I bet you do it enough with that Isobelle Frank!' she spat out, and was immediately ashamed of herself. That was not the way to win.

'Oh Sara,' Daniel crossed the room and took her face between his hands. 'It's not Isobelle that I want.'

'What do you want then?' she asked quietly, overcome by an inexplicable humility.

'I'll tell you,' he said softly, his eyes growing harder and brighter. He took both her hands in his and sat back beside her on the bed, pressing her hands feverishly, his eyes fixed on her. 'Sara, if you love me at all, try and understand what I am saying.' She nodded dumbly, unable to take her eyes from him.

'I want to restore an independent existence to our people.' He paused and looked away. 'I want to gather all the lost, unwanted, persecuted souls that are scattered over the face of the earth and make our people a nation again.' He looked at her intently. It was so important that she understand him, but he could not express himself easily. The difference between their ideas was so great.

'We can't create a homeland for our people in a system invented by outsiders. A land of our own is the Jew's one remaining solution and the only way to get it, the only way to be able to live together according to our traditions, is to hold a gun. If the Turk enters this war – and I believe he will – Turkey's days will be numbered. Britain will beat the Turk – must beat the Turk – and eventually will leave Judea to the Jews.' He paused again. 'I have to try and awaken this idea in other people's minds, renew people's hopes. I know it sounds like a dream – but it isn't.

Everything in this world was once nothing more than an idea. I am prepared to dedicate my life to this end – if necessary to pay with my blood. It fills me as no human being ever could – even you.'

There was a long silence. Sara felt her heart smash into a thousand pieces and knew she was defeated. She longed to break into sobs, but managed a small, wobbly smile. This touched Daniel more than any words could. He felt her pain reaching out to him and gathered her up in his arms.

'I love you, Sara. You know that there is no way I can hide that from you.' He kissed her eyelids and cheeks gently and then, brushing her lips with his, he whispered: 'You had better go now.'

She leaned her head on his shoulder, pressing hard to keep back her tears. Then, surreptitiously brushing her face with the back of one hand, she rose silently. At the doorway she paused for the briefest moment and turned back to him. She longed with every ounce of her soul to touch him just once more, but she squared her shoulders and with a last desperate glance left the room.

The door clicked. He was alone. Daniel pressed his hands to his face and was almost surprised to discover it was wet. But he knew he was right. He couldn't marry her, subject her to all the trials and dangers that a life with him might bring. The only thing he could do was to give her her freedom and with it a chance to make a good life for herself – with Chaim Cohen.

Suddenly filled by an intolerable depression, Daniel lit a cigarette and lay back on the bed, an arm behind his head and his eyes closed. He must stop thinking about her, he told himself, must fight against this melancholy mood. An image of Sara, her cloud of golden hair around her face, floated before him and he pressed the balls of his hands into his eyes, trying to block out the image. *Get out of my head, get out of my life, damn you.* He turned over on the bed and stubbed out the cigarette. Once again he closed his eyes and tried to shake off his thoughts.

Sara was as capable of handling the situation as he was, she was young and strong, he needn't worry. His throat tightened. *I love her*, he whispered to himself, *and you can't stop loving someone overnight.* He knew that time would lead her away from him, that the Turk would enter the war and his destiny would start to unfold. Then maybe he could begin to forget.

The first of the three o'clock cries arose from a nearby mosque and then another until the night was filled with the chanting that called the faithful to prayer. The voices rose from height to height and at last Daniel felt at peace. He loved Sara, but he had given her up. He would forget her in time. *I will, I hope so – Oh God, I hope so.*

Sara sat rigidly in front of the dressing table, the hypnotic chanting washing unheeded over her. Her eyes were fixed and staring, her whole body shaking with noiseless sobs. Like her heart, all her dreams for the future were now shattered. Daniel was lost to her – could never be hers. With a dim resignation she told herself that she must now accept the fact – the time had come to let go.

There is an answer, she told herself, *embark on a new life. Deliberately rebuild brick by brick until all the shadows of the past are obliterated. Get out – run away. The pain will lessen until you feel no more than a dull ache. Forget Daniel Rosen.*

Daniel could never be her husband but Chaim Cohen could. He was a good man, Sara knew that, decent like her father. She might just manage to be happy with him. It would not be the same, but nothing ever would be.

Then another truth gripped her and her throat swelled with pain. Daniel was right. She was selfish. She couldn't go on sacrificing everything for an empty love. She looked at her sleeping sister. Just because her own life was in ruins she must not spoil Becky's. Chaim would be a kind and loving father – she knew that. He would probably be a kind and loving husband. She certainly liked him more than anyone else she knew. How could she do better?

With a deep breath she picked up the hairbrush and drew it savagely through her hair. Under her breath she counted the strokes. By the two-hundredth, her arm aching like her heart, she had decided to marry Chaim Cohen.

BOOK TWO

CHAPTER TWELVE

Constantinople: February 1915

In the late autumn of 1914, after weeks of speculation, Enver Pasha decided to take Turkey's fate into his own heroic hands. On 29 October two German cruisers, which had arrived in Constantinople in August seeking protection from the British fleet in the Mediterranean, reflagged and, escorted by a Turkish squadron, steamed out into the Black Sea. Without warning or provocation the ships sailed to the Russian port of Odessa and attacked and sank ships lying in the harbour. Simultaneously, the Russian fortresses of Sevastopol and Novorossiisk were fired on by Turkish ships. It was a decisive act of war which no one could ignore. On 30 October the Russian, British and French Ambassadors to the Ottoman Empire requested their passports. For Turkey the war began on 31 October.

The Empire was barely four months into the war and, already, everything seemed to be conspiring against her – even the weather, Selena thought, pulling her black cloak closer around her narrow shoulders and shivering despite its thick fur lining. This winter was turning out to be the coldest in living memory but even the bitterness of the air could not deter Selena from her daily walk around the grounds of the Rose Palace. She valued this hour more for the privacy it afforded than for the exercise and would never give it up, slipping out every morning and losing herself in thoughts of the past and plans for the future.

Her small feet warm and dainty in red felt boots, Selena picked her way carefully down the shallow stone steps, still half covered with ice and snow. She went to the exquisitely designed Italian gardens that sloped to the Bosphorus, the mist swirling around her ankles in a ghostly embrace. It's like walking into the heart of an opal, she thought, marvelling at the strange beauty. She stopped in her tracks and admired the scene.

Selena sat on her favourite bench facing the Bosphorus. Only six months before, when she had first arrived at the Rose Palace, she would sit and watch the ships making their way up and down the straits, the shipping lanes always busy with the international traffic passing back and forth between the Black Sea and the Mediterranean. Now that the Turks had closed the waterway to the world, she rarely saw anything more than the local caiques or an occasional Turkish or German battleship floating silently by.

Her hands snug in the fur-lined kid gloves, she sat thinking once more about the problems of the orphanage and how best to solve them. Prices were spiralling, staple goods like oil and flour were already ten times what they had been only three months ago. With such inflation the orphanage could not have kept going had it not found a patron in the ever generous Annie Lufti. But other, more ominous, ideas were occupying Selena's thoughts.

For centuries the Moslem Turk had nourished a deep-seated and virulent hatred of the Armenians. This was based jointly on a superstitious fear of Christians and partly on jealousy, as the Armenians were the merchants of the Empire and controlled most of the trade from the Euphrates to the Mediterranean.

The anti-Armenian feeling was not just instinctive among the Moslem majority; it was backed by the Triumvirate, who regarded the Armenians with the gravest suspicion on two counts – their geographical position, dangerously close to Russia in the north-eastern reaches of the Empire, and the fact that most of them were Georgian Christians. Of all the non-Moslem minorities in the Empire (and the Turks viewed them all as potential traitors), the Armenians were the most suspect and most vulnerable.

Selena, who now attended services at the Armenian Cathedral and was deeply involved with the Armenian community, had begun to hear disturbing rumours of persecution and murder taking place all over the province of Armenia. This had followed the Turks' humiliating defeat after their first offensive against the Russian front. The campaign to encircle and defeat the Russian forces in the Caucasus had been, from the very beginning, a total disaster. The Turks, unused to the appalling winter conditions and already exhausted from their long march north, suffered a major defeat. Of the hundred thousand men sent into battle, only a third had survived. Bewildered, starving and without command the troops had been slaughtered in their tens of thousands with almost as many again freezing to death as they slept.

The Triumvirate had been quick to blame the Armenians and a new Moslem governor had been hastily despatched to the area to set about the task of ridding the Empire of 'its most subversive element'. All travel permits and post in and out of Armenia had been suspended but, despite this, reports from missionaries were reaching community leaders in Constantinople by sea. Whole remote villages had been wiped out in a series of savage pogroms. Men had been roped together and shot; women raped and slaughtered; children carried off into slavery. The new governor (nicknamed the 'Blacksmith' because of his predilection for nailing horseshoes on to his victims' feet) was carrying out his command with systematic relish.

She feared that unless international attention could be brought to the situation the pogroms would worsen and spread. The trouble was that nothing official showed that these reports were true. Nevertheless she must do something to try to help the Armenians in Constantinople. She was meeting Mrs Morgenthau tomorrow at the orphanage and would mention the matter to her first. Perhaps a word from her husband to certain people might be timely.

With a shrill cry a peacock broke cover and darted from a bush across the frozen grass. Selena started and came back to the present to find her feet were frozen. Stamping and blowing on her hands, she made her way to the house. She had promised Annie help with the flowers and had spent more time out in the air than she had intended.

'Ah, there you are, Selena darling,' Annie's urgent voice rang across the hall. 'I need your help with these wretched flowers.'

Selena handed her cloak to Akiff and followed the voice into the drawing room where Annie, dressed in a loose robe of pink Chinese silk, with her hair cascading down her back like a shawl, was stabbing a pine frond into a singularly ugly flower arrangement. Selena laughed and took the frond from her friend. She removed some of the hot-house flowers from the vase and with a few deft touches rearranged the blooms into a more harmonious pattern.

'They're perfect,' said Annie delightedly, sinking into a chair and lighting a cigarette.

'In which case . . .' Selena snapped off a particularly beautiful bloom and they laughed together at her superstition. Both women knew the Eastern belief that evil is trapped inside perfect beauty and both were happy to avoid bad luck.

Annie looked up at the clock and jumped up from the chair, scattering ash around her. 'Good gracious – what am I doing sitting here in my morning gown,' she said and, striding across the room, she rang for the maid to come and clear up after them.

'There are only five of us tonight. I've invited Frank . . . what is his name? . . . Walworth to dinner this evening. He's a reporter from the *Morning Journal*, you know, Hearst's newspaper.' Selena nodded. Whenever back copies arrived, Annie read them avidly, but as far as Selena could work out the *Journal*'s specialities were crime, underwear and New York society gossip. She lifted an eyebrow, and Annie laughed.

'Walworth is in Constantinople to cover the war, not to uncover my private life. At least I hope not. Anyway what could I do – it's a direct command from Hearst himself that I invite this journalist to dinner and introduce him round a bit.' Annie paused, her eyes rounding. 'Pity old Jemel Pasha's been pushed off to the provinces, he would have been perfect, of course.'

Jemel Pasha, one of the members of the Triumvate that Selena secretly called the unholy trinity had been made commander of Syria and Palestine and appointed co-commander of the Fourth Army with Count von Kressenstein. This, rumour had it, had not pleased him at all. He felt, and probably with good reason, that he was being fobbed off with the Syrian command and had only been given it to be out of the way of central power. With public smiles and private rage he stormed off to the Fourth Army headquarters in Jerusalem.

Annie sighed deeply. 'As it is I've invited Bedri Bey, the Minister of Police, and then there's the Major of course.' She gave Selena a wicked little smile as she led the way up the stairs. Annie had quite a few plans for Selena's future, most of them involving her marriage to the German Major. Unfortunately, Selena was not falling in with Annie's ideas, and her heart sank at the mention of his name.

'Really, Annie, you must not encourage Major Rilke.'

'My darling, you know perfectly well he needs no encouragement. The man is absolutely besotted wtih you.'

Selena took refuge in a silence that was broken by Annie's two spoilt Maltese terriers, Mitsi and Suki, racing across the slippery

168

floor towards their mistress. They were followed by an apologetic maid.

'No matter,' said Annie, scooping them up into her arms. 'I was just on my way up to change. Selena, come and talk to me while I get laced into my corsets. Do you know I have heard that in Europe they've started not wearing them. Can you imagine?' Annie dropped the two dogs on to the floor and the two women walked down the long corridor to her room, Annie talking earnestly about fashions and Selena wondering if Frank Walworth would be interested in her people's plight and, if he was, how best to bring the Armenian question to his attention without compromising anyone.

'Come, come, gentlemen,' Annie clapped her hands authoritatively. 'Spare me your political discussions. Here smoking is allowed – *la politique est défendue*.' She lit a cigarette and smiled impishly. They had moved from the dining room to one of the smaller sitting rooms where the coffee was set on low tables. Small bowls of oranges, fruit and nuts were laid out for anyone who could still possibly feel hungry, and the ubiquitous Turkish delight was there to go with the coffee.

During dinner Annie had managed to keep the conversation away from politics and the war; they had mostly talked about America. But now that they were relaxing the American had started holding forth about the wisdom of Turkey's decision to enter the war.

'You've got yourselves into a game that's far too big for you,' he announced, directing his gaze towards the police chief and shifting his large weight round on the ottoman. Selena secretly agreed with him, but cast her eyes demurely down and bit her lip.

Annie, with her usual eye for theatrical effect, rose to stand in front of the blazing logs. She was dressed in black velvet, her flaming red hair braided down her back and sprinkled with frivolous ornaments. The room was lit by the light of the fire and by the hundreds of candles scattered across the room in silver candlesticks.

'Well, we hear from all sides that victory is to be expected any day now,' she said with a radiantly confident smile, 'which will at least mean a return to normality. Frankly, I've never understood the theory that the best way to defend your own country is by occupying someone else's. If it were true, where would it end?' She had not meant this as a question, but, rather, as a bridge to cross from one conversation to another and was annoyed when Walworth piped up again.

'It ends,' Walworth said, as histrionically as Annie, and with a hostile glance at Hans Werner, 'in millions of human beings being uprooted and torn from everything they have ever known. They are left destitute, homeless, and often nationless.'

Walworth was a tired-looking man with an aggressive manner. He must have been quite attractive before his cynicism had scored the lines in his face and clouded his blue eyes. Selena liked him: he was clumsy, brash and utterly American, but decent in his straightforward way and she agreed with almost everything he had said that evening.

Hans Werner, on the other hand, disliked Walworth intensely and wished he were English or French so that he could punch the journalist's nose with impunity. Why on earth had Annie asked him, he wondered?

Bedri Bey coughed slightly and gave a charming smile, flashing golden teeth: 'Allow me, sir. I don't think you are taking into account the universal human need for an enemy. There is no conscription in England and yet I hear they are queuing up to "take the king's shilling", as they so picturesquely put it.'

'Yeah,' Walworth said, making no effort to hide his contempt for the bearded, bear-like Minister and wishing to hell he could get a proper drink. None had been served at dinner out of courtesy to the devout Moslem, Bedri Bey. Walworth, not a religious man himself, would normally have respected this but in this case he doubted the efficacy of the Police Minister's acts of devotion. Bedri Bey held a post that demanded a taste for assassination and murder, and he was widely known for his brutal excesses. 'Rumour has it that you are not so successful on that score. They say that Syrians and Arabs are chopping off their own right hands to avoid being called up.' Annie looked at him furiously, but he pretended not to notice.

Bedri Bey continued to smile blandly and faintly patronisingly.

'Rumour is always rife at these times, Mr Walworth,' he smiled. 'The Prophet has said that great power brings greater enemies.'

Walworth, who had been lounging back on the ottoman, was suddenly alert. 'And what of the rumours of murder and persecution in Armenia, must I suppose them to be untrue also?'

Both Annie and Hans Werner looked at Selena anxiously. Her

cheeks had blushed a dusty pink but otherwise she seemed not to have heard. This was an old trick she had learned in the harem and she was practising it now with a vengeance. Bedri Bey dropped his veneer of cheerful bonhomie and his eyes glittered unpleasantly, but he remained calm and polite.

'Murder? Persecution? Exaggerations, I assure you. We have admittedly taken certain precautionary steps to prevent the spread of Armenian nationalist feeling among the subject peoples. We have, of course, pronounced a ban on any activity calculated to endanger public order, but this hardly constitutes murder.'

'So what does this activity include?' Walworth asked sourly. 'I must assume it includes the subject people's drawing breath?'

Bedri Bey smiled faintly, as though to mock the foolish rumours, but he did not rise to the taunt. 'Certain acts are necessary to protect our society from the Marxist monsters who have allied themselves to those vile dogs in Russia, indeed some of them even wish to be part of Russia. We cannot allow these god-haters, with no respect for the Moslem religion, to infiltrate our society.'

'Baloney!' said Walworth so loudly and suddenly that everyone, including Bedri Bey, started. 'The Armenians are devout Christians. It's the same old story of religious persecution given a new twist. If it is the Marxist influence that bothers you why not confine yourselves to rounding up the ringleaders?'

'Because,' said Bedri Bey in measured tones, 'all Armenians are traitors.'

'So that is why you condone the rape and slaughter of children – they are potential traitors.'

Hearing this, Selena, despite her resolution to keep calm, could not hold back a low choking sound. She covered it with a tiny cough and briefly covered her mouth with her handkerchief, swallowing down a sense of outrage, which burned like acid through her brain.

Hans Werner, deeply distressed for Selena, leant forward on his low sofa: 'Really, Mr Walworth, must you be so graphic in front of the ladies?'

The room was silent for a moment as Walworth, looking smug, cracked a nut. 'Why sugar-coat the truth, Major?' he said, tossing the nut into his mouth. 'You know it is happening and it should not be.'

'I agree with you, Mr Walworth,' Selena said, joining the conversation at last. Everyone looked at her as if they expected an outbreak of hysterics but she pressed on, 'If there are perilous days ahead for Armenians, then I believe the world should be told about it.' Not daring to meet anybody's gaze she self-consciously shifted in her chair and gazed resolutely at her hands.

Annie, bewildered by Selena's sudden and uncharacteristic surge of forthright speech, was nevertheless the first to collect her wits. 'Would anyone like some more coffee?' she asked with strained gaiety. They all accepted with alacrity, pleased at the change of conversation.

The rest of the evening developed with surprising mellowness considering the explosive subjects that had been discussed. Walworth, with a journalist's inside knowledge and relish for gossip, recounted several stories about New York society's darker aspects and Bedri Bey was again all honey. Only Hans Werner was unusually quiet.

Selena, composed once more, even manged to smile sweetly at Bedri Bey over the rim of her coffee cup, successfully concealing what she truly felt in her heart for him and his team of thugs. She was, however, relieved when he rose abruptly, announcing that he must go. It was not easy for her to entertain the one man who now epitomised to her all that was cruel and evil in the repressive regime.

Bedri Bey gave a shambling bow to the company, begging that no one should get up. 'It has been a delightful evening, Madame Lufti,' he said, raising her hand to his lips. 'Mr Walworth – it was a pleasure to meet you, what a shame it did not happen sooner,' he paused as he caught Annie's eye and then read her message correctly, 'perhaps I can offer you a lift back to your hotel?'

'Thank you but I think I'll walk back,' Walworth said, rising to his feet. 'After lunch rest a while – after dinner walk a mile. That's my motto.'

Selena nodded goodnight to Bedri Bey and then turned to Walworth. 'Goodnight, Mr Walworth,' she said and then very quietly added: 'Might I visit you at your hotel one day soon? I have something I would like to discuss with you. It would only take a moment of your time.'

Annie and Rilke looked at Selena in astonishment and she, conscious that six months ago she would not have left the house without permission and yet now she was inviting herself to a man's hotel, blushed scarlet under their scrutiny. Walworth, however, smiled and nodded acceptance. Selena was grateful to him for not pursuing the matter then and there. Annie escorted the men out into the hall with some haste.

Selena and Rilke were left alone together and Selena, seeing that he made no move to go, asked him if he would like some brandy. He looked at her soberly: 'No, thank you. Selena, I want to talk to you about something very serious before Annie comes back.'

Selena sat down quietly and looked into his eyes. 'What is it, Major?'

He cleared his throat and frowned. 'I must be straightforward. The – er – political situation concerning Armenia – er – Armenians, could get unpleasant here.'

Selena smiled softly, 'Yes, I know.'

Hans Werner sighed and moved forward on the sofa. Just thinking about what was happening to women in Armenia made him shiver, and he knew that if events turned nasty here in Constantinople, Selena could find herself in danger. 'It is my belief that you should stop involving yourself with the Armenian community. I grant that your race has suffered – is suffering – enormous tribulation, but you are personally fortunate at this time. Don't, I beg you, try and force a confrontation with the authorities. It is unwise, worse than unwise.'

Selena turned her face away to hide her agitation. 'I must follow my conscience,' she said adamantly.

'Selena,' Rilke said, turning her face to his, 'I'm very serious. You must listen.'

'All right, I will.'

'Could you possibly limit your visits to the orphanage to when Mrs Morgenthau is also there?'

Selena shook her head and forced a smile. 'It is truly wonderful of you to show such concern,' she paused and looked into his eyes, 'but I could not do that. Mrs Morgenthau visits very infrequently. Major, I am almost ashamed to admit the deep satisfaction I find in being with the children.' She shook her head again and smiled, 'I am sorry, but I cannot give up my daily visits to the orphanage.'

Her smile was so lovely and so unaffected that Rilke felt his chest tighten. She moved him in the same physical way as a beautiful piece of music. Everything about her, her walk, her smallest gesture fascinated him, but he was after all no more than a friend and he feared to bring the carefully built walls of friendship crashing down around him.

'Then perhaps you will at least refrain from making political comments in front of other people. Especially men like Bedri Bey. He's a formidable man, hard as iron and sharp as an axe. It's not unlikely that the police already have a file on you, because of your time with Abdul Hamid.'

Selena sighed and absently smoothed back her hair. She liked Hans Werner very much, even found him attractive and she very much appreciated his concern. But she was determined that now she would live her life as she pleased. 'Please don't worry about me. I have always taken care of myself.' She gave him a wicked grin. 'But I do promise to – how do you say? – curb my tongue.' Hans Werner smiled back.

The room was dark now: the fire had died down and the candles were guttering with their last desperate flickers. Rilke leaned forward slightly in his chair.

Selena saw the look of adoration on the Major's face and, nervous of what might follow, spoke quickly to break his mood. 'Have you any news of your transfer yet?'

Hans Werner glanced away to hide his irritation. Frustrated by following the war only on the map, he was itching to see action and had applied to join Von Sanders's staff in Gallipoli, where he hoped the British Navy might attempt a run to Constantinople. He also thought that, if he were caught in the thick of battle, Selena's feelings for him might just change. He took a sip of the brandy and swirled it around the balloon glass.

'No, not yet. But I expect to hear any day now.' He gave Selena a curious little stare. She did not seem at all disturbed that any day now he might be whisked away from Constantinople at a moment's notice, and he felt a surge of fury that he should have allowed his feelings for her to become so deep.

Selena knew what he was feeling and consternation mingled with her compassion. It was with a sense of relief that she heard the returning rustle of Annie's skirts as she crossed the marble hall back to the sitting room. Rilke stood as she came in and made his farewells. As soon as Annie had seen him out, she turned to Selena.

'Well?'

'Well what?'

'Well, what did he say?'

'He said that the trouble in Armenia might spread here to Constantinople and that I should take care on my visits to Kum Kapu.'

Annie frowned. 'He may be right. I shall send Akiff with you in future.'

Selena blushed in the semi-darkness. 'Oh Annie, please, there is no need for that.'

'No, no,' said Annie, raising her hand to silence Selena's protests, 'I'm sure the Good Lord will watch over you, darling, but I shall feel much happier if Akiff does too.'

Selena laughed. 'Whatever did I do in my life to have such a wonderful friend as you,' she said, linking her arm into Annie's.

'God knows,' Annie answered with a laugh and, arms round each other's waists, they made their way to bed.

CHAPTER THIRTEEN

Her eyes closed, she felt the warmth of the sun on her skin. She lay under a lapis-blue sky chewing a blade of grass. Her inner eye still bore the imprint of the sun shining through the latticework of branches overhead, and her senses were overwhelmed by the droning of bees, the sweet smell of the grass and an undefined happiness.

Sara opened her eyes. With a familiar sinking in her heart she saw the high, shadowed ceiling and her throat closed as she breathed in the dank, cold smell that pervaded the house. Every morning began the same way; Sara would wake with an ache in her heart, wishing she could cry, but for minutes would lie staring blankly at the ceiling, her tears unshed. She knew that her disappointment was futile, that although tears would bring a temporary release they would not solve her sense of uselessness and impotence.

She sat up in bed and pulled the blanket up to her chin. For the past few weeks Constantinople had lain under a heavy fall of snow, but it was just beginning to thaw now. Perhaps she would feel better with the mild air and soft light of spring – if only it would arrive. She sighed. However tightly she tried to keep her thoughts in check during the day, her memories would always take over her dreams and every night she would be taken back to Palestine – back home.

She turned on her side, searching for the warm spot in the bed, and caught sight of herself in the mirror on the huge, dark wardrobe. She looked almost transparent in her whiteness, like a ghost but for the dark purple smudges under her eyes.

'Well,' she said firmly to herself, 'this is home now, and don't you forget it, Sara Cohen.' She gave a hard little laugh. 'Home!

What a joke. Although I suppose it keeps the snow out.' She looked round at the ponderous, grand furniture her husband thought suitable for her and imagined the room she would be happy in . . . a small room, whitewashed with a narrow iron bed against the wall. The window would open on to a view of fields and there would be a bunch of flowers in a glass on the plain wooden dressing table. It was a pure room that hid no lies and she knew too well which room she was imagining, but could not stop herself.

Since her marriage four months and eighteen days earlier, her life had become one long pretence. In fact, she supposed that the lies had really started from the day she agreed to become Mrs Chaim Cohen. She had known – or thought she had known – what she was letting herself in for, but she had not expected the dreamlike quality of a life in which she felt she was an actress in a miscast role.

She groaned and rolled over on to her back, her arms behind her head. She stared at the dark green wallpaper that was peeling in a corner of the room. Her surroundings did not help her overcome her feelings of anti climax. Once more she thought of all the chances she had had to change her mind.

Sara had agreed to marry Chaim the morning after her midnight conversation with Daniel. Chaim was suitably happy, but left Sara feeling that he had never had any doubt that she would accept him. They returned home that day and Sara had immediately told her father of her decision. He had sat in silence for a moment and then raised his eyes from his book.

'Sara,' he had said, 'you know that I have always tried not to interfere too much in your decisions, but are you in truth sure that you want to marry Cohen?' Sara's heart sank and she could not keep from blushing a little. She had hoped that her father would be pleased – Chaim was a good match and he had been anxious about her marrying. The last thing she wanted was to be cross-examined by him – he knew her too well. She looked at him as he sat there, his glasses perched on the end of his nose. He looked suddenly old and strangely vulnerable. She looked away.

'Yes, Papa,' she murmured. He looked at her dubiously and she added more confidently: 'I love him.' She felt the blush deepen and hoped he would take it for maidenly modesty.

'Well, I hope so,' Abram said, laying aside his book and taking her hands in his. 'Marriage is a life-long commitment. You must always remember that. It is not something to be entered into lightly. I know things have been – difficult – for you here recently, but that is not a reason to marry.'

Sara knelt down beside him and held his hand to her cheek. She had to make him believe her. 'I do love him, Papa. I know I have not known him long, but he is so kind, so – so easy to talk to. I will have a wonderful life.' She gave her father a bright smile and a quick hug. 'Please don't worry about me.'

Abram sighed and leant forward in his chair. 'Sara, what happens to you is important to me, and must be to you too. Don't do anything without consideration – this is no time for pretence.'

Sara looked down at her hands. She wanted nothing more than to put her arms round him, weep into his shoulder and tell him that she had to marry Chaim to cut the cord with Daniel, that it was the only way to start a new life and her only chance of happiness. But she knew that her father would not be happy unless he thought she was marrying Cohen with a heart full of love, and she had to convince him that she was. At the same time she was filled with a rebellious defiance. An inner voice was urging her to escape, to marry – anything to escape.

She shook her head. 'Don't worry, Papa. I know what I am doing.'

Abram looked at her, his eyes searching hers. 'Well, you're twenty and twice as stubborn as ever your poor mother was. You're like her – you always know your own mind and won't be shifted. I suppose you are aware of what you're up to.' There was a silence for a few moments. 'Well, there it is,' he said finally and patted her hand sadly. Sara hesitated for a moment, then slipped an arm around his neck and rubbed her cheek against his. She pushed his hair gently back from his face. There were so many things she wanted to say to him, had wanted to say for years. But the time had never been right and now it was almost too late and she still couldn't find the words. He patted her head again and the light came back into his eyes.

'Take no notice of me. I'm just a selfish old man and I hate the thought of losing you, that's all.' He got up stiffly from his chair, adding: 'Wait here a moment,' as he hurried from the room. He returned carrying a heavy white garment and smiled at her puzzled expression. 'It's your mother's wedding gown. Don't wear it if you'd rather have one of your own but I thought, as there was so

178

little time ... I know it's not very fashionable now, but ...' he tailed off, a hint of a tear in his eye.

'Oh Papa, I'd love to wear it.' Sara reached out and took it from him. The material was heavy and rich, the stiff, white satin creamy with age. The bodice was finely studded with tiny pearls.

On a wave of pious emotion, Sara thought: may God help her to be as good a wife to Chaim as her mother had been to her father. She would do her best. Her determination to be a good wife overcame her feeling that she was doing wrong in marrying a man she did not love and carried her through the next days. Her few moments of utter helplessness were followed by fresh resolve.

At dawn on the day of the wedding, the sky was a clear blue, but as the day progressed the weather seemed to reflect Sara's feelings of uncertainty. The sky turned yellow and dusty, the air was hot and suffocating and by ten o'clock the sun was an angry amber glow.

'*A Khamsin,*' said Aaron, sniffing the air. 'Let's hope we get a tepid breeze at least, not a scalding boiler of a day.' The wedding took place on the lawn outside the house and Sara took it as an omen when, as she left the house to walk towards the waiting Chaim, a hot gusty wind started blowing from the east, carrying clouds of desert sand with it. As if by magic, the sand covered everything with a fine layer of grit.

Alex, Sam, Aaron and Lev held the four poles of the chuppah, the ritual wedding canopy, and as Sara stood beneath it she tried to concentrate on the holy words Rabbi Goldman was intoning in a sing-song voice of prayer. But the heavy veil, the heat and the almost total dryness of the air made her feel as though everything were coming from a long way off.

Suddenly she was aware of Chaim and felt a slight pressure on her arm. Her body stiffened and a chill crept over her heart. She looked blankly at Chaim and realised Ruth was holding the glass of wine out to her to sip. She saw Rabbi Goldman staring at her, his eyes red-rimmed under the fur brim of his hat, and caught sight of her father's anxious look. She helped Ruth lift the veil, took the glass and sipped at the wine. An almost perceptible shudder of relief rippled over the company, like a giant bird shaking its wings. She heard the crash of glass as Chaim completed the ritual. She was married.

'*Muzel tov! Muzel tov!*' Her friends and relations gathered around her, congratulating and kissing her. Suddenly she was weak with relief. It was the relief of a man sentenced to death, who hears his sentence commuted to life imprisonment. She felt free and happy and for the first time that day looked like the bride she was. She was even looking forward to stepping on to the boat that would take her to her new life in Constantinople.

She turned this way and that, laughing, kissing and being kissed, when suddenly Daniel was standing in front of her. She hadn't seen him since that night in Jaffa. She stood stock still and stared at him as she heard Chaim say, 'Aren't you going to kiss the bride?' Daniel took an awkward step forward and kissed her cheek. Sara felt as though something were tearing inside her.

'Congratulations,' he said quietly. Sara nodded and gave him a shaky smile, avoiding his dark eyes that seemed to be looking into the very depths of her soul. She turned swiftly to greet the Vali of Beirut, a good friend of Aaron's, who was effusively wishing her luck and happiness. It was an honour to have him at the wedding as he was the highest authority in the area, and for Aaron's sake she wanted to be gracious. She tried to stay calm but then she heard Daniel say to Chaim:

'Look after her – she is very precious to me.' The effrontery of it took her completely by surprise, and for a moment she was full of love's mirror, hate. How dare he tell Chaim – her husband she thought for the first time, and with a burst of loyalty – that she was precious to him. Her fury with him – her hate for him – sparked off her first truly affectionate feelings for Chaim and carried her through the rest of the party.

Becky, Ruth and Fatma hugged her tearfully in her room as she changed to leave for Haifa. Fatma was wailing enough for all of them, pulling at her hair and clothes and making sure they all knew just how unhappy she was. Sam and Alex hugged her at the door; only Aaron and her father were to accompany them to the port.

It was not until Aaron held her very tight that she begun to fear she might not be able to stay dry-eyed after all. And then her father hugged her and she could not hold back a rising sob. 'I will miss you, Papa,' she said, her voice choking her, and then she took Chaim's arm and they both boarded the small boat that was to take them to the ship.

'Goodbye, God bless you. See you in the summer,' she heard her father's and brother's voices, half cheerful, half solemn, floating over the water towards her, and it seemed as though she could still hear them long after their distant figures had turned and walked away.

Sara strained her eyes to the shore until there was nothing more to see and then turned into the ship. It was a sturdy steamer that plied its way between Haifa and Constantinople. Chaim had tactfully left her to make her final private farewells to her home, so Sara made her way to their cabin on their own. She was relieved to find that he was not there; she needed some time alone. Locking the cabin door behind her, she threw her new hat off and lay on the bunk, crying. By the time Chaim knocked at the door, she was ready and waiting for him, nose powdered and no hint left of her bout of weeping.

Their cabin was on the promenade deck and was the only one with the luxury of a double bed and en suite bathroom. It was large and elegant, more so than the exterior of the ship would have led Sara to believe. She sat nervously on the edge of bed, sipping her champagne and thankful that at least the saying of the marriage vows had not turned her respectful suitor into a slavering wolf.

On the contrary her new husband seemed highly solicitous of her comfort. He took her on a tour of the ship and after their dinner at the captain's table introduced her to the joys of liqueurs. This was the life she had been expecting, and she even began to enjoy herself. After a last stroll round the deck they returned to their quarters. More nervous than she had anticipated, Sara went into the bathroom and changed into the cream lace nightdress that was part of her trousseau.

She felt warm with excitement; the drink had certainly helped. She checked herself in the mirror and smoothed an eyebrow with a finger. She looked pretty. 'You are pretty,' she mouthed at her reflection, and then giggled, surprised at her vanity. 'Let's get this virginity business over with,' she said gaily and with a bold click of her fingers she went into the cabin.

To her relief Chaim was standing by the window, dressed in a dark red silk dressing gown. He slipped into the bathroom and returned only moments later. Sara smiled at him weakly from the safety of the bed. He took off his robe and slipped into bed beside her. In that moment Sara caught a fleeting glimpse of his body; his flesh was surprisingly white and his arms, chest and even shoulders were covered in a thick coat of black hair. An image of Daniel's smooth brown chest rose unbidden before her and she quickly suppressed it, biting her lip to dimiss other thoughts.

'My lovely bride,' Chaim murmured, looking at her almost wonderingly. And he turned off the light.

She felt him move towards her and felt the harshness of his hair against her skin. Her body shrank from his involuntarily.

'Don't be afraid,' he said, misinterpreting her movement. 'I'll be very gentle.' He ran a clumsy hand over her thigh and peeling up her nightdress sought her mouth with his lips. He moved his body on top of her and she felt his arms tightening behind her back as he crushed her to him, her face hard into his chest. She felt a warm pulse beating between her thighs and with a plunge he drove roughly into her. A sudden pain as he thrust deeper into her made her gasp, then moan with pain. Chaim climaxed almost immediately with a grunt, leaving a wet stickiness between her legs. He pulled away abruptly and moved to the other side of the bed.

Sara opened her eyes and blinked. The pulse still beat within her and she felt mildly irritated and sore inside and out. She was also surprised; Ruth and Fatma had led her to expect much more pain. She turned over to look at her husband and saw that he was staring at her, his face pale in the dim light, his expression cold and fixed. There were frown lines on his face as he looked at her, his gaze never wavering, the only sound that of the ship moving through the water.

Bewildered, Sara pulled herself up on to one elbow. 'Is anything wrong?' she began tentatively.

Chaim gave her a hard look and sat up, moving his face until it was level with her, his expression suddenly distorted, lips pulled back against his teeth in a mask of anger. 'You're not a virgin,' he hissed.

Sara looked at him in appalled silence. Her mouth was suddenly dry and she felt completely breathless. How could he even suggest such a thing? How could he even consider it?

Chaim grabbed her arm, his fingers digging mercilessly into her flesh. 'You're a harlot – a whore. Did you really think you could fool me? No wonder you had to marry an outsider from your village, someone who didn't know the truth.'

'But it's not true, it's not true at all,' Sara burst out, pulling her arm free, her mind racing as she wondered how on earth she could prove such a thing. Blood! All at once she remembered how often her mother and Fatma had warned her against riding astride. Two summers ago she had jumped Bella over a high hedge and, coming down hard on the mare's withers she had felt a pain like a knife

182

shoot through her. She had bled a little but had thought no more about it until now. Her cheeks burned in a powerful mixture of embarrassment and anger.

She swung herself off the bed, feeling Chaim's eyes following her like a cat, a livid smile on his mouth. *I want to kill him*, she thought, *I want to kill him*. But she stood, trembling and feeling that she ought to try and explain. 'Chaim,' she stammered, 'I didn't . . . it isn't what you think. I ride a lot . . . perhaps . . .' She gave a short dry sob and rushed into the bathroom, locking the door behind her.

Sitting on the edge of the bath she sobbed bitterly, her jaws clenched on a towel. It was incomprehensible to her that she was trapped on a ship – in a life – with a stranger who had all kinds of rights over her, complete power over her from now on. The feeling of total helplessness left her aghast.

After a long while there was a rap on the door and Chaim, his voice low and courteous, apologised and asked her to come back to bed. 'I see I jumped to conclusions. It was foolish of me but . . .'

Eventually, Sara dabbed her tear-stained face with water and dragged herself back to bed. She fell back, exhausted, and Chaim, muttering words of endearment, assaulted his bride again.

Afterwards he rolled off her, took a deep noisy breath and began to snore. Sara lay awake, a heavy weight on her heart, tears trickling down her cheeks and into the corners of her mouth. She was filled with misery, a longing for home rising in her like a floodtide. Who was this stranger who could call her his wife and hurt her? But she knew she was not alone. She wondered how many other women had found themselves suddenly exiled from a world they knew with a man that they did not. *Perhaps all of them*, she thought, *all of us*.

Clenching her fist under the sheet, she stifled all thoughts of Palestine. Perhaps Chaim had been overwrought, behaved un-characteristically. *I am Mrs Chaim Cohen now*, she thought bitterly, *and like all women I must submit to my husband*.

The following day Chaim was, as he had always been, formal, attentive and courteous. So much so that Sara had to remind herself that this was the same man who had behaved so viciously towards her in the night. She gradually relaxed. Later that afternoon Mrs Chaim Cohen learned that Russia had declared war on Turkey and a cold chill spread over her heart.

*　　*　　*

Sara stepped off the boat full of trepidation. Her new life as a sophisticated city dweller was about to start. Chaim guided her through the crowds to a carriage and she leaned forward like a child on the journey to her new home.

The house was a shock. It was in the old Jewish quarter of Galata, just an alley or two away from the Bosphorus. The houses were crowded together on either side of narrow cobbled streets, and the whole area had the air of having come down in the world if not about to come down altogether. Paint peeled from the doorways and walls, and with a detached amusement Sara realised that if she had not been going to live there she would have thought the whole area charmingly picturesque. But she had never seen a ghetto before, never experienced the narrowness of ghetto life; when she walked through the tall, rusty gates she had no idea of the rules and suspicions that from now on would govern her daily life.

Inside the gates was a small enclosed courtyard through which Sara walked on Chaim's arm. She was silent as she took in the iron-barred windows and tightly-closed shutters. The house was dark and depressing and Sara felt wearily as though she were moving from one period of history to another.

Chaim took her into the house, but stayed less than five minutes before he gave her a perfunctory kiss on the cheek and dashed off, muttering that he had been away from his offices for long enough. He left her in charge of Irene, the elderly Greek housekeeper, who had been his mother's companion. Sara knew that she would have trouble with Irene from the moment she saw her; Irene's face was perfectly polite but her blank expression covered a not very well concealed hostility. She was short and squat with beady black eyes that seemed to miss nothing, and her upper lip was covered with a heavy layer of fine black hair.

Sara boldly asked for a cup of lemon tea, which was grudgingly fetched by Irene. After its soothing warmth, Sara felt the tension and disappointment, which had been accentuated by her physical weariness and all the excitement of the last few days, lift and she summoned up the courage to explore her house.

It was large but uniformly dreary. About a dozen rooms were all furnished with the same heavy, dark furniture, while the wall-coverings differed only in their degrees of ugliness. The ceilings showed signs of winter floods and summer dampness, and in most of the rooms the paper was peeling back from the walls. In many of the upstairs rooms the furniture was covered in dust sheets and, although it was only November, the woodwork already showed patches of mildew. Her eyes stung with the dust that hung in every room.

Disappointed with the main rooms, Sara went down to inspect the kitchens. The ancient stove was black with grime and shockingly rusted. The sink was chipped and had deeply engrained dirt – Sara wondered when it had last been cleaned. The most cheering moment of her tour of the house was when she came across Nasib, a pleasant-looking Arab boy who diffidently introduced himself as the errand-runner and household wood-chopper. He stood to attention and wriggled his bare toes with concentration as he talked to her. Sara liked him immediately.

The ground floor rooms where Chaim had been living since the death of his mother some four years before were the best kept but, although fairly clean, they were no less depressing than the other rooms. The sitting room was papered in a dark green with heavy red curtains. A straggling vine and a plane tree in the courtyard immediately outside the window shut out any light that might have shone on the heavy furniture and dark covers. A few oil paintings of Romantic landscapes torn apart by storms hung in unlikely corners of the room and a portrait of Chaim's mother gazed down at her.

By the time Chaim came home that evening Sara, full of her duties as a married woman, had made a very detailed list of all the cleaning to be done and most urgent repairs that needed doing.

'The roof must be patched before the rains start; I'm pretty sure the plumbing needs redoing entirely; we need a new stove and the sofa and chairs need recovering,' Sara said confidently.

'Yes, you are right. I suppose it does need doing. Give me your list and I will see it gets done.' Slightly taken aback, Sara handed the list to Chaim. The stove was replaced that week and not long afterwards Chaim, unasked, had had the piano retuned. Otherwise the house remained the same. Sara had asked him repeatedly when the other work would happen, offering to see to it herself, until one day he had turned on her and, with hostility, had said: 'Sara, I don't really think this is a time to be discussing such frivolities as chair covers. You are extravagant and wasteful. Everything is as my dear mother left it. She was a saint among women and if it was good enough for her it is surely good enough for you.'

After that she stopped asking.

The first week of Sara's life in Constantinople passed in a flurry

185

of activity. She and Nasib cleaned the whole house from top to toe, including the rooms that were rarely if ever used. Irene's contribution was to stand around watching and complaining about her old bones. Every morning Sara would wake when Chaim left early for work and tell Irene what to do in the kitchen. She soon found that Irene could produce nothing edible except stew. Sara decided that teaching her to cook would come next after cleaning up the dirt.

Every day the mess improved; Sara made Irene scrub the table with salt and scour every pot in the kitchen. She made her boil all the water before it was used for drinking or cooking, and inspected the dishcloths daily until she was sure they were being thoroughly washed.

Then she would drag Irene off to the local market to show her the stalls where they would haggle for bargains. Every day, when her tasks were done, she sat down for an hour or so to write letters home to Palestine. After her initial anxiety, the war seemed to have fallen into a limbo. Sara knew it was real enough but so far Turkey had made no offensives, nor had Russia attacked.

After the first week, Sara stopped taking Irene with her on her shopping trips. Irene, always sweet and docile when Chaim was near, changed drastically the moment he left the house. Her slow and complaining steps made Sara feel like an Arab pony yoked to an ox. Now that she knew her way around, she could move much more quickly, besides which she enjoyed being on her own outside the house. Sara loved the lively, congested quayside that was only a few moments' walk from her door. She would pause to watch the caiques, their bodies low in the water as they neared the quay. Each time Sara was sure they were about to ram into the quay edge they would drop the square sail and the seeming disaster was averted. She bought fresh fish, gathered gossip about the local personalities, and, more importantly for her, picked up little bits of information – or gossip – about the war. Until she left Palestine she had been totally disinterested in politics; now she wanted to know every tiny detail of the war's progress. Far from her family, she worried about them all the time and every letter she received from Palestine brought a sigh of relief.

Sara, used to the freedom of the countryside, was surprised at the strictness of the Moslems here in the city; the women, nearly always accompanied, flitted through the crowds like black phantoms and Sara wondered whether their voluminous robes helped keep off the heady stench of donkey and fish. As the weeks went by, Sara began to look longingly at the busy crowds crossing the Galata Bridge. Not so far away, either, was Pera, the smart, Christian part of the city. She had glimpsed the sophisticated Italianate houses on her journey to her new home. Pera was a different place, a city of smart carriages and fashionable women, theatres and culture. At night Sara could see it, all lit up, from her window, and she wondered when Chaim would take her there.

Before long Sara had begun to hate the neighbourhood she lived in. She hated the meanness of the streets, and the small mindedness of her neighbours, among whom she had made no friends. She often thought that all the faults of the Jewish race were concentrated here and the contrast with the open spaces and open faces of Palestine appalled her. Sara now realised how lucky she had been in her upbringing; she had never experienced the world of the ghetto Jew, although she knew of the oppression under which Jews lived in Poland and Russia, where the only way to survive was to cringe or bribe the authorities. The Jews here seemed to have similar attitudes. They walked through the streets as though they had something to hide; nothing but suspicion showed in their defensive expressions. At first Sara was taken for a gentile, which did not help relations with her neighbours. Two thousand years of persecution had left its mark on the Jews of Galata.

One evening, a few days after Sara had begun shopping alone, Chaim stood drinking his after-dinner coffee with his back to the empty fireplace, absently tapping his foot on the marble hearth. Sara wondered what was coming.

'Sara,' he began. She looked up from her sewing expectantly. 'It has come to my notice that you have been leaving this house unchaperoned, without asking my approval.'

Sara looked at him, stupefied. Chaim cleared his throat a little and continued with the air of an adult explaining something slightly complicated to a not very bright child.

'I know you were not brought up in a city, and maybe you are not aware of the customs of a more sophisticated society.' Sophisticated! Sara thought indignantly. Zichron was more sophisticated than this backwater. 'You are my wife, Sara, and must behave accordingly. Your reputation and mine are as one.'

'I never wished to do anything to jeopardise your reputation, but . . .' Sara began, her heart beating fast with indignation, but she was not given a chance to continue.

'I'm afraid the gossips are already buzzing about your excursions down to the harbour. In this part of the world married women just do not behave in that way.' Sara was angry now, her mind working quickly to find a good answer to his crass authoritarianism.

'Perhaps you will be happy if I wear a yashmak,' she retorted angrily.

'Don't be so silly, Sara,' he replied irritably. 'I live and work here – and was doing so long before you ever left Zichron. You must behave as other wives – to do anything else only attracts gossip and suspicion. Sara, believe me when I say that to act differently will only compromise your position.' He paused for a moment and looked at her sternly before adding: 'Sara, do you understand?'

Sara, hit with the full horror of what he was saying, wanted to scream. She would be trapped, marooned in this dim, dark world of narrow-minded bigotry. Her eyes were burning but the anger she felt took her beyond tears.

'I cannot and will not spend the rest of my days sitting in this house like an old servant.' She heard her voice rising. *I'm getting hysterical*, she thought, *calm down, Sara.* She drew a deep breath and in the short silence Chaim thrust his face into hers. It looked red, swollen and *ugly*.

'You heard what I told you,' he warned hoarsely. 'Don't you ever disobey me – ever!'

For the first time in her life, Sara felt afraid of another human being. Her head began to thud and her throat hurt so much that she could hardly speak as she felt a flash of pure hatred for this man. She must say something, she could not spend her life locked in this house, forbidden to leave it. 'Then may I take Nasib with me,' she stammered, 'for shopping?'

Chaim immediately relaxed and smiled the smile of a victor. 'Yes, of course you may,' he said, flicking an imaginary speck of dust from his lapel. 'Come, shall we go to bed?'

The hatred rose in her again as she looked at him. She knew he thought he was rewarding her by not disappearing into his study as was his custom. She clenched her jaws and nodded in assent. *Yes, my darling, how nice it will be to walk up those cold dank stairs with you and enjoy five minutes of your slobbering over m*

*breasts, pawing at my thighs and plunging between my legs. And
then listening to your snores.*

His 'little talk' filled her with foreboding; thoughts of the years
stretching ahead loomed up in her imagination, nuances of his
expression obsessed her. Her marriage had settled already into a
mould she had not anticipated and depression descended on her
like a black shroud. Sara only saw Chaim at dinner – and in bed.
With the war, business was booming for him, the Turks and
Germans were stockpiling in panic and making him richer than
ever. But to her dismay Sara discovered something about her
husband she could never have foreseen. Although as rich as
Croesus, he was mean. Going to the theatre was costly, food
should not be wasted, they should not accept invitations because
they could not afford to return them. The only time they ever went
out together was to the synagogue. Sara thought about speaking to
the Rabbi about her problems, but decided that if she told anyone
at all word might get back to Palestine; she would rather die than
have Daniel hear the true tale of her life in Constantinople.

Sara, used to speaking her mind and behaving impulsively, now
taught herself to be careful not to encroach upon Chaim in any
way. A curious indifference towards him took the place of her
anger and misery. She treated him with courtesy and attentiveness
and he never even guessed at the depression that had overtaken
her.

There was a sharp rap at the door and Sara jumped back into the
present.

'It's very late, madam, nearly eight o'clock and your water is
getting cold.' *Old bat*, thought Sara, but sat up anyway and said
nothing. She got out of bed, shivering in the cold, and went into
the bathroom. Dressing quickly, Sara went down into the sitting
room where a small fire was struggling in the grate. She sighed and
blamed herself for having taken pity on the ragged soldiers who
had straggled back from the Caucasus and to whom she had
surrendered most of her already pathetic stock of firewood. She
shivered a little and drew her shawl closer round her shoulders.
The tea Irene brought her was colder than it should have been, but
still warmed her a little.

Taking the tea Sara crossed the room to her desk to find the last
few letters she had received from home. They were all she lived for
now, the only light in her dreary life and Sara read every letter

again and again. They arrived dog-eared and almost illegible, the indiscriminate censor's ink blackening every page but, despite this, Sara would settle herself comfortably at her desk, carefully open the envelope and devour the letter's contents.

The post was becoming more and more infrequent and the letter she now opened to reread for the thousandth time had arrived from Ruth six weeks before – nothing at all had come since then. Something made her uneasy about this letter – and the one from Aaron she had received a few weeks before it. Judging by the small snippets of information the censor had left in, everything was as normal at home, but something rang false. There seemed to be something they were not telling her, presumably to keep her from worrying.

She folded the letter carefully and put it back with the others in the pigeon-hole in her desk. They had all managed to write to her – even Becky had sent her a few lines from Beirut – all except Daniel. Sara had written to him once, a cautious, sisterly letter, but there had been no answer. Her heart began its familiar downward spiral and Sara wearily rubbed her eyes to shake the feeling and her thoughts away. Daniel was now lost to her for ever.

She rose from her chair, glancing at the clock. Nearly ten o'clock, it was time she got on with her chores. She felt a very faint tremor in the air and the window panes rattled. Probably another storm blowing up, she thought vaguely, and then heard another distant rumble.

Some instinct clutched at her stomach and in a second she changed from listless boredom to tense excitement. She pulled on a shawl and ran down the stairs and out on to the porch. The bitterly cold air hit her like a blow, but she was to preoccupied to mind. Pulling the shawl closer, she listened with every nerve in her body. Then she heard it again – very distant, but in the open air, a more distinct boom.

A crowd of people had gathered in the street outside the gate and an unnatural silence had fallen on the whole area. People were staring out into the distance, listening hard while others whispered excitedly to each other. Nasib, his eyes rolling, came out on to the porch, followed by Irene whose coal-black eyes were filled with blank fear.

'Maybe it's the Russians,' she wailed, her panic-stricken voice breaking the silence. Sara motioned her to be silent and listened closely.

The rumbling came from across the straits – from the direction of the Dardanelles. A little flicker of hope rose in her and she held her breath with excitement until she heard the next boom.

'No,' she said, almost to herself, 'it can only be the British.'

At the end of 1914, there had been a few skirmishes at the entrance to the Dardanelles – once a British submarine had managed to penetrate the narrows and torpedoed a Turkish submarine before returning to the safety of the Mediterranean. They must surely be making another attempt.

Sara quickly turned back to the house and going to her desk pulled out a map on which she had been following the progress of the war. It had been pinned on the wall until Chaim, besotted with the Germans and irritated by his wife's open admiration for the British, had made her take it down. Falling to her knees Sara spread out the map on the floor and stared eagerly at it. Irene, had followed her into the house and stood over her, her hands on her hips.

'Where do you think they are?' she asked, squinting down at the map. Sara pointed at the Dardanelles. 'It's very close,' Irene said faintly and sank down on to a chair.

Not close enough, thought Sara, staring down at the map. The mouth of the entrance into the Dardanelles from the Mediterranean was wide enough, but further upstream the Dardanelles, which separated Europe from Asia, were no wider than any river, and steeply banked on each side by cliffs. The narrows were heavily defended and laid with mines. From their advantage, high on the cliffs, the Turks could fire almost point blank on any enemy vessel trying to pass through. If the ships could only get through the narrows to the Sea of Marmara, it would be an easy enough journey to the Bosphorus, and once there they could turn their guns on Constantinople.

Sara sunk back onto her heels, thinking hard. She doubted whether it would be possible for the Dardanelles to be taken by storm, but comforted herself with the thought that the whole world acknowledged the British Navy to be the best. She held her breath with excitement, her fists clenched on her lap. Then an idea came to her. There was bound to be fighting – perhaps right here in these very streets. She might be able to convince Chaim to send her home for safety: all the reports said that Palestine was safe. A picture of Palestine came to her mind's eye and for the first time in months she saw the harsh, austere landscape of home through a cloud of hope, not regret. Jumping to her feet she ran into the hall and pulled on her hat and coat.

She was at the gate before Irene caught up with her. 'Where shall I tell Mr Cohen you've gone if he comes back and asks?' she said slyly. Sara had completely forgotten Chaim's command about not going out alone, and she hesitated a moment. Then, in her exhilaration, she threw caution to the winds.

. 'It's Mr Cohen that I'm on my way to see,' she said coolly and, turning on her heels, she marched up the road without a backward look. The moment she was clear of the house she began to laugh – the look on Irene's face had been a pleasure to see.

The sun peeked from behind a cloud and slashed its watery rays on to the streets and rooftops. Sara felt all the misery of the past months fall away from her, leaving her buoyant and lightened. She hummed to herself as she made her way through the crowded streets. She had never yet visited Chaim's place of work, but knew how to find the offices and warehouses. She passed the counting houses of Galata and easily found the freighter docks.

'Chaim Cohen', a neatly-painted sign declared over a doorway. Sara stood a moment, undecided, wondering what his reaction would be, then summoned up her courage and walked in. Two clerks standing behind a long counter stopped talking in mid-sentence, their mouths agape. Women were obviously not seen here often. Sara asked for Chaim and was told he was expected back any minute. 'Who shall I say is calling?' asked the younger clerk, obviously intrigued. 'Mrs Cohen,' she answered, and sat down on a bench to wait.

Through the partition she could see a large, unadorned room. The walls were covered with pigeon-holes, hundreds of them, each one stacked with folders. She felt sorry for the pale-faced clerks bent over their desks. They were obviously cold, their breath rising in a steam like cattle at dusk. The offices were neither dirty nor sordid, they just smelled of dried wheat and something else . . . *Time passing*, thought Sara and shuddered, pulling her coat more tightly around her.

She began to lose the hope and confidence that her excitement had given her and was beginning to wonder about the wisdom of coming here unannounced and alone. She stood up, ready to make her excuses and leave, but an old man in wire-rimmed glasses came through the partition. 'Mrs Cohen?' he asked.

'Yes, I'm Mrs Cohen,' she said, summoning up a smile. He

looked at her for a moment, a question in his eyes, and then a look of understanding came into his face.

'I'm sorry, I didn't know Mr Cohen had a brother,' he said politely.

'A brother?' Sara repeated.

'Yes. Are you not his sister-in-law?'

Sara felt her colour deepen. 'No,' she said with an embarrassed laugh, 'I'm Mr Cohen's wife.'

'Oh dear Lord, I do apologise – Mr Cohen never mentioned . . .' he tailed off.

'We've only been married a short while,' Sara said, her cheeks fiery now.

At that moment the door opened and Chaim stepped in, chattering gaily to a tall, pleasant-faced man in a German military greatcoat. Chaim's surprise and disapproval at seeing Sara was immediately clear. There was a brief silence as he composed himself enough to be polite, then he beamed and hurried over to her. 'This is a pleasant surprise, my dear. Nothing wrong at home I hope?'

Sara, flustered, shook her head. 'No, I was just passing,' she blurted stupidly.

'Well, well,' he said, clearly at a loss, then remembered his manners and turned to the German. 'Sara, this is Major Rilke. We are old business acquaintances. Major Rilke, my wife, Sara.'

'*Enchanté*, madame,' the Major bent low over her hand. He had a nice smile and an even nicer manner, thought Sara. Chaim, who still looked anxious, excused himself and the Major and, moving out of earshot, they chatted briefly. Then, with a bow to Sara and a nod to Chaim, the German left.

The moment the door had closed Chaim took Sara's elbow in a firm grip and almost frogmarched her to the door. 'I'll walk you home, my dear,' he said, for the benefit of the clerks.

As soon as they had cleared the building he swung Sara round to face him. 'Now will you please tell me the meaning of this flagrant disobedience. Have I not made it clear that you are never, never to leave the house without my permission and without a chaperone?' His voice was calm but authoritative and Sara felt her hackles begin to rise.

She controlled herself by watching some Arab acrobats as they somersaulted near the quayside. *I must not lose my temper, I must try my best to make this marriage work* she told herself firmly. *He thinks I'm just a stupid feather-brained female, well that's what I must try to be.*

She looked up at him, her eyes soft: 'Please don't be angry with me, Chaim – I was frightened. I heard guns and well . . .' her throat tightened and tears began to stream down her cheeks. She tried to form more words but produced nothing but sobs.

Chaim fumbled for a handkerchief. 'My dear, I am so sorry. I should have realised that you might be worried. But let me assure you that there is not the slightest chance that the British will ever get through the Dardanelles, let alone arrive in Constantinople.'

Sara stopped crying immediately. 'What makes you think that?' she asked, all hope of escape dying by the second.

'Just take my word for it, my dear,' he said kindly and, taking her arm, patted her hand and continued walking. He sighed and turned to her. 'You must forgive me if I sometimes sound a little harsh with you, but I expect my wife to behave like a lady, with decorum.' He sighed again. 'I expect your background worked against you; I really must have more patience.'

He smiled sweetly and Sara felt rebellion rising in her again. Conscious that she was making difficulties for herself she could not resist asking, 'Have you ever mentioned our marriage – to anyone?'

Chaim cleared his throat. 'I don't generally discuss my private life.'

'Not even marriage?'

Keeping his eyes carefully in front of him Chaim said casually: 'It just didn't seem important.'

Sara walked on in silence. Not important! Well, perhaps to Chaim it wasn't. *Stop being childish and stupid*, she told herself. *It will be all right. It really will. It must.*

CHAPTER FOURTEEN

Palestine: February 1915

'It keeps crossing my mind,' said Alex with a hollow laugh, 'that if I die it will be without knowing if the whole thing was a tragedy or a farce.' A clap of thunder broke the silence of the valley and was immediately followed by warm torrential rain. The three men were silent for a moment.

It was early morning and Alex's bulky frame lay stretched out on the sofa in Aaron's room at the research station. He was raggedly dressed in the uniform of a Turkish regular soldier, and his blond hair was long and unkempt. Daniel, sitting astride a chair, and Aaron, who had paused for a moment in his pacing round the room, looked at him sympathetically.

Like most Ottoman subjects between the ages of twenty and forty Alex had been conscripted for military service. Daniel was exempt because he was his mother's sole supporter (which was just as well as he had decided that he would rather fight for the devil than the Turk) and Aaron was exempt because he was the head of an American institution. Sam, at nineteen, was still too young to be called up. Before the war it had been possible to buy exemption from military conscription but this had now changed and, towards the end of December, Alex had received the papers. Within a month he was seeing his first active service on the Suez Canal, and this morning he had returned on a supply cart on its way from Haifa.

Alex looked out at the thundery skies and went on with his story. 'It took us about ten days to advance across the desert from Beersheba to the Suez Canal – no mean feat I can tell you. I suppose that not counting the Bedouin we were roughly twenty thousand strong. We marched mostly by night, partly to avoid the heat and partly in the vain hope of concealment. I say vain, because at least ten times a day French sea-planes and the British Flying Corps flew lazily overhead on reconnaissance. They didn't seem to bother much about us, although what we looked like from above I would rather not imagine. We had about ten thousand camels carrying the ammunition and water supplies, and oxen were dragging the pontoons and rafts. The procession must have been miles long – we probably looked more like a trail of refugees than a so-called army.

'The attack against the British was to begin on the evening of the second but a thick sandstorm blew up, which brought everything to a standstill. Everyone, except the Germans, of course, stood round muttering that it was an evil omen from Allah but regardless of everyone's fears the troops of the Twenty-Fifth – which is an Arab division – were marshalled up and the attack was launched at about three in the morning.'

He paused for a moment and continued with a bitter laugh. 'If you can call it an attack. The Twenty-Fifth was halfway across the canal when the British gave the alarm and opened fire from the West Bank. A few reached the other side and were either killed or taken prisoner. At the first sign of failure the rest of the division deserted en masse. What a fiasco! The Arabs blamed the Germans, the Germans blamed the Turks and Jemel Pasha, who was there in person, went so far as to blame the Russian Jews, claiming they were treasonous –'

'That doesn't surprise me,' Daniel interjected drily, but Alex was not to be diverted.

'What they thought they would achieve by attacking the canal,' he continued, 'only a fool could know. Rumour had it that Enver and Jemel expected Moslem Egypt to rise in revolt against their British protectors and join us as we drew near. Well, all I can say is that we didn't see so much as one Egyptian, let alone an uprising.' He drew a deep breath and took an appreciative gulp of his lemon tea. 'Anyway, after a few more half-hearted stabs, the troops seemed to lose the stomach for it. Jemel went into a huddle with Von Kressenstein and put in the order to retreat so we all scuttled back through the dust to Beersheba. Frankly, we were lucky to escape so lightly – we should by rights have been completely annihilated.'

'Needless to say on the way back we ran out of food and water . . .' he rolled his eyes and threw up his hands, while Aaron and Daniel exchanged looks.

Ever since the outbreak of war Palestine had been threatened by the relentless approach of famine. Within weeks the troops of Jemel Pasha's Fourth Army had covered the land like a Biblical plague. Every road in Palestine was filled with Turkish and German convoys heading for their garrisons or moving south to the Sinai Desert. As they went, the patrols requisitioned food and livestock at random and very soon there was practically nothing left to put on the tables of the Palestinians.

The Levinsons, like all the settlers, were subjected to repeated searches by raiding parties of both soldiers and septieh. At any time they could expect a group of men to appear, swarm over the house in search of arms, food or money, and disappear again with their loot. Fatma, silent with impotent rage, would stand fuming, her arms folded as she watched them discover her latest hiding place and make off with her precious stores of grain and dried vegetables. The impoverished countryside was now expected to feed an entire, hungry army. Every day brought fresh catastrophes to the Palestinian settlements.

Atlit alone remained sacrosanct. It was widely known to be an American institution and respected as such. No one, least of all the Turks, wanted to antagonise the most powerful of the neutral countries, so the station, and Aaron himself, were left unmolested.

At the beginning of November the British had blockaded all Ottoman ports and the only ships allowed to pass freely were those flying under the American flag. Aaron was appointed to take charge of the relief that had started to pour into the country from American Jewish communities almost as soon as hostilities broke out. Food supplies were failing even in the first few months of the war and most people living in towns were quickly reduced to living off bread and olives.

Henry Morgenthau, himself a Jew, had succeeded in securing permission for American Naval vessels to bring relief shipments of food and money into Palestine. Aaron, along with Ivan Bernski, took responsibility for distributing the aid in Northern Palestine. Authority for the south was delegated to the various emergency committees set up by Jewish agencies in Jerusalem and the new suburb of Jaffa, Tel Aviv. This was, Aaron thought glumly, the one time when all the fragmented idealists pulled together for a common cause.

By far the most difficult of Aaron's problems was that of getting the relief supplies further into the country than the unloading bays at the ports. No sooner did the goods arrive than they disappeared into the hands of the Turkish officers and Hamid Bek's septieh.

Worse even than the threat of famine was the hostile attitude of the Turkish administration to the Jews. In December, Beha-a-Din, the ancient, irascible governor of Jaffa, had expelled the six thousand Russian Jews living in his city. With little warning, he had piled them all on to a steamer which, luckily for the passengers, was given permission to sail for Egypt rather than Russia. Had they gone to Russia, the anti-Semitic Tsarist regime would almost certainly have put them all to death.

Few Jews in Palestine had ever become Ottoman subjects; they had learned early on that they were better treated as foreign nationals but now, to stem the tide of what was feared would become a mass expulsion, religious and community leaders urged thousands to take up the dubious advantages of Ottoman citizenship. No sooner had they done so than Beha-a-Din, now Secretary for Jewish Affairs, drafted most single Jewish men not into the army but into a labour force that was all but penal. They were given the jobs of building much-needed roads or quarrying stone; those weak from starvation or illness were accused of malingering and imprisoned.

This led to another problem which Aaron, along with the majority of farmers, had to come to terms with – insufficient labour on the settlement farms. By December most of Aaron's key workforce (including Lev Salaman, Manny Hirsh, Robby Woolf and Alex) had been conscripted. The severe shortage of workers to produce the food needed meant that, without a miracle, the settlements would face a total famine by summer: Aaron did not believe in miracles and this grim fact was never far from his mind.

The final blow to Aaron's patience came when he found soldiers cutting down one of his precious eucalyptus trees for firewood. As he watched the desecration, he decided then and there to pay a visit to Jemel Pasha himself. Palestine was carved up into so many different administrative units that the various governors in Beirut and Jerusalem were continually issuing conflicting orders and edicts. The only thing to do was to circumvent the whole lot of them and see the top man himself. With his official support there was still hope for the Jews; without it, their days in Palestine were numbered.

Aaron's decision was a courageous one. Since his arrival in Palestine, Jemel Pasha had ruled like a king. His love of torture was indulged indiscriminately and he ordered hangings and imprisonments with complete capriciousness. Aaron knew all this but nothing could deter him.

Aaron forced the car mercilessly all the way to the gates of the former residence of the French Ambassador to Jerusalem. The palace was now the official headquarters of the Fourth Army and its commander, Jemel Pasha. The evening before Fatma had sewn a small American flag and it fluttered proudly from Jezebel's bonnet. The small dusty car flying an American flag was a sufficiently unusual sight to be allowed through the gates of the Headquarters of the Ottoman Fourth Army. Aaron parked ostentatiously close to the main steps and hurried through the magnificent doors into the marble hall.

Without looking around, he walked directly up to a sergeant standing on duty behind a desk at the far end of the hall and laid a business card down on the desk, carefully slipping a gold coin beneath it. He hoped that the combination of the name of the American research station and the large bribe would help smooth his way into Jemel Pasha's office.

'I should like this handed to His Excellency immediately. It is on a matter of the utmost urgency.'

The soldier picked up the card with a self-important scowl. 'His Excellency is too busy to see people without an appointment,' he muttered.

Aaron looked him in the eye. 'Try,' he said.

The sergeant rose resentfully, pocketed the coin and calling another soldier to take his place at the desk sauntered off down the corridor. Aaron waited impatiently, wondering if Jemel Pasha were indeed as terrible as his reputation, and telling himself to remember how easily legends are created around people in positions of power. He did not have long to wonder. The sergeant returned surprisingly quickly, his whole manner altered.

'His Excellency will see you immediately, Effendi Levinson. Please follow me.' Aaron had never seen such a quick change from surly to positively deferential, and smiled to herself. So now I'm going to find the truth for myself, he thought as he followed the soldier along the long passage. He himself was surprised at the ease with which the audience had been granted, and was almost suspicious of a trap.

They climbed an elegant back staircase and Aaron noticed

199

remnants of a European sophistication under the layer of scars left by military occupation. In a small ante-room Aaron was handed over to an aide, who led him to a large double door, at which he knocked, entered and saluted in one fluid movement.

The room in which Aaron found himself was grandiose, with a huge Venetian chandelier hanging from the beautifully-moulded ceiling. The marble floors were enhanced by fine Persian carpets and the walls hung with French watered silk.

Behind a desk stacked high with papers sat Jemel Pasha, in battledress. He was immediately recognisable by his sallow skin and thick, black beard. He sat with shoulders hunched into his bull neck as though he were supporting an intolerable burden. Behind him was the towering figure of his personal bodyguard, an impressive figure in scarlet tunic and gold turban, outlined against the high windows. Aaron appreciated the old Asiatic love of display coupled with the fear of death by assassination. For a moment Aaron lost his trepidation at the approaching interview. He could not be afraid of a man who was himself afraid.

Aaron took all this in as he stood in the doorway and heard his name announced. Jemel Pasha signalled to the bodyguard who pulled out a chair; then Jemel motioned Aaron to come forward and sit down. He did not say a word and barely looked up from his papers, staring fixedly at the uppermost document, busy with his own thoughts.

He disliked the Jews with all their sentimental rubbish about the return of the Messiah; he distrusted their fleshy lips and their moist, ever-moving eyes. Their leaders lacked both dignity and ceremony; half-humble, half-superior, they always had to prove how clever they were, how much they knew. The Arabs, mind you, were not much better, but at least they knew their place, were polite and obsequious to their masters. If they occasionally went a bit wild and rioted or fired shots at the Jews that was only to be expected from such poor uneducated fools. Oh, the devil take the Semites and their blood feuds.

Jemel Pasha shifted his sly black eyes to take a look at the Jew in front of him. Yes, this Jew was different, one of the new breed – blond and freckled with sturdy broad shoulders. He was a true Ottoman subject with none of the overbearing arrogance of the Europeans. Men like this were the sons of farmers and shared his own peasant's love of the land. Despite himself Jemel liked the look of this young man who sat in perfect dignified silence, without fidgeting nervously, as he waited until he was addressed.

Jemel Pasha already know about Aaron Levinson, and was impressed by what he knew. Even old Abdul Hamid had heard of Levinson and knew of his discovery of wild wheat and how he had reclaimed land afflicted with all the Egyptian plagues and turned it into a fertile plain. Jemel decided to like Levinson. He laid down the paper he had been pretending to study, lifted his head and spoke at last.

'You must excuse me, Effendi Levinson,' and he waved dismissively at the documents lying thick on his desk. 'This is a happy coincidence. I was on the point of summoning you to an audience when you presented yourself – an omen from Allah, surely?' and he beamed affably.

Aaron, who was totally unprepared for such a reception, was aware that his heart was beating heavily, but it did not take him long to compose himself. He returned Jemel Pasha's smile, and nodded.

'Surely,' he repeated.

Jemel Pasha's smile switched off like a light as he looked at Aaron speculatively. After a moment he reached across the desk and offered his visitor a cigarette from his elegantly-engraved gold cigarette case. Aaron hesitated, then gratefully accepted one. Jemel tossed the matches across the table and coughed slightly, shaking his head like a man deeply disappointed.

'But I presume you have come here with a complaint,' he said, with a sigh. 'I am like an ocean with the rivers of complaint that come to me. I find it very wearisome.'

'Your Excellency,' said Aaron, carefully polite, 'I have come here to address myself to you because I believe you to be a man of rare understanding – a wise man. And a wise man removes the grounds for complaint when it is to his advantage.' Aaron's choice of phrase in Turkish was so smooth that Jemel could not help but look pleased.

'I – we – have been known to do so under certain circumstances,' he smiled tightly and, his face thoughtful, put his elbows on the desk-top, pressing his fingers together.

The hands of an executioner, thought Aaron, but was nevertheless impressed by the man's tigerish charm.

'Well, tell me how I can help you.'

The General listened attentively while Aaron explained how

201

impossible it was for the settlements to produce enough food to feed the Army while their best men were randomly removed to cut stones for highways. These men were experts, he explained, and were not replaceable by the young boys who could provide the brute strength but none of the knowledge needed to coax the barren earth into fertility. Not only were the men being removed from the farms, but the grain for planting was being pillaged and desperately needed agricultural supplies sent from America were disappearing into the hands of Army and police officers alike.

'You must forgive me for bringing these matters to your attention,' Aaron concluded, 'but if something is not done then I am afraid the certain result will be a famine.'

'On the contrary, I am only too glad to be told of these things,' exclaimed Jemel, squashing his cigarette into an onyx ashtray and springing to his feet with an agility that was surprising in one of his bulk. 'This is the right time for us to come together. It is a disgrace that matters have gone as far as they have.' He began to pace back and forth behind the desk, his beard sunk on to his chest, muttering to himself.

Jemel Pasha might not have been a great soldier, but he was an excellent administrator. However, despite his efforts, all attempts to run things smoothly were bungled by the stupidity of those around him. By some lucky coincidence his overweening passion was agriculture and he felt enormous respect for a man who could make Palestine fertile. Odd though it may have been, he and Aaron shared a great love. Jemel Pasha's interest was further fuelled by the knowledge that an Army marches on its stomach, so his motives for listening to Aaron were two-fold.

Back at his desk again, he repeated, 'it's a disgrace', almost to himself. 'Something must be done to clear this matter up. I will have those responsible shot.'

He looked up at Aaron. 'Rest assured that the points you raised will be dealt with, Effendi Levinson. But I wished most particularly to see you about another matter. I believe you to be a brilliant agriculturalist, indeed your knowledge and your successes are legendary. I have some plans that I should like to put before you. If you have no prior commitment I would consider it an honour if you were to dine with me.'

Intrigued, Aaron nodded. 'The honour will be mine, Your Excellency.'

* * *

Aaron's meeting with Jemel Pasha had far exceeded even his wildest hopes. To have gained such an unexpected ally as Jemel Pasha was the last thing anyone would have dreamed of. The General's agreement to intervene was certainly Aaron's greatest success so far.

Only days after Aaron had returned from Jerusalem a new Captain of the septiehs appeared, an Armenian named Kristopher Sarkis. Everything about him was different from his predecessors; polite and cultured, with a dry sense of humour and warm brown eyes. He was slim and good-looking, but Aaron sensed a strength, combined with great self-discipline and control, which made him out of the ordinary. He also loved books and had gazed enviously at Aaron's magnificent collection until Aaron had offered to lend him some.

He had arrived apologising for the disappearance of a shipment of grain. 'It was rather hard to track down,' he confessed with a smile, 'but should be here in the next few days. I am afraid it's rather depleted; eaten by rats.' He smiled again and his double meaning was not lost on Aaron.

Not only did the grain and seed arrive, but a few days after that Lev, Manny and Rob arrived back with most of the Zichron men. To cap all, Alex had arrived at dawn a few hours earlier. Aaron brought his mind back to his brother's story.

'Of course,' Alex was saying, 'after the event Jemel and Von Kressenstein loudly announced that the idea of the attack was to secure a portion of the canal and destroy it, effectively stopping the flow of British shipping. Had that been the aim it would have been a perfectly good one, but it was most definitely planned as a serious invasion. Well that's what you get for trusting to Egypt.' The Biblical reference did not pass Aaron by – he knew The Book as well as he knew the *Larousse Plant Directory*.

'If a man trusts and leans on Egypt it will pierce him,' he quoted.

'It is curious that inferior troops were used for the initial attack,' said Daniel thoughtfully. He had been unusually quiet, but now he stood up and began walking towards the window. He stopped midway and looked first at Alex and then at Aaron. 'Why, tell me, didn't the British just walk into Palestine? There does not seem to have been much to stop them.'

Alex smiled a little. 'They did. A Cavalry Brigade crossed the canal, sniffed around a bit and went back. Reconnaissance I suppose. I think they were expecting us to attack again.'

Daniel's feelings boiled up inside him. 'God Almighty they could just walk in – sail in – the coastline is practically undefended!'

'Perhaps,' said Aaron quietly, 'they don't know that.'

Both Alex and Daniel were silent for a moment, and then Aaron continued: 'I believe that the reason the British don't attack is simply that there has been a breakdown in military intelligence. They have no way of knowing the extent of the Turks' strength and would of course presume that such an important stretch of coastline would be heavily defended.'

'So,' said Daniel, looking at Aaron questioningly, 'what do we do about it?'

'I don't know yet,' said Aaron.

'Meanwhile, I will get a stomach ulcer,' said Daniel impatiently. 'Two thousand years of impotence is coming to a head in my blood. I want action.'

Aaron looked at him with the deep blue eyes that were so like his sister's. 'Well, what do you propose to do about it? Break through the Turkish lines, cross the Sinai? It's nearly three hundred miles of desert. And then what? If we lived, we would be shot as Turkish spies.'

Daniel felt his frustration evaporate and sat down more calmly.

'No,' Aaron went on, 'apart from our own simple observations about the dispositions of troops and the whereabouts of the odd artillery site, we don't know enough to warrant any real attention. I propose that we wait and watch a little more closely. As the Prophet said, courage is patience.'

'He also said time is the air we breathe,' Daniel laughed softly.

'Good God!' Aaron exclaimed, looking at his pocket-watch. 'We had better be on our way. We have a meeting with the committee in Haifa,' he explained to Alex. 'Where are you going?'

'Up to Zichron to see father.'

'Of course – why don't you take Daniel's horse? He's coming in Jezebel with me. Thank God I changed all the livestock to American registration when the Vali of Beirut was here for Sara's wedding or they'd all have been requisitioned by now.' He put on his jacket hastily, checking his pockets for money and keys.

'So Goliath is American now, is he?' Alex said with a wry smile.

'Yes, I had a hell of a job teaching him English – even Fatma's quicker off the mark,' Aaron joked and he and Daniel rushed off, leaving Alex to make his own way to Zichron.

*   *   *

Daniel was silent on the journey to Haifa: the mention of Sara's wedding had brought her back to his mind and made him once more feel the pain of his emotional wounds. On the whole he had managed not to think of her but when he did the whole wretched tornado of feelings and memories would begin again. How could he have let her go? Why had he allowed it to happen? He vividly recalled the wedding, where everything had seemed confused and meaningless. 'That should have been you standing next to Sara,' Manny had said to him just after the ceremony.

Daniel had given him a cool look and carefully answered, 'I'd rather not discuss it.' Inwardly, though, Manny's words made him seethe with anger – they had echoed his own thoughts precisely. Being Daniel, he did not confide in anyone but found easy cures for his unhappiness – drinking and lovemaking.

For the first few days after Sara's departure with her husband, Daniel had spent his time in Haifa with Isobelle Frank doing just these things. He soon found that, although he could temporarily put Sara out of his mind, he only thought of her with a fresh force once the alcohol had worn off. But, as Daniel was brooding over Sara, war was declared and the storm clouds he had longed for began to draw closer. Little by little his ache faded and the weight on his heart was gradually lightened. He told himself that Sara would never come home now; she was married and that was that. As far as he was concerned she might as well be dead. And so he buried her in his heart and turned back to life. Aaron had noticed that, without being exactly depressed, Daniel was often thoughtful and preoccupied, but he said nothing; it was not his business.

Then a letter had arrived. Daniel kept it in his pocket for a long time without opening it; occasionally he would take it out and study Sara's fine, angular script. When he did open it he was irritated to notice that his fingers were trembling. The letter was friendly and non-committal and much like those she sent to Aaron or her father. She seemed happy and had obviously taken pains not to mention anything which would remind him of her feelings for him. The letter was cool, but his vague feeling of disappointment was soon overcome by one of relief. He did not reply.

By the time Aaron and Daniel had reached Haifa the weather had cleared up and the sky was now a pale, washed-out blue with the sun beginning to break through. Just as they came to a stop outside Ivan Bernski's house they saw Joe Lanski, mounted on a sleek white stallion whose trappings glittered in the watery sunlight. He was evidently just leaving.

He rode over to Daniel and Aaron as they climbed out of Jezebel and dismounted, tossing the reins to a small Arab boy mounted on a leggy chestnut. The stallion snorted at the car's fumes and Joe patted his proud, arched neck. 'Whoa there, Negiv,' he soothed him and gestured to the boy to lead the horse away from the car.

The three men shook hands. 'What a stroke of luck; I wanted to get in touch with you, but heard you were in Beirut,' said Aaron.

'I was, I came back last week. I trust the merchandise was up to scratch?' He was referring to some guns he had procured for Aaron.

'As ever,' Aaron smiled, 'but what I wanted to talk to you about was my sister Sara.'

'Really?' Joe's white teeth gleamed in his brown face. 'And how is the divine Miss Levinson? I hear she is married.'

'Well, that's just it. She is living with her husband in Constantinople and the post is so impossible that we haven't heard from her since the beginning of January. To be honest, I'm quite worried about her. I know you go to Constantinople occasionally and wondered if I could ask you to look her up when you're next there?'

'Nothing would bring me greater pleasure.' Joe's voice held a teasing note that Aaron did not quite understand. 'In fact, I am going next week. If you address a letter to her and leave it at The Hotel Pross for me I will see that she gets it.'

'I would be very grateful,' said Aaron, shaking his hand again.

'Well, gentlemen, I must be off – business calls,' Joe sprang into his saddle. 'I'll ride over with news of your sister when I get back.' He dug his spurs into his horse, who pranced from one foot to the other before galloping off, throwing up a spray of mud behind him.

'Arrogant bastard, isn't he,' said Daniel, watching Lanski gallop off. Although he would have bitten his tongue off rather than admit it to himself, he didn't like the idea of Joe Lanski visiting Sara. 'I wonder what he really believes in.'

'His own luck, I should think,' said Aaron with a smile. 'Well, here we go,' he turned towards the house. 'Prepare yourself for a severe case of committee-itis.'

Joe was in a very good mood as he rode off down the street. He was delighted with his commission and looking forward to his visit to Constantinople far more than he had been an hour earlier. There was a glimmer of secret amusement in his eyes and more than a suggestion of a grin lurked around his mouth. He broke into a cheerful whistle.

CHAPTER FIFTEEN

Constantinople: April 1915

As Sara approached her house she was surprised to see a sleek grey Mercedes flying the twin eagle standard of the German Empire drawn up outside her gate. The driver was busy fending off the small army of children that had gathered curiously round it. The moment he realised she was the mistress of the house he raised his cap in respectful greeting.

Sidestepping the mud-holes that pitted the alley-way Sara exchanged glances with Nasib. He rolled his eyes in wonder at the automobile and then they both stopped, astounded, at the unaccustomed sound that filled the air. Sara's piano was being played very loudly, very fast and very badly by whomever had arrived in this smart automobile. Not only that, but the music being played was most emphatically not usual for the area, which was used to the strains of Bach fatigues or Mozart sonatas, and not *Yankee Doodle Dandee.*

'Who on earth could it be?' Sara asked, hurrying ahead while Nasib extricated one of his slippers from the mud. He shrugged and jogged up to her. The raucous noise coming from the house had attracted the attention of the neighbours, who were peering furtively through their latticed windows, and Sara could not help but smile. Whoever it was had a certain style, and it looked as though her day was about to brighten up.

Before she was halfway up the front stairs the door flew open and Sara saw Irene, hands on hips and looking more flustered than Sara had ever seen her.

'Thank goodness you're back,' she said breathlessly. 'There is a man to see you.' It was obvious from her tone that men, like wild beasts and lepers, had no business in this house and that it was more than remiss of Sara to put Irene in a position of having to let them in. With an inward sigh Sara knew that the incident would be mentioned to Chaim.

'Who is it?' she asked sharply. Irene's continual air of disapproval irritated her intensely.

'He seems very impatient,' Irene ignored the question deliberately. 'He's been stomping round for at least half an hour. And then he started this – noise,' she waved her hand indignantly in the direction of the piano playing. 'I didn't want to let him in but he insisted.'

'Yes,' Sara shouted impatiently, trying to make herself heard over the strains of *When the Saints Come Marching In*, 'but who is it?'

The playing stopped abruptly and Sara started struggling out of her coat and gloves.

'He says he's a friend of your brother's,' Irene said, turning away without further elaboration.

For once Sara did not mind Irene's insolence; she was not listening to her any more. Tossing her hat on a chair and quickly checking her reflection in the hall mirror she dashed across the hall to the drawing-room door, her heart leaping. Lev? Manny? all sorts of names rushed through her head as she flung open the door. Then she stopped, completely taken aback. She was so surprised that it took her a moment or two to recognise the tall, well-built figure dressed in an elegant grey suit who was standing staring up at the grim portrait of Chaim's mother. Joe Lanski! Of all people! How odd that it should be him, she thought in a flurry of agitation, suddenly conscious of her muddy shoes and spattered hemline. Joe turned from the picture and gave her his lazy smile.

'So here you are at last,' he said and studied her for a moment with the same air of abstraction with which he had been looking at the portrait. 'I must say that the room has improved since you walked into it.' Sara, furious with herself for minding how she looked, managed a wan smile. A teasing look came over Joe's face as he took in her dark red suit and primly-buttoned white blouse. 'But I think I prefer the way you looked at our last meeting.' He sketched a mocking little bow in her direction.

Sara's mind flew back to the meeting in the dawn mist and the memory of his lips on hers caused a flood of anger to rise in her cheeks. Against her will she had remembered that kiss more than once with a mixture of guilty relish and furious resentment. She held herself in check. Why did Joe Lanski always succeed in irritating her so? She met his eyes and held the gaze.

'Indeed?' she said with a polite smile and a coolness she was very far from feeling. 'You do get about, don't you, Mr Lanski.' He crossed the room to where she still stood in the doorway and lifting her hand he brought her fingers to his lips.

'You don't know how hard it is to keep away from you,' he said teasingly. When he caught the look in her eyes he threw his head back and laughed. He has an attractive laugh, Sara noted, and extracted her hand quickly. She was determined not to like this arrogant friend of Aaron's.

'Your usual civilised self I see,' she said curtly.

Joe laughed delightedly. 'I see that marriage hasn't curbed your acerbic tongue. Are you going to come in and shut the door? Do – I won't take advantage of you, I promise. Besides,' he added, glancing at the hard, uninviting sofa, 'there's no chance of amorous dalliance here.'

Sara closed the door and sat down, thinking how true that was. Then she indicated the chair furthest from her own and tried to regain control of the conversation. After all, it was her house. 'Do sit down. I presume you have seen Aaron?'

'Yes, a week or so ago,' Joe answered, making himself surprisingly comfortable in the stiff, upright chair.

'Please,' she said excitedly, her cheeks flushing, 'tell me everything and don't leave a single thing out!'

Joe grinned, and fished about in his pocket and brought out a bulky envelope. 'I have this for you.'

Sara leapt from her chair and practically snatched the letter from him. Excusing herself hastily, she crossed the room and, standing with her back to Joe, tore open the envelope and smoothed out the pages of the letter. Joe, looking at her stiff back and feeling her excitement, felt a flash of sympathy. Her unconcealed eagerness to hear news from her family confirmed the impression the unpleasant serving-woman and the dull atmosphere of the house had already suggested. This was not a happy home.

Then Sara remembered her manners and offered Joe a drink. After she had poured him a brandy and herself a glass of wine, which she felt she needed, she returned to the letter. This was the first she had received for almost two months. Sitting at her desk, she read the letter through quickly, knowing that it would be reread many times.

Joe, turning the glass around in his hand, watched her thoughtfully. She was thinner than when he last saw her, and, he decided, even prettier. But her eyes disturbed him. Those brilliant blue cat's eyes he remembered so well were dull and resigned.

Sara refolded the pages with a little sigh and looked up to see Joe watching her. His face held none of its usual irony and, surprised at the expression she saw, she dropped her eyes. It was as though she had caught him naked.

'When did you arrive in Constantinople?' she asked to cover her embarrassment and returned to her chair.

'Yesterday,' he answered, the seriousness gone from his face and the veil of flippancy back in place.

'And what brings you here?' she asked warmly, for after all he must have gone to some trouble to bring her the letter.

'Business,' he said vaguely.

'With the Germans?' Joe nodded.

'But it's more interesting to know what brought you here,' he said casually, crossing one well-shod foot over the other.

'My husband,' Sara said simply.

Joe smiled ruefully. 'Yes. Well, I must admit I find it hard to understand how the upright Mr Cohen managed to capture the heart that I remember was so dedicated to another . . .?'

Sara felt herself blush. He knew that she did not love Chaim and was laughing at her. Well, it was none of his business. Joe gave her a curiously searching look.

'Is it a case of a marriage of convenience or of a heart too soon made glad?' He lifted one eyebrow, but receiving only a furious pink glare in response continued, 'I hope your husband will be back soon. It would be a pleasure to meet him again.'

'He's away for a few days on business,' Sara almost, but not quite, snapped the words.

Joe looked genuinely surprised. 'He leaves you alone here, with the British knocking at the doors of Constantinople? What would you do if they walked in?'

'Invite them in for tea,' Sara answered, with the glimmer of a grin. But then added helplessly, 'Not that there appears to be much chance of that.'

Ever since the first attack she had waited impatiently for something to happen. The British fleet skulked around in the Mediterranean just outside the straits and made the odd adventurous bombardment. They did succeed in destroying a couple of

211

forts in the Dardanelles, but basically they just sat and waited . . .
for what?

In Constantinople the whole thing became more like a farce
than a state of siege. The fashionable way of passing an afternoon
was to take a trip around the islands in the Marmara to look for
enemy submarines. It became more and more like an elaborate
joke which no one quite understood.

Then, in March, the British had made two full-scale attacks. The
second succeeded only in destroying mines cunningly laid parallel
to the Asiatic shore. Having failed to break through the narrows
the British had not followed up the attack but had limped back to
Egypt a few weeks ago leaving Constantinople in a state of
muddled confusion.

Sara had begged Chaim to let her return to Palestine but he
would have none of it. 'If and when the time comes to leave
Constantinople, we shall leave together,' was all he would ever say
before changing the subject. He had remained convinced that the
British would never reach Constantinople and he had been proved
right. Sara had remained optimistic until the news of the British
departure dashed her hopes.

'Do you think they will return?' Sara topped up Joe's brandy.

'Oh, they will be back all right,' he answered confidently. 'Although this time with support for a land advance. The
idea of a battle between a navy and an army was certainly
unique.'

'The sooner the better,' said Sara, almost to herself.

'So Daniel Rosen and you seemed determined to think.'

'What about Daniel?' Sara asked cautiously, aware that Joe was
watching for her reactions.

She had hesitated for only a fraction of a second before asking
the question, but it was long enough for Joe to know the answer to
his earlier question. So it was a marriage of convenience and she
was still in love with Daniel Rosen. For some reason he felt a keen
disappointment, but he answered her question coolly enough.

'He was with your brother in Haifa. They were visiting Ivan
Bernski.'

'Oh,' said Sara and looked primly into the glass that she was
holding firmly in two hands. It needed all her self-control to hide
the emotion that Daniel's very name still inspired in her. Daniel
was probably visiting Isobelle, she thought, well to hell with him.
To cover the silence she rose and poured herself another glass of

212

wine. Joe, as usual, seemed to find her discomfort amusing and was watching her closely through narrowed eyes.

'We had a long talk when I called to pick up your letter,' he said, and embarked on a selective account of the Jewish position in Palestine. Aaron had warned him not to let her know just how bad the situation really was. 'Daniel and your brother appear to share your confidence in British invincibility and justice. For my part I am not so sure.'

Sara eyed at him speculatively, remembering the German car outside, 'Just whose side are you on, Mr Lanski?'

'My own,' he replied glibly and then seeing her face laughed aloud. 'My dear Mrs Cohen . . . No, that's too unattractive,' he said thoughtfully, 'My dear Sara, you must know by now that I am by nature a gambler. One must have a cool outlook in war – one may have to back one side . . . then the other. So I keep my cards close to my chest.'

'Well, there will no doubt come a time when you have to lay them down,' she said with some satisfaction.

'That's as may be. But in the meantime I don't allow my personal views to interfere with my work.'

'That's what my husband says,' she replied contemptuously.

Joe looked at her thoughtfully. 'Ah, what a pity I missed the opportunity of meeting him again,' he said, rising. 'Well, I must be off.' And then with a small smile he added, 'Do you like beef?'

'If you're selling it, no thank you,' Sara answered firmly.

Joe threw up his hands in mock despair. 'I thought you might like to have dinner with me, that's all.'

'Dinner?' she said it as though she had never heard of the meal. A dozen thoughts were flashing through her mind, foremost of which was a longing to get out of the house, even if for a few hours.

'I am staying at the Pera Palace and we could dine there. They have excellent beef and I believe the wine cellar is pretty good too.'

Sara was torn between the joys of escape and the knowledge of how furious Chaim would be if – or rather when – he found out.

'Of course,' Joe began with an ironic little smile, 'if I'm tempting you . . .'

I don't care, Sara thought rashly. Why shouldn't I go out? I'm tired of sitting at home alone night after night and she found herself saying that she would love to dine with him.

'I'll pick you up at eight o'clock then.'

'I'll be ready.'

When the front door closed behind Joe, Sara stood for a moment in the hall, feeling vaguely at a loose end, then returned to the drawing room. It seemed different, colder and emptier now he had gone. There was something about Joe Lanski that Sara could not quite make out, but he had brought with him a sense of excitement, of power and adventure, and it had filled and transformed the dark, dreary room.

Joe had also brought to the surface her never very deeply-buried longings for home. Mindful of Chaim's declaration that he would try hard to understand her better, Sara had determined to do her best to be the wife he wanted. She would try to be undemanding, unquestioning – entirely passive. But Sara had soon found her intentions were not enough: the only change she found was that Chaim became more irascible; it seemed that the more acquiescent she became, the more demanding he was. The slightest thing now threw him into paroxysms of annoyance – a crease in a shirt, the dinner not on the table at the moment he had ordained. All of this was sapping her good intentions, but not, yet, her will-power.

In the last few months the stifling blanket of misery that had weighed on her physically as well as mentally had gradually lifted. There were still many days with no colour, but she constantly cheered herself with the thought that soon she would be able to return home for a visit. Chaim had promised her that much before their marriage. Sara knew there would be enormous difficulties in obtaining permits and travel documents, but she did not waver in her intentions. She would hold him to that promise.

She picked up the paper fan Daniel had bought her in Jaffa and fanned herself lazily. July – just three months away. She did not yet feel that she could raise the subject with Chaim but was happy to wait a little longer, just a little longer, until things were more settled between them.

Then thinking that by accepting Joe's invitation to dinner she might push Chaim into being more repressive, she stopped fanning herself. But *surely not*, she decided. *After all, Joe is a friend of my family – there can be nothing untoward in my agreeing to dine with him. I can hardly ask Chaim's permission when he is two hundred miles away.* Deep down she knew that Chaim would be angry, but she did not care. *All that matters is one evening's escape*, she thought. *What happens will happen. I will face it when the time comes.*

The clock on the mantelpiece chimed, reminding her of the time and for once she had something to get ready for. Her spirits rising at the thought of the evening ahead, she dashed up the stairs to her room and started pulling clothes out of drawers and cupboards, wondering what on earth to wear. She wanted to look stunning – with so few chances to dress up she was going to make the best of this one.

Finally, she settled on a strapless black taffeta dress that fell in a cascade of ruffles. It had its own stiff little jacket lined in pink silk, like the ruffles of the skirt. She had worn it only once before, at a reception the Morgenthaus had held for Chaim and her at the American Embassy soon after her arrival. 'You could do with an outing too, couldn't you,' she said to the dress as she held it against her. The black exaggerated the creamy smoothness of her skin and Sara knew she looked good in it.

Once inside the Pera Palace it was easy to forget the war, Chaim, even herself, Sara thought joyfully. She knew that the hotel was luxurious but was unprepared for the glittering kaleidoscope that met her from the moment she stepped into the hotel's entrance hall. The air was thick with the smell of scent, flowers, cigars and brandy and Sara looked about her without making any attempt to hide her curiosity. Pera, unlike Stamboul, was lit by electricity and to Sara the unaccustomed brightness was extraordinary.

Sara was so happy as she stepped down the few ornate marble steps into the dining room that she did not notice how every man in the room was watching her arrival. Joe saw it, though, and was pleased that he had followed up his impulse and invited her to dine. He too admired her as he took in her smooth, unswept hair, creamy skin and her naturally graceful movements as she followed the maître d'hôtel to their table.

'Champagne, Mr Lanski?' the maître asked knowingly and Joe nodded as he watched Sara looking round, fascinated. Huge crystal chandeliers were reflected many times over in walls of pink mirror, and the waiters, immaculately dressed in European style, carried trays deftly between tables set with gleaming crystal and hothouse flowers.

After six months of going nearly mad with ugliness and boredom, Sara found herself in a room which seemed to float on a sea of silks, satins and taffetas. This was the world Sara had promised herself when she accepted Chaim. In general the women were gaily painted and wore deep *décolletages* and jewels that vied with even the electricity in their brilliance. Behind an airy, voile curtain on a raised platform at the other side of the room an unseen band of musicians was playing a waltz and Sara swayed slightly to the music. The waiter arrived with the champagne almost immediately and Sara drank two glasses one after the other.

'Have the beef,' Joe advised with a knowing smile when the waiters handed them their menus.

'You choose for me,' said Sara, feeling happy at the joy of being alive.

'My, my, you have changed,' Joe laughed, his teeth showing white against his tanned skin.

'Don't count on it,' she replied quickly and watched him through lowered eyelashes as he ordered the meal. He was beautifully dressed in white tie and stiff shirt front and Sara was sure the pearls in his studs were real.

She wondered what Joe Lanski was really like, how old he was, where he came from. It was the first time she had really thought of him as a person and not just as a name. She realised with a start that he seemed just as much at home in these magnificent surroundings as he did on a horse out in the wilds. In spite of herself she found she was becoming interested in him. I'm drinking too much, she thought, but took another sip anyway.

'You must stay here often – everyone seems to know you,' she began brightly. 'Are you really very rich?' Joe laughed in amazement.

'What a question,' he smiled in surprise. 'But then you always were a girl who spoke her own mind. I've always found that attractive. Let's put it this way,' he took a sip of his champagne, 'for a Russian orphan I've done well.'

'Orphan?' It was the first glimpse Sara had had into what lay behind the sophisticated veneer and she was silent for a moment. 'What happened to your family?' she went on.

'Oh, the usual story,' said Joe, brushing the question aside.

'No, really, I'd be interested to know . . . if you don't mind talking about it.' Joe looked amused at the idea that any subject should be too painful to talk about.

'Well . . . I was born near Kiev, in the Ukraine,' he began in a mock story-telling voice, but seeing Sara's alert face he lapsed into his normal voice. 'When I was eight my parents were beaten to death in a pogrom. Most of the adults and many of the children in my village were killed. Clever little Joe Lanski already had his eye out for the main chance and hid in a pigsty until the danger had passed. The one place they would never think of looking for a Jew – I've had a fondness for pigs ever since.'

'So how did you get to America?'

'As always I was one of the lucky ones. My mother's brother had emigrated when the troubles started and he sent me money for the passage to America. I was brought up by him on the Lower East side of New York. He was unmarried and looked after me well. We lived there for eleven years and he became more and more involved in politics and Zionism. Finally, he decided he should go back to the land of our people and back we came. After only a few months he died of typhoid. That was fifteen years ago – and there you have it.'

Sara did a rapid calculation and worked out he must be in his mid-thirties. The waiter arrived with the food and a dusty bottle and Joe told the waiter to let her taste the wine. 'She's the expert,' he said with a grin and Sara realised he was glad of the interruption. She sniffed the wine's bouquet and held it up to the light with the concentration of a connoisseur. It was the best wine she had tasted.

'*Bon appetit,*' said Joe as the waiter gave them their beef. 'These days to eat well has become a rare pleasure.'

They did not talk much during the main course but shared a pleasure in the excellent food and wine. Sara realised that despite the silences this was not only the best, but the most companionable, meal she had eaten for a long time. This evening was so different from the gloomy meals she shared with Chaim where conversation, when there was any, was limited to his work or to complaints about the food. Joe had probably made her laugh more often during this one meal than Chaim had in all the months of their marriage, she thought.

'That was wonderful,' Sara said, patting her mouth with her napkin after the last delicious bite. 'I don't think I've eaten so well since the outbreak of the war – at least!' Joe smiled at her obvious sincerity and talked knowledgeably of food, books and travel. Sara enjoyed being with him; there was an excitement about him that charged Sara's own perceptions and kept her wits sharp. But however much she enjoyed his company, her instincts warned her that he was a man to be careful of, and she fully intended to be just that.

217

By the time the waiter brought a delicate flaky pastry steeped in honey, they had finished the second bottle of wine. Joe treated her with a gallant concern and made sure she had everything she could want. Why did Chaim never treat her like this? It never occurred to him to make any effort for her now they were married; he assumed that she was happy as his wife and the very idea that she should have any problems or longings of her own would have shocked him to the core. He had been brought up to have a good opinion of himself above all others: it was not the foundation stone of a successful marriage.

'Are you happy?' Joe asked over the brandy, echoing her thoughts.

'Of course,' she replied, carefully averting her eyes.

He loked at her for a moment in silence and then laughed.

'Mrs Cohen, you are a very bad liar,' he said, his eyes glinting with amusement. 'Marriage is like mushrooms. You never know if they are the safe or poisonous variety until you try them.'

This was so true that Sara could not help but burst out laughing. Once again he had turned her mood into one of gaiety and fun. And in spite of her own good sense she could feel her defences slowly being broken down.

'Come, Sara,' he said, taking a final swig of brandy, 'I'd better get you home before that witch who passes as a housekeeper turns you into a grasshopper.'

They were two-thirds of the way out of the room when a noise that sounded like a shrieking parrot echoed across to them. Waiters paused for a moment, even the orchestra missed a beat and Sara froze.

'Joe Lanski! You naughty boy! You're in Constantinople and you haven't even called to pay your respects!' Sara followed the voice and saw a painted and powdered woman whose magnificent red hair was dressed in the very latest fashion. She was covered in the most beautiful shawls and jewels Sara had ever seen and was imperiously beckoning Joe over to her table. Sara felt like giggling at the idea of calling Joe a naughty boy. He did not seem to mind. Grinning broadly, he took Sara's arm and led her to the redhead's table. She kissed and hugged him and then turned to Sara.

'What a beauty!' she said, with a bright stare as she shook Sara's hand enthusiastically. 'Well done, Joe. A woman worthy of you at last.'

'Thank you,' he said, with a small bow to Sara. Embarrassed, she shot a furious look at him, but he was not to be deterred. 'I would ask her to be my wife, but I'm afraid another lucky gentleman already has the honour of her hand.' Sara flushed a bright pink.

'Come, sit down,' said the woman, whom Joe had introduced as Annie Lufti.

With a shock of horror Sara realised that the tall, friendly German to whom Annie was introducing her was the one she had met in Chaim's office several months before. Uncomfortable at the memory, she felt her already glowing cheeks deepen to scarlet.

'Madame Cohen and I have already met,' he said with a warm smile.

All Sara's excitement suddenly collapsed as reality returned. Chaim would be furious when he learned about this. Feeling subdued, she sat quietly down between Annie and an exquisite beauty in Oriental clothes. 'My name is Selena Gabriel,' the beauty introduced herself. She had a fragile, faun-like loveliness and Sara took an immediate liking to her, but she turned to Annie who had focused on her as soon as she sat down.

'Now tell me all about yourself,' she was insisting. 'How do you know this rascal here?' She waved an enormous ruby ring at Joe who was talking earnestly to the Major.

Sara smiled. 'Mr Lanski is a friend of my family in Palestine.'

Annie looked at her keenly. 'And what are you doing here in Constantinople, so far from home?'

'My husband lives here.'

'Then I'm surprised we haven't met before.'

'I . . . my husband and I rarely go out,' Sara explained haltingly.

'That must be rather dreary for you.' Annie looked sympathetic. 'Who is this husband of yours?'

'Really, Annie,' Selena broke in with a laugh, 'you really must stop interrogating people.'

Annie smiled broadly. 'I suppose you're right, but I just love asking questions – I'm terribly nosy.'

'I don't mind at all,' Sara said quickly, realising that it was just this atmosphere of frivolous femininity that she missed so much. She liked these women, particularly Selena. Apart from her obvious physical beauty, the girl seemed surrounded by an aura almost of spirituality, and her loveliness seemed an outward reflection of inner grace. Sara relaxed, feeling at ease and happy again.

219

Conversation flowed between the women and Sara found herself opening out as she never had to anyone other than Ruth. She told Selena and Annie about her life in Constantinople, how much she missed Palestine and her family and how badly she wanted to go home. Annie's kind heart was always on the look out for a cause and she rose eagerly to this new challenge. Besides, she thought, Selena is getting far too deeply involved in this Armenian business and maybe having a girlfriend of her own age . . .

'Selena has some sort of a job in Stamboul,' she exclaimed.

Selena elaborated quickly. 'I help out in an orphanage in Kum Kapu,' she said, mentioning the Armenian area which was not far from Galata.

'They also have an agency for Armenian women,' Annie interrupted. 'Look at the embroidery on this shawl – isn't it beautiful? I have hundreds of them.' Sara admired it dutifully and then heard Selena's soft voice on her other side.

'I will be at the orphanage tomorrow. Perhaps I could call on you for tea? I promise not to try to sell you any shawls,' she added with a laugh.

'This is wonderful, we are all going to be the best of friends!' cried Annie, already rearranging Sara's life for her.

Joe left the car, which turned out to be the Major's, at the end of the road so as not to wake the neighbours, and walked Sara to her gate, where he said goodbye.

'I've really enjoyed this evening,' she whispered. Although used to wine, she was a little tipsy, but pleasantly so. 'It was a wonderful dinner – thank you.'

'I'm glad you enjoyed it,' Joe studied her for a long moment and then leaned towards her. For a split second Sara thought he was going to kiss her again, but then, to her surprise, he raised her hand to his lips and, looking into her eyes, wished her goodnight, gave her his old, mocking bow and disappeared into the darkness.

Sara watched him go for a moment before opening her front door. He really was a very attractive man and, to her irritation, she realised she had been disappointed that he had not kissed her. How stupid I am, she thought crossly as she pulled the door to behind her, and then nearly fell over Nasib who was asleep on the floor. He woke immediately and in a hurried whisper told her that Irene had had a headache and he had given her four times the prescribed dose of opium drops to make sure she slept well. 'Good thinking Nasib,' Sara said, patting him affectionately on the cheek. At least she had one ally in the house.

Sara lay in the big square bed, her mind full of what she knew she had no right to be thinking about. She considered Joe's eyes and the way they changed expression so quickly. She thought of his mouth and how his lips had lingered on her hand. It suddenly occurred to her that he would probably know how to please a woman ... he must have had enough of them, she reflected cynically.

She shuddered a little. I've drunk too much, she thought, turning over in her bed. What bliss it was to be between clean white sheets without Chaim pawing over her. What had begun as distaste had turned into repugnance. Sara now had to force herself not to recoil when she felt her husband move towards her. A shutter came down over her mind. *I've made my bed and now I'm lying in it,* she told herself miserably and turned down the lamp. She was bending her nature as far as it would go.

CHAPTER SIXTEEN

Palestine: May 1915

Aaron hit the keys of the Remington irritably, missed the letter and jammed his forefinger between the keys. 'Damn it,' he cursed for the hundredth time that morning. 'Where, oh where, is my darling sister when I need her?' and once again he thought longingly of Sara's mysterious skill with the temperamental machine.

He leant back in his chair and rubbed his eyes with his fists. Jemel Pasha's continued interest in him and the research station was proving to be a mixed blessing: the protection was certainly appreciated, but the daily letters from Jerusalem placed an extra burden on an already overworked system and took up more than their fair share of Aaron's time.

Aaron could not remember ever having felt so tired. For various reasons he had been forced to put in long hours in the fields and laboratory over the past weeks and the pressure of work was wearing him down as it never had before. Every night he would fall asleep on the sofa in his study only to wake a few hours later and lie worrying, staring into the semi-darkness.

Then, at about four in the morning, he would finally admit defeat and make his way to the laboratory where he would more often than not run into Daniel, who was suffering from the same problem. Working together in the early morning light they would tackle the latest project, the one most dear to Jemel Pasha's heart – the development of the oil rich sesame.

Aaron had isolated this new strain of the seed quite recently, and he was convinced that when it was properly exploited it would at least double the yield of the present varieties. He was now in the process of trying to 'fix' the seed, an experiment which had attracted a great deal of German attention which in turn further increased Jemel Pasha's own interest. Aaron was often tempted to ignore the letters, but under the present circumstances he knew he had no choice and the letters continued to fly back and forth between Jerusalem and Atlit.

This could not be said for the letters from Constantinople. It was more than a month since he had heard from Sara, and that letter had been delivered personally by Joe Lanski. Joe had not been very forthcoming about Sara's life in Constantinople, which made Aaron suspect that things were not going well. But although he worried, there was nothing he could do about it any longer and he knew that she was at least safer where she was than she would have been here.

One thing that was becoming increasingly clear to Aaron was that the British would never succeed in taking Constantinople from the Dardanelles. They had returned at the end of April and an apparently fierce battle was now being waged at Gallipoli, one which from all accounts they were not going to win. It would not be long now before the British were going to have to turn their attention away from the peninsula and take a serious look at Palestine.

And when that happened ... Aaron's thoughts turned to reports he had tucked away among his biology files: records of troop movements, ammunition dumps and any other pieces of information which had been picked up by Daniel, Alex or himself. It was surprisingly easy to garner little bits of news, which, if his instincts were right, might soon prove very valuable. Here in Palestine the Turk was desperately short of manpower and munitions and he, Aaron noticed as he wound a new sheet of paper into the typewriter, was becoming almost as short of paper for his endless reports. He looked blankly at the white paper, wondering where to start. There was a knock on the door and he looked up crossly as Frieda came in. 'Yes, Frieda, what is it?'

'Ahmed refuses to take the lunch out to the fields.' She looked at Aaron accusingly. 'He says that you told him to mend the aerometer and he won't budge until he's finished.' Ahmed was a Christian Arab who had what amounted to genius when it came to machinery and Aaron, secretly pleased at an excuse to get out of his study, got up at once.

'I'll take the lunch out myself,' he said. 'I ought to get down there and see what they are up to in any case.'

Frieda grunted, obviously cross at having come off the worse in an argument with Ahmed, and went off, shutting the door behind her with a bang.

Down in the stables, Aaron harnessed the mule Esther to a cart, enjoying the change from desk to manual work and relishing the feeling of the sun on his back.

Ahmed rolled a barrel of water for the animals and one for the men over to him and together they loaded them in the back of the cart. Frieda, still frowning, came out with her basket of food and Aaron, suddenly hungry, could not resist taking a look. There was pitta bread, still warm from the oven, some dates and olives and a huge steaming pot of *majdera*; a wheat and lentil porridge.

'It's nourishing and satisfying,' she assured Aaron as he took an appreciative sniff, and she smiled for the first time that morning as he urged the mule forward and set off. The mule plodded down the palm avenue and with no prompting took the usual turn on to the coastal road. Aaron was relaxed as he sat, an old straw hat on his head, savouring the short journey through the countryside he loved. It was May, the time when the uncultivated land was thickly carpeted with wild flowers – camomile, spurge, thistles, poppies and grasses – before the brutal heat of the summer withered them. Up to his left Aaron could see Zichron, set on its stony ridge among the vineyards and olive groves. Esther's hooves made a pleasant sound, backed by the noise of grasshoppers and the call of the bulbul bird. Had it not been for the flies that buzzed around his head he might well have dropped off and caught up with some much-needed sleep. As they reached the fields Esther broke into a trot. Before Aaron could see the men, he could hear the Arabs singing in rhythm to their work, *Ya hai lili, ya hai lili*, as they pulled up the couch grass between the almond trees.

The men shouted in welcome when they saw Aaron and, downing tools, turned gratefully towards the shade of some tall eucalyptus trees near the track. The Arabs dropped their baskets of couch grass and formed a separate group under another tree. The foreman came forward to help unload the cart. Ezra, one of the more successful of the new boys from Tel Aviv, ran to help, closely followed by Adam Leibovitz, who still carried a torch for Becky.

'Have you heard from Becky? Is she well?' As always, these were the first words he asked Aaron. The mail services from Beirut were still working erratically, but not too badly. Becky seemed genuinely happy but Aaron was working on a plan to get her and

Alex to America. He had already spoken to Jemel Pasha who had swallowed his story whole and promised to arrange Alex's travel documents. In fact there was nothing underhand about Aaron's suggestion. He really did need someone in America to liaise between the Jewish community there and himself in Palestine – and who could be better than Alex, who had accompanied him to New York many times? Naturally if he went he would take Becky, who needed to complete her studies there. Or so Aaron's story went.

'Still safe and well,' Aaron answered, smiling, 'although how much studying she's doing is anyone's guess.'

Adam, as always suddenly embarrassed at having made his infatuation so obvious, looked at the ground and scuffed it with his heavy boots before turning to unload the cart.

Aaron noticed that Ezra's hands were inflamed and the skin was broken in places. The boy was learning his skills the hard way, and he liked him for it. 'You had better ask Frieda to put something on those hands,' he said. One of Frieda's many skills was a wide knowledge of herbal medicine, and the boys at the station all swore by her.

But Ezra had all the nonchalance of youth and only shrugged, answering, 'Oh, they'll harden up in a couple of days.'

But only after they've got a great deal more painful, Aaron thought, although he forbore to say anything. He did not want to seem to nanny these new recruits who were proud of their first job and being one of the men.

'No news yet?' Aaron asked Robby. Robby grinned nervously. 'I was about to ask the same of you. There was no sign of it when I left this morning, but I'm afraid I've been spending a lot of time looking up the hill towards the village.'

Aaron laughed. 'You'll make up for it when the boy is born!' Robby laughed too, but even as he did so he craned his neck towards Zichron. Ruth's baby was due any day now and they had arranged a signal for when she started to go into labour. Their house was on the outskirts of the village and facing this way. When labour started a red blanket would be hung from an upper window. Down in the field, Robby would see it and know he was only hours away from becoming a father.

Paul Levy – slightly thinner but by a small margin – came forward and effortlessly unloaded the water barrel. Aaron was surprised to see him among the men, but soon realised the reason. Paul made his announcement as they all sat on the ground in a circle, dipping the pitta bread into the *majdera*. 'I'm leaving Palestine within the week,' he said, carefully not meeting Aaron's eye. 'I've got my marching orders – from Hamid Bek himself. I'm out on the next neutral streamer to Egypt. Odd, isn't it – that was where we were going when we decided to stop here. I'll get a chance to see the pyramids at last.'

'And Eve?' Aaron asked about Paul's wife.

'She's been ordered to go too – besides you don't imagine she'd allow me to go wandering off on my own.'

'Why not swear allegiance to the Turkish Empire and become a citizen?' asked Lev, his cropped dark hair turned even more earnestly than usual towards Paul.

'Because,' said Paul, lowering his voice, 'I am going to join the British Army over there and help fight to free the Dardanelles.' The men moved their heads together; all but Daniel who was leaning against a tree. He sat aloof, watching the others and lost in his own thoughts.

'I'll return through the back door and before you miss me will be here to liberate you all,' Paul joked.

'You won't – they won't find a uniform big enough to fit you!'

Daniel joined in the laughter but in his heart he was thinking how he would give anything to be able to do something to join the struggle actively.

'Don't you worry, I'll be back soon to proclaim liberty for the captives . . .'

'. . . and the opening of the prison to them that are bound,' said Daniel, pleased at capping the quotation. He looked at Paul, thinking how much he would be missed from the group. But then it occurred to him how potentially useful it would be to have Paul in Egypt – just in case.

'Do you have a contact address in Egypt, in case I ever want to pay you a visit?' he asked.

'Of course. Eve has relations there – the whole world is one enormous family to her!' They joined in with Paul's infectious laughter and the conversation had become more general when, suddenly, Aaron motioned for quiet. They all heard the approaching hoofbeats, and then round the corner came a group of septieh, who drew up at the edge of the field.

For a moment the workers looked at the septieh, and the septieh looked at the workers. Then Aaron detached himself from the group and walked towards the mounted men. He was surprised to see that the captain, who was dismounting, was not Sarkis, but a man they had never seen before.

The captain looked grim, his face unshaven and his movements hurried. He covered the remaining distance with swift, long strides and bowed his head politely.

'Effendi, Aaron Levinson?' he asked, looking past Aaron to the men sitting in silence in the shade behind him.

'Yes? I am Aaron Levinson.'

The captain looked at him respectfully and closed his eyes for a moment as though rehearsing what he was about to say. Aaron was not going to help him out and there was a short silence.

'I have ridden out from the station at Caesarea at the express command of His Excellency Jemel Pasha.' He paused again and his face contracted. 'His Excellency orders you to proceed to his headquarters in Jerusalem without delay,' he lowered his voice. 'Locusts have been reported coming in from the south.'

Aaron contemplated the implications of this fresh disaster that was about to descend upon them. No one knew better than he the destruction locusts could wreak – they could strip a field clean in a few short hours. The food shortage would be nothing compared to the famine which would follow a plague of locusts. 'God help us all,' he said, almost to himself.

With a jerky movement, as though he had forgotten it until now, the captain took a document from his pocket and handed it to Aaron.

'What is it?' Daniel came forward to hear whatever news the septieh had brought and then both men's eyes widened as they saw the paper Aaron unfolded. It was a pass, signed by Jemel Pasha himself, which entitled the holder to move freely anywhere in the Empire. If it had not been for the disastrous news of the locusts Aaron would have smiled. This was exactly what they had been praying for, but had never believed possible.

For a moment Aaron looked up at the sun, which was slowly crawling across the sky. Then, business-like, he turned smartly to the captain. 'I'll leave immediately,' he promised. 'Tell your men to help themselves and your horses to water.' He gestured towards the water barrels and began to walk back to the waiting group of men under the eucalyptus trees. The captain bowed deferentially and gave his men a sharp order.

'What is it?' Daniel asked again, walking beside Aaron, whose blue eyes were glittering strangely in his pale face.

'Locusts,' he answered quietly and continued walking as Daniel stopped stock still.

'Oh my God,' Daniel, as Aaron had, looked up at the sky as though questioning God.

'What was all that about?' Robby asked, his hawkish face glowering in the direction of the septieh. 'If they're here, it can only be trouble.'

Aaron looked around at the group. 'I'm leaving for Jerusalem immediately. It's locusts,' he said shortly.

'Where?' Lev asked quickly.

'The south. But I mustn't waste time talking. Manny, ride to Haifa at the gallop and warn Ivan Bernski. Tell him I'm on my way to see Jemel Pasha and I should be able to get everything we need while I'm in Jerusalem. Ask him to start organising the settlements in the north – this is one battle which they do need us Jews to fight.' He looked about and his glance fell on Ezra. 'Take Ezra with you – and a gun.'

Ezra, extremely proud of his mission, began to discuss which horses they should take.

'Daniel, you go to Hadera with Alex. Warn them and bring your cousins back with you. We'll coordinate this area from Atlit.' Aaron watched Manny and Ezra set off at a brisk pace and turned back to Lev and Paul. 'I should be back tomorrow. And Paul – if I don't see you – good luck.' He wrung his friend's hand, emotion briefly overtaking them both, before he turned back to the emergency. Briskly issuing further instructions, he told Sam to go and warn his father and the settlement at Zichron. Then he drew Daniel and Alex aside.

'This just might be the chance we've been waiting for,' he said quietly. 'Jemel obviously wants me to organise a campaign. A plague of locusts will finish off his Army quicker than any battle could – no food; no Army. Nothing could be more calculated to put the fear of God into them. With an anti-locust campaign as cover and a few more of these' – he tapped his pocket significantly – 'we can travel freely and pick up all sorts of useful information.' His final words before turning away were spoken almost to himself: 'And I plan to take every advantage of the situation.'

Aaron stood with his team on the edge of the field, waiting for dawn to break. About fifty men, women and children were spread over the land, holding pots and pans and all expectantly looking

228

out at the horizon for the first sight of the approaching cloud. Aaron, Frieda, Kristopher Sarkis and eight septieh stood on one side of the field, at the opposite side of which a ditch had been dug the night before. And far beyond the ditch were the waiting women and children with their pans and kettles. Aaron hoped everyone remembered – and obeyed their instructions.

The sky began to take on a pinkish glow and slivers of light shimmered through the harvested wheat stalks. Aaron called for silence. 'We will fire this field first,' he said, circling the men and looking at them earnestly, his face full of determination. 'The west wind is freshening and it will carry the flames towards the ditch.' He looked at Frieda, who was to be in charge of the women. 'Go and join the women now, Frieda. When I give the signal, marshal yourselves into a line and move forward making as much noise as you can. Shout, hit your pans, everything, but you must drive the locusts towards the ditch – towards the fire. Do you understand?' Frieda nodded and started to move off. 'Don't forget to keep your faces and hair covered,' he called after her, and laughed as she spun round with a frightened face. 'Don't worry, they don't sting or bite – it's just to keep them out of your mouths.' Frieda marched off across the field looking not in the slightest reassured and muttering to herself.

Aaron turned back to the men and started to organise the distribution of torches. Ezra, keen as ever, was one of the first to grab a kerosene-soaked torch and make his way to his post on the other side of the field, closely followed by Alex.

Aaron's face looked grey with exhaustion in the morning light. He sighed and looked wearily into the faces of his team. 'Well,' he said, 'you all know what to do.'

'That we most certainly do,' Daniel said to Manny as the two men walked together to their station on the far side of the ditch. 'We could do it in our sleep by now.'

For weeks they had worked ceaselessly against the almost Biblical plague that threatened every part of Palestine. They had each been assigned different areas, from Galilee to the Dead Sea and even into the desert. Men and troops were dispatched to every corner of the land in the fight to stem the swarms that were coming up from the south, but it was practically impossible and they were all feeling the strain.

Operations like this one were now a daily chore as Aaron and his men travelled from Arab farm to Jewish settlement and dug the trenches into which the hatching females would be driven. Once they had laid their egg packets the locusts would be torched before the young had developed their wings. But although they had torched fields and vineyards in every part of Palestine, this time it was different. This time it was Atlit they were protecting.

Aaron checked the various groups. Daniel waved to signal that he, Manny, Sam and Robby (now a proud father of a baby girl) were in position on the other side of the ditch. Beyond them Aaron could see that the women and children were all lined up at the far end of the field. The young oat shoots were showing clean and green above the chalky red earth. They were still damp with dew. In a few minutes they would be trampled to the ground by the approaching feet of the locust patrol, but nothing could be done about it. It was by far the lesser of two evils.

Sarkis and his troops were also at their stations, lining the perimeters of the fields and standing with shovels and water buckets, ready to douse the precious eucalpytus trees if they should catch.

Everyone was silent now and the fields were bathed in an eerie peacefulness. Even the birds and the grasshoppers seemed to have fallen silent, waiting uneasily for the first sign from the locusts. The relentless, unearthly humming of a million wings would be heard before they would become visible as anything more than an approaching storm cloud.

'Here they come,' shouted Aaron, and already his voice could scarcely be heard above the noise of the wings.

'Damn the bastards,' shouted Daniel, 'let's get them.'

In seconds the blizzard of locusts descended and all were caught in the whirl of insects around them. The men watched with a mixture of wonder and frustration as the green and gold was covered with a moving blanket of yellowy-green, all-devouring greed.

'Torch the field,' Aaron yelled, and Daniel passed the signal to the women, who began beating and moving slowly forward. Frieda screamed as she felt the locusts all over her, but she kept beating, encouraged by the women on each side of her.

Flames billowed along the edges of Aaron's field and then flared as they met the wheat stalks. The carpet of red flame advanced with a roar, burning wheat and locusts together and carrying the loathsome insects forward on a wave of heated air. A gust of wind from the sea turned the flames briefly towards the bank of eucalyptus that acted as windbreakers.

'The trees,' Daniel shouted as he smelt the pungent aroma of burning eucalyptus. Sarkis's men lumbered towards the trees and soon had the sparks under control. The air around Daniel and Manny was dense and suffocating now. 'Quickly,' Daniel coughed, 'torch the ditch.' The swarm and the fire were nearly upon them.

Manny struck a match and lit Daniel's torch. Then, in a shower of sparks, he lit his own from it. 'Oh damn,' he said, brushing the sparks from him.

'Quickly,' Daniel urged. Signalling Sam and Robby to do the same from their end, Daniel put his torch to the ditch. The noise was nightmarish. Behind him the women were getting closer, beating on their pans and shrieking hoarsely. In front of him were the squeals of burning field mice, the steady humming of the locusts and the roar of the approaching fire. Daniel and Manny watched as the ditch smouldered for a moment before blossoming into murderous, cleansing fire.

'This should do it,' said Manny gleefully. 'This should get them.'

The swarm had reached cooler air and had dropped. In no time the flames had risen from the ditch and greedily sucked in the locusts. Other locusts, driven forward by the women, flew straight into the flames and burnt.

'Keep them coming,' shouted Manny, running along the ditch and dousing it with kerosene. 'We must keep them away from the nursery.'

Daniel felt his heart sink as he saw a cloud rise and float off towards the station and nurseries. The others saw the direction in which he was gazing and fell silent. Then suddenly the inland breeze quickened and the cloud was carried out to sea. A huge cheer went up as the humming grew fainter and fainter and a great flock of screeching gulls swooped down to feed on toasted locusts.

The men and women huddled on the edges of the field, standing ankle-deep in burnt insects. There was a feeling of anti-climax and silence fell. Looking round it seemed as though there was very little difference between victory and defeat. They watched as the flames died down and the fields smouldered in the early morning light.

'At least we've saved the nurseries,' said Aaron, wiping his face with his arm. He crossed to Sarkis to thank him and his men for their help. Sarkis, his fair skin and blond hair black with smoke, nodded and turned to dismiss his men. He, like Aaron, knew that this was far from being the end.

Daniel heard a buzzing close to his ear and found a locust trapped in his keffiyeh. He caught it and it fluttered in his hand, panic-stricken. On its own it looked a pathetic creature, with no hint of the havoc it could cause when it moved in a swarm. Alone, it held no terror, and Daniel crushed it easily between his thumbs. This is precisely what we shall do to the Turk very soon, he thought with satisfaction. Between them, Aaron and Daniel had come up with a plan.

Aaron waited in silence as the men gathered round. They settled down, talking in subdued voices, impressed by Aaron's own solemnity. Most of them were exhausted by the never-ending struggle against the locusts and were intrigued rather than pleased at being called out so late at night with no explanations given. Not everyone was here yet and Aaron looked around the tightly-shuttered, candle-lit room, taking in the men's seriousness as he counted heads.

He had asked only his most trusted and closest friends and colleagues to meet him in his upper-floor study at the research station; men who had all worked with the watch group and later on the locust patrol and of whose loyalty he was already convinced. None of the men present was committed to any other Jewish organisation and none, apart from Robby, was married. The surly-looking Saul Rosin, at fifty, was a widower and had no children or other dependents. Ezra was the youngest at eighteen, and although Daniel and Aaron had had many discussions about the advisability of including him in their plans, they felt that he more than deserved their confidence. Alex had left a few days before to pick up Becky from Beirut and take her on to America, but Sam was there as well as Manny and Lev. Despite himself Aaron had a few worries about the men's reactions – what he was about to say was so desperately important to himself, Daniel and each and every one of them.

Ben and Josh were the last to arrive – they were the only ones who did not come from Zichron – and as they made their way into the room, apologising for keeping the others waiting, Frieda bolted the door behind them and went down to unchain Goliath, who would be sure to give the first warning of any strangers. Ben and Josh greeted the men nervously, immediately struck by the unusual air of tension.

'We're all here now,' Aaron said with a sweeping glance around the room. 'Good, let's begin.' He cleared his throat as though about to deliver a major speech. A rustle spread through the men as they settled themselves, like a first-night audience as the curtain goes up. For a moment Aaron looked straight into Daniel's dark eyes as if searching for inspiration for his words. Then he began.

'Perhaps I'd better recap a little on what we all know is going on around us – politically,' he opened, surprising his audience. They had all thought this was to be another meeting about strategy for the locust campaign. A few exchanged glances, but all remained silent.

'For weeks now we've been fighting the locusts and, between us, I'd say we'd travelled over the whole of Palestine – no questions asked and welcome wherever we go. Thanks to our friend Jemel Pasha' – a few sniggered at what they thought was meant to be irony, but immediately shut up – 'I've been able to send you, and others, wherever the locusts and I chose. Just think of the ground you've covered. You've been into Arab villages, munition dumps, even Turkish Army camps.'

'Which would have been impossible a few months ago,' Lev said wonderingly.

'Exactly,' nodded Aaron. 'And then think of the man-power we can command. We've used septieh, Turkish soldiers and Arab fellahin. When it comes to hunting out the locust eggs and grubs our worst enemies are our friends. This is important. But,' Aaron continued, 'I did not call you here to talk of locusts. I want to talk of the growing problems we are facing, not as farmers but as Jews. And this time, I want to do a great deal more than talk. I have a plan for action.' He paused for a moment. He must now tread carefully.

'Turkish oppression is increasing, not weakening. Zionist leaders are being exiled and Jewish soldiers are being transferred from the Army to the labour gangs. Even within our own ranks there is trouble. The Jewish community is split between allegiance to the Turks and to the Allies.' His eyes flickered unconsciously towards the filing cabinet where the botanical files were bulging with enough information to prove that there was little or nothing to stop the British from crossing the desert or even landing anywhere along the coast. There was no sign of any artillery or airplanes and the coastal defence was in the hands of an inept militia made up of local Arabs. Only Daniel noticed Aaron's involuntary glance and within seconds Aaron had recovered himself.

'I want to talk about how I see things developing for us in Palestine. We all know that we are as close to famine as a beggar is to poverty. Only the Moslem Arabs are perhaps in a worse condition – partly due to their own improvidence. But they have lost nearly everything, and are already having to fall back on the little they managed to put aside. The Jewish settlements might manage to hold out against actual starvation until the next harvest but,' he sighed, 'we all know the twisted labyrinths of the Arab mind – and it works on a short fuse.' The men nodded agreement. They were now wholly absorbed in what Aaron was saying and their eyes never left his face.

'In order to save their skins, the Arab religious leaders will use their same old strategy. They will stir up anti-Jewish riots and will storm our orchards, fields and storehouses and then have a party massacring any Jews they find. And, of course, will pounce on the weakest and most exposed settlements first.' Aaron crossed to his desk and picked up a flimsy piece of paper. Still in silence, the men's eyes followed him.

'This was brought in from Haifa yesterday,' Aaron said, waving the paper at them. 'It appears that the Turk is already encouraging anti-Jewish feeling.'

Lev, who was sitting nearest to Aaron, took the paper from him and began to read it aloud. After a few sentences he stopped. There was no point going on with it. It was the usual call to drive the infidel Jews into the sea, and was signed by Moslem religious leaders in Constantinople, Jerusalem and Jaffa. Lev shook his head and gave it without further comment to Manny, who read it and passed it round the room.

'All this only goes to prove that the noose is tightening round our necks. Even more dangerous, I have heard rumours of a new edict which will confiscate all Jewish property.' A buzz of indignation rose from the audience and Aaron waited until it had died down. Then he spoke slowly and forcefully.

'I am convinced that if the British don't put a quick end to this war it will mean only one thing for us – extermination.'

'And what in the name of hell can we do?' Saul Rosin burst out harshly. 'The British have quite evidently decided to hold their battle-front on the Turkish mainland – and good luck to them.'

Aaron, who had been pacing back and forth in the middle of the room, came to a halt and faced his friends. 'We can help them to realise their mistake,' he said simply. 'Each of us in this room knows how poorly defended Palestine is, but the British obviously don't. The powers granted to us by Jemel Pasha are almost unlimited. We have a unique opportunity to gather intelligence – with, ironically, support from the highest Turkish authority. That is where we can help. We know this territory better than anyone except God. With the locust patrol and the research station as cover we can travel freely and pick up all the military information needed to help the British to a swift victory in Palestine.'

There was a total silence in the room until Robby Woolf blurted out incredulously: 'Are you suggesting that we spy for the British?'

'Yes,' said Aaron firmly and looked round the room. 'What I am suggesting is that we supply information to the British in return for the promise of support for a Jewish homeland when the war is over.'

The silence broke as all the men talked excitedly to each other. Spies! The idea was anathema to the Jewish way of thinking. To Jews, spies were the cursed dogs that betrayed them to the authorities in oppressed countries in return for a slice of sausage.

'Are you mad?' Lev's voice rose above the others. 'Spying is against all our traditions, against all . . . moral scruples!' He brought his hands down on his cropped skull with a gesture of outraged despair.

Daniel rose from his chair in a single, smooth movement. He had known this question would arise and was prepared for it. Where Aaron had spoken calmly and matter-of-factly, Daniel spoke rhetorically.

'Did Joshua have any moral qualms when he sent out spies to Jericho? Didn't Jacob get his land and God's blessing through an act of deception? They both realised that there are times when scruples are a luxury. This is another such time.' Lev looked at him, patently unconvinced. 'What do you want to do, Lev? Save your integrity while thousands of others are starved or hacked to death? We know we will be comparatively safe here – we are protected by the research station being American-funded and by Aaron's reputation. But what about the others, Lev? Of course, no one would like to fight the Turk barehanded in the street more than I would – but that kind of action would be senseless. It would just give them the excuse for a massacre. In the end we have to use deception to save others from deception. It is the logic of the moment.'

'And what makes you think the British would listen to us – a half-starving bunch of Jewish peasants obviously smarting under Turkish rule?' asked Robby, taking a light for his cigarette from Sam. Sam had already heard most of the arguments from Aaron and Daniel and was in favour of the plan. 'What do they know about the Jews of Palestine – we don't exist to most people outside the Empire. How do we know they will listen to what we have to say?'

'We don't,' said Daniel. 'But we have to give it a chance.' There was silence as Lev and Daniel looked at each other solemnly.

'Oh hell,' said Lev helplessly, 'I know you are right but I just wish I had some choice.' Aaron imperceptibly relaxed; he sensed the battle was half won.

'Yes,' Robby added, thinking of Ruth and his daughter, 'so do I. Spying is a risky business.'

'Being a Jew is a risky business,' interjected Manny who trusted Daniel and had already made up his mind to go along with him whatever. A laugh circled the room for a moment.

'Say we do fall in with your idea,' said Saul, who looked preoccupied and was obviously thinking hard, 'and the British conquer Palestine. We still won't be free. The most that will happen is that we will exchange one set of rulers for another, will be owned and squeezed dry by another parliament, king or whatever.'

'Yes, but we will be a step closer to a Jewish homeland – a free state,' said Daniel urgently. 'Let me tell you something, I've had more than enough of living under the Turks' rule.' He paced the room excitedly. 'Right now I'd be prepared to bargain with the devil if he gave us a chance of ridding ourselves of the Turk. How much longer can we wait – another year? Another thousand years?' he waved an angry hand, gesticulating extravagantly.

Ezra, who had been listening in total silence, jerked eagerly to his feet. 'I don't want to wait another minute – I spit on the Turk,' he announced and spat dramatically three times. Then blushing bright red, he sat down as suddenly as he had stood up, looking as though his bones had been broken under him.

Manny burst out laughing, and the others could not help but join in.

236

'Hey,' said Daniel, 'I'm supposed to be the hot head round here!'

The tension in the room was broken and the men relaxed for the first time. Sam lit a cigarette and most of the others followed his lead.

Daniel's cousin Josh turned to Aaron, 'Do you have a plan?'

'Yes,' said Aaron calmly, not rising from his seat. 'Yes, we have a plan. The first step is to gather as much military information as we can and get it to the British in Egypt.'

'You would be the best man for that job,' said Lev, 'You're the one with a reputation outside Palestine. They would be most likely to listen to you. And you're the one with the contacts, the passport.'

'Of course, it can't be Aaron,' Sam interrupted, 'He has to report to Jemel Pasha every week. They'd miss him immediately.'

'Well, how is anyone to get out?' Ben asked. 'Through the Sinai Desert?'

'But that's impossible in summer,' Saul objected. 'Apart from the danger of having to pass through Turkish lines, the worst enemy would be thirst. The two unpatrolled routes across the desert are feasible only in winter. You know as well as I do that the water holes are very low, if not totally dried out, until the October rains.'

'And I suppose the sea route is as impossible,' said Lev, taking a drag at his cigarette. This was the plan Daniel had originally favoured – to sail a small boat out to the open sea at night and hope to be picked up by Allied ships on Mediterranean patrol. But a week or so before, the French had blockaded the whole Syrian and Palestinian coastline and announced that all boats would be sunk on sight without warning. So that option was now gone, as he explained to the men.

'So how?' asked Manny.

'On a neutral American ship out of Haifa, that's how,' said Daniel in a totally expressionless voice. 'The warship *Des Moines* is calling at Haifa next week to evacuate all neutrals expelled from the Empire. She's taking them to Egypt. I plan to go with them. I'll have a forged passport, thanks to a printer friend in Haifa, and there should be no problems.' He looked round the room at his friends' faces. They were all watching him intently.

'My God,' said Ben, awed, 'if the Turks find out they will kill every Jew breathing.'

237

Daniel shrugged. 'It's a chance we've got to take. If we do nothing we'll all be exterminated anyway – if things go wrong it will just be quicker.'

'What about the other Jewish communities – the Zionist and socialist groups – will they help?' Robby asked.

'I don't think we can count on them,' Aaron answered. 'I have put various feelers out, mainly to Ivan Bernski, but the impression I get is that, although they believe as strongly as we do in building up a nation of our own, they are not prepared to take such risks with their communities. They might come round later, when the situation changes. But I must admit I think it's a good idea to keep the group as small and as underground as possible.' There was a general murmur of agreement to this.

The room was becoming stuffy and cloudy with smoke and the men were infected with a sense of growing excitement. Aaron stood up. 'My life's work, and my life's ambition are here in the station, but I am prepared to risk it all. But this is my choice and I must not influence any of you. If you join us you will be risking your lives and if you want to leave now I will understand completely.'

There was a silence in which the men looked at each other through the smoke and did not move. 'We won't take any money,' said Lev firmly.

Aaron sighed at Lev's stubbornness. 'Of course not. We are patriots not spies. So who is in favour of throwing their lot in with the British?'

'Me,' said Ezra, rising again and standing to attention.

'Me too,' said Lev, 'and God help us.' One by one the men stood up to be counted, until only Robby remained seated.

'Are you with us, Robby?' Aaron asked gently.

Robby looked uncomfortable. 'I'm sorry, but I made a solemn vow to Ruth on our marriage – that we would never have a secret from one another. I would go to hell and back to cast my die with you, but I cannot deceive Ruth.'

Aaron looked at Daniel, who paused only a second before nodding. 'Ask her,' said Aaron, and turned to the others. 'But the rest of you, talk to no one. It will endanger not only us but them, remember that.' They all nodded solemnly.

Aaron became business-like and started to outline plans. They were perfectly simple: the men were to carry out their normal duties for the locust patrol while keeping their eyes and ears open.

Anything they learned was to be told to Aaron and he would pass the information to Daniel, who would code it and take it with him to Egypt.

'Those of you who would like to return to Zichron tonight had better leave here two at a time. The rest of us may as well stay here the night. Now are there any last questions?' Everyone seemed clear about their tasks. 'Well, well,' said Aaron. 'I thought I'd never see the day – a room full of Jews without questions.' The men laughed and relaxed, gathering their things together for their departures.

'I've got one,' said Manny waggishly, 'can we open the bloody windows now?'

Daniel laughed and, throwing the window open, breathed in the sweet night air. *This time next week I shall be in Cairo*, he thought and for the first time since before Sara's wedding a dimly-remembered feeling washed over him. He was happy.

CHAPTER SEVENTEEN

August 1915: Constantinople

'My feet are so hot and tired I can hardly stand,' said Selena as she walked into Sara's kitchen with a weary smile. Drawing a long breath, she flopped into a chair, kicked off her shoes and, toes wriggling with pleasure, put her feet on the edge of the old tin bath which Sara and Nasib had just filled with a huge block of ice.

Sara glanced anxiously across the room at her friend, feeling a rush of warmth and affection for her. They had known each other just over three months now and it had become a routine for Selena to drop in for a chat three times a week on her way home from the orphanage.

Those months had sealed a close friendship between the two women, based on an empathy and understanding – and bolstered by trust. Sara had soon discovered that behind Selena's delicate femininity lay one of the most indomitable characters she had ever met. She had an obstinate will, a strong intelligence and a warm, loving nature; it was the combination of these three traits that was the clue to her extraordinary appeal.

Even the misanthropic Chaim had fallen under Selena's gentle spell. Not that this had led to any relaxing of his tight control over his wife or made any real difference to their social life together. There had been just one visit to Annie Lufti and Chaim had reluctantly agreed to giving a small dinner party in return. He had been charming and convivial and the evening had been a success, but the moment they had said goodbye to their guests he had told Sara that that was to be that. These occasions tired him and that was not good for his business.

Sara had said nothing, not wanting to antagonise him. He had been furious over the evening she spent with Joe Lanski, but had seemed to accept Selena who, ever since, had been dropping in for a chat. With the advent of Selena's friendship Sara's life had changed for the better. Life was more bearable now that she had a friend in whom to confide, and the friendship had given Sara a new sense of security and even of independence.

She had told Selena everything. About her family in Palestine, about Daniel, about Chaim and their life together. Selena in turn confided to Sara, unburdening her heart in a way she never could to Annie. They were now as close as sisters – closer, really, thought Sara as she watched her friend easing her aching feet on the ice block. Selena seemed pale and deeply tired and something about her made Sara frown, feeling something heavy press her heart.

'Selena? Is everything all right?'

'Yes, of course,' Selena smiled at her. 'It's this heat, it's a curse. Everything is drooping and weary,' she said, gratefully accepting a glass of lemon sherbert from the hovering Nasib.

'Everything except the sun,' Sara put in with a light smile and took a long draught from her own lemonade.

Sara drew up a chair opposite her friend and lowered herself into it with a sigh. 'We spent the whole morning ironing,' she said wearily, 'which of course meant keeping up the fire for the iron. I haven't even had time to read the newspapers yet,' she continued, then leant forward slightly in the chair. 'Any important news from Gallipoli?'

Selena shook her head. 'Nothing beyond the fact that the Allies are neither advancing nor being driven away.' They both fell silent. As Joe had predicted, the Royal Navy had returned and landed British and Allied troops on the peninsula. Battles had been raging on and off for months now but the Turks seemed to be holding firm. Panic had broken out only once in Constantinople and that had been towards the end of May when a British submarine had surfaced in the Golden Horn. This time Sara had barely time to put on her shoes before Chaim, thinking it was the prelude to a serious attack on Constantinople, had rushed home telling her to pack. She did so with alacrity, but by the time they were ready to leave the submarine had disappeared and the alarm was over. They remained in Constantinople and the only sign of the war being fought practically on their doorstep was the occasional flashes of artillery fire at night.

'I just can't believe that the Turks might actually be winning,' said Sara very quietly.

'Neither can I,' said Selena and the two girls exchanged glances.

In their hearts both of them wished for a British advance. Selena because of the steadily growing threat of violence to the Armenian community in Constantinople, Sara partly because she was now also deeply concerned about the fate of the Armenians and partly for the purely selfish reason that she still wanted to go home and Chaim was adamantly refusing permission.

'Have you heard from Hans Werner yet?' she asked. The Major had left to join Limon von Sanders's staff at the Gallipoli front three weeks earlier.

Selena smiled. 'Yes, I had a letter yesterday. He seems to enjoy being in the thick of battle.'

'I suppose he would,' Sara said with a tiny shrug. 'Men are like that. Now tell me about the children.'

Selena's face was instantly illuminated with the brightest of smiles and she launched into an account of her afternoon at the orphanage. But, slowly, it began to dawn on Sara that Selena was hiding something – something important that was upsetting her deeply. Her eyes were curiously empty and her lovely voice flat. Sara looked at her thoughtfully.

'Selena, are you sure nothing's wrong?' she interrupted.

Selena gave a small start and shook her head, avoiding meeting Sara's eyes. Sara's whole attention was focused on Selena's distressed face and Selena, realising, turned her face away quickly, closing her eyes. She desperately wanted to unburden herself to Sara, but the words Frank Walworth had told her that afternoon stuck in her throat. Suddenly tears swam into her lovely dark eyes and her lips trembled. Sara's heart flew out to Selena in compassion and, rising quickly from her chair, she rushed to Selena's side and squeezed her arm. 'Selena, whatever is it?'

Selena brushed her eyes with the back of her hand. 'I . . . I . . .' she began but a sob broke and the tears splashed her cheeks as all the pent-up emotions of the day finally spilled out.

'Please, please tell me what is wrong,' Sara begged, her voice rising in alarm. She knelt down beside her friend and took her hand, patting it affectionately as she spoke. 'I'm your friend, remember.'

Selena pulled her hand free from Sara's and wiped her face with her hands, sniffing back the tears. 'I'm sorry,' she said, her voice shaking slightly, and she looked down at her hands while she regained her self-control.

Sara rose and pulled her chair round until it was next to Selena's, then waited. 'Is this anything to do with the troubles in Armenia?' she asked softly, after a moment.

Selena nodded and swallowed hard. 'I saw Frank Walworth – you know, the newspaper reporter – this afternoon. He came to the orphanage.' She paused a moment and cleared her throat. 'He has just returned from the Caucasus, and passed through Armenia on his way. Apparently, they are implementing systematic deportation of all Armenians from some of the villages.' The two girls locked troubled eyes.

'What do you mean deported?' Sara asked, bewildered.

'I mean that there are orders, signed by Enver Pasha himself, saying that the whole Armenian population, down to the last babe-in-arms, is to be evacuated from the towns and villages of Armenia.'

'No! That can't be true!' Sara cried, her eyes wide with shocked disbelief.

'I'm afraid it is. There is no doubt that the report is reliable.' Selena turned to face Sara. 'The town of Zeitun and several others have already been evacuated to . . .' she took a deep breath as if not wanting to go on, but continued in a steady voice, 'to Deir ez Zor – the Mesopotamian Desert.'

'The Syrian Desert?' Sara exclaimed, appalled. 'But there is nothing there – not even water.'

'I know,' said Selena very quietly. 'I can only think that the government is planning to destroy the whole nation.'

Sara straightened and looked squarely at Selena. 'Surely the Germans will protest. They would never tolerate persecution of fellow Christians,' she said firmly.

Selena smiled and said softly, 'You know about the Triumvirate, Sara. Can you imagine them allowing the Germans to interfere with their internal policy?'

Sara thought for a moment then jumped in again. 'Then you must inform Henry Morgenthau immediately. You must tell Annie to contact him tonight. He must be able to do something about this – this abomination,' she said fiercely.

Selena looked at her friend lovingly, her eyes full of sadness. 'The Ambassador knows about it already. Nothing has been made public yet in the hope that he will be able to do something to prevent further deportations. There is also the added fear of spreading panic in the Armenian population here. Naturally, they have heard rumours of the ghastly fate of our people but the moment rumour becomes fact they are likely to react in some unpredictable way. A few might seek revenge on the Turk and you know what that will mean.'

Sara nodded. It took very little to light the fires of religious fanaticism in the Moslem world and Sara had seen for herself the work of Armenian baiters scrawled in crude letters on walls. 'Armenians are swine, usurers, bloodsuckers,' and worse. The messages appeared overnight and were not removed. Yesterday she had seen an Armenian youth running through the streets with a bloodied head, pursued by a scruffy rabble yelling and pitching stones at him. He had taken refuge in a Jewish café frequented by Greek-Jewish stevedores, who had warded off the crowd.

Sara was constantly shocked that people could be hated just because of their race. Her own parents had, of course, been the prey of racialism but to Sara it was an unreasoned hatred which she could not understand. The Armenians, like the Jews, were intelligent, hard-working people. What had they done to arouse this kind of persecution? 'Oh, Selena whatever are we going to do?' she said. She hesitated, then added, 'Perhaps you should stay away from Kum Kapu – just for a while.' She spoke knowing full well how Selena would react.

Selena's eyes flashed. 'On the contrary, this is the time for our people to come together,' she said with fierce determination. She looked down a moment and a soft expression washed over her delicately beautiful face. She looked up and reached out for Sara's arm. 'Thank you, Sara, for being my friend and for wanting to help. I'm grateful for that. But this is something I should not like you to get involved in. Please try and understand.'

She put on her shoes and pushed herself to her feet. 'The Lord is sweet and gentle, but the way he sets for us is hard beyond telling,' she said with a smile. She glanced at the clock and her hand flew to her face. 'I'd better be going, or I'll be late for the meeting.'

'What meeting?' Sara asked with a frown.

'Just a meeting of community leaders and clergy,' Selena answered lightly.

'Is that wise?' A brief, dismissive glance was the only reply to Sara's question, then Selena kissed her affectionately on both cheeks.

'See you on Thursday,' she said, stepping to the door. Sara watched her get into the waiting carriage, relieved to see the threateningly large figure of Akiff in the dark interior. She smiled and waved. 'See you on Thursday,' she echoed and watched as the carriage rolled out of the alley before turning back into the house.

That evening at dinner Sara was distracted and thoughtful. From the moment Selena left, Sara turned over and over Selena's words in her mind, creating an ever-growing shadow of uncertainty. She was filled with a terrible despair for Selena's safety and for her own bleak future. She was hot, and had no appetite for the fried fish and boiled potatoes, which were Chaim's favourite supper. She pushed the food moodily round her plate until Chaim paused, his fork loaded with fish, and spoke with a frown. 'Sara,' he said, in that controlled voice that reminded her of a schoolmaster and never failed to irritate her, 'is there something worrying you? If so, please say what it is.' He put down his fork and waited.

Sara folded her napkin and said carefully, 'I was talking to Selena this afternoon. She told me several things I find hard to believe.'

Chaim grimaced. 'Such as?' he said, picking up his fork again.

That is scarcely an interested voice, Sara thought in agitation. 'She told me that there is a rumour that the whole Armenian population is to be evacuated,' she paused, watching him intently, 'to the Syrian Desert.'

Chaim snorted and shook his head. 'Nonsense,' he replied without looking up from his plate.

Sara pushed hers away. 'But it's true, Chaim – I know it's true. I have an awful feeling – it's terrible.'

He sighed and, with a world-weary shrug, reached across the table for another potato. 'Sara, this is 1915 and I do wish you would not persist in thinking the worst of the Turk. I for one have never met with anything other than friendship and civility. If the government finds it necessary to stamp out rebellion in the Armenian villages then there is nothing we can do to stop it. Just put it out of your mind.' He waved his fork in dismissal of the subject and turned his attention back to the plate. His face took on its familiar, closed expression.

A shudder ran down Sara's spine and her heart began to pound horribly. This man was not human, she thought in disgust. There was a long moment of silence during which she stared at him, longing to swear at him, use all the Arab gutter language and shriek abuse. Her flesh crept as she looked at his cold imperturbable face.

'The Armenians now. The Jews next. How long do you think it will be before they come for us? A month? Six months? A year?' This surprised him; it was sufficiently unexpected for him to put down his fork and look at her. Outwardly Sara was calm, inwardly she was boiling.

'Don't be ridiculous, Sara. We Jews have never been anything but loyal subjects of the Empire.' For once he looked unnerved.

'So have the Armenians,' she shot back, her eyes beginning to blaze. 'How many dissenters can there be among them?' Her voice was rising steadily now in agitation as she went on: 'How great could the influence of those few dissenters be? Not many and not much would be my answers. It does not seem to stop the Turk making the whole Armenian race the prey of its ancient hatred – so why not us – what's to stop them turning on us next?' Now the contempt was clear in her voice.

Chaim pushed his plate away angrily. 'Could you not find a more opportune moment to discuss these things? You have completely spoilt my dinner.'

Her eyes blazed at his words. 'Well it's certainly spoiling the Armenians' dinners too – all two million of them.' She jumped to her feet and looked wildly round the room. Then, in a frenzy of rage, she seized a plate and hurled it to the other side of the dining room. 'That's what I think of your dinner!' she shouted wildly, a sob rising in her throat. 'You make me sick. Yes, sick. I'm sick of your cold mechanical attitude to everything. Including me,' she was screaming now, almost hysterical.

Chaim stood, his face dark. 'Sara, will you be quiet. The whole neighbourhood will hear.'

'I don't care if they hear me or not,' she yelled. 'Let everyone hear what a mean, grasping miser you are!' She burst into loud sobs, 'Let them know how you treat your wife as a cross between cook, laundress and whore!' she screamed. 'How unfeeling and callous you are!' she was driven by demons, possessed.

In seconds Chaim was beside her and with one deft sweep of his arm he slapped her a stinging blow across the face. She lost her balance and staggered back against the wall, her breath driven from her lungs in a gasp. He grabbed her arm and swung her towards him with a savage triumph, thrusting his face into hers. 'You're a curse on my life,' he snarled, 'a curse!'

Sara was too shocked for tears, she began to swell in indignation. She hated him, hated this stranger who, by putting a ring on her finger, felt he could treat her as no person had ever dared treat her before. All her fear of him fell away, leaving only a chill steeliness, which crept icily along her flesh. For a moment she stared at him. This was the end, she knew it, the final and only end. 'If you ever – ever – lay one finger on me again I will ruin you,' she said with deadly coldness. 'Do you hear me, I will ruin you. I will telegraph my father to come and fetch me and demand a return of my dowry. I swear I will.' She stood very still, her heart pounding wildly.

Chaim blanched and stared at her stupefied, realising he had gone too far. 'Now let go of my arm,' she gasped with such venom that he looked at her, startled for a moment, before relaxing his grip.

'My God, Sara,' he began, 'I'm so . . .' The look on Sara's face silenced him quickly. He was suddenly aware that Sara was staring at someone in the doorway behind him. He spun round to see Nasib, his eyes cast down, his feet scuffling the floor.

'What the hell do you want?' he barked.

Nasib mumbled something inaudible.

'What?'

'Madame Lufti is here, master,' he said with frightened eyes.

Chaim turned to Sara. 'Annie Lufti . . . good God.'

They stared at each other, equally appalled at themselves and both feeling such shame at the idea that Annie might have overheard their brawling. Neither of them moved. Then Sara gathered her wits and rushed to the mirror on the wall. Quickly she pinned up the hair that had fallen around her face and touched her cheek, which was glowing a fiery red.

'Sara,' Chaim began hesitantly. His face was strained and wretched. 'What I did was unforgivable, I don't know,' he tailed off. Sara stared at him a moment. He seemed to have shrunk visibly and she felt a stab of pity for him. It was not only his fault, she thought sadly. They were both trying to mould the other into the partner they had hoped for and, failing, had lashed out in frustration. It had taken almost a year for the marriage to deteriorate to this abysmal point, a year in which they had grown increasingly hostile to each other. What had happened this evening should not really have surprised them, it had only been a matter of time.

'It's all right, Chaim,' she said quietly. 'We'll sort ourselves out later. Let's go to Annie.'

'Madame Lufti, what a pleasure.' Chaim's voice was cracked with forced enthusiasm but Annie, who was pacing the drawing room and wringing her hands, was not in a state to notice. She gave Chaim a dismissive look and turned directly to Sara. 'I was hoping Selena would be here – she isn't, is she?'

At the words Sara went cold, knowing instinctively that everything she had feared for Selena had come to pass. The blood drained from her face and she seized the back of the nearest chair for support. 'No. She left here at about half-past four.'

'Did she say where she was going?'

'To a meeting – with community leaders – Armenians.' Sara's face brightened for a moment. 'She was with Akiff.'

'She sent Akiff home without her,' Annie said dully, sinking on to the sofa. Pale and drawn, she rummaged in her bag for a cigarette and, lighting it, took a deep breath and looked Sara straight in the eye.

'There's been trouble in Kum Kapu tonight, looting and rioting. They've arrested Armenian leaders – from the Bishop downwards. Selena's disappeared.'

There was a short silence, then Chaim stepped forward. 'Madame Lufti, is your carriage outside?'

'No, Akiff is driving the car. I thought it would be faster.'

Chaim nodded. 'Good,' he said, almost to himself. 'Look, don't worry. I'll go to Kum Kapu and look into this myself. Don't worry, I'll find Selena,' and without more ado was out of the room.

But Chaim had not found her and neither had Annie, despite the political connections she had thought would be so useful. Annie pulled strings here and promised bribes there, but to no avail. Selena had vanished – disappeared without trace.

Over the next two weeks details of events that evening began to emerge. Everyone at the meeting Selena had attended (and attended it she had) had met one of two fates. They had either been shot trying to escape or imprisoned. But Selena could not be discovered among the listed, dead or jailed.

Chaim and Annie had explored every angle. A distraught Hans Werner, caught in the thick of Gallipoli, had sent several German officers to assist in the search but, as one of them had said, there were so many different authorities involved in the arrest of people suspected of anti-Turkish activities that not even they could help. There was a strong possibility that Selena was dead, shot and thrown into the Bosphorus, but neither Sara nor Annie could accept this. They had hoped at first that she was in hiding but daily this hope was diminished. They both felt that somehow Selena would have sent a message to one of them.

No, thought Sara sadly, standing looking out of the window as she did so often these days, *she is either dead or languishing in earthly purgatory in some dungeon.* It was not unlikely that she had been thrown into some prison and forgotten about. There were more prisons in Constantinople than Sara could ever have imagined. 'Perhaps I'll never see her again,' said Sara softly, and felt the tears prick at her eyes. Selena's appearance in her life had meant so much to her; her disappearance with such startling suddenness left Sara feeling totally bereft. She turned from the window and glanced at her trunk, open and standing half-packed in the corner of the room, for Chaim had finally given Sara permission to return to Palestine for a while.

On the day after Selena's disappearance Sara had received, after two months' of no mail, a sepia postcard of the Parthenon in Athens. It was from Becky and Alex and said that they were on their way to America, Becky to study and Alex to work for the station. The card was dated the end of July, which made it over a month old.

Sara had shown Chaim the card, saying how worried she was as to why they were leaving in the middle of the war. When she had said how much she wished she could go back for a visit, she had expected him to react as he had so often before when she mentioned Palestine. But he had looked at her for a moment and then nodded.

'Very well, if you wish to visit your family I will make no objection. I will help you sort out the details and obtain the permits. You must let me know how long you plan to stay – you are coming back, I hope?' He had said this with a slight smile, but Sara had noticed a convulsive twitch in his cheek as he spoke. She told him that she would return, and she had meant it.

Since that terrible night Chaim had become touchingly thoughtful, and he was as good as his word in helping her to arrange her journey home. Here, again, was the man she had respected and once thought she could grow to love. It was ironic that she should find him again now that she was leaving. It was also ironic that only two weeks ago the thought of her imminent return home would have sent her wild with happiness; now it just buoyed her sinking spirits a little. If only they could find Selena, if only she could leave knowing that her friend was safe.

Sara sighed and half-drew the shutters. She was as good as useless anyway, powerless to do anything as she was. Crossing to the dressing table she put on her hat and pulled on her gloves. She had one last document to be stamped – the police tax form that would allow her to cross the Turkish border. She stared at her reflection for a moment, wondering if she really could bring herself to leave Constantinople without any knowledge of Selena's fate – whatever it may have been. She doubted it but would go and get the stamp anyway. It was something to do, something to blank out her eternal worries about Selena.

Sara stood indecisively in the cavernous hall of the police headquarters. Men, women and children of every description – nomads, tribesmen, townspeople – stood around in knots or sat on the tiled floor gossiping, weeping or sleeping. To the left a large, stone staircase led to the upstairs offices, the wall in front of it covered with brass plates. Telling Nasib to stay by the main doors Sara threaded her way through the crowd to the plaques. *Typical Turks*, she fumed. The notice that read 'Tax Department' omitted to say on which floor its offices were found. But, on closer inspection, Sara saw an arrow pointing to the stairs to the lower floor.

Sara ran down the steps. It was far less busy in the basement and thankfully much cooler. Taking a breath of relief, she followed the arrows down a corridor. Several turns later Sara realised she was in the wrong part of the building. She retraced her steps but could not find her way back to the stairs and stopped, hopelessly lost, to try and find her bearings.

The light was very dim now and Sara felt a twinge of alarm. The building was an old fortress, the atmosphere far from reassuring. She turned another corner but, seeing a man being escorted down the passageway away from her, she stood motionless. The guards were punching and kicking him, pushing him along with their bastinados every time he faltered. Sara noticed that his hands were tied behind his back and that a thin wound oozed blood from his cheek on to a torn white shirt. Sara stood rooted to the spot, horrified at what she saw and convinced that she should not stay, nor be found here.

She spun round to leave the place, and found herself face to face with a police officer in a smartly-pressed uniform. Sara held back her instinctive cry of fright and looked at him as boldly as she could. The man stared back at her with calm brown eyes.

'Are you looking for someone, madame?' His tone was polite and his attitude not unfriendly, but Sara was flooded with panic.

She nodded, trying to collect herself. 'I'm looking for the tax department – a Captain,' she fumbled in her bag to find the name of the man who had already been bribed to stamp her travel paper.

'Capain Fardhi?' said the officer helpfully.

'Yes, yes that's it,' she stammered and managed a smile.

The officer smiled back. 'It's easy to get lost down here,' he agreed, stopping at the sound of doors being pushed noisily open. Sara wheeled round to see a young girl being dragged out of a room, her clothes ripped, her hair wild and loose around her face. The two guards laughed as she lost her balance and almost fell.

Sara froze. *It couldn't be . . .* The girl with the swollen face and long black hair regained her balance and walked forward. *It wasn't?* Sara, her heart pounding, let her handbag fall to the ground where it skidded along the hard, tiled floor, bursting open, its contents clattering down the corridor. The officer bent to pick them up and the two guards stopped a moment to look. The dark girl turned her head and for an instant their eyes met. Then the guards grabbed her arm again and with a push sent Selena stumbling through another doorway.

There was a small silence before Sara collected her wits enough to bend and mechanically help the officer to retrieve her things, forcing herself to resist the impulse to knock him on the head, steal his gun and take Selena to freedom. As she spoke platitudes to the man, stuffing everything back into the bag, she knew that she must do one thing: see Annie. And as soon as possible. Only she could pull the necessary strings to ensure Selena was released.

When the officer stood up Sara was composed. 'Thank you for your help. I'm always amazed at how much we women carry around with us,' she said with a weak smile and snapped the bag shut.

'If you would like to follow me, I will show you to the correct office.' Sara followed him meekly along the corridors until he left her on a corner. 'Just along there on your right,' he said, and with a nod and a bow turned back.

The moment he was out of sight Sara ran up the stairs and across the hall to Nasib. She grabbed the startled boy by the arm and pulled him to the exit. She had no time to waste. Selena's life depended on her.

Sara, who had been waiting impatiently for Annie all day, rushed to the door as soon as she heard the car draw up. As Annie walked into the hall, Sara gave her a questioning look. Annie smiled and Sara let out a huge sigh of relief. These had been the two longest days of her life.

'Is Chaim here?' asked Annie, and Sara nodded. 'Good, I need him,' she said, walking into the drawing room. She exchanged greetings with Chaim and sat down on the sofa. 'It's all arranged,' she spoke in an exhausted voice, 'but there are several conditions. The first is where I need you, Chaim – a Turkish citizen must become responsible for Selena while she remains on Turkish soil. I'm hoping you will sign for her.'

'Yes, of course,' Chaim said quickly.

'What do you mean about as long as she remains on Turkish soil?' asked Sara.

Annie sighed. 'I'm coming to that. The orders for release – the details – everything is in my handbag. We are going to fetch her now, but the authority to release her is given on condition that she leaves Turkey by the end of next week.'

'Next week? But where will she go?' cried Sara. 'She has nowhere – it is criminal.'

'There is nothing we can do about it,' said Annie wearily. 'However I have, with the greatest difficulty, managed to make the travel arrangements for her. She is booked on the train Sara is catching to Rayak – Selena will go on to Beirut and from there board a ship for America.'

'America?'

Annie nodded. 'I have friends there who will take good care of her. I've even managed to arrange for a special set of papers to be issued for her – at a price,' she added bitterly. She looked at Sara. 'I had to make a lot of decisions on the spot, without consulting you. I thought it would be a nice idea for you to travel together.

She might be very weak, and will need your help.'

'Yes, yes, of course, it's a good idea.'

'Right. We must go.' Annie said, standing up. 'What do the conditions matter? Getting her out is the only thing that counts.'

The police station was quiet, nothing like it had been two days before. A sergeant showed them into a small ante room and introduced a small, balding man who looked like a clerk. 'This man is dealing with your problem,' they were told, and they were left with him.

The clerk asked Annie to show him the papers, read them, turned to Chaim and asked: 'Are you the citizen taking responsibility?'

'I am,' he said.

'The lady is in there,' the man said, pointing at a door. 'Please will you identify her.'

Chaim walked quickly to the door and opened it. He looked briefly into the room and returned straight to the desk. 'Yes, that is Selena Gabriel.'

The atmosphere relaxed a little. 'Sign here please.' Chaim read the document carefully before putting his name to it while Sara watched, exploding with impatience, but knowing that for once Chaim was wise to be pedantic.

The clerk took back the document and stamped and folded it. 'That will be all,' he said.

Annie and Sara looked at each other, white with expectation. They took each other's arms for support and crossed to the door of the room which held Selena.

She was sitting on a wooden bench; stiffly, as though she were afraid to move without permission. She looked so small and childlike wrapped in a big, black cloak that both women felt tears swim into their eyes. They ran to her and held her. Only then did Selena attempt to rise. She said nothing as the women embraced her, smiling wanly. Some attempt had been made to patch her up, but the filth and the bruises were obvious. She looked sick, broken and afraid, her eyes staring emptily at them. Annie and Sara, appalled at her condition, could only hold her and murmur words of encouragement.

Selena was so weak that Chaim had to carry her to the waiting car. He held her with an unaccustomed gentleness, then propped her between Sara and Annie on the back seat. Selena sat between them, each hand in one of theirs, but she could feel only exhaustion as the car drove out of the gates that swung open before them.

CHAPTER EIGHTEEN

The Haidar Pasha station was a stinking, dirty, noisy mass of humanity. The platform was packed to overflowing with soldiers rushing in every direction, shouting a cacophony of orders and counter-orders at the tops of their voices. This was the entry to the war for troops, armaments and provisions for two battle fronts and, although Sara had known this fact, it was only now that she perceived its reality.

Her excitement at the impending journey had been building up all day and that, combined with the worries of the past few weeks, threw her into a high state of nerves, and she clung on to Chaim's arm for protection against the jostling crowd. A group of dervishes twisted and whirled to the monotonous tone of the shawn pipe, pushing through Sara's little group in their progress. Sara turned her eyes away from the sight of their faces, contorted with religious ecstasy. It made her feel uneasy and confused.

Sara had been so eager to leave Constantinople, to be reunited with her family in Palestine, that until now she had taken little heed of the fears expressed by Chaim and everyone else about the dangers of women travelling alone in wartime. Now, faced with the reality of the arduous journey across harsh, forbidding wilderness, she felt her confidence shrinking under the immensity of it all.

Shaking her head free of these sudden nagging doubts she told herself that everything would be all right. Annie had managed, God bless her and only she knew how she had done it, to secure a whole compartment for the two girls. Looking towards the carriage, Sara wished the station master would blow his first whistle so that she could finish these interminable goodbyes and set off at last. The trunks were stowed, Selena was tucked up in their compartment with their personal belongings; they were ready to go.

Selena's face was pressed up against the compartment window. Her eyes were closed, and she seemed to have fallen asleep. Sara realised that Annie was staring anxiously at Selena too, and exchanged a glance with her. Over the four days since her release from prison she had regained a little of her strength, but now they were less concerned with her physical than with her mental strength. The train snorted a cloud of acrid steam and smoke and Annie, dressed in red and purple, which outshone even the most resplendent of the officers' uniforms, turned and hugged Sara.

'Look after yourself, darling,' she said a little tearfully, 'and Selena.'

They looked at each other through the drifting clouds of steam, both reluctant to relinquish the close friendship they had formed over the last few weeks. 'Don't worry, Annie. I'll take good care of her. You know I will.' Her voice was barely audible above the hiss of steam, but Annie nodded.

Sara turned to Chaim. Although he was trying hard to put on a brave face he looked miserable about her departure. For the last half hour he had kept saying her name. *Perhaps he is more fond of me than I thought*, Sara wondered, remembering all the kindness he had shown her over the last few weeks. She studied him carefully and felt a pang of nostalgia she could never have foreseen. She could almost forget the snarling insults and general mistreatment; he seemed a different person. Her heart went out to him for a moment, as if he were in truth a loved husband.

She touched his arm gently. 'I think I had better get on now.'

Chaim assented and, taking her elbow, led her to the steps of the train. He looked worried. 'A pity there are no purdah compartments on military trains,' he said, nodding towards the soldiers who hung from the train doors openly admiring his willowy, blonde wife. 'Don't forget to keep the blinds down and lock the compartment door the moment the train leaves the station.'

'Don't worry, Chaim, we'll be fine,' Sara answered lightly.

'If you have any problems, don't forget Colonel Schmidt,' he said, indicating the next compartment.

Sara turned her head to glance at a German Colonel with a waxed moustache, who was hanging out of the window next to her. Hans Werner, still in the field hospital with his leg shot up, had gone to great pains to find a fellow officer who would be travelling on

the same train as the girls and would offer them some measure of protection. The German caught her eye and smiled. He looked
gentlemanly and wore the Iron Cross First Class around his neck, but
his travelling companion was a different proposition: a Turkish
Captain with a face the colour and consistency of pork lard, who
gave her a leering smile. Sara hurriedly averted her glance. Thank
goodness they're only going as far as Aleppo, she thought.

Chaim took her shoulder gently. 'I just want you to know things
will be different when you come back, Sara. Don't stay away too
long, will you?' He was gazing at her almost in supplication and
Sara listened to him with a sudden wild hope. Perhaps it could
happen: that they might come to love each other. She could not
accept that the marriage was, in any true sense, over, but in the
bleak honesty of her heart, she knew that things could never
resolve themselves differently.

'No, I won't,' she said quietly.

'Good, good.' Sara heard relief in those two words but also,
suspiciously, a note of triumph. 'Well, goodbye,' he said gravely
and kissed her awkwardly. 'I shall miss you.' He then reluctantly
released her shoulder. He sounded oddly, almost foolishly, doting.
Sara had to look down for a moment to hide her embarrassment
before gathering up her skirts and mounting the compartment
steps.

The train gave a roar and belched another cloud of damp steam
over their heads. The station master blew his whistle and porters
began to run the length of the platform, slamming doors shut. Sara
paused on the compartment steps and raised a hand in farewell to
Annie.

'Insist that Selena call all those people in the States,' Annie
bellowed, her voice hoarser than ever with suppressed emotion.

Sara nodded, smiling. If Selena lived another fifty years, she
would never have time to visit a quarter of Annie's friends. She
blew Annie a kiss and, with a last lingering look at Chaim, entered
the train.

Selena was hunched up tightly in the corner of the compartment.
She was dozing, her brow and cheeks flushed and a dewy
moustache of sweat hovered above her lip. The carriage was very
hot indeed but Sara, remembering Chaim's instructions, pulled
down the blinds to shut out the curious stares of the soldiers who
packed the corridors of even the first-class carriages.

She crossed to the window to let some air in, but the sash was stuck. She pulled at it irritably, then made a helpless gesture as the train lurched forward at last. She stood and watched until the train pulled out of the station, gaining momentum as the figures of Annie and Chaim grew smaller and smaller and finally disappeared.

Then, with a deep sigh, she unpinned her hat, tossed it on the food hampers stacked in the corner and sank back wearily on to the red velvet seat. She looked at Selena and her heart contracted with pity for her. Her lovely face was still swollen and covered with angry blemishes. When they had taken her home from the prison and undressed her, they had found cigarette burns all over her breasts and thighs. The realisation of what Selena had suffered at the hands of her gaolers made Sara sick to the soul.

Selena never mentioned what had happened during those two weeks. The day before Sara had tried to draw Selena out about it, but Selena's eyes implored Sara so despairingly that she had not dared to continue.

Sara's head fell back on to the seat as she let the sound of the wheels lull her into calm. The wheels gathered speed, quickening in their haste to take her back to Palestine – home. Joy rose within her and with it a terrible desire to be with her family again. And Daniel. She thought of him with an unexpected pang. She wondered where he was and what he was doing. Perhaps he was in love. Perhaps he was in bed with Isobelle Frank at this very moment. Only a year ago the very thought would have been enough to overwhelm her with jealousy; now she could smile at the concept. It was not so much that her feelings for Daniel had changed as that they had fallen into step with the grand order of things.

She closed her eyes. She would find out about Daniel soon enough, she supposed. But first there were hundred and hundreds of miles to cross. As she fell asleep the wheels seemed to be singing 'going home . . . going home . . . going home . . . going home . . .'.

CHAPTER NINETEEN

Cairo, Egypt

Nothing could have been further from Daniel's mind than Isobelle
Frank or any other woman. He was sitting, surrounded by dusty
palms, in an alcove between the lounge and the ballroom of the
Savoy Hotel, Cairo. Every week one or other of the hotels gave a
ball and tonight it was the turn of the Savoy. Daniel sipped
moodily at his drink and watched the mixture of expatriate hotel
society and British officers in their Egyptian Army mess kit
preparing to enjoy themselves. His eyes swept over the marble
floors, the huge gilt mirrors, the shining candelabra, the tables
loaded with delicacies. Were it not for the swarming military
presence one would never know that there was a war on, he
thought cynically and wondered how long Egyptian society could
live in such luxury, encircled as it was by potential battlefields.

A lovely dark-haired woman, whose supple body was poured
into a silver gown that left little of her charms to the imagination,
passed by and looked curiously at Daniel. She searched his eyes for
a moment and then her face was lit up with a spontaneous and
charming smile as she moved on. Daniel noticed but was not
stirred by her beauty.

He shifted his gaze to a group of Egyptian businessmen huddled
together in the lounge discussing the fluctuations in the grain
market and sighed. Nothing was going to lift this depression from
him, for that morning all his hopes had tumbled about his ears and
he knew that he was going to have to go home and admit failure.
He had been ordered out of the country at twenty-four hours'
notice on pain of imprisonment and the next morning he was
going to have to pack his bags and make his way back to Palestine
across the Sinai. He had never doubted his ultimate success yet
now he was forced to acknowledge defeat.

Everything had begun so well! The passage to Cairo had been so smooth that he had hardly noticed he had left Palestine before he was being waved through the officials at Port Said and was out on Egyptian territory. His luck held and he found Paul and Eve Levy's house almost immediately, where he was given a tremendous welcome.

Paul had been turned down for the army. 'Flat feet' he admitted disgustedly, but he had made many friends among the junior officers stationed in the city and introduced Daniel at once. Daniel knew that it was vital to see a top intelligence officer at the Arab Bureau; to do anything less would be to endanger the lives of everyone involved with Aaron and his plans.

It had taken Daniel almost a month of continuing and frustrating effort to secure the interview he had had that morning with Colonel Thompson of Staff Intelligence at the Arab Bureau. Everything hung on the few minutes the Colonel would give him, and Daniel had been determined to make the right impression at once.

But the two men had taken an instant and violent dislike to each other. Daniel had seen a red-faced Englishman (could none of them acclimatise to the sun?) with plastered-down, sandy hair and Colonel Thompson had seen a smooth, good-looking foreigner, who managed to look cool even in this atrocious climate. The Colonel had not smiled when Daniel walked into the room, but had studied him for a moment with cold grey eyes before motioning him into the seat opposite his desk. Daniel sensed the man's hostility and his optimism and good humour vanished in the face of it. Never mind, he was not here on a social call, he told himself.

The office was spartan: a broken fan whirred irregularly overhead; the desk was meticulously tidy and the walls bare but for a portrait of King George in court dress. A stern-faced woman watched over the interview from a photograph on the desk.

The two men had sat in silence for a moment, weighing each other up and waiting for the other to speak.

'Well, and what can I do for you?' the Colonel had finally asked, his voice clipped almost to incomprehensibility.

Daniel took immediate offence at the man's tone but was determined to curb his irritation. He needed this man's co-operation more than he had ever needed anything in his life, and he was not going to wreck his chances by hot-headedness.

'My name is Daniel Rosen,' he had spoken calmly and politely.

'I am an associate of Aaron Levinson, the scientist, who heads the American research station at Atlit in Palestine.'

The Colonel's pale eyebrows disappeared behind his plastered-down forelock. 'So you're a Jew?'

'Yes, sir, and I am here as a representative of a small group of Palestinian Jews headed by Aaron Levinson. We are in a unique position to offer you information about the Turkish situation in Syria and Palestine.' He had paused for a moment to see the Colonel's reaction, but a witchdoctor's mask would have been more expressive so, after shifting a little in his chair, he had continued undaunted.

'Recently Palestine and Syria were badly hit by a plague of locusts. Jemel Pasha himself ordered us to help stamp them out. As a direct result of this, our men have been in every military camp and,' Daniel had fumbled for the right English words, '. . . arms dump across the length and breadth of Syria and Palestine. With the locust patrol as cover we have collected a great deal of military information that could well be invaluable to you when you open the Palestinian front.'

The Colonel turned his hard grey eyes on Daniel. 'And how much would you fellows want for this . . . information?' It was easy to sort out the enemy agents by the prices they asked.

Daniel had frowned. 'You seem to misunderstand me. We do not wish for payment.'

Now the Colonel was at last surprised, but he carefully kept all expression from his face and eyes. 'Then what do you want?'

Daniel allowed himself a small smile. 'Freedom from the Turk and eventual independence,' he said simply.

Thompson wondered briefly whether he was dealing with a lunatic zealot and filled his pipe to give himself time to consider. It was not his job to think in broad political terms and he was not at all sure he believed a word of what this young man had told him. A load of cock and bull, it seemed to him. Rosen – German name, wasn't it? God knew what the Bosch would think up next.

Under Daniel's steady gaze he had shuffled his travel papers on the desk in front of him and had glanced over them again.

'So your name is Rosen and you are a Palestinian Jew?' he had barked out.

Daniel had nodded, feeling suddenly apprehensive. Although the Colonel was maintaining a cool politeness, Daniel could sense his hostility and had not missed the sudden change in mood.

261

'It says on your papers that your name is Ramones and you are a citizen of Spain,' the Colonel had coolly observed.

'I borrowed those, sir,' Daniel had fought against the sinking feeling which threatened to overwhelm him. He must keep control of the interview or all was lost.

'Why don't you carry your own papers?' the Colonel had asked.

Daniel looked at him, exasperated at the man's stupidity. 'With my own papers I would never have got here,' he had snapped, the anger showing in his voice.

Insolent puppy, thought the Colonel and continued with his questions. 'No one is allowed to travel without their own papers. You, as a Palestinian, are a citizen of an enemy country. You have also flagrantly broken the law. Now would you please show me your own identity papers?' and he had reached an autocratic hand across the vast desk.

The sweat broke out on Daniel's back as he faced the fact that this barbarian did not believe him – had decided not to believe him – and would not change his mind. He told himself to keep calm but was finding it increasingly difficult.

'Now tell me,' the Colonel had continued with nerve-wracking politeness, his small red-rimmed eyes fixed firmly on his prey, 'what you have really come for.'

Daniel had desperately tried to contain the panic and anger that was sweeping through him. 'Colonel, in the name of God I have told you the truth . . . you don't understand.'

'I fear it is you who do not understand,' the Colonel had broken in. 'I could have you arrested for travelling without proper identification,' he paused for a moment, still watching. 'But I have decided against that. I will give you twenty-four hours to leave Egypt. If you are not out of the country by this time tomorrow, I will have you thrown into jail. Now good day, Mr – er Rosen?'

In seconds Daniel's last vestiges of self-control had vanished. Rising to his feet he had snatched his papers from the startled Colonel's grasp. To have travelled so far, risked so much, only to be faced with such blind stupidity was more than he could bear. Shaking with rage, but aware of the staff in the outer office, he kept his voice low as he said, 'I have heard it said that the British are lions led by donkeys but this is the first time I have fully appreciated what that means. *You are a donkey, Colonel Thompson*. Upon your back you carry many British lives – they might have been safe if you had listened to me with the faintest glimmer of intelligence. Good day.'

Swinging round, he had collided in the doorway with a young officer. Angry as he was he could not help but be arrested for a moment by the man's extraordinarily pale blue eyes. Daniel had the feeling that the young man had heard – and enjoyed – his speech at the Colonel's expense.

'Excuse me,' said Daniel and skirted round the soldier.

'Rum beggars these Jews,' were the last words he heard as he strode away from the office.

Rum beggar indeed, thought Daniel, still angry at the memory.

'D'you mind if I sit here a moment – I've just got to jot a few things down.' The American accent startled Daniel and he swung his head to see a large, heavy-set civilian lower himself into the chair next to him.

Daniel stared blankly at him for a second before coming to his senses. 'No, of course not,' he said quickly and watched the American pull a small writing pad and pencil from his pocket. Daniel bent forward. 'You're a reporter?'

'Correct. Frank Walworth's the name,' said the American, looking up with a wide grin. Then he put on the eyeglasses dangling from a chain round his neck, leafed a few pages through his pad and, licking the pencil butt, bent over to write.

'A drink, sir?'

Daniel looked up to see a tall Nubian waiter in an embroidered monkey jacket and red tarboosh standing in front of him with an empty tray in his hand. Out of the corner of his eye he noticed a familiar-looking British Lieutenant-Colonel enter the lounge alone and thought he might as well make a last ditch attempt to collar someone of importance before he had to leave. 'A raki,' he said to the waiter without taking his eyes from the officer.

'Make that two, there's a good chap, Abdul,' said a pleasant voice with a clear-cut British accent. 'And a dose of bourbon for my friend Walworth here.'

Daniel turned to see the officer he had bumped into on his way out of Thompson's office taking the chair on his other side and sprawling comfortably into it.

'Not for me, Lawrence, I've got work to do,' said the American without looking up. 'Next time, maybe,' he added with an anxious glance at his watch. 'I've got a line booked to New York – can't miss it.' He stood, snapping his notebook shut, and ambled off. Daniel watched his bulky form dodge round a palm and disappear, then turned back to the Englishman.

'You're the Palestinian who gave Thompson what for this morning, aren't you?' said the officer. 'What an ass that man is – gives me constipation just mentioning his name.'

Daniel laughed, liking the man's irreverence (which extended to his sloppily done-up uniform) and hypnotised once again by those astounding blue eyes. 'My name is Lawrence and my rank is friend,' said the officer, holding out his hand for Daniel to shake.

'Good, I badly need a friend right now,' he said earnestly.

Lawrence smiled. 'Bit of bad luck landing with old Thompson. Mind you the Bureau's stuffed full of chaps like that, sitting on their nice, warm, incompetent shelves bungling everything they touch. Exasperating!' The Nubian arrived with two glasses of clear liquid and set them on the table with a jug of iced water. Lawrence thanked him in fluent Arabic and poured water into the two glasses. Daniel watched in silence as the clear liquid turned a milky white. 'To friendship,' Lawrence said and Daniel raised his glass in the toast.

'Certainly – if our interests are the same,' he said and took a gulp.

'I should think they might be. I heard something of your story. Rather romantic it seemed to me. Where in Palestine are you from?'

Daniel was instantly on his guard. However friendly this man appeared, he was a complete stranger and Daniel did not want to fall into any traps.

Lawrence smiled. 'So you don't trust me. Well, you're probably right not to. God knows this city is a hotbed of intrigue and confusion – on every level.' He hesitated a moment and took a sip of raki. Daniel's mind ticked over furiously. He might be foolish, but something in this blond stranger's manner inspired trust.

He smiled back and held out his hand. 'I'm Daniel Rosen, I was born in Hadera and my story – well whatever you heard of it, is all true.'

Lawrence grasped his hand and shook it cordially.

'I thought it was. So you're a friend of Aaron Levinson's. I met him once a few years ago – a brilliant chap. Had a very pretty sister as far as I remember.'

'Sara,' Daniel said, amazed.

'That sounds right. It must have been five or six years ago. When I was at Oxford I went on a tour of Syrian and Palestinian Crusader castles to get material for a thesis together. I've hated the Turks ever since,' he added confidentially, knocking back his raki in one gulp. 'Care for another?' and he signalled for the waiter.

Daniel nodded, but his mind was not on drink. After so much disappointment, he thought he could see a glimmer of hope. 'Why are you interested in my story?' he asked.

'Because, old chap, it seems to me you're genuine and could be of some use to us against the Turk.'

'Do you have sympathy for the idea of a Jewish State?' Daniel's eyes shone with excitement.

'Personally I think it's a lost cause – there aren't enough Jews,' Lawrence said. 'But I do think Palestine should be a self-governing Jewish province under Arab sovereignty.'

Daniel shrugged helplessly. Here was yet another Englishman fallen under the spell of the Arab – why were they all so fascinated by them?

'But we'll leave all that to the politicians,' Lawrence said lightly.

'Ah, there is honour among thieves, but not among politicians. I have a feeling we'll learn that to our cost,' Daniel answered.

Their second drink arrived and Lawrence drained his in one again. 'I must go,' he said, rising to his feet. And in a low voice added, 'Go and see Lieutenant Woolley at Port Said. He's in charge of naval intelligence. Tell him I sent you. He's a great chap and a rarity over here – he's not afraid to act on his own initiative.' He chuckled. 'He'd rather die than live in Tunbridge Wells.'

Daniel wondered what was wrong with Tunbridge Wells and stood, grinning, to shake hands. 'Thank you very much for everything. You were heaven sent.'

Lawrence laughed. 'Not many round here think of me that way – oh and by the way, if you get a chance, take a look at the map I drew of Sinai. The War Office asked for it. Some of it is fairly accurate, but some shows my imagination! Pretty though – three colours!'

Daniel laughed. 'I won't give you away,' he promised.

'Well, see you in Jerusalem some time,' said Lawrence and left with a wave.

'Next year in Jerusalem,' Daniel repeated softly in Hebrew, echoing the time-honoured prayer, and sat down again, watching the fair-headed officer until he was out of sight. He felt optimism returning. Tomorrow he would go to Port Said and find Lieutenant Woolley. Tonight . . . the loose-limbed brunette in the silver dress crossed his line of vision again and this time Daniel felt himself respond to the invitation. He stood up and smiled back.

'Would you care for a drink?' he asked.

Sara, sitting in semi-darkness behind the tightly-shuttered windows of this shabby train to which they had transferred the night before, felt no closer to home than she had when she had steamed out of the Haidar Pasha station almost eleven days earlier. By now Selena should have reached Beirut and Sara should have been well on her way to Haifa. But they had not yet crossed the Syrian border and, apart from anything else, it was now clear that Selena would not be boarding a ship bound for America. In fact, Sara was praying that she would live long enough to reach Aleppo.

Sara stared anxiously at Selena who was sunk into the corner of the wooden bench, the milky light filtering through the cracks in the shutters making her seem more pallid than ever. Sara felt the now familiar wave of worry and sorrow that weighed continually like a heavy black stone on her heart. Last night, after having been transported across the Amanus Mountains in a cart and then carried on to yet another train, Selena had fallen from a fever into a coma-like stupor.

After the first four or five days of travel, it had become clear to Sara that what she had taken for the symptoms of shock was something much more serious. Selena sat, her face quiet, her hands folded neatly in her lap, saying nothing for hours on end. When she did speak she stumbled over the simplest words, her huge brown eyes glazing over into an odd, vacant stare, her face looking smaller and whiter than ever. She barely ate, tasting the food only when Sara's coaxing came close to force. If Sara tried to speak to her she would shake herself, and close her eyes as a bar to further conversation.

Sara already knew that there was no hope of Selena's travelling to her ship alone and had made up her mind to accompany her to the port. Once on the ship she would be looked after until her arrival in New York, where Annie's friends could be trusted to take over.

But when the fevers began, Sara's hopes sank. Selena was seriously ill — and Sara was now convinced that she was suffering from one of the two epidemics raging at the moment: cholera and typhoid. The two words had beaten at each other in her brain as she tried to remember what she knew about them. Sara's mother's and Fatma's words came back to her over an unimaginably long distance. High fever following a pattern – up and down in stages until it reached a climax from which a patient recovered or died. So Selena had the dreaded typhoid.

When Sara realised this, they were only a day's journey away from Muslimie Junction, just north of Aleppo, which was the only town where Sara could be sure of finding a European doctor and sanctuary. Sara had immediately appealed to the German officer recommended the by Hans Werner, and he had done all he could to ease their journey, responding to her request with calm efficiency.

The railway system was ridiculously complicated. They had already had to porter themselves with their luggage three times across the mountain ranges where tunnels, started years before, had never been completed. Each time Sara had been grateful for the existence of Colonel Schmidt, although she grew increasingly wary of the Turkish Captain. Selena shrunk in fear from the Turk from the first time she saw him while Sara, noticing how much more frequently his short rap came at the door of their compartment, had quietly transferred a sharp knife from the food hamper to her travelling bag, which she always kept near her. But now the obviousness of Selena's illness kept the Turk, and all other travellers, well away from their carriage.

It seemed to Sara that the train had stopped every five minutes for days. And now, with the sea blockade preventing the movement of coal, the train was crawling along on an odd mixture of wood, cotton seed and dried camel dung. She was still sitting in semi-darkness, blinds drawn against the unrelenting morning heat. The Colonel had told them that they were only forty miles from Aleppo – *Aleppo*, thought Sara longingly, *city of fountains, orchards of sweet apricots and doctors. Above all, doctors.* She looked at Selena in worried desperation. *If only we could move*, she thought, her fingers pulling restlessly at her clothes and praying for the train to move, promising God all manner of things if only Selena would live. The train gave a shudder, a whistle and a roar.

'Thank God,' Sara breathed as the train rattled into action. She rested back on the bench again, her eyes closed. After what felt like only a moment or two Selena woke with a little cry. Sara moved over to her and took her hand. To her joy, it felt cooler than before and, although she still seemed feverish, her temperature was obviously dropping. Sara whispered a prayer of thanks. It would be so much easier once they reached Aleppo. She dampened a handkerchief from the water bottle and gently wiped Selena's forehead. 'Don't speak,' she said tenderly. 'We must be nearly at Muslimie Junction. Colonel Schmidt will arrange transport for us to Aleppo. I'll find you a doctor there. Everything will be all right – I promise.'

Selena gave her a faint smile and closed her eyes. She no longer cared about living, and had already prepared herself for the blessed relief of death, but she found that her body had acquired a will of its own. 'Water,' she mumbled through chapped lips, her voice thick and slurred.

Sara lifted the water bottle and held it to her lips while she sipped weakly. Then she laid Selena's head carefully back on the seat. The carriage was airless and a nauseating stench had begun to seep into the atmosphere. Sara rose and moved to the window, hoping that the breeze now they were moving might alleviate the stifling atmosphere. She raised the shutter and blinked as the sun blinded her eyes. She blinked again at what she thought she had seen and stifled a scream in her throat.

The sight that met her eyes on the other side of the glass was so shocking that it was to remain engraved on her mind until the day she died. Sara closed her eyes and opened them again, hoping against hope that what she saw was some sick fantasy produced by her over-tired brain.

On every side of the carriage, as far as she could see, was an undulating stream of stumbling, shifting, half naked men, women and children. There were thousands, perhaps tens of thousands of them, bent, wretched and skeleton-thin. They moved forward in near silence, more like some sub-human race than human beings. Men scuffled along, roped together until one fell, when the septieh would ride over and club viciously before cutting him loose and leaving him to die. Hundreds had fallen dead alongside the track, their swollen tongues protruding between caked, cracked lips. Hundreds more lay half-dead, moaning in the dust or waiting passively for the inevitable end. Children, some no more than babes in arms, lay dead and dying while their half-demented mothers shrieked wildly beside their tiny bodies. Turkish and Arab women wandered among the dead and dying, picking the rags from their bodies. Wild dogs sniffed round, waiting for their turn to scavenge the dead and high above buzzards and vultures circled in the warm air currents, wary of the train but patiently waiting for the feast below.

Sara grasped the window frame, her head turned giddy and her stomach heaved in sickening waves of nausea. A terrible tormented groan escaped Selena, who had risen beside her and was clinging heavily to her arm. Some part of Sara wanted to face Selena and turn away from the horror. How she wanted to look away – block out this evil – but she was held spellbound, haunted and terrified in a way she had never known before.

As the train went on, the scenes became more and more violent and obscene. A woman, babbling like a half wit, kept pace with the train for a short while, her huge blue eyes staring blankly into Sara's carriage, before a septieh rode up behind her and rained blows on her head with the flat of his sword. At that sight something flexed in Sara like a muscle ready for action. It was not pity, nor even fear, but an anger so hot that it seared her brain, made her heart drum wildly, then exploded inside her. She began shaking hysterically. She was almost ready to leap from the train and attack the septieh with her bare hands, but a cool voice spoke quietly from some distant corner of her brain. *Don't be a fool. Keep calm. There is nothing you can do. You are as helpless as a wave dashed against a rocky shore.*

Sara knew she was witnessing all the horror Selena had envisaged in Constantinople: the ordeal of the Armenians. Once it seemed so unlikely but here she was, looking from the safety of a carriage window on to helpless droves of humanity. The Turks were keeping their promise to 'exterminate the subversive element' and, as she watched, Sara knew that the irrevocable horror would stalk her soul to the very end.

And then she realised that the Germans must know about this damnation. Surely Christian morality bound them to put an end to this horrendous denial of God's word?

A sharp pain in her arm made her turn to Selena, who was clutching her fiercely, her fingers pressing her flesh to the bone. Sara's heart gave a lurch as a new horror seized her. Dear God, Selena was Armenian. If this were known, she would be forced to join the multitude of her fellow damned – forced to share their hideous fate. She could do nothing for those thousands of wretched innocents, but she could do something for Selena.

Suddenly invigorated, she tore Selena's hand from her arm and threw her back on to her bench. Then she closed the window with a bang and pulled down the shutter with clumsy, trembling hands. The weakness and shaking in her legs increased and she sank on to her seat in a dizzy, nauseous spell. She dropped her head between her knees and clapped her fists over her ears, eyes tightly shut. She had to keep her brain clear to think – think constructively. Tears ached behind her eyes but she would not release them. She must concentrate.

She dug her fingers into her hair. Nothing in her life had prepared her for this horror. She needed a vision, a sign to tell her what to do. *There is no problem that doesn't have an answer. There is a solution to everything.* She kept telling herself. *All I must do is hold on to my reason and find the answer and everything will be all right.* But then despair overtook her again – *this is the East, here there are no sure answers to anything.*

She dropped her hands and raised her head. Selena was sitting on the edge of the seat, her eyes closed and her face so still and pale that for a sickening moment Sara thought the shock had killed her. She knelt on the floor beside her friend and feverishly searched for Selena's pulse. It was faint, but it was there. 'Selena, Selena,' she whispered, gently stroking her clammy forehead.

Sara rose unsteadily and began to rummage through her travelling bag for smelling salts. She was shaking so badly that everything slipped from between her fingers. The sense of her own inadequacy began to overpower her and once more she struggled against the threatening tears, and angrily tipped the contents of her bag out on to the seat, the desire to weep growing stronger.

Why was all this happening to her? Why did the train have to stop? Why was she the one who had to witness such a terrible sight? *I just can't believe it, I just can't believe I saw such a thing with my own eyes*, she thought, close to hysteria now. The smelling salts rolled on to the floor and Sara was shocked from her self-pity by Selena, who had begun to moan softly, beseeching the Holy Mother to help her. Sara almost joined her in prayer, but would not appeal to a God who had obviously forsaken this terrible land. It was the Devil who ruled here. Suddenly resolute again she took hold of the bottle, had a quick sniff herself and then waved it to and fro under Selena's nose.

Selena choked a little and weakly pushed it away. All the memories of the terrible things the Turks had made her do – things

270

she could never tell anyone – had reverberated in her skull until she thought she would go mad. Now, although she felt desperately ill and the fear, so much fear, was still inside her, she felt that she was returning from the hell into which she had fallen. Her anger raged within her like a cleansing fire and wiped clean all the terrible shame she thought she would not be able to live with. The great weight which had been almost too heavy to bear had lifted at the sight of the anguish and agony of her people – the horrendous mockery of God and the Saviour.

For the first time in days she no longer wished for death. She could let herself lie down and die with her people but she would not. She wanted to live – to live for them.

'Selena!' Sara's voice brought Selena slowly back from her thoughts. Her eyes fluttered open, and Sara saw they were no longer dull and glazed and that there was a little colour in her cheeks.

Selena looked steadily at Sara and gave her a faint smile. 'Don't worry, I'm all right now,' she whispered, her voice still hoarse. 'I'm going to live to repay the Turk for what they have done to my people.' She closed her eyes again and Sara had to bend forward to catch her words: 'Living is the only way I know how.'

Sara looked at her, stunned. The Selena she knew and loved had been transported back to her. Hope welled up in her as she patted Selena's hand and then put her feet up on to the bench. 'Here,' she said, tucking a shawl around her, 'you'll be more comfortable like this. Now sleep – we'll be at Muslimie Junction soon and you'll need all the strength you have.'

She watched Selena for a few moments until she was sure she was asleep, then sat on her own seat and looked out between the cracks in the shutters. There was only a flat sun beating down on a parched countryside. The thousands had vanished from view. She had a notion that perhaps she had dreamed it all, but she remembered the Armenian woman's blue eyes gazing into hers and knew it had really happened.

I'll never forget that sight. I'll see it every day of my life, she whispered to herself and with an effort she pushed the thought away. *Sara, don't*, she told herself. *Don't think about it. Don't let yourself think about it. Not now.* She got up and straightened her skirts. She paused for a moment to check Selena's sleep. Then, shoulders squared, she picked up her travel bag and began preparing for arrival.

*　　*　　*

Sara and Selena sat close together, wedged between their trunks, in the station square at Muslimie Junction. All around them was chaos and bustle, but they were very still: Selena because she was half asleep; Sara because she was trying very hard to remain patient.

This station where the Turkish railway ended and the Syrian began, was also the site of one of the largest garrisons of the Empire. Everywhere Sara looked there were reminders of the vast military presence nearby; bawdy troops swaggered along the platform, singing noisily on their way to or from their leave. Carts and wagons loading their burdens of supplies and provisions throwing up a cloud of dust as they moved; and everywhere the hens scratched and squawked, between the soldiers and water sellers. A large consignment of horses – as many as three hundred, including some beautiful thoroughbred stallions – had just arrived and were being unloaded from the train. The noise as their hooves scraped the ground and as they snorted at the white dust they raised drowned Sara's thoughts. But as she watched them a new idea came to her. If the Captain did not return with the promised cart soon, she would have to lay her hands on one of those horses – by bribery or even, if need be, by theft. A group of soldiers walked by making jokes at the girls' expense. They were the only women in sight and were attracting a lot of undesirable attention. Sara began to feel increasingly uneasy. The soldiers gave a roar of laughter and moved out of the way for a German cavalry division.

Sara looked at Selena who had dropped off into a fitful doze again. Against the black of her cloak, her face looked all the whiter and, although she had not complained once, Sara knew how ill she must be feeling. At the moment her fever was down, and Sara hoped desperately that she would be able to get her to Aleppo and a doctor before it rose again. Where was that Captain? He had seemed at last willing to be helpful, surely he could not have deserted them? They had been sitting at the station for an hour now, with almost no protection from the sun and none at all from the leers of passing soldiers.

Sara fanned herself irritably. She wished she could find some better protection than their sun hats. She began to fidget again, pulling anxiously at the fingers of her gloves as she searched the platform. The Captain could not have run out on them. Colonel Schmidt had ordered him to commandeer a cart and take them both to Aleppo. But perhaps he had not found one and just given

272

up, she thought, half relieved as she remembered the sly looks and knowing grin he had given them behind the German's back. If only she knew he wasn't coming, she could look after herself and Selena, she was sure of it.

She gathered her wits together and decided to try to bribe the sergeant in charge of the horses. Folding the cloak securely round Selena, she stood up to find the man, her money tucked ready in the palm of her glove. She was just about to cross the station platform towards the horses when she saw the Turkish Captain, accompanied by a sergeant in a cart urging a tired-looking horse through the crowd towards her. Sara sat down with a sense of relief.

As the two drew nearer, her relief faded a little. The sergeant accompanying the Captain was very unprepossessing indeed: his eyebrows met fiercely over small, piggy eyes, his forehead was low and ape-like and his head appeared to be fixed without a neck on to broad shoulders. Looking at him, Sara felt a sharp twinge of unease, but a low murmur from Selena reminded her that she had no choice: they had to reach Aleppo.

The Captain jumped down from the cart and addressed her politely, almost obsequiously. But this did little to abate her gathering disquiet. Sara was just on the verge of informing him that they had found alternative transport when suddenly a clatter of hooves rang out behind her and she turned to see a troop of septieh riding into the station. She caught her breath with fear. Even the Captain with his animal sergeant friend was a better bet than facing the septiehs. Having made her decision, Sara turned to the Captain with a sorry attempt at a smile.

'Thank you for coming to our rescue, Captain,' she said politely. 'We'd have been lost without you.'

'At your service, madame,' he replied. Then he looked towards their trunks: 'What about your luggage? We can't possibly fit it all in.'

'I've arranged to have everything kept until we send for it,' Sara answered.

'Then if you ladies would be good enough to get into the cart,' he said, with a dubious glance at Selena.

'I'll help my friend if you could put these in the back,' Sara said, passing him their hand luggage. He took it and slung it unceremoniously into the back of the cart.

Sara bent over Selena, and put a hand under her elbow. 'Come

Selena, we must go now – we're going to Aleppo. Do you think you can manage?' She spoke rapidly and low, into Selena's ear. Selena nodded and rose leaning heavily on Sara.

The two girls walked slowly to the cart and the Captain swung Selena in. Sara declined his offer of help and clambered in by herself. She helped Selena settle, resting her head against some sacks lying on the floor of the cart, and made herself as comfortable as possible next to her. The Captain climbed in the front and motioned to the sergeant who shook the reins over the horse's back. As they lurched slowly forward Sara sat uncomfortably on a pile of sacking in an agony of impatience. The horse was old and much thinner than it should have been. Mind you, the cart had seen better days too, she reflected morosely as they jolted out of the station square on to the road that would take them straight to Aleppo.

The road was busy with columns of marching soldiers and tangles of horses and carts. Every now and again a car would wheeze by, reminding Sara of Jezebel at home. She watched the flat, parched countryside go by; the only vegetation was dried-out scrub, the only sound was from crickets singing optimistically as the soldiers trailed past.

Selena was in a deep sleep, her face flushed and her hands very hot. Because Sara was afraid she had an aching longing for her home, her family and even for the solid presence of Fatma. She wanted to bury her head in her vast, comforting bosom and weep and weep. She dropped her face into the crook of her arm and felt tears threaten. She was tempted to give into them, but the thought of Selena held her back. As soon as they reached Aleppo everything would be all right, she told herself. It could not be much further. Within minutes she had fallen into a deep, dreamless sleep.

Sara came to with a bewildering suddenness and froze. With stony horror she realised that the Turks were taking the cart down a dusty, white track, which seemed to lead into the flats. Her eyes flickered desperately around; the track was deserted and even the fields seemed empty of human life. She leaned forward and tapped the Captain on the shoulder.

'Why have we left the main road?' she asked. She recognised the hysteria in her voice and bit her lip to stop it.

'It's a short cut,' the sergeant said calmly.

'Then why doesn't anyone else appear to be taking it?'

The sergeant shrugged. 'Only Allah knows.'

Panic rose in Sara's throat and she swallowed desperately.

The Captain turned and smiled at her. 'Don't worry, honourable lady,' he said, 'I promised the Colonel to deliver you to Aleppo and by the beard of the Prophet I will. My friend Sergeant Mustapha comes from this region and knows it like his mother's breast. He will take us the best way.'

He spoke so sincerely that Sara was calmed a little, but nonetheless she pulled her bag towards her and felt for the reassurance of the knife. She held the smooth handle between her fingers, then closed her eyes and counted slowly to ten, feeling herself steadying as she did so. She opened her eyes again and stared longingly at the Captain's gun, wishing she had one with her too.

They lurched on down the track for another five minutes and then came to a halt. Sara instantly leapt to her feet and saw that the track had petered out and come to a dead end. A thousand terrifying images ran helter-skelter through her head. A wave of fear seized her as for the first time she grasped the full impact of what was happening. They had brought them here to rape and kill them, of that she was certain. She gulped down a breath to steady herself.

'I demand to be taken back to main road. The sergeant was obviously mistaken.' Her voice was a croak and she swayed on her feet; her legs felt as though every bone and muscle in them had dissolved into milk.

The Captain and the sergeant exchanged knowing glances and Sara, the knife clutched behind her back, did not take her eyes off them for a moment.

The Captain's eyes narrowed. 'Get out,' he ordered.

Sara looked down at him, trying to maintain an air of dignity against impossible odds. She had to keep calm – keep her head. 'If we are not in Aleppo by this evening we'll be missed. Everyone saw us leave with you – the Colonel knows you took us. You'll be hanged if you touch us – hanged.' She shouted the last word in spite of her resolutions.

The Captain, his eyes glittering malevolently, jumped from the cart and in an instant had reached up and seized her arm. As he pulled her towards him, she whipped the knife from behind her back and slashed it across him. It caught his arm and with a surprised bellow he released her, grabbing at his coat sleeve where a spreading red stain appeared. Sara reeled and, losing her balance, half jumped and half tumbled from the cart. The knife fell clattering to the stony ground a few feet away.

'Bitch! Whore!' he spluttered as she staggered to her feet. She tried to back up towards the knife, but the sergeant was behind her and grasping her by the arms began dragging her towards some bushes. Sara wasted no energy in screams, but fought bitterly as he wrestled her to the earth. She pulled one arm free and twisted on the ground to get up, but he caught her by her hair and pulled it with such force she thought she would be scalped. Facing defeat, Sara screamed for the first time with the full force of her despair.

'Regular wildcat, aren't you?' said the Captain, standing before her as the sergeant pinned her to the bare earth by her shoulders. She tried to kick out at him, but he just laughed as he unbuttoned his trousers and took out his penis. 'A shame you don't carry a bit more meat on you,' he said, standing right above her, 'I like a woman to give me a little comfort,' and he was down on top of her, fumbling at her clothes, tugging her skirt up to her stomach and forcing his hand in between her legs. She screamed again as he pulled viciously at her body hair, and clawed and struggled, trying to hold her breath against his disgusting smell.

He drew back and hit her squarely across her mouth and the strength of the blow shocked all her fear from her. It was as if a mist had been blown from her head. Her eyes felt burning hot, not with tears but with a fierce, consuming rage. She stopped fighting. Even if she had to die he would never do this again to another woman. Slowly she began to slide her hand down his belly. The Captain, thinking perhaps that she was giving in, relaxed his hold and moved one of his hands to her breast, which he grabbed greedily.

'What did I tell you, Faris,' he muttered to the sergeant, who was still holding her shoulders, 'these bitches can't get enough.' He laughed coarsely. 'Look at this wildcat. Purring like a kitten, she is.'

Sara's questing hand reached the Captain's testicles and with the last of her strength, fuelled by despair and rage, she squeezed . . .

The Captain let out a roar and pulled away from her, rising to his knees and then staggering to his feet. Sara saw the anger on his face and knew that he would kill her. Then suddenly everything froze. The Captain was about to kick her but stopped in mid-air, his eyes suddenly dazed and surprised. As Sara watched, disbelieving, a slow moan escaped his lips and he thudded to the ground. Silhouetted against the hard blue sky stood Selena, swaying as she looked white-faced at the man at her feet. The ivory handle of Sara's knife stuck out from halfway down his back; the sharp blade had sunk in deep.

It took less than a second for Sara to react. Fighting to her feet, she twisted round and grabbed at the dazed sergeant's pistol. 'You bastard,' she spat, struggling against his grip, her whole body arching with her arm towards the gun. Then out of the corner of her eye she saw Selena with the Captain's gun in her hand, pointing it with a trembling hand before she fired it. It only grazed the sergeant's temple, but it was enough to knock him to the ground. Sara looked wildly round. She saw a white rock at her feet and in one movement had bent and picked it up. With all her strength she brought it down on the sergeant's head. The bone cracked and he was still. She saw the skull had collapsed under the blow.

Sara and Selena stared at each other, paralysed by the reality of what they had done. Sara dropped the rock and sunk to her knees beside the sergeant. She was breathing so hard she was almost choking and had a sharp, stabbing pain at the base of her neck.

With shaking fingers she felt the sergeant's throat for any sign of a pulse and then, hesitating, raised her head to look at the woman who had saved her life. Selena was still standing, staring in horror at the smoking gun.

'He's dead,' Sara said, her throat muscles so tense she could hardly speak.

Selena dropped the gun as if it were a stinging jellyfish and fell to her knees beside Sara. 'God forgive me,' she whispered, 'but there was no other way.' She began to cry softly. 'I've killed a man . . .' She stuffed her knuckles into her mouth, wracked with sobs that shook her entire body.

'We've killed a man. Two in fact,' Sara said in a very low voice.

'I had to,' Selena sobbed, her vision blurred with tears of fear, horror and remorse as she looked back and forth between the bodies of the two men.

Sara pushed herself to her feet and stood unsteadily. Her body felt battered and very weak and the longing to sink down on her knees again was overpowering. They had to get away from here – as far away from here as possible – and quickly. Bending down she grasped Selena by the elbow and helped her to her feet. 'We must go,' she said gently. Selena nodded and brushed the tears from her face with her arm. Sara supported Selena back to the cart, stumbling several times over the rocky ground.

'I feel sick,' Selena said suddenly and leant against the cart with Sara supporting her head as she vomited violently. 'I don't think I'm going to make it,' she whispered.

'Oh yes you are,' Sara replied and, gathering her strength, pushed Selena into the back of the cart. 'We've survived everything else that's happened to us and we'll survive this,' she said with firm resolve.

As she was about to climb up herself, she remembered something and ran back to the sergeant's body. Flies were already crawling thickly over his bloodied head, his features almost obscured by them. Sara felt her stomach lurch but looked away as she bent and retrieved his gun. Slipping it into her pocket, she ran as fast as she could back to the cart, clambered into the driving seat and with an anxious backward glance whipped the poor horse so hard it moved at once into a shambling gallop. She urged it on so fast she could barely keep her seat.

She did not pause until they reached the main road and then she drew into the side, and rummaged in her carpet bag for another cloak. Selena was almost unconscious again now, but Sara wrapped her up tightly in the cloak, tucking her hair into the hood and putting the sacks around her more comfortably. Now any passer-by would assume they were just two Moslem women on their way to market in a cart.

Slumped over the reins, her arms and back so weak she could hardly hold them, she set the horse's head at Aleppo and hoped she could trust it to keep walking. Her head throbbed and a mist swam before her eyes in which floated alternating images of the long columns of shuffling Armenian exiles and the sergeant's bloody head.

She shut her eyes tightly against the memory. All the horrors of the journey built up inside her until her body convulsed in a huge, dry, heaving sob. Hunched over the reins she felt sick, shaken and very alone. The loneliness washed over her and another wrenching sob escaped.

But just when she thought her courage was failing her she felt a spark of anger, which grew into overpowering wrath. She straightened up angrily and ran her hand under her nose. She felt no remorse, no pity for the dead Turks, but only triumphant pride. *I hate the Turks, hate them*, she thought, glorying in this primitive reaction to her own terror. They had wanted to rape and kill – but they had been the ones to die.

She fixed a fierce gaze on the blank blue sky. 'Why are you doing this to me?' she croaked, shaking an angry fist at the beyond. She watched a moment, half expecting some answer – a clap of thunder, perhaps. Silence met her query. She let out a savage moan. *There is no God*, she thought, and her heart leaped in fear at her blasphemy. Her mother came to mind and suddenly seemed very near, watching over her almost. The thought gave her a renewed strength.

They were not far from Aleppo now. She could just see the outline of the castle rising out of the horizon. On the outskirts of the town, she would abandon the horse and cart and find an inn – a Jewish inn and a Jewish doctor.

The road was practically deserted, the sky hurting her exhausted eyes with its brightness. Her head was pounding and with every jolt of the cart the pain in her neck worsened. As the tears built up behind her eyes she knew she should pray for strength but could not find the words. 'God help me . . . please help me save Selena,' and then the prayer petered out.

An open-topped car appeared over the brow of a hill. It was careering towards them, spraying a cloud of dust in its wake. Sara narrowed her eyes and shaded them from the sun with one hand. As it drew closer she could see that two men were sitting inside it, and that a flag – the American flag – was flying from its bonnet. Americans! There was an American mission at Aleppo! Americans were civilised – they would help – Aaron . . .

With a gasping sob she jumped wildly from the cart, waving her arms as new tears of hope slid down her cheeks. The car veered past her. 'Stop!' she shrieked. 'Please stop!' *Oh God*, she prayed. *Please make them stop.*

The car skidded to a halt forty paces away. Sara began to move towards it. Through swollen eyelids she made out a red-moustachioed man at the wheel and another, slimmer man, jumping lightly to the ground.

'Thank you, God, thank you,' she blurted as she broke into a run, stumbling blindly.

'Please help us!' she gasped, and then stopped dead in her tracks, the shock knocking all breath from her. She took a shaky step and peered at the man standing before her – unable to believe that such a thing was possible, she must be mad, hallucinating.

'Sara?' said Joe Lanski, his voice choking with surprise. 'Sara?'

She heard the familiar voice and everything around her swam into a blur. 'Oh, Joe,' she croaked, and burst into helpless sobs. Joe reached out and she collapsed against his chest, weeping with an unbearable relief. 'Oh thank God, thank God,' she sobbed as she felt Joe's arms close protectively around her.

The ship was less than a mile away from the Palestinian coastline now and, by the light of the waning moon, Daniel could just make out the bulk of land which was his beloved country. With any luck the moon would set in another half hour and they would then be able to move closer to the shore. Heavy rainclouds sailed across the sky, but for November the evening was balmy and the sea low. A perfect night for sea bathing, Daniel thought with a grin as his eyes strained to see the ruins of the Crusader castle, which dominated the shoreline.

'Another thirty minutes, would you say?' he asked anxiously.

Captain Jones nodded. 'Less if we're lucky,' he answered. 'We'll anchor directly in line with the castle – it'll give us good cover from the shore.'

Daniel looked at the Captain with admiration. His respect for him had grown ever since they met. Captain Jones was a short, swarthy Welshman who ran his small ship regularly between Egypt and the Phoenician coast of Lebanon. He picked up intelligence gleaned from cells in Tyre and Beirut and from now on he would also be calling off at Atlit once a month.

Thinking back on the last few weeks, Daniel thanked his stars for Lieutenant Woolley. Anyone less like Colonel Thompson would be hard to imagine: thoughtful, interested and intelligent, he was also a man who could listen and he and Daniel had got on from the start.

A few days before Daniel's arrival in Port Said, the Lieutenant had received word that the British High Command had decided to start another offensive against the Turk. The plan was to drive them out of the Sinai Peninsula and defend Egypt from the Palestinian borders rather than from the Suez Canal. Nothing could have suited Daniel's plans better. The Army would now need more information and Woolley's brief was to find field intelligence behind Turkish lines. Daniel's arrival was therefore fortuitously timed and within days a code had been drawn up and a ship organised to take Daniel home and to familiarise the Captain with the coastline.

'Drop anchor as soon as we've drawn level with the castle,' the Captain ordered one of his officers.

Daniel's heart rose with joy as he heard the anchor splash into the water. In twenty minutes or so he would be back on his native land and he was as happy as though he had been away for years. He felt like singing as he watched the crew move silently around the deck.

The bridge door opened behind him. 'Permission to lower the sea boat, sir,' came a voice through the darkness.

'Permission granted.' Jones turned to Daniel. 'A few more minutes and you should be on your way,' he said cheerfully. 'Good luck and I look forward to our next meeting. Are you sure you have everything?'

Daniel patted the oilskin package tied to his belt and nodded. 'Yes, sir,' he said happily. 'And thanks for everything.'

A seaman on deck looked up at the bridge and gave a thumbs up sign. 'That's your signal,' said the Captain and put out his hand. 'See you next month. U-boats permitting,' and he grinned as they shook hands.

In seconds Daniel was scrabbling down the rope ladder and climbing awkwardly into the little boat that bobbed on the waves, pushing itself away from the ship. Daniel sat tense with excitement as the sailors rowed silently towards the shore. They were only four hundred odd yards from land, but Daniel would have to swim the last fifty. He was stripped to the waist ready for it and shivered in the cool night breeze.

The boat stopped. 'This is as far as we go, sir,' whispered one of the men and handed Daniel a flask. 'The Captain suggested you have a swig of this before your dip.' Daniel took a gulp of the rum and felt it warming his body then, checking the bag with his clothes, papers and the gun that Woolley had given him, was secure around his waist, he lowered himself into the water. The cold bit into his bones and he gasped, but after a second he began to swim steadily towards the shore, stopping only when he felt land under his feet. Shivering with cold, he stumbled over the rocks, his feet so numb he could hardly feel them.

Overcome with giddiness he sat on the beach, the air searing into his lungs. Then he opened his package and dressed himself as fast as he could, tucking the revolver into his belt. Keeping close to the rocks, he set off along the deserted sea front towards the research station.

CHAPTER TWENTY

Does it happen to everyone, Sara wondered idly, her eyes fixed on her book, but her mind aeons away. Does everyone have someone like Joe Lanski, a person who, for no rhyme or reason, miraculously appears at just the right moment to save one from disaster? Twice Joe had come to her rescue when she was desperate. The first time, in the wilderness which now seemed so trivial. And the second time, she was only too aware that without Joe they would probably be dead by now, or rotting in a Turkish jail. Had he appeared on the road to Aleppo because she had prayed for help? Had God really sent him to save her and guide her home?

They had been travelling for five days now, but despite the dust and grime Joe managed to remain rakishly elegant. He looked perfectly at ease in the jolting railway carriage, one booted leg swung over the other and his face creased in concentration as he jotted notes into his little green book. The idea that this sophisticated adventurer was a guardian angel made her smile. She should know better – he was the last person to belong in heaven.

Joe looked up and smiled. 'Good book?' he asked pleasantly and Sara nodded and shifted slightly to hide the cover. It was a romantic novel she had found at the American mission and she knew that if Joe recognised the author's name, he would tease her about her choice of reading matter.

Joe had observed her ploy and leant across the carriage to turn the spine of the book towards him. 'Ah,' he said, the mocking expression returning to his green eyes. 'Ouida. I would never have dared recommend her to you – very fast!'

'I am a married woman and may read what I wish,' she replied so curtly that he burst into a laugh.

'Oh I do beg your pardon, Madame Cohen, but I had quite forgotten your marital status.'

Sara could not help a brief smile. The truth was she had almost forgotten it herself. So much had happened in the six weeks that had passed since Chaim had kissed her goodbye at the station that her married life seemed little more than a hazy recollection.

'I love to see you smile,' Joe said with the new gentleness he had shown during the weeks in Aleppo. 'Fleeting though it may be,' he added with a grin as she turned her head to look out of the window and end the conversation.

God almighty, he can be irritating, Sara thought. *He is the most complex person I have ever met. If we travelled for months I would be no nearer knowing him.*

Abandoning the vexed question of Joe Lanski she turned from the view to see how Selena was, wrapped in the travel-stained black cloak, shadows over her lovely face. Her fine skin stretched like tissue paper over her bones, but at least there was a little colour in her cheeks and her sleep seemed peaceful.

It had been as though she had given in to her illness the minute they had been rescued by Joe Lanski. When they had arrived at the mission her temperature had soared and she had tossed and turned in the clean, narrow white bed with a furious energy. The old Greek doctor that Joe had called in had taken one look at her and diagnosed typhoid, thus confirming Sara's worst fears.

'Will she get well, Doctor?' Sara had pleaded but the old man would promise nothing.

'Keep her as hot as possible – plenty of blankets. And keep giving her liquids, as many as you can get down her. Force feed her if necessary. That's all we can do.'

Selena had lain between life and death for three days while Sara, regardless of the danger of infection, had hovered over her bedside, wiping her brow and pouring drinks down her throat. Every time the fever fell Sara hoped it would be for the last time although she knew it was just another symptom of the disease that was devouring her friend before her eyes. On the third night the doctor shook his head sadly and asked what faith the patient was.

'Christian,' Sara had whispered, knowing what the question meant.

'Then I think you had better call in a priest.'

Joe had come back to the mission less than an hour later with the Greek Orthodox Archbishop himself in tow. Sara looked at the bearded figure in his tall, brimless hat, black veil and voluminous black robes edged in purple, an ornate cross hanging from his neck, and shivered involuntarily. To her tired and aggravated eyes he seemed more like an agent of some dark force than a man of God. But only hours after he had administered the last rites, Selena's temperature dropped and did not rise again. In the days that followed she had gradually recovered consciousness and strength, although the doctor had not pronounced her out of danger for ten days. She had been too weak to do anything for herself, even eat and Sara had continued to act as her devoted nurse.

And Joe – Joe had been wonderful, appearing at meals or at odd hours through the day with trays of tempting delicacies or presents for the patient: an exquisite little music box; an extravagantly beautiful silk shawl; and, finally, a couple of days before they left, two velvet cloaks, blue for Sara and rich dark red for Selena. The last gift Selena had refused, saying she had accepted too much already and begging Joe to give it instead to the mission that had helped her to recover. Surprised, Joe had given in, but had laughingly begged Sara not to double the blow by refusing hers. Sara, thinking of all the clothes locked in the trunks at Muslimie Junction, and remembering the bitter chill of the nights, had not been able to turn the gift down.

Joe had decided it was safer for them to jettison their luggage when he realised the news of the murder of two Turkish soldiers was all over Aleppo and the septieh were on the alert for two women, a Palestinian and a Turk, 'enemies of the Empire and of Islam', it was being said, 'who had lured the two soldiers to their deaths'.

'Lured them?' Sara had sputtered, aghast. 'Lure them! Those dung-eaters! I'd rather lure a camel!'

Joe had laughed. 'You don't know the best. The Arabs believe you to be two djinn in the form of sirens. It's just as well no one saw you in the car; the general story is that you both turned into wolves somewhere along the road to Aleppo and disappeared into the desert.' He was laughing, but Sara was still too angry to be amused.

'I'm glad you think it's so funny. I wish I could turn into a wolf

285

– it would have been a very useful accomplishment back there on the flats!'

While Selena pined in guilt at having killed, Sara's nightmares were of a different nature. Try as she might to rid herself of the picture, she was haunted by the memory of the thousands of Armenians wandering over the Syrian desert to their certain deaths. And as she dreamt, the Armenians became Jews and the woman running alongside the train was herself. Every night she would no sooner close her eyes than the images would float in front of her mind's eye and night after night she would wake, crying out in the dark, her body bathed in a cold sweat.

The first night it had happened she had gone in search of a glass of water to steady herself and had met Joe in the corridor. His breath smelt of alcohol, his clothes of cigars and some strong, musky scent. She stood in her nightgown, shivering with cold, and glaring at him in disgust. 'Been out gallivanting with your Turkish friends?' she said with consummate scorn.

Joe looked at her calmly, a hint of a smile playing round his lips. 'Perhaps it would be wise to remember,' he had answered, 'that if it had not been for my business with my friends the Turks I would not have been in Aleppo at the right time to be of service to you.'

'Yes,' she spat, 'selling them horses so that they can herd helpless women and children like cattle across the desert, selling them guns so that they can one day turn them on us – after they've solved "the Armenian problem", of course. Don't you see that after the Armenians it will be us – the Jews?' Her control snapped and her voice rose sharply. 'Will you still sell them guns when they start forcing us into the desert? You wouldn't care if they came and took me right now as long as there was a quick profit in it for you – would you?'

Her anger had taken her over completely as she felt Joe grasp her by the wrist and hold her roughly. 'You stupid woman, don't you know that everything that happens to you concerns me?' Sara stared at him, stupefied. He held her hard by the shoulders, looking earnestly into her face. 'Do you really believe I am a friend of the Turk? It was swine like them that massacred my family for no other reason than they were Jews? Do you think I have forgotten that? Do you really believe that I could be on their side?'

The look on Joe's face made Sara blush with shame and she lowered her eyes, unable to meet his. She wanted to ask his forgiveness, but instead burst into huge, gulping sobs. Joe put his arms round her and held her close.

'Sara, Sara,' he said soothingly, stroking her silky hair. 'Terrible things are happening round us but you must not torture yourself over things you can do nothing about.'

'But why can't I do something? I feel so helpless,' Sara sobbed, her body shaking in his arms.

'Sara, I know you do,' Joe said softly. 'I understand your wish to do something dramatic, something splendid. But you must get your priorities right – the time for killing Turks will come later. Look to the future. That we can do something about.' His voice sounded so strong and sure now that Sara's sobs were checked, her mind fumbling for his meaning. Then she sighed and rested her head against his chest. 'Oh, Joe, take me home. I want to go home. Please take me home,' she said in a tiny voice.

'Sara, trust me,' he whispered. 'As soon as the doctor gives permission I will take you both back to Palestine. Back home. I promise. Trust me.'

Joe had been as good as his word, although how he had managed to organise Selena's travel Sara could only guess. Now, at last, they were in Palestine. They had crossed the border the evening before and spent the night at Afula. Sara had hardly slept with excitement and thoughts of all the things she would see again. Palestine! The pure air, the space, the pepper trees and bleached eucalyptus, her mother's roses. And the people – her father, Aaron, Sam, Ruth, the new baby which she had not yet seen. Even Fatma's scolding would be music to her ears. How she longed to be back in her room overlooking the vineyards that rolled for acres into the distance. To see the sea smacking in the loop of the bay, to be able to ride Bella over the windy, scrub-covered wilderness. Home was once again a reality, not a wished-for dream. Palestine. Her land that she would never again leave or betray.

'Look, Selena, look!' she cried, reaching for her friend's arm and shaking her awake. The heavy grey roof of sky that had followed them all day suddenly lifted and they could make out the apricot-coloured coastline of the Carmel ahead of them.

Selena moved across the carriage and looked at Sara, her eyes shining so blue with emotion that tears welled up in her own. 'You are home,' she said with a look of total understanding.

Sara took her arm and smiled proudly. 'We are home, Selena. We are home. You'll love it – wait and see.'

Joe watched them both gazing out of the window, Sara exclaiming and pointing out landmarks, Selena responding with animation. Once again he was caught by Sara's beauty and his heart stood still for a moment, clasped in an unexpected grip of pain. He had steeled his heart to be as cold as granite, but it was going to hurt to leave Sara. Irritated by the thought, he pushed it out of his mind, shaking his head as though to shake off a fly. Damned woman with her unspoken demands and her unshakeable beauty. Well tomorrow he would be shot of her, and rid of this story-book passion. Still cursing her he rose, stretched and began taking the luggage down from the racks. They were nearing the station.

Sara was the first on to the platform, leaping from the train as though she had been travelling for one hour in luxury rather than seven weeks in dirt and danger. Her eyes searched the platform for Abdul, the ancient porter – more for old time's sake than for help with their pitiful baggage.

Then she saw him and her heart leapt into her throat. She stood stock still, her eyes round with amazement, trembling with joy. How could he have known she was on this train? Then she saw Joe, smiling broadly and triumphantly at her expression. Oh he was a saint after all . . . he must have sent word somehow last night.

'Aaron!' she screamed and ran through the crowds, pushing and shoving until she found herself in his arms hugging him as though she would never let go. 'Aaron, thank God, I've missed you so much.' She was half-laughing and half-crying as he hugged her to him.

Aaron was as relieved to see her as she was him. He had been surprised, then deeply concerned when he received a letter from Chaim asking if Sara had arrived safely and suggesting he use his brotherly influence to persuade her to write. How the letter had reached him at all was a mystery, but the fact that it had taken several weeks and there was no sign of Sara was even more disturbing.

Then came a hand-delivered note from Sara in Aleppo, saying not to worry as she was on her way home and safe with Joe Lanksi. No explanation, just the fact. Then nothing till that morning when a rider from Afula had brought word from Joe that they would be on the train.

Not until he had seen her jumping from the train had the feeling of unease that had hung over him for weeks at last disappeared. 'I've missed you too, little sister,' he said gruffly and then turned to Joe saying, 'What on earth where you doing in Aleppo with this rogue here?' The two men shook hands, smiling affably.

'It's a long story – Sara had better tell you,' said Joe. 'Where's Selena?' he added.

'Selena!' Sara exclaimed, turning back to the train and explaining to her bewildered-looking brother; 'she's my friend from Constantinople. I've brought her home with me.'

Aaron's misgivings at this sudden announcement melted as soon as Selena was introduced to him. The first thing that struck him when her face was turned up to his was how very small and delicate she was. And then, when she smiled, it was the smile of a madonna. Their eyes met and both knew at once that they would be friends. Aaron smiled a smile of acceptance.

'It is an honour to meet you, Mr Levinson,' said Selena returning his smile.

'The pleasure is mine. And please – Aaron, not Mr Levinson,' he answered. He turned to Abdul, instructing him to take their bags out to Jezebel. 'Welcome to Palestine,' he added.

Her beautiful smile flickered across her face again. 'Palestine comes most welcome to me,' she said. It did. For this was God's land, the land of Jesus, where her Church had sprung up. For the first time in weeks Selena felt a flicker of optimism, a tiny flowering of hope.

Sara lay back in the big white bath, her head, wrapped in a towel, resting on the edge, her whole body revelling in the luxury of heat and cleanliness. Outside, rain was pouring down, beating steadily at the windows behind the thick, cotton curtains. The wind and rain only added to her pleasure in the steam-filled room, fragrant with the smell of lavender oil and burning eucalyptus logs from the woodstove in the corner.

Selena lay foot to foot at the other end of the bath, musing in the comfort of the warm water. From the moment she had walked into the Levinson house she had felt a wonderful sense of peace envelope her. In some ways it reminded her of her own childhood home in Armenia, and Sara's father sometimes seemed so like her own.

Abram Levinson had stared gently at her and, holding her hand, had squeezed it for a moment. 'I think,' he had said, 'that I've just got myself another daughter,' and he had kissed her gently on the cheek. Selena smiled to herself softly, the tears not far away. She had forgotten how it felt to be a part of a family, where love was given unquestioningly and without words. What a miracle that she should find herself in such a home. It seemed a hundred years since she had experienced anything quite so wonderful.

'Are you all right, Selena?' Sara cast her a searching glance from the other end of the tub.

'I'm fine,' she murmured. 'It's just that everyone has been so good to me – I hope I will not be a burden on your family.'

Sara looked at her fondly. 'You'll soon be making yourself useful around the place, don't you worry. God only knows that there's so much to do around here we wouldn't ever let an extra pair of hands be idle.' She pinched Selena's slender calf affectionately. 'But first you must get well, put some weight back on and recover your strength. Fatma will help you with that, wait and see.'

'I still don't know how to find the words to thank you. Do you know this is the first time I have felt safe since . . .' She shivered and left the sentence unfinished.

'I know how you feel,' Sara assured her. She felt so utterly happy – so utterly content – just lying in the steaming water revelling in the sensation of being at home.

They had arrived in Zichron to be met by a grinning, gaping Fatma, tears pouring down that marvellous broad face and laughter ringing out between the sobs. Sam was there too, Sam who had grown up and filled out since she had seen him last, but who still hugged and kissed her with the spontaneity of a child, showering her face and hair with kisses and pausing only to gaze at Selena with spaniel-like devotion. Abu had almost broken Sara's back with the slap he gave it to express his joy while her father, older and thinner, had clutched her to him as though she were about to break away and head straight back for Constantinople.

Within the first half an hour home, Sara knew that Alex and Becky had arrived safely in America and that Alex was successfully co-ordinating the relief to Palestine from American Jews all over the United States. Becky, meanwhile, was happily living with some cousins in Brooklyn and due to begin college in January.

On their way towards Zichron, Aaron told Sara and a sleepy

Selena all about the locust patrol and the work they were doing at the station; he told her of the enormous changes that had swept Palestine in the year since she had left and about the scarcity of food and fuel.

'And Daniel?'

Sara's heart thumped so hard when she mentioned his name she had been afraid that Aaron would hear it above the put-noise of the car engine. Daniel was out near Gaza where some locusts had been sighted, but he was expected back any day now.

The bathwater was cooling and Sara shifted slightly, thinking it was time to leave its womb-like comfort and get dressed. She looked at Selena and, noticing the tiny lines between her brows and the dark circles shadowing her eyes, felt a rush of affection for her friend.

'Come on, time to dress for dinner,' she said, smiling and sitting up in the bath. 'Tomorrow we can go through my mother's clothes and make ourselves some new ones from them.'

'What did you say?' Selena tried to return the smile, but it was an enormous effort just to keep her eyes open and not fall asleep where she lay.

Sara looked hard at Selena. 'What you need is some rest. You look very, very tired.'

'I am,' Selena said drowsily. Sara pinched her calf again, but gently. 'Come on, tonight we'll eat and sleep. Tomorrow we can start planning.' She leapt out of the bath and wrapped herself in a huge towel, which had been warming near the woodstove. Selena lay back for a second longer, her eyes closed. Then she snapped them wide open. The old bravado was briefly back in her as she looked at her friend.

'Damn the Turks. Damn them. I will curse them all the days of my life. I will not let my fear overcome me. I swear it, Sara. I swear it.'

Sara stared at her stupefied, then laughed and held out a hand to her friend. 'Now I know you're really your old self,' she said, and pulled her from the bath.

'Pour me another brandy,' said Joe, leaning across the table with his glass stretched out. Aaron filled it and Joe sipped, appreciating the warmth that flooded through his body as he swallowed. They were in the outbuilding that had served as Aaron's study and lab before the research station was built. It was a large room, draughty but curiously comfortable in an untidy, masculine way.

'Sorry about the cold, but I'm conserving kerosene wherever possible,' Aaron apologised and Joe, warm with brandy, nodded. Aaron gestured to the bed, piled high with blankets: 'It should be warm enough once you're in it,' he added.

Joe grinned. 'I could do with a woman to warm me up.'

'Couldn't we both,' Aaron answered with a laugh, and drank the brandy back in a gulp. He suddenly realised the truth of what he had said and wondered when he had last had a woman. He had been so busy lately that he was particularly celibate since his parting from his mistress, Hanna. He cleared his throat and held the bottle up to Joe, who shook his head. 'So what Sara witnessed was only the tip of the iceberg?' he asked.

Joe stood up and crossed to the window. He was silent for a moment as he watched the raindrops make their way down the pane and tried to articulate what he felt. No one could know how hard he found it to speak of the massacres, of the mindless, bloody, killing and persecution, of the ignorant, deadly hatred. No one could know how the memories of the past returned to haunt him or how clear, so many years later, the pictures still were: the warm kitchen in the Ukraine, the peace broken by Cossacks bursting through the door in a drunken frenzy, a cacophony of hatred spilling from fat, white faces; and then the salvoes of gunfire, the heavy reek of gunpowder hanging in the air, the smoke clearing to reveal his father slumped over the table, kitchen knife held uselessly in his hands; his mother sliding slowly down the wall, leaving a trail of blood on the whitewash, her face blown away and her arms holding his two sisters so tightly that even in death they could not be loosened and the three had been buried together in one miserable grave.

In spite of the cold Joe felt the sweat break out on his forehead and he wiped it away with his forearm before turning back to Aaron.

'The Armenians are to be resettled in Deir ez Zor, in the heart of the Syrian desert,' he said slowly. 'Although this is, of course, the term being used for mass murder. The apparently enlightened government in Constantinople sees fit to banish the whole race to the desert. The plan has been worked out down to the finest detail and personally directed by Enver Pasha himself, they say. The Empire is to be rid of the entire race, and they are doing it systematically and without mercy. Given a few hours to leave their homes the Armenians are sent, unequipped and defenceless, to march several thousand miles without food or water. Even the youngest and strongest succumb to disease on the march, or just die of starvation or thirst. If those do not kill them quickly enough, the thrashings from the septieh does, and thousands of them commit suicide rather than continue. The roads are lined with hundreds of thousands of dead and dying; the living are too weak to bury the corpses, the septiehs do not care to. Not one of them will live to reach Deir ez Zor. Enver Pasha is showing a genius for savagery unmatched by the worst excesses of the Sultans from whom he delivered us.'

A deep silence fell on the room. Aaron felt as though he had been punched in the stomach. He took a deep breath and pressed his fists into the base of his stomach. 'Genocide,' he said slowly.

Joe looked him straight in the face and nodded. 'I'm afraid there's no other word for it.'

There was another silence as Aaron tried to regain his breath. 'But the Germans?' he finally asked. 'They're Christians – surely they cannot allow this to happen!' he cried out.

Joe gave him a cynical half smile. 'They care for nothing but winning their war. What is the fate of two million people they have never seen compared to the greater glory of world domination? Besides,' he added, 'I trust the Hun as far as a camel throws dung.'

Aaron's stomach was a tight knot of tension, and he pressed it again with his fists. 'Are we next?' he asked, his voice sounding strange even to his own ears.

Joe took a cheroot from his pocket, bit the end off, lit it and returned to his chair before answering. 'Not as things stand,' he said, studying the glowing tip of the cheroot, his lips compressed in a tight smile. 'Right now our banking brothers in Germany are far too important to the war machine to risk displeasing them. As long as they are on the winning side, at any rate.'

Aaron nodded. 'Yes, of course,' he said and paused for a moment. 'Strange though that there has been no attempt to round up the Armenians here in Palestine.' There was a large Armenian population in Jerusalem and Jaffa, among whom were many friends, particularly the kind Captain of the septieh, Kristopher Sarkis. 'I have friends – should we warn them?'

'I don't know. The majority of the Constantinople community is still apparently untouched,' Joe answered. The room fell into silence again, broken by Fatma calling from the kitchen door.

'Master Aaron? Dinner.'

The two men rose and crossed the room to the door. Aaron, with his hand on the knob, turned and, not quite meeting Joe's eyes, asked, 'Did those two Turks ... er ...'

'No,' said Joe, and a smile hovered over his lips. 'They killed them first.'

Dinner was not the happy affair Sara had imagined it would be when she made the long journey home. Aaron was preoccupied and silent, hardly touching his food. Sam and her father were both quiet as though they sensed the atmosphere. Selena had retired to bed, pleading exhaustion and Fatma, who could normally be relied upon to make any amount of noise, had followed her up with a bowl of soup and a lot of good advice. Even Joe was subdued; not one cynical remark had passed his lips and neither had very much of the simple but wholesome food. On the other hand, both Joe and Aaron drank a great deal, knocking the wine back in a moody silence.

Near the end of the meal the door was thrown open and in rushed Ruth, her pretty face alight with happiness at seeing her friend and her boisterous good spirits finally breaking the tense atmosphere. The two girls flew into each other's arms, shrieking and weeping and both trying to talk at once but incoherently. Ruth shared a glass of wine with the family, but finally had to go back to her baby, after Sara had promised to come and see her first thing the next day.

After she had gone the nervy silence fell back on the company and Sara was actually relieved when Aaron, followed by Sam, made their excuses and went to bed. Then Joe stood and bade everyone goodnight, bending to kiss Sara's hand with his usual grace. 'Good night, Sara,' he said, and as he looked at her his face was so expressionless he could have been a stranger. He turned and walked to the door, but before he could reach it Sara had jumped from her chair and intercepted him.

'Joe,' she said earnestly, holding on to his arm and looking up into his face. 'Joe, I will never be able to thank you enough for all you did for Selena and me.' She hesitated. Why was it so difficult to say anything nice to him? For a moment they stood looking at each other, and then his face changed and Sara saw the green eyes glitter in their old, mocking challenge.

'I'm confident that one day you will find a way, Mrs Cohen.' His voice was low and slow and something in his tone made her heart beat faster. His eyes moved lazily over his face and down her neck. 'Good night.'

Sara stood stock still as the door closed between them, the blood flooding her face. She had no doubt what he had meant and had her father not been there she would have given him a good kick. But, irritated as she was with his insinuation, she began to smile. His reversion to his old ways made her feel better, made her feel really home.

'As you're up, could you get me a glass of water, child?' her father's voice came from behind her.

'Of course, Papa,' she answered and, throwing some dead vine sticks into the fire as she passed it, she filled a glass and returned to the table, her spirits restored. She was home. The light from the oil lamp glowing on the whitewashed walls and the crackling of the vines added to her sense of homecoming and cosy happiness. Everything would be all right now, she knew it.

Her father took her hand. 'Did Cohen mistreat you in any way?' he asked gently. Sara smiled, her heart full of love for his quiet tact.

'No, Father,' she said honestly. 'But I was homesick, so very, very homesick.'

'Then you were right to come home. The house lost its heart when you went away.' Sara put her arms round her father's neck and leant her head contentedly on his shoulder. She was back.

Alone in her bedroom Sara studied her reflection as she brushed her hair the prescribed hundred strokes. In the last year her face had changed, had begun to develop, subtly altering the expression in her face and eyes. She was beginning, she thought, to look like herself.

Sara woke twice in the night, shaken and terrified by the same recurring nightmare. The second time she must have cried out in her sleep for when she woke it was to see Fatma, a worried expression in place of her usual cross one, bending over her with a candle. When she saw Sara was awake she put the candle on the bedside table and sat on the small bed, her still enormous weight making it creak and groan in protest.

She gathered Sara into her arms, almost suffocating her between her huge breasts. Rocking and clucking she enveloped Sara, crooning softly. 'Sleep, sleep my golden child, my golden minaret, you are safe here with old Fatma. So you have night stories of the dog-turds, who tried to dip into your well of sweet waters? So now you are safe.' Sara could not help but giggle weakly into Fatma's chest. How on earth had she heard already? But it was pointless to tell her that her night fears had a far more horrifying theme.

Sara managed to free herself. 'I'm fine now, Fatma, go back to bed, you'll catch cold.' Fatma peered at her suspiciously for a moment and then her forehead cleared and giving her old charge one more kiss she hauled herself from the bed. Before leaving the room she gave Sara another searching look.

'You go back to that husband of yours?'

'No,' said Sara. Fatma turned her head away in a show of disapproval but not before Sara had glimpsed her look of delight.

'It is the will of Allah,' she said piously.

'Yes, it is God's will,' answered Sara, knowing that that would end all questioning in the Arab mind.

'Now you sleep,' Fatma said gruffly, and waddled out, closing the door gently behind her.

Like hell it was the will of Allah, Sara thought, sitting up in bed. The will of Sara Cohen – Sara Levinson – more like. She knelt on the bed and pulled the curtains back. A splash of amber daubed the horizon and Sara knew that there was no question of her going back to sleep. In spite (or because of?) all she had been through recently she hardly felt tired these days, on the contrary as she looked from the small window over the countryside she loved she felt filled with exhilaration.

Shivering, she lit the candle and rummaged in the wardrobe for something to wear. She found an old riding skirt and jacket, a shirt and a thick, warm shawl. The cold made her hurry and within minutes she was dressed and, blowing out the candle, crept down the stairs, through the kitchen and out of the house.

It was still almost dark, although the sun was just appearing over the hills. A light wind had dried off most of the night's rain and the air was thick with the smell of wet earth. Leaving the house behind her she wandered into the garden to see how her vegetables were doing without her. The garden had been extended, new types of vegetable planted and they were growing. The grass, too, had grown long and, although the vegetables themselves seemed well cared for, the rest of the garden was neglected. Anyway, there was plenty of time to put that straight.

The dawn was rising quickly and it was already nearly light. Sara skirted the barn and Abu's hut and turned into the courtyard to be almost pushed to the ground by Sultan, wagging his tail and nearly frenetic in his welcome. 'Some guard dog!' she laughed, hugging him muddy paws and all.

When Sultan had calmed down a little she straightened up and gave a little whistle between her teeth. It was answered immediately by an excited whinny from the third stable. Bella had not forgotten her! She ran over to the stable door. 'Hello, my beauty,' she whispered into the mare's warm neck. She felt in her pocket for the sugar she had taken on her way through the kitchen and felt Bella's velvety nose nuzzle her hand for the treat. 'I'm back, my pretty, I'm back and I shan't ever leave you again.'

A restless stamping in the next loose box and a series of angry snorts made Bella break away from Sara and prance about. *Aaron's stupid Apollo*, Sara thought and opened the top half of the stable door. The magnificent head of a white stallion shot out and arched round towards Bella. *Joe's horse! Negiv!* Sara thought in amazement. *How on earth did he get here?* She put out a hand to stroke his nose and nearly jumped out of her skin when a voice from inside the stable hissed: 'What do you want, lady?'

Peering into the gloom she saw a skinny Arab boy with a coal-black face pointing an old Bedouin horse rifle almost as big as himself towards her. Her eyebrows shot up and she suppressed a smile. The small boy had bravado, but he presented a more comic than menacing spectacle.

'More to the point,' she said with mock sternness, 'what are you doing here?'

'I am guarding my master's horse,' he said with a solemn face. 'Many an evil devil has tried to steal him but none has ever got past me,' he thumped himself proudly on the chest, the gun wavering dangerously.

'I see,' Sara said thoughtfully. 'Well, I suggest you put that gun down and come into the house for breakfast.' The boy hesitated, torn between breakfast and duty. 'He'll be quite safe here, I can promise you,' Sara nodded encouragingly.

He moved closer to the door and peered up at Sara. Yes, he had thought as much. This was the she-devil that his master had found tangled in the thicket like a goat, then tracked at a distance wasting half a sun. He shook his head sadly; he worried about his master, who was the wisest man on earth except, he suspected, where this she-devil was concerned.

Sara unbolted the stable door. 'What's your name?' she said formally.

'It is Ali, slave boy to master Joe Lanski, whom I would follow to hell and back if he so commanded me,' Ali said in one breath with a big grin across his face.

Sara looked at him, horrified, while he, delighted at her reaction, grinned more and more broadly. 'What did you say?' she asked, aghast, her mind returning to the Bedouin camp and the slaves used as mounting blocks.

'Slave to Master Lanski,' the boy repeated happily.

Sara snatched the gun from him, leaned it against the wall and grabbing his shoulders frog-marched him across the courtyard towards the house. 'There are no slaves in my house,' she said firmly, clicking the gate to behind them.

'You will not let him beat me, lady?' Ali said forlornly, pulling against her grasp.

Sara stopped for a moment and looked at Ali with the fury of a she-devil aroused. 'Are you telling me he beats you?' she demanded.

Ali feared he had gone too far. 'Well, only a little,' he admitted, shuffling in the mud.

'Well, we'll soon see about that,' Sara announced and grasping his wrist continued to march towards the house. 'Joe Lanski!' she muttered to herself furiously, and wondered how many other slaves he kept – perhaps he even had a harem! In her mind's eye she pictured the magnificent harem Selena had told her about, the fabulous odalisques, rippling seductively on silken cushions with Joe in the middle of them, engulfed in cascading folds of velvet and flesh, a fire raged in her brain as she stormed on with Ali in tow.

'Lady, you hurt Ali's arm,' he whimpered and, as she loosened her grip on his arm, Joe came round the corner, dressed in breeches, boots, a keffiyeh round his neck and carrying a riding whip in one hand and a leather saddlebag in the other.

'Good morning, Sara,' he began cheerfully.

'Good morning, *Pasha* Lanski,' she flared.

Joe looked at her, surprised. 'You look as though you want my head on a plate,' he remarked with no loss of good humour.

'A good idea. With an apple in your mouth,' she retorted.

Joe threw back his head and laughed, stopping when he noticed Ali trying to break away from Sara. With one twist of his arm he was free and scampering back to the stables.

'So what has the little devil been up to now?' he asked.

'Are you referring to your Arab child slave?' Sara asked coldly.

This time Joe laughed even louder. 'Child slave? Ali? Arab? For heaven's sake he's as Jewish as you are!' he roared.

Her jaw dropped. 'Jewish?' she echoed and swung round to look at Ali, who was innocently saddling up Negiv. He rolled his eyes at her and sniggered.

Sara turned back to Joe, struggling between anger at having been made a fool of and laughter at her own gullibility.

'And did he tell you I beat him mercilessly?' Joe asked, still laughing.

'No, just now and again,' she admitted and could not help but join in his laughter.

'You really believed I kept slaves?'

'Yes,' she giggled, 'and a harem.'

Joe laughed all the more. 'Well, he's a convincing little scallywag,' he admitted and then sobered up and looked at her seriously. 'I wonder why you always have such a good opinion of me,' he said and Sara flushed and looked down at the ground.

'So he's Jewish?' she asked, changing the subject and making her way towards the house.

'Yes, he's a Bedouin Jew from the Sudan,' Joe answered, falling into step beside her. 'He got lost tracking a horse stolen from his tribe and was captured and sold, then resold. I found him in Syria three or four years ago and bought him his freedom. Fate saw fit to send me the son before the wife,' he finished with a grin.

'He should be in school,' Sara said.

'Try keeping him anywhere for long,' Joe answered with affectionate irony.

'And what happens to him when you're away?' she persisted.

'He's well looked after by servants, by . . . friends,' he said and Sara felt an odd twisting somewhere inside her. His remark had opened up a whole new train of thought, and one she did not like too much. It had not occurred to her that he would have a mistress tucked away and she was about to ask him when an inner instinct

299

told her to leave well alone. What did it matter to her anyway.

Joe watched her, the gentle winter sunshine lighting her face, her hair ruffled slightly in the light wind. All of a sudden he felt his heart pounding – what was it about this woman that had such a devastating effect on him?

'Joe? We go now?' Ali appeared, leading Negiv, the gun slung across his back and impatience written all over him.

'Well, this is goodbye,' Joe said cheerfully. 'No tears I beg,' he added, raising her hand to his lips with a flourish. Then he turned to the jittering stallion and mounted him in one easy swing. Bending over, he pulled Ali up behind him and looked down at Sara. 'Goodbye,' he smiled.

Bella whinnied excitedly in her stall and Negiv turned towards the stables, throwing his proud head up with an answering cry.

'We should get those two together some day,' remarked Sara.

'We shall – when the time is right.' Joe grinned and then, his spurs pricking the stallion's sides, he wheeled and cantered off out of the gate.

Sara leant against the barn wall watching them go, feeling suddenly empty. She would miss him.

Irritably she pulled the shawl tightly round her and walked slowly back to the house. There was so much to do – Ruth's baby to see, clothes to sort out, the garden to pull back into shape. And all the men looked as though they could do with new shirts. And then tomorrow was the first day of the Channuka holiday, so doughnuts must be baked and potato pancakes made. She wondered if there was any white flour.

So much to do, she thought, suddenly cheerful and whistling for Sultan she walked back into the kitchen.

Aaron stood in the doorway of Sara's room, smiling at the feminine confusion he saw there. Ruth and Selena were on their hands and knees sorting through mounds of clothes, which lay in a sea of colour around them. Ruth's baby was wedged between two pillows on the bed and gurgling quietly to itself. Sara, her hair dishevelled, was rifling through a wooden box full of dress patterns and cheerfully bemoaning how out of date they all seemed. How pretty and girlish they looked, he thought, standing unobserved as he wondered once more if he was about to do the right thing.

300

Ever since Sara had returned home he had been turning the question over and over in his mind and this morning had been spent almost entirely in weighing up the possible consequences of what he was about to do. He sighed. In his heart he had known all along that he would tell her; after all Ruth already knew and Sara would have to know sooner or later anyway. This was no time to procrastinate. Apart from anything else he needed Sara, he needed her moral support but more than that he needed her help.

He stepped into the room and the three heads whipped round. 'You girls are so industrious that I hate to disturb you,' he said with a smile, 'but I'd like to talk to you, Sara, if you can spare the time.'

'Of course, Aaron,' she said, getting up and putting a hand up to hair to gather together the stray strands that were falling round her face.

'Bring a shawl and put your boots on – it's cold outside,' he said as he left her room and Sara sobered. She was very close to Aaron, deeply attuned to his moods and something in his voice worried her. Without wasting time she grabbed an old black shawl from the wardrobe.

'No slacking while I'm gone,' she said, wagging a stern finger at the girls. 'And that goes for you, too, baby,' she added, unable to resist kissing the rosy cheek as she passed, and she ran down the stairs and joined Aaron on the veranda.

'Let's walk out to the vineyards, I'd like a little privacy,' Aaron said and Sara nodded and put her arm through his.

'You seem very worried, is it anything serious?' she asked after a moment.

Aaron squeezed her arm. 'Come, I want to discuss a new development with you.'

They walked in silence until they reached the first terraces. Weak sunlight bathed the rich damp earth, lighting up the newly-pruned vines. A faint sea breeze ruffled their hair. Aaron stopped and looked round, scanning the landscape for any eavesdropper then, when he was sure they could not be overheard, he sat on one of the long, low, stone walls. He motioned Sara to sit beside him and took her hand, looking closely at her. She, still at a loss as to what was happening, looked straight back at him, her gaze meeting his fearlessly but with an unspoken query.

'I'll come straight to the point,' Aaron said, 'I know you have common sense and I know I can trust you – but I have had to think deeply about involving you. The consequences of anyone finding out what I am about to tell you would be disastrous so I must have your total discretion. You must not tell a soul.'

Sara nodded, her heartbeat quickening. 'Aaron, what has been going on?'

Aaron told her, keeping nothing back. After twenty minutes she knew everything that had happened since she had left for Constantinople and her heart was almost bursting with pride as she realised what her brother had done.

'Of course, the risks are enormous, Sara. That is why I had to think so hard before confiding in you. If anything were to happen to the group you would probably have been safest if you were ignorant – as it is you're in deep waters now.'

Sara's blue eyes danced with excitement. 'I can swim,' she said bluntly and her eyes went out to the horizon as she thought about what she had been told.

For months now they had been doing something positive about this wretched war and the cursed Turk. And now perhaps in some small way she could contribute! She turned back to Aaron, 'I want to help.'

'Sara, spying is not a role I relish – for you or for me. But if our actions bring liberation from the Turk forward by so much as a week that will be justification enough.'

'Thank you for telling me,' Sara said, her voice intense. 'I want to be of use. What happens to you happens to me.'

Aaron helped her to her feet. She moved stiffly, the damp had seeped into her bones, and he linked arms with her and slowly began walking back to the house. 'Are you sure?'

She laughed. 'God knows how sure I am.'

'Good. Then this is what I'd like you to do . . .'

Sara sat up in bed, an eiderdown wrapped round her as she went once more through the list of instructions Aaron had given. They were beautifully simple. In two days from now she was to keep watch from the round attic window for a ship. If it stopped opposite Atlit, signalled with black smoke, then turned sharp right towards the open sea, she was to hang the scarlet eiderdown she was now wrapped in from the window. When those at Atlit saw that signal they would, if the coast was clear, hang a white sheet up as signal to the ship to return that night. The ship would then increase smoke to show that the message had been received:

simple. If visibility was poor Sara, in her eyrie on the mountain top, would be in the best position to see any approaching ship.

Sara shivered with excitement. Here at last was her chance to do 'something dramatic' as Joe had said to her. Well, it was dramatic – and helpful. Even better, Aaron was going to teach her to code the material that came into his hands every day so that he would be free for other work. She had wanted to be allowed to meet the rowing boat on the shore, but had finally given in to Aaron's insistence that she should only do jobs of minimum danger.

She had also agreed to his demand that Selena should not be told anything about the network. 'I'm not passing judgement, but for the moment let's keep it in the family, eh?' and Sara, understanding his concern, had agreed. Selena was to use her considerable secretarial skills drafting and typing up Aaron's agricultural reports.

Sara snuggled down in her bed, determined to go to sleep, but too excited for any such thing. She lay another ten minutes, then, unable to stand being so wakeful, she slipped out of bed, lit her candle and, wrapped in a warm dressing gown, went down to the kitchen to make herself a cup of herb tea.

The kitchen was still warm and when she threw a handful of vines on to the fire it blazed up almost immediately. Putting the kettle on the hob, Sara settled down to wait for it to boil. Now that the kitchen was the only room in the house that was heated, some of the armchairs had been moved in from the sitting room. On the table beside the chair Sara found her father's Bible and, picking it up, opened it at random. The page opened at *Joshua* and she began to read how after the death of Moses the Lord had said to Joshua to get ready to cross the Jordan river into the land he was to give them – to the Israelites.

'I will give you every place you set your foot, as I promised Moses. Your territory will extend from the desert to Lebanon and from the great river the Euphrates – all the Hittite country – to the Great Sea on the west. No one will be able to stand up against you all the days of your life. As I was with Moses, so I will be with you, I will never leave you or forsake you.'

Then Joshua secretly sent two spies across the Jordan river to look over the land, 'especially Jericho.'

So they went there and lodged in the house of Rahab the harlot. The King of Jericho was told that some of the

303

Israelites had arrived to spy out the land and he sent a message to Rahab telling her, 'Bring out the men who came to you and entered your house, because they have come to search out all the country.' Rahab told the king's messengers that indeed the men had been there but at dusk they had left. 'Go after them quickly. You may catch up with them.' But Rahab had hidden the two spies under stalls of flax drying on her roof, there-by saving them.

So the king's men set out in pursuit of the spies and as soon as they left and the city gate was shut behind them Rahab went upon the roof to the two Israelites. 'Our lives for your lives,' the men assured her. 'If you don't tell what we are doing, we will treat you kindly and faithfully when the Lord gives us the land.' So she let them down by a rope through the window, for the house was part of the city wall. Then the men said to her, 'Behold, when we come into the land, thou shalt bind this line of scarlet thread in the window through which you let us down.' They told her to bring her father and mother and all her family into her house. 'As for anyone who is in the house with you, his blood will be on our head if a hand is laid on him.' Rahab agreed. 'Let it be as you say.' So she sent them away and they departed. And she tied the scarlet thread in the window.

She looked up blankly, '*Scarlet thread — scarlet eiderdown.*' How strange that it should have fallen open on that particular page. Rahab was most likely the first woman spy in the Bible — perhaps in history.

The sound of footsteps on the terrace outside snapped her out of her reverie. Her heart began to thump as the handle turned and the door was opened quietly. A tall man with dark hair and a thick, black beard stepped carefully in and stood a moment in the doorway, looking at her. For a second she did not recognise him and then she was flooded with the same irrational excitement she had felt the first time she had ever seen him.

With a cry she jumped from her chair and flung herself across the room at him. '*Daniel!*' Her heart was pounding as she flew into his arms. He held her so close, so tight she could hardly breathe. She let out a small protesting squeal as he loosened his grip. Looking up at him adoringly she laughed again and threw her arms round his neck. 'Oh Daniel! I love you so much,' she had to say the words and oddly enough had no reticence in expressing her feelings. He meant so much to her.

Daniel smiled down at her and hugged her again, smoothing her golden hair lovingly.

'Sara!' he whispered, kissing her hair, her cheeks, her eyes. Then, drawing back a little, he looked at her carefully for the first time. He caught his breath and smiled softly as he spoke. 'Sara, for God's sake, never leave me again, ever!'

BOOK THREE

CHAPTER TWENTY-ONE

June 1916

On afternoons like this it was easy to forget all she had been through since leaving the safety of the harem; easy to forget the war that was tearing the world apart and ravaging Palestine like a plague. It was even easy to put her own private frustrations and griefs behind her and laugh at the very idea of cares. On days like these Selena could almost feel something strong and wild emanating from the earth itself and, although she laughed at her fancy, she felt protected.

The Levinson house was full of quiet and sunlight. Papa Levinson, whom Selena had grown to love as her own father, was taking his after-lunch nap; Sam was helping Abu make rabbit traps in the barn; and Sara was closeted in her attic room where she had been all day. She had not even come down for lunch and when Selena had taken her a bowl of soup she had opened the door a crack, said she was not hungry and locked herself in again.

Selena, getting ready to go out, smiled to herself. She would have to have the brain of a sheep not to know that something was going on, and she had a very fair idea of what it might be. But she respected, rather than was offended by, their secrecy and did not harass them with questions. Every time she did make some small comment Sara would beg her: 'Selena, for your own sake, for all our sakes, don't ask questions. Just trust me,' with such a smile of knowing pride that Selena knew whatever it was was good. Selena was sure that the Levinsons were involved in some sort of action against the Turk and was glad of it. If she had been allowed to help, she would have and gladly, but until they asked her she sat patiently by, watching.

In her own way she too was harbouring a guilty secret. Next to the writing machine on the table was an old leather-bound copy of a French novel and between its lines she was writing her own story. It had become almost a sacred act to pour out all she had seen, thinking it through and writing it down made her feel better. She patted the book proprietorially and was just tying the veil around her sun bonnet when she heard flying footsteps in the hall and the door flew open. Sara appeared, her face alive with excitement.

'It's Daniel – I've just seen him riding up the hill. Do me a favour, wait for him in the garden and tell him to come straight up to the attic, will you?'

Selena nodded and the two girls exchanged secretive smiles, their silent communion more explicit than words could ever be. 'I was just going to the garden anyway, to check up on my children,' she said with a smile. The vegetable garden had become Selena's province and she had proved to have a green thumb which could cultivate a huge range of food; there was always something to eat from the garden now that Selena was in charge. Not that they were always the recipients; every now and then the Turks would descend on them like sudden rain and rape the garden of its offerings.

Sara smiled her thanks and felt a sudden stab of sadness. More than anything she wished she could confide in Selena, whom she trusted completely, but she must keep her word. She sighed and ran back up the stairs to the attic.

She closed the door of the attic and leaned back against it. Thank goodness Daniel was coming: her frustration at the day's events was growing too much to bear alone. She crossed to the little round window and picked up her field glasses. For a moment she watched Daniel, riding his shiny black colt, as he turned the bend in the road and was hidden by bushes. Then she trained the glasses back on to the horizon where the sea and sky merged into a watery smudge of blue and her face darkened.

What in the name of God was wrong? The question was exploding in the minds of every member of the network. For three months the British ship had appeared like clockwork, signalled according to the code and returned under the cloak of darkness to send the rowing boat to shore to exchange pouches with Daniel and Manny. This contact with the outside world and the feeling that something positive was being done gave them all extra strength to cope with the shattering blows falling on the Jewish community in Palestine.

Jews were being arrested on endless minor charges: desertion; hiding food or animals; speaking in Hebrew. Maps of any kind were forbidden as was the blue and white Hebrew flag. But worse than the arrests were the terrible hunger and disease. Winter had been glorious for the Turk: the British had been routed at Gallipoli and, as they fled back to Egypt, the Turkish troops released from the Peninsula began to pour into Palestine, stealing what food and transport they could on their way south and spreading spotted fever and cholera caught from the corpses of Armenians, which rotted along the roadsides. The Turk was not only squeezing the Jews dry; he was breaking their spirit and every day events grew worse.

Then the German blockade in March effectively prevented the relief shipments from America reaching Palestine and the settlers were faced with sharing what little food and medicine were left. Even the Bedouin had stopped their raids on the settlements – not out of respect but because they knew there was nothing to be had. By Aaron's reckoning, the Jewish community was declining at the rate of one per cent a month; if the British did not invade soon there would be no Jews left to lead a Jewish revival.

When Aaron's group learned that U-boats did not attack ships under a certain size they passed the information on to Cairo, and at the end of March, a tiny ship appeared with news that gave them all fresh hope. The British had set up a new strategic base at Katia, twenty-five miles east of Suez. It was officially there to defend the canal, but the network took it as a sign that the British were preparing for invasion. It was near there, Aaron reminded them (not that any of them needed it), that Napoleon had struck camp ready for his advance into Palestine. With renewed fervour the patrol group sent all information requested back to Cairo, plus anything else that could come in useful to the General Command.

At the end of April the ship appeared as usual on patrol on the horizon. But this time the signal given was different. They replied with the code Woolley had given them, but the ship had not signalled back and the rowing boat did not arrive, neither that night nor the next. For three nights Daniel and Manny had stayed on the beach until dawn, and nothing happened. Yesterday the ship had again appeared on the horizon, and once again the signal was different. Sara was so frustrated she could have run down to the beach and swum out to the ship, demanding an explanation. Today at lunch time she had seen it returning from its patrol in Tyre and it had not even paused.

And now the horizon was still clear. She put the glasses down with a sigh and returned to the letter she had spent most of the day trying to write to Chaim. That was hopeless, she had too much on her mind and nothing to say to her husband.

The feelings of loss and frustration after the months of hope were more than she could bear. To Sara, her part in the struggle against the Turk was in the nature of a Crusade: even her passion for Daniel had slipped down a notch in her emotional scale compared to the passion she felt for the cause.

She was amazed at her calmness towards Daniel. She was no longer in a hurry. Oh yes, her head swam when he kissed her, and her senses still clamoured with heady joy when he touched her but she no longer fought to weave an invisible and binding web round him. She felt the languid pleasure of a woman who knows that the man she loves has surrendered himself to her, and that soon, very soon, they would be lovers.

There was a knock at the door and she leapt up to let Daniel in, immediately aware of the tension in his lean, bronzed face. Daniel touched her cheek for the briefest moment, then crossed the room and threw himself into the old leather armchair. He covered his face with his hands for a moment and then looked up at Sara. 'You saw it too.' It was a statement more than a question, but Sara nodded, her expression bleak.

'Yes, at about noon. It didn't even stop, just carried straight on back to Egypt.'

Daniel jumped out of the chair and began pacing the small room. 'Why doesn't it stop? It has worked beautifully for four months – what are we doing wrong now? We've risked our skins getting the information asked for – and then the bloody British desert us!' He sat down again and Sara watched him in silence.

There was nothing to say; they had all analysed the situation endlessly. She took a deep breath. 'The most feasible explanation is that they have changed their signal and Woolley's Arab spies have decided not to pass the information on to us – probably to knock out the competition,' she added sourly.

'But that's just the point,' Daniel burst out. 'Don't you see it's all my fault. Making contact with the British was the most crucial act of my whole life and I was stupid enough not to have arranged some back-up system with Woolley and Captain Jones.'

Sara shook her head. 'Daniel, it's easy to be wise after the event. The question is, what do we do next?'

Daniel sighed deeply and stood up again. 'That's why I'm here. You're to get your things together and come with me down to Atlit. Aaron has a plan he wants to discuss with you.'

Sara felt a stab of apprehension. Daniel had talked Aaron into allowing him to do something foolhardy and Aaron was going to break the news to her. She kept her face composed as she asked lightly, 'You're not going to try and smuggle your way back to Cairo again are you?'

Despite her care not to show feelings, Sara's face was so full of anxiety for him that at last Daniel's face relaxed into a smile. 'No Sara, I'm not,' he promised. 'With no more neutral ships in the port and the ever-active Colonel von Kressenstein trying to rout the British in the Sinai even I realise it would be suicide.' He smiled again at the relief that flooded her face. Crossing the room he pulled her to him and held her possessively. 'Sara, I haven't yet told you how much I've missed you in the last few weeks,' he murmured.

Work and her family had kept them apart and now she clung to him. 'I've missed you too, Daniel,' she whispered, the longing shining out of her eyes.

A thrill ran through him. Soon he would possess her utterly. When Aaron's new plan was put into operation, the obstacle of her family's presence would be removed and they would at last be together in every sense of the word. 'I know, my darling, I know,' he said. He kissed the silky crown of her head. 'It won't be long now,' he said hoarsely.

Sara drew back, her heart racing, and looked up at him. 'What does that mean?'

Daniel smiled. 'You'll understand when you've talked to Aaron. Now get your things together. It will be too late for you to come back here tonight.'

Sara nodded. 'Give me five minutes,' she said, her eyes glowing. Delighted at the prospect of action, she disappeared through the door, smiling to herself.

Selena was kneeling happily on the sunbaked earth between the rows of vegetables, her bonnet lying on the ground beside her. The air was cool enough to make the warmth of the sun on her back pleasant and the breeze brought her the smell of drying pumpkin and white roses. For Selena the time she spent in the garden was used in the same way as her daily walk around the Rose Palace gardens. It was a time for privacy and secret thoughts; right now her thoughts were on Sara, who had run into the garden, her eyes filled with a radiant light to tell her that she was off to spend the night at Atlit. 'I think Daniel has adultery in mind,' she had whispered with a nervous giggle, 'just like King David.'

Selena shook her head, smiling to herself, but feeling a stab of envy at her friend's happiness. Why was she destined to have men fall in love with her for whom she could feel nothing but friendship? She thought with a pang of guilt of Hans Werner. How she wished she could have returned his love.

Selena scratched the trowel into the soil, thinking how far away her soft Constantinople life now seemed. She hardly ever thought of it, and certainly would not want to leave this life, despite the hardships. *It's the summer*, she thought. *That's what is making me maudlin.*

Getting up, she crossed to the sacking where figs were drying in the sun. Today there would be nothing for Fatma to preserve or pickle, her latest mania. No wild fruit or berry had escaped Fatma's experiments and no corner of the house was safe from a jar of this or a bottle of that being tucked away for safe storage. Sara said it was a wonder they were not poisoned by Fatma and her experiments, and teasingly assured the old woman that one morning they would all be dead!

She turned the figs over, but her attention was diverted by Sultan, who came tearing round the corner in hot pursuit of a tiny kitten which shot past Selena and up the mulberry tree. Sultan stood at the bottom of the tree, whining, his tail wagging with pride.

'Bad boy, Sultan. Kennel,' Selena said sternly, pointing back towards the stables. With a last longing look up at the shivering black and white kitten he mooched off in the direction he had come from.

Selena turned her attention to the cat, clinging desperately to the wood and mewing faintly. It was too frightened to move, so Selena readied herself for a rescue attempt. She climbed on to the stone bench under the tree and stretched her arms out, making soft, coaxing noises to calm the frightened animal. It was just out of her reach. Selena considered the lowest branch and wondered if by climbing on to it she could reach the cat. She was so intent on the problem that she did not hear Captain Kristopher Sarkis coming slowly down the garden path, a book tucked under his arm.

He, however, did notice the slim figure standing on the bench, her arms raised to the skies as though in prayer to some ancient gods. He stopped and looked up. 'The blessings of God upon you,' he said in formal greeting.

The girl turned round in surprise and as soon as she saw him her lovely face was flooded with rank fear. He looked at the oval face and the world changed.

Climbing unsteadily down from the bench, Selena tried to contain her terror at the sight of a hated septieh. Images of the Armenian dead and dying came flooding into her head. She saw only the uniform that was inextricably woven into the fabric of her nightmare. To her this man standing in front of her was just a part of what the whole septieh represented – rape, terror and destruction.

She felt her face blanch and prayed her voice wouldn't tremble and give her away. 'And upon you too,' she answered. She stumbled over the words. Her heart was pounding and she had to fight not to cry out and run. Had he come to question her? Or was it the Levinsons he was after?

The Captain's brown eyes locked into hers. He had never seen such beauty and could not take his eyes off her as she stood, graceful and trembling like a fawn on the edge of flight. Sarkis felt his heart thumping; the girl had an effect on him that he had never experienced before. 'I'm sorry,' he said, pulling himself together. 'I didn't mean to frighten you. I thought you were a dream . . . an apparition . . .' he tailed off, feeling foolish. He could see from her face that she was so frightened she could hardly hear.

A faint miaow floated down from the mulberry tree and, looking up, Sarkis saw the reason for the girl's predicament. He smiled. 'Shall I get her?' he said, looking back at her. Selena looked at him, this time seeing beyond the uniform to the man. His eyes were gentle, his voice soothing and calm. She felt herself relax a little, and told herself not to be afraid.

Sarkis saw her chin lift a little higher and the huge brown eyes brighten slowly.

She nodded. 'Yes, please.' Her voice was so soft it was barely more than a whisper.

The Captain unbuckled his sword belt and pistol and jumped lightly up on to the bench. The kitten took immediate fright and scrambled further up the tree, with Sarkis in pursuit. Selena, who had been standing ready to flee back into the safety of the house, suddenly felt her fear was unnecessary. The Captain looked like a real person, she thought, and there must be some decent men in uniform. Hans Werner, for instance. And this man didn't look Turkish, she realised, noticing his thick blond hair and long, slim body.

At last he tore the kitten from its hold and brought it safely back to ground. 'Thank you,' Selena said, taking the kitten from him and noticing how warm his smile was. She pressed the furry, trembling body to her and looked up at him. Sarkis felt his heart stir as he looked into those huge eyes staring into his so seriously. He stood uncomfortably, trying to tear his gaze from her.

'Is anything the matter, Captain?'

'Sarkis – Kristopher Sarkis,' he said with a bow. 'I just, well – you're the most beautiful woman I've ever seen.' He was amazed at hearing himself say the words and Selena blushed, dropping her eyes to the kitten. She sat down on the bench, aware that her heart was pounding again. Captain Sarkis was throwing her into a turmoil and it was nothing to do with panic. Sarkis? The name somehow seemed familiar.

Telling himself to stop acting like a fool Sarkis buckled his belt back on. 'I brought my horse up to Abu,' he explained, 'he's injured his hoof and is in pain.' Selena nodded, many people brought their horses to be cured by Abu's expert touch. 'And I also want to pay my respects to old Mr Levinson. I don't come to Zichron much these days, since it's not on my patrol.' He trailed into silence again, brushing a lock of hair from his forehead and admiring the pretty picture of Selena with the kitten already fast asleep on her lap.

Selena picked up the book Sarkis had been carrying. She wanted to know more about him. The book was in Arabic, a collection of poems by an eighth-century Sunni writer. 'The Prophet Mohammed was not in favour of poetry,' she said with a tiny smile that offered Sarkis some hope.

'He did not approve of many of the things I enjoy, such as the wines of Zichron,' he responded with a grin and sat next to her on the bench. *So he drinks wine – perhaps he's not a Moslem, not even a lapsed one*, Selena thought, and for some reason was very happy.

'Then you are not a Moslem,' she ventured.

'A Christian, from Armenia,' he answered simply, fearing that the woman he had so suddenly fallen in love with was a Moslem or Jewess. *My first great love – doomed like that of Romeo for Juliet*, he thought dramatically and then, *Mother of God, what is happening?* He could not believe his ears. 'What did you say?'

Selena was staring at him in amazement. Of course Sarkis was a common enough Armenian name – that was why it had rung a bell. 'I said that I too am Armenian,' she repeated softly.

Sarkis was staring at her, wondering what quirk of fate had brought them together here. Then he laughed. 'I knew there was something different about you from the moment I saw you. What are you doing here with the Levinsons?'

She hesitated a moment, aware how his warm, honest eyes were watching her. 'I'm a friend of Sara's – from Constantinople,' she felt her heart race with nerves.

'They are a remarkable family.'

Selena nodded. 'Yes, they are very special people.'

She looked frightened, and Sarkis wanted to put his hand out to reassure her, but felt that if he moved towards her she would run.

'Where in Armenia are you from?' For an instant she just looked at him, then decided to tell him everything about her life. Why not? He was an Armenian like herself.

Speaking in their native language, Selena poured out all that had happened to bring her here, from her childhood in the mountains and her kidnapping onwards. She went on until she had told him everything, keeping nothing back and finishing at the moment he had found her praying to a kitten in a tree.

For almost two hours they sat in the afternoon sun, talking and learning about each other. She told him of the horrors she had seen on her journey to Zichron, horrors she had heard rumours of but had not wanted to believe. There were tears in his eyes as he listened.

He had taken her hand without being aware of making the movement, and he held it tightly as she told her tale. 'And what will you do now?'

'I shall wait until the Turk is beaten and then . . .' Her hands flew to her mouth and she stared at him, helpless with terror. She had said the unforgivable – and to a septieh. It was all over, her hopes, her life . . . the end had begun. She closed her eyes in anguish, and felt the Captain squeeze her hand.

'It's all right, Selena. There are many of us who think that way.' The huge brown eyes opened again. 'War is a terrible thing,' Sarkis continued reassuringly. 'Little by little everyone goes crazy and forgets God.' He sighed deeply. He was not unaware of what was happening through the Empire but had been stupid enough to think the reports exaggerated, to hope that the anti-Armenian purge would stay confined to the vilayets. Perhaps it would, but he would have to listen more carefully now.

The evening was setting in, long fingers of shadow reaching out from the orchard, the garden striped with shade and smudged with apricot and gold. Sarkis looked at the kitten in Selena's lap, now totally at ease and purring like a tiny motor. Then he looked up at Selena. He felt bonded to her as he had to no other woman. 'I am a simple man,' he said, his eyes serious as they searched her face. 'I fell in love with you the moment I saw you and I am going to marry you.'

Selena looked at him in amazement, her eyes widening slowly. Then she laughed gently. 'But Captain Sarkis,' she said. 'I hardly know you.'

Sara threw Bella's reins to a waiting Arab boy and, hat in hand, took the steps to Aaron's study two at a time, eager to know what all the fuss was about. Dinner at the station was at six and the sounds of table-laying and the dinner bell ringing in the fields warned her that she did not have much time for a private word with her brother. Dinner at the station had become more and more like a meal at a military camp as, since the return of swarms of locusts from the south, Jemel Pasha had told Aaron he could use any soldiers he thought he needed in his campaign against the pest. Aaron had used his new authority with enthusiasm and now, with ex-soldiers stationed in strategic positions all over Palestine and Syria, there was always a constant stream of newcomers passing through.

'Come on,' Sara said, tapping her riding whip impatiently against her skirt as she waited for Daniel to catch her up. Daniel, carrying a kerosene lamp, smiled but did not hurry his step. Sara opened the door for him to pass, rushed in to the study to kiss her brother and back across the room to lock the door behind them, while Aaron locked the windows and drew the curtains. Daniel lit another lamp and sat on the sofa and Sara, trying to restrain her inquisitiveness, sat down beside him, watching Aaron as he checked the windows and returned to his desk.

'Well?' she asked after a moment's silence. 'I'm dying of curiosity. What is this all about?'

Daniel and Aaron exchanged smiles and then Aaron's face grew serious again and he leant across the table, looking solemnly at his sister. 'I'm leaving next week for Germany,' he said, and smiled at Sara's startled reaction. 'Don't worry – it's all official. I've had my travel documents signed by Jemel Pasha himself,' and he tapped a pile of papers in front of him at the desk.

Sara stared at him, her eyes wide with surprise. 'Germany? But what for?' she stammered.

Aaron held her gaze, and lowering his voice answered: 'Ostensibly to visit my scientific colleagues at the university in Berlin. I've told you how interested the Germans are in my new strain of sesame seed, and now I've convinced them that a trip is necessary for consultation. In fact,' he added with deep satisfaction, 'we set the seed some while back.' And he chuckled drily.

Sara still could not understand what he was driving at. 'Then why go?'

'Because from there I plan to smuggle myself to England through one of the neutral countries. I've done some research – it could be done.'

Sara drew in a horrified breath. 'Dear God, you can't be serious.' Throughout the ride down to the station she had been puzzling over what could be in Aaron's mind, but had not imagined anything a quarter as dramatic as this.

Aaron ignored her remark and lit a cigarette, his expression highlighted in the flare of the match. Sara realised he was not even worried, just totally confident of the success of his plan. 'I've been planning this for some time – ever since Daniel came back from Cairo. Once Woolley realised our aim was national independence rather than sacks of English gold, he suggested we get someone from the network to London.'

Daniel interrupted. 'London is full of important members of the Jewish community, including our old friend Baron Rothschild, who are keen to bring about a Jewish revival in Palestine, under British auspices. When Aaron sees them . . .'

'If I can reach Britain,' Aaron corrected, 'and bring the attention of the powers that be to our network, I can see no reason why contact with Atlit should not be re-established. I am sure that half our problems in Cairo are because we are dealing with low-grade intelligence officers – they have no real influence and certainly no political authority. If we can impress the War Office in London, they will force those unimaginative buffoons at the Arab Bureau in

319

Cairo to take us seriously.' Aaron stubbed out his cigarette and looked from Sara to Daniel. 'And I fully intend to be taken seriously.'

Sara looked at him for a moment, filled with pride at her brother's bravery and logical reasoning. She knew that, while Daniel might rush headlong into something with no real thought, Aaron would have worked everything out before making up his mind and telling anyone what he meant to do. 'It's a brilliant idea, Aaron. But are you really sure you're not being too ambitious?' she said.

'As our Arab brothers say, a falcon which hunts mice is worthless,' he answered with a smile. 'I don't pretend it's not going to be tricky – and challenging – but I believe I can pull it off.'

Sara nodded and laughed, with Aaron in this frame of mind, few could doubt him. Then another thought occurred to her. 'Who's going to run the station? You can't let that go to seed!' Daniel grinned at her unintentional pun, but Aaron looked at her gravely.

'You are.'

Sara looked at him, surprised that he should joke about something so important, and then broke off in mid-chuckle, staring at her brother. From his face she knew that he was deadly in earnest.

'You can't mean it – why not Daniel?' she asked incredulously.

'Daniel will take over the locust patrol and liaise with Jemel Pasha, while secretly running the network. If you are willing – and confident that you can do it – I would like you to assume control of the day-to-day running of the station. Everyone here knows and likes you and the fact that you are my sister will wipe out the possibility of petty jealousies and squabbles.'

'Sam?' she queried.

Aaron grinned. 'Frankly, Sara, you're the best man for the job.'

A wave of exhilaration swept over Sara. This was the kind of challenge she had longed for in life and never thought possible. This was a chance she must seize, and prove herself worthy once and for all.

'Well, do you think you can handle it?'

'I can do my best,' she answered proudly, trying to hide her excitement and resisting the urge to throw her arms round Aaron and hug him in gratitude.

'I know you will,' Aaron said warmly. 'Now to details. I have put back enough supplies and gold to last the station until

November. By that time relations with Egypt should have reopened and with any luck the relief and gold from Alex in America should be stacking up nicely in Cairo. Until then I'm relying on you to keep the station going and balance the books.'

Sara nodded. 'Of course. And I already know how the books work – you can trust me, Aaron.'

He looked at her dubiously for a moment. 'Sara,' he said, a note of warning in his voice, 'I want to make it perfectly clear that you are to have nothing more to do with the network than you do at the moment. Continue the coding work, but you must promise me to do nothing else.'

Sara rolled her eyes to the ceiling in mock despair at the seriousness of his tone. 'I promise,' she said, and then added in a hurry. 'Aaron, I know what you feel about Selena – but may she join me here? I can't just desert her in Zichron. Besides she will be an enormous help to me here. And I won't tell her a thing she doesn't know already.'

'I've already thought of that,' Aaron said. 'Yes, of course, she can come. But I have a feeling she already knows too much for her own good, so be sure to be discreet. The fewer people who know the better.' Lighting another cigarette, he tipped back his chair and stretched his legs. 'There is one other thing I am counting on you doing for me,' he said and waved his arm at Daniel. 'I don't trust our impulsive friend here not to take it into his head to dash across the Sinai to Cairo if he doesn't hear from me in the first week. We know how limited his patience is, and I'm not sure he'll be able to keep quiet for two months without trying something of his own.'

'Nonsense,' Daniel retorted, furious at having Sara ranged against him. 'I've given you my word – I'll have the patience of Job.'

'From your mouth to God's ears,' Aaron quoted with a chuckle.

Sara leant back on the sofa and turned to Daniel with a smile. It was at that moment that the full reality of what he had said to her at Zichron really sunk in. With Aaron gone they would be as good as alone in the station. Her family, the obstacle that stood between their becoming lovers, would be safely at Zichron.

She laughed a little nervously. 'I'll keep a close eye on him – I'll be his guardian angel,' she promised, feeling oddly embarrassed and giggling slightly. She felt vaguely superstitious at the fact of all her wishes being suddenly laid at her feet. She had Daniel, she had the responsibility she had craved, she had freedom – would fate one day turn on her with avenging power, seeking retribution for all her good fortune? She had never queried the right and wrong of loving Daniel before now; it was as if a newly awakened conscience was unfolding inside her. But she knew she would not step back: she wanted what lay ahead too badly to falter now.

It was a magically still night, the air heady with the scent of the tobacco plants and young grasses and flowers. The full moon cast its light through the open window, dappling Sara's room with silvery light and milky shades. Sara lay, stretched on the bed, watching the play of the shadows on the wall. These first few days of her new responsibility had been punishingly hard, but tonight she felt no fatigue, had no desire for sleep. All evening a feeling of anticipation had been rising within her and now, naked and still, she lay content to rest and wait until Daniel came to her.

In the last couple of days Sara and Daniel had built a temporary bridge between them, knowing that they needed time to make the step between expectation and fulfilment. Working closely together, they had for the moment needed no more than that. But this evening they had said good night as usual, and their eyes had locked in a gaze so full of passion that for a split second Sara felt she had seen into Daniel's soul and she knew with total certainty that tonight he would come to her.

She heard the clock strike ten and then the sleeping house was silent once more, the stillness broken only by the sound of the breeze in the trees and the sea lapping the shore. There was no hurry; Sara lay, still and patient.

A stair creaked and Sara sat up on her elbows, listening with all her senses, her heart quickening in anticipation. Light footsteps came down the corridor and stopped outside the door to her room. It opened and Daniel stepped swiftly inside. Locking the door firmly behind him he stood back, staring at her. The moonlight had transformed her into a silvery statue; she seemed unreal, like something out of a dream.

'My God, you're beautiful,' Daniel said, his voice low and husky with long-suppressed desire. She said nothing, a slight smile on her lips and her eyes half-closed, basking in his admiration. Daniel caught his breath, and irresistibly drawn by the sheer sexuality that flowed across the room to him, moved towards her. He undressed quickly, his eyes never leaving hers, the blood rushing through him. Never had he wanted a woman as he wanted Sara now.

Sara held her breath, her brain dizzy with excitement. She had been fantasizing about this moment for years and now it was here. *My God, how I love him*, she thought, entranced at the sight of his tanned, smoothly muscular body looming over her. Every part of her was tormented with longing, straining towards consummation as his face closed slowly on hers.

In seconds he was ravaging her mouth, his tongue probing until it found hers. His hand slid down her body and covered her breast, his fingers caressing her nipple, which rose taut and erect to meet them. She gasped, overwhelmed by the thrilling sensations which swept her body as the pulse deep inside her became a fierce throb.

Daniel was half mad now, the heat raging in him soaring as her passion mounted. The desire he had held back for so many years swept through him with a strength and potency greater than any he had experienced before. She was his – always had been, always would be. And he wanted her instantly. Now.

He covered her and felt her body, liquid fire beneath his, arch to meet him. He paused a moment and gently ran his fingers through that marvellous hair, pushing it away from her face as he looked into her eyes. He wanted to see her face as she became truly his, he truly hers.

Then he gripped her, bringing her to him, her hips thrusting as he plunged inside, deeper and deeper, his body beating against hers faster and faster, his eyes watching the surprised pleasure in hers as she grasped, then clung to him as they fused together in a fierce, burning heat.

Sara lay awake for a long time afterwards, filled with a languorous weakness, as though she were floating some way above her body. She was happier than she could ever remember being. She moved slightly towards the heat of Daniel's body and he moaned in his sleep, reaching out and holding her to him, one hand clasped around her breast. She watched the brown fingers on the whiteness of her skin and covered his hand with hers.

When the war is over, she thought, *once I have sorted out my problems with Chaim* . . . She shivered, suddenly conscious of exactly what she had done and of its implications. Her mood sobered. Sara had analysed the situation between Chaim and her countless times before, but at that moment, her emotions high and her body still warm from Daniel's loving, a sudden remorse overcame her and she felt a surge of guilt at the thought of Chaim.

She moved nervously in the bed, struck by a new idea. What if she were to become pregnant by Daniel? A thrill of panic ran through her, compounded by the thought of how disappointed her father would be if he knew what she was doing. She cheered herself at the thought that she had not, after all, become pregnant by Chaim, and it was certainly not for want of his trying. She shivered. Constantinople now seemed a bad dream and she carefully kept out all memories of her married life. She would not go back – she could not. A soft sigh escaped her. This was really not the time to start worrying about proprieties, reputation, family and adultery.

Daniel murmured something in his sleep: soft, unintelligible words, and nestled closer to her. Pulled out of her troubled thoughts she smiled as she felt his body warm and smooth against hers. Daniel was once again the most important thing in the world to her, more important than life itself. She would take each day as it came. It would require a certain amount of courage, she was aware of that but – *the rest of the world doesn't exist* she told herself, her eyes closing sleepily at last.

But it did, and she knew it did.

CHAPTER TWENTY-TWO

November 1916

The next few months passed in a blur of almost perfect happiness for Sara. There was no doubt that the Turk's brief moment of triumph earlier in the year was really over. The war had certainly gone well for them so far; at Gallipoli the Turk had repulsed the most determined efforts of the British Army; at Kut in Meso-potamia the British were held at siege for one hundred and fifty-six days before surrendering unconditionally at the end of April. But there were now clouds on the blue of their horizon.

According to information gathered from the Bedouin who, even in the thick of war, moved freely between Turkish and British lines, the ever-active Bavarian Colonel von Kressenstein had in August attacked the British at Romani, twenty miles east of the Suez Canal. They were soundly trounced and apparently Australian-mounted Anzac troops were now scouring the desert, in their element and eager to kill any lurking Turk they might come across.

It also became increasingly obvious that cracks were beginning to appear in the German Army and that Germany itself was in trouble. Food was in desperate shortage and rationing had been introduced.

Then came some surprising news: Husain Ibn Ali, the Hashemite Shareef of Mecca, called to the Arabs to revolt and rid the Middle East of the Ottoman Turks and their infidel allies the Germans. 'Although he seems to be doing it under the protection of the infidel British,' Daniel remarked cynically. Britain, desperate to enlist support for the Army effort from all sides, appeared to be making promises to all and sundry and had now told Husain Ibn Ali its Army would back an independent Arabia. The hope was that proclamation of the Arab Revolt would induce Arab soldiers fighting in the Turkish Army to change their allegiance.

Sara took an active interest in the progress of the war, but her heart and mind were totally involved in the station – and Daniel. Her entire life until now seemed a pale introduction to the present. The work was hard and the pressure enormous, but she barely noticed that she needed only a few hours' sleep, or that a handful of figs and a slice of bread kept her satisfied for a whole day. The unsparing demands on her left no time for hunger or tiredness.

There were crops to sow – as many and as much as possible – and once sown to be watched and cultivated. The men had to be organised and rotas were drawn up to try and salvage the grape harvest, although they had to accept that the shortage of hands meant that most would be lost. Even Kristopher Sarkis and a few of the septieh helped out, glad of some food in payment for they had not been paid for months and had to supplement their meagre rations with whatever they could pilfer from the horses' fodder. Meals were increasingly difficult to organise, but she and Frieda between them managed to convince everyone that there was enough food to keep them all from starvation. So there was – but how long would it last?

And when the last meal was finished and night fell, the day was not over. Then she would study Aaron's maps and collate all the stories pouring into the station. She would follow up the information, making enquiries and asking for more facts until she felt she understood everything happening on the Egyptian and Russian fronts.

She was amazed at the coverage Aaron and Daniel had worked out between them: the intelligence scheme was more thorough than she had ever imagined. Despite her promise to Aaron within a few weeks of his departure she was running the network almost alone. Daniel, with Manny, Lev and Robby, was often away touring the country with the double-edged purpose of exterminating the locust and destroying the Turk. 'And when we've done that we will have perfected the best insecticide in existence – two plagues of pests down in one!' they chuckled among themselves.

The network now had considerably more scope than it had at first. Gradually more informants, on the whole relatives and friends of the nucleus group, had made it clear that they would like to help rout the Turk, and as time went on new contacts, mostly

Jewish Army doctors and engineers, with access to high places came forward with information.

Sara found fitting the pieces of information together rather like attempting a jigsaw – something she had never been very good at before. But now, instead of producing a picture of a tree or some rural scene from a faraway European country, the pieces joined together to produce an almost comprehensive plan of army movements and supplies. The satisfaction she felt when two pieces slotted together outweighed anything she had known. She began to know what details to ask for and soon became adept at getting the answers she wanted. Although the ship did not return, Sara continued to work towards what she thought the British would like to know and, proud of her work, she longed for them to turn up and ask for fresh intelligence.

She was not rash, though, and never took an unwarranted risk. One slip and the wrath of the Turk would descend on the Jews. She had glimpsed what might follow and that she should be in any way responsible for such horror filled her with terror and caused her to be cautious.

Another of her anxieties was that Aaron would not reach England and that the contents of the ever-filling tin box, gathered at such enormous risk and lying buried in the cellar, would never be decoded. She would shied away from that fear, feeling there was something almost sacrilegious in even considering it. There had been no word from Aaron since he was in Constantinople due to leave for Berlin the following morning. Since then – and it was ten weeks – they had heard nothing but Sara did not expect it and remained convinced that he would achieve what he had set out to do.

As Aaron had warned, Daniel was beginning to have doubts. Sara could almost hear his mind ticking over, working out the time it would take Aaron to get from Constantinople to Berlin . . . from Berlin to England . . . England to Cairo. She knew that he struggled against these uncertainties, but was not blind to his growing restlessness, to the undercurrents that rose nearer to the surface with each day that passed.

Almost imperceptibly, it became clear from their intelligence that the British were gradually shifting from an entirely defensive position in the canal to what appeared to be an offensive one. They were balanced on the brink of an invasion of Palestine. Daniel was driven nearly to despair by the knowledge that they had information which might push the British towards offensive action and help them avert possible calamity – save them precious time and lives.

Sara shared Daniel's frustration at seeing the fruits of their labour, gathered at risk to their lives, withering in the cellar, much of it becoming useless as positions in the Sinai shifted. She also shared his feelings of impotence in the face of their country being savaged by incomprehensible acts of violence. They could now see signs of starvation in towns and cities, while in Jaffa and Jerusalem the prejudice against the Jew, which had lain dormant for so long, was now open and rampant. Sara, like Daniel, wanted to be able to do something, to take the world as it was and turn it on its head, but she retained her faith in Aaron even as she watched Daniel gradually losing his.

Daniel's desire for positive action seemed to eat into his soul. During the day the crushing load of responsibilities left him no time to think but at night . . . there was time to think then. He still came to her bed every night that he spent at the station, and Sara had no doubt that she was loved, but she was under no illusion as to where she stood in Daniel's emotional priorities. 'When you choose me, you choose my struggle,' he had once told her. 'Your personal feelings, your desires, must all be secondary to that.' The concept sounded very noble but the feelings his statement aroused in Sara were anything but that.

She had the distinct suspicion that, whenever she tried to curb his impetuosity, to express her fears that he might do something rash, he looked on her as he might a spoilt child. But she was eaten up with worry that in his wish to rewrite the rules he would take risks, which would bring the network down with him. It would not take much for him to become addicted to risk, to take the final, damning step . . .

In spite of her unease in the dark reaches of the night, Sara felt useful and important for the first time in her life, and her strength and confidence increased daily. She had moved Aaron's desk to the window and would look up from her work, searching the horizon, knowing that, if not this month, then the next she would see the ship signalling its arrival.

It was a hot, still, restless day that reminded Sara of her wedding, and the thought prompted her to sit down and write to Chaim. She did so once a month, not caring whether the letters ever reached him, and happy to be able to salve her conscience so easily. She no longer regarded herself as a married woman and although, out of respect for her father's feelings, she still wore her wedding ring, she had lost so much weight that it was now on her middle finger.

Bored with writing the letter and unable to summon up the enthusiasm to continue it, she sat staring out of the window, watching Selena and Kristopher Sarkis walking slowly up the path between the apple and fig trees. It was obvious how deeply in love they were, and Sara knew that it was a love that would never be altered by time or circumstance. Founded on rock, they would wait patiently for the moment they could marry and then, with hands joined and hearts united, would face together whatever the future brought.

It struck Sara that she and Daniel would never be like that. Theirs was a passion built on flame and sand and dreams, not rock. Their kind of love was not a foundation on which to build a life. Sara sat up with a jolt, the sudden realisation confusing her. Perhaps she had known this unconsciously all along . . .

There was no emotional dishonesty in Daniel's love for her. He had never told her that he loved her more than anything else on this earth; he had never said that he wished to cherish and protect her with his life – for all his life. No, he had always admitted that he would willingly sacrifice her happiness and his own for his beliefs. But love – the need to be emotionally as well as physically fused – demanded just those commitments.

Another thought occurred to Sara. She loved Daniel. There was a strong bond between them, but now, looking deep into her heart, she realised that the love she had for him had subtly changed. Her love for him was different – because she was different. With a flash of unprecedented objectivity, it came to her that Daniel was no longer the centre, the *raison d'être* of her life, that other things – life itself – had altered her emotional outlook, shifted its balance away from Daniel.

A rap at the door broke into her not very pleasant conclusion and she looked up to see Manny walk in. He seemed to be in a state of barely contained excitement and as Sara jumped up to welcome him and close the door it was with the sinking feeling that he brought bad news.

'I was arrested,' he said abruptly, throwing himself down on to the sofa and looking up with a broad grin.

'What?' Sara gasped, clasping the arm of the battered leather chair opposite him. 'Where?'

'At the garrison in Beersheba,' he answered, dabbing the sweat from his upper lip with the sleeve of his shirt. 'Got any water?'

'Of course,' Sara said and crossing to the desk poured him a glass, which he drank in one, long gulp.

Manny put down his glass with a gasp of satisfaction and looked at Sara with a smile. 'But as you see I managed to extricate myself – or rather you did it for me.'

His grin grew broader as he watched Sara's puzzlement grow. 'I did?' she repeated, her dark brows shooting up her forehead and she sat down again heavily.

Manny leaned forward on the sofa and nodded delightedly. 'I was on my usual tour of inspection and decided to pop into the Beersheba garrison on the way back. There had been a lot of movement in the last few days and I thought I should check out what they had in the way of artillery.'

Sara shook her head in resignation. Manny was over-confident and daring and she had always suspected he took too many risks.

'Well,' he continued, 'I managed with ease to work my way through the various security rings until I was actually in the fort's arsenal – my military passport impressed everyone so much they did not even question me.' He paused for a moment, savouring his triumph. 'Sara, I counted seven . . .'

'Later, Manny. Tell me what happened next.' For once Sara was more interested in the story than the intelligence he brought.

'I was busy chatting away to a couple of Turkish guards and doing my best to memorise everything I could see when a German officer appeared out of the blue and began questioning me. What did I want, who was I, how come I could speak German – all that sort of thing. I told him I was a member of the locust patrol and showed him my papers. He couldn't read Turkish and passed them to one of the guards. He was clearly illiterate and passed them to another guard who looked at them upside down for a few minutes before admitting that he couldn't read either. Honestly, Sara, it was a farce! Finally, they called over a Turkish officer, who translated it for the German. So then I was told that my pass limited me to areas where there were locusts and he asked me sarcastically if I could see any there as he certainly couldn't. I told him a Bedouin had told me that he had seen some moving in that direction . . .'

'Was that true?' Sara interrupted.

Manny gave her a look. 'Of course not, Sara, but I had to say something. Anyway he looked at me in that arrogant, disbelieving way the Germans have and told me was I aware that I was in an area of high military security and I had no business being there. So it started all over again. What did I want, who was I working for, did I know the penalties for spying and that if he chose he could take me to the square and have me shot then and there. I must admit I was beginning to feel nervous . . .'

'Scared to death I'd have thought,' Sara put in with a grin, and Manny laughed agreement.

'So I realised that I was getting nowhere explaining my case to him and demanded to see the commanding officer. Our little argument attracted the attention of another officer, a Lieutenant-Colonel with a limp, who came over and asked what was going on. We both told him. He seemed very interested in Aaron's name and took my papers and gave them a good look. Then he asked if Aaron Levinson was Sara Cohen's brother. You can imagine I grabbed on that opening like a beggar with a slice of bread. So he told the Captain he could handle the matter and took me to his office. Apparently, he knows you from Constantinople. Lieutenant-Colonel Rilke.'

'Hans Werner?' Sara said, greatly surprised. 'Tall, blond?'

Manny nodded. 'He seemed nice enough as Germans go. He gave me this for you.' He rummaged in his back pocket and pulled out a letter. 'He gave it to me and told me I could go. I decamped pretty quickly, I can tell you.'

Sara had stopped listening; she took the letter and read it at her desk:

Dear Sara,

I have been meaning to get in touch with you ever since my arrival in Palestine two months ago. Now chance has presented Mr Hirsh to act as messenger between us. After Gallipoli I was lucky enough to be posted on to Colonel von Kressenstein's staff – and have been promoted to Lieutenant-Colonel to boot.

I understand that with your brother away in Berlin you now run the research station, which I have heard much about since arriving in your country.

If you are not too busy with all the responsibilities this must entail would you consider coming to visit me in Jerusalem? I have a few weeks' leave from 4 November and will be staying at the Hotel Fast. Please do try to come and see me: on the Saturday there is a small dance you might enjoy.

Let me hear from you soon – and come.

Affectionate regards,
Hans Werner Rilke

Sara carefully folded the letter back into its envelope and sat thinking for a moment. What an amazing stroke of luck! The Hotel Fast was the German military headquarters in Palestine. At a dance with the drink flowing, she could find out any amount of information that could be useful to the network. It was an opportunity she had no intention of passing by.

'Another man smitten by your charms?' Manny asked.

'No, nothing like that,' said Sara delightedly, 'but he has invited me to a dance at the Hotel Fast.'

'Good God, Sara, you're not thinking of going are you?' Manny said with a dark look.

Sara did not answer. She had no intention of arguing with Manny – she knew she'd get quite enough of that with Daniel. But going to the dance at the Hotel Fast was exactly what she was thinking of doing.

Sara had good reason to suspect that Daniel would have a great deal to say about her travelling unaccompanied to Jerusalem to go dancing with a German army officer. He had used every angle and argument open to him except the one which she suspected motivated him – jealousy.

'I won't hear of your going,' he told her dictatorially. 'I gave my solemn word to Aaron that I would not let you take any unnecessary risks and if ever I saw one this is it. God knows what would happen to you – the place is full of soldiers.'

'Precisely! That's why I'm going.'

'I'd have thought you'd had enough of them,' Daniel came back.

'That's not fair,' Sara said quietly, not wanting to provoke an all-out fight. 'Hans Werner is a gentleman and I trust his friends are the same. Besides, I am prepared to take my chances. This might be the best opportunity in a long while for us to hear how the war is going in the Sinai – and in the rest of the world come to that. I'm going!'

The arguments had continued until the last possible moment, but nevertheless Sara had left the research station immediately after breakfast on Saturday, promising to be back the following day. Daniel refused to drive her to the station so Manny took her in Jezebel. She arrived in Jerusalem feeling vaguely disloyal but as soon as she saw Hans Werner, smiling and waving, all guilt vanished. Rilke rushed over to her, his limp barely perceptible, and kissed her hand. Sara eyed his leg. 'I hope the wound is not too serious,' she said, 'or painful?'

'No, not at all,' he replied, grinning hugely. 'We'll go straight to the hotel if that's all right,' he said, guiding her expertly through the crowds.

Sara tidied herself after the dusty journey and went downstairs to find Rilke waiting to take her into lunch. After the deprivations all round, the hotel was like an island of plenty. Civilians might be starving and the Turkish soldier wretchedly fed but the Germans were apparently cared for splendidly. Before the meal even arrived there was white bread and tinned butter which, despite feeling she should not enjoy such luxury, Sara could not resist. Meat – even camel meat – was now very rare in Palestine, but here, although the Germans were officially rationed, there were patties of lamb grilled over charcoal and a wealth of fresh, green vegetables. The wine, from the Rishon l'Zion settlement, was good and after a glass or two Sara overcame the awkward feeling of being out of place and relaxed. Rilke, who had been worried to see how slender Sara had become, grinned happily as he watched her eat mouthful after mouthful.

As they ate they talked; Rilke told Sara that it looked almost certain that America would join the war. Although she had tried to stay neutral, the sinking of passenger ships and the subsequent deaths of American civilians was angering the country more and more. The Armenian massacres had held the front pages of the American Press for months now and Morgenthau was finally insisting that Annie return to the States. Rilke asked Sara if she had heard from Selena – a letter, a postcard, anything! Sara lowered her eyes and lied convincingly, although knowing how much he cared made her, at first, feel uncomfortable. She had to keep reminding herself that Rilke was a German and therefore the enemy.

They took a stroll in the city after lunch, but for once Jerusalem depressed her and the miseries of the war were so marked that she was happy to go back to the hotel for tea. Sara noticed a few Turkish officers mingling with the Germans. 'We're allies, but at heart they still resent us,' Rilke explained. 'They're welcome to come here, but most won't mix with us.' He ordered a plate of cakes and was amused to see Sara devour them as eagerly as she had lunch.

By dinner Sara felt she had relaxed enough and must now get to work. She skilfully manoeuvred Rilke into talking less about Annie and the past and more about himself and the war. At first he was reticent but soon the wine and Sara's honest gaze loosened his tongue and as he talked Sara began to feel less of a traitor and more of a heroine. Rilke talked about a new machine, a 'tank', that the Allies had introduced into the battlefield. Immune to machine-gun fire it could move almost anywhere and he was clearly more worried by the implications of this machine than he was about the possibility of the Americans joining the Allies. Sara, sipping at real Turkish coffee, thick and sweet, kept her eyes on the table, sure that Rilke would read the delight flooding her eyes.

As the sound of music and laughter filtered into the dining room Hans Werner suggested that they make their way to the ballroom. Sara stood with some relief. She had been concentrating hard on everything Hans Werner said, trying to remember the smallest detail that might be of value to the British and filing it away in her brain. The effort had been draining and she had determined that once dinner was over she was going to put aside the worries and tragedies of the outside world and enjoy herself.

The ballroom was ablaze with light, humming with gaily-raised voices and vibrating with the festive 'noise' of a German military band. As Sara walked in on Rilke's arm she felt her spirits rise as the atmosphere caught her. She could not help but notice the attention she was attracting. For a moment she felt a rare emotion, vanity, stir within her. She felt pretty this evening, for the first time in months. She had spent the last few nights restyling her finest dress, a green evening gown, to make it look as good as new. The colour deepened the blue of her eyes and, against the emerald of the silk, her blonde hair, drawn up at the sides, but tumbling in rich curls down her back, looked a shining, burnished gold. In the last few months she had barely had time to brush her hair properly and now, as the music washed over her, she remembered how good it was to feel young, pretty and desirable.

As Hans Werner guided her into the ballroom he gave her arm a gentle little squeeze. 'You look lovely, Sara.'

'Thank you,' she gave her warmest smile and held on to his arm as they made their way through the undulating sea of bodies. Sara was surprised to see how many people there were at this small dance. The room was crammed with women in evening gowns and men in evening dress or uniform with gleaming boots. As they made their way through the crowd Hans Werner introduced her to a few officers, until at last they reached a table next to the dance floor. Several of his friends and their wives were already seated; Hans Werner introduced her round, and they all smiled welcomingly. After a minute a waiter appeared with glasses bobbing with fruit. Sara gave Hans Werner a rueful glance.

'It's Bowle,' he explained with a laugh, 'a punch made with Rhine wine and fruit, with a bottle of champagne added to give it fizz. Go on, have some, it's very refreshing.'

The whole table laughed as Sara's face puckered after the first sip. 'It's so . . . sweet,' she said, laughing with them.

'Come,' Hans Werner knocked his glass of wine back in one gulp and stretched his hand out to her. 'Would you care to dance with the wounded warrior?'

Sara nodded and smiled. 'Anything to keep our valiant soldiers happy,' she quipped, giving him her hand.

The men gave a bawdy cheer at her remark and the noise followed them on to the dance floor. As they circled slowly to the strains of *La Belle Hélène*, she felt a stab of pain in her belly. *Paying for all that rich food* she thought sardonically and, gritting her teeth, shrugged it off. Goodness only knew when she would next be asked to a dance, so she closed her eyes for a moment, determined to enjoy the almost pre-war atmosphere and the luxury of music.

She suddenly thought of the dance at Zichron. Two years ago! It seemed so far away now. She was a lifetime older than the girl who had danced with Joe Lanski in a white muslin dress. Not for the first time she wondered what had become of him. She knew that Aaron had seen him several times in Haifa before he left the country, and he had sent letters to both Selena and herself. Well, hers had been more of a brief note than a letter. She thought how curious it was that she had felt vaguely disappointed – cheated even – by his brevity.

The music swung into a foxtrot. 'I'm afraid this is where I must bow out,' said Hans Werner with a sheepish smile.

'No matter,' Sara fanned her flushed cheeks and took his arm. 'I think I'd like another glass of Bowle to cool me down.'

'Look, there's Joe Lanski,' Rilke exclaimed, beaming with pleasure and waving an arm as he started towards the entrance. Sara's heart gave a little jump and she swung round to see his tall, suave figure making its way into the room. He looked staggeringly handsome as, with that familiar teasing look on his face, he inclined his head towards the woman hanging possessively on to his arm. She was ravishing, with a superb face haloed with flaming red hair. Her sloe-eyes looked coquettishly up at him as she laughed at something he said and nestled closer to him. Sara suddenly felt dowdy in her remodelled dress, like a heroine out of one of the novellas she used to read.

'Let's go and say hello,' Hans Werner said brightly, smiling down at her. 'I intend to claim at least one dance from the voluptuous creature hanging from his arm.' And he looked at Joe's glamorous partner with a gleam in his eye.

They had only taken a few steps when Sara was seized by an irrational panic, and she stopped abruptly. Hans Werner turned to her, startled. 'I'm sorry,' she said breathlessly, 'but please, I should like to sit down. Would you mind?'

'No – no, of course not,' said Rilke, his expression immediately concerned and he led her solicitously back to the table.

Sara sat down next to the large, blonde German wife of a smiling Major and thankfully accepted another glass of Bowle. She felt flustered and rather foolish, baffled as to why she had fled from meeting Joe Lanski. Collecting her thoughts, she began chatting with the Major's wife who, although friendly, failed to enthrall her with long-winded complaints about the laziness of Arab servants. Sara clenched her jaw and agreed with false enthusiasm.

She overheard a remark from the next table about the garrison in Beersheba and tried hard to listen, but her attention kept wandering. The German and Turkish flags draped over the walls of the ballroom no longer looked decorative; they seemed suddenly threatening. She shivered uncomfortably.

'Madame Cohen?' Brought out of her disquieting thoughts with a start she looked up and saw a face she recognised. Her pulse began to race in anguish and her heart sank like an anchor. 'Standenführer Schmidt,' said the German Colonel from the train with a gleaming smile. The men at the table stood up, but he waved them down again with a hand. 'What a pleasure to meet you again, Madame Cohen, in more congenial surroundings.'

Sara's face had paled and her thoughts were in chaos but she forced herself to smile and fluttered her fan to cover her distress. 'Far more congenial,' she answered with a laboured laugh, which rang false even to her ears.

'And your travelling companion?'

'Oh she is fine,' Sara dismissed the question smoothly with a quick, sidelong glance at Hans Werner, to whom she had said nothing about Selena's illness. Fortunately, his face did not register a question mark.

'Ah, Rilke,' said the Colonel, turning to Hans Werner. 'I know this lady is with you, but I would be honoured if you would entrust her to me for just one dance.' Rilke nodded, Schmidt bowed again, but this time to Sara, and led her away.

Sara relaxed a little as they moved out on to the dance floor. It was obvious that he had heard nothing about the two sirens that had lured the Captain into the Mesopotamian flats. He had commanded the soldiers to take them to Aleppo and had then probably forgotten all about it, but she felt her skin crawl at the memory of that ghastly day.

As they swirled round the dance floor the Colonel chatted to her about his new station at the Palestinian-Arab headquarters in Damascus and Sara felt her tension slip away with the rhythm of the music. The buoyant mood of the beginning of the evening returned to her and she started to enjoy herself again.

As the Colonel swung her around the floor she saw Joe dancing with the redhead. He looked as though he was having a good time and then caught her eye and grinned merrily. Sara found herself smiling back, and realised that their gaze was fast locked, and for some reason she could not look away. She blinked and felt her cheeks burn again as he gave her that old, appraising look before inclining his head back to his partner.

'I see you know Joe Lanski,' said the Colonel, following her gaze. 'A friend of yours?'

'Oh, more of an acquaintance,' she said casually, but her heart was for some reason several degrees lighter.

As the waltz came to an end they heard some disturbance coming from the back of the ballroom. The Colonel stood on his toes and turned to Sara with a pained expression, taking her arm protectively. 'The usual German-Turkish conflict,' he said in a low voice, as he led her back to the table. 'All to do with this precedence problem I expect,' he added with a heavy sigh, then pulled out her gilt chair, bowed, clicked his heels and told her he hoped they would meet again soon. Sara smiled and watched him go with a contented feeling of triumph.

As German officers were accorded one rank higher than their equivalents in the Turkish service, there was no end of friction between the two 'allied' armies. *They will never manage to pull together*, Sara thought happily. *Like oil and vinegar they will always go their own separate ways.*

A couple of Hans Werner's friends came to the table, eager to be introduced, and Sara smiled and chatted happily to them for a few minutes until out of the corner of her eye she saw Joe approaching her table, loping through the crowd with his assured stride.

His eyes were green and laughing as he drew closer, his teeth white against the dark sunburn of his skin. In his immaculate evening dress he looked every inch the gentleman, and the perfect rake. Sara greeted him with a warm smile and, feeling a fluttering in her stomach, realised for the first time that she had, in fact, been waiting for him to come over to her all evening.

'My dear Sara, what a lovely surprise. Why, I don't believe we have met since Constantinople,' he said urbanely, lifting her fingers to his lips. Their eyes met and smiled in secret amusement. She knew she need have no qualms that Joe would let anything slip about Selena.

Sara watched Joe greet Rilke and the rest of the company and was struck by the panache with which he seemed to do everything. He took the seat offered by Hans Werner, and Sara settled back in her chair, fascinated to notice how he was already the centre of attention. He was so completely at ease and in control of himself and the company around him that he carried everyone along with him effortlessly. Discussing the merits of horseflesh, Joe skilfully interested the German Captain in a gelding he had in stock. 'He certainly has a great eye for horseflesh,' said Hans Werner, 'and beautiful women,' he added.

And they for him, Sara thought contemptuously. All the women at the table were in one way or another vying for his attention. The blonde Heidi was behaving like a simpering schoolgirl, hanging on to his every word and to her annoyance Joe was giving her that particularly attractive, rakish look of his. Sara felt a flash of irritation. *He's an arrogant, conceited womaniser*, she decided. *Insufferable!*

However, when a moment later he stood up to leave, she felt

disappointed. 'I must go,' he said with a smile, and then turning to Hans Werner added, 'but first I should like to claim a dance with Mrs Cohen – if I may.'

Hans Werner nodded and Joe held out his hand, his eyebrows lifted questioningly. Sara saw the furious look Heidi shot her and stifled a laugh, pleased to have annoyed the pompous bitch. She smiled up at Joe. 'How could I resist,' she said teasingly and, rising, took his arm, and followed him to the dance floor.

The minute he held her in his arms he bent his head and whispered in her ear, 'What in the name of heaven are you doing here alone?'

Sara did not falter in her dance step nor change her expression but she hissed back furiously, 'I am not alone, I'm with Hans Werner.'

Joe pulled back and stared at her. 'Good God, Sara, surely you of all people know the dangers – and it's a very dangerous game you're playing.'

Surprise flickered over her face. 'And what game might that be?' she asked suspiciously.

Joe's eyes blazed brilliantly. 'I'm not entirely ignorant of what is going on at Atlit. I had several long talks with Aaron before he left for Berlin and some instinct tells me that your presence here this evening has more to it than might meet the eye.'

'Hans Werner invited me so I came. That's all there is to it,' she bristled. First Daniel, and now Joe, why were men always telling her what she should or should not do? She glared at him, hoping to convey her annoyance. 'And besides,' she added sweetly, 'it is none of your business what I do or where I go.'

Joe laughed and shook his head in mock bewilderment. Unfortunately, that was true, he thought ruefully. Joe had felt something like a stab of pain when he had first seen her standing with Hans Werner – and then bolting like a frightened filly. For months now she had danced round in his mind like some malignant djinn and now, seeing her again so unexpectedly, he was filled with an excitement he had not known since adolescence. He half believed himself in love with her although, thank God, she was unaware of his feelings. It had taken all his willpower not to rush over to her the moment he saw her and sweep her in to his arms. Instead he had held himself back and waited.

But now he was holding her so close, her body swaying to the music, the luxuriant hair against his cheek, the shining blue eyes so close to his own, and he regretted the lost time. The woman had woven some kind of spell over him and he marvelled not just at her beauty, but at the effect it had on him. He decided he did not want to know if she were still in love with Daniel Rosen. 'You're quite right, of course, Sara – it is none of my business,' he said with a grin. 'And besides, I know that your actions are always entirely above reproach.'

Sara caught his eye and could not help laughing. 'You are impossible Joe Lanksi!' she scolded without much conviction and allowed herself to be swung into the Viennese waltz that the band had just struck up.

Without taking his eyes from hers, his arm wrapped round her waist, Joe swirled and whirled her around the dance floor. They moved in perfect synchronisation, the room was a dreamy haze and the only thing in focus were Joe's eyes, set in an intent gaze. Sara was lost in the startling brilliance of those eyes swimming above hers as they went faster, faster, faster until the music stopped and, breathless and dizzy, she clung to him laughing.

'That was wonderful, Joe,' she gasped, smiling up at him. 'When I dance like that it's such a glorious feeling . . . how I wish I could feel like that – always,' she ended, laughing again.

She saw Joe's eyes change as if they were focusing on something inside her and she was aware of the smile fading from her face as she felt the heat of his body radiating through the thin silk of her dress. She had an almost unbearable desire to press her face against his crisp white shirt and breathe in the virile smell of his body. She felt weak and confused, but managed to tear her eyes away from his a moment before she was lost.

Joe bent his head towards hers. 'I've missed you, Sara,' he confided softly. 'I'll be passing through Atlit in a week or two. May I come and call?'

Sara looked back at him. His smile was laconic but his eyes were warm and soft. 'Yes, please do. I'd like that. I'd like that very much indeed.'

Sara left by train the next morning and settled into her compartment with a wonderful, contented feeling that she could not shake off. Not only had she really enjoyed herself, but had gathered some very interesting information. She could return feeling, not only warm with the memory of the evening, but satisfied that she had been proved right. She now knew that German forces in Palestine numbered 50,000, that the monastery at Afula was most likely an arms dump, and that the Turks were disbanding the Arab cavalry units due to their political unreliability. On the lighter side, Hans Werner had told her that Turkish uniforms were so scarce they were rotated among soldiers at different inspection sites. So the same uniforms were endlessly being inspected on the backs of different soldiers.

And, to add cream to her coffee, she had carefully tucked a pound of tinned butter, a box of sugary biscuits and a large bag of real coffee beans into the bottom of her suitcase. She had forgotten life could hold such riches.

Sara jumped down from the train, holding her precious suitcase tightly, and looked around for Daniel. But it was Manny who stepped forward and put out his hand for her bag.

'Daniel had to meet Ivan Bernski,' he explained and added with a cheeky smile, 'you look as though you've had a good time.'

Sara laughed. 'In more ways than one,' she agreed, with a wink. She wondered briefly about Daniel but was in far too good a humour to be concerned with petty jealousies over whether or not he was with Isobelle Frank. She would see him soon enough and, in the meantime, Manny could fill her in with developments at Atlit.

'I'm worried about Selena,' Manny said, putting Sara's bag into the back of the cart and helping her up. 'She hasn't come out of her room since Sarkis left yesterday. When I took her a tray she looked – well, unstrung.'

Sara felt uneasy and a pang of worry disturbed her buoyant mood. As soon as they arrived at the research station she rushed up the stairs to Selena's room. She knocked on the door but there was no answer. She tried the handle, but the door was locked. This behaviour was so uncharacteristic of her friend that she was at once apprehensive. 'Selena? It's me, Sara,' she said, knocking again. 'Please let me in.' The key turned in the lock and the door opened.

Sara felt her heart stir at the sight of Selena. She looked so tragically unhappy, everything about her ringing with despair from the slump of her shoulders to the pink tear stains blurring her lovely eyes. 'Thank God, you're back, Sara,' she blurted as Sara followed her into the room.

Sara leaned back on the door and stared at her friend aghast. 'Selena . . . what's happened?'

Selena ran a hand over her drawn face and, shaking her head, slumped into the armchair by the window. Without thinking, Sara crossed the room and dropped to her knees beside her, her arms outstretched. Selena surrendered herself to them and wept softly as they embraced. They said nothing for a few moments and then, snuffling and wiping her eyes, Selena pulled slowly away.

'Is it Kristopher?' Sara asked, her eyes seeking and holding Selena's.

Selena nodded and drew a deep, desperate breath. 'They are all . . .' she could not bring herself to go on and tears slid silently down her cheeks again.

Sara waited for a moment, then, taking her friend's hands in hers, spoke softly, 'Tell me – perhaps I can help.'

Selena tilted her head back and blinked. 'I'm counting on the hope that you can,' she said, wiping her eyes and composing herself. 'Kristopher,' she began, 'has heard reports that all Armenians in the Turkish service are to be disarmed and sent back to their native villages.' Her eyes looked fearfully into Sara's. 'And we know what that means, don't we?'

Sara went pale. She still had the nightmares caused by the sight of the doomed columns of Armenians dragging themselves to exile in the far reaches of the desert. She now saw Kristopher Sarkis added to that number, hauling himself along at the end of that abysmal vision and her heart pounded. 'When?' she asked, gripping Selena's hand tightly.

'They don't know. Kristopher has a close friend, an officer in the Turkish army. He found this out and has promised to warn Kristopher . . .' Selena pulled a hand free and searched for a handkerchief to blow her nose on.

Sara sighed deeply and stood up. 'We shall have to hide him,' she said in a businesslike way. 'We shall hide him and, when the moment is right, spirit you both away from here.' She looked straight into Selena's eyes, trying to see if she understood the implications, but Selena's tiny face seemed more distraught than ever, tears welling up yet again.

'I haven't told you the worst yet,' Selena spoke again. 'I promised I wouldn't breathe a word but . . .' She gripped her hands together and closed her eyes, clenching them shut for a moment. 'But Kristopher is the reason my heart still beats, my blood still flows.'

Sara sat down, never taking her eyes from her friend. 'Yes I know, I understand that,' she said gently. 'Now tell me the rest.'

Selena looked at Sara bleakly. 'Kristopher has a plan,' she whispered. 'He and two fellow Armenian officers in the septieh are going to assassinate Jemel Pasha.'

'What?' Sara was stunned.

'They are going to smoke enough hashish to dull their fear and then shoot him – murder him in revenge for what he is doing to our people.'

Sara stared at her, her eyes full of terrible understanding. 'But that will change nothing, surely he knows that.'

'Of course. He is bringing death on his own head. Oh, it is all so foolish, so gallant and so . . . so . . . futile.'

Sara rose and, crossing to Selena, bent down and gripped her by the shoulders. 'Selena, is Kristopher coming here today?'

She nodded. 'Yes, this afternoon.' She looked up at Sara. 'I haven't pried,' she said soberly, 'but I do think you might be able to give him some other, less direct way, to wreak his revenge.'

Sara smiled and squeezed Selena's shoulders. 'I promise I'll do all I can. Now go downstairs and help Frieda in the kitchen. It'll help take your mind off things.'

Selena smiled weakly. 'When Kristopher comes, tell him I should like to see him,' Sara said, her hand on the door knob. 'I'll go to my study and wait. I shall need some time to think this out.'

Sara had an hour to consider how she should approach Sarkis before the knock she was expecting interrupted her thoughts. 'Come in,' she said, standing as the door opened. She looked at him curiously as he approached her desk. He shook Sara's hand with his habitual courtesy, but she could see the agitation and anger beneath the politeness.

'Selena said you wished to talk to me.' His voice sounded strangely calm despite his underlying rage.

'Please sit down, Captain Sarkis,' Sara said, lowering himself into her chair. 'I believe we have some common goals and perhaps we should discuss the best way to achieve them.'

Surprise flickered over his features, then he sat down and looked at her questioningly. 'Selena had heard reports that you are soon to be disarmed and sent into exile?' Neither of them stirred for a moment until Sarkis drew a breath and gave Sara a small, wintery smile.

'I must suppose Selena has also told you what I plan to do about it?'

Sara nodded calmly. 'Yes.'

Sarkis turned his head away from her gaze, 'I have no choice – it is the only honourable course.'

'You mean you have no other choice but to kill Jemel Pasha?'

Sarkis turned back to her, his eyes glowering. 'No other honourable choice.'

'And what about Selena? Have you considered the consequences to her?'

Sarkis winced. 'Don't, please don't. I love Selena to the depths of my soul, and I know she would be lost to me for ever, my life would be ashes. If I survive, I should have to scuttle like a cockroach into hiding. I know that.' He raised himself stiffly in the chair, his face as though carved from wax. 'But it is my duty as an Armenian to end this madness.'

'Do you really believe that assassinating Jemel Pasha will in any way end it?' Sara's voice was calm, reasonable. 'If you want to die a hero go ahead and shoot him. But if you really want to help . . .'

'Holy Mother of God!' Sarkis cried, jumping to his feet in fury, intermingled with despair. 'Help! There is only one way that I can help and that is by ridding the Empire of those who wish to grind us into the dust. Without Jemel Pasha the Turkish Army would be leaderless, demoralised and disorganised. It may not be the best way, but it is my only way.'

'There might be a way to help,' Sara said, unmoved by Sarkis's oratory.

'How? Our people are dead and dying, our leaders under arrest and now our soldiers are to be disarmed. Unless we act soon there will be no one left to save!'

'We can open the door to the enemy of the Turk,' Sara answered in the same calm voice. Sarkis, suddenly quietened, swung round and stared at her. 'You are not the only minority with reason to hate the Turk,' she said, a flicker of a smile playing around her lips.

'How about a nightcap?' Daniel asked, pushing the papers away and brushing the hair from his forehead with a weary hand.

'I'd love one,' Sara answered, her face softening into a smile as she looked up at him.

Daniel rose from the chair close to hers at the desk and gently stroked her cheek. 'Stop worrying,' he said.

'Easier said than done,' Sara threw after him as he went out of the room in search of wine. She heard him chuckle in agreement. Her chin cupped in her hands, she slouched across the battered desk, looking through the window into the dark outside. Out at sea a wind was blowing, whipping into the land, and there was a steady fall of rain. The last of the summer had gone.

That evening she and Daniel had spent several hours talking about the situation. He was in one of his crazy moods, vacillating between hope and despair with no rationality in either state. He had been visiting Arab friends who owned a café in Nazareth and returned with stories about the Arab revolt led by his friend Lawrence. Full of envy and frustration he had pointed out gloomily that Aaron had been gone for four months now and they still had no idea where he was or if he had succeeded in persuading the British to open up contact again. Although he had never said so, Sara knew that Daniel regarded every day that passed as wasted. Carefully, Sara continued to do her best to reassure him that Aaron would achieve his aim.

'It's simply a question of patience,' Sara said again and again. 'Patience.'

'If I hear that word from you once more I'll strangle you,' Daniel would answer irritably, but Sara ignored him. All that mattered to her was that Daniel had given Aaron his word that he would not attempt another crossing to Egypt and she would make sure that he did not break his promise. But his attitude and growing restlessness irritated her. She had more than enough problems without Daniel souring her thoughts.

The money she had been left to run the research station was running pitifully short and Sara was worried that she would not be able to keep paying the men's wages. There had been so many unforeseen extra expenses – like the gold pound it had cost to keep Robby out of jail when he punched a Turkish officer for making a pass at Ruth. She knew that, if the ship did not arrive at the end of the month with relief supplies and money, she would have to lay off the majority of her work-force. Sara was filled with compassion for the workers and their families and was wearing herself out trying to make ends meet, but if the ship did not arrive she had no alternative.

It would arrive. She knew that. She knew that Aaron would not let them down, and could only pray that the others would share her confidence for a little longer. Aaron had promised that he would be in contact by the end of November at the latest and Sara clung to the words. In ten days' time the moon would wane and they could begin to watch for the ship.

Outside in his kennel, Goliath barked a few times. He had interrupted Sara's train of thought and she pushed aside the bundle of bills on the desk and stretched her arms behind her head. She lowered the flame on the gas lamp and crossed the half-dark room to the sofa.

Daniel reappeared with a tray carrying a jug of wine, two glasses and a bowl of olives. 'We're more likely to die from drink than starvation,' he said with a grin, and poured the wine. He sat beside Sara on the sofa and they sipped the wine in silence, both savouring the feeling of relaxation the first sip brought them.

Suddenly, there was a sound of pebbles hitting the window and they both sat up instantly, their bodies taut with expectation. They looked at each other anxiously.

'It must be someone we know or Goliath would have gone on barking,' Sara said and, crossing to the window, peered out. Down in the garden a man stood silhouetted against the sky.

'Mrs Cohen, it's me. Captain Sarkis,' came a voice full of hushed urgency.

'Come round to the side door. I'll be straight down,' she whispered back and, closing the window, turned to Daniel whose hand was wrapped firmly round the Browning pistol. 'It's Sarkis,' she said tersely, grabbing a candle and lighting it awkwardly. 'I told him to come here if the Turk began confiscating arms from the Armenian septieh – I promised to hide him.'

'You what?' Daniel exploded.

'Shush,' Sara motioned him to be quiet. 'He came to see me a few days ago, he wants to help . . . oh, I'll explain later.'

She sped to the door, tiptoed down the stairs and quietly unbolted the door, beckoning the Captain in. She signalled quiet and led the way upstairs to her study before speaking.

In the light of the room Sara could see he was soaking wet, his face drained of all colour and his eyes unnaturally large and bright. There was a significant pause as he recognised Daniel and stared at him anxiously.

'It's all right,' Sara said soothingly. 'Take off your cape, it's sodden.' She took it from him and hung it over the back of a chair. 'We were drinking some wine, will you join us?'

'I – yes, thank you.'

'Here.' Daniel refilled his glass and passed it to Sarkis. 'You look as though you need it.' With a crooked smile Sarkis took the glass and drained the wine at a gulp.

'Now what's happened?' Daniel spoke calmly to cover his concern at the risk Sara was taking. 'Have they ordered you to hand in your arms?'

'No – it will be on Saturday, we think,' Sarkis answered. 'I have brought you something.' His fingers, still trembling slightly, went into his jacket pocket and came out clutching a small black book. He handed it mutely to Sara. She took it and, carrying it to the lamplight, studied the first few pages for a moment before turning with a frown to Sarkis.

'What is it?' she asked, puzzled.

'It's the Turkish General Staff code book,' he answered quietly.

Daniel almost snatched the book from Sara and, eyebrows soaring in amazement, he flicked through its pages. He looked up at Sarkis, his eyes wide and lustrous in surprise. 'My God,' he said at last. 'Who did you have to kill to get hold of this?'

Sarkis smiled. 'No one. I just took it. It was lying on the desk of an officer friend of mine, and I slipped it into my pocket when we left his office.' He began pacing the room, his eyes moving from Sara to Daniel as he spoke. 'I just had to do something,' he said passionately. 'Mrs Cohen, you were right. I can't bring the massacred back from their graves, but maybe I can help send the cursed Turks to theirs.'

Sara, perched on the desk, looked at him steadily. 'You must take it back,' she said very quietly. Both Sarkis and Daniel looked at her as though she had lost her mind. 'You will have to return it,' she continued, 'because if you don't it will not take them long to realise that you and the code book disappeared together. They will be suspicious and will probably change the code, which would render what Daniel holds in his hands useless.'

Sarkis looked at Daniel, who nodded. 'Sara's right. We must copy it and somehow you must replace it.'

Sarkis sank heavily into a chair and laughed humourlessly. 'Of course. How stupid of me.'

Sara crossed to him and sat on the arm of his chair, a hand on his shoulder. 'Do you think you can do it?'

He managed a ghastly smile. 'I got it out – I'll get it back in.'

'Good,' she said, suddenly business-like, and stood in front of the meagre fire. 'Then this is what we'll do. I'll copy it as I write the fastest. Then you must take it back and leave it in your friend's office . . .'

She broke off, looking at Daniel who, absorbed in the black book, was suspiciously quiet. Normally, he would be formulating the plans, or at the least arguing with her ideas. She thought quickly. Tomorrow was Friday. She had promised her father to spend the Sabbath in Zichron, and knew she would have to go . . . perhaps it was just as well . . .

'Meet us in my father's house in Zichron around this time tomorrow night. You will have to cross the Carmel by foot – they could track you to us if you bring your horse again. I will tell Abu to expect you. Make absolutely sure no one sees you and don't even breathe a hint of this to anyone – or none of us may ever breathe again,' she added with a smile, hoping to lighten the atmosphere. She turned to Daniel, who was still sitting deep in thought; she could almost hear his thoughts grinding away against each other in his brain. She knew he was planning how to get the book to the British and felt a terrible foreboding as she watched him.

She squashed her fear and exasperation with him – she was only showing her vulnerability, she told herself. 'Do you agree with my plan, Daniel?' she asked sweetly.

He looked up with a start. 'Yes,' he said hurriedly and stood to pour out some more wine. Sara waved her glass away and turned her thoughts back to the Captain.

'Are you hungry? Would you like some figs, or bread?' she asked.

'No, thank you. But may I see Selena?'

'I don't think it would be a good idea to worry her so late at night,' she answered reasonably. 'I'll tell her we saw you and to expect you tomorrow night.'

Sarkis nodded agreement. 'Yes, you're right, of course,' he said and Daniel handed him some wine, which he accepted gratefully.

Sara took the code book to her desk and took out her ink. 'It shouldn't take me too long, but I'd better get started,' she said, dipping her pen into the ink, and then stared aghast at the white paper. In her agitated state she had taken the red ink by mistake. It dripped from her pen like blood, staining the virgin paper. She shivered with dread, then took a deep breath and silently cursed herself for her superstition. Omens! – she was becoming as bad as Fatma.

Picking up the black ink and a new sheet of paper she wiped the nib clean and dipped in her pen.

'You're looking very thin – are you sure you're managing down there?' Ruth asked, watching Sara play with her daughter, Abigail.

Sara looked up with a smile. 'Of course I'm managing – I'd be going mad if I weren't down there being useful.'

They were sitting on the veranda at Zichron, neatly combed and dressed for the Sabbath and enjoying the fragile warmth of the winter sunshine. Last night's rains had washed the earth and air and the ride up from Atlit had cleared her head. Sara had sat up most of the night copying out the code book and fighting a vague feeling of unease, but now she was home the niggling worry was at last dispelled. Sitting in the rocking chair, with pretty little Abigail on her knee, she felt almost festive. Abigail pulled at her sleeve and restarted the game of clap-clap, which was keeping them both amused. Robby, Sam and Abram, who spoilt the child dreadfully, were looking on, smiling indulgently at the small girl's screeches of delight. Ruth, satisfied that her daughter was being looked after, leant back in her cane chair and closed her eyes.

Sara suddenly realised that only Daniel was keeping aloof, looking over the lawns engrossed in thought. He had been silent ever since the episode with Sarkis the night before and even on the ride up had hardly said a word. Sara looked across at him, her eyes soft and, putting Abby down to play on a rug, she walked quietly over to him. 'Is anything the matter, Daniel?' she murmured.

His eyes met hers and he smiled. 'No, nothing, nothing at all. I think I'll get some wine,' he answered, and strolled off through the double doors into the dining room, ruffling Abby's hair as he passed. The table was laid with a white cloth and all the best china. A bottle of burgundy had been decanted and stood by the Kiddush cup, which had been placed ready for the Sabbath blessing, but Daniel went instead to the heavy dresser and absently opened a bottle. The room showed no sign that a war had changed their lives – the silver was hidden away, but the copper gleamed against the wood and, however little food there was, Fatma always made it look like a feast.

Daniel poured himself a glass of wine and leant against the dresser. He had been thrown into a dilemma by the priceless treasure Sarkis had brought them the night before. Daniel already knew that the British had established an active defence round El

Arish, only twenty-five miles south-west of the Palestinian frontier. The fact that the British were there, and in considerable force, could only mean that they intended to make a push to take El Arish itself – and the next step would be Gaza. If the British could be given the German-Turkish code it would be like handing them the keys to Palestine.

Daniel had decided the night before that he must attempt a crossing into the Sinai: the question that had haunted him all night was how? It was winter now, the water holes and wells would be full, and the British were much nearer than the last time they had considered a land crossing. On the other hand, the Turko-German Army was far more organised and active than a year ago and Gaza would be well patrolled.

He sipped his wine and determined that the best answer would be to travel as a Bedouin, skirting the main areas of military activity, and aiming for the British where they camped south of El Arish. But even travelling as a Bedouin he would need a companion – one man would attract attention, two would pass unnoticed. Besides, the desert had soaked up more blood than water, two would be safer.

Who should he take? The problem went round and round in his mind as he considered the possibilities. It should obviously be a member of the group, but every man he thought of had something against him. They were either too young, spoke Arabic with accents or, like Lev, just did not look the part. Only Robby passed on all counts, but Daniel was almost sure Ruth would veto the idea. Sara would have something to say, too, he could be sure of that. But Daniel would not be put off; circumstances had changed and he was convinced that Aaron would want him to go. He would just have to make Sara see that getting the code to the British was more important than keeping his word to Aaron.

A faint, throbbing noise broke his train of thought. As he listened the throbbing grew louder and, going out on to the veranda, he saw the others were gathered on the lawn, staring up at the sky.

'There it is,' said Sam excitedly, as the dark smudge took form.

'It's a German spotter plane,' said Daniel, listening to the engine. 'I had heard they'd brought a few in.' This was the first aeroplane most of them had ever seen and they stared at it as it swiftly crossed the skies, the engine noise growing louder and louder until the plane altered its course and veered back towards the coast.

They stood in silence, watching the vanishing dot and listening to the receding sound of its engine. Then, chattering excitedly, they made their way back to the veranda. Sara, feeling the chill in the air, ran into the house to fetch some shawls for herself and Ruth and arrived back on the veranda to hear the unmistakable noise of an approaching cavalry unit.

Everyone was discussing the reason for its arrival. 'Perhaps it's just passing through,' Sam suggested.

'And perhaps not,' Daniel added grimly. 'Any unlicensed guns around?' The men shook their heads and Ruth swept Abigail into her arms, cradling her tightly.

Looking down the road towards the valley they began to distinguish the scarlet jackets of a large troop of septieh marching up from the valley in a long, orderly line. They instinctively noticed that the troop was not announcing its arrival with the customary drum beats and bugle calls, so it was more likely than not that they were just passing through.

Sara held her breath, waiting for them to go past, but as they turned into the lane leading to their courtyard her heart sank. 'You don't suppose this has anything to do with Kristopher Sarkis?' she whispered to Daniel, a note of panic in her voice. Daniel looked at her, worried, but her eyes were calm enough and he was sure he could trust her.

'I don't know, but I pray to God in heaven not,' he answered, giving her arm a reassuring squeeze.

Robby walked over to them with an inquisitive lift of his eyebrows and Daniel smiled and shrugged fatalistically. 'We shall just have to see,' he said and then, narrowing his eyes, muttered, 'Good God, I can't believe it!'

Walking across the lawn from the courtyard came the chief of police himself, Hamid Bek. Sara felt suddenly weak and giddy as she saw the thin, bloodless face contort itself into a parody of a smile as he neared the group on the veranda. If it was Hamid Bek something serious must be wrong; she felt the fear swell in her heart, but struggled to give nothing away. Only this morning they had been discussing the latest tales of his legendary cruelty and, as Sara looked at the police chief, she saw pictures of Kristopher Sarkis and prayed he was safe. She was sure he would give nothing away to the Turks – if only because of Selena – but how hard had they tried to get information from him? Sara clenched and unclenched her hands in the folds of her dress. Thank God Selena was safe at Atlit. There was nothing compromising in the house. *I have nothing to fear*, she told herself and relaxed a little.

The group stood in an unmoving tableau, watching Hamid Bek approaching with several officers of Bek's gendarmerie until Daniel made as though to step forward. But old Mr Levinson motioned him to stop and moved stiffly forward to the top of the veranda steps.

Hamid Bek climbed the steps, his face beaming benevolently on his stony-faced hosts. He greeted Sara's father with becoming deference and, to Sara's surprise, recognised her, acknowledging her with a crooked little bow. 'Ah, Mrs Cohen, we have not met for some years now. How is your esteemed husband?'

In spite of her nervousness, Sara managed a pretty smile and answered sweetly: 'I believe my husband to be well, Your Excellency, and will convey your greetings in my next letter. The war has unhappily separated us.'

Bek made a commiserating little noise in the back of his throat and replied with a sympathetic shake of his head, 'War is unkind to women, I fear,' he remarked and turned abruptly to Daniel, his expression changing at once to one of marked hostility. 'Daniel Rosen, isn't it?' he seemed pleased with himself. 'I told you I would not forget your name when last we met.' His tone was light but the meaning distinctly menacing.

Daniel inclined his head respectfully and forced a smile in spite of the hatred that hit him like a physical blow. Unaccountably, an old saying of his father's came to his mind: 'The word you have said is your master: the word that remains unsaid is your servant.' The memory gave him strength to remain uncharacteristically silent.

Sara pulled the shawl closely round herself, wondering how Hamid Bek knew of her marriage. Had he just picked up the information in passing or had he been taking a special interest in the Levinsons? What else did he know about them? Sara felt another wave of panic wash over her. *What did he want here?*

Colonel Hamid Bek stood for a moment, tapping his riding whip on the tops of his mirror-bright boots and then, with another startlingly fast change of mood, he switched his attention to little Abigail, who was still nestled in Ruth's arms. 'What a lovely child,' he positively cooed and before anyone realised what he was about he had lifted the child from Ruth's arms and was fondling her dark curls. Chatting to the child he strolled unconcernedly to the veranda steps. Ruth gave a stifled moan and made towards her child, but Robby put a restraining arm round her shoulders. He could feel her shaking with fear and her struggling to control it.

Abigail, meanwhile, lay quite happily in the Colonel's arms, gazing up at him and talking her nonsense babytalk. Hamid Bek seemed genuinely enchanted with the little girl. 'What is her name, madame?' he asked Ruth politely.

Ruth, almost paralysed with fear for her child, muttered something inaudible so Robby, looking at her anxiously, answered for her. 'Abigail, Your Excellency,' he said evenly, although his tanned face had blanched to the colour of creamy coffee.

'Well, Abby, say hello to your nice new Uncle Hamid.' Everyone was silent, watchful, waiting for the next move in the Colonel's cruel game. 'Perhaps when I visit again,' he continued, the smile vanishing from his thin face, 'I shall take you with me to visit my doves in Caesarea.'

Sara's heart was suddenly sheathed in ice. Everyone had heard of Hamid Bek's doves – killing one was punishable by death – but his words carried a subtly veiled threat. 'Such pretty birds,' he cooed at the baby and then, tiring of the game, he tickled her under the chin and handed her back to Ruth, who almost snatched her from his arms. The relief emanating from the company was practically tangible. With it was a sense of weariness. The whole scene was too contrived, too carefully controlled. *What was he here for?*

Ruth was clutching Abigail so tightly the child began to cry. Muttering an excuse Ruth turned and fled along the veranda to the back of the house.

'Children – I do love them. They are so . . . innocent,' Hamid Bek said, following Ruth and Abigail with his eyes and flicking his whip against his boots again.

Abram, impatient of these theatrical games, was the first to collect his wits. 'May I offer you a seat, Your Excellency – some tea, perhaps?'

'Thank you, Effendi Levinson, but no.' And now at last he made his first sortie. 'I regret that my visit here is not a social one and my time these days is sorely pressed.' He glanced viciously at Daniel and continued, 'Unfortunately, there is a minority bent on causing mischief in this land. Recently, for instance, we found Arabs carrying large amounts of gold. The fools were under the pay of Feisal and his British dogs – and were hanged, of course. Our own leaders were born from revolution and we know how it is done and how to quell it.' He stood silent, watching them all as his words sunk in. Then he smiled again and seemed relaxed and almost jovial.

Sara folded her hands to stop them from trembling. This man was like a wild animal. One moment he purred and the next he snapped his jaws – what was he leading up to?

'Forgive me, I digress – these affairs are of no interest to you,' Hamid Bek went on, with a little bow to Abram. 'The innocent have nothing to fear, so it is written in the Koran. No, Effendi Levinson, I am here to give you sad news of your son, Aaron.'

'Aaron?' the old man blurted out, his face whitening.

'We have received news that he was taken off a neutral ship by the British and is now in a prisoner-of-war camp in England.'

'England!' There was no mistaking the genuine amazement on the old man's face. 'Surely, there must be some mistake!'

'There is no mistake, Effendi, the information came to us via the Red Cross who are always admirably correct.'

'How long ago did this happen, Your Excellency?' Daniel asked, truly flustered.

'Two months ago, I believe,' Hamid Bek answered and then turned to Sara. 'What do you think your brother was doing on a ship bound for the USA?' he snapped so fiercely everyone jumped.

He's done it! He's reached England! And this is his cover, Sara thought, almost sagging with happiness, and she answered with complete calm. 'I have no idea, Excellency. We have heard no word from him since he left Constantinople for Berlin on business for his Excellency Jemel Pasha.' Hamid Bek's look of annoyance at Jemel Pasha's name did not escape Sara, but she continued smoothly. 'Whatever his reasons may have been you can be sure they were patriotic – you know the Levinson family has always been loyal to Turkey.' Daniel glanced at Sara, feeling a little uplift of pride for her.

Hamid Bek's eyes narrowed, but he said nothing. Their astonishment had seemed so genuine that he was forced to admit to himself that this was the first they had heard of Aaron's whereabouts. His instinct told him to keep his eyes and ears opened – the Levinsons were not as straightforward as they seemed, he was convinced of it. He looked round them all again but saw nothing amiss.

'Effendi Levinson, please accept my sympathy for your son's incarceration. If you hear anything more I take it you will report it to me immediately.'

They all nodded and Bek gave the order for his horse to be made ready. Clicking his heels together, he bowed to Sara who smiled.

'We are grateful to you for bringing the news personally. Perhaps you will do us the honour of visiting again soon.'

'Perhaps, dear lady, perhaps.' Straightening his jacket he clicked his heels again and raised his arm in a salaam to the company. 'The blessings of Allah upon you,' he said and, followed by the soldiers, made his way back to the courtyard.

They waited in the falling dusk in silence until the cavalry unit had disappeared from view, then Daniel spoke. 'Thank God,' he whispered, 'thank God Aaron is safe.' Sara nodded, wrapping her shawl to her and feeling weak and chilly.

Abram shook his head and pulled at his beard. Looking directly into Daniel's eyes he asked, 'What do you suppose that boy was doing on a ship to America in the middle of the war?'

Daniel glanced at Sara and Robby. None of them had any idea how much the old man knew or suspected, but it was best to keep quiet. 'Perhaps he was planning to bring back some relief gold and supplies from America,' he suggested.

Abram grunted thoughtfully, but it was clear he did not believe it.

'I'm going to Ruth,' said Robby, still thinking only of what might have happened to his daughter. It was clear he had been terrified and he seemed to have shrunk into himself.

'I'm coming too,' said Sara, and Sam and Abram followed them in.

Daniel stood alone for a minute on the veranda, watching the door close behind Sam. After today's scene Robby would never consent to leave Ruth and the child and Daniel would not blame him. Thank God he had no children. It was clear to Daniel that the British had not believed Aaron's story and had locked him up as a spy. The same thing had nearly happened to him, and he knew the small-mindedness of some of the lower-ranking English officers.

Daniel's thoughts turned to Sara and his heart almost quailed at the thought of the responsibilities he would be leaving with her.

But he had no doubt that she would be more than equal to them, and he could not afford to waste any more time. It was up to him now. Tonight he would get Sarkis down to Atlit and on Monday he would set out for Egypt.

Alone, God help him. But so be it.

Sara closed the barn door behind her and paused for a moment, breathing in the musky smell of hay and dried grain and waiting for her eyes to accustom themselves to the gloom. She was glad of the dim light, knowing it would be easier to talk and knowing that she could no longer put off the moment of confrontation. She made Daniel out, sitting on the other side of Jezebel, which, propped up on blocks, had not been driven for months and probably would not be again until after the war. Light from a small, high window fell on Daniel, stippling his face with uncanny patterns. He was concentrating on his work, buckling some tack together with practised fingers.

'Daniel,' she said haltingly. He raised his head quickly, looked at her fleetingly, and lowered it again. Sara stood in silence, watching him and then, taking a deep breath, made her way through the obstacles to his side. There was no point in not discussing it any more, they were both sharing the same thoughts. She knew what was in his mind, had known it since the moment Sarkis brought them the code book.

Standing beside him, she looked down at his bent head, the nape of the neck so ridiculously vulnerable. He did not look at her, but continued making a bridle out of odd bits of leather. So he was going to sell his black colt.

'When are you leaving for Egypt?' she asked abruptly, clenching her hands and feeling a sense of release as at last she broached the subject.

'Tomorrow,' he said quietly, still not meeting her gaze.

Sara heard the answer she was expecting, but a surge of anger and panic swept over her as though she had been totally unprepared. She fought to control her emotions and, after a pause, she bit her lip and said softly, 'Daniel, please, please, don't leave me here. I can't manage on my own. I just can't.'

Daniel heard the catch in her voice and put the bridle down with a sigh. He had known this battle would come and was well prepared, but he was not going to enjoy the next few minutes.

He looked up at her and she was shocked at the coldness of his eyes. 'You know perfectly well that that is not true. You are strong, Sara, possibly the strongest person I have ever met. Certainly,' he added with a thin smile, 'the strongest woman.' Then, as though he had answered everything, he picked up the bridle again and calmly continued working on it.

Sara could not speak and could barely see for fury. How dare he – one minute she was a woman incapable of a simple journey to Jerusalem without an escort, the next she was some kind of contemporary Deborah leading the Israelites against their enemies. 'What exactly do you mean by that?' she snapped.

'I mean that you are good at taking charge – that you like responsibility. God knows, you're much better at it than I am, Sara. I saw how you handled Sarkis, and Hamid Bek. You rise to a challenge. Besides,' he added impatiently, 'Manny will be back from Akco in a few days. If you want to give up, he can take over.'

'You're crazy, Daniel.' Sara's rage began to get the better of her. 'Crazy! Why can't you wait? Another week – eight days at the most – and the moon will be down and the ship will be in. Why take such a dreadful risk, why not wait . . .' Her eyes blazed with fury and the determination to persuade him.

'Because,' Daniel exclaimed heartily, 'because I have to go now!' He sighed and with an effort put aside his anger; he knew he owed her an explanation. 'Listen to me, Sara,' he said, reaching out and drawing her on to the bale beside him. 'Crazy I am not. I have considered what I must do from every angle.' He took her hand and looked into her eyes. 'In another eight days the holy month of Ramadan begins – then for the whole of December nothing, not even a lizard, will be able to cross the Turkish lines undetected. If I don't go now,' his tone had become wheedling, persuasive, 'it will be the end of January before the moon wanes and I can try.'

Sara withdrew her hand and dropped her gaze, thinking over what Daniel had just said. She had to admit it made sense. Ramadan was the Islamic month of fasting and celebration when the Moslems gave thanks for God's gift of their holy book, the Koran. They fasted totally during the hours of daylight and then, at sunset, when a white thread was indistinguishable from a black one, they feasted and celebrated through the night till dawn.

She lifted her head and set her jaw. 'Then why not wait until January. All that about Aaron being a prisoner of war – don't you know it's just a cover to protect us here in Palestine.' Her voice was rising now in her effort to convince him. 'Aaron *told* us to

357

expect something like this – he warned us to be prepared.' Daniel looked at her unmoved and after a pause Sara allowed a pleading note to come into her voice. 'January is only a few months aw . . .'

Daniel leapt to his feet, snorting in irritation. 'Only a few months,' he mimicked furiously as he turned his back on her. Sara stood up and reached for his arm, but he shook her hand off roughly and swung round to face her. 'You know as well as I do that reports are showing a massive build-up of troops on the Turkish lines. They will soon become impassable.' He gripped Sara's shoulders and as they faced each other she was stunned by the light that had suddenly flamed behind his eyes. She was instantly reminded of the obsessive fanaticism she had witnessed on his return from France and she watched him in dismay.

His fingers dug deeper into her shoulders, his eyes impaled hers. 'And what happens if they don't come in January – or ever? That could happen, too, Sara. Every day history is being forged on the anvil of war. Everyone in the Middle East is vying for a better position. I can't stand and wait while other people snatch their own futures. I want us, the Jews, to have our rightful place too.' His hands relaxed a little and a new, gentler note came into his voice. 'I believe I have a duty – a sacred duty – to Palestine, to my people and to myself.'

Sara stared at him, tears starting behind her eyes and swallowed a large lump that had come to her throat.

Daniel flinched under the intensity of her gaze and, turning away, he continued: 'I've copied the code on to maize paper and rolled it into cigarettes. If I'm arrested the Turk will most likely smoke the evidence.' He turned back to Sara, a look of anguish clouding his features.

Sara gazed at him with damp, sorrowful eyes, then dropped her head. 'Daniel, please don't go – I'm sorry – I can't be strong about it.' Tears spilt through her dark lashes as she spoke.

'Sara, please . . .' He took her in his arms and held her. He wanted to be perfectly honest without hurting her more than was necessary. 'I love you, Sara, don't you understand that? You have meant as much to me as any person will ever, but I have never deceived you into thinking that I would put my love for you before my love for my country. You know that is true, you know that nothing, not even you, can ever come before that.'

The fight in her drained away, leaving her feeling weak and strangely resigned. She breathed out wearily, then straightening her shoulders said, 'You can't blame me for being annoyed and unhappy. I have an awful sense of foreboding – a feeling that if you go, something will happen to you . . . to me . . . to both of us.'

Daniel looked into her long, blue eyes. 'Sara,' he said softly, 'we are ultimately responsible for our own lives – for our own destinies.' He was smiling gently and she saw at once that his eyes were calm again, all hostility washed away.

She returned his smile and shrugged. 'I've never been able to make you see things my way, or to prevent you doing anything you wanted to do before.'

Daniel took her hand and kissed her cheek with a broad smile. 'Nor I you, Sara,' he said, 'nor I you.'

Sara came out of the barn, feeling terribly alone. She closed her eyes and leaned for a moment against the wall. How foolish of her to have imagined for a moment that she could influence him in any way. Daniel was his own man, and always had been. She smiled in exasperated admiration; he was so obsessive and idealistic. He did not belong to her and never had. He belonged to Palestine and his people. Was love ever a good thing? she wondered. She had no answers.

She straightened herself, determined to harden herself against him. Let him do as he pleased, she thought coolly and a curious sense of ease came over her, as though she had shrugged off a heavy burden.

Daniel had failed her. Worse than that, he had failed Aaron and therefore the network. She had spent months – and years before that – making excuses for his behaviour, but the excuses had run dry. She would think, but she would stop feeling. She knew her responsibilities lay not with Daniel, but with the station and her family. This little episode in the long saga of the war was not going to break her spirits.

'Mrs Cohen, madame? Are you well?' Sara jumped and opened her eyes to see Ahmed peering at her anxiously. She stood away from the wall and nodded, smiling wanly. 'Yes, fine. What is it?'

'I need more grease. It's for the aerometer.'

Sara sighed. And now back to routine. 'Come with me,' she said and set off for the storeroom in the courtyard.

It was the rainy season and so very little work was done on the land. As usual the time was spent in repairing and servicing the farm machinery and Sara was constantly being pestered for the nuts and bolts that were so carefully saved up and stored. She handed a tin of grease to Ahmed. 'We only have a few left, so use it sparingly and bring back whatever's left,' she told him and then, hearing the lunch bell ringing, looked towards the station.

She was just crossing the courtyard when she heard Bella, loose in a nearby field, whinnying and neighing excitedly. She ran to the gate and saw her mare galloping slowly along the fence. Looking down the palm avenue Sara made out a couple of horsemen riding towards her. She squinted in the sunlight and shaded her eyes with her hand. It was Joe Lanski, accompanied by his little devil Ali. Sara's heart lifted unaccountably and she smiled, delighted to see him.

Sara put a hand up to her hair, which was tumbling loose from its pins, and then opened the gate. Joe rode through with a smile and in one, smooth movement dismounted and threw his reins to Ali, who was giving Sara furtive, and not very friendly, looks. *I wonder why he doesn't like me*, Sara thought idly. *It's almost as though he's jealous of me – but that's ridiculous.*

'If you hurry you might catch some lunch,' she told him but Ali just smiled cheekily.

'Thank you, honourable lady, but I am carrying my own,' he said and led the two horses across to the hitching post.

Sara raised her eyes to Joe who smiled and shrugged. 'The awkward age,' he said ruefully and then looked at her questioningly. 'You're very pale. Nothing wrong, I hope?'

'No, nothing at all,' she lied, and then smiled with honest pleasure. 'What brings you to Atlit?'

Joe raised his eyebrows and set his face in a perfect parody of injured pride. 'Have you forgotten that I said I would be calling by? Surely not?'

'Oh, Joe, I'm so sorry it's just that . . .' Joe laughed at her pained expression.

'Bang goes another fanciful notion – Ah women; soft silk but wound like the sharpest steel,' he grinned. 'Actually I came to see Daniel – is he about?'

Wondering what he could want with Daniel, Sara pointed Joe in the direction of the barn. 'He's in there. Are you hungry or did you bring your own as well?'

'I'll have something later perhaps,' he said and strolled off towards the barn.

Sara, brows knitted in puzzlement, watched him until he

disappeared inside the barn, then turned back to the main building. She had better prepare something for Sarkis, he would begin to think she had forgotten him.

Sara, balancing the heavy tray carefully, made her way up the stairs to Sarkis. She had been cautious and had laid the tray for only one person – one very hungry person. It was quite usual for her to take her own lunch to the study, and no one would be suspicious if they saw her carrying a tray upstairs.

She knew the enormous personal risk she was taking in hiding the Armenian Captain but try as she might she did not care. They had ridden back from Zichron together the night before with no problems, and Sara had even enjoyed the feeling that she was doing something positive – and cocking a snook at Hamid Bek. How she hated that animal, and thank God that she did not fear him. That was probably her greatest strength.

Pausing on the landing, Sara checked the corridor cautiously. Sarkis was hidden in a small room at the end, which had been used as a storeroom for the laboratory. Now that they had had to stop experimental work nobody ever used the room and Sara knew that Sarkis would be undisturbed there. It was on the same floor as the study and the girls' bedrooms and, best of all, had a trap door on to the roof, which meant that if he ever had to leave in a hurry he could do so perfectly safely. With any luck Sarkis would be safe there until the ship arrived. Unless, unless America joined the Allies and the station became enemy, rather than neutral, territory. Sara shuddered at the thought. Things had already become harder – the locusts had moved further south and with Aaron a prisoner of war in England, the station was of no more interest to Jemel Pasha.

Sara shook off her thoughts. There was enough to worry about without panicking about future problems. Seeing that no one was about, Sara went to Selena's door and tapped lightly. Selena, a half-made man's shirt in her hands, opened it eagerly.

'What kept you?'

'Joe Lanski turned up. And there are a few other developments I'll tell you about later.'

Selena followed Sara down the corridor. She could not get over her relief that Kristopher was to be kept safe and sound only a few yards from her. Sara handed Selena the tray as she searched the ring she always wore at her waist for the right key. Looking up, she caught Selena's intense gaze. 'What's the matter?' she asked, her hand on the door knob.

'I was just thinking how very much I owe you.'

'Let's write the debt on ice, shall we?' she said and opened the door.

Sarah had been back in her study for an hour before Joe knocked at the door. He came in carrying a yellow box printed with flowers, which he put on the desk in front of her. 'I've brought you a small token of my esteem,' he said, smiling and sank into a chair beside her.

Sara found herself blushing as she opened the box. Inside it were three circles of soap, wrapped in delicate tissue paper. It was so long since she had even seen anything so trivial, so feminine, so entirely useless and perfectly lovely that tears rose in her eyes. She lifted a bar to her nose and breathed in the fragrant smell of jasmine. 'You cannot believe how much more delicious this is than Fatma's home-made soap,' she said, trying to lighten her emotion with a smile. As she inhaled the sweet aroma she was suddenly and painfully reminded of the days before the war when the world seemed secure and dependable, when this soap would have been just a good bar of soap.

She looked up and met Joe's eyes, how kind he could be sometimes. 'Thank you, Joe. It is so thoughtful of you.'

He waved his hand deprecatingly. 'I have something else for you,' he said in a low voice and, taking a folded sheet of paper from his pocket, put it down solemnly in front of her. Then he leant back, sprawling his long legs comfortably and added: 'Daniel said you would know what to do with it.'

Sara smoothed out the paper and stared at it, perplexed. It seemed to be a sketched map of something.

'What is it?' she asked, looking up at Joe.

'It's a map of the fortifications in Jerusalem, including positions of the Turkish and German batteries and arms slicks.' Joe's voice was casual but triumph shone out of his eyes.

Completely startled, Sara looked from Joe back at the paper. *I'll never understand this man*, she thought, *who is he?* She raised frightened eyes to his.

'I have a friend,' he said with a grin. 'The wife of a German officer. Her husband is away a good deal.' The grin broadened and Sara looked away in irritation. Her eyes fell on the box of soap and narrowed into slits as she looked from it to him. Her cheeks reddened. He really was utterly detestable – but what should she care? Why should it matter to her where he found anything – soap, maps – why think about it? She felt confused and unhappy. Somehow the present had lost its magic. She looked up at him and spoke calmly. 'Why are you giving me this?' she asked.

The grin vanished and Joe answered seriously. 'You are quite right to be wary. Espionage is a very dangerous business.'

Joe waited a second for this to sink in and then stood up. 'Come down to the gardens. I'd rather talk there.'

They walked in silence until they were well away from the station, and then stopped on a grassy hill overlooking the sea. Sara had been busy with her thoughts, with a new wave of hope. Perhaps Joe would see sense and help persuade Daniel to wait a little longer. She dismissed the thought almost as soon as it came into her head. Deep inside her she knew that Daniel would go tomorrow no matter who said what. Then her thoughts wandered towards Joe. Should she ask him to stay a while – until the ship came in maybe?

She looked at him from beneath lowered lashes. He was lost in thought, gazing out at the sea, his expression giving nothing away. *He is the most masculine man I have ever met.* Sara was surprised at the thought. *Always a man. Nothing of the boy in him.* She followed his gaze and stared at the sea, wondering how to broach the subject of his staying. The light was very clear and bright, a few rain clouds flirting with the horizon.

'I never tire of the sea,' Joe said, without taking his eyes from it. 'It's so peaceful, so undisturbed. Nothing to remind me of the war.'

With his mention of the war Sara saw an opening. Now she had to find out what Daniel had told him. 'Did Daniel say anything to you about his going away?' she asked innocently.

'Yes. I'm going with him.'

Sara looked at Joe wildly. 'You're what?'

'I'm going . . .'

'You're mad. You'll both get yourselves killed,' she cried angrily.

'I shouldn't worry. The devil looks after his own.'

Once again the irritation Joe aroused in her so often came to the surface. This was not a moment for flippancy.

'I would have thought that you had more sense. But I see you're as crazy as he is . . .'

Joe laid an urgent arm on her hand. 'Do be quiet, Sara, or the whole world will hear you. Calm down.' He thought how beautiful she was when blood rose to her cheek and her eyes were that bright, hard blue. Sara shook her arm free and turned away from him.

'Honestly, Sara. Daniel's idea is not as far-fetched as you think.'

Sara turned back to Joe and answered passionately: 'For heaven's sake, Joe, why can't you wait just another week or so. That's all I'm asking. I'm convinced that Aaron is not a prisoner of the British but . . .'

'And if he is? What then?' Joe interrupted. 'What's going to happen to Sarkis and Selena if America enters the war, which I think will happen sooner, rather than later. What will you do? Just sit the war out and watch as the Turk tears all you have built here to pieces? Well, I've had my bellyful of the Turk and death and destruction everywhere you look. The country's going to hell and we Jews will be the first to go with it.' Joe regarded Sara closely with those keen, intelligent eyes. 'Daniel is right you know. The situation in the Sinai is heating up rapidly. If we wait, it could well become impassable.'

They faced each other, Sara searching for an answer and furious to find that she could not put her finger on a flaw in Joe's reasoning. Unable to think of a retort, she turned the argument neatly. 'Well, well,' she said mockingly. 'You're singing a different tune now, aren't you? It's the first I've heard of your being interested in anyone's fate but your own.'

As she said the words she regretted them, but Joe just looked at her with a grin. 'Like all women you have a genius for selective memory.' Sara dropped her eyes under his challenging stare. 'But you are right, of course, I cannot lie. My motives in accompanying Daniel are entirely selfish. I enjoy our little meetings,' he laughed, 'and it would quite take the spice out of them if you were dressed in black and weeping holes in your handkerchief for a dead lover.'

'He is not my lover!' Sara burst out, and Joe laughed again, this time with a harsh note.

'Come on, Sara, don't insult my intelligence by denying something that is so patently obvious to the dullest brain.' He caught her chin roughly in his hands and lifted her face to his.

'However, I should like to think that while we are away you might spare the odd thought for me.'

Sara's blue eyes met his hard green stare and, for a moment, she felt her whole self drawn to him. Gathering her wits, she wrenched her head away. 'I'm sure you have more than your share of women worrying over the fate of your bones,' she said cynically.

He laughed again, more softly. 'Perhaps you're right,' he said and the mood between them relaxed again. Sara looked at him coolly for a moment.

'If you'll excuse me I had better start preparing food for your journey,' she said and, gathering her skirts together, she turned on her heels and marched off across the grass to the station.

Joe stood alone for a moment, looking back out to sea in an effort to calm his thoughts. Why in hell had he so readily agreed to accompany Daniel Rosen? The Russian Jewish poet Bialik's words came to his mind, raging words written after the Kishinev pogrom:

Now go outside the town where none shall see you
Sneak quietly to the place of burial
And stand beside the martyrs' new-made graves
And stand and let your eyelids fall –
And turn to stone.
Your heart shall fail within you, but your eye
Burn hot and tearless as the desert sand
Your mouth shall open to shriek aloud for revenge
And quiet as the tombstones you will stand.

Joe was suddenly full of more hate in his heart than he would ever have thought possible. Hatred for the Turk, for the Jews' silence in the face of the Turk's hatred. It was time to fight back. He did not share Daniel's faith in the British but something had to be done to stem the tide of persecution rising against the Jews in Palestine.

Looking back towards the research station he caught a glimpse of Sara disappearing between the greenhouses and his anger dropped as swiftly as it had arrived. He shrugged his shoulders and laughed to himself. Then, turning back to face the sea, he said aloud, 'I guess I just can't resist a challenge.'

Cairo did not seem to have changed much since Aaron had last visited the city nearly ten years before; soldiers in British khaki strolled the streets, but the atmosphere was as relaxed and chaotic as it had ever been. The noise was horrendous, pedestrians elbowed each other viciously in their attempts to make any progress, cars hooted in warning blasts, horses' hooves clattered and hawkers called out their tuneless cries. Aaron strained his eyes through the all-pervading dust; Cairo was a city bred in dust, with rain falling only a few weeks a year and the desert lapping daily closer towards its outskirts. The stench from a nearby alley made his eyes water and he pulled a handkerchief to his nose, not for the first time congratulating the Bedouin on their foresight in plugging their noses with cotton whenever they came into the city.

At that moment a car jerked out of a side street, its gears shrieking in protest and, had it not been for the speed of Paul Levy's reflexes, it would have driven straight into Aaron. With a nimbleness that belied his enormous weight, Paul shoved his shoulder into Aaron's side and sent him reeling to safety as the car slithered to a halt in a bird-seller's shopfront. The caged birds squawked, their wings fluttering frenetically and scattered pedestrians cursed as the shopkeeper emerged, wiping his hands on an old rag and pronounced the driver a leprous son of a dog. A crowd gathered, small boys appearing out of dark corners to try and catch the freed birds as Paul pulled Aaron to his feet. 'Sorry about that – everything happened so fast.'

'I'm fine,' Aaron answered with a smile, dusting himself down and readjusting his Panama hat, 'but something tells me we should get out of here quickly.' The driver, a bearded, swarthy man, had fixed his eye on Aaron and was beginning to shout over the crowd.

'Have you no eyes, you dog-turd?' He made as though to struggle through the mass towards them but then, catching sight of Paul's six-foot-two, twenty-one stone frame, thought better of it and went back to shouting nameless obscenities at the small boys who still clustered around the car.

Paul and Aaron exchanged smiles and, pushing through the few people staring at them curiously, they continued up the road, neither fast nor slow, but confidently. Suddenly, as so often in Cairo, the squalid alley gave way to a busy street and they slowed their pace.

'A few weeks ago I would have squashed that chap like a fly – and gladly,' Paul said, glancing wistfully over his shoulder.

'But now you have rather more important challenges,' Aaron reminded him, patting his friend's shoulder. 'The possibility of a broken arm does not bear thinking about.' And Paul, smiling, nodded agreement.

He was the only man apart from Aaron in Cairo who knew the Atlit coast well enough to attempt a landing on a dark night. It had been decided that Aaron, with his unique knowledge of Palestine, was too important to risk and Paul had been elected to sail on the contact ship due to leave Port Said in a few days' time. Aaron was furious, but the British High Command, who at last recognised his worth, just would not give him permission to go – either on his own or with Paul.

The two men came to a busy intersection where an Egyptian traffic policeman, his eyes blank with either the fatalism of the Moslem or the trance of a hashish smoker, observed the chaos around him. Paul and Aaron crossed the road as best they could without him, dodging the clanging, hissing trams and lunatic drivers and then walked at a leisurely pace up the street until they reached the synagogue. Paul pointed at a large restaurant on the corner opposite where waiters in short white jackets and red tarbooshes were busy serving sizzling kebabs to the diners, who had already collected on the terrace.

'I'll wait for you there if you don't mind,' Aaron smiled, his blue eyes gleaming at his friend.

'Yes, I expect you're hungry,' he answered, remembering the breakfast Paul had already eaten – the equivalent of half a cow, he had teased at the time.

Shaking Paul's hand, Aaron walked on past the synagogue, the brim of his hat pulled down over his forehead and his eyes fixed on his shoes. In London Aaron had been given a new name and identity, to protect the family if anything should go wrong. The Jewish community in Cairo was vast, further swollen by the men Jemel Pasha had thrown out of Palestine. These had banded together to form the Zion Mule Corps, so called because its members had been in charge of delivering the supplies and equipment by mule from flatboats on the beaches to the trenches of Gallipoli. It was unlikely he should bump into anyone he knew, but it was not a risk worth taking. Next to the synagogue was a large, crumbling, plaster and stucco building with a Union Jack hanging limply over the door. This was the club and Aaron turned smartly up the steps and through the front door.

The *Boab*, an old Egyptian with a squint and a glass eye, was on duty at the door and Aaron nodded at him, handing his hat to a servant in a red tarboosh hovering at his side. 'Major Wyndham Deedes,' he said.

'Ah yes, Major, this way please,' said the *Boab*, opening the door.

'No,' Aaron said slowly, 'I am not Major Deedes. I am John Williams and I have a lunch appointment with the Major.' His experiences of the last few months had left him with the patience of Job.

'Yes sir, yes sir, please to wait in the bar,' the *Boab* said agreeably and Aaron went with a sigh through to the dim Mecca of male military leisure. Looking at the clock over the fireplace Aaron saw that he was early and picked up a freshly-ironed copy of *The Times*. Dated 11 November, it was nine days old but Aaron settled down with it happily.

Aaron ordered a gin and tonic and glanced at the front page. Rumania looked as though it were about to join the fighting in the Balkans and it appeared as though the British Prime Minister Asquith's Ministry were teetering on the edge of collapse. The military situation was, to say the least, gloomy. The horrendous sacrifices of the Somme had been followed by a winter mud, which bogged down any hopes of movement and there did not seem to have been any noticeable improvement in the Allies' strategic position in France.

Aaron sipped at his drink, unable to concentrate on the complexities of the report. His mind was on his forthcoming luncheon with Major Deedes. He had one last request to make of the British before the contact ship sailed and he had chosen to present his petition to the Major.

Although Brigadier-General Gilbert Clayton was first in rank at General Staff intelligence, Aaron was convinced that his right-hand man, Wyndham Deedes, was his superior in initiative and intuition. He was a brisk, no-nonsense man with a dry, perceptive humour and it was thanks to him that Aaron had at last broken through the endless layers of bureaucracy, which cloaked the mess that passed for military administration in Cairo.

Aaron had arrived in Egypt from Britain six weeks ago with a letter of recommendation from General MacDonough himself. Having been passed by the Chief of Military Intelligence in London, Aaron felt totally confident that he would now be taken seriously by the underlings in Cairo. But that had been far from the case. Despite his London backing he found himself treated with much the same offhand suspicion as had greeted Daniel. It was admitted that the intelligence they had sent during the few months that contact had been maintained between Atlit and Egypt had been superb, but there was no cutting through their rules and regulations.

If Lieutenant Woolley had been there to help it would have been easier, but Aaron had heard the Lieutenant's fate while he was still in London. The Englishman had been taken prisoner by the Germans, which had been the main cause of the breakdown of communication. Apparently Woolley, suspecting that the Arab cell in Tyre were either double agents or had quite simply not passed the change of code on to Atlit (either through incompetence or in an attempt to squeeze out the competition), had decided to sail with Captain Jones and discover for himself. The ship was torpedoed by a German submarine and Woolley taken prisoner. All his paperwork had been passed on to Daniel's acquaintance Colonel Thompson at the Arab Bureau. Thompson, the only other man in Egypt with direct knowledge of the group and its work, had neatly filed everything away and considered the episode closed.

It had taken Aaron a month of interviewing by junior officers and filling in as many questionnaires as if he were applying for a post as a junior bank clerk before the Bureau had sorted to the bottom of the files and he had been allowed to meet the Major, the first real man of influence he had been near.

'What it really boils down to,' the Major had explained over a brandy and soda, 'is the well-known lunacy of our race as far as foreigners are concerned. There is a deep-seated fear in most British minds that all foreigners are only there to get one over on them. Add to that the fact that British government servants in Egypt – and India, come to that – are numberless groups more or less working against each other, each with their own particular theories about how to run things and it easy to understand the deficiencies of British organisation.' Even though he had fallen victim to just such incompetence, Aaron had to laugh. Here, at least, was a man he could trust.

Ostensibly, the sole objective of the British in Egypt was to protect the Suez Canal – 'the gateway to England's jewel in the crown, India' – but as the war continued the British representatives had broken into rival groups, each championing a different cause for control of the Middle East. One group supported the claims of Abdul Azzis Ibn Sa'ud, who had emerged from obscurity a few years earlier to conquer the Arabian peninsula. Another section was for Husain, the Shareef of Mecca, and his sons, who were locked in bitter enmity with Abdul Azzis. Abdul Azzis considered Husain nothing more than an ambitious upstart and was furious with the British for supporting him.

Luckily, Major Deedes did not believe in cutting up the skin before they had killed the bear. He was for trapping the bear first. Within an hour of his and Aaron's meeting, they had both gained the other's complete confidence. Best of all, as far as Aaron was concerned, was the Major's ability to give commands. As soon as he had listened to Aaron's case he had rounded up everyone concerned and issued immediate orders to renew contact with Atlit. Over the last few days they had painstakingly gone through every eventuality that might arise and worked out a new, more complex code. With the Major in control, Aaron's frustration and disappointment had fallen away, leaving only worry about what was going on at Atlit. Try as he might he could not rest calm about what Daniel might be up to by now. Well, he thought, draining his drink, in eight days' time – ten at the most – he would know the best and the worst.

Aaron refocused his eyes on the by now crowded bar and made out the tall, spare figure of Major Deedes bearing down on him. He stood to shake hands. 'Another drink?' the Major offered. 'Or shall we go straight in to lunch before the place gets too hectic?' Aaron, eager to come to the real reason he was seeing the Major, chose to go into lunch at once.

As they settled into their places a waiter handed them menus with a bow. 'Choose something simple,' Major Deedes advised. 'The waiters here have a singularly imperfect knowledge of English and asking for anything much more complicated than a steak nearly always leads to very unexpected results.'

Aaron bore this in mind and ordered the same as the Major; brown Windsor soup and the recommended 'slice off the old leg', which translated into roast leg of mutton with onion sauce. They talked pleasantly but generally over lunch and the Major showed a great deal of interest in the history of the Jews in relation to Egypt. He was clearly a cultivated and intelligent man, but although Aaron enjoyed their conversation he could not for long forget his reason for wishing to see Major Deedes.

At last Major Deedes folded the napkin on to the table beside him. 'Shall we adjourn to the smoking room for a cigarette?'

Aaron nodded. The hovering presence of the waiters excluded

any private conversation and he was now eager to raise the matter in hand. They were lucky to find the smoking room empty and both lit up, settling into chairs on each side of the empty fireplace. The Major smiled. 'Now then,' he said, 'I have the distinct feeling that you want to tell me something of great importance. Am I right?'

Aaron looked at the Major with serious eyes. 'Yes, it's about the gold. I have had an idea that I think might change the mind of the High Command.'

A quick look of irritation was replaced by one of scepticism as the Major raised his brows questioningly. They had been over and over the question of how to send the relief gold to Atlit but it had been impossible for him to gain permission for it to be carried on the contact ship. The ship was a spy ship, sent to gather information from spies – foreign spies. And the gold was not British gold but American. This was where the shifting world of politics met that of espionage – and the result was deadlock.

There was another reason why permission had been refused, a reason Major Deedes was not inclined to disclose to Aaron. Large sums of gold channelled illegally into Palestine would add considerably to the likelihood of the network being uncovered. The British High Command now considered Aaron a valuable asset to the Allied cause and had a mounting confidence that the information Atlit could provide might prove priceless. Personally, the Major would have given permission, but he had to abide by his orders.

He drew smoothly on his cigarette and studied its tip before looking back at Aaron. 'What exactly do you have in mind?'

Aaron had been infuriated by the British refusal to allow the gold to be transported on the contact ship. Thanks to Alex's work in the States and the generosity of the American Jews, the gold had been piling up in the fund set up in Egypt. Aaron knew that if the gold did not go on the ship it could be a month before there was another chance. Now he had come up with an idea which could, if he were tactful, make the British change their minds.

'As you well know, Major,' he began, 'Palestine is the Holy Land to more people than the Jews. There are numbers of Christian institutions here, all supported by the heads of their denominations around the world. Yesterday I had a meeting with the chief representative of the Church of England and that of the Vatican here in Cairo. They also have relief funds piling up which they are keen to get to Palestine where orphanages and other establishments are reported close to starving.' Aaron took out a letter addressed to the Commander-in-Chief of the British Forces in Egypt and handed it to the Major.

The Major took it thoughtfully.

'Naturally,' Aaron added, 'I said nothing of how the aid would reach Palestine. I only asked them to trust me and promised that this letter would reach Sir Archibald Murray.'

Major Deedes, balancing the letter on the tips of his fingers, turned his attention back to Aaron. 'I must say,' he laughed softly, 'I hope for the sake of Britain that you are all you say you are. If not, with your intellect and your talents for persuasion, you could well prove to be the most pernicious, deep-seated traitor in our island's history.'

The men's gaze met and they both smiled. Major Deedes stood and shook Aaron's hand in farewell. 'I cannot promise anything but I will do my best to have an answer for you tomorrow.'

'Thank you, Major,' Aaron said warmly, grateful that his idea had at least passed the first barrier.

They strolled to the front door together and shook hands again as the Major waved away the duty car waiting for him. Muttering something about a constitutional he strode down the street and Aaron watched him until his lean figure was swallowed into the crowd.

Aaron smiled, convinced that his strategy would bear fruit. The British High Command might care little for starving Jews: but starving Christian children would be another matter. Aaron had been through a great deal but he could not suppress a rising satisfaction at the knowledge that at last the tide was turning in his favour. As long as there had been no disaster at Atlit. Try as he might, he could not rid himself of the feeling that something was wrong.

Daniel had more than once had good reason to be grateful for Joe's company across the desert. It had been years since his childhood experiences with Sheik Suliman's tribe and he had fooled himself when he thought that his brief forays into the desert since then had kept him fit for a longer journey. Since they had left Beersheba, the last patch of fertile ground before the desert, he had come to rely on Joe more and more. Joe had spent years travelling the desert, trading with Arab tribes and his rich store of experience told in his favour. Secretly Daniel wondered whether he could have made it on his own. Without Joe he doubted whether he would even have been able to buy himself a camel.

Ali had ridden with them as far as Beersheba, and then they had sent him back with the horses which would not have stood a chance in the journey ahead. Left without transport, Joe and Daniel found Beersheba almost empty of dromedaries, as the wily camel traders had sold them all to the British in the Sinai before they were requisitioned by the Turk. Joe had had to call up a lot of favours, but it had still taken them days of intricate ritual bargaining before two medium-sized and reasonably well behaved camels had been found for them.

The Arab reluctance to part with the beasts was understandable; although Daniel had never been able to drum up any affection for them, they were of a great deal more use to the Arabs than land. A camel was a valuable commodity that could move around under its own power, that fed its owner with its milk, and whose urine was used by the women of the tribe to wash their hair in. Camel's meat made up ninety per cent of the Arab diet. In times like these its value almost tripled. As Daniel relaxed in the smooth, rhythmic movement of the camel's walk, he thanked God again for Joe's influence and persistence.

They had left Beersheba the day before, an hour after dawn, and had been riding gradually south through the changing landscape. The first few rains had fallen and in the Negiv desert splashes of bright orange broomrape and sprouting winter grasses contrasted with the surrounding austere vegetation. But the further south they rode, keeping clear of the heavily-patrolled coastal routes, the hotter it became and the more stony and arid the land. There were fewer and fewer landmarks and Daniel knew that before long they would face the endless sameness of the desert.

Tonight they were going to try and cross the Turko-Egyptian border that officially ran (although the Turk still considered the Sinai his) from Rafa on the Mediterranean coast to the Red Sea. They had decided to take a route that Joe knew was used by Bedouin trading Palestinian oranges to the British. To avoid any confrontations they must keep well east of Kossaima, a route which was below sea level and meant heat, no villages, no water and, with any luck, no landmines.

It was late afternoon now, nearly time for a break, and they had made steady progress. They had passed only one Turkish Army camel patrol, which had given them only a cursory glance. The incident had given them both a boost of much-needed optimism. The sun was still beating down on them, but it was visibly slipping lower in the sky and they knew they could look forward to some relief. When the sun sunk below the horizon, the temperature would drop almost immediately.

Daniel pulled at his camel's headrope and, pushing his keffiyeh back from his face, turned in the pack saddle to wait for Joe. Joe's camel was the more cussed of the two and proceeded as though she had her own route mapped out in her mind. Joe, the more experienced rider, had elected to ride her but however much he urged her on, her shorter stride kept her permanently behind Daniel's more eager mount. Joe kicked his heels into his camel's shoulders and tapped her with his stick, encouraging her with clicks of his tongue to catch up with Daniel.

Daniel, watching, wiped the sand from round his mouth and licked his lips. His tongue and throat were so dry he could barely speak. 'How much further?' he croaked, choking against the dust in his mouth. Joe blinked the sweat out of his eyes and checked with the compass hanging around his neck. That and a torch were the only non-Bedouin equipment they had allowed themselves – a map would, of course, have been out of the question. He squinted ahead and pointed at a stunted tree growing on the left of the horizon. Daniel looked at him questioningly. Distances were impossible to gauge in this wasteland; the horizon appearing sometimes an infinity away, sometimes so close that you could almost touch it. Daniel had long since given up trying to guess at distances. 'An hour, perhaps two,' Joe said and kicked his camel on. It took two.

The place Joe elected to stop had a single waterhole with sour, brackish water. But there was enough scrub for the camels to eat and although they could go for weeks without food it was worth keeping them good-humoured and fit with a meal a day.

They dismounted and couched the camels under a tamarisk tree. The light had faded almost completely and the desert had taken on the strange bluish tinge that always covers it in the early hours of the night and that is such a relief to the sore eyes of desert travellers, in a white daze after hours crossing the pale sands. They carefully unloaded the heavy waterskins and guns and hung them on the branches of a caper bush. In this merciless land water was not treated lightly, and always kept close beside one. Together Joe and Daniel unpacked some rugs and a few pots from the saddlebags, laid the pack-saddles carefully under a tree with the guns and then, hobbling the camels securely, set them free to graze. Not until then did they allow themselves a pause, their eyes at last adjusting to the softness of the fading light.

Joe quickly poured two bowlfuls of water and stirred in a little flour and sugar with a twig. Handing a bowl to Daniel they both drank deeply and in silence, all their senses responding to the wonderful drink, so much more refreshing than plain water. They sat a long moment, enjoying the luxury of stillness. Daniel's muscles ached from the unaccustomed strain of riding a camel and he felt deadly tired, but he had no intention of showing or succumbing to his exhaustion.

The air began to feel damp and chilly and Daniel put his hand out for a rug, wrapping it round him and checking with his torch that the camels were still nearby. Joe passed him a cigarette and the two men lit up, breathing the tobacco into grateful lungs. Only then did they talk for a while in desultory tones about banal matters. Neither spoke of what was foremost in their minds.

'I'm going to scout for camp fires,' said Joe after a while and rose to his feet with an effort. 'Bring up the camels and couch them, would you. I don't fancy searching for them in the dark.' And he strode off out of sight.

The moon was very low and in a few hours would be down altogether. They would need the darkness later, but now he wanted to pinpoint their position. Joe found a rise in the ground and looked over the surrounding land. In the far distance was a dim glow, orange against the night sky. He made a fix with his compass and went back down to Daniel, who was couching the second camel by the tree.

'Dead on course,' he said in a pleased voice and Daniel looked up with a tired smile. Joe pulled a string of dried dates from the saddlebags and handed some to Daniel, who joined him on the rug. 'We should leave at about one o'clock,' he said, biting into the fruit, and Daniel nodded. By then the moon would be very weak, allowing just enough light for them to make their way onwards without giving too much away.

Daniel stuffed the remaining dates in his pocket, wrapped himself in his rug and lay back with closed eyes. Suddenly, a great crashing boom of thunder shocked the two men into alertness, both of them sitting up and straining their eyes in the dark.

Seconds later, brilliant forks of metallic yellow light reflected over the sky in a magnificent display. In less than a minute it had disappeared as quickly as it had appeared and the men lay back again, their minds pulling against the exhaustion that overcame them.

Daniel must have drifted into sleep as the next thing he knew he was being shaken by Joe. He gasped awake, pulling himself out of his sleep with an effort. 'Come on,' Joe whispered. 'Get your camel ready and mount up. It's time to move on – to Egypt.'

Moving quickly, they saddled the camels who groaned at being disturbed in the middle of the night. Just before they mounted Joe took hold of Daniel's arm with a smile. 'Here's to luck – it's all we need now.'

Daniel shook Joe's hand formally with a grin. 'Good luck, Joe.'

Joe walked over to his camel's head. 'Do me a favour – stand on my camel's front legs while I mount her. She's a bitch for getting up before I'm on her.'

The two camels plodded on through the sand, the only noise a soft crunching from under the padded feet, as they walked rythmically onwards. Joe and Daniel sat alert, the adrenalin rushing through their veins as their eyes looked ahead into the dreary monochrome. They continuously urged their camels forward, pausing now and again for Joe to check the compass.

Suddenly, Daniel's camel came to a halt and Joe, just behind, heard Daniel swearing softly. 'What's up?' he whispered, bringing his beast up beside Daniel's.

'Wire! Bloody wire. A curse on those goddamned Germans – the Turks would never be bothered to be that organised.'

They looked bleakly at the thick line of barbed wire which stretched out in front of them, into the darkness in each direction. Then they exchanged blank looks.

Joe turned his camel's head and spoke in a forcedly optimistic voice. 'This can't be across the entire desert. Let's go further east.'

Joe's optimism proved right. An hour later – they had begun to fear it would be more – they came to a ravine, where the wire came to an abrupt end. Both men heaved a sigh of relief. The limestone of the ravine would mean it was almost impossible to mine and from now on they should be safe.

Their animals slipping on the loose rock and sending little shoals of stones down in front of them, they passed slowly through the gorge and only then did they stop for a drink. Their mouths were chalky from the dust and the tension, and each took a long draught from the goatskin. The water was oily and tainted with the taste of the skin but neither man complained; to them the cool liquid in their mouths was as refreshing as nectar. A splash of red appeared on the horizon and both men watched it gratefully for a moment: never had a dawn been more welcome.

'A morning of goodness, brother,' Daniel said in Arabic to Joe.

'A morning of light,' he answered and together they moved on into the slowly growing sunrise that glowed crimson in front of them, sending oranges, yellows and turquoises up into the sky. They both felt a surge of hope; with any luck their only enemy now would be the desert itself.

The next few hours passed in a vacuum. They did not exchange a word; lulled into a calm silence by the rocking of the camels as they moved on through the dry, almost featureless Sinai. They travelled for mile after mile while around them nothing changed; nothing soothed or frightened them until Joe, turning, saw eight camel riders bearing down on them at a fast trot. Their camels were small and quick and as they drew nearer it was obvious their riders were Bedouin but, despite their own disguises, Joe sensed danger. Both he and Daniel instinctively felt for their weapons as one man broke from the group and urged his mount into a gallop. The man drew close and pulled his camel to a rude halt in front of them. His face was mean and foxy and he greeted them with none of the friendship they might have expected from a Bedouin.

'Where are you going?' he asked aggressively.

'To Hassana,' Joe replied with no deference in his voice.

'So why do you travel this way? The wells are dry, there is no water.'

Joe did not answer but gave him a glowering stare which the Bedouin would recognise as a warning. The man seemed to change tactics and spoke again, his voice a little less frosty.

'What is your people?' and, his eyes missing nothing, he looked appraisingly at the camels, the saddlebags and guns.

'Ikaban.'

'Perhaps you have come to spy out the land for the Turk?'

Daniel gave a growl of laughter at this irony and Joe grinned menacingly, his fingers feeling for the grip of the pistol hidden in the folds of his shirt.

For a long moment the men looked at each other and it seemed that neither would back down. Daniel, his own pistol in his hand, was ready to fire at a moment's notice. But the Bedouin turned his camel's head towards his men, who were waiting some yards away. 'Go in peace,' he said and rode off.

'Go to hell,' Joe rejoined under his breath as he watched him go.

'I reckon they're bandits,' said Daniel, riding forward.

'I agree,' Joe answered uneasily. 'He definitely had his eye on our camels and probably our lives would be well worth their price.'

'We had better keep a careful watch, although they seem to be going,' said Daniel, looking at the group, which was riding north behind them.

For several hours they rode on, keeping a look-out for the bandits, but by midday they concluded with some relief that the Bedouin must have decided against an attack. The land was very open, and their spokesman had seen they were well armed.

The day drew on and they plodded monotonously forward, the heat beating down on them mercilessly. Daniel found it harder and harder to keep his mind from wandering. The lassitude, which had begun to creep up on him at midday, known as the Demon of Noontide, grew progressively worse. His mind was increasingly out of control; for minutes at a time he was plagued with nothing but jumbled, illogical thoughts and then he found himself considering the most profound and philosophical arguments with a clear, well-ordered head.

Daniel was half aware of what was happening to him, but was unable to fight against it. In normal circumstances thoughts are constantly intruded upon and influenced by the peripheral. Out there, in the unchanging wilderness with a featureless horizon, no middle distance and nothing more than a few pathetic patches of scrub to relieve the eye, the mind is left to its own resources. In one sense the nothingness all around liberates the traveller's thoughts, in another it entraps them, dragging them into the desert's own emptiness. Time slowed down until it stopped and Daniel's mind was thrown into a hopeless state of confusion.

But he could cope. He would survive. This was the land in which his ancestors and wandered and grown strong: the land of Genesis where centuries before his people had first been enslaved by the Egyptians. Out here in the desert he could, for the first time in his life, feel at one with his ancestors, with Abraham and Isaac and Jacob. Perhaps Sara had been right when she had said that in another religion he would have become a priest. How close his people's past felt to him now. How close he felt to God. How magnificent, how all-encompassing was his love for God. And in comparison, how petty, how earthbound, his love for Sara. How easy it was in this great wilderness to surrender to the idea of God's omnipotence. This could never be mastered. To master one had to fight and there was no fighting this cruel environment. How fitting it was that this should be the throne of Allah. No fertile ground could give Islam that all-embracing belief that required no questions, no great thought, merely the acceptance that there is no God but God and Mohammed is his Prophet. In Islam pleasure is to suffer and true satisfaction comes only from abstinence. A religion made for a desert life.

And how beautiful, after a life in this desolate hell, to die: 'There shall flow in it rivers of unpolluted water and rivers of milk for ever fresh. Rivers of delectable wine and rivers of clearest honey.' Yes, the Koran's Paradise was sweet indeed: honey, wine, milk and water.

Water. He was thirsty. Was it his second or his third thirst? If you drank before your third you became insatiable. He could not remember. With a great effort he pulled his mind into the present and tugged on the camel's headrope, waiting for Joe to catch up with him. It was only then that he noticed the wind that was sweeping the sand over the floor of the desert in little gusts. The sky had taken on a sickly yellow tinge, the sun was a pale imitation of itself. The atmosphere was uncomfortable and as Joe reached Daniel the two camels drew together with an instinct as old as time.

Joe had been keeping an eye on the weather and was worried. 'I think a sandstorm is blowing up,' he said soberly.

Daniel turned this over in his mind for a moment, disturbed by the possibility. 'Any ideas?' he asked, grappling with his fatigue.

Joe looked around quickly and pointed ahead to where the flat land became rolling sand banks, and a few thorn bushes might give a little cover. 'I suggest we make for those bushes,' he said. 'It's better than nothing. But we'd better do it fast.'

The camels knew the dangers of the sandstorms and were restless and unmanageable, zigzagging in their determination to keep their tails into the wind. The wind rose and with it the desert. Its surface, normally so calm, lapped and danced round the camels' feet. The men wrapped their headcloths tightly over their faces to protect them from the sharp stinging of the sand. By the time they were within five hundred yards of the scrub, the wind gusts had become sharper and more powerful. Ghostly dancing djinn blew up and swirling dust clouds, like the sacred pillars of cloud that led the Israelites out of the wilderness, roared around them. It was a sight both frightening and magnificent.

Joe looked ahead. Only four hundred yards further. Then something moved on the edge of his vision. He remembered the tribesmen they had met earlier in the day. He shouted a warning to Daniel, but his voice was drowned in a volley of gunshots that cut through the wind. A jolt in his leg, that sent him reeling back against the camel, told him he was hit. Ahead of him he saw Daniel slump in his saddle and then slip in slow motion to the desert floor. 'Oh God, no,' Joe groaned as Daniel's camel galloped off in fright.

Another volley of shots rang out but went wide – deliberately, Joe was sure. These men knew what they were doing and did not want to harm the camels. Joe looked round desperately. There was no advantage to be had from his position, he was as vulnerable as a wasp in a beehive.

In an instant he had made his decision. Pulling his knife from his belt, he sliced through the strings holding the waterskins to the saddle and jumped after them to the ground, keeping the camel's headrope in one hand and reaching for the gun with the other. In the desert there are two things without which man cannot survive – water and a camel. Out of the corner of his eye he saw Daniel stir. So he was not dead, thank God. The pain in his leg was threatening to overcome him, but Joe gritted his teeth against it and thought quickly. From the sound of the shots there must be about six of them. There was no point in trying to fight it out. His only chance was to let the second camel go and hope that that would be enough for them. They would have to follow the brutes before the storm blew up any more, so unless the camels were not the cause of the attack, they should be safe. He had no choice but to set the animal free, beating its haunches with the rope to send it galloping off into the sandstorm.

Joe dropped to his belly and picked up his shotgun, peering through the haze. If they did come to get him he could at least make sure of taking a few of them with him. He looked round for Daniel, who lay fifty yards away from him, the sand beginning to pile around him. *I must get over there*, Joe thought. *If he's not dead the sand will drown him.*

380

He waited a moment more and then began a slow belly crawl towards Daniel, dragging the waterskins and gun with him. There was no sound but the whistling of the wind, which threw handfuls of stinging sand into Joe's eyes as he crawled painfully across the desert. He was sure now that the camel thieves had taken off after their booty and that they would be safe from further attack.

Joe forced himself to his feet. He could see nothing of the Bedouin. The pain in his leg was like a living thing now. Staggering against the wind and the pain, he reached Daniel and fell down beside him in the sand, which had built up a foot high against his back. His face was still free of sand and, as Joe looked at him, Daniel opened his eyes.

Then Joe saw the gaping wound in Daniel's chest. *Dear God, help us*, he prayed as he took Daniel's hand and gazed into his eyes. 'I'm going to try and get us over to the sand dunes. Is it bad?' Daniel shook his head in denial, but could not speak.

Joe took off his keffiyeh and tore a strip from it, which he tied round Daniel's chest. He tied another strip on top of his own leg and watched as the red blood seeped straight through.

'Water,' Daniel whispered, 'water.'

Joe paused, hating himself for his hesitation. No one could survive a wound like that. Unless help came very soon Daniel was a dead man. Then Joe unscrewed the top of the waterskin and held it to Daniel's lips, waiting as Daniel choked in his haste to swallow. Carefully closing the skin he tied it to his belt and tried to find his footing against the wind, ignoring the pain in his leg. He took hold of Daniel and, with all his might, began dragging him towards the sand banks. He would never have believed he was capable of such reserves of strength. His breath screamed in his throat and his sight went dark as he reached the dunes and pulled Daniel into the lee of a bank that, although small, would give them vital protection. The wind was a devastating force that howled and swirled the sand round them in a yellow blur. Despite their protection the sand piled against them, threatening to bury them. As fast as Joe pushed it away it moved closer again.

Suddenly, the wind dropped and everything was still. There was no sign of the power that had torn through the wilderness only seconds before. A few grains of sand floated down through the air to mingle with the sands of the desert.

Joe sat up and dug through the sand for the waterskins. To his horror he found one must have been damaged when he cut it from the camel as it was now nearly empty. He dug frantically for the second, holding his breath until with a sigh of relief he found it intact.

He loosened the keffiyeh from Daniel's face. His friend was totally white, sweating badly and breathing with difficulty. Joe poured a little water into his hand and held it against Daniel's mouth. He took Daniel's hand and squeezed it, hoping to give him strength. The wound was bleeding again, a darkening stain spreading across his chest and down to his belly.

Daniel opened his eyes and whispered, 'It's bad, isn't it?' Joe nodded, looking away.

'I can't breathe,' Daniel gasped.

Joe gently pillowed the sand behind his head and Daniel seemed to breathe a little more easily. 'Take the code from my pocket,' he gasped and, without arguing, Joe took the tin of neatly-rolled cigarettes from Daniel's pocket and transferred it to his own.

Then he looked back at Daniel. To his surprise there was no fear in Daniel's eyes, even a hint of a smile. 'Looks like I won't be coming with you,' he panted and lay silent again.

Joe turned away to hide the tears he was surprised to feel rising to his eyes. He gripped Daniel's hand, hoping that human contact might comfort him and was silent, leaving Daniel's last moments on earth for his soul.

Daniel's mind was floating as it had earlier when the Noonday Demon had reached him, but more comfortably. *Lucky Jew who has seen the Promised Land, who has breathed in the air of Israel and Judea. Lucky Jew whose bones will join those of his ancestors, buried in the sands of the Sinai where they had wandered with Moses.* Then, briefly, he raged. *There is so much left to do, this is not the time to die . . . no time left . . . Oh Sara . . . Oh Zion . . .*

Sara sat at the window, her eyes sore with searching into nothingness. Outside the sea and the sky met in a relentless grey blanket, which seemed to cover the whole world. A strong wind was blowing inland from the sea, tearing with wicked fingers at the trees and smashing like a battering ram at the walls of the research station. For the third day running, torrential rain fell almost horizontally from the skies but however much moisture the sky gave out there was more to come. If the ship were out there, Sara knew that the stormy seas would prevent any landing at Atlit this month, but still her gaze was locked on the eerie grey seascape beyond the study window.

The afternoon had dragged out its listless hours and soon it would be dark. Maybe then she would be able to tear herself from the window and make herself do something constructive. If she didn't move soon she would surely freeze to death for, on top of all her other troubles, it was bitterly cold. Sara sat like an old lady, bundled up in layers of clothes, looking uncomplainingly out of the window for hour after hour and thinking her bitter thoughts.

She had too much to worry about; sometimes she thought it was too much to bear. She was not sure they could survive another month if their hopes were once again dashed. She was worried about Daniel and Joe, and spent hours imagining the worst, sure she had been wrong to let them go without a further fight.

Three days ago she had received the first mail for months. Several letters arrived at once; a few from America, one from Aaron in Germany saying he was about to leave for Denmark to meet up with some academic colleagues, and one from Turkey. Sara had opened the Turkish letter last. The writing was familiar, but not Chaim's. It looked like the writing of someone not accustomed to using a pen very often and as Sara's eyes flew to the signature at the bottom she was surprised to see it was from Irene.

She had barely thought of Irene for months; the old housekeeper had faded into the back of her memory of her unhappy married life and they had never corresponded since Sara's departure. Puzzled, she read the letter through slowly, and then again to grasp its full implications. Irene was asking for permission to stay in poor Mr Cohen's house until the war situation made it possible for Mrs Cohen to come home and settle her husband's affairs.

Chaim was dead. How or why Irene did not say – letters must have been sent to Sara months ago, but she had received nothing. Aaron had seen Chaim four months before and said nothing about his being ill, so Sara could only hope that it had been a quick and painless death.

Sara was surprised that her first reaction had been for Chaim, not for Daniel and herself. She had shed tears for her husband, wished she had been a better wife to him and recalled his better points. They would never have been happy together, she knew that, but the fault was hers as much as Chaim's. Her fault lay in having agreed to marry him.

The news of Chaim's death had made Sara consider her relationship with Daniel. She was a widow now, free to marry him. But did she still want to? She remembered how thrilled she had been when she first saw Daniel riding into the stableyard at Zichron. She remembered standing on the hill overlooking Galilee, her heart aching as he told her he was leaving Palestine. And she realised how her whole relationship with him was balanced on his side; he always leaving, always talking of sacrifice, his love for her always lagging behind his greater love for Israel and Zion. And for the first time this knowledge did not hurt. Her love for him had changed. She still loved him, but the passion was spent. Her love was now a deep and abiding affection, no longer twisted by childish infatuation, combined with an adult sexuality. Madly she had married Chaim, and as recklessly deserted him. She realised now that Chaim had needed her love; it only served as a torment to Daniel.

How stupid she had been. How incredibly stupid and selfish. She had tried to channel fate for her own designs, and had only hurt those closest to her as she had pursued her fantasies. And now she was left alone. No Daniel, no Aaron. Even Chaim was beyond helping her now. She was marooned with her thoughts and her dwindling hopes that the ship might yet come.

She stared out through the gathering dusk. The weather was unrelenting – a landing would be out of the question. And tomorrow the moon would be up. She quelled the last flicker of optimism and put her head in her hands. She would just have to wait another month. And admit that Daniel and Joe had been right to go. Darkness fell on the room as she brooded, feeling exploited, useless and as angry with herself as with the absent men.

Joe narrowed his inflamed eyes and stared at the amber flash on the horizon. Was it dawn or sunset? His mind struggled as the silence of the desert dinned in his ears. Whichever it was, he needed to rest. He would make for a tree not far off and rest a while. At least he hoped it was not far off; his eyes were playing tricks with him now. His eyes and the compass. Something had thrown it and it was wrong, he was sure of that. That could not be north, not if this was dawn. But was it sunset?

Totally disorientated, he staggered on towards the tree, the burning pain in his leg the sole thing keeping him conscious. It was only when he reached the tree that Joe saw the giant vulture perched on a high branch, glaring down at him with the confidence of a sure victory. Joe smiled wryly. He did not need a vulture to tell him that this was most probably his last day – or night – and he would soon be nothing more than flesh for carrion to fight over.

How long had he been plodding aimlessly through this vast wasteland, this sea which had dried up in prehistory and left not one drop of water to save him? Days? Weeks? A month? The only thing he knew as he picked up the waterskin was that this was the end of the water.

His hands trembling with weakness he tipped the foul, greasy water down his throat drop by drop. He sucked in the last and grinned stupidly. 'Chateau Lafite 1906' he mumbled to himself, but the effort hurt his cracked and swollen lips.

He raised his eyes to the horizon again and with relief identified the time of day. It was sunset. A few stars dusted the sky and the dying sun was putting on a spectacular show, sending out streamers of crimson, pink and liquid gold out into the backdrop of lapis and turquoise blue. Joe had never seen anything more beautiful ... except perhaps Sara. His tired mind relaxed into bizarre fancy and, as his physical eye took in the glories of the sky, his inward eye saw Sara, her long eyes as blue as the lapis of the sky, her mass of hair cascading in a prism of sparkling colours, golds, reds, blues, greens ... black.

Joe woke with a start, fear clawing at his entrails. Peering into the dusky light, he saw the grotesque outline of the vulture which, attracted by the blood oozing from his leg, was sitting less than two feet away. Fear gave him new energy and almost without effort Joe was on his feet, his mind once again lucid. The vulture flapped away to a safer distance.

The sky was now a deep blue, the light almost gone. The cool of the night would help him survive – he had no intention of dying, not yet. Behind him he saw some bushes which he had not noticed in his semi-conscious state earlier. He crawled over to them and grabbed handfuls of branches of the dry, white broom, which he then spread over a patch of ground his size. When he had prepared a thick layer of the broom he set it alight and waited until the flames had died down to embers. Then he covered the embers with a layer of sand. The fire would smoulder inside and guarantee him a warm mattress through the night.

He wondered if he were near a wadi, a dry river bed – perhaps his compass was working after all. The compass is always right, *the compass is always right*, THE COMPASS IS ALWAYS

RIGHT. He repeated the words to himself like a litany as, a few feet from the tree, he dug a hole in the sand, threw in a pile of torn-up leaves from the acacia tree and put the silver cup from his long empty brandy flask into the hole. Then he placed the empty waterskin on top of it and scrabbled on the ground under the tree until he found a small stone which would make an indentation in the skin above the silver cup.

The job took an enormous amount of effort and left him exhausted. He crawled back to the bed, grateful for the warmth that seeped through him as the night air turned cold. Then the dreadful loneliness that had fallen on him like a blanket after he had buried Daniel shrouded him again before he passed into a heavy, death-like sleep.

It was just before midnight as the rowing boat, pitching and tossing on the dark water, came into the bay. Paul could just distinguish the outline of the castle looming out of the windy darkness ahead. At least he hoped it was the Crusader castle at Atlit and not the Roman ruins of Caesarea. Two strokes further and he could see the tabletop rocks: thank God it was Atlit.

The sea was much calmer than it had been on the way here. For two days they had been holed up in Famagusta waiting for the storms to pass but finally Paul, desperately anxious to reach Atlit, had persuaded the Captain to take the chance. Now, with the wind's icy fingers clawing his courage from him and the waves looming so much higher than they had seemed from the ship, Paul felt his heart beating hard with fear. The sailors rowed in closer and closer, but still not close enough for Paul.

'Clear your mind of worries,' said Calib, the Christian Arab who had accompanied him in the rowboat. 'Contract, then relax all your muscles – it'll help.'

'It's not so easy – I have plenty of worries,' said Paul grimly and was silent, looking out into the vast darkness swelling around the boat to the shore, which still seemed so far away.

'Ready to jump?' came Calib's voice. Paul's heart beat even faster and, before answering, he felt under his blanket for the oilskin package strapped around his middle. It seemed secure.

'I'll give it a go,' he said, trying to sound lighthearted.

Calib thumped him on the back. 'You're a brave man, Mr Paul.'

Bravery had nothing to do with it now, Paul thought. After all Aaron and he had been through in Cairo, he would have to be braver to go back and face Aaron without having attempted the landing. He pulled off the blanket. 'Hang around a bit if you can, just in case,' he said. 'Where's the damn whisky?' A sailor silently passed him a flask, which he drained at a gulp. He almost choked as the liquor stung his throat and rushed down to warm his stomach instantly. 'Good luck,' whispered Calib, and the oarsmen echoed him. Trembling with cold and fear Paul nodded and threw himself over the edge of the boat into the blue-back void. For a few seconds Paul felt nothing. Only when he realised that the undertow was carrying him to the rocks did his brain begin to function. On the second swell he would have to grab on to the rock, or he would be dashed to death. He threw himself on to it and frantically searched its slippery surface for a hold as the wave tried to suck him back into the sea. Only his incredible strength saved him from being crushed like a cockroach against the rockface. As the wave receded he pulled himself further up the rock, knowing that he must find a good grip before the next wave came to claim him. And then, shivering with the numbing cold, he scrambled to the safety of the shore.

He threw himself exhausted on to the beach; he had done it. Suddenly remembering the Turkish patrols he sat up wearily, half-naked and nearly drowned. Panting for breath and almost choking he muttered to himself, 'Turkish patrol my foot. Only a bloody Englishman would be out on a night like this.'

It had become a habit for them all to gather in the study every evening for company. Tonight they sat in silence, sunk in various stages of despondency. Manny, who had been on stand-by at the station for the last few days in hope of a ship, sat looking gloomily through a gap in the curtains into the darkness. Lev stared at the floor, cracking his knuckles every now and again, and Sara and Selena barely spoke except to beg him to stop it. Only Sarkis was comparatively cheerful, and that was because he looked forward so much to the few hours when he could come out of hiding for a wash and a shave and some company.

Each was preoccupied with his own thoughts, mostly irritation with Daniel. Manny was furious that he had left for Egypt without waiting for him to return from Nablus; Lev was angry with him for leaving Sara alone. Sara was concerned not only at the continued non-appearance of the ship but at the fact that Ali had still not returned from Beersheba with the horses. And Selena, now fully informed about everything that had happened, was worrying about everything and everybody.

'So what do we do now?' Lev asked, cracking his knuckles again and apologising as he saw Sara's annoyed wince.

The room was quiet and then Manny stood, rubbing his hands wearily over his eyes. 'I suggest we call it a night. Tomorrow I'll ride to Hadera and rustle up Ben and Josh and we'll go and search for that little beggar Ali.' He looked round, and everyone nodded agreement. It was a relief to come up with any sort of plan of action.

'You'll need some money,' Sara said, making to rise from her chair, but Selena was already on her feet and pushed her gently back.

'I'll get it,' she said, crossing the room.

'Better make it a couple of gold pieces in case he's run into any kind of trouble,' Manny said.

'The least we owe Joe is to keep that monkey out of prison,' Sara said with a smile.

Joe had, without telling Sara, left Selena with enough money to pay the workers and see them through the next few months. He had told Selena it was a loan – repayable after the war. This thoughtful act and tactful way of doing it had touched Sara deeply and, as she watched Selena leave the room, she wondered if she had not misjudged Joe.

Manny and Lev began another moody discussion about what Daniel could have done, when suddenly a harsh and insistent barking broke into their argument.

'Goliath!' Sara whispered as they all stared at each other, frozen.

'Who in the hell can it be at this time?' Manny whispered. Sara turned to tell Sarkis to get back to his hiding place. He was already at the door.

'Tell Selena to keep to her room, will you?' Sara said and Kristopher nodded and disappeared.

'Perhaps it's Ali come back with the horses,' Lev said optimistically.

'Pray God you're right,' Sara answered, her nerves straining towards any noise. She crossed to the window and looked carefully through the curtains. The wind had dropped but a thick mist hid even the nearest trees. There was a bang on the main door and everyone jumped. Sara's eyes swept the room for any giveaway sign.

'I'd better go down,' said Manny, his eyes glittering in expectation.

It seemed hours but it was only seconds before they heard heavy steps on the stairs and Manny burst the door open, almost gibbering with excitement. No one understood what he was saying at first until the mountainous, dripping form of Paul Levy appeared behind him. He stood, like a shivering Neptune, a pool of water forming round his feet and bits of seaweed sticking to his beard. In place of a trident he carried a gun which, after a quick look around the room, he laid down.

Everyone stared, disbelieving. One moment all hope had gone and the next . . . Paul stood, his teeth chattering, and then sunk heavily into the nearest chair which protested loudly under his weight. 'B-bloody m-marvellous,' he broke the silence. 'I s-swim all the way from Egypt and no one even offers me a d-drink.'

Sara marshalled her senses. 'Find him a blanket,' she told Manny, 'and tell Kristopher and Selena they're safe.' She fetched their last bottle of brandy and poured Paul a generous measure. She was so excited that she poured herself a tot to steady her nerves. Everyone was shouting, demanding news, trying to ask their questions first. There was so much noise they were in danger of waking the whole station.

Only Paul was saying nothing. He was trying with chilled fingers to undo the leather straps that still bound the waterproof package to his chest. His fingers fumbled and the leather dug into his flesh. 'Give me a knife someone,' he said. Lev produced his pocket-knife and they watched as with a few slices Paul freed the pouch, which fell to the floor with a thud.

Lev bent to retrieve the package. 'God in heaven, what have you got in here?' Lev asked, weighing the pouch in his hand. 'Gold?'

'Got it in one,' Paul answered simply and, gathering the blanket more tightly around him, took a swig at the brandy.

A new round of questions was volleyed at him: 'where did you get it?' 'how did you get here?' 'where's the ship?' 'what of Aaron?' Paul watched them, amused and then said, 'If you all shut up for a moment I'll tell you. Has anyone got a cigarette?'

Manny produced one and Lev held a match to it. Paul inhaled deeply and checked the clock on the wall. 'I don't have much time. I have to be back at the beach by three o'clock at the latest, before the moon reappears. Otherwise I'm your guest for the next month. So first things first.'

He took the package from Lev and unwrapped it carefully. It contained a thick sheaf of papers, a heavy canvas bag and a torch. He handed the papers to Sara. 'These are for you. There is a lot of material about the change of code, information needed and such like. And there's a long letter from Aaron explaining the situation in Cairo and how he got there. Burn it the moment you've all read it.' He looked at her seriously, stressing the words and Sara nodded silently, holding the papers tightly in her hands. Then he tossed down the canvas bag. 'This is twelve thousand francs in pre-war gold coins. It was the most I could carry without risking drowning. God willing, the sea will be down next month and we'll be able to get more to shore. Instructions about its distribution are in Aaron's letter.'

Sara nodded again, in a frenzy of impatience to read the letter but knowing it must wait for Paul. 'How long ago did you leave Egypt?' she asked.

Paul calculated quickly. 'Five days.'

Sara thought for a moment. 'So you haven't heard any news of Daniel?'

Paul gave her a quick look of surprise. 'Daniel? No, why?' Sara told him in a few words. 'They what?'

She smiled softly in agreement. 'I know, I know, but there was nothing I could do to stop them. Let's just pray that they are there when you get back.' She was a little calmer now, her thoughts more in order. 'Paul, it's most urgent that Selena and the Captain get to Egypt as soon as possible. The longer they stay here, the more danger they – and we – are in. What are the chances of getting them away tonight?'

Paul pulled his beard reflectively, looking more and more like a Biblical prophet. 'Small, but they're there. The wind from the sea was dropping as I walked up.' He looked at Sara quickly and gave a slight shake of his had. 'Whether they'll be allowed on to the ship is another matter. You have no idea of the problems we had getting permission to carry the gold, never mind two contraband passengers.'

'We'll just have to risk that, won't we?' she said with a tight smile and turned to Manny. 'Go to the cellar and get the tin box. You, Lev, go and make some hot tea. I'll help Captain Sarkis and Selena get their things together.'

'I've only been back a few hours and I'm already homesick about leaving,' Paul joked as he fitted the oilskin round himself again. Sara had a confused feeling that something else had to be done and was going over everything again and again in her mind.

Paul did up the last strap and looked round once more. Selena and Sarkis, dressed in the darkest clothes they could find, were ready. Selena bit her lip, her face very pale against the black hood of her cloak. Paul picked up the torch and jammed it into his belt, and Manny and Lev picked up their rifles. 'Then it's time to go,' Paul said briskly. 'We may have to waste time at the Haifa Road if there are any troops around.'

It was only then that it really struck Sara that Selena was going, was already almost gone from her and she hugged her friend to her with a terrible ache in her heart. Selena's eyes were filling with tears and her voice shook as she spoke. 'I'll always love you, Sara. We'll be back — as soon as the war is over, we'll be back,' she searched for Sarkis's hand and held it tightly. 'We both will, won't we?'

Sarkis looked into Sara's face and he too had tears in his grey eyes. He seemed to hesitate a moment, then bent and quickly kissed her cheek. 'Thank you seems so little to say after all you have done for us but . . .'

Selena stepped forward and hugged Sara again. 'Goodbye. Give my love to Joe.' And then she added in a low voice, 'There is a great deal in him to love, you know, Sara. Sometimes I think that you have missed the real person in him,' and then she hugged Sara again and stepped back, avoiding her friend's surprised stare. 'I shall pray for you, all of you, every day,' Selena finished.

Sara caught the look on Paul's face and squeezed Selena's hand for the last time. 'You must go now,' she said, her voice husky with supressed tears. She was longing to go with them to the shore but Paul would not let her — he said he had promised Aaron that on no account would she go near the beach. They filed silently down the stairs and Sara eased back the big bolts one by one. She had no idea how she was going to bear the next hour until she knew they were safe, but she had no choice but to be left alone with her fears. One by one they stepped out into the night. Selena turned and gave Sara a last lingering look and then was gone.

I've got to get up, I've got to get up, Joe mumbled to himself, not realising that no sound came from between his cracked lips. *Must get up, got to get up.* The patches of darkness grew deeper every time he slipped back out of consciousness. He had been lying on his bed, floating in and out of blackness since first light, his mind reluctant to face the trials the day would bring. But the raging thirst tormented him and pursued him even to the depths of his sleep. He dreamed of rivers and lakes, rain and pools of ice-cold water, but every time he reached for them they vanished. Perhaps death would be a blessing . . . if it were not for the thought of that vulture tearing his flesh from his body he would almost have given up, but he must live on . . . he must. If it was the final thing he did he would outlast that bloody vulture.

Painfully, he forced open his sanded, mucus-encrusted eyes. The light pierced his brain like a burning needle. He pushed himself into a sitting position and a horde of flies flew up from where they had clustered round the blood on his leg. Even the pain was not enough to revive him completely.

He sniffed. It was said that some Bedouin could smell water at a distance of many miles, and suddenly he believed it. He could smell water. Thank God. It had not been a dream. On hands and knees he dragged himself towards the still he had made the night before, his throat convulsing painfully. With shaking hands he lifted the canvas cover and peered inside. A damp, leafy smell hit him in the face and he breathed in deeply. After the dry, desert air the very smell was an elixir. Evaporation from the foliage had condensed in the boiling heat and had run down the underside of the canvas to the silver cup. It was half full. *Dear God, half a cup of water!*

Joe was trembling so badly that he did not dare pick up the cup for fear of spilling the precious liquid. Then slowly, slowly, he raised it to his lips and with all his self-control he forced himself to take one tiny sip only. His throat ached with the effort of swallowing, but it was instantly rewarded. Sip by blissful sip the moisture trickled down his throat, recharging his wasted strength as his dehydrated tissue sucked in the water like blotting paper. And then he dipped his finger into the empty cup and ran whatever remained round his lips, enjoying what he knew would be only a brief respite before the thirst returned again.

He looked up at the tree. The vulture had now been joined by another two and the three of them sat watching him balefully. 'Invited a few friends round for the feast, eh?' he croaked. They stared back at him, disdainful and brooding, and Joe read their resentment to mean that breakfast might have to become lunch after all.

Joe replaced the cup and readjusted the canvas. He knew that all he could do was stay alive. As long as he lived, the hope remained, however small, that he would be found. He made an effort to stand but his legs would not respond to his will. His whole body was too stiff and weak to stand so he had to crawl back again to what little shade the tree could offer. As he lodged himself against the twisted trunk, he felt his mind begin to become hazy once again, and wondered if this time he were finished.

At every minute he felt the blackness creep closer and his powers of fighting weaken. He felt the presence of the boundless, immense plain of sand and, opening his eyes briefly, saw the burning sky filling with patches of wheeling shadow, approaching slowly but purposefully. *The vultures. It's the vultures. Take the knife . . .* but his hand lay motionless beside him. The shadow was right above him now and was speaking, the voice soft and caring. Why should God speak English?

With a small shock of surprise Joe realised it was a man, leaning over and holding out – *dear God, he was holding a water bottle*. With the last of his strength Joe reached out both hands and grabbed on to the water bottle, gulping and gulping at the sweet water until he felt it run down his chin and slosh in his belly. He drank and drank in desperation, *thank you God, thank you* ringing in his brain and drowning out the voice that urged him to drink more slowly, to go easy.

The bottle was removed from his lips. 'More,' he croaked. 'More water,' and he reached out towards the only thing in the world that he wanted, that he would ever want again.

'Don't talk, mate. Save it. We've got to get you to a hospital pretty damn quick. Bloody lucky we came along when we did. Another hour and you'd have been a gonna.'

Joe found it hard to understand his words. He wanted desperately to say something . . . something very important . . . but what in the name of God was it . . . ?

Oh yes. Of course. He took a deep breath and croaked painfully 'Don't smoke the cigarettes. For God's sake don't smoke the cigarettes,' before passing out on the sand.

The ring of the telephone rose above the monotonous whirring of the fan and jolted Aaron in some semblance of wakefulness. As usual, it took him a moment to remember he was in a hotel room in Port Said and he reached wearily for the receiver. His sleep had been restless, torn with dreams about the ship and its journey.

'Hello?' he mumbled.

The brisk English syllables of Major Deedes cut clearly through his brain's fogginess. 'Mr Williams?'

'Yes, Major Deedes. Good morning.'

'One of your men has reached here through the desert. He was picked up by an Australian patrol near El Arish.'

Daniel! The shock jolted Aaron upright in his bed. *The bloody fool, what did he think he was doing?* 'Where is he?' Aaron bellowed.

'In the officers' hospital,' the Major answered, and Aaron felt a stab of apprehension.

'Is he all right?'

'He was badly dehydrated and wounded in the leg, but is quite comfortable now. Damn fine man – for an American,' he finished with a chuckle.

'An American?'

There was a significant pause before the Major answered. 'He says his name is Joe Lanski,' he said in a worried voice. 'Don't you know the chap?'

'I'll get over there right away,' Aaron said, hanging up almost before he had finished speaking.

The duty nurse tapped her way briskly down the corridor ahead of Aaron. The air was hung with the sweet smell of blood mingled with disinfectant and Aaron wrinkled his nose fastidiously as he followed her. The nurse was obviously smitten by the charms of her newest patient and her face had lit up when Aaron asked for him.

'Are you a relation?'

'No, a – a business colleague.' She had looked dubiously at him, but had led him off towards Joe's room.

There was a soldier on duty outside, who checked a list before he waved Aaron inside. Joe had a small room to himself, and he lay still, his hands brown against the crisp white sheet. His face was deadly pale and covered with crusty sores. One leg was bandaged to the knee but apart from that Aaron was pleased to see that he seemed lucid and all in one piece.

'You have a visitor, Mr Lanski,' the nurse said and Joe forced himself back from the edges of sleep. He opened his eyes and exchanged a very long look with Aaron while the nurse made herself busy patting pillows under his head and propping him up higher in the bed. He managed a smile. 'It's almost worth the pain to be looked after so well by Nurse Suzy.' She beamed her pleasure at them both. 'Be a good girl, will you, and get us some coffee?' The nurse nodded and with a last smooth of the sheet left the room.

The expression on Joe's face changed immediately. He hoisted himself higher and looked into Aaron's face.

'Aaron – damn it – it's hard to say. Aaron, Daniel – Daniel is dead.'

Aaron flinched. The news pierced him to his depths. He walked slowly to the window and looked out, seeing nothing as the tears welled in his eyes. Then, like an old man, he walked to the chair beside the bed and sank into it, covering his face with his hands. His throat tightened and he swallowed. He raised his head and stared blankly at the ceiling. The first shock began to recede.

'How?'

In a whisper Joe told him everything from when they decided to leave the station and set off for Egypt. 'Am I making sense?' he asked after a while.

'Unfortunately, you are,' Aaron said bitterly.

'Aaron, I did what I could to ease his way. And I buried him to save him from the carrion.' Joe shivered at the memory of the birds waiting for his own flesh.

Aaron sighed painfully. 'Yes. Of course. Thank you.' There was a brief silence and then he burst out with all the anger and pain he felt at his friend's death. 'Why? Why? Why?' He looked at the ceiling again, trying to master the emotions that flooded through him. 'What a bloody trivial way to die – the bullet from a stinking camel thief! I knew something like this would happen. I knew it!' His rage bordered on tears. 'Daniel needs – needed,' he forced himself to speak in the past tense, 'needed . . .'

'Action,' Joe put in, and Aaron nodded glumly.

'Yes, as much as an alcoholic needs his liquor.'

Joe looked at Aaron, whose face reflected the agony of a man facing an unpleasant reality.

The nurse came into the room with steaming cups of coffee, and the two men waited without speaking until she had gone. Then Joe fumbled beside his bed and handed the tin box of cigarettes to

Aaron. 'The code,' he said simply. 'I'm sorry it had to end this way but at least his death was not in vain.'

Aaron turned the tin over in his hands. Daniel's death was something new to be borne and presented them with endless difficulties. Who could safely be told? Sara? His father? Daniel's mother?

Aaron pulled himself together. There was a great deal he must do.

'Do you have compass bearings on Daniel's grave?'

Joe nodded and produced a small green notebook from beside the bed.

'Thank you. I'll request a patrol be sent to try and find his body.'

There was a silence in the tiny room. Then Aaron looked at Joe with a new respect, and gently touched his arm. 'Thank you. I will leave you now, but I'll be back this evening when I've sorted some things out. Get some rest,' he said, rising and walking out. 'We need you fit and well.'

CHAPTER TWENTY-THREE

January 1917

Paul's midnight visit to the research station had given everybody fresh hope and for the next few weeks the group threw themselves into a frenzy of activity. Now that they knew the British were resuming contact, they worked hard to streamline the network and consolidate all the information they had gleaned over the long, lean months. One of the major problems was that their chief informants were nearly all Jewish doctors or engineers, who were liable to a change of post at the shortest notice. Lev, always one of the most methodical of the group, had been hard at work relocating the agents and inspiring them again with enthusiasm for the work. His task was doubly difficult as the locusts had made themselves scarce and Jemel Pasha's protection was, at this vital time, significantly lacking.

Towards the end of December the British had advanced to take El Arish, the Turks retreating before them to Rafa and Magdhaba. After a costly attempt to hang on to their last remaining foothold in Egyptian territory, Colonel von Kressenstein withdrew the Turks and at last the Sinai was free from Turkish occupation. Now, in the middle of January, the British were at the gates of Gaza, the gateway to Southern Palestine.

As the news filtered through, the little group at Atlit seethed with a quiet glee. All they heard convinced them that Daniel and Joe had made it to the British and had handed over the precious code book. Rumour had it that Jemel Pasha was complaining that the British seemed to anticipate his every move, and the group could only hope that they were in part responsible for that.

Part of the small amount of gold Paul had been able to carry in to them had been taken to Ivan Bernski in Haifa. Bernski had asked a few questions about where the gold had come from and accepted it with a smile and offered Sam a weak cup of tea. Bernski had reported the latest news. Russia was crumbling, he said. The country was in an uproar and the last days of the Tsar had surely come.

Sara had taken some of the gold to Dr Ephraim in Zichron for the hospitals and for the children. She told him that the money was an advance of her inheritance from Chaim and that, as she was not in any need at the moment, she wished to help the community. Not a natural liar, she found it hard to keep her composure as Dr Ephraim gazed at her fondly, blessing her for her generosity.

Explaining Daniel's absence to her father was an even harder task. Aaron's arrest, followed by Daniel's conspicuous absence, had aroused every one of the suspicions he had been forcing to the back of his mind for some months. In the end he had to believe Sara's excuses and she, loathing herself for lying to her father, comforted herself with the thought of the worry she was sparing him.

Added to all these problems were Sara's own, more private, anxieties. Since the reappearance of the British, Sara had worked tirelessly at learning the new code, reorganising the network and keeping the station running. Her mind was kept occupied throughout the day and evening. But at night, when at last she went to bed, her thoughts would return to Daniel, Selena and Joe as surely as rivers ran to the sea. She missed Selena desperately, realising for the first time how much Selena had contributed to life at the station. When she caught a lingering hint of Selena's attar of rose scent the pain she felt was almost as keen as though she were mourning a dead friend. But despite this she never once doubted that Paul, Selena and Sarkis had made it back to Egypt.

Her feelings about Daniel were quite different. Every bone in her body, every bit of woman's intuition in her, told her that something was very wrong. She would lie awake at night, staring into the darkness and seeing picture after picture of Daniel and reliving the recent past. Her mind went over and over the last morning before he had ridden off into the desert with Joe. Daniel, mounted on his black colt, had made no attempt to conceal his eagerness to leave and his dislike of farewells. He had never been good at the business of parting, but Sara had hoped that this time it might be different. He had looked down into her face for a moment, his eyes bright and restless.

'Please be careful, Daniel, please,' she had whispered.

'Don't worry,' he had answered lightly and, bending down in his saddle, had planted a brief kiss on her forehead. It was the casual kiss of a long-married husband. Sara had said goodbye quietly and calmly, but with a feeling of foreboding and disaster.

Now, when she thought about him, he already seemed to belong to the past. Somewhere deep inside her she knew he was dead, but she recoiled with horror each time she tried to confront the thought.

And then there were the images of Joe, which would flash unbidden into her mind and distract her with their frequency and the effect they had on her. With a bitter-sweet pleasure, she thought of Selena's last words to her and wondered what Selena had really meant by them. It was almost, she realised one morning, as though she were in love with Joe, which was a ridiculous notion. But she could not control the demon in her mind. Her sleep was broken night after night by strange, tortured dreams, and then the nightmares started once more. The same nightmares that had plagued since Aleppo, but the people in it changed and each time the terror mounted. Now it was Daniel who ran by the train, looking up and begging for salvation, then it was members of the group who ran, silently crying for hope, once it was even Chaim, poor, forgotten Chaim, who ran alongside the train. She would often wake exhausted at sunrise and, knowing there was no hope of more sleep, rise wearily to face the problems the day would bring.

Ali had been a big worry to her after Joe and Daniel left. He had turned up with the horses just as they had given up hope. Sara had welcomed him to the station, but he remained morose and taciturn, frequently disappearing for days at a time. When asked what he was doing he would say he was foraging for food and it was true that he always returned with some food – grain or vegetables. Every day he provoked a row and every day Sara debated sending him back to Jaffa. But she had promised Joe to look after the little devil and so she resigned herself to waiting for Joe – if he ever did return.

Sara had brought Abu down from Zichron to look after the horses at the station and drive her round and he and Ali formed an odd union. The old man had kept the boy under some control until a week earlier when Ali had disappeared again for the night, returning the next day with a sack full of drawn, plucked chickens. Looking at the dead birds with a sinking heart, Sara knew that they could have come only from the German garrison on the other side of the Carmel Mountains, and that the Germans would regard the pilfering as a very serious crime indeed. All they needed was a German troop riding in this direction in search of their dinner.

Sara set off in a high dudgeon to look for Ali, and when she found him she marched the unrepentant boy off to her study for a serious talk. *About time*, she thought grimly. *If he can't be made to understand I'm in charge he will have to go. Whatever Joe says when he comes back.*

'Ali, I know where you got those chickens, so don't even try to lie to me. But why did you do it? Are you hungry? Don't we feed you enough?'

Ali just scowled and looked at his toes. He hated it here. Everyone was always trying to push him out of the way, to keep secrets from him. And worse still was this she-devil in charge and the old witch in the kitchen, Frieda, telling him to be grateful and to wash himself every day – even Joe, who was bad enough, was not as strict as that. If he hadn't promised Joe that he would wait for him here, he would have run away to Jaffa by now. But he had promised and he would rather die than break his word to Joe.

Thinking of Joe, he began to sniffle and wiped his nose on the back of his hand. He loved Joe more than anything in the world – even his horse – and had begun to worry that Joe was not coming back, that he was dead. Tears pricked the back of his eyes, but he would not cry, not in front of anyone, particularly this woman. He gave one, big sniff and blinked back his tears, looking the woman firmly in the face and squaring his little shoulders defiantly.

Sara, watching him, was struck by the dignity of his gesture and was touched in spite of her anger. The poor child was lonely. He missed Joe, who was probably the only secure thing in his life. After all, however tough he acted, he was only a boy. She softened and spoke to him more gently than before. 'Look, Ali, if you want to forage that's fine by me – I won't pretend it's not a help. But you must stay away from the garrisons. You are endangering all of us and using up your nine lives. If anything happened to you Joe would never forgive me. The last thing he said to me before he left was "look after my son Ali".' She spoke very solemnly, looking at him closely.

'He did?' Ali asked cautiously, not yet ready to believe her because he had never heard Joe refer to him as anything but 'the little devil'.

'Indeed he did,' Sara answered, keeping back a smile as she remembered his real farewell. What he had in fact said was, 'Is the departing hero allowed a kiss?' and then, seeing the look on her face, laughed and kissed her full on the lips anyway, before riding off in a flurry of dust.

Ali's joyous look brought her back to the present and more than compensated for the deception. 'He made me promise,' she continued, 'to see that no harm came to you. And that is why I ask you *please*, to stay out of trouble.' She smiled and held out her hand, but Ali thought for a moment before answering. Well, it made sense to him. He took her hand and shook it firmly.

'All right.' He retreated towards the door and then turned back to her. 'He did really call me his son?' Sara nodded her head gravely. The last traces of stubborn resistance left his face and his teeth flashed in a wide, white smile. Then he looked at the floor again. 'And the chickens?' he murmured.

Sara smiled. 'Give them to Frieda. We had better eat the evidence tonight.'

The incident had cleared the air and Ali was now more obedient, if still occasionally a little wilful. But no sooner had that trouble resolved itself than another, far more serious, appeared. It was time to expect the British contact ship and Manny, Lev and Robby had joined Sara at the station in readiness. They were all tense with expectation, eyes constantly straining to sea. The weather had turned – and stayed – dry and sunny and the sea was as flat and smooth as a lake. It was perfect. All they had to do now was watch and wait.

Then, late one afternoon, their hopes were dashed. Lev spotted a German U-boat wandering up and down the coast. He watched it for a moment or two, almost hypnotised with disbelief. Ready to weep with vexation, Sara ran to hang out the white sheet in warning to the British and spent the rest of the afternoon watching the boat winding, turning north, then south, then north again. Was this a coincidence, or did they have information and were lying in wait for the British boat? Sara thought she would go mad with waiting.

Later that evening the ship had finally left and now at last there was nothing to be done but wait and hope that the submarine had not put off the English ship. It was Manny's turn to watch and he yawned and rubbed his eyes. It was a tiring job keeping his sight focused on the endless, unchanging sweep of sea and sky.

Boredom, frustration and concentration were a bad combination and they had all agreed that each turn should not last longer than an hour.

Manny was just about to call to Sara to take over when he saw a small white blob a few miles out to sea, just rising over the horizon. Tense with excitement at the thought that this could be the British ship, without moving his eyes, he felt behind him for the field-glasses. 'Quick, hand me the glasses,' he muttered, unable to find them and unable to take his eyes from the blob. Sara heard the excitement in his voice and leapt up, scattering rota papers around her as she grabbed the glasses from the chair and, edging round the desk, passed them to Manny. There was a long silence as Manny peered through the lenses.

'It's the British. I know it is,' he gasped. Sara watched, her knuckles white on the window sill as the small ship edged slowly nearer. Then, when she was almost level with the station, the ship let off a few large puffs of black smoke before lazily turning back to the open sea. Manny and Sara stared at each other for a moment before Manny gave an elated whoop and they hugged each other wildly with happiness. 'Sara, they're here. It really is the British!' he cried.

'Thank God,' she answered, her cheeks flushed with elation and ran out of the room to hang up the red blanket. A few minutes later she was back, panting as she ran to the window. They watched as the ship returned the signal that all was clear and they would be back later that night.

'I'll go and tell Lev and Robby that it's on for tonight,' said Manny, making for the door.

Well, I'm damned if I'm going to sit here at the station while the others go down to the shore, Sara suddenly thought.

'Manny, I'm coming with you tonight.'

There was a short silence while Manny looked at her dubiously. 'I don't think,' he began and then grinned. 'Oh hell, what can I do if you want to come?' and he headed out of the room, banging the door behind him.

By ten o'clock that night Sara, Manny, Lev and Robby were safely ensconced in one of the cave-like rooms of the ruined castle. The atmosphere was one of suppressed glee and expectation as they sat huddled together behind a vertical slab of sandstone. The smell of damp and rotting seaweed hung thickly in the air and the old walls projected a strange chill, but none of them felt the cold or minded the fetid smell.

Ezra, who had the sharpest eyesight, was on look-out duty so all they could do now was wait for the moon to come up and the rowing boat to appear. They did not dare talk and the time seemed to pass very slowly. The only sounds were their shallow breathing, the lap of the water on the shore and distant, high-pitched squeaks of bats. They all sat, deep in their own thoughts.

Sara, sitting close to Robby for warmth, thought back to the day – it seemed a lifetime away – when Daniel had come home and had kissed her here in the castle. How simple life had seemed then, how black and white the choices she had to make. Suddenly she heard something and jerked her head up swiftly. 'What's that noise?' she whispered. They all strained forward, listening intently in the darkness.

'Just a lizard,' said Manny and eased his grip on the gun, which was at the ready across his lap. They relaxed again until a few minutes later came the distinct croak of a frog. Everyone jumped. The croak was Ezra's warning that something or somebody was on the beach.

'Probably a patrol, damn the buggers,' Manny muttered.

Something was coming towards them, a rustle rising above the noise of water and, peering into the darkness, they made out Ezra's spindly form moving cautiously towards them.

'What is it?' hissed Lev.

'Something moving north along the beach. A camel caravan, I think. If only there were a moon I'd be able to see,' Ezra complained.

'Count yourself lucky. If there was a moon they'd be able to see you,' Manny countered grimly. 'Wait there, I'll come with you.' And he crawled out of the castle ruins towards Ezra.

'A camel caravan?' Lev asked.

'Hashish probably,' Robby answered. 'Taking the same advantage of the low moon as we are.'

There was a great deal of hashish smuggling from south to north, the hashish made into flat slabs and hidden under the luxurious hair around the camel's hump. The Germans were trying to clamp down on this timeless traffic and more and more of the travelling was done by night. The tension in the ruin rose to a peak as the caravan passed silently. It seemed a long time before Manny reappeared.

'They've gone. Quick, give me the torch, the British have just signalled. They're coming in.'

Everyone stood up and they stretched their stiff bodies with relief.

'Wait here until I can see them,' Manny ordered and took off his shoes, hiding them behind a boulder. Down at the beach, with the cold water lapping at his ankles, Manny carefully pointed the light out to sea and flashed the two signals, counting to twenty between them. Three thin fingers of light probed towards the beach in answer.

He had no feeling in his feet by the time he saw not one but two rowing boats coming out of the murk towards him. He motioned Ezra to fetch the others. Sara was the first down, the others close behind her. The little group stood excitedly on the beach, waiting as the boats became more visible. It was so calm that they could make their way close into the beach.

Sara's heart was thumping and her breath coming in shallow gasps as out of the darkness before them came darker figures, arms above their heads, water to their shoulders at first and then gradually – oh so slowly – they emerged, dripping, on the shore, dropped their packages on the beach and looked around apprehensively.

Quickly, the group gathered round the sodden newcomers. 'Manny?' said the shadowy figure next to Sara. It was the unmistakable voice of Joe Lanski. They had made it! Thank God they had made it! Sara threw herself into Joe's wet arms. 'Thank God you're here. I was so worried. Is Daniel with you?' That was the question Joe had been dreading, but now was not the time or place to answer it.

'Later,' he said, hugging her so tight she could hardly breathe. 'There's little time and we must unload the boats. By the way – Lev – Manny – Robby – this is Mohamed and his two sons. They are Egyptians and totally loyal. In future they'll be meeting you on the beach.' They all exchanged hasty greetings. 'Who's this?' he asked, peering at Ezra who was practically standing to attention.

'Ezra, sir,' he answered briskly.

'Well, Ezra, keep your voice down and come back to the boats with us – you're tall enough. You too, Robby. The rest of you get these sacks up to the castle and pile them up there.'

There was a flurry on the beach behind them, and they all

jumped and looked round in sudden fear. Then they stared incredulously at a large canvas-covered case lying on the beach. Muffled flappings and cooings emerged from it.

'What's that?' Robby asked, horrified.

'Pigeons!' Joe announced proudly.

'Pigeons?' Lev repeated.

'Sshh, the British thought they might be useful for getting any urgent messages to Egypt.'

'We can always eat them,' Lev joked.

'Come on, let's not waste time,' said Ezra, wading into the icy water.

They moved into action. 'Here,' said Sara, thrusting a bulging leather pouch into Joe's hands. 'You'd better take this back to the boat now in case we're disturbed.'

'Good thinking,' said Joe, taking the package; then added, 'What are you doing here anyway? I thought you were under orders to stay at the station?'

'I wanted to come and so I came,' she said simply.

Joe laughed. 'Better get to work then . . . but first – a kiss?'

For the first time Sara responded and quickly kissed his salt-laden lips before picking up a sack and heading towards the castle. Joe touched his lips and watched her recede into the darkness, his heart heavy with apprehension. The pain in his leg was growing and he felt a creeping dread. How on earth was he going to find the words to tell them Daniel was dead? With a heavy sigh he turned back to the sea.

They had worked fast and by the time the horizon was glowing a pale yellow the little group had gathered, damp and sweating, in Sara's study. Sara stared from the heap of sacks piled on the floor to her hands, which had been rubbed raw in heaving the small, heavy bags of gold up the hill to the station. Ezra had been sent to find a temporary home for the pigeons in the old barn, and Mohamed and his sons had left as quietly as they had arrived, so the nucleus of the group was left together at last.

'How much money is there?' Sara asked Joe, rubbing her aching arm and shoulder.

'About fifty thousand dollars in assorted gold coins. There will be another consignment next morning. Aaron tells me the fund holds around half a million at the moment, so you had better start thinking how you are going to spend it.'

Robby whistled in amazement. 'Half a million! We didn't expect nearly as much.'

'It will take every penny of that and more to save all the Jews here from starving to death,' Lev said dourly, and everyone looked crossly at him. Trust him to put a dampener on their spirits.

'I suppose we had better start digging a hole in the cellar to hide all this,' Sara said. 'Where's the pouch?'

'Here,' Joe began to walk to the desk, but stumbled as a white hot pan shot down his leg.

'What's the matter?' Sara asked swiftly, conscious of his white face and realising for the first time how much weight he had lost in his absence.

'Nothing,' said Joe, but he spoke too quickly and Sara searched his face, looking for the real answer. Their eyes met, blue locking into green, and Sara could read the torment behind his vague expression.

'Joe?' she almost whispered. Something was very wrong, every instinct in her body told her that.

'Perhaps I had better sit down.' Joe spoke with a weary resignation. 'Perhaps we had better all sit down.' Everybody stared at him as he crashed heavily into the chair beside the desk. A sudden, dreadful feeling of doom overcame them all and no one moved a muscle, waiting for him to speak.

Sara was the one to break the silence. 'Sit down, everyone. I think Joe has something to tell us.'

Joe looked up at Sara and saw in a flash that she knew. How in the hell he had no idea, but put it down to that dangerous instinct called intuition. Women always knew things like this. Joe felt very tired, so tired he wondered if he could speak. His wound was playing up badly and, now that the risk of getting to the station was over, Daniel's death returned to prey on his mind. *Better get it over with*, he thought, and spoke with a sigh.

'Sara's right. I have got something to tell you.' Steeling himself he took a deep breath as they all sat down awkwardly. He raised his eyes to the ceiling and began in a voice so low that they had to strain to hear. 'Daniel and I were a few days' journey into the Sinai when we ran into a gang of camel thieves. I was shot in the leg. Daniel . . .' The words would not come. He tried again. 'Daniel was badly shot up and . . .'

'He's dead, isn't he?' Sara said flatly. The others stared at her

406

astonished, and then looked back at Joe who, with his eyes on Sara, nodded soberly.

'Yes,' he said finally. 'Yes, he's dead.'

'But – but that can't be true,' Manny burst out in angry denial.

Joe turned from Sara to look at the motionless figures slumped in chairs around the room. 'I'm so sorry . . . so sorry. But it is true.' He looked at each of them turn, and they gazed back, faces white with shock and blank from the emotional jolt he had given them. Joe ran his fingers through his hair and burst out: 'Please stop looking at me like that. The cards have been dealt already; I'm just turning up the faces.' He could not help thinking that they all wished it was he that had died and not Daniel.

Manny stood, murmuring an apology, and crossed to the window, blinking away the tears pricking his eyes. Lev and Robby lit cigarettes, trying to disguise their shaking hands, remembering so much they had done with Daniel, so many arguments they had had together.

But it was Sara who concerned Joe most dearly. Despite his own pain and desperate fatigue, he was overwhelmed with compassion for her. He looked at her, and found her face an unreadable mask. Her hands were clenched in her lap and her eyes closed tightly.

She was battered by stronger emotions than she had thought ever possible. Anger, hatred, love and longing washed over her, meeting in an explosion of feeling that left her drained and weak. And then, in their place, came a white rage that pierced to her very soul. She took a deep breath and opened her eyes. 'Joe, I think we ought to know how it happened, however painful it will be.'

Everyone looked at her amazed. No one had expected such calm control, especially Joe who had steeled himself for an outburst of weeping or recriminations. He looked at her seriously, then sat back in his chair, forcing his muscles to relax. He began from the day he and Daniel had left the border town and struck into the desert.

Manny stood by the window, moaning occasionally as Joe told his story. Lev and Robby sat on the edges of their chairs, chain-smoking and stoically keeping back their tears. But Sara sat rigid, staring cold-eyed at Joe, every now and again asking him to repeat a fact.

'The patrols the British sent out did not recover his body?' she persisted.

'No, I'm afraid not. I was – not well – myself. Totally

disorientated, I guess. I must have got the bearings wrong.' He shook his head. 'I'm sorry.'

Manny looked at him, dazed as the senselessness of Daniel's death hit him again. 'If only I'd been here, insisted he did not go. He'd be alive, I know he would.'

'Manny, that's not true. You must never think that,' Sara said firmly. 'It's not your fault. No one could have stopped Daniel. No one. His death is nobody's fault but his own, and you know it. He would have admitted it himself. You know he would.'

Manny's eyes, soft with pain, looked into hers and he asked in a shaken voice, 'Why? Why did this have to happen. A bloody camel thief, for God's sake! Why?'

'Come on, Manny. What did you imagine might happen?' Sara said harshly. 'What do you think might happen to any of us? God in heaven, who in the world is safe? Do you think our lives are for some reason charmed – we'll never get caught, get sick, get murdered? Daniel's death is the price, the true price, of what we have got ourselves into and anyone who hasn't realised that by now is a fool.' She stood up with a determined strength, and faced them, her fists clenched. 'Daniel knew the risks and took them. But there is a palliative for our pain,' and her eyes moved from one to the other of them; 'there is a way we can cauterise it. Revenge!' she hissed. The colour was back in her cheeks as she stood like a defiant fury. 'What else?'

Nobody answered. There was no answer.

Everyone at the station, from Manny and Robby, to Frieda and her kitchen help, was worried about Sara in the days following Joe's return. She went about her jobs in the same efficent way as ever, but her eyes were distant and lacklustre. Although she moved almost mechanically, there seemed to be a grim purpose in her every act. Only Joe had any realisation of what she was going through, and he understood and shared her pain. He had lived with death all his life. His mother and father, sister and brother had died and, later, the only other woman he had ever really loved.

He knew Sara was deceiving herself in her belief in her own strength, but he also knew that her own obstinate pride was helping her to bear the loss bravely. They were so alike in so many ways, it only amazed him that Sara had not noticed it herself.

Sara insisted that she should ride to tell Daniel's mother herself and, although both Manny and Joe accompanied her, Joe knew that it was another way of helping her face and then exorcise the grief that numbed her. Mrs Rosen had taken the news with resigned calm. Her silent dignity was more heartbreaking than a million tears would ever have been. She had not even asked why her son was travelling across the Sinai in the middle of a war. She had just blown her nose a little shakily and said, 'Let's not talk about it any more. I knew this would happen one day. Thank you for coming, but I should like to rest now.' She had closed her eyes and leaned back in her chair and even Joe had had to swallow a lump in his throat as he led Sara out of the house.

For almost a week Sara remained mute and tearless about Daniel. They all tried to talk to her about him, to break down the reserve she was building up, but she seemed not to hear. And then Joe, who was impatient to leave, finally told her that he would be going the next day – for a while at least. He had a great deal to do and his disappearance might already have aroused suspicious gossip.

'Where are you going?' she asked, her eyes a brighter blue than ever.

'To Jaffa.'

'For how long?' Sara asked nonchalantly, wanting to hide her sudden awareness of how much she would miss him.

'I'm not sure.' He looked at her and felt that he had hurt her in some way. 'Be very careful, Sara. If there is the slightest hint of anything going wrong, be sure to contact me.'

Sara nodded and looked swiftly away, not wanting him to see how vulnerable she felt, how frightened she found herself at the idea of his leaving. Her mouth tightened as she looked back at him, her eyes direct and clear. 'We are careful and nothing will go wrong. So don't worry on our behalf.' She said with a frosty regality that made Joe want to smile.

He looked down at her, noticing once again how the events of the last year had made seem her stronger and at the same time more fragile. And he did worry. Very much indeed.

Concern about what would happen while he was away kept Joe awake on his last night at the station. Every time he turned down the lamp and closed his eyes for sleep they snapped open a minute or so later. His mind and emotions were in chaos. He knew he must get back to Jaffa and sort out his affairs, above all the question of his American citizenship. The threat of America entering the war on behalf of the Allies was now very real and it was crucial that he use all his connections and became an Ottoman citizen as soon as possible or leave the country. And that was unthinkable.

On the other hand, he was worried about leaving Sara in her present state of mind. He would not be surprised if, in her emotional condition, she took unnecessary risks. She could well not only destroy herself, but take them all with her. His feelings towards her were desperately confused. On the one hand he felt a violent jealousy at her love for a dead man, on the other he was filled with tender sympathy at her distress. And at the same time he was consumed with longing for her. He knew that staying near her now would achieve nothing, and only wished that he had the strength of mind to walk away from a relationship that did nothing, as far as he could see, but make his life difficult.

The other complication was his love for his country and its people. He had never realised until the outbreak of the war quite how much Palestine had come to mean to him. He had always believed that mankind, not any particular race, owned the world. Now he found himself something he had always considered with contempt: a nationalist. He turned angrily in his bed, pulling the bedclothes closer around him. The room was cold and still had a faint hint of Selena's attar of roses. Well, at least she and Sarkis were safe now, happily ensconced with Paul and Eve Levy in Cairo and making plans for their wedding.

Suddenly, a scream of pain tore into his thoughts. He sat bolt upright for a second before realising where it came from and then, pulling on his trousers, he rushed into Sara's room. She was standing, wide-eyed with terror, in the middle of the room. Her heavy flannel nightgown was drenched with sweat, but when he took her hands they were icy cold.

'Sara, Sara, don't be afraid. What is it? Was there someone here?'

Sara shook her head violently. 'It's the nightmare . . . they're chasing me . . . it's horrible . . . horrible . . .' Her speech was disjointed and she seemed still to be in the grip of the dream. She took a short, sobbing breath and let Joe lead her back to the bed.

'It's just a dream, don't be frightened,' he said gently. She sat up against the pillows and took hold of his hand tightly.

'Stay with me, Joe, just for a moment . . . I'm frightened.' Joe sat next to her, holding her hand in both of his. They sat silently for a while, her grip never weakening, as though she were afraid he would slip away.

And then the first tears since Daniel's death slipped slowly down her cheeks. 'Hold me, Joe, hold me,' she whispered as all the pent-up emotions of the last week suddenly broke free in her.

'Sara,' he murmured as, naturally and lovingly, he at last held her in his arms. She clung to him, sobbing, her breath coming in gasps, her shoulders heaving. He rocked her gently, smoothing her hair and murmuring inarticulately until at last her tears subsided.

Eventually, she extricated herself from his embrace and, wiping her eyes with both hands, tried to smile. 'I'm sorry,' she began falteringly. 'It's just that . . .'

'Don't be sorry,' he mumbled. 'I know what it is to lose someone you love.' He clamped down the jealousy that was stirring in him and smiled at her gently.

Sara wanted to confide in him, to tell him that she had somehow known Daniel was dead and had been prepared for it. She wanted to tell him that the affair had really been over long before Daniel left for the Sinai, that it had finished almost as soon as it had begun. That she was angry with Daniel, even now he was dead. But she couldn't. It was all too much to say, too difficult to explain and somehow too revealing, too humiliating. She sighed and slid down into the warmth of her bed. Joe stood up, but she reached out and laid a restraining hand on his arm. 'Would you mind very much staying with me until I fall asleep? Please?'

Joe looked down, touched by the helplessness in her voice and the trust she placed in him. 'Of course I'll stay. Sleep. You're safe now, believe me.' And, as her eyes at last closed, he muttered to himself, 'I'll make sure of that.'

411

CHAPTER TWENTY-FOUR

March 1917

With the pouch from Cairo the group had received further instructions and requests for information that far exceeded anything they had done before, and they all had to work hard to find new sources and informants. Their intelligence had led them to believe that the British Army was now standing in the green and grassy land before Gaza and Aaron's letter had confirmed this welcome piece of news. According to him, however, the Army was to stay there for some time as General Murray was now hampered by lack of water. 'I have been trying to convince the High Command here,' he wrote, 'that water is plentiful only two or three hundred feet underground, but they will have none of such advice and continue to lay their wretched pipes. It's a slow, slow business.'

Aaron also asked the group to begin sounding out young men who could be used as scouts for the British if and when the attack began. Sara decided to ignore this particular request for a while as they were by now all overwhelmed by the demands the British were making on them. The group, although it had grown since its tiny beginnings, was still not large, and they were trying to operate with only about twenty-five active members and informants. These had to cover an area that spread from Gaza on the Egyptian border to Damascus in Syria and they were so short of messengers that it was more or less left to Lev, Robby and Manny to collect the reports from the outposts.

As the demands on the network expanded, Sara became more and more engrossed in its work. She was intellectually and emotionally excited by what they were doing and was more and more keen to be actively involved. One of the things the British had asked for additional information about was details of the railway gauges over the Empire and after some thought Sara decided to go to Afula herself in the hope that she might persuade a distant cousin to open a café at the railway station. Afula was an important depot for the main stockpiles of food, weapons and ammunition and was also a major station through which the troops travelled. With a social centre like a café, the group should be able to pick up a great deal of information about the numbers of troops and arms being moved to Beersheba.

Sara's cousin reacted at first with horror to her idea, but after some persuasion had at last agreed. It took a further week and a great deal of gold to find the materials needed to build the café. This use worried Sara constantly. She had not forgotten Hamid Bek's pointed remarks about Arabs caught with gold – 'a hanging matter' – he had sneered and his words were deeply etched on her memory, and everyone else's. Whatever they did they must be very careful not to alert the authorities to the fact that the Jews were in possession of large amounts of gold.

When the second shipment of gold arrived in March, they buried a large fortune in the cellar at the station. The time had come now to contact Meir Dizengoff in Tel Aviv. They had more money than was within their means to move and so they must now ask for support from the Hashomer, whose organisation alone could distribute such a large sum. So three days after the March shipment arrived Lev and Sara set off together for Jaffa. Sitting in the train, looking out blankly at the passing countryside, Sara had time for her own thoughts at last. Lev was deep in a book and she had nothing to do but think. This was the first time she had gone to Jaffa since the day – so long ago now – when Daniel had insulted Hamid Bek and later spurned her naïve, embarrassing advances. The next day she had accepted Chaim Cohen. Now Daniel and Chaim were dead and Aaron, Becky and Alex were far away. The fan Daniel had bought her in the fair was long since lost, abandoned in the trunks at Muslimie Junction. Sara remembered that day so clearly, the browsing among the stalls, the coffee house. And the fortune-teller. 'You will save many souls,' the woman had told her and, remembering, Sara gave a shaky laugh. So far she had helped dispatch two, with any luck, to their own Moslem hell.

'Are you all right?' Lev asked, looking up from his book.

'Fine,' she answered, jumping back into the present. 'And you?'

'Paying the price for all I drunk last night,' he said with a smile,

413

and they exchanged conspiratorial looks. Lev had spent the night before buttering up a Captain from what was rumoured to be a crack new coastal patrol, and had found to his great relief that this patrol sounded as inefficient and disorganised as all the others.

Sara touched Lev's arm. 'After we've seen Dizengoff we can go back to the hotel and rest.'

Lev shook his head. 'I thought I'd go and see Joe Lanski. He might have something of interest for us.'

Sara nodded, but did not reply and looked out of the window again.

Joe had called at Atlit only once in the last six weeks, explaining that he had just happened to be in the neighbourhood, but bringing with him several important maps showing the Turko-German defence entrenchments. The visit had been very short and they had had no opportunity for any kind of private talk. Sara was longing to ask whether the maps came courtesy of the German officer's wife and felt an impotent and totally unreasonable fury at the very idea. Exasperated with herself, she fell back into the old barbed way of talking to him, which only encouraged the familiar, cynical laughter. Despite this he brought with him the same aura of excitement, which had persisted long after he left.

The memory of that night in the wilderness came back to Sara and with it all the emotions that his first embrace had aroused in her. She tried to push away the memory of his lips as she felt she was in some way being disloyal to Daniel . . . but it stayed with her and came back to haunt her at inconvenient moments.

She suddenly felt a burning curiosity to see how he lived – and with whom. 'I think I'll come with you,' she said, turning back from the window casually.

Lev looked at her appalled. 'I really don't think that's wise . . . I mean what about your reputation, you really have no idea . . .'

'Reputation my foot,' Sara snapped, her mind made up, and unsure whether to be amused or impatient at Lev's regard for proprieties. Since her widowhood and Daniel's death Lev's old hopes towards her had revived and, fond as she was of him, his constant interference with her wishes drove her mad with annoyance. 'Besides I should like to see Ali,' she added unnecessarily.

Lev sighed. He had more than a suspicion that it was Joe she wanted to see and felt a sinking in his chest at the thought.

It was one o'clock by the time they arrived at the inn near the church and monastery of Saint Peter. They had followed a small Arab boy through the maze of streets and, although Lev was pushing Sara's portmanteau in a wheelbarrow, they both felt hot and thirsty when they arrived.

Sara threw open the shutters of her room and looked out at the bright blue of the port and the domed rooftops of Jaffa. The town had grown in the last three and a half years, swollen with new inhabitants, who had fled from starvation in the south to the security of the town. If Sara stretched her head out, she could see the squat white houses of Tel Aviv nestling in among the sand dunes to her right.

She closed her eyes, feeling the warm sun on her face, her heart several degrees lighter than it had been for weeks. They must see Dizengoff first, but later this afternoon she would take the opportunity of visiting the piece of land Chaim had bought when they became engaged and would then go and see Joe. The plan cheered her and, with a whistle, she set about unpacking her bags and tidying herself up. She looked at herself in the mirror and her heart sank as she realised how, from total lack of care for herself, her face, neck and hands were brown from the sun. It was her first moment of pure vanity for more than a year.

An hour later Sara had finished unpacking and was ready and impatient. Taking her hat with her, she went to Lev's room and knocked at his door.

'Who is it?' came feebly from inside the room.

'Me, Sara,' she answered. 'Are you ready yet?'

A low moan came through the door and she was about to go in when the handle turned and Lev's face appeared through a crack. He was very pale and looked as though he had been fast asleep when she knocked. 'I'm sorry,' he said, standing aside to let her in and then winced and held his hands across his stomach. 'I feel awful, Sara,' he groaned. 'It must have been that tin of sardines I ate last night.'

Sara looked at him crossly. 'That or the drink. Oh, I suppose I'll just have to go to Tel Aviv without you.'

'I'll be better tomorrow,' Lev said weakly and Sara bit back a sharp remark as she saw how ill he really looked.

'Tomorrow's too late,' she said mildly. 'I'll get you some of that magic medicine Aaron sent us. Doctor Collis something's elixir. I brought a bottle in my portmanteau just in case.'

A minute later she was back with the bottle of medicine, which she slammed down on Lev's chest of drawers with a rattle. 'Here, that should have you raring to go. Now,' she said casually, turning to pin her hat on, 'where does Joe Lanski live? I'll ask him to accompany me to Tel Aviv.'

'I really don't think you ought to go wandering around Jaffa looking for Lanski. The city isn't safe, Sara,' Lev protested.

'I don't care if it's safe or not,' she insisted. 'Where does Joe live?'

Lev, too weak to argue, told her. 'Any diligence will take you there.'

'Thank you,' Sara said and swiftly left the room. She heard Lev shouting after her but paid no attention and rushed on down the corridor. It was already nearly half-past two and she would have to hurry if she was to find Lanski and get to Tel Aviv in time to see Dizengoff. Sara easily found a diligence and, as Lev had promised, the driver knew exactly where Joe lived and took her there within ten minutes.

Joe's house was in the beautiful old Turkish section of the town and was long and low, built from mellow sandstone, the walls covered with bougainvillea. The building formed a compound, with a high wall surrounding it and an iron gate built into a magnificent archway at the entrance. In the middle of the courtyard behind the gate a fountain played, the noise cooling in the afternoon sun. Sitting in the carriage, Sara smelt the damp, salt scent of the sea and realised that the house backed on to the Mediterranean. It was a beautiful and peaceful spot, a house that looked like a home, with the wonderful, peaceful aura of a house that was loved and looked after.

Sara stepped out of the carriage and asked the driver to wait before she pulled the heavy, iron bell-chain. She waited, feeling a little less sure about the idea of just dropping in, but she felt that to go back now would be foolish. The house gave her a glimpse of a side of Joe she had not seen before, and this made her feel uncomfortable. And curious.

A barefoot youth came to the gate and let Sara in without asking her name. *He's obviously used to letting in endless streams of women*, Sara told herself, and could not help feeling prickly at the thought. She strode truculently across the courtyard, her heart beating fast, her face flushed with self-consciousness and . . . excitement? A tall, dignified manservant appeared in the doorway and bowed. 'May I help you, honourable lady?'

Sara straightened her back, looked him in the eye, swallowed and found her voice. 'I should like to see the master, Joe Lanski,' she said firmly.

'The master is out at lunch. Would you care to wait?' and he motioned into the inside of the house.

Sara flushed. 'No, I'm in a hurry. Er, please tell Mr Lanski that Sara Cohen called.'

She was just turning on her heels to go when Ali came speeding across the courtyard, coming to a breathless halt in front of Sara. 'Joe is not here, he's,' he paused for a moment, his brow furrowed, then his face cleared and he grinned broadly. 'He's out at lunch, but I know where he is. Do you want me to take you?'

The Arab servant looked uneasy and gave Ali a sidelong warning glance, which the boy ignored. Sara, looking earnestly at Ali, lost the old man's look and was thinking quickly. She would have to go through Jaffa to get to Tel Aviv, so she would be losing no time. She briefly felt a flicker of misgiving at whether it would be really wise to chase across the town to find him, but the moment passed. She needed someone with her. It was worth a try. She nodded at Ali. 'I have a diligence outside. Shall we go? I'm in a hurry.'

Once outside the safety of the compound Ali felt less certain about his trick and paused as his courage deserted him. Joe could get damned mad sometimes, worse than a bull camel even. He fidgeted uneasily.

'Well?' said Sara, holding the carriage door open for him. 'What's the matter? Get in.'

Ali scowled at her cross tone. Well, serve her right. All the other women in Joe's life spoiled him mercilessly. Ali had seen her arrival at Joe's house as a danger signal. The last thing he wanted was this woman as a 'mother' – why at the moment he had dozens and Joe more or less to himself. He smiled up at Sara looking positively cuddlesome. Giving the driver swift instructions, he climbed into the carriage and they rode off in silence.

When they arrived, he settled back in his seat. 'It's on the second floor,' he said, looking upwards with sharp black eyes. 'I'll wait here with the carriage.'

Sara ran up the two flights of stairs and knocked quickly at the door at the top. For a moment there was no reply and she knocked again impatiently. The door still did not open, but a soft woman's voice came from behind it. 'Who is it?'

Sara felt a twinge of panic and looked around uneasily to see if there was another door on the stairwell.

'Who is it?' the voice repeated, slightly more loudly.

'I'm – I'm looking for Joe Lanski.'

As if the words were a secret signal the door opened and for several seconds the two women stared at each other. 'One moment,' the woman said and disappeared, leaving the door ajar. She had not gone too quickly for Sara to miss the beautiful white face and tumbling mass of dark red hair. It was Joe's dancing partner from Jerusalem. She stood, wondering what to do next, suddenly aware that she was interrupting something rather more than a friendly lunch. She wanted to turn and run down the stairs and wring Ali's neck, but told herself that to flee was beneath her dignity.

The door was pulled back open and Joe appeared, his loose-sleeved white shirt open at the neck, but otherwise immaculate in boots and breeches. 'Sara! What the devil are you doing here?' His surprised expression changed to concern as he saw her face, and noticed her shifting uncomfortably from foot to foot. He lowered his voice urgently 'Are you in some kind of trouble?'

She gave a fleeting smile. 'No – well, yes, but nothing serious.'

Joe grinned at her, the familiar gleam back in his green eyes. 'Well, how kind of you to call. You know I am always at your service.'

Sara bit back the barbed answer that came to mind. 'For heaven's sake, Joe, I'm in a hurry. I don't have time for your jokes.' Quickly, she explained the reason why she had come looking for him and he listened attentively.

'Joe?' the woman called from inside the apartment.

'Go down and wait in the diligence,' he said, walking with her to the stair head. 'I'll be down in a minute.' Turning to go inside, he paused. 'How did you know where to find me?'

'Ali brought me. I'm sorry – I had no idea.'

Joe gave a thin-lipped smile. 'I appear to have an embryonic Machiavelli on my hands,' he said and turned back into the room.

More like a Borgia Sara thought furiously as she stamped her way down the stairs and then stopped in mid-flight. Her chin dropped and a stunned expression washed over her face as an idea occurred to her for the very first time. She drew in her breath in an astonished gasp. From somewhere deep within her had come the idea that it was not Ali she was furious with, but Joe. *God help me*

418

I'm jealous, she thought. *I'm jealous of Joe Lanski. Dear God – I can't be in love, not with – Joe.* 'Nonsense,' she said out loud and walked firmly down the stairs.

Pushing all unbusinesslike thoughts away from her she picked up her skirts and marched to the diligence, betting herself that Ali would be nowhere to be seen.

Dizengoff, sitting behind his office desk in shirt sleeves, put down the paperknife he had been fiddling with as he listened to Joe's story. Joe had spoken cautiously, but had given the salient facts – that a hundred thousand dollars in pre-war gold coins had been sent by sympathisers in America and were now buried in the cellar at Atlit. They were now asking the Jewish National Fund to take the gold away and distribute it.

Dizengoff looked at the paperknife in silence for a moment before raising his clearly disapproving gaze to first Joe and then Sara. Sara had not said a word during Joe's explanation, but her mind was raging with fury. Dizengoff had made his contempt for them clear as soon as he realised what they were saying: despite the offer of more money than he had probably seen in a long time, he wanted them to see how much he disapproved of any activities that did not involve the official organisation. He leant back in his chair, folded his hands over his little paunch and studied Sara.

'Now let's talk sense. You have a hundred thousand dollars in gold that you would like us to distribute?' Sara nodded. They had made that much perfectly clear. 'Where does the gold come from?'

Sara felt a nerve throbbing in her temple. 'I am not at liberty to tell you.'

Dizengoff was silent for a moment, then looked at her sharply. 'Does your brother Aaron have anything to do with this, by any chance?'

Sara lowered her eyes, but answered calmly: 'I am sure you know that Aaron is detained by the British.'

'Huh!' snorted Dizengoff. 'I don't believe that story and neither, let me tell you, does most of the executive here.' He leaned across the table and spoke almost cajolingly. 'And your father? Does he know about the gold?'

'No,' Sara answered quickly, her eyes hardening and meeting his full on. 'And I do not wish him to do so.'

Dizengoff sat back in his chair. 'The fact that some of the money is to be distributed to Christian organisations only reinforces my belief that the gold has been smuggled in from Cairo. Has it?'

Joe interrupted smartly: 'My dear Meir, you may believe what you wish. The question is – do you want the money or not?'

Dizengoff sighed. 'Yes, don't misunderstand me. We will, of course, take the money and thank you for it, but I don't want it to cost us the life of one member of our Jewish community. You know as well as I do that the relief fund can operate only with the good will of the Turk. If there is a suspicion, however faint, that any member of the Jewish community is involved in rebellion or spying of any description then,' he looked at them solemnly; 'then this land will flow with more blood than at any time since the Crusaders. Do you understand that?'

Joe nodded, making no attempt to hide his irritation. 'Yes we do. Our understanding of that is precisely the reason why we have come to you. Now when can we expect the Hashomer?'

'Within the week,' Dizengoff answered wearily. 'Just one more thing, Joe. I will accept the money on behalf of the relief fund but please understand that I will not sanction espionage.'

Joe threw back his head and laughed. 'Neither do I, Meir, neither do I.'

Sara launched herself angrily into the bright sunlight outside and marched down the wooden planking that served as a pavement. The streets were busy with workers on their way home from jobs in Jaffa, with women shopping at the crowded stores and stalls. It was the first Jewish town to be built since Biblical times, and now a throbbing, vibrant city.

'Damn, damn, damn them,' she muttered furiously and Joe, keeping pace at her side, smiled at her ill-temper. 'They've always hated the Levinsons and never given Aaron the public status he deserves. And now they treat us like runaway schoolchildren. Damn them to hell.'

Joe caught her by the elbow and swung her around to him. 'Then stop behaving like one and calm down. We're one people, don't forget that. We're bonded by the same blood, the same dreams. We are just different people taking different paths to the same goal. Think of his position, Sara, not just yours.' His eyes as they met hers were serious and caring, and his expression deflated some of her anger.

'Yes, of course. Joe, I'm tired, hungry and cross. Would you take me back to my hotel?'

'No, I've a better idea. Why don't you come home with me? The food is better.'

'Joe, I'd rather . . .'

'I'll have you safely in your hotel before the nine o'clock curfew, I promise.' He grinned at her serious face and held his right hand up. 'Promise,' he repeated.

The thought of sitting alone in the hotel eating salt herring and beans while Lev retched upstairs suddenly lost its appeal, and Sara nodded. With no further resistance she let Joe steer her towards the waiting diligence.

Back at the house, Joe dismissed all the servants for the evening, telling Sara they would then be able to talk confidentially. Sara was not convinced it was a good idea, but was too tired to argue, and sat back with a cool drink while Joe prepared the supper himself. They ate a delicious dish of rice, chicken and olives and Joe produced a bottle of wine from the Zichron vineyards with a flourish. 'To make you feel at home,' he told her, adding that this was a small celebration – he had become a citizen of the Ottoman Empire at last. Now all the red tape had been cut through, he would be free to come and go from Jaffa again.

As Sara ate and drank she did begin to feel at home in Joe's house. The room suited her completely. It was a charming, simple room with four windows all looking out to sea. The walls and high ceiling were painted a crisp, clean white. One wall was hung with a remarkable carpet of great age and breathtaking beauty. As Sara looked at it, it seemed literally to glow. The room was furnished casually, with rugs scattered on the floor and low sofas piled high with soft cushions. Small, intricately-patterned brass tables and niches in the walls held books and a few *objets d'art*. The room was altogether peaceful, uncomplicated and tasteful.

After the sunny day, the night was remarkably warm for the end of March and all the windows were open, letting in the smell of the sea, the jacaranda and almond blossom. Sara sat on her own, waiting for Joe to make the coffee, and was distantly aware of the sound of the waves beating on a low ledge of rock below the house. Far away a dog bayed madly.

Her chin propped in her hands, her eyes half closed, Sara realised how much she had enjoyed the evening. Joe appeared quite the domesticated male in his own home, but at the same time

Sara was always acutely conscious of a restrained masculinity about him that disturbed and excited her. They had talked with an easy, intimate fluency and Sara felt more relaxed and happy than she had for a very long time. It suddenly occurred to her that she had never had such a calm, intimate evening with either Chaim or Daniel, and she felt a shiver in her soul. What sort of person was she? Could all her problems have been caused by her own follies? Dare she really hope that after two mistakes she could build a new life. She pushed the thoughts aside, feeling disloyal to Chaim and Daniel. They were both dead, and comparisons should not be drawn. *But what about me?* whispered the part of her that she spent her life trying to suppress. *Why shouldn't I start again?*

A wave of exhaustion overtook her. What was she doing sitting here like this? Lev would be out of his mind with worry already.

'You work too hard.' Sara started and looked up. Joe was leaning against the door jamb gazing at her thoughtfully. How long had he been there? Sara blushed at the idea of having been watched. *Don't be a fool*, she told herself and glanced away.

'You ought to stay here for a few days,' Joe continued; 'you need a break. Look at you – rail thin, your clothes are falling off your back. And apart from anything else I've just found out I can't make coffee,' he looked ruefully at the watery slop in the jug he was carrying, and went to sit beside her on the sofa.

Sara laughed a little nervously. 'Do I really look that bad?' she asked, smoothing her hair back defensively. Joe looked at her. How he loved her eyes, so blue, so dauntless.

'You always look lovely,' he said gently. 'But I fear that one day soon you're going to crack under the strain. Stay here a few days, Sara. Relax.'

'I can't.' Her voice was strong as she looked him straight in the eye, shaking her head. 'It's Passover next week – my father – and besides I must be back at the station to deal with . . .'

'Damn it, Sara,' Joe interrupted harshly. 'What more will you do? Wear a hair shirt – sackcloth and ashes? Daniel is dead. That's the hard truth and you must face it. One day I'm going to die and you're going to die but in the meantime we should fight like hell to keep alive. Stop trying to bury yourself with him. It's not fair on yourself – or anyone around you.'

Sara stared at him, amazed. 'That's not true. I'm not!'

'Of course it is, but you'd rather bite your tongue off than admit it.'

The muscles in Sara's face tightened.

'You just don't understand, do you? You don't understand that my devotion to the station and – and the other work – has nothing whatsoever to do with Daniel's death. I worked before he died, before he left, and his death has not changed a thing.' Her voice was taut with emotion, it was so important to her that Joe should understand. 'I believe in what we are doing deeply, with every fibre of my being, every breath in my body. I'm not willing myself to death, and don't you dare think it. I'm willing the network to life, to success.'

She glanced down at her hands, considering for a moment, before she looked up at Joe again. 'My relationship with Daniel had died some time before he did,' her voice faltered and she stopped. Joe looked at her hard and saw from her face that she was being totally sincere.

As their eyes met, searching, questioning and answering, Sara, with a swift flash of insight, admitted the truth she had been fighting against, the truth of which she had only become gradually aware. This was more than a physical attraction. She had fallen in love with him. The tension between them was suddenly unbearable and Sara looked down, covered in confusion. She felt weak, as though she were bleeding to death, but she knew she must move.

'I must go,' she said, rising unsteadily to her feet. 'It's nearly nine.'

Joe rose swiftly with her and, after a tiny silence, spoke in his usual light-hearted tone. 'Of course. I'll get your hat and coat and raise the driver.'

'Thank you,' she said with an abstracted smile.

Joe looked at her quickly. She seemed suddenly very young, almost child-like. He wanted to reach out and take her in his arms. But her eyes were subdued, her expression serious. He could feel that she was pulling back from him. Her gaze was so cool that for a moment he thought he had imagined the look in her eyes that had told him she felt the same way about him as he did her. But he knew in his heart, with a certainty untainted by arrogance, that he had not been wrong. He remembered what he had told her about Dizengoff. 'We are bound together, but we are separate people going different ways to the same goal.' He now knew that the same was true of Sara and him. They were heading in the same direction, and very soon now their two paths would become one.

*   *   *

423

Joe was lying in a hazy stupor in the big steam room of the hamam. He had taken Sara back to the hotel and then asked the driver to stop at the Turkish baths. After twenty-five minutes there he felt all the tension had evaporated: the damp heat had penetrated to his bones, the steam had gone deep into his lungs, and he felt as though he were in a dream.

A few dismembered voices occasionally came through the steam, disturbing his lazy thoughts. Most of the clientele at the baths were Turks, and from their educated voices these three sounded as though they were well-placed socially if not politically. It was not until he heard the name of Hamid Bek that he jerked himself out of his steamy dream and began to listen in earnest.

He sat up on the wooden bench and tied the towel round his waist, as he peered into the steam, trying to find figures to match the voices. One was elderly and querulous, the second cynical and sneering, the third young and cocky. Joe could not make out all the words but listened hard, hoping to hear something of interest.

'. . . the English . . .' came the old voice.

'. . . it's probably only a rumour . . .'

'But he's a close friend . . . it's a very good source,' insisted the old man.

'But why . . . ?'

The third, young voice burst into laughter. 'Because the Jews are traitors and will welcome the British with open arms.'

Then there was a period of more muttering which Joe could not catch until the old voice said: '. . . it's to be posted by government order . . .'

'Yes, at midnight . . . Hamid Bek . . . beat the dog and the lion will behave itself.' And the know-it-all voice burst into laughter again.

His heart beating wildly, Joe jumped to his feet and rushed through the cooling room. His attendant, who was waiting to pour bowls of warm water over him before kneading and pummelling his flesh into relaxation, stared in surprise as Joe brushed past him and sped along the white marble tiles into the dressing rooms. Rubbing himself hastily with a towel Joe dressed as fast as he could, praying that Lev and Sara had brought their army patrol passes with them. He had his own securely with him. *Beat the dog and the lion will behave itself.* The word echoed through his mind. *Well, Hamid Bek and Jemel Pasha are going to*

*have to learn that this pack of dogs still has its teeth — and more
importantly its cunning.*

Sara woke from a deep sleep to a quiet but persistent rapping at
her door. She lay a moment, struggling out of her sleep, but as she
hesitated she heard a voice coming through the keyhole.

'Sara, it's Joe. Please open the door — it's urgent.'

'What do you want?' she whispered back, feeling for her
dressing gown and sticking one arm into it. 'It's very late.' She
crossed to the door, fumbling with the braid that tied her hair up.

'Open the door and I'll explain,' Joe hissed. There was a
moment's pause as Sara tied her dressing-gown belt. 'For God's
sake, I'm not here on an attempted seduction. It is important.'

Sara turned the key in the lock, standing back to let him into the
room. Joe closed the door gently behind him and looked at her, his
face serious. 'Forgive me for intruding so late, but it's an
emergency. I've come to get you and Lev.' Joe was whispering, and
Sara looked at him, waiting for an explanation. 'Sara, have you
got your patrol passes — the ones signed by Jemel Pasha?'

Sara was still tussling with the dream-like quality of the scene.
What was Joe doing here, she wondered as, trembling, she tried to
strike a match to the candle. She felt strange and ill at ease, with a
fear of the unknown prickling at her spine. She waited until the
wick flared up, casting odd shadows over the room, before she
answered.

'Yes, of course we have. Why — what's happened?'

Joe took the candle from her and put it down on the chest of
drawers. He took Sara firmly by the shoulders and looked into her
eyes, his face more serious than she had ever seen it. A feeling of
dread swept over her as she returned his look. 'Joe?'

He spoke before she could go on. 'Now listen carefully. Get
dressed and ready to leave. I'll be back in ten minutes. I'm going to
wake Lev — which is his room?'

'Eighteen, just down the corridor — but why?'

'This is why,' Joe said harshly, pulling a flimsy white paper from
his pocket and thrusting it into her hand. 'Remember, you've only
got ten minutes. I've got everything planned so don't worry, just
get dressed.' He slipped out of the room, closing the door quietly
behind him.

Sara looked curiously at the paper and began to read it.
Halfway through she found herself shaking so much she could

425

barely hold the pamphlet still enough to read it. It called for the immediate evacuation of all civilian Jews in Jaffa and Tel Aviv. The deadline for their departure was noon on the 28 March. Any still in the town after that time must face the death penalty. The 28 March! Sara gave a horrified gasp. That was now, today. They had fewer than eight hours before they must all be out of the city. Hamid Bek must have had the signs posted after curfew, knowing full well that they would not be seen until six in the morning at the earliest.

Dear God, she thought. *First the Armenians and now us!* Her worst fears were being realised. Sara's head was throbbing and swimming, but she forced herself to be calm.

She sat on the bed and looked at the pamphlet once more. The expulsion was by direct order of Jemel Pasha and Hamid Bek. The reason given was to protect the citizen from a sea attack on the towns. British ships were now shelling the city of Gaza, their troops moving in from Egypt, and Jaffa was expected to be the next target.

Sara felt a quiet satisfaction at the knowledge that at last the British were moving closer, but she was scared by the danger signals: the signals bred in her from generations of ancestors who had fled in the face of persecution of their race. The burning hatred she felt for the Turk drowned any fear that might otherwise have made her incapable of action. She hated the Turk's cruelty, his inhumanity but, almost as much, she hated his stupidity. Were they really meant to believe that this expulsion was for their own safety? Why should the Turk pick out the Jew to protect? The province was filled with Arabs, Turks, with every minority race under the sun – and the Jews alone were to be protected? Sara could almost have dropped everything and howled her rage aloud. But that would have been self-indulgent.

Within seconds she pulled herself together and began to pack her case. *What happened to the Armenians is not going to happen to us*, she muttered through clenched teeth. *It will not!* She fumbled with her hair, tying it back with the same length of braid that she had hastily removed on Joe's arrival. This was no time for vanity. In seconds she was dressed, and had just fastened the clasp on her portmanteau when there was a knock at the door and Joe and Lev came softly in.

'I always knew you were the kind of woman to have around in an emergency,' said Joe, looking absent-mindedly round the room.

'You said you had a plan. What is it?' asked Sara.

'You and I will drive to Tel Aviv and rouse Dizengoff and the Hashomer. We will need to arrange and synchronise the evacuation very carefully. No one must be forgotten. The municipal hospital and orphanage will need clearing and men must be organised to carry the sick and protect the groups of refugees against thieves – and kidnapping,' he added, giving Sara a knowing look. 'Now I've worked out that the majority of the Jewish farming colonies are to the north – there are forty-five from Mikveh to the Sharron and lower Galilee so nearly everyone will have to trek north. South we have only sixteen farming communities, with a few extra around Gaza, which in the present situation is no safer than here.' He paused for a moment, thinking hard. 'The best thing is to say that only those with relatives in the south should go south, the rest head north.

'Lev here is going to race north with Ali and alert the settlements to the crisis. He'll send every available vehicle, horse and donkey towards Jaffa to meet those on foot. I've already sent couriers south.'

'What about the railways?' put in Sara.

'And the diligences. Maybe we can hire those,' added Lev.

The three of them talked earnestly, exchanging ideas and making plans. Their minds worked with extraordinary speed and clarity and they talked on until they heard a clatter of hooves outside and a long, low whistle.

Joe looked out of the window, peering sideways towards the front of the hotel. 'Good boy – it's Ali with the horses.'

A thought suddenly came to Sara. Joe was safe, rich and comfortable – by helping them he was surely involving himself with nothing but trouble. 'Won't this jeopardise your position here – with the Turk – with Hamid Bek? You've only just got your papers.'

'Maybe,' Joe said dismissively. 'But this is my land and I'll be damned if any Turk is going to usurp my right to live here in peace and dignity.' Turning abruptly he caught sight of Sara's portmanteau. 'You'll have to jettison this,' he said, lifting it off the floor for a moment. Then the familiar grin appeared. 'We Jews are always boasting about our brains,' he said lightly. 'Now we'll have to prove we've got them.'

By eleven o'clock the ten thousand Jewish inhabitants of Jaffa and

Tel Aviv were gathered in groups throughout the city. The largest collection, of over seven thousand men, women and children, was massed on the wide, empty space beyond Zagwill Street, where the houses gave way to the sand dunes. The air was heavy, the only noise the crying of children and babies and the occasional bark of a dog. The adults stood silently, heads bowed against the visions of the Armenians' fate and the dread that those scenes were to be repeated – with themselves as victims. The atmosphere was dead, the scene like a dream where nothing is real but the emotions behind it. The smell of fear hung solidly above them all.

With difficulty Sara threaded her way through the people sitting huddled among their possessions. They had all been told to carry nothing more than food, water and warm clothing, but how could a child be separated from its doll, a tailor from his machine, a woman from her Sabbath candlesticks? Of the seven thousand, not one soul had come empty-handed. All had brought some reminder of their home. Sara, and most of the other organisers, had given up trying to persuade people to abandon their possessions.

She felt exhausted, but they had achieved almost everything they had set out to accomplish. Each person wore a label with his name and destination pinned to his front. Each orphan had been placed with a family, each patient from the hospital laid in a canvas-covered cart. Bands of men were mounted and ready to ride out and protect the evacuees. All they were waiting for now were Hamid Bek's men, who were to escort them out of the province.

Sara shaded her eyes and looked up at the flat roof of the last house in Tel Aviv. It would make an excellent platform for addressing the crowd. But where was Joe? She was gradually becoming more and more worried about his disappearance. He had set off with Dizengoff over two hours before to meet Hamid Bek, and had not been seen since. Meanwhile, the most fantastic rumours were circulating: Dizengoff had negotiated an agreement whereby the Jews could stay, Dizengoff had been sent into exile in Damascus; Dizengoff was dead. Dizengoff, Dizengoff on every side but *where was Joe?* As time went by the stories became wilder. All men would be hanged, all women raped, all boy children castrated and sent to slavery. *Why didn't he come?*

Then there came the distant muffled beat of the drums and a

bugle blare that heralded the imminent arrival of the septieh. A low moan swept through the crowd as panic and frustration overtook them. Voices rose in wails. There was movement on the roof of the house and Dr Arthur Ruppin, a well-known and respected member of the community, came forward and talked to the crowd through a megaphone. After he had begged for silence a few times, an uneasy hush settled on the crowd. Here was the father figure after all, strong and benevolent. Let him speak.

'People,' he raised his voice like a schoolmaster in class; 'People. In moments the septieh will be here.' Another moan drowned his words, this time one of fear. 'I beg of you for the sake of us all – do not defy or antagonise them. It would be senseless to arouse their blood lust.' Murmurs of assent greeted his words and he paused for a moment to let them die down. Then he held up his hand and continued: 'Rather let us leave in a sane and orderly fashion. Already our people in the north are on their way to meet us with transport and water.' A ragged cheer interrupted him again. 'In their villages we will find food and shelter. Do not fear, or despair. We will keep together.' His strength seemed to push outwards from him, and the crowd's spirits seemed to lift. 'As the mountains are around Jerusalem so the Lord is around his people.'

'We will be back!' someone cried from the back and the shout was taken up by a thousand throats, echoed and re-echoed with energy and hope.

Then people began getting up, gathering themselves together in preparation for moving on. By the time the mounted patrol of septieh arrived, firing guns into the air, the spearhead of the long column of exiles was already heading north along the red, rutted road.

Sara watched for a while, feeling strangely detached from the scene. The people walked past, pushing carts or wheelbarrows piled high with their possessions. Some of the eastern women had tied their things in blankets and carried the bundles on their heads, infants were strapped in shawls on women's hips, children carried caged birds or clutched a cat. They stepped solidly forward, their faces worried and sad, their lips repeating *don't look back, don't look back, remember Job.*

Sara gave a last look round for Joe and asked one or two of the mounted guards if they had seen him. The answer was always no. She went towards the house which had been, until last night, the workers' club. She had volunteered to take charge of a travelling first-aid post and had been given two carts and donkeys. She must prepare her helpers to leave.

A discussion about what to paint on the torn sheet that was to serve as a standard was in full swing and threatening to end in anger. Sara listened for a moment and then joined in. 'Look,' she said; 'if we paint a Star of David, even if it's red, some block-headed septieh is going to think it's a Jewish flag and will shoot us.'

'Well, what shall we put?' asked a small, round woman with a 'kerchief round her head and a paint brush at the ready.

' "Doctor" in Turkish and Yiddish,' Sara said promptly.

'But I can't write Turkish,' the woman wailed in dismay.

'Here, give it me.' Sara took the brush and quickly sketched the letters. She was concentrating so hard she did not notice the crowd around her falling silent and it was not until she had finished and heard her name that she turned.

'Madame Cohen?' She jumped and turned to see Hamid Bek, a tight-lipped smile on his face, looking down at her from a magnificent horse. 'What a delightful surprise to see you here.' The police chief raised his eyebrows and waved a careless hand at the crowd. 'I am personally very sorry about this, but it is for your own protection.'

With an effort Sara kept her self-control but her eyes flashed the truth of her feelings at him. 'No matter,' she said, her eyes caught like blue glass in a shaft of sunlight, 'being a Jew has always meant that we are a wandering people.' Her voice was tart and she thought too late of Ruppin's words to the crowd.

'Now, now, Mrs Cohen,' Hamid Bek shook his head in mock despair. 'You are trying to provoke me. Let us not spoil our friendly relationship.'

Sara swallowed her repulsion and smiled slightly. 'No, I should not wish for that.' She lowered her eyes for a moment, wondering how she could find out what had happened to Joe without mentioning his name. 'Perhaps you could tell me the whereabouts of Effendi Dizengoff?' she asked politely.

Hamid Bek's eyes took on the glassy stare of a boiled fish.

'That traitor has the disobedience of a mule – and its stupidity. The mayor will be doing Tel Aviv no more of his favours. If I ever see him here again, he will hang in the middle of this town of his.' Sara gasped and Hamid Bek smiled patronisingly. 'I have sent him to Damascus – for the moment.'

'But, Hamid Bek, Effendi Dizengoff is no traitor,' Sara began, shocked at his exile but relieved he was alive.

'All Jews are traitors,' he interrupted easily, with a little smile. Her stomach rose in a sudden, sick lurch. How much did he know? His cool look gave away nothing, but she knew better than to take such a man at face value. He could not know about Aaron, or there would have been trouble already – but Daniel? She forced herself to meet the policeman's gaze. His eyes travelled down to her bosom and then back up to her face. 'Although I could wish that all traitresses looked like you. It would make my job a great deal more pleasurable.' He tipped the brim of his hat lazily. 'Well, Madame Cohen, I'm sure we will meet again soon,' he said, kicking his horse forward, the crowds before him parting like the Red Sea before Moses.

Sara made a point of returning to her job with the pennant, but her fingers were trembling. She had sensed the warnings behind Hamid Bek's flippancy, and like an animal she read the signals and was on guard. She knew she was under suspicion – in danger – and knew instinctively that Hamid Bek had something in mind and was just biding his time. What she did not know was how much he knew and how much he just suspected.

She raised her head and stared after Hamid Bek, watching his neat, dapper frame in blue and scarlet as it bobbed, ramrod straight, above the crowd, stopping now and again to greet people, with all the ease of a host at a successful dinner party. She remembered the insulting scrutiny of her breasts and hatred for him burned like fire at the back of her throat. Straightening her shoulders, she stared after him with defiance. She would not be afraid – she was not afraid. Sara looked round one last time and would have given a piece of her heart to have heard some cynical bantering remark in Joe's light, familiar voice. But he was nowhere in sight. Disappointment flooded her heart and she rubbed her eyes wearily.

'Come on! Move along!' The jostling of the crowd broke into her thoughts and she turned back to the cart. They were moving now, all together, all so different, but all linked with an incredible closeness. Seven thousand different souls with nothing in common but their Jewishness – and their pride.

By three o'clock that afternoon it seemed as though the long line of evacuees had made no progress at all. From the very beginning wheels had fallen off carts, donkeys had stood, heads hanging and refusing to move an inch, army traffic had driven them from the highway into the sand dunes. They had passed through many Arab villages, but without incident. In this province the Arabs and Jews were traditionally friendly, and had worked amicably for decades – in the case of some families for centuries. The travellers were greeted with customary Arab warmth: even those at the back of the convoy were met with friendliness and water. The villagers were moved by the spectacle of thousands of Jews on the march: they themselves were terrified at the prospect of being caught in a major confrontation between the Turk and the English infidels. The terrible butchery of the Crusaders, so many centuries earlier, had left an indelible scar on the Arab memory. In some cases the Jewish leaders had great difficulty in stopping the Muktars of the villages from leaving their houses and fields to join them. 'The Turk is not moving us for our own safety, as they say, but in the hope that hunger, thirst and disease will rid them of the Jew,' they promised. The Arabs looked sceptical but stayed at home.

Soon only the whirling dust paid tribute to the passing thousands. The sky was a pale blue above them, the sun shone bright as gold. As they passed the occasional citrus grove, the people raised their heads and breathed in the fragrant scent of early orange blossom. And in among the sand dunes white broom, bright scarlet crowfoot and pale yellow groundsel bloomed in defiance of the pain that walked solidly by.

Sara had placed herself and her carts at the back of the convoy, where she could gather up lost children until a frantic parent appeared. It was not a pleasant position. Thousands of feet had drummed up billowing dust clouds that mixed with the sand thrown up by the bad-tempered septiehs. As it was mostly the weak and weary who, unable to keep up, were falling to the back of the column, they were an easy prey to the septieh. If they noticed someone stopping to catch their breath or wipe their eyes free of the dust the septieh would ride over and prod the 'lazy dog' with their rifles, or kick them from their mounts. Sara, tired and irritable herself, stopped in horror as she saw bullets spraying round the feet of an elderly couple pausing by the roadside. As the couple clung together, paralysed with fear, the septieh laughed coarsely and fired another couple of rounds.

Sara looked desperately around, wondering how to stop such rank viciousness. More and more of the men were beginning to gather together, whispering as they marched on. She could see the danger signs. Any violent action – any defiance – now would lead to bloodshed.

The beat of galloping hooves coming from behind made her swing round. It was Joe at last. Her relief was so intense that she felt the tears sting at her eyes. With him were three men who, from their clothing – boots, breeches and keffiyehs – looked like members of the Hashomer. They rode up to the two septieh and Sara felt her heart swell in pride as she saw the easy smile on Joe's face as he sat comfortably astride Negiv. The other three men, slightly behind him, sat their mounts and stared blankly at the septieh. The septieh stopped laughing and stared back.

The tension was unbearable. Everyone nearby froze and watched quietly. Then, like young wolves backing away from the pack leader, the septieh lowered their pistols and casually replaced them in their belts. Like the last of the air being expelled from a bellows, there was an audible sigh of relief from those witnessing the little scene.

Sara dashed forward and put her arms around the hunched shoulders of the old couple, who were still clinging to each other, breathing shallowly. Someone came forward with a cup of water for the old man, who passed it immediately to his wife.

Joe, watching the scene, caught sight of Sara and, meeting her eye, raised a brow and grinned jauntily. The septieh followed his gaze. 'Just the person I'm looking for – my sister,' Joe said with a lewd wink. The innuendo was not lost on the septieh and, as they guffawed, Sara flushed scarlet, then coughed to cover the embarrassment caused by the stares and whispers of the crowd round her. Joe reined in his stallion beside her and bent over the saddle. He reached down and, before she realised his intention, he had whipped a powerful arm around her waist and swung her up behind him on to Negiv's rump.

Sara squealed in surprise and her blushes turned a deep angry red. She snatched at her skirts and came close to falling from Negiv as the stallion side-stepped nervously. She grabbed hastily at Joe, who laughed and turned to her, smiling in his infuriating way. 'Hold tight, sister, I must see you home as soon as possible,' he laughed and, nodding to the two septieh, added; 'have I permission to proceed?'

The septieh, noting the predatory gleam in Joe's eye, hooted with laughter and nodded. 'There is no refusal.'

'Then, please excuse us, gentlemen,' Joe said with the same lazy grin. 'I'm in rather a hurry,' and, winking again, he urged Negiv smartly forward.

Sara instinctively wrapped her arms around his lean, hard body and moved closer. She felt utterly breathless and tried to shut off the rising sensations that sent a fierce heat through her body. Her breasts ached . . . her whole body ached . . . for Joe. The desire to press herself against his loose white shirt so shocked her that she relaxed her grip and wriggled back slightly.

'Hold tight, Sara,' Joe warned; 'they're still watching us.'

Sara leaned closer and hissed in his ear, 'What in the hell is all this about. A fine spectacle you made of me back there.'

Joe laughed and looked at her sideways, his cat-green eyes dancing in amusement. 'I could hardly tell them that I need you to show me where the gold is hidden, could I? Now hold tight – tighter. We're going to ride hard to Atlit, pass on the gold and let Aaron know what's happening.'

'Pigeon post,' Sara whispered softly.

'Got it in one,' said Joe and, wheeling away from the long column of refugees, he spurred Negiv on and the four horsemen rode off at a flying gallop.

CHAPTER TWENTY-FIVE

Cairo: March 1917

Towards the end of March, Aaron was given the rank of Major and ordered to shift his headquarters from Port Said to Cairo. He obeyed the command willingly. The constant travelling between the port and the capital had been time consuming and tiring, and in Cairo he was near to the top brass. The GHQ was now comfortably ensconced at the Savoy Hotel and Aaron soon found himself enjoying a considerable success. General Murray often called him in when he needed clear and immediate advice about the lie of the land and the positioning of waterholes. Aaron admired the English General, appreciating his great ability for logistics and administration as well as the foreigner's recognition of the fact that the battle for Palestine would involve conquering the elements as much as the desert forces of the wily von Kressenstein.

To date, the English General's achievements had been very impressive. The Sinai had been conquered, which relieved the threat to the Suez. A system of pipes had been imported from America and laid across the length of the Sinai, pumping water from the Nile to within ten miles of Gaza. Before that a railroad had been laid across the desert, and there was even a sort of road, made of pegged-down wire netting, which eased the agony of the marching infantry. This unhospitable avenue led the Army straight to the walls of Gaza.

The word Gaza meant fortress and the British had cause to sigh at the aptness of the name. Throughout history would-be conquering heroes had battled at its walls for, not only did it command all the roads leading into southern Palestine, it jealously guarded the most essential element in desert warfare: water. After Gaza the next water source lay twenty miles further on, in Beersheba.

Aaron had tried to prove that there must be other sources of water, but all his arguments fell on deaf ears. He had painstakingly drawn their attention to the previous existence of long-buried villages, but the logic of his theory was disregarded. 'They could not have existed without water supplies. And they are all around Gaza and Beersheba – the same water that feeds those two cities must run underground between them. All we must do is drill.' He pleaded vainly. The British were polite, but ignored him.

Well, let them take Gaza first, he told himself, but niggling away at the back of his mind was the ever-present doubt whether Murray was really the man who would carry away the gates as Samson had done in the Bible, or whether he would even be able to carve his name on the scroll of triumphant generals. Murray was a brilliant administrator, but he was no Alexander the Great, Saladin or Napoleon.

Despite these worries Aaron was, until the end of March, almost a happy man. The ship was once again running smoothly to Atlit, bringing back valuable field reports from Sara. His rooms at the Continental Hotel were large, old-fashioned, very British and extremely comfortable. And, at a cocktail party Major Deedes had persuaded him to attend, he had met Deana, an amusing dark-eyed Jewess from Alexandria who brightened his life a great deal. He was surprised at the force of attraction and the amount of time and thought he gave to the Alexandrian. Everything about her was warm and humorous, and to his delight Aaron discovered that she shared his belief in Palestine as the Jewish homeland.

But on 29 March came the news of the first British defeat at Gaza. The report fell on incredulous ears. The strategy had been inspired. Aeroplane reconnaissance by both the Royal Flying Corps and Von Kressenstein's airborne units had discounted any possibility of a surprise attack. Until, in a dense sea fog on the night of the 26th, General Dobell succeeded in massing his five divisions in an almost complete semi-circle around Gaza. When the fog began to lift and the sky lightened into dawn the Turks were dismayed to discover enemy cavalry had silently swept over their outposts. By that evening, after hours of bitter fighting, the 53rd Welsh Division had secured much of Ali Muntar, the hill that dominated Gaza, and by nightfall some units had linked up with the Australian Anzacs on the coast.

Then the trouble started. The staff of both sides instigated a series of miscalculations and simple mistakes that crippled their armies. In the confusion both Dobell and Von Kressenstein believed themselves beaten. Von Kressenstein halted his men and guns while the men of Dobell's Desert Column listened in disbelief as the orders arrived to retreat. In a moment of pure farce the German Commandant of Gaza, believing the battle lost, blew up his own wireless station. By the next day, von Kressenstein had consolidated his position and there was no longer any hope of taking Gaza.

The defeat shook Aaron badly, but then came news which was if anything worse. The pigeon post arrived, telling of the mass expulsions of Jews from Tel Aviv and Jaffa. As he read the flimsy paper, Aaron felt a cold, heavy weight settle on his heart. Half mad with worry he waited for news from Sara, but her April report was curiously cheerful and optimistic. The Hashomer had taken over the distribution of the gold, she wrote, which left her free to concentrate on the espionage work – and of course the station. Atlit no longer seemed isolated as a thousand refugees were crammed into Zichron. They had refused to take any refugees into Atlit, which had aroused the suspicions of the Zichron council, especially as their best excuse – the American ownership of the station – had vanished with the American entry into the war. Atlit was now, technically at least, confiscated by the Turk.

The wonder of it was, Sara continued, that Hamid Bek and his septieh had not as yet visited them. She made a fleeting reference to her meeting with the police chief in Tel Aviv, and mentioned that she was wary of him. Although she had glossed the incident over, Aaron had felt a wave of apprehension at her admission, which he tried to quell. The Turk was hopeless at intelligence, but surprisingly capable at counter-intelligence and Aaron could not help but wonder how long it would be until the Teutonic thoroughness of the Germans led them to suspect a nest of rats in their midst. Only the fact that Joe had returned to the station relieved him a little, as he trusted the American to protect the network from making mistakes through over-confidence. Sara's letter had been full of depressing news, but somehow it was not depressingly written. There had not been one word of gloom in it, and Aaron wondered if the light tone had been anything to do with Joe. Perhaps the very fact that he was there strengthened her sense of security: if so his presence was an added bonus.

When he learned that Murray planned to make another attempt

437

at Gaza in April, Aaron decided that if it were successful he would break up the network. The amount of intelligence they had managed to supply to date was staggering: the fall of Gaza would be a timely call for a halt.

But it had not happened. Dobell had launched his Eastern Force augmented by the punching power of eight Pincher tanks but after a day of bitter fighting had called off the second battle of Gaza. He had lost six and a half thousand men in return for minimal gains. The Turk held high the laurels of victory. London was not pleased at the loss and recalled Dobell to England. Rumours began to circulate that Murray too was to be replaced. In the first few weeks of May sweeping adminstrative reforms were implemented and Aaron looked forward to his weekly meeting with Major Deedes.

The ship was due to sail for Atlit in a few days' time and Aaron went to see the Major armed with all the meticulously coded orders in the 'information required' file. Each month the British demands, far from lessening, grew alarmingly. Aaron's only mistake was perhaps to present the job as one easily done, but the mistake came from an eagerness to prove his group's loyalty and competence.

Aaron sighed and rubbed his clean-shaven chin thoughtfully. There could be no question now of disbanding the group and the feelings of foreboding clutched at his chest again. Dragging his mind from his negative thoughts he lit a cigarette and sat at his desk, pulling the Arab paper *Muktari* towards him and avidly skimming the pages in the hope that there was news of who Murray's successor might be. All he could see of interest was a speech by England's Lloyd George, in which he declared that the government intended to give the Holy City of Jerusalem as a Christmas present to the British nation. Well at least that showed there was no intention of their calling off the Palestine campaign as yet, unless this was just a moral boost to a nation still locked in a bloodbath in Europe.

Aaron folded up the newspaper neatly and checked his watch, impatient for the Major's arrival. He rose and crossed to the double windows, shutting them to block out the deafening din from the street below. He switched on the ceiling fan and watched it abstractedly for a moment and then, as though he had not just looked, checked the time again. It was two minutes to nine. Smiling, he made a bet with himself that Selena would arrive at precisely nine o'clock and, as he had so often before, he blessed the gods of fate that had brought her into his life. His mind went briefly back to the railway station at Haifa, when she had first stepped shyly off the train behind Sara . . . it was hard to recognise her as the same woman today.

She and Sarkis had married a fortnight earlier, as soon as they had received official papers of residence. They had moved from Paul and Eve's house to their own tiny flat in the centre of the city. Kristopher had begun to study photography – a profession undertaken by many Armenians here – and Selena had begun to work as Aaron's secretary. Poised, groomed and startlingly efficient, she had already become indispensable to him.

On the first stroke of the clock there was a light tap on the door and Selena walked in, her arms full of flowers. 'Good morning, Major,' she said, her smile as bright as the flowers she held as she looked at him through the spikes of scarlet gladioli. 'I thought that perhaps your room could do with a brightening up.'

'You do that yourself by being here,' Aaron answered with genuine admiration.

Selena had at last abandoned the eastern clothing she had worn for most of her life, and today she looked wonderfully smart in a crisp white summer frock, a little straw hat perched on her smoothly drawn-up hair. Sarkis was a lucky man, but Aaron had no doubts that he knew it. Selena put the flowers down on a side table, took off her hat and put it with her bag on a chair beside her own small desk and, looking round, found a vase. 'I'll just get some water,' she said, going to the bathroom.

Aaron nodded and, unlocking the steel filing cabinet, took out of it two red folders and put them on his desk. Selena came back with the vase and with quick, deft movements began to arrange the flowers expertly. Aaron watched her for a moment, wondering at the quality of gentleness that touched everything she did. Even Major Deedes seemed to soften when she was in the room, his voice dropping a degree or two in her presence, a foolish smile often lightening up his face when she came in.

She stood back to check the flowers and then turned to Aaron. 'Do you think Major Deedes would mind if I included something personal in the despatch this month?' she asked.

'No, I shouldn't think so – what is it?'

'Well, it's Sara's birthday this month' – Aaron felt a pang of guilt at not having remembered himself – 'and I wanted to send her a gift from Kristopher and me.' She took an envelope out of her bag and opened it. 'Look,' she said proudly, pulling out a photograph, 'Kristopher took it himself – it's good, don't you think?'

Aaron looked at it, wondering what set it apart from other photographs he had seen and then he realised. Selena was smiling frankly out at the camera, her pose totally relaxed. It was the most natural photograph he had ever seen.

'There's also a lace collar,' Selena went on, pleased at his admiring silence. 'Sara was always complaining that hers were all full of holes.' She replaced the photograph in the envelope, which she put beside the files on Aaron's desk.

A sharp tap at the door announced Major Deedes. Selena let him in and the two men saluted formally before greeting each other warmly.

'Everything ready?' Deedes asked, settling his neatly-pressed figure into the chair opposite the desk and eyeing the two files eagerly.

Aaron nodded. 'Any last minute additions?'

'Only a few.' Aaron grinned. It was always the case that more had to be slipped in at the last moment and the two men briskly exchanged information, Aaron making notes directly into code.

'And one other thing,' Deedes announced just as Aaron thought they had come to an end. 'A simple thing is puzzling our chaps in the flying corps. When dropping propaganda leaflets over Arab villages they have noticed that the villagers almost fall over each other in their efforts to run away from the paper. What can you suppose the reason is?'

Aaron smiled grimly. 'Most probably the Turk has announced the death penalty as a punishment to anyone reading the leaflets.'

'Good God!' the Major said, genuinely shocked. 'Surely not?'

Selena, who had been sitting working quietly at her desk, raised her dark head and exchanged a glance with Aaron. Would the British never understand that the Turk did not regard human life as sacrosanct, that no individual human life was priceless?

'I could be wrong, but I suspect not,' Aaron said matter-of-factly.

A silence fell as Deedes chose a cigarette, tapped it on his silver cigarette box and lit it. Then he looked up at Aaron, a hint of a smile on his lips. 'I believe I know who is to step into Murray's shoes,' he said. 'Interested?'

Aaron laughed. 'You know damn well I am. Who is it to be?'

'Well, I'm not yet certain, of course, but the word is that it's going to be Allenby.'

'Who?' Aaron asked, thoroughly intrigued.

'General Sir Edmund Allenby,' Deedes repeated. 'Apparently, Smuts was asked to replace Murray, but turned down the offer. Stroke of luck for us if we do get Allenby. He's a cavalry general and most of our troops are mounted.'

'What's he like?'

Selena was also listening with open interest to the news.

'Well,' Deedes said thoughtfully; 'I don't know him personally but his nickname is "The Bull".' Aaron lifted his eyebrows in surprise. This man must be very different from the administrator Murray. 'He supposedly does not suffer fools gladly. He insists on straight answers to straight questions. Got a bit of a temper, they say.'

'Allenby,' Aaron said quietly. 'Is he English?'

'English as Coleman's Mustard,' Deedes answered, chuckling at his analogy. 'He's an earnest student of the Old Testament and a keen botanist and ornithologist.' He stubbed out his cigarette and rose to leave. 'You two should get on like the proverbial house on fire.'

Aaron rose too, and shook Deedes's hand in warm farewell. After he had seen the Major out, he turned back into the room to see Selena looking at him fixedly.

'Allenby,' she said slowly. 'The Arabs are bound to make much of that name.'

'Why?'

'Because Allenby, translated into Arabic, could be read as Allah-en-nebi. Prophet of the Lord.' Selena looked pleased with her lateral thinking.

'Well, I'll be damned,' said Aaron. 'Allenby — Allah-en-nebi,' he repeated, smiling as the meaning became clear. 'And isn't there some kind of prophecy . . . ?'

'Yes. In effect that the Turk would be driven from Jerusalem only when a Prophet of the Lord brought the waters of the Nile to Palestine.'

'Murray's pipeline!' Aaron chuckled. His spirits rose again, although his head told him that old prophecies had little to do with modern warfare. But still . . . Allah-en-nebi . . . there could be something . . . He sat at his desk, looking at the telephone thoughtfully for a moment. He had been planning to spend the evening at home, going over some old maps Paul had found in a bookshop. But with the thoughts buzzing in his head like a colony of bees he would be too restless to concentrate. With a smile he came to a decision and picked up the telephone. One hand fiddling idly with the telephone wire he asked the operator for Deana's number.

The operational room in the Beersheba garrison was small and stuffy, filled with over thirty officers sweating gently in the heat. Jemel Pasha was at a low table, facing them: even sitting he dominated the room. His eyes were stony as he listened to reports by German members of the staff and Hans Werner at least could feel how strongly the Turk hated the German. Colonel von Kressenstein sat beside his commander, his long aristocratic features wearing an attentive, set expression. And behind the two men, dwarfing the seated officers, was the exotic frame of Osman, Jemel's bodyguard.

The Germans and Turks had unconsciously separated themselves into two groups like sheep and goats. Despite the victory at Gaza a month before, relationships between the two were if anything deteriorating. Hans Werner, like all the Germans, felt nothing but contempt for the Turkish HQ staff. All the wrong people were in charge, the right ones being sent to inconvenient outposts. From the beginning of the war the Turkish badge of rank had been synonymous with bungling inefficiency. They could not even run a war properly. Supplies were not getting through, their troops were suffering from undernourishment and as a result deserting in alarming numbers – it was reported that as many as three hundred thousand so far. Gasoline was also in cripplingly short supply, which meant the planes were grounded uselessly. The Turk seemed incapable of or unwilling to understand twentieth-century warfare.

It had just been pointed out that raw recruits were being sent to the fronts and Hans Werner could see Jemel Pasha's face darkening in fury. There was an uncomfortable shifting in the room, broken only by the clicking of the telegraph machine in the corner. Jemel Pasha fought down his temper. Anyone would think that it was his fault that that little war god Enver Pasha was sitting on his throne in Constantinople refusing to send trained soldiers for the Fourth Army, bullets for them to shoot and food to feed them.

442

He stood up, then sat down as abruptly, realising there was no room to pace round in. Looking over the officers' heads at a stain on the wall the shape of Italy, he waved an arm above his head and burst out. 'Apply to His Excellency Enver Pasha. The War Minister alone has the power to redress the situation.'

There was another silence, in which the German staff officers stole furtive glances at one another. Jemel's mention of Enver Pasha's name made them feel apprehensive. Everyone present knew full well that the War Minister was slowly divesting Jemel Pasha of all political and military power. The recent arrival in Constantinople of General von Falkenhayn had been taken by Jemel Pasha – and others – to mean that Enver was about to try to neutralise him by placing the German General above him in Syria and Palestine.

Colonel von Kressenstein wisely chose to change the subject. Crossing one long, booted leg over the other he turned to Hans Werner, 'Lieutenant-Colonel Rilke here has something to report that you might find of interest.'

Jemel looked down at the table and tried, not very successfully, to stifle a yawn. They had been here over three hours and it was past lunch time. Didn't these infidel satan-worshippers ever get hungry?

Hans Werner rose swiftly. 'With respect, Excellency, German intelligence has reason to suspect military leaks to the British.'

Jemel Pasha said nothing, but pulled irritably on his black beard. German intelligence. It was always German something or other. How he would enjoy stripping these arrogant bastards naked and trundling them through the streets on a dung cart. With an effort he met Rilke's eyes and kept his voice low. 'In which case, why doesn't your military intelligence do something about it? Espionage is not my business.'

'With respect, Excellency,' Kressenstein leapt in; 'anything that affects the Fourth Army which marches under your glorious name . . .'

'Very well, yes, yes.' Everyone heard the little gurgle his stomach made, and he coughed to cover the noise. 'So what is all this about, Rilke?'

In crisp, neat words, Rilke summed up how it seemed that the British had an almost uncanny knack of knowing their next move, and outmanoeuvring them. They were also bombing, with pinpoint accuracy, the gasoline and ammunition dumps. It was all more than coincidence could explain. 'There is no hard evidence that an espionage operation does exist,' he concluded; 'but there is enough circumstantial evidence to cause us some disquiet.'

He looked at Jemel Pasha for some sort of response, but the Turk was staring fixedly at his pocket watch, which sat open on the table in front of him. It was nearing the sacred hour of kif-siesta. It appeared that these infidels did not eat or sleep. He clapped his large red hands together, his sharp eyes darting round the room. 'If there is such an operation I guarantee we will find and destroy those running it. By Allah and the Prophet, if such a disgrace exists it will be run to ground and torn up by the roots. On that, gentlemen, you have my word.'

And before anyone had a chance to bring up another subject he rose to his feet and, followed by the devoted Osman, strode to the door. 'Espionage indeed,' he muttered to himself as soon as he was safely out of the door. 'They always thought themselves so clever. Clever indeed – they managed to blow up their own wireless station, didn't they!'

This thought cheered him considerably through his late and hasty lunch, but, later, lying on his uncomfortable bed unable to enjoy his kif, his thoughts turned again to Rilke's words. What if such a network did exist and was discovered by the Germans? He'd look an unutterable fool. As he shifted his bulk in the narrow bed, doubts began to nag him. What Rilke had said made sense; Jemel hated coincidences, just didn't believe in them.

'A curse on them all,' he muttered and, giving up the hope of a sleep, rose and quickly scrawled a note to Hamid Bek in Jaffa. There was a man with a nose sensitive enough to sniff out any subversion. Jemel trusted the policeman and, more importantly, his methods, completely. He sealed the envelope fiercely and called for Osman. 'See this gets to the chief of police immediately – top priority,' he said, pushing the letter into his bodyguard's hands.

Then he lay back on the bed and, having done all he could, closed his eyes and promptly forgot all about the subject.

Hamid Bek folded the letter from Jemel Pasha into a neat rectangle and leaned back in his chair, bending his bastinado whip almost on two and smiling in grisly satisfaction. 'I want the most rigorous inquiry . . . do everything necessary . . . I want to hear no more about it until those responsible are hanged.' And nor would he.

The police chief crossed to the window and looked out, the

444

whip tapping rhythmically on his boot. He had no evidence at all. It was instinct only that told him the Levinsons and their locust patrol were not all they seemed. However good an egg looked, if it stank there was something wrong. The Levinsons stank. But they looked good. His thoughts returned to the woman, her heavy breasts straining against the confines of a demure blouse. One day soon, very soon now, he would rip off the fabric and see those breasts tumble like ripe peaches into his waiting hands. His features coarsened and he felt himself swell and harden as he experienced an almost religious glow at the fantasy. Oh yes, it would be soon now. He checked his erotic thoughts and returned to the desk. First he must search for some tangible evidence.

All haste is the devil's, he reminded himself. All haste is the devil's.

It was a warm, breathless June evening. The air hung still and heavy, sweet with the scent of roses and lavender from the garden. Sara had given herself a holiday for this one day, her birthday, and, leaving all responsibility behind her at Atlit, she and Abu had saddled the horses and ridden up to Zichron in the middle of the morning.

The flower gardens had been left to run wild over the past two summers, but now that Zichron was filled with over a thousand refugees from Tel Aviv and Jaffa there were plenty of volunteers willing to show their gratitude in some way, and the gardens were gradually being tidied back to their former glory. Sara had not minded the lush wildness, but she knew how it pleased her father to see the gardens brought back to civilisation.

Zichron's numbers had doubled overnight: every house had taken people in and the wine cellars and school house served as dormitories to the rest. Abram Levinson had taken into his house a young widow with her two small boys. Sara liked Rachel Abromovitz and now they were sitting together on the veranda, Rachel quietly patching one of her son's trousers while Sara watched the two boys playing leapfrog on the lawn and Ruth helped Fatma lay the table behind her.

At the other end of the veranda Sara's father and her brother Sam were as usual bickering in a companionable way with Doctor Ephraim. He had called in to wish a happy birthday to the girl he had delivered twenty-five years before, but her day had not been a happy one – or, at any rate, having started well, it had threatened to fall around her. An hour ago she had realised that Joe was not going to turn up for the celebratory dinner, and ever since she had been moody, her heart restless.

Joe had left for Beirut two weeks before, just after the visit of the contact ship. His trip was partly on his own business and partly in answer to a request from the British to find out how many submarines were kept in the German base there. Although both of them knew he would be hard-pressed, Joe had made a point of mentioning to Sara that he would return in time for her birthday. Silently watching the sun move west, Sara sighed inaudibly and gave up the last hope. She closed her eyes and leant back in her chair, feeling the last rays of sun warming her lids. Instantly her mind focused on Joe and she felt a sharp stab of pain twist her heart. Hesitantly, and against her will, she accepted that she had fallen in love with him.

Since he had left she had been in the grip of an aching longing for him: without him her life seemed eerily empty. She missed his smiles, his warmth, even his teasing. Joe's very presence at the station, and his involvement in so many aspects of her life was having a profound effect on her. They worked so well together, understood each other so fundamentally, responded to each other's unspoken questions and worries. For the first time in her life she had found herself dependent on a man.

This feeling surprised Sara, even vexed her, and she fought to suppress it. She valued Joe's opinion and listened to his advice – at his request she had even given up going to the shore to meet the boat. She was now at that stage of love where passionate joy, total despair and self-indulgent analysis followed each other in a frenzy. The despair came because, although she understood Joe's intellectual thought processes, she did not understand him. He was still a complete enigma to her, a playing card lying face down. For all his rakish posture he had made no attempt to seduce her, had never even suggested anything untoward. He remained charming, friendly and totally relaxed with her, like a brother – damn it.

She shivered, remembering his lazy cat-eyed smile. Sometimes she caught him watching her thoughtfully and had to stifle the impulse to reach out and touch him – tell him what was in her heart. But her pride intervened, and she shrank like a snail from taking the first step. The real source of her trepidation was her fear that Joe did not share her feelings – had lost interest in her. Her heart froze at the thought. *Oh Joe, where are you*, she thought, wishing that she could open her eyes and see him standing there, magically transported from goodness knows where. But she knew he would not come now, and struggled with the disappointment which threatened to engulf her. She was lonely without him, lovesick and lost.

She opened her eyes, determining to shake off all thought of Joe Lanski. *Stop being foolish, Sara Cohen*, a small voice nudged at the back of her mind. *He'll be back tomorrow, or the day after.* A deep glow of happiness spread over her heart at the thought and she stood up, deciding that even if it was a holiday it was time she lent a hand in the kitchen.

'Sara!' Doctor Ephraim's voice stopped her in her tracks and she waited as he crossed the veranda to her side. 'Sara, I believe we must talk,' he said, laying a hand on her arm and looking at her with a mixture of pity and concern.

She felt a pang of anxiety. 'Of course,' she said. 'Is it do with Papa?'

'In a way,' he answered. Then, gesturing discreetly at Rachel, said, 'Can we talk alone?'

Sara nodded, puzzled, and let the old man lead her to the front of the house. As soon as they were out of earshot he stopped and faced her.

'I have been asked by the Zichron council to have a word with you about certain rumours they have heard,' he looked extremely serious. 'Rumours that a British ship is calling monthly at Atlit bringing gold and medical supplies in exchange for military information.'

Sara stared at him blankly, her heart racing, her mind telling her to *say nothing, keep calm, give nothing away*.

'We have heard,' the doctor continued, 'that you are a part of the group supplying intelligence.'

'That is preposterous,' Sara said fiercely. 'The very idea is ridiculous. It's just thoughtless, malicious gossip – and very dangerous gossip at that. I'm surprised you listened.'

Don't overplay it, her inner voice warned. *Careful.*

Doctor Ephraim looked at her, his gaze direct and unwavering. 'That is as may be,' he said. 'But it does not take away from the fact that people are talking and the council is naturally worried that a daughter of the village might be involved.' He breathed out heavily. 'If these rumours reach the Turk, it will not only be you that is in danger. Your father and brother, of course, but the whole village would be called to trial. Do you realise that?'

Sara tried desperately to collect her thoughts. How much did they really know? Did they have facts or was it just gossip? They must have facts, she concluded desperately. This is a warning to hold off. Her heart sank. She would just have to try and bluff her way out of trouble. 'Really, Doctor Ephraim,' she said with a wry laugh; 'me a spy for the British! Does it seem likely?' she gave another little laugh, but it caught in her throat.

Doctor Ephraim looked at her sharply. 'I hope for all our sakes that you are speaking the truth. Espionage is not the business of Jews, and now of all times it is imperative that we keep the Turk's attention away from us. If there is any truth at all in these rumours then, please stop this work at once. You know what it will lead to, Sara. More hangings, more massacres.' There was a small pause. 'I'm sorry, Sara, but I had to mention this to you,' he concluded wearily.

'That's all right, Doctor,' Sara said, covering her disquiet with a smile. 'Of course I understand the council's concern but rest assured that if there is such an espionage group it has absolutely nothing to do with me – nor, as far as I know, anyone else at Atlit. Now tell me,' she changed the subject quickly and took his arm; 'are you staying for my birthday dinner?'

'Thank you, my dear, but I still have a few patients to visit. What a pity none of the refugees was a doctor, eh? I could do with a helping hand now.'

They walked back to the veranda, where he kissed her cheeks, wishing her a happy year again, and said his goodbyes to the rest of the company. Sara watched him, feeling so heavy with worry that she could barely breathe. If only Joe would come home! She felt a desperate need to unburden herself to Sam and Robby but, forcing herself to think straight, she could see no point in frightening them yet. She could not see that there was any danger – unless Hamid Bek or one of his minions had heard the rumours. She began to feel sick. But no, no Jew informs on another. Not to the Turk.

The big question was whether the British intended to launch another attack soon. If not, perhaps they should suspend their work for a while, halt the ship for a few months until suspicion died down, and then take up where they left off. She must write to Aaron, he must decide. And meanwhile Joe would help, whenever he came back.

'Come on, everyone. Dinner's ready,' Ruth called cheerfully

from the double windows, and with a heavy heart Sara led the way in.

Sara barely touched her dinner, but drank more than usual. She tried to shake off her mood and chat to Ruth who, pregnant again, was sitting next to her making fine work of Fatma's cooking. But try as she might she could not forget the doctor's words and could not help worrying as she looked at her family and friends sitting so happily around the table. Was it really necessary to endanger their lives and probably the lives of everyone living in Zichron? She did not fool herself into doubting for a moment what the Turk would do if they discovered spies behind the lines. She took another sip of wine, and gave her father a sidelong glance. What would his attitude be if he knew? Anger? Pride? Disapproval? She dared not tell him, and could not begin to guess at his response.

'Are you ill or just daydreaming?' Ruth nudged her. 'Fatma just asked you what was wrong with the food.'

Sara straightened herself in her chair. 'Nothing, it was delicious, Fatma, but I'm not very hungry.' Fatma clucked and scowled, but held her tongue.

'Are you all right?' Ruth asked quietly, gently touching Sara's arm. 'You look – well, upset.' She waited expectantly, her brows puckered.

Sara drained her glass: the wine was at last beginning to relax and cheer her and she gave Ruth a real smile. 'I'm fine, really I am. Just a little . . .'

Footsteps on the veranda outside stopped the conversation and everyone looked expectantly at the French windows. Sara felt her heart skip a beat, then a rush of happiness surged through her. He had come – he was here. She was secure again, protected from the Turk and the Zichron council alike.

'Anyone would think I'd just woken up from the dead,' Joe said, standing in the doorway and smiling widely. He greeted everyone, apologising for being late, effortlessly the centre of attention. A moment later he was by her side, his green eyes reflecting his own obvious delight at seeing her. She felt the slow, burning heat that always surfaced whenever Joe was close to her and struggled to maintain her composure.

'A happy birthday, Sara. Until a hundred and twenty,' he said, kissing her cheek lightly as he spoke the Jewish birthday wish. She felt her cheek flush under his lips, and stood up quickly.

'I'll lay you a place, you must be very hungry.'

'Thank you, but I'll just have a drink.'

'Come and sit over here,' said Sam, pulling a chair forward between Rachel and himself. 'I'd like you to meet the prettiest mother in Zichron.'

Joe grinned, raised an eyebrow at Sara and moved down the table.

'So what's going on between you and Joe Lanski?' Ruth whispered, watching Sara carefully.

'Nothing,' Sara said, calmly refilling her glass.

'Come on – the way you looked at each other, I thought you were about to fall into each other's arms.'

'Nonsense,' said Sara, sipping the wine and shifting uncomfortably in her chair. She was relieved she was sitting down. The impact of seeing him had thrown her and she was spinning with the stars.

Ruth chuckled. 'You, my friend, have never been any good at masking your emotions. Well, I hope there is a romance going on – I think Joe Lanski would be the best thing that could happen to you.'

'Well, I'm sorry to disappoint you, but we are just good friends,' Sara said stiffly. The look on her face made Ruth burst out laughing.

'What's so funny?' Robby asked, putting an arm round Ruth's shoulders with a friendly look at Sara.

'Just girl talk,' Sara answered swiftly.

It was over an hour before Sara and Joe were by themselves in the kitchen, the Woolfs gone home and everyone else was in bed. The house was quiet. Sultan whined in the kennel outside and the clock ticked noisily.

'How was the journey?' Sara asked at last.

Joe shot her an amused look. 'Lonely. Did you miss me?'

'Not a bit,' she said with a slow smile.

He laughed softly and reached across the table to squeeze her arm. 'Come on, let's go for a walk. We'll talk outside.'

They walked slowly out of the house and towards the courtyard. The moon was bright and a faint breeze had blown up, bringing the salt smell of the Mediterranean with it. Sara told Joe what the doctor had said, the warning behind his words. As she spoke, she felt immeasurably relieved. They stopped beside the white wicker gate, Joe's face pensive.

'If they want to talk, let them,' he said at last. 'I don't believe they have any facts, otherwise the council would have approached your father. They were shooting in the dark, hoping to frighten a confession out of you.'

'Do you think so?'

'I hope so.' He said quietly. 'But we had better move with extreme caution from now on. The Turk seems to be clamping down on travel – Bek's men are stopping everyone for their permits.'

He looked at Sara and broke off abruptly. She looked so young, so vulnerable and so stunningly lovely that his heart clenched. He realised that he was so wildly, so passionately in love her that he could contain his feelings no longer. Before he could stop himself he pulled her towards him and, tilting her face to his, gazed down into her eyes. He had to know if she loved him, wanted him, as he did her.

She made no attempt to avoid his eyes: she was mesmerisingly, heart-stoppingly in love with him and could not pretend otherwise any longer.

Spellbound, they gazed at each other and saw the desire of the other so clearly that it was as though they had exchanged a vow. With a low moan Joe pulled her close to him, and then his mouth was on hers, his kisses long, slow and passionate. Sara clung to him, responding with such wild longing that it took them both by surprise. On the verge of losing control, Joe pulled away from her. They stared at each other breathlessly, shaken by the intensity of their feelings.

Regaining some measure of composure, Joe looked down into those blue eyes that had captivated him for so long and smiled that lazy smile she knew so well. 'I was just remembering the first time I saw you . . . at that dance. I said to Ivan Bernski that you had eyes worth hanging for – and I'll be damned if that doesn't turn into a prophecy!'

Her face changed, became stricken, hurt. 'Don't say that, for God's sake please don't say that,' she whispered urgently. Responding swiftly to the panic on her face he laughed softly and drew her towards him again, gently now, kissing her tenderly, deeply, until she was caught up in another blissful wave of desire.

Joe's kisses suddenly stopped and he grasped her arm, peering into the darkness behind her. Sara stared up at him dizzily.

'What is it?' she asked. Sultan began to bark and Sara pulled reluctantly back from Joe.

'Someone is riding up the hill,' Joe said and turned back to Sara, caressing her cheek as he spoke. 'Wait for me in the kitchen. I have a feeling they're coming here.'

Fifteen minutes later Sara, waiting in the unlit kitchen, heard the door squeak open. She jumped to her feet as Joe walked slowly in and ran swiftly to his side. Even in the half light she could see from his expression that something was very wrong. 'What is it? What's happened?' Her tone was flat with dread.

Joe looked down at her for a moment and took her hand. 'Lev's been arrested.'

Sara felt her knees turn to jelly and slumped into the nearest chair. 'Oh, my God,' she gasped, sinking her face in her hands to ward off the images of arrest, of prison, of worse. 'When? How?' she faltered, in a tiny, tinny voice.

Joe answered matter-of-factly. 'Two days ago. He was heading for Jerusalem when a Turkish patrol stopped him and asked him for his travel papers.' He paused for a moment, then continued wearily. 'He was searched. They found several gold sovereigns hidden in his boots – one dated 1916, minted, therefore, during the war. They believe it comes from Britain – Arab revolt gold – and have arrested him for spying.'

There was a small silence and Sara lowered her hands from her face, making a stupendous effort to control herself. 'What shall we do?' she asked helplessly.

'I might – just might – be able to get him out. It will cost, of course. With luck I could get some Turkish acquaintances of mine to get him moved to another prison – and we can try to kidnap him on the journey. I don't know. It's going to be hard, perhaps impossible. It depends a great deal on what he's said so far.'

Sara shuddered. 'Lev wouldn't mention names,' she said, and tailed off into doubt. It was a forlorn hope; they all knew how few people were capable of withstanding torture.

'Sara,' Joe spoke gently; 'I don't doubt Lev's courage for a moment. But we both know the Turk's methods.'

Sara jumped up, horror at last giving her the energy she needed. 'Joe! Don't talk like that! Lev . . .' Her eyes unexpectedly filled with tears and her lip trembled.

With one step Joe was beside her and his arms round her. 'I'm sorry,' he muttered, pressing her face to his chest and stroking her hair. She clung to him willingly, closing her eyes against the reality of what had happened.

'I'm scared, Joe. Frightened . . . not just for Lev . . . for all of us.'

'You, frightened? Nonsense!' Joe said soothingly, and tipped up her face, searching for her expression. 'This is a difficult and troubling situation. But I think you can manage it – can't you?'

Sara nodded and sighed. 'Yes. I can handle it. At least I think I can.' Her throat was so sore with restrained tears that her voice was only a whisper.

'Good,' said Joe approvingly and he fished in his pocket and found a handkerchief. 'Here, blow your nose.'

Sara sniffed into the handkerchief and handed it back with a wan smile. She pulled her fingers through her hair and nodded. 'There. I'm all right now. What do you want me to do?'

It was Joe's turn to sit at the table, head in hands as he thought hard. 'Well, the first thing to do is to send the pigeon post to Egypt. Let Aaron know what has happened and see if he can arrange for the contact ship to arrive twice a month. We might have to evacuate our key members in a hurry. Have you got that?'

Sara nodded dumbly.

'I must go now. Above all, we must know if Lev has broken and if so how much he has said. I'll let you know any news as fast as possible.' He stood and gently brushed a stray lock of hair from her cheek. 'If there is any hint of a problem leave the station and come back here to Zichron. And please, I beg you, be careful.' He took her hand and kissed it briefly. With a glimmer of a grin he added, 'I'm not saying that I can't live without you, Sara – but I would prefer not to have to.' Then he had vanished through the door into the night.

Sara stood where she was, rooted to the spot, until she heard the faint clopping of his horse's hooves fade down the road to the valley.

After four hours of unconsciousness the cold stone of the cell floor penetrated through Lev's pain and he woke. He lay still, in a sea of unimaginable pain. They had meticulously broken each bone in his right hand and beaten his feet to a bloody pulp. He vaguely wondered whether he would ever walk again.

He had not spoken. But he knew that soon they would come for him again and a wave of pure fear wrenched at his innards. What next? His other hand? His testicles? He did not know how much longer he would be able to hold out against the pain, how long it would be before he would lose the images of Sara, of Manny and Aaron ... and with them all sense of reality. He did not think he could find the reserves of strength to survive much longer without squealing like a pig. His heart almost cracked in despair.

Lev forced himself to fight the pain and dragged himself into a squat. He crawled to the wall and pushed himself up against it. Rats shrieked as he interrupted their feasting on the loaves that were thrown in to him. His eyes were too swollen for him to see the rodents, the pain too great to know if they bit him as he shuffled past. The food meant that someone was passing money around, but Lev knew by now that the only response to the bribes would be the bread. They were not going to let him go, no matter how much illegal money they tucked into their boots.

Then, in the foggy wasteland of his mind, he made a connection. He remembered the shard of glass hidden in today's loaf. He had not understood then, thought it was a new torture, but now ... On his knees, his right hand tucked protectively close to his body, he felt round the floor with his left hand. Then he found it, cold and sharp against his fingers. Suddenly the pain receded and he was at peace.

His life for Sara's.

His soul for hers.

It was not too late.

Sara always had one answer to worry: work. In the days following Joe's departure she worked harder than ever before, finding jobs from nowhere if necessary. Anything was better than having time to think. And there was plenty of work to do. Without consulting her or anyone else Sam had joined her at Atlit. The news of Lev's arrest spread like fire within the Jewish community and as soon as it reached Manny, he returned, keeping himself well within the confines of the research station.

Although they all shared the same thoughts, the worry was so intense that none of them was able to discuss Lev or his fate. Nor could they meet each other's eyes without seeing their own agony mirrored. None of them could forget that while they were free Lev was lying bound and beaten – tortured – maybe dead, and they could not push aside the fear of what was to happen if – when – Lev cracked.

Sara was not the only one to try and wear herself out with work: there was plenty to do in the fields and Sam and Manny organised, worked, and accounted themselves into deathly, unrefreshing sleep every night. And Sara worked on the farm and in the house, at the cleaning, accounting and paperwork. The rugs must be beaten, the curtains washed, Bella needed a grooming and her tack must be polished. There was always more to be done. Others urged them to slow down, to take a break, to pause, but a pause was the one thing none of them could face.

The likelihood of Lev remaining silent was minimal: they knew that. But they also knew that even if he did not speak, the Turk would be suspicious. It was well known that Lev worked at the station. If he was under suspicion, so would be his working mates and friends. From now on they were all in permanent danger.

Sara, under hourly fear of a raid, changed all the hiding places in the middle of the night. She could have done it by day, but despite her hard work she could never sleep for more than a few hours and was grateful for a job she could do without waking anyone else. Her dreams had come back. The nightmare of the train journey to Aleppo and the running, desperate woman. For, however hard she tried to numb her brain during the day, she could not force away her panic in the night. And so she would go to bed, sleep restlessly and dreamlessly for an hour or two and then, sinking deeper into sleep, fall back into the old nightmare and wake, screaming and drenched with sweat.

Despite this, despite all their fears, they had agreed that now was not the time to call a halt to the group's work. If they sent out word to stop now it would spread only panic and confusion, and matters were unsettled enough in the wake of Lev's arrest. So they decided to work on, waiting for news from Joe and hoping against hope that he would have organised Lev's escape.

Five days after Joe left, Ali arrived at the station. Alone. He brought with him the news of Lev's suicide, and broke it to Sara as she stood alone in her study. She grasped the chair in front of her for support, her mind a screaming blank as it refused to take in Ali's words. But she looked at the boy's face, normally so cheery and cheeky, and now peering at her half afraid, half anxious, and she knew that he was telling the truth.

'Dead? Lev dead?' her voice was an unrecognisable croak.

Ali took a step forward and gently touched Sara's arm, and the small compassionate gesture finally broke her control. With a choking cry she sank to the chair, her face in her hands. Lev. Poor Lev who had courted her from her childhood, who cracked his knuckles when he was excited or thoughtful and whose love and protectiveness towards her had done nothing but madden her. Lev was dead. He had killed himself to save them. To save her. To save them all.

She did not hear the door open, hear Ali's garbled explanation or Manny's quick step crossing the room. She did not feel Manny taking her shoulders or hear him saying her name. She stared up at him with unseeing eyes, the blue darker and more intense than ever before, and she said over and over again: 'I hate them. I hate them . . . I hate them . . .'

The news of Lev's death made each of them doubly determined to carry on with the network. The only way they could exact retribution for Lev was through ultimate success. But at the same time they began to work out plans for escape against the day when it was impossible for them to stay in the country. The planning took a great deal of thought: too many people could not be evacuated together, or suspicion would fall on the inhabitants of Zichron.

Sara was determined that the first to leave should be Robby and his family. Robby was equally determined that Sara should leave with Ruth and Abigail while he stayed behind. 'You are in the most danger, Sara, because of Aaron and Daniel. The minute anything goes wrong you should go.' Sara smiled but did not answer. There was no chance of her leaving and she was now so consumed with hatred that she felt no fear. She knew that nothing would ever persuade her father to leave the land that he and her mother had brought from stones to fruition, and she knew that for her to leave without him would confirm all the Turk's suspicions and be the death blow to Zichron. And aside from anything else she wanted to be there when the Turk was crushed; she wanted to see the English march in victorious, and know that she had played a part in that victory.

It remained to be seen who arrived first: the English or Hamid Bek. As Sara waited she was almost detached, curious.

The afternoon was blazingly hot; the heat brutal and hard. Sara crossed the courtyard, bending by habit to pull up grass and weeds that had pushed their way up between the cobbles. She paused at the sound of running feet, and looked up to see Ali hurtling towards her from his post overlooking the road to the station. Her heart lifted. For one moment she thought that Joe was back; she needed him so desperately it hurt.

One look at Ali's face told her it was not Joe returning, and she pushed back her disappointment and asked mildly, 'What is it?' She immediately thought they were being raided, and felt the alarm rising in her, but did not want the boy to see it.

'There is a man with a wagon and two horses,' he panted. 'He is coming up the palms.' Sara relaxed and straightened her straw hat. The septieh would never arrive in a wagon. She smiled at Ali affectionately and patted his shoulder. 'Come on, let's go and see who it is.' They walked together to the gate, Ali hovering attentively at her side. Ever since her return to the station his attitude to her had changed, and Sara wondered whether Joe had said something to him or whether he had drawn his own conclusions about the dual role of the station. Whatever the reason for the change, she was grateful for it and pleased with Ali's usefulness and affection.

She leaned against the gate and stared down the road, smiling when she saw that the visitor was Natan Shapira. He had a long way to come to the station, so his visit must be important, but she was always pleased to see him. He was a carter with the Army around Beersheba and was in the extraordinary position of having free access everywhere. He was one of the few civilian carters not to desert when the pay began to dry up – but he did not need the Army's money, only its cover. He was a key member of the information gathering group.

Sara took him up to her study and then sat him down with a cup of fig tea. Looking into his eyes, she said, 'Lev is dead – did you know?'

The young carter lowered his head a moment, then nodded. After a second he looked at Sara again and said softly, 'Don't lose heart, Sara. They will pay for this one day. If I have anything to do with it the day will be soon.'

Then he opened a bag of salt he had brought with him and feeling inside it found a small square of folded paper, which he handed to Sara. 'I know the ship is expected in a couple of days so I travelled here non-stop to bring you this. I felt it was too important to wait for the next ship.'

Sara smoothed out the sheet and stared at the map drawn on it. She recognised it instantly as a roughly-drawn but accurate plan of

Turkish Gaza. 'What do those circles show?' she asked with a puzzled look.

A slow smile spread across Natan's face, the first she had seen since his arrival. 'They are the top-secret dug-outs of the Turkish machine guns,' he answered proudly. Sara gazed at him in amazement, and looked back down at the map in her hand. There were literally dozens of them. She jumped to her feet and ran round the desk to kiss Natan on the cheek. 'Bless you,' she said warmly and shook her head with a smile. 'But you shouldn't have taken such a risk.'

'Oh,' he answered dismissively, 'nothing ventured nothing gained with those snakes. Besides,' he added as he stood up, 'it made me feel better – you know, Lev and everything.' Sara nodded. She understood only too well.

'Will you stay the night?'

'No, I'd better be off. I'm on my way to Haifa.' He kissed Sara shyly on the forehead. 'Take care of yourself. You're looking tired.'

He gathered his things together but then paused for a moment. 'There is something else,' he said. 'I don't know but it may be important. The Turks have just caught two Christian Arabs in Nazareth – they were spying for the French. Apparently, they were brought in from Egypt a month or so ago and dropped at the old Phoenician Harbour outside Haifa. They've confessed everything, including the date the French ship is due to pick them up. The Turk intends to sink it.'

Sara felt a rush of anger at the French stupidity. They should have known that the communities in Palestine were small and any strangers would be marked men. 'Damn them,' she muttered to herself; and asked Natan, 'When is the ship expected?'

'Tomorrow night, I think.'

As soon as Natan had made his farewells and left, Sara went into the now unused laboratory and rummaged round in a tin at the back of a drawer until she found a tiny metal cylinder. Then she returned to the study and carefully wrote out in code all that Natan had told her about the French ship. She rolled the paper up neatly and fitted it into the cylinder. It was nearly four o'clock: in half an hour the station should be clear of workers. If she released the pigeon at five it should reach the British Headquarters in Egypt by half-past seven, when it was still light. Good. She would send the pigeon and trust to the wind and its speed.

Sara sat for half an hour in unaccustomed laziness, looking out of the window and watching the workers gradually set off home. Then she walked slowly out of the station and took the path that led to the back of the buildings, where the pigeons lived in a cot among wooden sheds that housed old agricultural equipment. Few of the workers ever came this way and the spot overlooked the sea.

It was too hot to rush, and she had a little time in hand, so she dawdled along, breathing in the beauty round her. A sense of peacefulness filled her, calming her for the first time in days. In the burning July sun the land had a hypnotic quality and Sara could not avoid falling under its spell. The still air was full of the noise of grasshoppers and birds and she heard a sudden rush of wings as a flock of purple heron flew overhead. Sara loved this land with her heart and with her soul. It was not the fertile green of ancient Eden but, as her eye swept the landscape from the sea to the blue inland hills of Ephraim, her heart rose in response to the austere beauty of her country. And in among the untamed wildness was the ordered softness of the land on which man had made his mark, neat fields and rows of vines.

' "And the Lord said unto him," ' Sara quoted softly; ' "this is the land which I sware unto Abraham unto Isaac and unto Jacob saying I will give it unto thy seed." ' She smiled at her sentimentality and pulled herself together, moving forward intent on her purpose.

There were only three birds left in the dovecot, and Sara was careful to latch the door behind her. The pigeons had on the whole been more trouble than they were worth, several of them returning a few days after their release with the cylinders still attached, others wandering miles from their destination. Ruth had seen one drinking at her water tank at Zichron, and they had no idea how many others had chosen freedom rather than making the journey to Egypt. Sara had decided that they were more dangerous than worthwhile, and had asked Aaron not to send any more, but now she was glad of them. She considered the three birds, and her eye fell on Alice, who sat quietly on her perch in a corner of the cot. Sara picked her up and counted her flight feathers. They were all there, and intact. The message would be entrusted to Alice.

Holding the pigeon to her chest, Sara attached the cylinder to the bird's leg. Then she took the bird out of the cot, quickly checking that they were not being watched. She stroked Alice's head for a moment and threw her into the air, hands outstretched to send her on her way. Alice circled once as though to check her bearings and then flew away, along the coast to Caesarea. Sara watched her go, shading her eyes from the sun. Then she turned back to the house, mentally running through the list of things she must get through before bed, and praying that Alice would not fail them.

Alice flew for about thirty miles south, her instinct for home unerring, when something in her homing mechanism snapped. Suddenly confused, she wheeled and circled in the air like a bird of prey until, drawn by the cooing of other pigeons beneath her, she moved inland and floated down on an air pocket, wings outstretched. She fell in a long swoop from the sky to a courtyard where, fluttering her wings and calling, she joined a flock of pigeons being fed corn by an old Arab.

Selim Hamid eyed the newcomer with expert interest. The bird had a good, bold head and dark mahogany legs set strong and low in her body. The old man had often noticed birds flying south overhead, but this was the first to join his flock. He was sure that it was no wild bird, but a pet. Clucking softly, Selim Hamid crept up on the happily feeding bird until he was close enough to sweep her up in one hand. He felt something cold and hard among the feathers and, turning her over, he found the cylinder attached to the leg. He took it off and opened it to find a piece of paper covered in squiggles. Selim Hamid could not read and looked at it perplexed, wondering what to do next. Then he replaced it in its cylinder and put it in his pocket. He would show it to his master Hamid Bek on his return from Jaffa next week. He smiled happily. Who knew? This bird in the hand might bring him a reward. He went back to feeding the pigeons.

Sara had taken to spending an hour or so in the evening with Frieda in the kitchen. Life was very quiet at the station these days, with the workers going home in mid-afternoon and the others away – or dead. Sara was worried that Frieda might become lonely and was loath to admit to herself that she was more lonely than she had been since the early months of her marriage in Constantinople. So after dinner at six, eaten with Abu, Ezra and Ali, Sara would take her workbox to the kitchen and chat before going up to her study for more paperwork.

Tonight the two women sat in silence, Sara darning and Frieda sprawled in her chair beside the open window. The clock struck eight and Frieda sat up with a jerk. 'I must have dropped off,' she mumbled.

'Don't worry, Frieda,' Sara said, putting down the nightgown she had been working on, 'I'll lock up. You go to bed, you look exhausted.'

The sound of a horse's whinny brought her head up sharply. Goliath barked once, then listened: suddenly he was whining. There was only one person he would make that sound for, Sara suddenly thought. Joe!

She was overcome by a dizzying wave of first relief, then excitement. Sara tore up the stairs to her study, her heart singing and soaring with joy. She threw open the windows, breathing in the cool night air and then, realising she must look a mess, ran to her room, unpinned her hair and roughly brushed it. She pinned it back up with practised fingers, studying herself in the mirror. There was no denying that she was not at her best. She bit her lips and pinched her cheeks until they were a glowing pink, sprayed herself with some of Fatma's home-distilled lavender water. She walked more sedately back to the study, closing her eyes for a moment and willing herself to stay calm. Her head pounded, and she could hear footsteps on the stairs. She opened her eyes and told herself not to be silly. The door creaked open and her heart seemed to stop before racing even faster.

Joe stood in the doorway, larger than life and staggeringly handsome. He smiled at her, his slow, lazy smile. She tried to say something, but the words died in her throat as their eyes met and spoke in a language much older than words.

'Joe . . .' Her heart thumped in her ears as she flew across the room into his arms. He pulled her tightly against him, in an embrace that would never end, so close she could barely breathe.

'I wanted to see you so desperately,' he said swiftly; 'I've been nearly mad with worry about you.' He lifted her face to his, his eyes flickering over her face, drinking it in. 'I love you, Sara, I've always loved you. If you let me, I'll love you as much as ever a man loved a woman.'

'And I love you,' she whispered, knowing with full certainty that she wanted to spend the rest of her life with this man.

He moved his hand up her back and held her by the nape of her neck, his eyes searching hers. 'Say it again, Sara,' he commanded. 'Tell me again.'

461

'I love you, Joe,' she whispered, her breathing so quick that she could hardly speak. 'I love you,' she repeated as, slowly and with infinite tenderness, he began to pull the pins from her hair. Released, the honey-blonde thickness cascaded down her back.

'And?' he asked, running his fingers through the silky length.

'And I want you,' she gasped, the desire flooding through her, melting her bones with its heat. She brought her face up to his and their lips met, his mouth demanding and relentless on hers. Then, pulling back, he smiled down at her. 'Let's make up for lost time,' he said, bending to pull her into his arms. He carried her along the corridor to his room, talking low and sweet into her ear.

As he kicked the door shut behind them, Sara knew without any doubt that she belonged to this man and that Joe Lanski was to be the violent and devouring passion of her life.

Sara woke as the first faint light filtered through the window, and eased herself up in bed. She looked down at Joe, lying beside her on the crumpled sheets, and felt a wave of love stronger than anything she had ever known wash over her. She had never been this happy in her whole life before: never before had she been in love and been happy at the same time. She loved the blue of growing beard on Joe's chin, she loved his warm, fresh mouth, his extraordinary passion, his sexuality, his tenderness. Over the last six days he had become part of her blood, of her life. In Joe's arms she could forget everything else: Lev's death, Daniel, Hamid Bek, it all gave way before the overpowering sexual magic between them and the discovery of their growing love.

She resisted the urge to run her fingers over the tanned muscles of his chest and cover him with kisses. She must go back to her room. She watched him for a moment longer, counting her blessings. Even the ship had brought the good news for which they had all been waiting. A strategic plan of attack had been formulated and a major new offensive would begin towards the end of October. The war must finish soon.

Aaron had written ecstatically: 'In Allenby we at last have a commander who will lead us to victory. His qualities of common sense, military logic and relentless energy are so great that he has already stamped his personality on us all and the Army's morale has risen almost overnight.' The news gave them all a boost too: within a few months they would be able to break up the network and join forces with the conquering army. After the blow of Lev's death this hope gave them the spirit to carry on.

Joe moved slightly in his sleep and Sara felt a slide of dismay. Today he was leaving the station. The ship had brought more gold and medicine with it, but the Hashomer had not come to collect it. The medicine was desperately needed and it was dangerous to keep the gold hidden at Atlit. Presumably, the leaders of the Hashomer had decided that, in the wake of Lev's arrest and suicide, it would be too hazardous to be seen at Atlit, but Joe had come up with a novel way of carrying the gold across the country.

The Turk was terrified of disease so, bearing this in mind, Joe had asked Abu to knock up a cheap, false-bottomed coffin. Ali was to lie in it and play the part of a corpse, dead of cholera. The coffin was to be loaded on to a cart which Abu would drive to the Italian hospital in Haifa – one of those in most urgent need of medicine. The cart was leaving today, with Joe riding alongside as guard.

Sara sighed and pushed her worry about the trip to the back of her mind, sliding carefully out of bed. Her movement woke Joe, who opened his eyes and lay still, his face awash with pleasure, as he watched her move naked across the room to where her dressing gown lay tumbled on the floor. She was beautiful. But, for the first time in his life, a woman's beauty was a bonus, not just the reason for seeing her. He felt that her voice alone, her eyes, her hair, would be enough to make him love her just as entirely.

'Madame,' he said in a sleepy, bantering voice; 'you are the most beautiful woman I've ever known.' He grinned as his eyes swept over her body. Sara blushed and laughed, pulling on her gown and tying it tightly round the waist. 'I love you and want you,' he went on and then commanded; 'come back to bed this minute, woman.'

Sara hesitated a moment, torn between the need to fulfil the desire she felt for him and worry at being caught in Joe's room. Then she shook her head, 'I can't, Joe. If I stay any longer it will only mean trouble.'

'Won't you ever do anything I tell you without arguing the point?' he asked, in mock crossness and Sara laughed and tossed her head. 'No.'

Joe chuckled and jumped out of bed, totally at ease with his nakedness. He folded her in his arms and hugged her tenderly, his beard scraping her neck, pressing little kisses on her shoulders. He rested his chin on her hair, looking over her head to the early morning outside the window. 'We're going to have to do something about all this creeping round,' Joe said. 'I'm going to abduct the next Rabbi I pass and bring him straight back here. What do you say?'

Sara pulled away, and stared up at him in amazement. Was he asking her to marry him? Joe Lanksi, who had once told her that to be a bachelor was to be a sultan?

'Married? Us?'

Joe chuckled again and touched her cheek gently. 'Yes. Married. Don't look so shocked. Not all my intentions are dishonourable, you know.' He held her chin and looked gently down at her. 'You do love me?'

'Yes.' She saw the beginnings of amusement in his eyes.

'I'm not just a passing fancy for a merry widow?'

'Of course not, Joe Lanski!'

'Then marry me.'

'We could just live together,' she said, pretending to consider her options.

'Why, Sara!' he protested. 'That's the most improper thing I ever heard!'

Sara giggled and hugged him tightly to her. 'Of course I'll marry you,' she said, her eyes sparkling. 'I want to more than anything else in the world.'

'That's as well,' he said; 'because I mean to give you lots of fat bouncing babies with long blue eyes.'

'Green,' she put in firmly, but he kissed the word from her mouth.

'Come on,' he said, pulling her back towards the bed; 'let's get into trouble.'

Hamid Bek sat behind his desk, glaring at the old Arab servant who stood shakily before him.

'You say the pigeon flew in from the north?' he asked, tapping a pencil against his teeth.

'Yes, Your Honour.' All Hamid Bek's servants were terrified of him, and with reason, so the old man hesitated before adding: 'I have seen others before.'

The words were music to Hamid Bek's ears. North? Hadera was the nearest Jewish settlement to Caesarea, then Alona and then Atlit. He smiled and looked down at the coded scrap of paper before him. The letters in the code were Hebrew: the pigeon must have come from the Jews. Scum – sons of dogs, all of them. Now the only thing he had to do was get the paper deciphered and he would know everything. This would make up for not getting to that Jew they had held in prison before the coward killed himself. He had been part of the locust patrol, and therefore from Atlit, but this . . . this was the first tangible proof that a spy ring did exist inside the Jewish community. He had them now!

He banged his fist on the desk with glee, making the Arab jump in fear. Bek looked at him irritably, and waved his hand in dismissal. 'You can go,' he said, with no word of the reward the old man had expected. 'And you,' he added, passing the paper to a Captain who stood by the door, 'take this to Army Headquarters in Beersheba. Tell the chief code officer to sit on it until he breaks it. Stay with him until he does. This is a priority.'

The Captain saluted smartly and left. Bek sat for a moment, thinking, then rose to his feet. He would take a patrol and ride along the coast from Caesarea, stopping at every Jewish homestead until he found dovecots. He would have to tread carefully: the Germans had become touchy about the Jews ever since they had been driven from Jaffa, but if he visited a few Arab villages as well they would not be suspicious.

He called a sergeant and ordered him to have a patrol unit prepared to leave immediately. 'It'll not be long now,' he swore to himself. 'I'll make those filthy camel turds wish they had never heard of England. One day soon.' Swearing viciously, he picked up his whip and strode from the room.

Bek and his men rode into Hadera with their customary noise, but once they arrived were alarmingly restrained in their dealings with the villagers, asking them almost politely to assemble in the square. The people were shown an unhappy-looking pigeon in a wicker cage, and each man had to file past, inspecting the bird, while septieh stood around with guns. If everyone were not so terrified, they might have found the scene funny.

'Does anyone know this pigeon?' Hamid Bek asked in a reasonable voice. 'To whom does it belong?' The farmers shook their heads. 'Then please look at it again.' He said impatiently, and once more they all trooped past. 'I am sure you realise the penalties exacted on those caught protecting spies,' he said menacingly, but was met once again with a chorus of denials.

Bek called Nissim Aloni the blacksmith forward, prodding him with his bastinado.

'And you? Perhaps you know this pigeon well, Effendi, perhaps

465

you would like to send a message to your British friends? Maybe you ought to see if another look will refresh your memory.'

The blacksmith peered into the cage and apologised to it in Arabic, saying he was sorry he did not speak German and could not help it find its way home. The crowd laughed at his cheek and Bek, furious at the implication that the bird was German, cursed and gathered his men together to leave.

When the septieh rode off, the tone of the conversation changed. Jew would not betray Jew to an outsider, but most of the villagers were bitter against the few Jews who selfishly pursued their dreams at the expense of them all. Some began to accuse Sara and the group based at Atlit, gossip flourished as they put their heads together trying to find a way to stop any spy network. A few of the men went to see Daniel's mother, while some of the others began discussing whether they should begin to draw up a list of names – just in case anything happened. Ben and Josh, listening without saying much, where aghast at how much was known about the network and thanked their stars that their names were not mentioned. As soon as they could leave without drawing attention to themselves, they saddled their horses and rode as fast as they could to warn Sara at Atlit.

Sara saw them riding up the palm avenue and waved at them gaily. She hung on the gate, enjoying the hot August haze which hung, still and fragrant, over the Sharron plain, and waited for them to reach her. It was not until they dismounted that her pleasure turned to anxiety. They had no smiles for her, their faces were stark and worried. They hurried over their story and within minutes she had heard about Bek, the pigeon and the tide of feeling that was turning against them.

'Oh, my God,' she said, clutching a fence post for strength as she tried to sort out the chaotic thoughts whirling round in her head. How long would it take the Turks to decipher the code? It was a difficult one, a complex mixture of Aramaic and Latin, which changed every month. But how good were their code breakers? The main question was whether they would be able to break it before the ship she had requested arrived on the 12th – seven days away. With luck they would give the message to their own men to break, rather than to the Germans, who were more competent.

After a second she realised what she must do. She would send off the remaining two pigeons with messages to Aaron, telling him what had happened and asking him to make doubly sure the ship arrived on the 12th with two rowing boats. They must then destroy the cot and every sign that the pigeons or the network had ever existed. And she must send out the code word to all the key members, telling them to gather on the beach on the 12th.

Everyone involved had already been briefed and would know what to do. They must just bank on the code remaining unbroken a little longer.

'What in the name of God are we to do?' Ben asked.

Sara looked at him and he saw her face tighten and her eyes grow cold. 'Come,' she said, turning on her heel; 'we have work to do.'

Aaron sat nervously in the staff waiting room at Allenby's Cairo headquarters. He was angry, discontented and, worst of all, guilty. He knew now that he should have made a rescue ship a condition of the network's working for the British. But he had overlooked the obvious need for it and now everyone in Palestine might have to pay. His anger at himself and the Turk subsided in the face of his guilt.

Three weeks ago a pigeon had arrived with news of Lev's arrest, and Aaron had immediately requested that the contact ship stop off at Atlit twice a month from now on. Deedes wrote the request in the day book, but the first pigeon was swiftly followed by Sara's monthly report with the news of Lev's death. Lev, who they had affectionately mocked so often, who had irritated them with his eagerness and nervous habits, had sacrificed himself rather than risk talking. That was when Aaron's guilt had begun, and when he had reached a grief greater than any since the war began.

Now, three days ago, another pigeon arrived with news of the coded message falling into enemy hands. Aaron remembered that during the First Crusade, when the murderous Christians were camped at Caesaria, a messenger pigeon had been felled by a hawk. That pigeon had been carrying a message from the governor of Acre, who was trying to persuade the Jews and Moslems of Palestine to rise together against the invaders.

Aaron, Paul and Selena were horrified by the news: the more so as they had not yet received confirmation that the rescue ship would be sent. Aaron began to feel that they were not being treated the way that they would have been if they were English spies, rather than just spies for the English. Once again, he was convinced that they were being penalised for the Englishman's basic xenophobia. Timing was now of crucial importance. The rescue ship must leave within the next four days if it were to arrive at Atlit by the 12th. Along with the request for the ship to be sent, Aaron had asked that he might accompany it. He knew he was the only person who would be capable of making his father leave, and he also knew that neither Sam nor Sara would leave without the old man. Deedes understood Aaron's personal situation, but the request had been apologetically but firmly refused. All this was before the rescue ship itself was definite.

'I'm sorry, Aaron, but we just can't let you go. You are now an officer in the British Army and your first responsibility is to us.' The rational part of Aaron understood that this was right, but he could not keep himself from fuming with rage and worry. His problem was that he had been so keen to inveigle himself into a position of trust with the British, many of whom had not even realised the large Jewish presence in Palestine, that he had made himself indispensable to them. The leaders now knew considerably more about the Zionist cause than before, but the more they knew the more they felt they needed someone on hand.

Allenby, the new Commander-in-Chief, relied on Aaron a great deal. Now that the plans for Z-day were being finalised, he often called Aaron into headquarters to acquaint the commanders with the territory they would have to cover. Aaron's knowledge of the country was practically encyclopaedic and the military authorities were happy to pump him dry of all he knew. No detail was too small, too insignificant, for Allenby: the seasonal occurrence of malignant malaria, which they believed had nearly destroyed Richard the Lionheart's Army, keeping him from reaching Jerusalem; records of air pressures for the Air Force; rock formations for the engineers. Sara had pulled any data that might be remotely relevant from the files and sent them by the contact ship. At last Aaron was being listened to, and respected.

The new plan still had the old worry – water. Allenby and Aaron pored over maps and Allenby, who knew his Bible as well as any man, knew just where Aaron meant when he referred to old wells. Aaron's instincts were so often proved right about which wells had survived and his talent for discovering and divining water proved so great that he was nicknamed 'Moses' by the English.

Until the disastrous news arrived from Palestine, Aaron felt that the situation was changing for the better. In July Lawrence and

Feisal had captured Akaba, the once fabled port of King Solomon that lay at the tip of the gulf fed by the Red Sea. Akaba, only a hundred miles off Allenby's right flank, would protect the British from any counter-attack in that direction from the Turks. Allenby himself was the biggest stroke of luck for the British. He was a great leader, a remarkable and compassionate man. It was Aaron's knowledge of this last quality that had led him to where he now sat, waiting for an interview with the Field Marshal. It was strictly against regulations for him to request a private audience, but what he had to say was so much more important than the small breach of security involved that he would not miss any chance to win his way.

'Major Levinson, sir,' Aaron looked up sharply; 'The Field Marshal will see you now.' Aaron rose and the adjutant ushered him in.

Aaron saluted neatly, and Allenby smiled and rose to shake hands. Even when relaxed he was an imposing figure, with his broad shoulders and large, hooked nose. His bright blue eyes rested on Aaron quizzically. 'Be at ease, Major,' he said, after the formalities had been observed. 'Sit down if you like.'

Aaron took the chair offered by the adjutant. 'I am sorry for the lack of protocol . . .' he began, but Allenby waved his hand in dismissal of the subject.

'I'm sorry to hear you lost one of your men to the Turk . . . Deedes told me what happened.'

Aaron nodded, accepting the formal words of sympathy, but for a moment a shadow fell across his eyes. 'Thank you, sir,' he said quietly and cleared his throat. Then found he had to clear it again. 'It is not about him, but about the fate of the rest of my family – and friends,' he added significantly, 'that I have come to see you. Sir, I fear very much that their days may be numbered . . .' His voice was gruff and he found he had to clear his throat again.

'Forgive me for having broken protocol, sir,' he went on, 'but I believe you will be able to understand my wish to save my family and friends.' He paused a moment for emphasis. It was well known that Allenby had lost his only son in France a few weeks before, and the Field Marshal flinched slightly then looked back at Aaron with keen eyes. 'I am not sure, Major, what this is all about. Perhaps you had better explain yourself.'

Aaron did so in a few brief, but well-chosen words. 'We have been waiting three days for confirmation of this ship, sir, but you have got to send her – sir,' he concluded harshly, his normally florid face flushed further with anger. 'And, sir, I request permission to sail with her.' The words, more forceful than any normally used to the Commander-in-Chief, hung in a silence.

Allenby looked down at his desk and then back at Aaron.

'I understand your feelings,' he said at last. 'You have every right and, I admit, every reason to be irked. Your people in Palestine are performing a valuable service for us. I owe you both thanks and an apology.'

'You owe us neither,' Aaron cut in. 'It is our war too. But maybe you do owe us that ship.'

'Hear me out,' the Field Marshal said peremptorily, and looked at Aaron a moment before continuing. 'I will make sure that a ship is sent for those who wish to leave.'

Aaron let out his breath in a burst of relief. 'Thank you, sir. And permission to sail with it?'

Allenby shook his head. 'But . . .' He raised his hand. 'I believe your aims in helping us are – political?'

Aaron looked at him warily, then nodded. 'Yes,' he said simply. 'It's my life.'

'Then let me tell you something you don't know.' Allenby turned to the adjutant standing by the door. 'For the next few minutes you will hear nothing.'

'Sir,' the adjutant answered crisply.

Allenby turned back to Aaron. 'I believe it is only a question of a month or so before the British Government openly declares its support for a Jewish National Homeland.' Aaron straightened up in his chair, his mouth dry. He was too shocked – too disbelieving – to speak. This was why he had worked, the reason for his hopes and dreams. This was why Daniel and Lev had died. The single idea in his life to which he had clung throughout everything and for which he would die. Allenby's words rang in his ears, growing sweeter each time he heard them. The British Government was to support a Jewish National Homeland. He sat in silence, trying to fight back the tears that pricked the backs of his eyes.

'The formation of a Jewish State,' Allenby continued drily, 'will be a massive undertaking and there will doubtless be opposition in one form or another. In London, as here, there are those who are not too keen on Zionism; let me assure you that anti-Zionism and anti-Semitism do not necessarily go hand in hand. The large majority is simply uninformed. It will need special men, dedicated and persuasive men like yourself, to show this majority that the ideas of Zionism are just and fair. I have spoken to Sir Reginald Wingate, the British High Commissioner here in Egypt, and he would like an interview with you in the next few days. He wishes to send you to London for certain work in connection with the forthcoming British declaration.'

He looked at Aaron for some sign, but Aaron could only clear his throat and nod. 'That, Major, is why I am refusing you permission to accompany the ship to Atlit. What you are doing here is, and will continue to be, vital to the eventual well-being of your land. Now do you agree?'

Aaron felt almost suffocated with joy. Daniel's and Lev's deaths and the appalling risks he had allowed Sara and the others to take were being justified now. But his practical mind returned to the present. 'And the rescue ship?'

'You have my word,' said Allenby solemnly. Then, to Aaron's amazement, his stern features softened in a sympathetic smile as he rose, passed him a handkerchief, and left the room. Aaron looked at the closed door and felt the tears well up in his eyes. He did not need the handkerchief but it was a close-run thing.

The last few days, Sara thought grimly, were probably among the worst in her life – though the nights the best. Yesterday was the very worst. Her father had arrived in the middle of the morning demanding, in his own quiet way, to know the truth about what was happening. He led her into the kitchen, sent Frieda on an errand, looked Sara in the eyes and told her why he had come. He had heard the story of the pigeon – everyone had – but he was not worried until a deputation had arrived at Zichron from the executive council. They were convinced that the pigeon had come from Atlit and that Sara was the leader of a spy network working for the British. He had heard that Aaron, far from being a prisoner of the English, was running the enterprise from Cairo with the sanction of respected Zionists. He said that he had confronted Sam, who refused to say more than that he should speak to Sara. So here he was.

Sara watched his face as he told his story, amazed to see that he seemed neither horrified nor angry, just painfully anxious.

'Well, Sara? Is it true?' he said when he had finished.

Sara thought about lying, but he knew too much now. Her father was no fool and, although he had said nothing since the day when Hamid Bek had arrived with news of Aaron, she knew that he had remained suspicious. Apart from anything else, he was in danger too. It was time to tell him at least a part of the truth – too much would be dangerous, for him and them, but now the opportunity had come she found she needed to lift the weight of the secrets between them. She bent her head and shook it slowly. 'Yes, Papa, it's true.' She spoke as evenly as possible, but felt her throat tighten. 'It's a long story, please – don't ask any more.'

She looked up at him. He was watching her with a frighteningly expressionless face. 'Aaron – is he in Cairo?'

I can't tell him, she thought, *I can't*. He nodded as though the look on her face was all the confirmation he needed. Sara sunk into a chair and leaned her head in her hands for a second, her heart stricken at the thought that he deserved care and love from his children in his old age, not this, not to be put in a position where at any moment he could be arrested and tortured by those brutes.

'Bone of my bone, flesh of my flesh,' he murmured. 'Dear God, what have you done?' Tears welled up in Sara's eyes, and she covered them with her hand.

She heard the chair next to her creak as the old man lowered himself into it, then she felt her hand taken in his strong one. 'I'm sorry, Papa,' she said, wiping away the tears. 'But we are certain that, no matter what the risk, our future in Palestine lies with the British. The Turk cannot be allowed to win. What we would gain by sitting back and thinking of the war as an interlude is the only thing the Jew has ever gained in the past – a stay of execution for a month, a year, bought at the price of whatever is best in us. Our pride, our hope, our self-respect. Whatever happens in the end we need those things. The Turk has us like rats in a barrel. I saw what they did to the Armenians, Papa, and that fate would be ours in a matter of time.' Her voice trembled slightly and she paused for breath. Then she straightened her back and looked ahead, her eyes hard and flinty. 'Papa, we have a different vision of the future. A vision of our own land – Israel. And I'm proud of it.'

Abram was quiet for a moment, and Sara turned to look at him. She saw in his eyes such blind love and pride for her that the tears came rushing back to her eyes. He patted her hand and said softly. 'You are right to be proud of your vision, daughter. And I am right to be proud of you.' He kissed her cheek. He sat back in his chair and his face fell back into its old, long-suffering lines. 'You must promise me one thing, Sara. The moment there is any hint of trouble you will come straight to Zichron.' His words were wrung from him like a plea from the heart, and Sara promised him. She had had no other intention.

Then, Joe's trip to Haifa had gone badly. First of all Ali had become claustrophobic and banged on the lid of the coffin. It was opened to find him so hot and sweaty that a heat rash had broken out and the corpse was quickly transformed into a smallpox carrier being taken to hospital. The medicine had arrived safely at the hospital, but there was more trouble when Joe delivered the gold to Ivan Bernski. Bernski had taken the gold, but had demanded that all further espionage work cease and told Joe to stay away from Haifa until suspicion died down. He told them that they had no right to continue as they had without the central committee sanctioning their work, and that they were putting all other Jews in mortal danger.

It was true that, since the pigeon episode, the Jews were again living in an atmosphere of worry and fear. Hadera, Caesarea and Bat Slomo had already been searched – why not Zichron and Atlit? Was Hamid Bek playing some sort of perverse game with them?

Sara would not be able to relax until the following night – if the ship came. She was so concerned about the safety of the network's key members that she could barely keep her mind from them and would feel a huge weight of worry drop from her shoulders as she waved them all goodbye. Sara had decided that she was not leaving. Her mind was made up. She had told no one of her intention, pretending that she would leave on the rescue ship with the others. She feared that if she told the truth Manny and perhaps even Robby and Ruth might refuse to go, and God knows she had enough guilt to contend with already without being responsible for their missing an opportunity for safety.

The only problem would be Joe. He was to stay at the station with Saul Rosin and slowly pay off the workers, winding things down slowly to keep up appearances. He had runners out, who would let him know as soon as anything happened to jeopardise his position – the code being broken or someone denouncing them – and he would then hide out until the end of the month when the next ship would come and pick him up. He made it all sound very simple. But Sara knew otherwise.

She had at first insisted on staying behind with Joe, but he had been adamant. 'Sorry, Sara. You're leaving on the 12th and that is all there is to it.' After a while Sara had given up mentioning the subject, only smiling sweetly when it was brought up. They could think what they wanted but she had no intention of leaving her father, brother, lover and country to the mercy of the Turk. Like hell she had.

Joe was not fooled by her sudden capitulation, and watched her carefully. This morning he had come up behind her and pulled her into his arms, whispering, 'I don't know how I'm going to bear being away from you.' He caught sight of her face in a mirror on the other side of the room and seen her give a tight, smug little smile. So his suspicions were well founded, he thought, and had to hide his laughter in a faked coughing fit. As usual the scheming little minx had no intention whatsoever of doing what she was told.

He wondered what he should do with her – at one stage hitting her over the head and throwing her into the boat seemed a good idea. But as he thought about it he realised that her argument against going did make some sense. Unless the code were broken or they were betrayed, they were as safe here as anyone else. If and when the septieh did come to search the station, the first person they would want to talk to was Sara. If she were missing, it could lead to serious repercussions for the Zichron community. And, after all, she was a grown woman with a right to make her own decisions. He had no right to use force against her – and he knew she would never forgive him if he did.

Joe looked at her carefully. It was time to end this game – nothing ever went to schedule here and it was better to admit it. Sara felt Joe looking at her and hesitated self-consciously before turning to meet his eyes. 'What is it?' she said after a second's silence.

'What?'

'You've been looking at me oddly all day. Is something wrong?'

Joe took a breath as though to speak, then strode across the room to the window and looked out at the view. He suddenly turned back, a decision made, and walked across the room to her.

'We're going for a ride. We need to get away from the station for a bit – it's too claustrophobic. Go on and change, I'll saddle the horses.'

474

He sounded so serious that Sara wanted to tease him, but as she looked at him she knew there was no point. She shook her head and smiled: 'I really shouldn't, I've so much work to do.'

Joe pulled her towards him and gently touched her cheek with his fingers. Sara's eyelids fluttered closed and she instinctively swayed towards him. Oh how she loved him, the idea of being without him was unendurable. Joe bent and kissed her lightly on the lips, then pulled back and looked down at her with a grin. 'Do as I say, get dressed at once,' he said with mock sternness.

'I'd rather get undressed,' Sara said with a wicked grin.

'Later,' he promised. 'Now come on.'

They rode in silence until they reached the beach, Sara enjoying the sense of freedom that riding always gave her, and realising for the first time how claustrophobic life in the station had indeed become. Bella needed no pushing, but pranced along, doing her best to keep up with Negiv. Joe kept the pace sedate: the horses were showing far more bone than they ought and should not be pushed, but when Negiv felt the sand under his hooves he reacted like a true Arab and flew across the beach to the water's edge. Joe gave him his head until they reached the water, then reined him in and turned to watch Sara catch up, her cheeks glowing pink under her hat.

They encouraged the horses into the water and splashed along for a while, murmuring endearments to the willing beasts. The afternoon sky was a deep azure, and against it the Crusader castle rose like a mirage. Sara sighed and wished she could ride like this for ever, going with Joe wherever fancy took them. The war, the Turk, seemed so far away now, like another era.

Joe pointed to an outcrop of rocks. 'Let's leave the horses in the shade there and take a walk down the beach,' he said, and Negiv trotted out of the shallows along the hot beach until he reached the cool shade.

Sara followed and slipped down from the saddle. They fastened the horses to a tree and, hand in hand, set off along the seashore. There was no one else in sight as they walked across the sand ribbons; only a few sandpipers pecking about for titbits in the calm, shallow water. Sara breathed deeply, relishing the salt in the air and the peace.

Joe gave her a sympathetic look, and, stopping, took her other hand in his so that she faced him. He looked at her carefully. 'You don't intend to leave tomorrow, do you, Sara?' he asked. She paled and looked at him in sudden panic, but said nothing. Joe was not convinced by her silence. Suddenly angry, he took her by the shoulders and shook her until her hairpins fell free and her hair tumbled around her shoulders. 'The truth,' he demanded, his face painfully anxious. 'I must know the truth. I must know what you have planned.'

Sara tried to shake herself loose, but her self-control was weakening and his grip was firm. 'No, I'm not going,' she cried fiercely, her eyes glaring defiance. 'If I go – leave – it will be as good as killing my father, my brother – and God knows how many more from Zichron. I will not go.'

His hands dropped from her shoulders as she stared proudly at him, waiting for his reaction. *Why did I tell him*, she wondered. *It will confuse everything*. To her unspeakable surprise, she saw Joe's face crease into a smile and heard him begin to laugh.

'Did you really suppose that you could hide that from me until the last moment?' He asked, his face serious again. 'You silly fool, do you really think I know so little about you?'

'I won't change my mind,' she warned, unsure of what he was about to say.

'I don't expect you to,' he said. 'I've thought about it. You're right not to leave. I love you and am proud of your bravery. But Sara, do you have any plan in mind?'

Sara dropped her eyes and shook her head. 'All I know,' she said, looking him in the eye again, 'is that if I leave – I of all people – the Turk will take a terrible revenge on Zichron. My mind keeps going back to the Armenians. I just couldn't live with myself if I did one thing that helped precipitate that sort of cruelty.' She sighed and thought for a moment. 'With the others gone they might believe the network has broken up, its members flown. After all, I am a woman. They might just think they were wrong about me.' Even to herself the idea sounded weak, but there was none better.

Joe took her hand again and they began walking slowly back towards the horses. 'I want to establish a plan for you, so you will know what to do if something goes wrong – if something terrible happens.' He looked at her soberly. 'I'm very serious and you must listen carefully. I want you prepared at all times now.' She nodded and Joe explained his ideas as they strolled along.

Sara stopped dead. 'You can't do that, Joe, for God's sake. What if the British postpone the offensive? What if they decide to hang you there and then? What if . . .'

Joe gave her a rueful smile. 'Danger always brings out the best in me. I've always been something of a gambler in more than the cards. My luck will hold.' He pulled her into his arms. 'Sara, I respected your decision; you respect mine. We won't talk about this any more until the times comes. Until then we will think of the present, only the present.'

Sara did not argue. She knew Joe too well, and knew that his stubborness outmatched even her own. She looked at him, the sunlight reflecting the sea in his eyes and felt a faint stirring of optimism. Perhaps his luck would hold – she could only pray that if the crunch came it would hold long enough.

In the muted light of the barn Sara was sorting out some of the chaos left by Bek and his septieh after their visit a week ago. They had arrived with trumpets blaring and drums beating and departed, leaving havoc behind them. The mess had still not been righted. *God in heaven, what a disaster*, Sara thought, wiping the perspiration from her face and looking round at all the work still to be done. 'Damn the Turkish bastards,' she muttered for the hundredth time that week, but with a small smile of triumph. Although the place looked as though all hell had erupted, the Turks had not found a single piece of incriminating evidence against them. Nothing, not a pigeon feather or the tiniest scrap of unexplainable paper. And, meanwhile, the contact ship had been and gone, taking with it Robby and his family, Ezra and, after much persuasion, Manny. Frieda had been sent to her sister's house in Haifa and most of the workers had been paid off with the excuse that the station had no more money.

When Bek arrived they were prepared, but his expression when he saw Joe there showed his surprise. Sara stood, seemingly calm, Joe's presence bolstering her courage. But when they had wreaked their destruction and ridden out, she almost fainted with the relief. Nothing disastrous had happened. The code had been sent to Damascus, where the Germans had a decoding machine, but so far it had apparently baffled it.

Sara straightened up and pinned back a loose lock of hair. She walked over to Jezebel, the old car they had once been so proud of, which now sat in the barn gathering dust and rusting. She patted the car's bonnet, remembering the day it had brought Daniel home and how much she had loved him. Her love for Joe was so different, almost inexplicable, earthy and sacred at one and the same time. Joe was everything she had ever yearned for in a lover and she loved him more than life itself but she never denied her past love for Daniel. Joe was her life but she would cherish the memory of Daniel for a lifetime.

'Sleep well in your sandy grave, Daniel,' she murmured. 'One day, when all this is over and the land is ours, we will find you and bring you home to sleep in the earth you loved so much.'

Her musing was interrupted by Ali, rushing in with the announcement that a *Bedu* was riding towards them. 'Very fast, beating his mount like a rug!' he said excitedly. Sara wrinkled her brow in puzzlement. A Bedouin? Then she realised it was probably a member of the Hashomer and a flash of irritation crossed her face. They had stayed well clear of Atlit since the search for spies had begun, forbidding their members to mix with any of the group. They had been buying up arms and transporting them to the isolated settlements in Galilee. The Turks had made no bones about their intention of destroying those farming communities as they retreated, and the Hashomer blamed the network for the fact that most vehicles were now being stopped and searched. Of course, if it were not for the gold that the network had brought into Palestine they would have no money to buy the arms. But they chose not to remember that.

Sara crossed the yard and watched the rider, dressed in a black burnoose, sweep through the gate at a great speed, pulling his horse to an abrupt halt in a flurry of stones. He pushed back his keffiyeh from his face and Sara looked up with a gasp. She was looking into the beautiful, insolently haunting, face of Daniel's old flame, Isobelle. What could she be doing here, for God's sake? A dreadful feeling of impending disaster struck Sara and, alarmed, she clasped her hands together tightly.

Isobelle leaped from the horse, throwing the reins to Ali. 'Take the horse and bring me another,' she ordered in her distinctive, husky voice. Ali scowled and looked at Sara and she, responding to the urgency in the woman's voice, nodded to the boy. 'Saddle up Bella,' she said faintly.

Ali's eyebrows shot up in amazement, but he did not move. 'Do as I say!' she almost shouted, and instantly regretted her tone.

Isobelle walked over to Sara and held her arm in a grip that belied her tiny frame. 'Come over here,' she said, leading Sara to the side of the courtyard, 'and listen very carefully. I will have no time to repeat myself. There is a crisis. This morning Hamid Bek paid Ivan Bernski a surprise visit in Haifa. He had the safe forced. Inside they found the gold Joe brought. He immediately had all the leading members of the Jewish community rounded up and threatened to shoot them unless Bernski told him who had brought the gold.' A deep shadow fell over her eyes. 'He had no choice,' she said calmly. 'He told him.'

Sara stared at her in stunned disbelief. What had she just said? For a moment Sara thought she had misunderstood but then the horror of the truth sunk in. Isobelle shook her arm roughly. 'You have understood, haven't you?' Sara could not think straight, but she nodded her understanding. The implications of the news were shattering. *Bek knew Joe was here at Atlit*. He might arrive at any moment.

Suddenly her brain snapped into action and she shouted at Ali to bring Bella immediately. She gave Isobelle an impulsive hug. 'Thank you,' she said. The other girl mounted Bella. 'I'd better go. If I'm caught here, I'll swing for it,' she said with a glimmer of a smile. 'Tell Joe I'm sorry,' she said with a great gentleness.

Sara nodded and, her heart like a block of ice in her chest, she ordered Apollo to be saddled and a cart to be harnessed up. Then she turned towards the house. She knew that the time had come and went very carefully and very quickly in search of Joe.

As soon as Joe saw her standing in the doorway he knew that the time he had been dreading had arrived. They looked at each other silently, overwhelmed by love and regret. Then with a cry like a wounded animal, Sara flew across the room and almost fell into his arms. He hugged her to him with a tenderness born of distress, but after a second she pulled back and told him what Isobelle had said.

'You must leave, Joe. You must go now. There's no time, they could be here at any moment.' She forced back the sobs and closed her eyes, but the tears slipped through her lashes and fell unchecked into the corners of her mouth. With a supreme effort she opened her eyes. Joe's face was calm: only his eyes showed his anguish. He was suddenly swamped with despair. How was he going to find the strength to leave her, do what he must do for everyone's sake? He hugged her fiercely, and they clung together

479

for one last moment before pulling apart. 'I'll get the things ready,' he said, and strode from the room.

When Sara and Joe arrived in the courtyard Apollo was already saddled and waiting, pawing the ground impatiently. Ali was holding the horse, tears making tracks down his grubby little face as Joe gave him his last-minute instructions.

'You are not crying, are you, Ali?' he asked softly.

'No, Joe . . . I've got something in my eye,' Ali managed to say in a choked voice, turning his face away.

'Both of them?' asked Joe and, smiling, bent down and took the boy gently by the shoulders. 'Now you are to do everything Sara tells you – everything, you do understand that, don't you, Ali?'

Ali sniffed and nodded, bending his head, ashamed of his tears. Joe pulled out a handkerchief and wiped Ali's face.

'Joe, oh Joe, I am fearful for you,' the boy cried with a tearing sob, and clung to Joe's legs, all self-control gone.

'Nonsense,' said Joe. 'I'll be back in no time.'

Ali looked up anxiously, the tears still brimming in his eyes. 'You speak the truth?'

'Would I lie to you?' Ali thought about this, then shook his head.

'Mind you,' said Joe, 'I wouldn't be so pleased about my coming back if I were you. I'm putting you straight into school – I'm not having any son of mine unable to read and write.' Ali's head shot up, tears forgotten as he was torn between the joy of Joe referring to him as his son and horror at the idea of school. Joe ruffled his head and laughed, reading Ali's thoughts exactly.

He turned to Sara and the smile was gone. Sara could not meet his eyes, knowing that if she did she would lose her control.

Joe put his arms round her and hugged her. She was his life. After this he would never be parted from her again, not as long as he lived. He held her back from him a moment and lifted her chin, whispering, 'I love you, Sara. And I promise you that no matter what I will be back, I will hold you in my arms again, I promise.'

Sara looked at him and nodded mutely. He took a step back, and only then did she whisper. 'Goodbye, Joe. I love you. I'll be here. God be with you.'

Joe smiled. 'You had better be,' then, turning away from her, he mounted his horse swiftly.

He looked down at her. 'Please go,' she said, hoarsely. Despite her iron will, her voice shook. 'Go now or I won't be able to let you.'

Joe leant over and taking the white 'kerchief from her neck smiled and put it in his pocket. 'I appear to be short of a handkerchief,' he said, and put his heels to Apollo, making the horse skitter in the dust. Then he bent over, took Sara's hand, and kissed it. It took all his strength not to pull her into the saddle behind him. She moved closer, holding the stirrup for a moment and looking up into his face.

'Sara?' Joe said.

'Yes?'

'Remember when I told you I could live without you?'

'Yes.'

'I was lying,' he said, with his old, mocking grin, and kicking Apollo's flanks he galloped off.

Sara was left standing, watching him go through the tears that were now streaming down her face. Her fists and jaw were clenched until they ached. She must keep her nerve. The important thing now was survival. That above everything else. She felt Ali tugging at her sleeve. His eyes red and swollen with sorrow, he peered anxiously up at her.

'We must go, Sara. Or death will surely have us by the heel.'

She nodded and, with one last lingering look in the direction Joe had taken, mounted Negiv and kicked him forward in a trot towards Zichron.

Sara crept down to the kitchen with the candle, and sat down heavily on the chair, burying her face in her hands. There was no hope of sleeping with her turbulent thoughts and fears chasing each other round her brain. Joe had left at four thirty in the afternoon: it was now three in the morning. They would be here soon.

Her heart began to beat rapidly; she could feel the tension rippling through her, and once again she was overwhelmed by the number of things that could go wrong. She sagged back against the chair. *Oh God, stop driving yourself crazy*, she told herself furiously. She must not allow anything to sway her from her course, to weaken her determination. For the next two days she would be single-minded of purpose and must trust herself not to give Joe's destination away. He must reach Beersheba; everything depended on that. Only two days – and some luck.

The house was silent – silent as a graveyard, she thought with a small, cynical smile. Rachel, her boys and a reluctant Fatma and Ali had been moved into Ruth's empty house. Sara wanted no one more than necessary here when Bek arrived with his men. She thought of Sam and her father and was flooded with sorrow and guilt. She and Sam had gone into this with full awareness of what the consequences might be – but her father . . .

There was a rustle in the hall and Sara jumped. It was Sam. She quickly lit the lamp with her candle and saw him peer at her, anxiously pushing back the red locks from his face. Sara felt a warm rush of love for him and adopted a light-hearted tone to cover her feelings.

'Can't sleep, then?'

Sam shook his head, a wry smile playing on his mouth. 'You neither.'

She forced a smile and shrugged. 'Would you like some tea?'

She was halfway out of her chair when she froze, gripping the back of the chair in sudden fear at the sound of Sultan's barking. They looked at each other. 'It's the septieh,' Sara said, her voice clear and crisp. 'Better lock up Sultan and tell Abu to make himself invisible – knock him out if you have to.' Sam nodded and disappeared out of the door.

Sara went to the door, every nerve in her body straining to hear. Then her heart started to pound, knocking frantically against her rib cage. It was them. They would be here in another ten to fifteen minutes. Panic raced through her. Ten to fifteen minutes. Oh God, they were coming to question her – but they knew nothing. Not yet. And she must not tell them. So many lives were at stake, those of men, all over the land who had brought them information, trusting them – trusting her. She pressed her hands to her mouth, terrified of the demands that would be made on her courage and that she would not be able to meet them. Desperately afraid, she turned to see her father standing in the hall doorway, fully dressed and looking at her with seeming calm.

'The septieh? Hamid Bek?' he asked, and she nodded, taking her place at the table again. 'Don't do anything foolish, Sara,' he said, sitting beside her. 'Just remember the Armenians.' He did not look at her but picked up his Bible and, finding his glasses in his pocket, bent the wire round his ears and began to read. Sara turned her head away so that he should not see the tears she shed at the thought of his anguish. She groped for his hand and sat, strangely comforted by the feel of his familiar strength.

Together they waited for the septieh to arrive.

It was nearly half an hour before Sara, Sam and Abram heard the septieh outside, their boots heavy on the veranda, their feet kicking down the door that hands could easily have opened. Sam stood as the men swept into the room; the old man sat still holding his daughter's hand protectively.

A sergeant marched into the kitchen and gestured to his men to leave him with the Levinsons. They waited in silence, hearing the boots marching through every room in the house.

'What is going on, sergeant?' Sam asked, his face deathly pale. The sergeant muttered something to his guard and Sam backed into the table as the guns turned on him. There was a crash of breaking glass from somewhere in the house, and the sound of the cellar door being axed down.

Abram squeezed Sara's hand as he felt it begin to tremble, and her father's calm helped soothe her distress.

'Please tell me what is happening,' Sam repeated nervously. 'Why are you doing this? We have done no wrong.'

'Sit down,' the sergeant said, ignoring Sam's question and gesturing menacingly to a chair at the table.

Everyone was silent, waiting for something. Waiting for Hamid Bek. It seemed as though an hour passed, but it was not long before they heard the footsteps of a group of men crossing the veranda. Hamid Bek led three men into the room, his bastinado tapping against his long brown boots.

Abram Levinson rose to his feet. 'Thank God you're here, Your Excellency,' he said. 'There seems to be some terrible mistake . . .'

'There is no mistake, Effendi Levinson,' the police chief remarked; 'and until this interrogation is over you will say nothing unless first addressed.'

'What do you mean?' the old man began, but was roughly pushed back into his seat by a septieh.

'We are talking about spying,' Bek said with an easy smile. 'A subject I'm sure your charming daughter could tell us something about.'

Sara met his gaze, her eyes as unflinching as his. 'You can't be serious,' she said in a voice so level she hardly recognised it as her own. He smiled thinly and walked round the table to face her.

'You will soon see how serious I am,' he said, and before Sara could move a heavy slap sent her reeling sideways from her chair, her nose spurting blood.

'No!' the old man shouted, rising to his feet only to be pushed back down by the septieh.

Sara sat up, dazed, and put a hand to the back of her head. She felt blood in her hair and knew there was worse to come. A sudden fury at her own helplessness gave her the strength to pull herself back into her chair and sit straight, breathing hard.

'Do you see how serious I am now, Madame Cohen?' Bek asked politely, his eyes glittering malevolently into hers. 'Now tell me, where is Joe Lanski?'

'I don't know,' she said, wincing as she felt her lips begin to swell. Bek laughed mirthlessly, his face darkening with rage.

'Do you think I am a fool?' he said.

'No,' said Sara truthfully.

'Then let's talk about Joe Lanski again. Where do you suppose he could be?'

'At the research station perhaps?' She shrugged: 'How should I know where he is.'

Hamid Bek sighed theatrically. He was enjoying himself more than he had in weeks. He looked at the three captives one after the other, deciding who should go first. Not the Jewess, that pleasure would come later, he decided, feeling a pleasant warmth spread down his belly and into his loins. No, not the Jewess. 'Your denials are pointless and stupid,' he said; and then added to the sergeant, 'take the old man.'

'No!' Sara screamed and both she and Sam jumped to their father's rescue.

One of the guards swung his rifle into Sam's belly and he doubled up, gasping in pain. Bek nodded and Abram was pulled from the room.

'Please don't hurt him. He's an old man,' Sara heard herself plead in a whisper. She had to fight to keep the tears from her eyes. Tears of horror, grief and guilt.

'Then tell me all about Lanski and we'll forget this unpleasant incident,' Bek promised. He eyed Sam, who had been propped against the wall and was trying to regain his breath after the blow. Then he pushed his face into Sara's. 'Tell us all about Daniel Rosen, and Joe Lanski, and your clever brother Aaron. And the rest of the traitors. Or your brother's pretty face just won't be so pretty.'

A long scream echoed round the house. Dear God, how they must have beaten her father to make him scream like that. They are killing him, Sara thought in panic, but then she felt raw fury flare within her and take over.

'Shut up,' she screamed, barely knowing what she was doing. 'Shut up, you filthy Turkish pig.' Her hand reached out and her nails tore a scarlet path down his cheek. Bek tried to push her away, but in her rage she was almost a match for him. Until she felt a sudden blow on her head and sank to the floor.

They kept her awake all night, promising her that if she so much as sat down her father would be beaten again. She walked round and round the room, sometimes sleeping for a second or two before the downward jolt of her body awakened her. By daylight she was exhausted and disoriented. She no longer had any real idea of the truth — where could Joe be by now? With no sense of time, she had no idea.

They tied her to the kitchen table and left her for a while. Sara cried now, her hands tied above her head and her tears running unchecked into her nose and mouth. She was very afraid. But she told herself she would not give in, must not give in.

The door opened to Bek. 'Have you remembered anything?' He asked.

'I don't know anything,' Sara croaked, trying to keep her eyes from the bastinado he was twitching in his hand.

'It is a pity your stableman lacks a tongue. But he seems to think you have something to tell us.'

Bek gave Sara just long enough to shake her head before bringing the whip down hard on the soles of her feet. Sara could not have imagined such a level of pain. She moaned and gasped, 'Please, no more. Please. Stop.'

Mercifully enough, he did. He reached over her and hooked two fingers into the sodden shirt that clung to her sweating body. With one swift movement he ripped the material, exposing her breasts to the staring eyes of his men. Sara would no longer plead or beg. Through a haze of agonising pain she lifted her head and spat at him, instinctively ducking from the expected blow. But it did not come. Sara heard a growl from the corner of the room, and hazily saw Sultan, his teeth bared and his eyes gold with rage as he lunged for Hamid Bek's arm. Sara could not see what happened next, it was all so quick.

There was a silver flash of steel behind Bek and a cry, 'A knife, he has a knife!' Then Sam lifted the knife and struck once, then again and again. The room seemed to be filled with blood and curses. Septieh poured into the room, fighting to pull Sam back, but he seemed possessed with a demoniac strength. Then he lurched and fell away from the men on to the wall. Shots followed, mingled with Sara's screams until at last something cracked in her head and she sunk into merciful oblivion.

Joe sat on the thin straw pallet staring up at the tiny window of his cell. He had spent most of his two months in prison with his face stretched up to the small opening, breathing in the fresh air and staring out to the edge of the city and the hills beyond.

He was in the grand part of the jail, reserved for those with enough money to pay for its comparative comforts, but still a stinking hole of a place. Not that it made much difference to him now. He was to be hanged that morning. He had already had a two-week stay of execution, granted because he had been ill with a fever on the appointed day. It had been typical of the civilised behaviour of the Germans to wait until he had recovered before hanging him, he thought cynically. Not that that mattered much either now. His plan had gone completely wrong.

Joe had ridden safely from Atlit to Beersheba, where he had easily found Hans Werner Rilke. He had walked into the Major's room, taken his hat off politely, and requested to be arrested and imprisoned. 'There will be no need for torture,' he had promised. 'I will confess everything.'

Rilke had looked at him in amazement. 'But why?'

'Because Sara is being held, and I am foolishly in love with her. Besides which, she is innocent,' he had added, looking Rilke straight into the eye.

'But why me. Why come to me?' Rilke had persisted.

'Because you are a German and a gentleman. In giving myself up to you, I know what to expect. If I were to give myself up to the Turk, I would only know that he would do whatever I least expected.'

Hans Werner Rilke chuckled and shook his head with admiration, then looked at him earnestly, before asking quietly, 'Lanski, it is very important that you are not lying.'

Joe had taken a breath and then calmly told the tale that signed his death warrant. The evidence he gave was, of course, pathetically incomplete. He only named those who were safe or dead. At the end of his story he had looked at Rilke and asked. 'Well? Do we have a deal?'

Rilke had shaken his head. 'What are your conditions?'

'I want you to radio your men at the Carmel garrison and order them to go to Zichron and release Sara. But quickly – time is passing and she is in danger.'

And time continued to pass, but the British did not come. Joe was still in his prison cell, and although he could hear the sound of falling shells and sometimes even see gunsmoke, he feared it was too late. 'And I always thought the British were punctual,' he murmured with a rueful grin.

It was a Tuesday, the day on which the Moslems hanged all their criminals. Oddly enough, it was supposed to be a lucky day for Jews – the day on which God made everything twice. Oh well, he thought, it could make very little difference now. Joe was prepared. He had given the governor of the prison his money for a decent grave and had offered to pass messages over to the other world. The thought raised a prickle of fear on the nape of his neck, a fear he despised. He had had everything a man could ask for in life. And, with Sara, so much more.

Joe touched Sara's silk handkerchief and sighed. He was dirty and unshaven, but he had kept the handkerchief scrupulously clean, in an uncharacteristic act of sentimentality.

The grey light of dawn came through the window and with it the first boom of the guns. The Turks were due for a busy day today, Joe thought with satisfaction. The British were too late for him, but they were getting closer. Suddenly, a bomb exploded so close that Joe felt the building tremble. He jumped from his pallet and took the step to the window, his leg chains clanking behind him. He could see two workmen in the courtyard below, putting up the hangman's scaffolding, and he shivered. But there was more than that: guards were running to and fro, cursing and swearing. Officers poured out of their mess, stumbling in the dim light. The noise grew louder and more frantic. Then came the unmistakable whistling of a shell and Joe, flinging his hands over his head, closed his eyes and breathed a frantic prayer.

The world exploded in red, ear-splitting violence that shook the foundations of the building and vibrated deep in his chest. Coughing as dust and smoke filled his lungs, Joe cautiously dropped his arms and opened his eyes. The courtyard below him had been destroyed. A dense cloud of smoke rose from the rubble and stones that had been walls. Even his cell had not withstood the force of the bomb. Falling stone and crumbling mortar lay strewn around him. Joe began to laugh, then to whistle the English national anthem. God Bless King George. The Turks would not hang Joe Lanski today.

Maybe Tuesday was a lucky day after all.

CHAPTER TWENTY-SIX

January 1918

Sara opened the gate to the Levinson plot in the small Zichron graveyard. She crossed to her mother's grave and knelt beside it, eyes half-closed in thought. She often came here alone in the afternoons, to sit by her mother's grave and draw strength from her memory. The graveyard was so peaceful, set on the hillside overlooking the sea. There was a new grave here now, Lev's. It did not yet have a headstone and, as was usual in Jewish custom, would not have one until a full year had passed. Sara would plant some of her mother's roses beside the grave; in the summer they would bloom and bring comfort. If only Daniel could be here too, she thought, instead of lying lost under the desert sands. He had always loved her mother's roses.

Sara winced and rocked back on her heels, then sat on the smooth, pink, Jerusalem stone slab that covered her mother. She still limped when she walked but the wound was less painful every day. The flesh had healed quickly and she could now walk without the help of a stick. Her father's recovery had been nothing short of miraculous: Doctor Ephraim's expert work had been painstaking, but even he was amazed at the speed with which the old man's bones knitted together.

Only Sam was still in need of all the care and attention Doctor Ephraim could give him. Her brother had been near death from the wounds inflicted on him by the septieh, but slowly and with steely determination he was recovering, although still in prison for the murder of Hamid Bek.

Sara rested her head on the gravestone behind her, a small sigh escaping her lips. Sam, like the research station, was now in the hands of the Turk, but not for long, she knew. Retreating soldiers had brought news of the British victory in Beersheba in

November, swiftly followed by their conquest of Jerusalem. For the first time in almost four hundred years Jerusalem was free of the Turk.

The villages and settlements in Sharron and Galilee were still in Turkish hands and likely to remain so for the next few months, although there was no longer any noticeable Turkish presence in the area. The Germans and Turks had more important matters to worry about than this little pocket of land, and so the only military to be seen was the odd soldier, lost and humbly asking for water or a little food. Nearly all troops had been moved to Syria and the Russian border in a desperate effort to stop the Russian conquest.

The Turkish Army was still between Sara and the British, but she knew they were there now, knew they were coming closer. Allenby was in Jaffa, waiting for the fall of Syria, so the land between Jaffa and Zichron remained Turkish. But there was no fear now; all could rest in the certainty that once the British turned their might on them, the Turks would vanish like smoke. The jails were still full of prisoners, but the torture and executions had stopped: the Turks, sensing defeat, feared that positions would be reversed all too soon. Sharron and Galilee were left to fester and look after themselves as well as they could.

Sara lifted her head and looked out towards the sea. The late afternoon sun shone on the Crusader castle, turning its ancient stone to liquid gold and her eyes lingered on the scene for a moment before travelling on to the station. Resting her chin on her knees, she stared at it for the longest time. There was no sign of human life near it now, it slumbered in the sun, the palms lining the avenue still miraculously intact, the station and aerometer still standing. But around the buildings, nature was reclaiming her own: the land, once so carefully cultivated, was overgrown with weeds. Time and the Turk had wreaked their havoc, and now the land was returning full circle to its beginnings. And so would its people. When the British arrived, Sam would be released, Aaron would come home and so would Manny, Robby and Ruth and Selena and Kristopher. Alex and Becky would return from the States. And Joe . . .

'Oh Joe, how I miss you,' Sara said aloud, the longing breaking in her voice. Where was he? The question, never far from her mind, rose to the surface again and with it came the doubt, the fear. She had heard so many rumours . . . The jail in Beersheba had been liberated by the British . . . And then that the prisoners

490

had already been moved to Damascus by the Turks ... The jail had been bombed to the ground ... Or, worst of all, Joe had been hanged. Sara's mind floundered at the thought. Joe could not be dead – he just couldn't. She would not be able to bear it.

Sometimes she had to face the fear that he would not come back, but she struggled valiantly against it. Joe must be cut off from Zichron by the Turkish lines, and he was far too well known to attempt a crossing – he would be arrested on sight. She sighed and sat watching the clouds drift by and darken the sky. *He'll be back, I know he will*, she told herself firmly and rose clumsily to her feet. She picked up two stones and placed one on each grave, making the traditional mark of a visit from family or friend.

Sara picked up her basket and left the graveyard, surprised not to see Ali at the gate. He barely left her side these days, but Sara smiled, knowing his superstitious dread of cemeteries. She paused for a breath at the top of the road leading down to the house, and noticed that it was unnaturally still. Normally, her father would be sitting on the veranda as he did at this time of day. And Abu should be somewhere in sight. But the house looked deserted. Sara felt a stab of apprehension and opened the gate quickly.

A few steps up the path she saw Fatma, standing in the doorway of the veranda, peering out at Sara with arms akimbo, and Sara's worry gave way to irritation. Fatma's mollycoddling would drive her mad in the end. When Fatma saw her she gave a shriek and covered her mouth with both hands. Then she jumped in the air, picked up her skirts, and to Sara's blank astonishment ran, a little wobbly, but *ran* into the house.

'What is the matter?' Sara muttered, staring after the fleeing Fatma. She pulled herself together and walked briskly towards the house until something made her stop and drop her basket in the pathway. She listened again. Her piano was being played very fast, very loudly and very badly. As she identified the strains of *Yankee Doodle Dandy*, comprehension suddenly flooded her and she thought for a moment that her legs would buckle under her. Then a smile washed her face with a radiance and a beauty she had not had for months. She began to run, feeling no pain as her entire body concentrated on reaching the drawing room. Faster and faster she went, not limping, just running. To him.

She threw open the door and there he was, standing in front of her with that wonderful, lazy smile and the old roguish expression on his face, just as she had imagined him so often in her dark hours. She flew across the room and into his arms and was so close that all she could see were those green, green eyes swimming above hers, and all she could feel was the strength of his arms and his heart thudding in time with hers.

She tried to speak but her voice was shaking too much between laughter and tears and she buried her face in his chest, sobbing with relief.

He lifted her face and looked at her. 'Sara. My beautiful Sara. Didn't I tell you – didn't I promise – that you were my destiny and I would be back?' His eyes searched her face and she nodded, laughing through her tears.

'I'll never doubt you again,' she promised, clinging to him with all the anguish of the past few months.

The smile left his lips and he put her gently away from him, looking at her with a question, with alarm, with hope. 'Sara? My God, Sara, you're . . .'

Sara laughed with joy. At last she had made him speechless. 'Coming back was not the only thing you promised me,' she said. 'Don't you remember all those fat babies with long, green eyes?'

'Blue,' he said firmly, his hand moving slowly down her body to their child.

'Green,' she said, laughing back.

'You're still arguing with me, you crazy, contrary woman.'

'Yes, Joe.'

He bent over her, 'We'll see about that,' he said. 'Life is going to be different now.' He kissed her with all the passion he had been storing for her for months and she, her arms round his neck, thought happily that he was right. Life was about to change. It already had.

EPILOGUE

In 1931 a Palestinian Jew employed by the British to lay telegraph wires across the Sinai heard local Bedouin tell of a date palm grove known as the Jew's Grave. Suspecting this might be the site of Daniel's grave he informed the Jewish authorities in Palestine. They were refused permission to investigate further by the British Governor of the Sinai.

In 1967, after the Six Day War, Daniel's remains were sought for and found in that very spot. The lonely palm grove had sprung from the dates Daniel carried in his pocket. His remains were transferred and buried with full military honours in the sandy soil he loved so much.

THE AFTERMATH

On October 31 1918 Allenby effectively forced Turkey out of the war. Eleven days later the Germans sued for peace.

The Great War was over.

British victory spelt the end for the Triumvirate. In November 1918 Enver, Jemel and Taalat were secretly spirited away from Constantinople by a German torpedo boat.

In 1922 Enver Pasha was killed leading a cavalry charge in Russia. Both Jemel and Taalat were assassinated in the 'twenties by Armenians.

Mustapha Kemal, the hero of Gallipoli, became Turkey's first President. He was known as Attaturk: the father of Turkey.

The Sultanate was abolished.

In 1918 Abul Hamid died peacefully in the arms of his favourite, Kadine. Mûzvicka was the only member of his harem to remain with him to the end.

Captain Leonard Woolley survived his internment by the Germans and returned to his great passion in life – archaeology. In the 1930s he excavated one of archaeology's greatest treasures, a succession of ancient cities, which he believed to be Abraham's biblical city of Ur, at Tell el Mukkayer in Mesopotamia. He published the result of his excavations and was knighted.

The progressive and courteous Major Wyndham Deedes was appointed Chief Secretary to the British Mandatory Government of Palestine.

Major T. E. Lawrence, 'Lawrence of Arabia', remained in the Middle East for a short while as Political Advisor to Winston Churchill. He wrote the *Seven Pillars of Wisdom*, then dodged the limelight and profit that publication brought. He enlisted under assumed names in the RAF and Tank Corps, preferring a life of obscurity to one of fame and fortune. After surviving guerrilla warfare during the Arab revolt and countless plane crashes, he died in England in 1935 after a motorcycle accident.

For Allenby the rewards were swift and deserved. For his outstanding military achievements he was created Viscount Allenby of Meggido and Felixstowe and received a Parliamentary grant of £50,000. Allenby never campaigned again. He became British High Commissioner in Egypt (1919–1925) and died in 1936. One of the main streets in Tel Aviv is named in his honour.

THE PROMISED LAND

When the fighting stopped, the great land masses of Syria, Western Turkey, Palestine and Mesopotamia were under British control. At the same time the Yemen, Aden and indirectly the Arabian Peninsula were freed from Turkish rule. The map of the Middle East was about to be redrawn.

In 1919 Palestine was made a mandate where the British were legally committed to honour the Balfour Declaration of 1916 and establish a national home for the Jewish People. Syria and Lebanon went to the French and Armenia to the Russians. In 1920 Trans-Jordan (75% of the Palestinian Mandate) was christened the Emirate of Trans-Jordan and given to Abdullah, the eldest son of Husain, the Shareef of Mecca who had instigated the Arab revolt. Mesopotamia was renamed Iraq and given to another of Husain's sons, Feisal, under British tutelage. Both men were strangers in the lands they now ruled. Their father, the Shareef, was acknowledged as King of the Hijaz and foolishly became involved in a war with the powerful desert Prince, Abdul Azziz ibn Sa'ud. In a trice he was defeated, deposed and fled to exile in Cyprus. Out of the conquered tribal Arabia, Abdul Azziz ibn Saud, carved the modern kingdom of Saudi Arabia.

In 1947 the problems Britain encountered in trying to reconcile Arab and Jewish aspirations in Palestine proved insurmountable. Over the passage of years, oil was discovered on the Persian Gulf and British interest began to shift towards the Arabs. They reneged on the Balfour Declaration and the whole issue went to the United Nations where the General Assembly voted 33 to 13 in favour of the only feasible solution, partition. Under the final plan the new Arab state of Palestine would embrace 4,500 square miles, the new Jewish state of Israel 5,500 square miles, most of which was desert.

The surrounding Arab states flatly rejected the vote and an Arab Liberation Army was organised. On May 14 1948, the eve of Israel's declaration of independence, the united Arab Armies, intoxicated by their own rhetoric, marched into Palestine convinced of an easy victory. But the new Jewish Republic, outnumbered by the Arab Armies by at least 5 to 1, waged fierce warfare of its own. 'War is war,' declared Ben-Gurion, Israel's first Prime Minister, 'and those who declared war upon us will have to bear the consequences after they have been defeated.'

When the hostilities ended there were 538,000 Arab fugitives from Israeli controlled territory. Denied work and herded into camps by their brother Arabs, it was the beginning of the refugee problem that continues to consume Middle Eastern politics to this day. Over the following years almost 500,000 Jews living in Arab and Moslem lands were forced to flee their ancestral homes. They sought and found refuge in Israel.

TO LOVE A HERO
Suzanne Goodwin

There were few mysteries in the life of Sorrel Scott's
mother. So when death came to her during the blitz, there
was little in her effects to arouse Sorrel's curiosity – except
the identity of 'George', the man who had been
inexplicabably sending her money.

Taking leave from the WRNS, Sorrel embarks upon a
search that takes her to Evenden Priory and its owner,
George, Lord Martyn, the mysterious benefactor. There
too she meets Toby, his darkly handsome son and heir,
already a war hero with an MC to his name. And there is
no mystery about Toby and his feelings for Sorrel . . .

After a whirlwind courtship, they marry, only to be
separated by Toby's overseas posting. And then disaster
strikes; Toby is reported missing in action. Overwhelmed
by grief and the violent aphrodisiac of war, her new love
is destined to change her life for ever . . .

0 7474 0296 5
GENERAL FICTION

TOO DEEP FOR TEARS
Kathryn Lynn Davis

1879. Three strangers, each haunted by the father she has never known, now drawn together by the tortuous threads of fate . . .

AILSA ROSE, the wild Highland beauty torn by her twin inheritance – her mother's passion for her native hills and her father's wonderlust – she forsook the voices of her heart for the man who offered her a world beyond.

LI-AN, a blue-eyed outcast at the proud and suspicious Chinese court, her father's legacy a constant reminder of her shame and of her danger: Li-an briefly forgets her past in a passion more dangerous still . . .

GENEVRA, the gentle English girl with a scandalous past, abandoned by both her parents amid the splendour and squalor of India, with only her painting for solace – offered the chance of joy, can Genevra dare to love?

Three women, with three dramatic stories to tell – in one captivating, evocative and sensuous novel of fathers and daughters, of love and hate, of sorrow and joy *Too Deep for Tears* . . .

0 7474 0548 4
GENERAL FICTION

All Sphere Books are available at your bookshop or newsagent, or can be ordered from the following address: Sphere Books, Cash Sales Department, P.O. Box 11, Falmouth, Cornwall TR10 9EN.

Please send cheque or postal order (no currency), and allow 60p for postage and packing for the first book plus 25p for the second book and 15p for each additional book ordered up to a maximum charge of £1.90 in U.K.

B.F.P.O. customers please allow 60p for the first book, 25p for the second book plus 15p per copy for the next 7 books, thereafter 9p per book.

Overseas customers, including Eire, please allow £1.25 for postage and packing for the first book, 75p for the second book and 28p for each subsequent title ordered.